FLIGHT OF THE

SETTING SUN

The Life and Adventures of Captain Jake Martin

A Novel by

MARVIN
ARNOLD

Samco Publishing
www.storydomain.com

Flight of the Setting Sun
2nd Edition

This is a fictional story. Use or mention of historical events and places or the names of famous persons is dones solely for placing the story within a given historic time period and geographic region. Any similarity of this story to persons or events that actually took place is coincidental.

First published by AuthorHouse 01/25/2007
 ISBN: 978-1-4259-8646-9 (sc)
 ISBN: 978-1-4259-8645-2 (hc)

Second Edition printing by CreateSpace 12/26/2011
 ISBN-10: 0615580335 (sc)
 ISBN-13: 978-0615580333 (sc)
 ASIN: B004PLNLBO (Kindle)

Samco Publishing   CreateSpace   Amazon Books

Contents

THE FLYING M RANCH

Outside a small Texas town between Sherman and Wichita Falls laid one of the largest working ranches in the Red River Valley. John Martin settled in North Texas south of Oklahoma Indian Territory in the late 1800s. The brand for the Martin ranch had a bar dash in the upper right corner of the M, hence the name Flying M.

Only the most rugged of individualists put down roots and survived on this hard land. Many came from back east to settle, but gave up after a few years. Droughts ruined the crops, water holes dried up and cattle died off. John stuck it out and bought up spreads for ten cents on the dollar from the settlers who moved on. John Martin became a legendary figure in those days held in the same high regard with the likes of John Chisum and Charley Goodnight.

The indigenous people of the area, those of Spanish descent and the Indians who traced their ancestry to the Tejas, still outnumbered the settlers. First and second generation Europeans, primarily German Lutherans, settled the early white man communities. Like John Martin's parents, they came to this country to escape religious persecution.

Water wells were an essential to survival in the arid climate. A couple of miles east of the Flying M ranch, underground water seeping from the sandy bottom of the Red River provided such a well and the ranchers built a cattle chute alongside the railroad tracks. The small town of Pottsburg grew up on the site.

Most folks knew of no particular reason for the name Pottsburg, but when the railroad built the trestle bridge over the nearby creek, the workers unearthed a large amount of old broken Indian pottery along the creek banks, a clue to the many Indian prayers for rain. The native Indians customarily broke a piece of pottery when offering a prayer.

For many years the economy centered on cattle ranching and farming, but with the oil boom of the early 1900s stretching from Tulsa Oklahoma to Midland, Texas, the area found itself in the middle of a vast undiscovered and undeveloped oil rich field.

John stood fast against allowing oilmen on his ranch, but with the discovery of oil in the vast Electra Field southwest of the Flying M, it became obvious the oil rich veins also passed directly under the Martin lands. Finally, John relented under the condition that his son would manage the oil holdings.

Born on the ranch in 1880, Jacob Teel Martin, Sr., became the only son and heir to John Martin's cattle and ranching empire. A broad-shouldered figure of a man, he stood six foot two and for obvious reasons, everyone called him Big Jake.

Big Jake Martin volunteered for duty with the American Expeditionary Force in Europe during the First World War. He served in an artillery unit earning a battlefield promotion to captain. Local citizens regarded him and those from Pottsburg who served with him as war heroes, but Big Jake seldom spoke of his war experiences.

Big Jake reached middle age slightly overweight and his thinning hair had a trace of gray at the temples. He wore high-heeled cowboy boots and a narrow-brimmed, light gray Stetson hat, all of which made him seem even larger than life. A quiet, unassuming and honest man, he was well liked and respected by all who knew him.

Big Jake founded the only bank in the small town, but spent most of his time managing the oil business. He soon built the Martin oil ventures into an even larger empire than the ranch holdings. Big Jake's most trusted friend, the Flying M foreman Travis Swanson, largely ran the ranch. Travis, like Big Jake, had also been born on the ranch.

Through a deal negotiated with the senior Hughes of Hughes Tool Company, the Martin Company produced oil well drilling equipment at a manufacturing facility in Gainesville, Texas. With large oil reserves being discovered in the California basin, Martin Company planned to expand its oil well drilling equipment business by building a new factory on the west coast.

Big Jake's wife, Florence Melinda Parker was born in 1884 on the Parker ranch. She never knew her father, a Scottish immigrant who was killed while working on the railroad. Her mother also died very young.

Florence took the Parker name from her mother's family. Her mother's brother, George Parker and his wife Wilma raised Florence. George and Wilma had one son, Dan, born in Florence's early teens.

Most with the family name Parker in this part of Texas descended from Cynthia Ann Parker and thus, had some Comanche Indian blood. Florence's great aunt Cynthia, the daughter of a Baptist preacher, came with her parents to Waco to found a church and start a Christian college.

A handsome Indian brave, Coda Nocona, kidnapped Cynthia as a young girl, but those who knew her best claimed she voluntarily ran off with him. Nocona Park, a town west of the Parker and Martin ranches, bears his name to this day. Coda and Cynthia's son, Quanah Parker, turned renegade and raided settlers along the Red River for years until agreeing to cease his outlaw activities. The small town to the south, named after Quanah, honored him in a 4th of July parade before he died.

Florence, a strikingly pretty, full-figured, raven-haired young girl whom everyone affectionately called Flo, grew up on the Parker ranch, which adjoined the Flying M.

Big Jake took notice of Flo at a Lutheran church ice cream social the summer of Flo's sixteenth birthday. He vowed to marry her on her eighteenth birthday and he did.

After ten years of marriage, slightly heavier and still a fine figure of a woman, Flo retained her well-known sense of humor and easygoing manner. Flo rose early every morning to tend to her chores around the ranch house and always wore a neatly pressed print-pattern dress and apron with her long, coal-black hair wound tightly in a bun on the back of her head.

Flo and Big Jake thought they might never have children, but finally in 1912, Flo gave birth to a son and named him after his father. Big Jake called his boy Son. Everyone else called the boy Little Jake for obvious reasons, except Flo who always called her son by his given name Jacob. Flo's world centered arnound her husband and son, whom loved more than life itself.

Flo and Big Jake nearly lost their son at age three. He remained sick for several months and the doctors suspected it was possibly scarlet fever. Little Jake was smaller than most boys his age until his early teens when he caught up or outgrew the others. Big Jake tried, mostly unsuccessfully, not to spoil the son Flo had given him.

Little Jake heard the stories of the Parkers and the exploits of Ol' John Martin many times growing up. An excellent horseman and a fine judge of stock, Jake's grandfather exemplified the rugged individualists and the true cowboys of the old Wild West. Two things Jake remembered most about his grandfather were his long-winded stories and that he was an avid hunter.

Jake did not care for killing things. When his grandfather took him hunting and Jake had a buck in his sights, even though an excellent marksman with a rifle, Jake would intentionally miss the shot. Jake would fire to scare the elk or deer away and claim to have missed. He respected the freedom of the large animals and admired the ease with which they went airborne to clear a barbed wire fence. Jake developed a strong will and his own opinions at an early age.

John passed away in the fall of the year after Jake's tenth birthday. At John Martin's funeral, folks came from miles around to pay their respect. Herbert Hunt, an oil well wildcatter, came up from Dallas and Robard Hughes, the inventor of the rotary bit drill head, traveled all the way from Houston. When introduced, Jake remembered Hughes saying he had a young son about his age.

John's wife, Big Jake's mother, died giving birth to a second child and Big Jake's sister died of pneumonia in January of 1900. John was laid to rest beside them on the far northeast section of the ranch where he and his wife had built a small cabin when first starting the ranch.

By the third decade of the twentieth century, the ranch stretched for miles over great open pastures. Patches of woods, mostly blackjack oak, clustered at the edges of the fields and cottonwood trees grew in narrow rows along creek beds and near underground streams. Windmills checkered the countryside pumping water into stock tanks and ponds for the cattle to drink.

The wide sandy bed of the Red River ran nearly dry in the heat of late summer as it meandered through the rolling hillsides. The river passed north of Pottsburg and through the northern sections of the giant Flying M ranch. The center of the rust colored river became the official border between Texas and the new State of Oklahoma.

By August, everything green turned a golden brown and the temperatures hovered above one hundred degrees for weeks at a time, but a spot of shade and the gentle breeze that usually hung in the air would cool and dry the sweat of those working in the afternoon heat.

Electrification of these rural areas had not yet been accomplished. Kerosene lamps and smokehouses served as the utilities of the day. Dirt roads dominated the countryside and one of those dusty dirt roads crossed an old wooden plank bridge leading from the Martin ranch into town.

Dedicated To

**The China Clipper crewmen
who flew the world and to
all the airmen of WW II.**

**This story is about choices.
The choices that each of us
make that change the course
of our lives forever.**

Dusty Road In Texas

Several months had passed since the Japanese air attack on Pearl Harbor. A nice looking man in his early thirties pulled his two year old, canary yellow Continental Cabriolet into a parking space in the lot out front of the Martin oil well equipment manufacturing company at Culver City, California.

The man exited the car, which was covered with a light coating of dust from having been in storage. He reached back through the open car door for his dark blue, double-breasted suit jacket and put it on over his white shirt, matching slacks and tie. Placing a large brown, accordion folder under his arm, he shut the car door and headed for the main entrance to the factory administration building.

He carried himself with the apparent self-confidence of a man on a mission, but a keen observer might have detected a slight limp, which the man disguised very well as he moved hurriedly across the parking lot.

Entering the lobby, the receptionist greeted him.

"Good morning, Mr. Martin."

"Good morning. Annie, isn't it?"

"Yes sir. Thank you for remembering."

A dull roar from the factory machinery could be heard in the background as he passed Dan Parker's office.

"Hey Jake, there you are," Dan called out. "I'll get with you this afternoon. Snowed under this morning!"

Jake Martin paused at Dan's open office doorway.

"No problem, Dan. Got some things I want to get started on anyway. Enjoyed dinner last night, great place to eat. Thanks for the invite."

Jake climbed the wide brass-railed staircase from the lobby up to the second floor of the building, the location of his new office. As he entered, his newly assigned secretary, Gertie, stood with folded arms watching as two workmen remodeled the smaller room adjoining Jake's office.

Gertie, a slender prim and proper middle-aged spinster lady, took very little nonsense off of anyone. She wore black dress suits with high-necked white lace blouses and rarely, if ever, deviated from that style of professional businesswoman's attire. Gertie glanced at her watch as Jake approached, ten o'clock.

"Good morning, Mr. Martin."

"Good morning, Gertie."

Jake stepped over some temporary phone wires strung across the floor to enter his office.

"Should I always expect you to arrive this late of a morning?" Gertie inquired as she followed him into the office.

"Great Scott, no! I had some shopping to do."

Jake placed the large brown accordion folder, stored in his car with some other personal belongings since his return from Asia, on the newly delivered desk.

"I'm sure you did. I mean, needed to do some shopping. I almost didn't recognize you this morning. Yesterday you arrived unshaven and your clothes… well, they looked like you slept in them," Gertie commented tartly.

"I had!" Jake smiled and turned to look directly at Gertie. "Clean up pretty good, don't I?"

Jake removed his new suit coat and went over to the wooden hall tree in the corner to hang it on a hook next to his tattered leather flight jacket he had hung there the day before.

Two workmen in coveralls entered the office with a large leather couch.

Gertie pointed to a place along the far wall. "Over there," and looked at Jake to see if he agreed.

Jake nodded his head yes.

"Thank you. That'll be all," she told the two workmen as they sat the couch down.

One of them tipped his hat to Gertie, nodded and said, "Ma'am."

She gave the workman a stern look and turned her attention back to her new boss.

"Some of the furniture's used, but it's the best I could do in wartime 1942, Mr. Martin. You'll just have to be satisfied with it."

"You did great," Jake said noticing the table in the corner, "and you saved the old drafting board for me, too."

Gertie took a good look at Jake for the first time since having seen him for only a few minutes the day before when Dan assigned her as his new secretary. A strikingly impressive figure-of-a-man she thought, tall with thick dark brown hair and steel blue-gray eyes. Her new boss exhibited a certain take-command style of arrogance and yet his pleasant demeanor seemed to set people at ease.

Jake stood at his new desk, unfastened the tie-string from around the large brown, accordion folder and removed an assortment of well-worn black and white photographs.

"Do you know any of these fellows?" Jake asked holding up one of the photos for Gertie to see.

"Clearly, the one in the middle is you and I think the man on your left is Lawrence Wilcox, one of the company attorneys from Texas. Of course, he's a lot younger in the picture than when I saw him on his last visit here."

"Right on, Gertie."

"I don't believe I know the other two gentlemen."

"This one's Red Henderson," Jake pointed to the young man in an undershirt with a dress tie around his neck. "You'll get a chance to meet him one of these days. He's still off flying in the Pacific somewhere for Pan Am. The fellow on the far left is Charley Armstrong. He died in a crash at the Bendix Air Races in 1938. The monoplane behind us is a Fairchild, my first plane. Charley helped me rebuild the ol' plane from the ground up."

The telephone in the outer office rang and Gertie excused herself to go answer it.

Jake plopped down in the brown leather desk chair, propped his feet up on the desk and leaned back. As he thumbed through the pictures, he came across an early photo his mom had taken of him as a boy in coveralls back on the Flying M ranch.

Jake stared off into the distance and his thoughts drifted to a hot July afternoon in 1923 when as a young boy he was walking down a dusty dirt road...

***

The small North Texas settlement of Pottsburg with its Spanish-style town square and Sittler's General Store lay at the end of the dirt road. The boy had three cents in his pocket he had earned doing odd chores all morning and he planned to purchase a cold soda pop.

He occasionally kicked at the sandy ruts in the road causing small dust clouds to drift off in the direction of the nearly calm wind. The boy stopped and crossed his ankle over his knee once to pick a cocklebur from his toe.

Jacob Teel Martin, Jr., whom most called Jacob or Little Jake, preferred to be called only Jake. His dirt-smudged, freckled face peeled from sunburn and his sandy hair that needed cutting a week ago fell in his eyes. The dirty gray, pinstriped Roundhouse bib coveralls he wore were ragged at the knees.

To look at the boy, no one would have guessed he was the son of one of the wealthiest men in those parts, Big Jake Martin, Sr. Young Jake loved and respected his father and mother very much, but never gave any thought to his family's extensive business holding. He was a typical young boy off on a new adventure every day.

Things mostly mechanical fascinated him. He liked the challenge of figuring out how they worked and took things apart even at the risk of not always being able to get them back together exactly right.

The sun melted like molasses in the western sky. Dark green trees sharply outlined the golden blue horizon. The yellowish green pastures seemed to stretch to where the earth must end and heat waves made the low-lying land appear like large bodies of water off in the distance.

Turning to march backwards for a few steps, Jake gazed out toward the western sky. The afternoon sun would be setting late this time of year, he thought as he conjured up images of far away lands where the first rays of the rising sun might be cresting the distant eastern horizon.

He had read a book entitled *Land of the Rising Sun* and figured out on his own that when he looked out over the western sky of Texas, morning dawned on those distant lands the other side of the world.

If Japan was the land of the rising sun, did they think of us as the land of the setting sun? He often daydreamed of those strange distant lands wondering about the people there. How would their strange language sound if he heard it, would he be able to talk with them and pondered whether he might someday see such a place.

The droning sound of an engine could be heard faintly in the distance, but Jake paid no mind to the sound at first. The wind often carried the familiar pacaka-ta-pacaka sound of a pump-jack in the oil field for miles.

Jake picked up a rock and threw it in the general direction of some crows. The large crows squawked and took to flight. Jake did not care for crows, but he never tried intentionally to hit them. He accomplished what he had intended, to scare them away.

Again the sound in the distance and this time it distracted him. The sound was different. Standing very still in the middle of the road, he listened intently until the sound of an engine came closer. Jake stood spellbound as he looked up into the blue sky to see a biplane coming directly at him.

The sound emanated from the engine of a Curtiss JN-4 biplane, affectionately referred to as a Jenny. These sturdy old biplanes were the best the United States had when it entered the-war-to-end-all-wars, but most never saw before the armistice.

Easy to obtain and inexpensive to maintain, these old surplus biplanes became the airplane of choice for rogue pilots known as barnstormers. These experienced flyers roamed the countryside finding ways to finance their passion for flying.

Coming in low above the treetops, the pilot of the Jenny circled low over the town, a popular ploy used by the barnstormers to drum up interest. If the town people came out to see the biplane fly over, the pilot would land in a nearby pasture to offer rides aloft for a few dollars.

The Jenny circled back from town so the low pass, referred to by flyers as buzzing, must have met with some success. The pilot turned into the wind and pointed his biplane for a large open cow pasture just beyond the barbed wire fence where Jake had stopped on the road to watch.

Airplanes occasionally flew high over the ranch and Jake had seen photos of them, but never before had he seen a real one up close. He could hardly control his excitement when he suddenly realized the pilot intended to land in the nearby pasture.

As the biplane descended towards Jake, its shadow moved across the land in slow motion bobbing up and down as it traversed the uneven terrain. The shadow of the Jenny darkened the sun for an instant as it passed directly overhead. With the biplane's engine idled, Jake could hear the whine of the rigging wires and the rush of air past the wings as the plane passed over. The sound reminded him of standing beneath a flock of low-flying Canadian geese.

Assuming a nose high attitude, the biplane settled onto the ground with the ease of a giant bird. As the wheels touched the ground, they caused two small puffs of dust to drift off in a vortex.

Jake ran down the road, through a gate and into the pasture to watch the biplane taxi back towards him. The noise of the engine quit with a cough and the propeller kicked half a turn backwards coming to a sudden halt. Stillness once again permeated the surrounding countryside.

The pilot of the red and yellow Jenny climbed down from the lower wing of the airplane. He removed his flight cap with goggles attached and stretched slowly as though having been cramped up for some time. Younger flyers often referred to these veteran aviators as Old Hands.

The pilot wore a tattered leather jacket, high-waited jodhpurs and riding boots like a cavalry officer's. Except for the black leather patch over one eye, which Jake assumed the flyer lost in the war, the aviator looked exactly like those he had seen pictures of in magazines.

Jake ran up to the flyer and stood speechless looking up at the larger-than-life figure in front of him. A man of average height and build, to the excited youngster, he represented a towering icon.

The flyer's white silk scarf floated in the gentle breeze drifting across the open field. Jake's imagination allowed him to fantasize the scarf had been presented to the flyer by some genteel European lady in gratitude for his having bravely defended her country.

Jake finally mustered enough courage to speak.

"Will you take me for a ride in your biplane?"

Obviously anticipating the boy's question, the pilot replied, "Sure kid, but not without your parent's permission. Rides are five dollars. Same price for two as one, so best to go get someone to split the cost with."

Spectators from town began to arrive on the scene. They came by automobile, horse-drawn buggy and even a couple on bicycles. A small crowd gathered around the flyer and his Jenny as he began to drum up business.

"Waldo's my name, flyin's my fame! For the small sum of only five dollars, I'll show you fine folks the wonders of the sky. You can pick out your house or farm as it can only be seen from the air. Who'll be first?"

Jake had not made a lot of hard choices in his young life. Everything mostly came too easy for him. Now he would have to make a choice. Stay and watch all the excitement or go try to obtain his father's permission. Failing to go flying in the barnstormer's Jenny was not an option. He stepped slowly backwards out of the crowd and reluctantly removed himself from the midst of the euphoria.

A wiry young farmhand with a pencil-thin mustache purchased the first ride for himself and his girlfriend. The farmhand removed a calfskin pocket purse from his overalls and paid for the ride with a well-worn five-dollar bill.

His girlfriend, a slightly overweight, jovial blonde-haired young lady smiled and giggled with anticipation. The barnstormer ushered his first two passengers up onto the wing of the biplane and stuffed them into the front seat.

The flight controls and instrument panel in the front had been removed and the bucket seat replaced with a wooden bench seat. These modifications and a lighter fuel load allowed the Jenny to carry two passengers instead of only one in the forward open cockpit.

The barnstormer walked to the front of the Jenny, grabbed the propeller with both hands, kicked his right leg high into the air and pulled down hard. Known as propping, this turned the engine over and it started. The well broken-in engine of the biplane fired off easily and the pilot ran to climb into the back seat.

"Hold on, you all," Waldo hollered out, "here we go!"

The barnstormer's amateur theatrics pleased the gathered crowd that cheered and waved.

Jake watched as the biplane took off with its two passengers and then took off running for home.

***

Jake ran into the house and through the living room with the screen door slamming behind him. He raced up the stairs to his room, grabbed a pair of toy motorcycle goggles and a leather cap with earflaps, then back down the stairs through the kitchen and past his mother.

"Slow down young'un," Jake's mother, Flo, hollered at him as he ran past.

Out the back door Jake went.

Flo shook her head and mumbled, "I wonder what's gotten into that boy this time?"

Out back near the barn, Jake's father stood with one foot resting on the bottom rail of the corral fence talking with the ranch foreman Travis and a couple of the ranch hands.

Jake came running up.

"Pardon me, Dad. I got to ask you something really important!"

Big Jake turned his attention to his son.

"Dad, please let me go flying. I really wanna go. I just gotta go flying in that biplane!"

"What biplane's that, Son?"

"You know, the one landed in our south pasture."

Big Jake and the ranch hands had not seen the biplane come over as the barnstormer had approached from the direction of town, not passing over the ranch house.

"Whoa there, Son. Just calm down long enough to tell me what in the fool tarnation you're talking about."

Jake stood looking up at his father with great anticipation, trying to catch his breath and gather the right words to explain.

Travis made it his business to know everything that took place on the Flying M and he said, "Little Jake, I don't think we know anything about something landin' over there in the pasture." Turning to Big Jake, Travis asked, "You want me to go over there and check it out?"

"No, Travis, I'll tend to it. You boys go on back to work."

Big Jake put his hand on his son's shoulder to walk with him back to the house.

"Wouldn't mind seein' a thing like that myself."

Jake walked with his dad back up to the house where Jake's mother came from the kitchen onto the back porch drying her hands on her print apron.

"Flo," Big Jake explained, "We're going to go have a look at this flyin' machine that has alighted itself on one of our pastures."

Flo protested several times for various reasons. "Supper'll get cold before you two get back," she said using up her last valid objection.

Big Jake assured her the matter posed no danger and went into the house to get the keys to his automobile.

Jake, with cap and goggles still in hand, followed behind his dad like a shadow.

The two went out the front door onto the large wooden front porch of the Martin ranch house and the screen door slammed behind them.

Big Jake paused for a moment to stare out over the front yard from the high porch. The view looked out onto a nearby orchard and to a golden cornfield beyond. He looked down at his son and could see the excitement in the boy's eyes.

"Well, why don't we go see what this flying machine's doing in our cow pasture."

Jake ran down the front porch steps and jumped into the passenger seat of his dad's Lincoln Model L Touring car parked on the grass in the front yard.

Big Jake climbed in the driver's seat.

"Which field again did this here machine land in?"

Jake thought his dad should adopt the usage of the new terminology aero-plane or airplane instead of referring to them as flying machines, but he was not in the habit of correcting his father.

"The southeast pasture, sir. The one towards town, not too far from the old creek bridge."

On the short drive over to the field where the Jenny landed, Jake realized his dad only agreed to go investigate and had not yet given permission for him to go flying. Jake would need to do some fast convincing to get a ride in the barnstormer's biplane. Worse yet he would have to ask his dad for money, five dollars to be exact, something Jake seldom ever did.

***

The canvas-topped open Touring car with no side curtains turned off the sandy dirt road and into the cow pasture as the barnstormer's Jenny touched down with its last passenger of the day.

Jake jumped out of the car to run on ahead and meet the biplane where it shut down, but thinking better of it, he returned to walk with his dad.

"I really want to go up in the aero-plane. It's something I've always wanted to do. I know I was meant to fly, I mean get a ride in an aero-plane. Please Dad!"

"Aero-plane, not flyin' machine. Is that right?"

"Yes, sir."

"Guess I need to remember to call them aero-planes in the future." Big Jake looked off in the distance and smiled, his terminology having just been tactfully corrected by his young son.

As they approached the biplane, Jake recalled the farmhand and his girlfriend rode together.

"Dad, I want to go flying, but I don't want to ride with anyone else. I want to go by myself. I'm big enough, I can handle it."

Waldo thanked his last paying passengers for the day and turned to greet Jake and his dad.

"I'm sorry folks, I'm through for the day. Maybe I can catch you all the next time I come by."

Jake felt his heart drop. He knew the barnstormer had never passed through here before and most likely would not be back this way again.

"My name's Martin," Big Jake said offering to shake hands with the flyer.

The pilot returned the handshake with a firm and friendly grip.

"Name's Waldo, at least that's what everyone calls me. You live around here, Mr. Martin?"

Big Jake smiled.

"Well, kind of. Seems your flyin' machine, I mean your aero-plane, has taken a liking to roosting in my pasture."

Waldo, perceiving he had created a problem for himself by trespassing on the Martin property, began to try to talk his way out of the situation.

"Well you see, I mean, most folks…"

"No, no, it's quite all right. That's not why I'm here, Mr. Waldo."

"Just Waldo's fine, sir."

"Now then Waldo, it seems to be good entertainment for the folks. People around these parts don't get to see machines like yours very often."

The two men walked together away from the biplane over to the shade of a nearby oak tree and continued to talk.

While his dad and Waldo visited, Jake circled the Curtis biplane inspecting it as he went. He overheard his dad and Waldo refer to the Maginot Line and Lafayette Escadrille, but those words held no meaning for Jake.

As a doughboy, Big Jake served in France in a field artillery unit and some of the local men still addressed him as Captain, but Jake knew nothing of his father's military exploits.

As the two men talked, they seemed to have a shared experience in common. In a few minutes, a deal must have been struck because Waldo smiled, stepped back and gave a casual salute.

"Consider it taken care of, Captain Martin."

Big Jake walked back to the Touring car and sat down on the running board. He folded his hands with his elbows resting on his knees as though planning to watch something.

Jake, left standing about halfway between Waldo and the biplane, waited as Waldo approached.

"Let's go flying, kid!" Waldo said as he walked past Jake and slapped the now grinning boy on the shoulder.

Jake ran to scramble onto the wing of the Jenny. When he looked down into the open cockpit of the front seat he froze like a possum.

Waldo climbed onto the wing behind him.

"Where are my controls?" Jake demanded.

"You don't have any. I took them out along with some of the other stuff to make the ol' girl lighter. Why do you need a control stick?" Waldo chuckled, "Oh, were you planning on flying us today?"

Reasonably sure Waldo knew he could not fly an airplane and was only kidding him, Jake replied, "Well no, but I thought I could see how they worked."

Jake climbed into the front cockpit seat.

Waldo checked to see his young passenger's seat strap was fastened and climbed into the rear cockpit of the tandem seated biplane.

Earlier, Waldo had shown a husky young fellow how to swing the prop and he motioned for the helper, waiting under the shade tree to be paid for his day's work, to come over to start the engine. Waldo turned the fuel selector on and yelled, "Contact!" as he held the brakes and switched on the magneto.

The Jenny's engine puffed a small black cloud of smoke out the exhaust stack that drifted down the side of the fuselage and disbursed. The engine fired off with a loud pop, but soon smoothed out to run on all cylinders and the engine noise faded into a pleasant drone.

The wide, wooden bench seat in the front cockpit, big enough for two large people, posed a minor dilemma for Jake. He slid first to the left and then to the right of the seat, finally deciding the right side suited him best. He took the leather cap with earflaps out of his pocket and put it on. The toy goggles went back into his overalls as they might cause him to miss seeing something.

The sun hung low in the western sky and a light breeze drifted across the grassy field out of the northwest. Waldo waited for his helper to stand clear and added power. The biplane moved slowly forward in a wide circling turn to face into the wind, bounced as it taxied over the rough cow pasture and reminding Jake of riding in a buckboard wagon on a washboard road. He hung on with the side of the cockpit tucked under his right arm and waved to his dad with his left hand as they passed by.

Big Jake, still seated on the running board of the Touring car, took off his gray Stetson hat and waved it back at his son. He wiped the sweatband of his hat with a large red bandanna handkerchief from his pocket and put the hat back on his head.

Waldo stopped the Jenny for a moment to reconfirm the wind direction and eased the throttle forward to the full power position.

Big Jake stood up to watch the takeoff with its precious cargo on board.

The biplane bounced forward moving Jake firmly against the back of his seat. The wing strut wires tightened as lift generated over the twin airfoils. Her wings rocked to the left and to the right like a barnyard turkey trying to lift off and fly. In a second or two, the rocking stopped and the biplane became stable.

Like a giant homesick bird, the old lady-of-the-air made the transition from her strange and clumsy lumbering place on the ground to a world she knew far better how to handle. She was headed for flight. With one last thud the bumping from the landing gear stopped and she broke contact with mother earth. Once again the Jenny had entered the realm of three dimensions.

Jake sat captivated as the ground moved faster and faster under them. The windblast became strong like riding in the Touring car at high speed. He almost lost his cap, but caught it and buckled the leather strap under his chin.

Jake could not see over the nose as the biplane climbed skyward into the air. He strained upward in his seat with no success and settled back content to look out between the wings. They rose above the cows in the pasture, then over the fence and above the treetops. The ground seemed to have fell away from them instead of them lifting off of the ground.

The Martin ranch house loomed just ahead. The shadow of the Jenny moved up over the barn roof, back down again and across the corral. The barn passed under the leading edge of the lower wing and out the backside. His mom, hanging out the wash in the backyard, left a sheet hanging by only one clothespin to stop and wave a cup towel as the biplane passed over.

Jake waved back and the wind pressure pushed his arm backwards. He slid over to the left side of the seat to see what he might be missing over there.

In the hot air of the late summer afternoon, the Jenny climbed very slowly. At about a thousand feet above the ground, Waldo eased back on the power and lowered the nose to level flight. Jake could see through the spinning propeller forward over the engine radiator to the far horizon. The engine ran quieter, but the wind noise increased. Jake slid to the center of the seat to allow the windscreen to deflect the stronger air. The cooler air had already dried the sweat on his shirt.

He was flying, but he could not quite figure out why he did not feel lighter. He studied the matter for a bit and decided he must weigh the same seated in the biplane as he did in a chair on the ground.

About the time he settled on this as his permanent theory, the Jenny hit a strong heat thermal and it pushed him down into his seat as the biplane rose. Coming out the other side of the air pocket, it lifted him off his seat as the biplane settled onto the cooler side of the thermal.

"Whoa," he yelled out. Maybe there still remained a few things he did not yet quite understand about flying.

Waldo, from the rear cockpit, laughed out loud when he heard Jake yell out and banked the Jenny easy to the left so his passenger would have a better view of the ground.

Jake reasoned the biplane must be going faster, but the ground seemed to stand still under them, so he picked a spot on the ground and watched as it progressed slowly under the wing. They were moving after all.

He leaned back in the seat, closed his eyes and listened to the sounds around him and discovered he could tell when the plane flew faster or slower by the singing of the rigging wires between the wings.

Waldo allowed the heat thermals to carry the Jenny up to around three thousand feet.

"I can see for miles!" Jake hollered, "I can see the Red River that runs to the north of the ranch. That's the first time I've ever seen further than the bend in that river!"

He saw the afternoon train moving westward along the railroad tracks headed for Estelline and Amarillo. Jake always thought those Baldwin steam locomotives were the biggest things he had ever seen, but as they flew over, it looked like a toy train.

Jake expected the biplane would bank more when it turned, but the stable old Jenny was built like a box kite and most barnstormers learned from experience to make shallow turns so as not to make their passengers sick.

Waldo made a shallow turn to the east to get the sun out of his eyes and circled out over Pottsburg. Waldo's deluxe air tour usually included a circling view of his passenger's home or a nearby town.

Jake could not read any of the signs from that high up nor could he make out the barbed wire fences separating the property lines. He wondered if this might be the way God saw the world. Passing over the town square, Jake pretended to broadcast over a radio station.

"Now coming to you from high above beautiful downtown Pottsburg is the famous flyer, Jake Martin. Come in Jake!" he said into a make-believe microphone.

Waldo turned the Jenny to head back to the landing field. The ride became smoother as the afternoon sun reached the western horizon and settled like a giant golden ball sinking into an ocean of land. Jake would always remember this day as the flight of the setting sun.

Waldo retarded the throttle a little, played off the airspeed and started a long slow descent into the wind for a straight-in approach to a landing on the cow pasture. As they approached the landing spot, Waldo pulled the throttle full off and the engine went to idle. The Jenny seemed to hang suspended in midair as it slowed to a glide.

Jake could almost count the blades of the propeller as it turned in front of him. The ground moved faster now and he saw his dad's car parked at the far end of the field. He felt a momentary sadness realizing his first flight neared its end, but hey, making a landing might be the neatest part of the whole flight.

The nose of the Jenny rose higher and Waldo broke the Jenny's rate of descent. Everything happened so fast, but at the same time seemed to happen in slow motion. With a cur-chunk, the Jenny plopped onto the pasture, rolled about a hundred feet rattling Jake's teeth as they slowed to a stop near Big Jake's Touring car.

Jake sat mesmerized in his seat. He had done it. He had actually flown in an airplane! Flying was everything he had imagined it would be and yet, nothing like he thought it would be.

The engine stopped and Jake bounded onto the wing and jumped to the ground. He ran to meet his dad walking towards the Jenny.

Waldo climbed slowly out of the rear cockpit onto the wing and grunted as he stepped onto the ground.

"Thanks, Waldo, for taking my son up in your aero-plane. Oh and I paid your helper so he could go on home to his supper."

"You're one good egg, Captain," Waldo said and turned to pay attention to Jake who had asked three questions in a row about the Jenny. "Another time, kid. Me or someone else will answer all your questions or at least try to, but not now. It's been a long day."

"How would you like to come home to supper with us? Flo, my wife, always cooks plenty."

A Jordan Roadster with the top down waited not too far away in a clump of shade trees and two young ladies dressed in the popular fashion of flappers waited patiently. Waldo looked over his shoulder at the two ladies in the Roadster.

"Thank you, but no. I'm pretty sure I've made other plans for the evening. I appreciate your hospitality though. There's one favor I might ask, would it be all right for me to leave my biplane parked here in the pasture for the night?"

"Don't see as how there would be any harm in that."

This meant the Jenny would be there in the morning and Jake planned to watch Waldo depart.

"Thanks again, Captain," Waldo said to Big Jake and gave Jake a couple of scrubs on his sandy haired head. "See ya kid."

Waldo smiled and took off in a slow trot towards the Jenny to secure the biplane for the night.

Big Jake and his son walked to the Touring car.

"Your mom was right about one thing, supper'll be cold by the time we get home and wash up."

"Ah, Dad, you know Mom will keep it all warm for us."

"Yeah, Son, I know.

Jake continued to look back at the Jenny as they pulled out of the pasture and onto the dirt road headed for the house.

Waldo removed a rope and some tools from a compartment behind the rear seat and drove a steel stake in the ground near the rear of the biplane to tie the tail down. The Roadster pulled up to Waldo and he climbed in.

The evening turned to dusk and the tree-covered dirt road was even darker. Jake could not come up with all the right words to describe the experience of his first flight, but Big Jake listened patiently as his son tried.

The Roadster passed Big Jake's Touring car in a cloud of dust headed for town. Waldo, seated in the middle of the two flappers, waved with the back of his hand as they sped past.

Talking and laughter could still be heard over the quiet of the countryside as the Roadster disappeared out of sight. A double thump-thump sounded in the distance as the Roadster's tires crossed the wooden bridge of the creek on the way into town.

***

Jake dressed before dawn and hiked the two miles over to the pasture to watch Waldo takeoff. The corner of the pasture where the Jenny had been parked, contained only a few grazing cows. The barnstormer, who brought all the excitement with him the day before, left early that morning at first light.

Jake wondered why he had not heard the biplane takeoff and then he noticed the wind was out of the south. Waldo had taken off a different direction from yesterday and not flown over Jake's house.

Jake tried to overcome his disappointment as he sauntered slowly back down the dirt road to his house. His mother was in the kitchen preparing breakfast as he came in the back door letting the screen slam behind him and plopped down in one of the kitchen table chairs.

Normally, Flo would have told him not to slam the door, but she sensed her son bore more serious matters on his mind this morning.

"Mom," Jake began, "do you have any idea how I felt when I looked down and saw the whole world below me like I did yesterday from the biplane?"

Flo came over to the table, sat down and took her son by the hand.

"No, Jacob, I don't and I most likely never will, but I do remember the words to a hymn I love. 'Oh Lord of earth and sky, the heavens are Thy cathedral,' I believe is how it goes. I've always believed the heavens were God's tabernacle and if for no other reason, they should be held in the highest regard by those who enter there."

Not exactly the answer Jake had expected, but a good answer and his mother's words made him feel better.

***

A book young Jake had read, *The Land of the Rising Sun*, contained a cryptic phrase he did not fully understand. It read "Beware, for there be dragon out there and he who hunts for them, may find them!"

Sometimes, a heavy spring rain will change the course of a stream. A simple choice of trails at a fork in the road will take the traveler down a different path. There are seemingly insignificant choices that each of us make in our lives that change the course of our destiny.

Jake's first adventure into the realm of flight in that old Jenny biplane had given him the resolve to someday become an aviator. He now wished for this more than anything else in the world.

The history of the world recorded no particularly notable events on that hot July afternoon, but young Jake Martin on that dusty dirt road in Texas had experienced a genuine life-changing epiphany.

The Lindbergh Effect

Big Jake had the main house on the Martin ranch built for Flo the first year they were married. The home was a large two-story frame with a massive shake-shingled roof and a high, wide porch on the south and east sides. The back of the house faced north to the corral, a large barn and the carriage garage. The house had been repainted several times a bright white, but the Texas west winds had a way of sandblasting it dull again in a few years.

The place was quite an impressive structure, such that people would come from miles away just to view the house from the road. There were ten rooms in all. Flo kept the six high ceiling rooms downstairs immaculately furnished with the antiques she collected over the years. The heavy white lace curtains that draped the large pane glass windows were washed and starched regularly.

Big Jake's father, John Martin, lived out his last few years in the main house, sharing the upstairs in a bedroom down the hall from Jake's room.

Jake's was the largest of the upstairs rooms and had windows that faced to the north and the south. His room was always cluttered with half-built projects and magazine cutouts pinned to the walls. Jake never thought much about the house being large, he had grown up there and the place was home to him.

Like most ranch kids, Jake learned to ride well at an early age, but never took the same liking to animals as his dad and his grandfather. Of the dozens of saddle horses on the Martin ranch, Jake only claimed personal ownership to one, a spirited gray stallion he named Robey. The horse was just plain mean and threw every rider who attempted to break him, but for some unknown reason, the horse would let Jake ride him.

The only animals Jake ever spent time with were his two dogs Scout, a black and white cow dog, and Prince, a brown and tan part German shepherd. The two dogs seldom-left Jake's side and would wait for him outside the one room schoolhouse Jake attended.

Jake did not care much for cats. When he could catch one of his mother's cats, he liked to hold it upside down by its four paws and let go of it in order to see it amazingly rotate and land on its feet. Jake's mom would get all over him when she caught him doing it and call him by his full name, Jacob Teel Martin, Junior, which he hated.

Jake's two best friends were Zack and Sarah. Zechariah Washington, a young colored boy about the same age as Jake, was the son of a cotton field sharecropper who farmed the creek bottomland. Zack lived with his parents, an older brother and two sisters in a small frame shack not far from the Martin ranch house.

Flo, not without influence in the community, made arrangements with the teacher at the one room school for Zack and his sisters to attend with the white kids.

Zack's older brother worked the cotton fields with his father and never attended school. Jake did not see any difference between Zack and the other boys. He whupped the tar out of one big ol' boy for calling Zack a nigger and put a stop to that sort of thing. Zack was a loyal, devoted friend and hung out with Jake whenever Zack's dad did not have him working in the fields.

Sarah Ann Swanson, the only daughter of the Flying M ranch foreman Travis Swanson, was a slender freckle-faced, young girl with reddish brunette hair her mother braided into two long pigtails. Sarah was a year younger than Jake and very much a tomboy. She followed the two boys everywhere they went. Jake treated Sarah more like a sister than a girlfriend even though Sarah had a crush on Jake since long before she could remember. She remained content to accept that role in order to be included in on the activities of the two adventurous young boys.

***

In late spring, almost a year after Jake had flown in the old Jenny, he decided to build the tree house he had planned to start last summer. He recruited Zack and Sarah to help with his new and most ambitious project to date. His two friends considered it at least something to do and quickly became willing participants.

A small stream, a tributary to the Red River, ran north not far from Jake's house and may have had a name, but with no abundance of streams in the area to confuse it with everyone nearby just called it The Creek. The shallow creek ran completely dry in some places during late summer, but ran bank high during the spring rains. At a place where the creek took a slight bend, the water swirled up to form a pool deep enough to swim in.

Growing on the south bank near the swimming hole, a giant cottonwood loomed higher than all the other trees. Last spring, Jake tied a large hemp rope to one of the high limbs hanging out over the deepest portion of the water so he and his friends could use the rope to swing out over the swimming hole, let go and splash down into the water.

When perched on even one of the lowest limbs of the giant cottonwood, a fantastic view overlooked the valley with breathtaking panoramic vista of the western sunsets. The large cottonwood was the undisputed tree of choice for building the new tree house.

An ample supply of old weathered lumber piled up behind the barn adjoining the horse corral provided the material the three young builders needed for their project. One board at a time, they toted the scrap wood to the site on the creek. Jake liberated a long rope, a hammer and a tin can full of rusty nails from the ranch supply shed.

Transporting the materials and designing the tree house consumed most of their first day on the job. Jake sat Zack and Sarah down in the late afternoon to explain how they would build the tree house.

"We'll nail the short boards to the trunk of the tree for steps. Then I'll loop this long rope up over a limb above where we'll build the platform for the tree house."

"What's my job?" Sarah asked.

"You'll stay on the ground and use the rope to hoist the boards up to me and Zack in the tree."

"Right," she said resolutely, "I'll be in charge of the ground."

"Zack, you'll help me nail the boards to the tree."

Sarah and Zack shook their heads yes, they understood.

Jake really did not think they did because he knew he did not know exactly how to build it yet himself, but he guessed they would figure it out along the way.

A pleasant spring morning and the second day of the project the trio began work early.

Sarah waited patiently at the foot of the cottonwood, daydreaming and waiting for her assistance to be requested. She picked through clumps of clover in the field looking for one with four leafs.

Jake, perched about fifteen feet up the tree with Zack seated on the limb across from him, hollered down, "Sarah!"

"Yes?" she answered and jumped to her feet.

"Tie the rope around that two by six."

Jake pointed to the board on Sarah's right.

Sarah pointed to the board.

"Yeah, that one."

Sarah did not know the size of boards, but tried hard to learn, because being a part was important for her. Sarah's father had taught her how to tie a double half hitch or a good firm square knot and she knew how to handle a rope.

Sarah hoisted each board, one at a time on request, up the tree to where Jake and Zack nailed them in place. One by one, a platform of several boards slowly began to span the two large limbs.

Travis rode by on his saddle horse about noon on the way out to the north pasture and brought the kids a packed lunch Flo prepared for them.

Their second day's work on the tree house grew short. They were having so much fun time had passed quickly. At the end of the day, Sarah received an invite to climb the tree to join the two boys on the platform.

The three tired workers sat quietly watching the Texas sunset, not saying a word. They watched the evening sky slowly changed from gold to magenta, a deep purple and time to go home.

The tree house, completed on three sides by mid-summer, needed a roof. Large cane stocks, Jake called it bamboo, grew along the creek bank and he fashioned them into a makeshift thatched roof. One wall they neglected to finish, the west wall, would block their view of the setting sun.

The three co-workers spent many hours up in that old cottonwood tree sitting on the floor staring out over the countryside from their castle in the sky.

"It's the best view in ten counties," Jake claimed, but Sarah knew he made it up because Jake had only been in three counties in his whole life.

"I can see all the way to Europe from here," Sarah added. She was looking south at the time.

They took turns telling stories and talking about what they might want to be when grown up.

Zack, the best storyteller of the three, learned from his dad how to tell a good yarn. He entertained Jake and Sarah for hours with the humorous stories about the antics of his older brother and sisters Molly and Violet. Zack had a way of embellishing an ordinary story from a funny viewpoint.

"Zack, how come your brother can't get work in town?" Jake asked.

"I doesn't knows for sure, but I thinks it's the color of our skin. My bud got real upset about it one time, but 'yous plays the cards yous dealt' is what my pappy told him."

"Not me," Jake boasted. "I'd make 'em deal me a new hand."

"And I believe you could too," Zack said smiling.

"Yeah," Sarah added, "Jake could do anything he set his mind to."

When Jake's turn came to tell a story, it would usually be some variation on his flight in the old Jenny biplane. Zack and Sarah heard it all before, but they listened intently as Jake told it one more time because he told it with such enthusiasm.

Sarah talked all the time, except when it came her turn to tell a story. Then she could never think of anything.

***

Jake, Zack and Sarah could always be found in the loft of the barn adjoining the corral when not down at the tree house by the creek. On one particular afternoon, the trio played tag in the hayloft jumping from bale to bale until they fell exhausted and flopped down in front of the open loft door to rest.

Suddenly Jake sprang to his feet.

"Wait here, I'll be right back," he ordered.

He returned with a large, tattered old black umbrella he obtained from the hall closet at his house.

"You spectin' it to rain?" Zack asked.

Sarah laughed.

"Nope, got something I want to try out."

"What's that, Jake?"

"Parachuting."

"Oh no!" Sarah sighed anticipating events to come.

Below the second-story loading door of the hayloft, a pile of loose hay had been thrown down for the stock in the corral, a distance of about three times Jake's height from the loft to the top of the haystack. Zack and Sarah sat down on each side of the open hayloft doorway with their feet dangling over the side and waited.

Jake stood in the center of the open door. He opened the umbrella, gripped it firmly with both hands, hesitated for a moment, took a deep breath and jumped. The umbrella folded upward as if caught in a windstorm and Jake hit the small pile of hay with a thud. He landed on his feet, his knees buckled under him and he sat down hard on his backside.

Two startled, wide-eyed, saddle horses turned in time to see Jake land and backed away.

Zack slapped his leg and laughed hard.

Jake let out a grunt when he first hit, but said nothing after that.

Sarah grinned at first, then ran for the hayloft ladder to go down to see if Jake was hurt. When Sarah reached him, Jake stood up still holding the collapsed umbrella in one hand and brushed the hay from the seat of his pants with his other hand.

"Are you hurt?" Sarah asked from the edge of the haystack looking up at Jake.

"Well, except for my pride, I guess not!" Jake said with a smirk on his face.

Then and only then did Sarah laugh.

Retiring to a nearby shade tree, the three sat down Indian fashion in a tight triangle to discuss Jake's landing. As they talked, Jake pulled the black cloth off the umbrella's broken and bent metal fasteners. After he removed about half of the cloth, he held it up.

"Remind you of anything?"

"Looks like an ol' broken umbrella to me." Sarah said.

"Bat wings!" Zack exclaimed.

"Doesn't your older sister, Molly, take in sewing?"

"Sure she does, Jake, but what do you need her to sew? You can't fix that old umbrella. It's broke too bad."

Jake laid the umbrella cloth down on the ground.

"Wait here, I'll be right back."

Jake ran to the house and this time came back with a lightweight red cotton windbreaker jacket.

"Let's go to your house, Zack. I need to see Molly about this idea I've got."

"Here we go again. Wonder how this one's going to turn out?" Sarah mumbled as she got up slowly and ran to catch up with the two boys.

For the better part of the mile over to Zack's house, Zack and Sarah questioned Jake as to his plan.

He remained tight lipped.

On the unpainted wooden kitchen table in the Washington's small house, Jake laid out the red jacket and the umbrella cloth. He showed Molly exactly how he wanted a quarter of the umbrella's cloth cut and sewn under each of the jacket's arms.

"See, like bat wings under the arms."

Sarah watched as Jake laid out the sewing job for Molly. "Just what I was afraid of. He's going to try to fly again."

When Molly completed the hand-stitch work on the bat-wing jacket, Jake tried it on. He extended his new webbed arms like a bird in flight and ran around the room.

Molly, Zack and Sarah laughed at him.

"Just what I wanted. Thanks, Molly!"

Jake became more enthusiastic and confident about his ability to fly as they traipsed back over to the barn to prepare for his next attempt at flight. Even if not able to fly, he would glide to a soft landing.

Arriving back at the corral, Zack took a pitchfork and piled more hay on the stack at the bottom of the hayloft. In spite of Jake's confidence, Zack thought a softer landing spot might be in order.

Zack and Sarah took up their positions on each side of the open hayloft door. Jake, with his bat-wing jacket on, stepped to the edge.

A slight breeze blew through the open loft door and Jake felt it a definite assist to his takeoff. In that regard, the twelve-year-old self-appointed, aeronautical design engineer showed some rudimentary comprehension of aerodynamic lift. Unfortunately, he possessed not even the slightest concept of more complicated theories like weight-to-lift ratios.

Two old saddle horses, Jake's stallion Robey and a couple of prize calves in the corral anticipated the coming descent this time and retreated to the far corner of the corral to wait and watch.

Jake spread his arms and with one grand jump assumed a belly flop attitude as he descended onto the haystack. He hit so hard it rattled his teeth.

Sarah believed Jake invincible, but as he lay motionless on the haystack, she became less certain.

"Not again," Zack sighed.

"Jake, you all right down there?" Sarah yelled.

Jake did not answer.

Zack joined Sarah this time to run down and check on Jake. When the two reached Jake, still laying face down on top of the haystack, it seemed once again it might be only Jake's pride not allowing him to speak, but Sarah decided he must be hurt.

The fall only knocked the wind out of him, but temporarily unable to speak, he finally took a big gulp of air and gasped, "Wow, that really hurt. The last time I did that was when I got throwed offen ol' Robey."

Zack and Sarah tried not to laugh, but they could no longer help themselves and fell onto the haystack with Jake laughing.

After resting for a few minutes, Jake stood up, brushed the hay from his clothes and climbed down from the pile of hay. He removed the bat-wing jacket and threw it down hard on the corral ground. The jacket landed in a pile of horse manure.

"That's about what that dang things worth," Jake said when he saw where the jacket landed. "I guess I need to rethink this whole flying thing."

The trio headed off to the tree house down by the creek for what would inevitably be a lengthy and detailed discussion of their most recent adventure.

***

The year Jake and Sarah finished grade school, the old one room schoolhouse on the dirt road into town closed. Students from the Martin ranch and nearby farms began attending school in town.

Jake and Sarah started their freshman year at the newly constructed Pottsburg High School. Segregation of the races being the order of the day, Zack and his sisters' education ended with the eighth grade. Zack spent the next few years working the cotton farm with his father and older brother.

The Majestic Theater movie house, located on Main Street downtown across from the National Guard Armory, offered the only social activity for teenagers in Pottsburg, other than ball games played against nearby towns. On Friday and Saturday nights, Mrs. Wilson, who taught piano from her home during the week, provided the background music for the silent picture shows. Rumors of movies that talked circulated, but no such modern display of movie technology had yet come to Pottsburg.

A typical weekend for Jake began on Friday night when he would meet Sarah at Sloan's drugstore. Sarah and Jake would have a soda at the fountain before going to the picture show. Zack usually waited for them on the sidewalk outside the drugstore. At the theater, Jake always bought three tickets and handed one to Zack who was required to sit in the balcony.

A double feature and a selected short subject could be seen for the price of ten cents. One of the features generally included a cowboy movie. Jake wondered why the stagecoach wagon wheels appeared to turn backwards and would bug Sarah, an honor student, by talking about it during the movie.

"Why do you think that happens, Sarah?"

"Hush, I don't know."

"You're an A student in science, why don't you know?"

"Do you have to over analyze everything? It's just one of those things you have to use your imagination to overlook."

"I'm sure it's a technical problem that could be fixed," Jake concluded, but he would need more information.

After church on Sunday, Jake and Sarah often went horseback riding. Jake and his two dogs would wait with Robey on a hilltop above the river valley for Sarah and her black charger to ride out and meet up with them.

They did not go up into the old tree house anymore. The wind and the rain had pretty well dilapidated what remained of their old hideaway.

One weekend went mostly like the one before, until the week before school let out for the summer Jake's junior year. Harold Donaldson, the son of one of the Flying M ranch's top hands and quarterback on the high school football team, asked Sarah to go to the picture show with him that Friday night.

Jake pretended not to be concerned about the matter when Sarah told him about Hank asking her out.

Sarah became rather upset with Jake over his attitude and declared, "Very well, if our going out on the weekends didn't count as dating, I'm going to accept Hank's offer and go out on a real date."

***

With school out for the summer, Big Jake decided the time had come for his son to learn the ranching business from the ground up, literally.

On Monday morning at breakfast, Big Jake informed his son, "Starting today, I want you to work for Donaldson, our lead wrangler, on the north sections."

"I know what's expected of me, Dad, and I'll do what you say, but I'd really rather work for Travis, if it's all the same."

"No, Travis is always too easy on you. Donaldson will teach you what you need to know."

"I guess I'll play the hand I'm dealt," Jake mumbled.

Big Jake, reading his paper as they talked, asked, "What's that you say, Son?"

"Nothing, Dad, just something Zack said one time."

"Mr. Donaldson's a good man," Flo commented. "He's worked for us many years and next to Travis, he's our best hand. I think you know his boy Harold from school?"

"Yes, Mom. I know Hank," Jake replied politely.

Not bad enough Hank had stolen Jake's girl, to add insult to injury, it looked like he would be spending the summer working for Hank's dad.

Jake went to the corral after breakfast and had just finished saddling Robey when Big Jake walked up.

"Son, you ought to make a gelding out of that stallion, no one can get near the horse except you. He tried to bite one of the wranglers the other day."

Jake smiled.

"No, don't want to, Dad. It'd destroy his spirit. I don't think he really wanted to be a saddle horse in this lifetime anyway. We get along fine the way he is. I talk to him and he seems to understand."

Big Jake laughed. "You will let me know if he ever talks back, won't you, Son?"

Jake exited the corral gate trailing Robey and walking with his dad. He closed and latched the gate behind them.

"Dad, I'm fine with working on the ranch this summer. Like Mom says, 'I was born to it.' So guess I best learn how it all works."

Big Jake placed his hand on his son's shoulder and walked along with him for a ways.

"You see, one of these days you're going to inherit this place like I did from your granddad and I still recall the difficulty of figuring it all out when I took over."

"Sure, I understand. Honest, I'm all right with it, Dad. It'll give me something to do this summer. Like Travis says, it'll keep me out of the pool halls."

Jake mounted Robey to go catch up with Donaldson and his wranglers on their way to round up strays.

"That's the ol' Texas can-do attitude, Son."

Big Jake started to slap Robey on the hindquarter, but thought better of it. Big Jake waved.

Jake waved back as he rode off.

***

Jake would never be quite as large in stature as his father, but stood six foot tall, a slender and nice looking young man. His light sandy hair had turned a darker brown.

Jake traded in his school clothes for a pair of blue jeans, boots and a Panama straw cowboy hat. He was a hard worker, rode well and knew as much about ranching as anyone on the place, but Jake never considered himself a cowboy.

As one of the wranglers put it, "Little Jake's a good hand, but he don't rodeo."

Donaldson, for whom Jake worked, pushed himself and his wranglers hard. The daily routine on the north sections involved rounding up strays that wandered off into the underbrush, branding new calves and the occasional doctoring of an unwilling sick calf or cow.

Riding fence and patching the breaks in the barbed wire usually fell to Jake, the youngest and a gray-bearded wrangler named Jeb. Jake liked working along side Jeb, an uneducated but clever old fellow.

"There're a few benefits to cowboyin', but very few," Jeb often remarked.

When Robey wanted to graze on the tops of some tender new grass shoots, Jake would rest with one leg crossed over the saddle and watch with amazement as a hawk or an eagle circled effortlessly overhead riding on the heat thermals high in the sky. Truly, it must be an amazing thing to fly free like a bird, Jake thought.

Winter set in and Jake continued to help out on Saturdays, thereby allowing one of the hands a day off. He and Robey would ride out to bust the ice off the top of the water tanks so the cattle could drink.

There were those rare moments out on the snow-covered prairie when the stillness made Jake feel like the voice of God could be heard if he listened hard enough.

The Canadian geese migrated south in the fall and returned north in the spring passing over the ranch. Their distinctive honking telegraphed their arrival miles ahead and the sound echoed over the quiet prairie. There would be a thousand or more flying in dozens of V-shaped formations.

Jake would always pause to watch them as they flew overhead and listened to the swish-swish of the rush of air over their powerful wings. If they arrived early of an evening, the whole flock would circle and land to spend the night in the marshland along the Red River.

***

A goodly number of new producing oil wells sprung up across the ranch. When Jake's old gray cowpony needed to rest a spell, Jake would stop at one of the oilrigs. After loosening the cinch on Robey's saddle so he could breath easier and telling Sport and Prince, "Stay boys," he would go up on the rig to visit with the roughnecks.

Jake learned to hit the third step on the rig stairs, as a rattlesnake or two quite often nested under the first step. The rig crews had plenty of spare time to visit when not pulling rod to change a bit or setting casing pipe. Jake asked a lot of questions about drilling and the roughnecks gladly obliged, if they knew the answer.

"Woo-ee, Little Jake," one driller told him, "sometimes you plain ask too complicated a questions."

Before long, Jake came to know as much about how a drilling rig operated as any hand around, even the engineers and geologists.

The rowdy bunch of hard-working roughnecks Jake befriended toiled year round in the heat of summer and through the coldest days in winter.

Jake learned first hand the meaning of, "Colder than a Texas well driller's ass in January," and the code these rough and physical men lived by, "If you could whip the driller, you got to be driller the next day."

After a well came in ready to produce, the roustabouts, mostly Mexican laborers, set the pump jacks, laid the pipe and connected the crude oil tanks. When completed and producing, the job of keeping the well running fell to a man they called the pumper.

Mickolene O'Brien, an old Irishman called Mick was the pumper for the north sections and taught Jake a lot about oil field work.

"Don't go near one of them wells at night with a lit kerosene lamp when its quit pumpin'." Mick warned Jake, "Them that does, blows 'emselves up!"

Jake understood a stopped well could leak natural gas that settled along the ground and would explode when ignited.

"My biggest problem's not being able to tell when a pump jack shuts down in the middle of the night," Mick complained to Jake.

"You know Mick, that seems like a solvable problem to me. Let me work on it."

Jake studied the problem and came up with an idea. He attached a magnet to the pump's counterweight, which passed over a coil, a simple magneto that flashed a light bulb mounted on a pole.

Jake demonstrated it to Mick.

"All you got to do is scan the horizon at night and where one of the light's not flashing, the pump's quit."

"Gull-darn," Mick said, "if that there ain't the best dang invention I ever seen."

Mick soon rigged all the pump jacks in sight with Jake's magneto-lights and never missed an opportunity to tell anyone who would listen, how well Jake's setup worked.

Jake's job on the ranch soon evolved from junior cowhand to one of resident Martin Company oil production manager. With Big Jake's blessing, Jake's short-lived career as a full time cowboy was concluded.

Jake bought a Model T Ford flatbed pickup truck from one of the cowhands for ten dollars cash and a chrome-handled pocketknife. The truck sat where it had quit in the pasture two years ago. The trick would be to get it running. Everyone else who tried soon gave up on the old Tin Lizzie. Mick helped Jake overhaul the four-cylinder flathead engine.

"How tight do you want these cylinder head stud nuts?" Jake asked Mick as they worked on the engine.

"One thread before they strip," Mick replied.

Mick had a way of explaining complicated concepts in simple terms. Jake learned more about engines from Ol' Mick then he could have at the best engineering school.

***

During Jake's senior year in high school and the following summer, he often drove his old truck over to the factory at Gainesville to pick up spare parts. He always stayed over for a while to learn as much as he could about the equipment-manufacturing end of the Martin Company business.

When Jake had two dogs, they always rode on the bed in the back of the truck, but Jake's black and gray German shepherd, Prince, now rode up front in the passenger seat. On a snow covered moonlit night last winter, Scout took on a pack of coyotes that came too near the house and before Jake could get out there with his rifle, they killed Scout. With Prince getting a little older, Jake understood he missed Scout.

On a Saturday afternoon in late May of 1927, Jake had spent the day helping Mick repair a valve in a pipeline pump and worked through dinner. Jake stopped at Sittler's General Store to get a candy bar and a cold drink on the way home.

As Jake visited with Mr. Sittler, he overheard one of the other customers say, "Well, ol' Lindy made it."

"Guess they'll be calling him Lucky Lindy after this," the other customer replied.

Jake asked Mr. Sittler, "What are they talking about?"

Mr. Sittler pushed the Wichita Falls newspaper over in front of Jake.

"You must be the only one in town who hasn't heard. Charlie Lindbergh flew the Atlantic and did it solo!"

Jake picked the paper up off the counter, went over to an old wooden bench against the wall and plopped down to read the story.

Paris, May 21 – Lindbergh did it. Twenty minutes after ten o'clock tonight suddenly and softly there slipped out of the darkness a gray-white airplane as 25,000 pairs of eyes strained toward it. At 10:24, the Spirit of St. Louis landed and lines of soldiers, ranks of policemen and stout steel fences went down before a mad rush as irresistible as the tides of the ocean. Well, I made it, smiled Lindbergh, as the little white monoplane came to a halt in the middle of the field and the first vanguard reached the plane.

The story went on, but Jake laid the paper down and stared off into the distance. At that very instant, every ounce of rancher and oilman drained from his body. From the day Jake flew in the old Jenny, he wanted to be an aviator.

Jake paid Mr. Sittler for the newspaper, folded it under his arm and headed for home.

That evening, Jake cut the Lindbergh headline out of the newspaper and tacked it to his bedroom wall above a picture of the Spirit of St. Louis.

***

Jake and several high school boys hung around out front of Sloan's Drug Store after church on Sundays. Small groups of girls past by, spoke and exchanged a few pleasantries.

On this particular Sunday afternoon, three young Mexican girls stopped to visit. The youngest Garcia girl, Dolores, knew Jake from school and Jake often admired her from a distance.

Dolores, a slender, dark-haired beauty, wore a full black skirt with fine Chantilly lace at the hem. Her off-the-shoulders white blouse allowed her smooth light-tan skin to glisten in the sunlight.

Dolores watched Jake as the girls visited, but quickly looked away when Jake made eye contact with her.

"Have you seen my old truck since I painted it, Dolores?" Jake asked.

Surprised when Jake addressed his question directly at her, she did not answer for a moment.

"Well, no. The last time I saw your truck, seemed to me was the same ol' rusty black color."

"It's still black, but I repainted it, with a brush. Come on, it's around the corner. I'll show it to you."

Jake smiled and held out his hand to Dolores.

Dolores glanced over at her sister talking to one of the older boys and impulsively took Jake's extended hand. Dolores soon let go of Jakes hand as they walked, but continued along beside him around to the side of the drugstore where the old truck sat.

"There she is," Jake said pointing with pride to his Model T Ford flatbed parked on a slight downhill grade.

To Dolores it looked like any other old truck, but because Jake seemed to consider it some kind of prize possession, she pretended to admire the old rattletrap.

"I park it back here because it's downhill and I can let it roll forward to jump the clutch and get it started."

Jake leaned back against the front fender and braced himself with both hands.

"You think you might like to take a ride with me?" he stammered. "Maybe even go on a date or something?"

"I didn't even know you were interested in me, Jake."

"Well, would you?"

"I'm not sure what 'or something' is? But yes, I would like to go out with you. I have to go home with my sister for now, but you can come by my house after supper. I'm sure it will be alright, but I'll ask my mother to be certain."

Jake knew Dolores' father, Senior Garcia, the local blacksmith. A stout man with a large black mustache that curled around both sides of his mouth, he often came out to the ranch to shoe the saddle horses. Jake's dad commented one time, "Garcia is a proud and honest man, a fine craftsman."

That evening at supper, Jake hurried through his meal hardly eating much. As soon as politely possible, he excused himself from the table and left to go pick up Dolores at her house.

Dolores' family lived in a small provincial hacienda on the street behind the Garcia Blacksmith Shop. Dolores waited in the front yard with her sister and her sister's girlfriend for Jake. When Jake pulled up, she ran to jump in the truck with him and he pulled away.

Jake headed out a county road to a hilltop overlooking Pottsburg, a quiet place where the lights of town could be seen as they came on in the early evening. He parked the truck pointed downhill and put his arm across the back of the seat. The worn leather bench seat in the truck, with the springs coming through the cushion, served as a rather poor couch for courting.

Dolores, noticeably uncomfortable, said very little.

Jake tried to ease the situation by nervously making conversation. He could not keep his eyes from returning to Dolores' low cut blouse and her very beautiful bosom. Finally, he mustered enough courage to take her in his arms. After one or two awkward kisses that seemed to improve slightly with practice, Jake slipped her blouse down below her breasts. His heart pounded like it would jump out of his chest any minute and his hand trembled as he moved slowly across them.

Dolores, also very nervous, did nothing to stop Jake's advances. That was, until Jake started to ever so slowly raise her skirt.

"It's not hard for me to guess what's on your mind," she whispered and gently pushed his hand away.

To save his dog-gone soul, Jake could not think of anything to say.

"You know Jake, you can have any girl in this county and I'm flattered you're attracted to me, but if we do what you're thinking and I got... Well, my father would kill me. In fact, he might even kill you!"

That sudden sobering thought caused Jake's physical passions to wane rapidly.

"Well, maybe you're right about that!"

Dolores pulled the white blouse back up over her shoulders and straightened her skirt.

An evening chill hung in the air and the lights of town twinkled in the distance as the two sat quietly for a spell.

"What if the truck won't start?" Dolores asked.

"Oh, it will. If it don't, I can hand-crank it. You ready to go home now?"

Dolores, without looking directly at Jake, shook her head yes.

Jake released the handbrake to allow the Model T Ford to roll down the hill a ways, popped the clutch to start the engine and headed back to town.

They pulled up in front of Dolores' house where her mother left a light burning for her.

"I know you probably won't ask me out again, Jake,"

Dolores put her arms around him and gave him one passionate kiss.

Jake grabbed for her, but she moved back out of his reach.

"What was that all about?" Jake gasped.

Dolores stepped out of the truck.

"Just wanted to give you something to miss," and she waved goodbye as she left to go into the house.

Jake sat for a minute, smiled and shook his head. He looked around for his hat Dolores had knocked off. He found it on the floor, put it back on his head and drove off.

***

Flo and Big Jake, seated at the kitchen table talking, looked up when Jake came down to breakfast the next morning. Flo got up to go over to the stove where some bacon and eggs simmered in the frying pan.

"Understand you got a new girlfriend, Jacob?"

Jake only looked down at his empty plate.

Flo returned to the table and placed a large helping of bacon and eggs on Jake's plate. She smoothed the corner of the red and white-checkered oilcloth table spread with her hand and strolled back to the stove half humming and half singing a little tune she made up.

"Pretty little senorita, big fat senora."

Jake stared into his eggs that glared back at him like two giant orange eyeballs.

"Darn it! Dang small town gossips, anyway!" he mumbled.

Big Jake chuckled from behind his newspaper as he turned the page of the evening paper he had fallen asleep reading the night before. He did not look up, so it might have been something he read, but more likely in response to Flo's kidding her son.

Flo turned, smiled at her son and waited.

Jake started to grin and finally laughed.

"Jacob, your dad and I been discussing your future. He'll explain it to you," Flo said smiling.

She tossed a cup towel over her shoulder and went to tend to her kitchen duties.

"Guess it's time for me to stop goofing off and get back to some serious ranching. Is that it dad or do you want me to go to work over at the Gainesville factory?"

"It's more than that, Son. You know our businesses well enough to choose what best suits you. From now on you're going to have to start making your own decisions."

"So what's next?" Jake asked.

"You can start by getting' those work clothes off and put on your Sunday-go-to-meetin' duds. I'm driving over to Wichita Falls to meet with some fellows today and I want you along with me."

Jake had taken a bite out of a biscuit from the pan on the table and he mumbled, "Great, anything to get out of punching cows all day sounds good to me."

"What'd you say, Son?"

Jake swallowed the large bite of biscuit in one gulp.

"Sounds good to me. I'll be ready in a minute."

Big Jake had waited in the backyard for Jake and the two walked down to get Big Jake's Lincoln Model L Phaeton out of the carriage barn.

The first automobile Big Jake ever owned was a Leland Cadillac. Henry Leland had built Liberty engines for airplanes in the war and started the Lincoln Motor Company in 1919. Big Jake, an admirer of Leland, bought one of the first Touring cars Leland manufactured. After Edsel Ford bought the company, Big Jake remained a customer.

Big Jake bought a new Lincoln about every other year and had recently taken delivery on a new Phaeton Touring sedan. The smoothest riding automobile he ever owned, Big Jake claimed.

Jake never missed an opportunity to ride in the car, but his dad had not offered to let him drive it yet.

From the dirt road leading from the ranch, they pulled onto Highway 82, the only paved stretch of highway to Wichita Falls. Big Jake kicked the Phaeton up to about sixty on this beautiful Indian summer morning. Too windy with the side curtains off to hold a normal conversation, they sat back and enjoyed the drive. Occasionally, they saw a small herd of deer or antelope grazing in among the cattle and pointed them out.

Arriving in downtown Wichita Falls, Big Jake parked the Phaeton out front of the largest hotel in town. To the side of the main hotel entrance, a rather elegant brass plaque on the brick wall near another door read "*Petroleum Club.*"

"Come on, Son, this is where we're meeting our guests."

When they entered the club, the manager who had been watching for Big Jake to arrive, came to greet him.

"Good to see you again, Mr. Martin. Your associates are already here. I'll show you to your table."

In a private corner of the dining room, two men sat at a large round table covered with a white linen tablecloth set with fine china and silver. The two men stood to greet Big Jake as he and Jake approached.

Big Jake did the introductions.

"Jake, this is Noah Dietrich. He manages all of the Hughes Tool Company affairs and a close associate of the young Howard Hughes who inherited the company from his father a few years ago."

Jake stepped forward and shook hands with Dietrich.

"A pleasure to meet you, sir."

Big Jake turned to the other gentleman.

"And I think you know Randall Wilcox, our lawyer for the Martin companies."

Jake recognized Wilcox who often came over to Big Jake's office on business. Jake shook hands with Wilcox trying hard to be on his best behavior as this might be a world he would have to someday learn to master.

"Yes, good to see you again Mr. Wilcox."

The group took their seats at the table and waited for lunch to be served.

"I understand you met Mr. Hughes, Sr. one time," Dietrich said to Jake,

"Yes sir, I did. He attended my grandfather John's funeral. Someone told me at the time Mr. Hughes invented the multi-head drill bit."

"That's right he did, but you're one up on me, Jake. I never got to meet the man. I've only worked for his son, young Howard."

"What does his son do now? I've heard of his interest in aviation."

People seldom inquired about Howard's other interests and Dietrich did not reply. He turned to listen to what Wilcox was saying.

"My son, Lawrence, is only a year older than you, Jake. He attends college at Southern Methodist University in Dallas and plans to go on to law school. I hope to eventually bring him into my firm. Wilcox and Wilcox has a nice ring to it, I think."

After lunch, Big Jake concluded the small talk and directed the group's attention to business matters.

"As you know, Martin Company plans to build a new oil well equipment manufacturing facility in Culver City. The recent major oil discoveries in the California basin lead us to anticipate an ever increasing demand for drilling equipment out there."

Jake sat quietly through the discussion memorizing as many of the details as possible. An agreement was soon reached for Martin Company to produce equipment under a licensing agreement with Hughes.

Dietrich and Wilcox excused themselves to go over to Wilcox's office located upstairs across the street and draw up the contracts.

Big Jake called Wilcox back.

"Put Dan Parker, Florence's cousin, down as president of the new company, but keep me as chairman of the board like always."

Wilcox nodded he understood Big Jake's instructions. He also clearly understood the heir apparent to the Martin oil and cattle empire had been seated at the table with them.

"Good you could join us today, Master Jacob."

For a moment, Jake did not realize it was him that Wilcox was speaking to.

"Oh, yes sir. Thank you, Mr. Wilcox," Jake replied.

The waiter brought a box of cigars to the table.

Big Jake selected one and prepared it to light and turned to Jake.

"Now's as good a time as any for us to discuss what your mother and I talked about this morning. You'll be out of high school soon and we're wondering if you want to go to college. You've always shown a keen interest in mechanics. How about some kind of engineering."

With Jake's father bringing up the subject of college, how was he going to explain that he wanted to go to flying school and learn to be a pilot. Maybe the best thing to do would be to change the subject.

"Dad, you know some of the guys I go to school with are joining the National Guard. Considering joining up myself. What do you think?"

Big Jake took a long drag on his cigar and paused to think for a moment.

"I'm aware they're starting to build up the Guard, but I'm not sure it's the best thing for you. Not saying you shouldn't serve your country if the need arises, but from time to time, those politicians have a way of getting us involved in things we have no business meddling in."

Jake succeeded, at least for the moment, in diverting his dad's attention from the subject of college.

Big Jake leaned forward, put his elbows on the table as though preparing to tell Jake something very profound.

"I'll tell you bout soldiering, son! War is not a good thing, not all the glory it's cracked up to be. When I shipped over to France in the last war, I saw things I wished I'd never witnessed. Those old cavalry officers would run our young men into the Hun's machinegun lines…"

Big Jake choked up and paused for a moment, but he pretended it had been the cigar smoke.

"They didn't seem to understand how terrible a piece of machinery the modern machinegun was. In one day alone, I saw five thousand of our brave young men killed in battle trying to take one lousy hill. A friend of mine, who I grew up with, stood beside me in this artillery battle and an incoming shell hit close and a fragment cut him in half. How I came out of that living hell without a scratch, I'll never know, Son, but I can tell you war's a terrible thing, avoid it if you possibly can!"

At that point, Jake regretted changing the subject, but one thing for sure he did not think he would be joining the National Guard anytime soon.

"Maybe you'd like to go down to Bryan and attend A&M. Old Sul Ross helped found the college there and a lot of fine Texas families send their sons there to be educated. You see, no one in our family ever went to college, let alone got some fancy degree. Your Grandpa John wanted me to go to college, but the war and the demands of the ranch kind of got in the way."

"Who was Sul Ross, Dad?"

"A captain in the Texas Rangers and governor of the State when I was a young boy."

"Oh," Jake said. "Dad, I'd really like to learn to fly. I know you want me to go to college, but aviation's my only real interest. According to ol' Mick, I'm a pretty darn good engineer now and I don't know any college offering a degree in aeronautics."

Big Jake was well aware of Jake's long held interest in flying. The pictures on the walls of his bedroom and the books he bought more than confirmed his son's interest in aviation.

"How would you go about learning to be an aviator?"

Jake's enthusiasm increased as it appeared his father actually might be willing to listen to what he wanted to tell him.

"There's a flight school that trains airline pilots down at Fort Worth. The school's called American Flyers and they teach you everything you need to know. The school has a real good reputation for training pilots."

Big Jake took some bills out of his wallet to pay the check the white-coated waiter placed on the table. The waiter smiled and thanked Big Jake as he always left a large gratuity.

Big Jake got up to leave and Jake followed.

"Maybe we can work something out, Son. If you go to this here flyin' school, which I'm assuming shouldn't take over a year, then would you consider going on to college?"

"Sure, Dad. I'll get the information about the flying school. I think they'll mail me a brochure if I write to them."

Flying School

Jake sat on the back porch of the house enjoying the beautiful spring morning. Today he was both excited and melancholy. This coming July he would be nineteen and he pondered what the months ahead would bring. In his hand he held the dog-eared brochure sent to him from the flight training school in Fort Worth that he must have read a hundred or more times.

Along with the brochure Jake held a letter dated last month accepting him for enrollment in the beginning pilot flying course at American Flyers.

Big Jake came out the back door and down the wooden porch steps where Jake sat.

"On your way to work at the bank, Dad?"

"Yes, got an early morning meeting. Listen, Son, I want to wish you all the best on your new adventure. I kinda envy you taking on a new challenge. Your mom and I are here for you if you need anything."

"I know, Dad. You always have been."

Big Jake shook his son's hand and headed off to work.

Flo had packed a small suitcase for Jake and it sat on the porch beside him. She came to the screen door.

"Are you going now, Jacob?"

Jake stood up, went to the door and hugged his mother.

"If you'll have Dad run a telephone line out here from town, I'll call you once in a while."

"I'll work on him, but you write for now and come home when you can. It's not that far."

"I will, Mom. Love you."

Jake picked up his suitcase and went over to the Model T truck parked on the grass under a shade tree and threw his suitcase in the back.

Flo hollered after him, "How you gettin' to the bus station?"

"Zack will take me," Jake hollered back.

Jake's old dog followed him and tried to climb into the passenger seat.

"No, Prince, you're not going along this time." He gave Prince a good scratch behind the ears. "Stay, boy!" and climbed in the truck to leave.

Flo waved goodbye from the porch as Jake drove away.

Jake pulled up to the nearby field where Zack toiled with his dad and older brother chopping cotton. He stepped out of the truck and motioned for Zack to come over.

"Tell your dad you'll be back in a short while. I need you to run into town with me," Jake yelled out to Zack.

Zack turned to his dad with a questioning look. His father nodded his approval and went back to work.

Zack dropped the hoe where he stood and ran to go with Jake.

"Why you let that boy runs off in the middle of the work day?" Zack's older brother asked his dad.

Mr. Washington did not answer his oldest son or look up from his work. He just kept on chopping the cotton row.

When Zack jumped in the truck, he saw Jake's suitcase in the back.

"Where you headed?" Zack asked as they took off down the dirt road trailing a large cloud of dust behind them.

"I'm off to Fort Worth to begin my flying career, but first I want to stop by Sarah's house to say goodbye."

Jake pulled up in front of Sarah's house and Zack waited in the truck as Jake went up to the house.

Sarah heard them pull up and stood waiting just inside the front door as Jake got out and came up on the porch.

"Hi, Jake. What're you doing out running around the countryside all dressed up this morning?"

Jake looked down at his boots instead of looking directly at Sarah.

"I guess you know how many times I've talked about learning to fly."

Jake looked up at Sarah as though asking her blessing.

"I'm off to the American Flyers flying school at Fort Worth."

Sarah stepped out onto the porch and closed the screen door behind her.

"You ever coming home again?"

Jake tried hard to be cheerful.

"I'll be home on weekends from time to time and when I get to flyin' regular, I'll come and take you for a ride."

Sarah's forced smile turned to a frown.

"Why don't you go tell your little Mexican senorita instead of coming and telling me?"

"Aw, come on Sarah, don't be like that. You know you're my best girl and always will be."

Sarah's expression softened. She started to go back in the house, but paused, came back and gave Jake a kiss on the cheek.

"I'll be right here, Jake. You know where to find me."

Jake started for the truck, but stopped and turned to look back at Sarah.

Sarah stood holding onto the screen door like she needed something to hold on to as she waved goodbye.

As Jake climbed behind the steering wheel, he sat motionless for a moment. The strangest feeling came over him, like if he changed his mind at this very moment about leaving his whole life would somehow turn out very different. Was this a choice he had to make?

At the gas station on the corner of the highway crossroads where the Greyhound bus stopped, Jake left the engine running on the truck and stepped out.

Zack slid over into the driver's seat to take the truck back to Jake's house for him.

Jake lifted his suitcase out of the back and walked around to the driver's side. He reached in his pocket for a piece of paper and handed it to Zack.

"Here, I wrote this out last night. This here paper says you're the legal owner of this old truck and you didn't steal it from nobody."

Zack reluctantly reached for the piece of paper Jake held out to him.

"Go on, Zack, take it. The truck's yours now. I'm gonna be flying everywhere I go from now on!"

Zack smiled and took the paper from Jake.

"I does appreciate you thinkin' of me. I'll take good care of her in case yous ever wants her back."

Jake offered his hand to Zack. The two young men had shaken hands a hundred or so times over the years to confirm a bet, but the first time they had ever shaken hands to say goodbye.

"I guess I'll be here when you come home, Jake. Still chopping that damned old cotton, I suppose."

"I'll see you, Zack."

Jake picked up his suitcase and went to meet the bus.

***

Jake sat by an open window watching the countryside roll by on the long hot bus ride to Fort Worth. The bus stopped at every little town to take on and let off passengers. If the stop happened to be a county seat, the bus would make a short layover. In Denton, at the bus station on the town square, the driver announced a twenty-minute stop.

Jake walked across the street to the small cafe on the corner, as it had been a while since breakfast. He seated himself at the counter and ordered a piece of cherry pie and a cup of coffee.

A pleasant rotund lady in a starched, white cotton waitress uniform served it up promptly.

Jake listened as some old men at a table talked about the weather and what they might expect from the cotton crop this year.

In a few minutes, the bus driver sounded the horn on the bus parked across the square. Jake went to board with the other passengers.

"Can you let me off at the airport north of town?"

The driver shut the door behind Jake with the long leaver handle from his seat.

"You mean the new airport they named after ol' Mayor Meacham?"

"Yes, sir, that's it."

Jake took a seat a couple rows back and the bus driver raised his head to look in his rearview mirror to see where Jake had taken a seat.

"Sure, I'll holler at you when we get there, but you'll have to walk from the road. The bus doesn't go up to the air terminal."

Late that afternoon, the bus headed down far North Main Street in Fort Worth. Meacham airfield was located northwest of the stockyards district where the drovers stayed over when they brought their cattle to market. The locals called the area Cowtown.

Jake could see the airport coming up on the right-hand side of the bus as the driver pulled over onto the shoulder of the road.

"Meacham Field," the driver announced.

Jake grabbed his suitcase from the overhead rack and stepped out of the bus. The door to the bus closed behind him and pulled back onto the highway.

Jake stood on the highway shoulder at the gravel road leading up to the terminal building and some large wooden hangars about a quarter mile away.

He might as well have been standing at the edge of the known universe. Never before had he been this far away from home and never before had he felt so alone.

American Flyers was painted in large letters on one of the hangars and beneath it the words Learn To Fly. Jake made his way to the hangar and the flight school office.

A young lady, seated at a desk filing her fingernails, looked up as he entered. She smiled and asked politely, "Can I help you?"

Jake approached the counter and sat his suitcase down.

"Yes, ma'am. My name's Martin and I'm here to enroll in the flying training program."

The young lady, dressed in the popular style of a flapper, got up from her desk and came over to the counter with a folder in her hand. Her bleached blonde hair was cut in a bob and a chemise dress draped her slender, shapely figure. Long beads tied in a knot dangled from her neck almost touching the counter as she leaned over.

"We've been expecting you Mr. Martin. My name's Elsa Bowles. I'm the secretary for the school here. Would you fill out these forms and sign all of them for me, please."

Jake took the forms and the pen Elsa handed him.

"Pleased to meet you, Elsa. What are these forms for?"

"Basically, they say that if you kill yourself in one of our airplanes, you're not going to blame it on us."

Elsa returned to her desk and Jake couldn't help watching her as she walked back to the desk, seated herself on the edge of her chair and crossed her legs in a rather provocative manner.

Jake glanced through the forms only long enough to see where he needed to sign.

"What the heck am I going to do about it if I kill myself anyway?"

Elsa answered the telephone when it rang and spoke with someone about picking her up after work. She hung up and came back over to the counter to look through the forms Jake signed.

"Where're you planning on staying?" she asked.

"I don't rightly know. I was going to look for a room to rent nearby."

Elsa placed Jake's paperwork back in the folder with his name on it and put it in a large oak filing cabinet. She returned with a small bound book with a black leatherette cover and handed it to Jake.

"This is your log book. You'll use it to record your flights." Elsa paused to look Jake over. "You're a healthy specimen, aren't you?"

"Beg pardon, ma'am?"

"Never mind," Elsa said smiling. "There's a widow lady down the road with a large house and she rents out rooms to some of our students. I'll call her and see if she has a room available."

Anxious to have a look at the trainer aircraft he would be flying, Jake went out the side office door that opened into the hangar.

A rain shower had moved in from the northwest and Jake watched as a Stearman CMB-3 and a Douglas DM-2 were being pushed into the hangar.

A big fellow in one-piece coveralls with graying hair and a Van Dyke beard was helping a mechanic bring the last of the two trainers into the hangar. When they finished, he walked over to Jake, removed his leather glove and extended his right hand.

"You must be Martin. Our owner, Mr. Allen told me you'd be arriving today. Name's Theodore Gobles. I'm one of the instructors here. Everyone calls me Ted. Some call me Teddy Bear behind my back, but I prefer Ted. That wiry ol' fellow over there's Tinker, our mechanic."

Tinker gave a two-finger hand salute to Jake and Jake waved back.

Ted spoke with a thick accent and seemed not given to smiling easily. This might have been his nature or maybe only the way his beard curved down around the corners of his mouth.

"Pleased to make your acquaintance, sir. I'm anxious to get started."

Jake followed his new instructor to the back of the hangar.

Ted took a shop towel from the workbench and dried the dampness from his forehead and arms. The light rain, which had moved across the airfield, had wet him down.

"Soon enough, Martin, but the weather's got us shut down for today. Be here at eight o'clock in the morning and be prepared to start with the rest of the students. We do a daily mix of flight training and ground school."

A large, gunmetal gray Packard sedan with dual spare tires mounted in the front fenders pulled up out front of the hangar and the driver honked the horn several times.

Elsa stuck her head out the office door.

"Come on, Mr. Martin. That's my boyfriend Dutch. We'll give you a ride down to the rooming house. Mrs. O'Leary says she has a room for you."

Jake ran to get his suitcase from the office and went out to the waiting Packard.

Elsa jumped in the front seat and slid over close to the driver. Jake shut her door and climbed in the backseat of the suicide door sedan.

Elsa turned and looked into the backseat at Jake.

"This is my boyfriend Dutch McCoy. What's your first name anyway, what do they call you?"

"Jake, everyone just calls me Jake. Thanks for the ride, Dutch."

Dutch grunted, "Yeah sure, you're welcome."

Jake settled back into the soft camelhair upholstery of the large backseat as the Packard pulled out of the airport and headed south on Main.

"What do you do, Dutch? I mean what line of work you in?"

Dutch looked at Elsa who laughed.

"Me? Oh, I'm a trucker."

Jake wondered why Elsa had laughed.

"What kinda truck you got? What do you haul?" Jake asked, attempting to make friendly conversation.

This brought an even harder laugh from Elsa.

Dutch looked at Jake in the rearview mirror.

"Got a couple of Rios. Mostly haul Texas Tea out of Canada."

Jake did not understand.

"Tea? I thought tea came from China."

With that, Dutch even laughed and Elsa came unglued.

Jake decided to give up trying to make conversation at that point and remained quiet for the rest of the short ride into the north part of town.

Dutch stopped the sedan in front of an older two-story white frame house.

"This is the place," Elsa said composing herself. "Just tell Mrs. O'Leary you're the new student I called her about. See you tomorrow, Jake."

A large middle-aged lady came to the door when Jake rang the bell.

"You Mr. Martin?"

"Yes, ma'am. The lady at the flight school said you had a room for me."

Mrs. O'Leary ushered Jake upstairs and showed him to a single bedroom.

"Fresh towels are there on the bed and the bathroom's at the end of the hall. You share it with three other young men like yourself."

Jake looked around the clean, well kept, but otherwise drab boarding house room.

"Rent's five dollars a week, I'll need to collect a week in advance."

Jake paid her for a month.

"Thank you, Mr. Martin. Goodnight."

Mrs. O'Leary closed the bedroom door behind her as she left.

The day had been a long one, not to mention he had not eaten any supper. He threw his suitcase on the floor, took off his boots and trousers and fell into bed.

***

Along about first light, someone knocked on Jake's bedroom door.

"Anybody alive in there?" a young man's voice called out.

Jake struggled to wake up and sit on the edge of the bed.

"Yeah, I think so. What is it?"

The door opened and a young redheaded fellow about Jake's age stuck his head in the door.

"One of your fellow students, Elliott Henderson, but call me Red for short. You want to go get some breakfast?"

"Sure," Jake replied.

"Meet me downstairs in about five minutes. There's a place down the street that has good home cooking and I know a fellow who eats there every morning who works out at the airport and we can hitch a ride with him."

A cooked meal sounded real good right about then. Jake hurried to get dressed, but did not take time to shave.

By eight that morning, Jake, Red and six other pilot students gathered in the small classroom adjoining the American Flyers hangar. Two instructors, Ted and Mike, came into the classroom with the school's owner, Robert Allen.

Mike, Allen's nephew, was a quiet unassuming young fellow who helped teach ground school and made the longer flights with the advanced students.

Allen was a dapper, well-groomed, middle-age man of less than average height. He wore a double-breasted, navy blue blazer, the style of jacket often worn by airline pilots. Intelligent talking, Allen meticulously selected his words as he spoke. Obviously Allen intended to set a standard for the students by his own example.

"Good morning gentlemen. Looks like another fine day for making aviation history. Most of you here know our instructors, Ted and Mike. I'm your chief pilot, Robert Allen, but you will address me as Mr. Allen."

A couple of the new students chuckled, but Jake did not. A quiet pause went across the room as the two who had laughed realized Allen was dead serious. Then Jake and the rest of the class laughed at the ones who had laughed.

"I'll be testing each of you by flying periodic check rides with you. Today's schedule calls for rotating four of you into the Douglas DM-2 trainer. Mike and one of our senior students will be gone all day on a cross-country training flight in the Stearman. When you're not flying, I want you hitting the books. Any questions?"

There were none and Allen left the classroom.

Mike picked up a piece of chalk and wrote the number 24 on the blackboard.

"Turn to section twenty-four in your training manual. Today you will be studying the section on aerodynamics."

The students opened their textbooks and began to read.

Ted left to go out to the hangar to check with Tinker, the flight line mechanic, about the flight readiness of the Douglas biplane.

Jake had not been issued a manual yet, so he sat quietly.

In a few minutes, Ted returned to the classroom.

"First up this morning will be Mr. Martin. He's our zero flight time man. The rest of you keep hitting the books and Jake you come with me."

Ted directed Jake to the rear of the hangar where some lockers were located.

"Select a jacket, a cap and some goggles that fit."

Jake grabbed his gear and ran to catch up with Ted already halfway out to the orange and white Douglas biplane parked on the apron in front of the open hangar.

Ted began, "This is an airplane."

Jake spoke before he thought, "I know that."

"Well then, Martin, why don't you tell me what you do know about this airplane?"

Not being exactly certain what Ted was asking, Jake began to recite everything he remembered having read about the plane.

"This plane's a Douglas model DM-2 biplane built in California. Designed along the lines of the deHavilland DH-4 biplane first built in 1925 for airmail service and has a 400 horsepower Liberty engine. This model's a two-seated tandem trainer, but they also make a model for one pilot with a cargo compartment in the front capable of carrying a twelve hundred pound payload."

Ted showed no outward expression, but apparently had not expected Jake to have any knowledge of the DM-2.

"And how is it you come to know so much about this aircraft, you been around them before?"

"No, sir, but I read about them in a magazine I used to subscribe to called *Wings*."

Tinker placed a stepladder at the leading edge of the upper wing beside the biplane's engine. Ted began his pre-flight, walk-around inspection instruction on how to check the oil, the gasoline and inspect the airframe.

Jake followed Ted around the plane. As Ted completed each check, Jake repeated it back to Ted.

"From now on this will be your responsibility, but I will check everything you do. Don't miss anything! I call that a crash-and-burn. One C-n-B and you're grounded until you commit the preflight checklist to memory. Two C-n-Bs and we start over at lesson number one. Three C-n-Bs, well you don't want to know."

Ted motioned for Jake to climb onto the wing and sit in the front seat. Ted stepped onto the wing and positioned himself where he could look over Jake's shoulder into the cockpit.

"This aircraft has rather sparse instrumentation, but it's quite adequate as a basic trainer."

Using his swagger stick as a pointer, Ted named the instruments as he pointed them out.

"Airspeed, altimeter, compass and a turn-and-bank indicator used to show slip and skid. The one in this airplane isn't much better than a carpenter's level, so you'll have to learn to tell by feel when you're not making a coordinated turn."

Next, Ted went over the engine switches, flight controls, brakes and a small rear view mirror mounted on the upper wing where the student could view hand-signals from the instructor in the back seat.

"This cone looking thing here behind your headrest is a megaphone through which I can yell instructions at you."

Jake made the mistake of saying, "I already figured that out."

"Fasten your safety belt," Ted announced sternly and climbed in the rear cockpit seat. "Clear," he yelled as he started the engine.

Ted taxied the plane to the north end of the north-south runway and pushed the throttle forward. The lightly loaded DH-2 rolled a short distance down the runway and lifted effortlessly into the air.

Jake sat motionless in the front cockpit as the plane rose to an altitude of about one hundred feet off the runway.

Ted took his swagger stick and from the rear seat, punched Jake firmly in the left shoulder as he let go of the controls and over the megaphone yelled, "You got it, cowboy."

Jake came suddenly to the realization he had let his overconfidence and big mouth overload his capability. He struggled to level the aircraft still at a full power setting and climbing. Rocking to and fro with the nose bobbing like a porpoise on the horizon, Jake tried desperately to control the airplane. Actually, he was over-controlling the aircraft and worse yet, Jake could hear Ted laughing heartily at his expense from the rear seat.

After a few minutes, Ted returned the Douglas biplane to level flight and retarded the power.

"I got it," Ted decreed still laughing. "Now, let's go learn how to fly an airplane. Maybe you don't already know the rest of this stuff."

For the next hour and a half, the instructor took Jake through climbs, descents, coordinated turns and most of the basic maneuvers. When Ted needed to explain something, he would pull the power off to reduce the engine noise level and add the power back when through speaking. Mostly, they worked on staying level in a turn for this first lesson. Ted performed a maneuver and then turned the controls over to Jake for him to duplicate the maneuver.

They returned to the airfield and Ted landed the plane. Jake was exhausted. He had puckered so tight he figured he had left a permanent crease in the canvas cushion on the bucket seat.

Ted pulled the DH-2 up in front of the open hangar door and ran Jake through the shutdown procedure.

On the ground, after Jake climbed down out of the cockpit, Ted commenced to critique their flight.

"I'd like to compliment you on your coordination and your newly acquired willingness to learn. However, when you show up tomorrow, I expect you to be clean-shaven. We train airline pilots here, not bums. I expect to see you in a neatly pressed shirt with a tie. Oh, and those cowboy boots, lose 'em. Those heels can get caught in between the rudder pedals and spin us both into the ground. Get you some soft leather, lace-up high tops."

Ted turned away to his next waiting student.

Jake thought to himself, next waiting victim!

Jake ambled over to where Red and a student named Dale Harkins were taking a break from class. They had overheard Ted's dressing down of Jake.

"Boy! You got a taste of the ol' Teddy the Bear's wrath first time out of the barrel," Dale said.

"Ol' Teddy is one of a kind. You're not the first and you won't be the last to get it from Ted," Red added.

Jake smiled.

"Yeah," Dale said. "That thick accent of his will scare the hell out of you!"

Red and Dale walked along with Jake to the hangar lockers to return his flight gear.

"I think he's Polish," Dale commented, "an officer in the army and he flew fighters during the war in Europe."

Red chuckled and said, "Just not sure which side he fought on?"

Red's last wisecrack cheered Jake up a little. The three student pilots returned to the classroom. Jake spent the rest of the day studying his newly issued training manual. Allen came into the classroom from time to time to review the lesson and quiz the students.

The other students took their turn flying with Ted. Two of the more experienced students would not fly today. They were waiting to fly a check ride with Allen. The Stearman CMB-3 had departed on a long cross-country flight and was not due to return until evening. Late that afternoon, one student scheduled for night flying remained and the rest of the class was dismissed.

"Come on, Jake, I know a bar over in Cowtown where we can get a beer and a steak at a good price."

Dale's young bride of two months, Peggy, waited in their beat up old Studebaker out front of the hangar.

Dale hollered to Red and Jake, "Come on guys, we'll give you a lift over to the stockyards."

Dale pulled over to the curb to drop Jake and Red at the Main Street entrance to Cowtown.

"Thanks for the ride, Dale. Nice to meet you, Mrs. Harkins," Jake said politely as he and Red piled out.

"Who's he talking to?" Peggy joked looking at Dale.

"It's Peg to you, Jake! You boys stay out of trouble tonight, you hear," she hollered back as they pulled away.

Red motioned up the street a ways.

"The White Horse saloon's not far."

Jake noticed the stores where still open.

"Hold up a minute, Red. I need to pick up a couple of things."

Jake went in a leather goods shop, purchased a pair of ankle-high lace shoes and from the outfitter next door, he bought a navy blue dress tie.

At the White Horse, Red led them to a table in front of the large gilt-edged, pane glass window.

"We can watch the ladies of the evening and the drunken drovers on the street from here," Red explained.

After dinner, Jake and Red got into a long-winded philosophical discussion about whether or not God meant man to fly. Red had been raised a good Catholic and had even considered becoming a priest when he was younger.

Another flying student and a couple of drunken cowpokes wandered by and joined the conversation.

These discussions, a strange mix of H.G. Wells, Jesus Christ and Buck Rogers, would become a regular part of many a future evening activities down at the White Horse.

Jake and Red walked back to the rooming house. In his room, Jake laid out clean clothes from his suitcase, his new tie and his new shoes. He shaved before going to bed.

***

The weeks wore on. More and more holes were bored in the sky and Jake learned, as all beginning pilots soon do, he could pucker only so long and then he began to relax in the cockpit.

Jake's student pilot tunnel vision soon cleared up. He sharpened his awareness of things going on around him and to use all his senses. He learned to keep his eyes on the horizon and his ears tuned to the many changing sounds of the aircraft. He developed a keen sense of balance, jokingly referred to by the students as center-of-ass.

If ol' Ted caught one of his students not paying close enough attention, he would chop the power and announce, "You have just lost all power in your engine."

The student was then expected to establish a normal glide speed and set up an approach for a safe landing in a nearby open field.

Ted would not come back in with the power until this was accomplished and if the student failed to select a good landing spot or tried to stretch his glide, Ted would declare, "You just killed the both of us. Take us back to Meacham and land. This session is over."

A worst-case scenario would be when Ted took the controls to prove to the student he could have landed the plane three times in the field the student pilot had missed. Fortunately, this never happened to Jake, but he heard horror stories from other students who had made the mistake.

After two months of stalls, takeoffs, spot landings and basic aerobatics, Jake had soloed and logged a little over thirty hours of flying time. The day finally came for Jake to take his check ride with Allen for completion of phase one of his fight training.

Jake waited patiently on the ramp for Allen to come out to the aircraft. Allen arrived with his flight gear and clipboard in hand. He sat his gear down on the ramp and went over what he wanted Jake to demonstrate.

"One of the maneuvers I want to see done well today is a Chandelle. Explain it to me."

"Yes, sir. A Chandelle is a climbing power-on turn, an evasive maneuver that requires good coordination and timing to execute properly. The maneuver is named after the fighter pilot who perfected it during the war."

"Very good, Jake." As always, Allen ended with, "Any questions?"

Jake decided to take a shot and asked, "How about a question off the subject, sir?"

"Sure, but let's talk on the way out to the aircraft."

Allen picked up his gear.

Jake grabbed his flight gear and caught up with Allen.

"Where'd you learn to fly?"

Allen grinned and continued walking to the aircraft.

"Ah, the ol' how'd-you-come-to-be-a-pilot question. Not much of a story. My grandfather was a Naval officer and my father was a Naval officer. I was sent off to military school at an early age and when I graduated from college, of course I joined the Navy. At the time, they were offering to train young officers like myself as pilots, so I volunteered. Thought it might keep me off a Tin Can, that's a destroyer escort to you, Jake."

"That must've been really neat. Learning to fly in the Navy, I mean."

Jake put his gear in the front seat of the tandem trainer. Allen tossed his stuff in the rear seat.

"Well maybe, but it didn't keep me off a ship like I planned. I ended up being assigned to a battleship. Flew a reconnaissance plane, a single-engine floatplane. They fired us off of the deck with a catapult and then hoisted us back aboard after we landed on the water."

Allen slapped the side of the fuselage with his calfskin leather-gloved hand.

"Okay Jake, let's do the pre-flight so we can get this ol' bird in the air. I used to let the Navy try to kill me, but now I reserve that privilege for you guys."

***

Jake managed to log about a hundred hours of total flying time by late summer and now worked towards building his solo flight time and on his cross-country navigation skills. Jake moved ahead of the other student pilots in his class in total flight time, as he made himself available to fly anytime an aircraft was not being utilized.

Allen purchased another used Stearman biplane like the one he started the school with. The new yellow trainer had wide red lightening stripes down each side of the fuselage and red scallops along the trailing edges of the upper wing.

The addition of the third aircraft made it easier for the advanced students like Jake to schedule a plane for overnight cross-country flights. Now he would be able to fly home over a weekend for the first time. The advanced student pilots shared weekends on a rotating basis and the second weekend in September, it came Jake's turn to use the plane.

He took the yellow and red Stearman on a standard triangle cross-country navigation flight to Amarillo and then to his home at the Flying M ranch. Jake landed in the same pasture Waldo landed in that fateful summer day eight years ago.

Sunday, after church and after one of Flo's excellent fried chicken dinners Jake had missed so much, he excused himself to go see Zack and Sarah.

Big Jake walked to the door with him.

"How you plan on getting over to Sarah's house?"

"Ol' Robey, I guess or maybe use one of the ranch trucks. Why, Dad?"

"Robey's nearly lame now, Son. He's been in a lot of pain lately. We're gonna have to put the old stallion down before too much longer."

"I know, but I don't want anyone else doing it. I'll take care of Robey myself, when it's time."

Big Jake reached to get a set of keys off a hook on the kitchen wall and handed them to Jake.

"Why don't you drive the Phaeton? You always liked that car. Besides, it needs a good running. I don't drive it much since I bought the new Model K sedan."

"Thanks, Dad."

Jake headed for the garage with Prince running along beside him to go pick up Zack.

The Washington family was not home from church yet. Jake drove on down the road to what some called the darky's church. Jake could hear the singing a quarter mile away before he got to the old white frame church at the crossroads.

Jake parked the Phaeton and went in quietly. He found Zack seated near the rear of the church and sat down with him. Jake stayed for a couple of songs.

"Dry bones, dem bones," the congregation sang out and "Ain't gonna study war no mo," shook the rafters of the old church.

Jake punched Zack. "Lets go," he whispered and the two slipped out.

When they stopped at Sarah's house, Zack pushed Prince over to climb in the backseat, but not before Prince gave him a big wet lick right on the face.

Sarah heard them pull up and went out to the car.

"Where're you two going?"

"I've got the airplane, Sarah, and I'm going to take you flying like I always promised I would."

At first, Sarah resisted, but after years of listening to Jake brag about his first airplane ride, she decided the time had come for her to decide firsthand what she thought about flying.

"I'll do it, but I want to ride by myself and in the front seat like you did the first time."

"Wouldn't have it any other way!" Jake replied and thought to himself that it seemed like old times as the three drove off together.

Arriving at the pasture where Jake had left the Stearman parked, Sarah insisted Zack go first.

"I want to watch you takeoff. You two go on!"

Sarah sat in the Lincoln Phaeton and watched them circle the field. Jake came in low and buzzed her once. Jake flew Zack around for about twenty minutes, returned for a landing and did not shut down the engine.

Sarah ran for the plane, holding the skirt of her calico dress with one hand against the prop wash. Zack gave her a hand up onto the wing and helped her climb into the front cockpit. Sarah, a wiry little thing, accomplished all of it with ladylike grace.

Not only had Sarah never ridden in an airplane, this was as close as she had ever been to one. Knowing this, Jake flew the powerful radial engine Stearman at a reduced power setting and made shallow turns. They flew low out over the ranch land and down the Red River following the sandy riverbed for miles.

Sarah soon gave up trying to hold her hair in place and let her long brunette hair trail in the wind. She leaned back against the headrest and smiled as she watched the countryside roll by beneath them.

From the rear seat, Jake noticed how the sunshine gave Sarah's brunette hair an auburn glow. He had almost forgotten what a natural beauty Sarah really was and how good it made him feel when she smiled.

Sarah was experiencing for the first time what Jake had always tried to explain to her. He thought he heard Sarah say something over the noise of the engine and was almost certain she had said, "Now I understand."

After they landed, the three old friends sat in the Phaeton under the shade of a large oak tree in view of the biplane parked on the grass. They talked for an hour or so about everything and nothing. Sometimes, they sat without saying a word like they had when they were kids, but mostly they talked about memories they shared growing up together.

Sarah's friendship with Jake had long ago turned into a deep abiding love for him, but in her heart she understood Jake's love of adventure and that he would always be going off to see what lay over the next horizon.

Jake cared more for Sarah than any other woman on earth, save for maybe his mother, but he held Sarah in too high a regard to think of her as just another girlfriend.

Late that afternoon, Jake took Sarah and Zack home. He returned to the ranch house, put the Phaeton away in the carriage garage and went into the house to tell his folks goodbye. He reassured them he would get home again as soon as he had a chance.

Jake walked the dusty dirt road back to the pasture and to the Stearman. He did a quick pre-flight inspection and took off to return to Meacham Field. The evening air was cool and the flight back pleasant. When Jake touched down on the unlit runway, the sun had already set. Only a faint glow of daylight remained on the western horizon.

Tinker came out of the hangar to greet Jake when he taxied up. The two pushed the Stearman into the hangar and chocked the wheels.

"There's still one airplane out, so looks like it's going to be a long evening for me," Tinker said, "but if you want to wait, I'll drop you at your rooming house when I'm done."

"Sounds like a good deal to me. I got nothing better to do."

Jake and Tinker went over to sit in a couple of old metal lawn chairs. They talked about flying and generally enjoyed the pleasant Indian summer evening while waiting for the last plane to return.

***

Jake completed basic flight training in early spring of 1932 and continued on into the optional Advanced Pilot's Training at American

Flyers. The APT class would officially graduate in the fall. All the students having logged two hundred or more hours of flying time and having received their Bureau of Aeronautics pilot's certificate from the government examiner's office would graduate.

In an informal ceremony, Chief Pilot Allen presented each pilots a diploma suitable for framing and a letter of personal recommendation stating the pilot met the highest standards for the completion of the flight-training course at American Flyers. The new pilots could present the letter to a prospective employer when applying for a flying officer position.

After the ceremony, Allen asked Jake to stop by his office to discuss Jake's plans for the future. Allen's office was cluttered with years of flying memorabilia, photos of his old Navy squadron and various flying events.

Allen seated himself behind his large oak desk and packed a well-worn old wooden pipe with tobacco.

"Sit down, have a seat. You smoke, Jake?"

"No sir, I don't."

"Good! Nasty habit I picked up in the Navy, don't ever start. Jake, you're one of the best pilots to ever come through this school. You're a natural. Some got it, some don't. Some are born with it, some learn it, but you have one of those rare natural instincts for flying."

Jake was somewhat uncomfortable with the compliment and shifted in his seat several times.

"Thank you, sir."

"I don't say that to many of our students and never before they graduate. Most pilots have got an ego a mile wide already. There's no sense in throwing fuel on the fire."

Jake laugh.

Allen smiled and asked, "What're your plans?"

Jake moved to the edge of the leather chair.

"Mostly, I want to fly and right now the best opportunity I can see would be to get on with one of the new startup airlines."

Allen relit his pipe a little better as they talked.

"Most copilots start out doing all the grunt jobs, loading baggage, dumping the puke-bags and stuff like that."

Jake nodded his head yes in agreement.

"Since the crash of '29," Allen went on, "there haven't been a lot of new jobs out there for pilots. Heck, the airlines still haven't convinced the public it's safe to fly."

"I know you're right, sir. I've talked to some of the pilots who graduated earlier and they've all told me the same thing. Some of the old timers are still doing stunt work at county fairs."

"The flying circus days are over! The airlines will put the passenger trains and the long haul buses out of business one of these days, but right now the public is not exactly beating a path to their door."

Allen sat thinking for a moment.

"Tell you what I'm going to do, Jake. I got a few contacts and I'm going to send a personal recommendation to some of the people I know in the business. Like you've heard, there're some new airline ventures trying to get off the ground."

Allen stood up. Jake rose to his feet and reached over the desk to shake hands.

"I do appreciate all you've done for me and the other students trying to teach us how to fly right and all. I'm heading home to the ranch to help out with spring roundup. I'll check back with you from time to time."

"Good luck to you, Jake."

Jake went to the office to find Elsa.

"Oh, hi Jake. Thought you were gone by now," Elsa said as he came in.

"Not yet. I hoped you'd still be here. I didn't want to leave without saying goodbye."

"Just waiting around to lock up. I told Mr. Allen I didn't mind staying late this evening. Dutch is out of town picking up another load of Canadian whiskey in those old trucks of his. I've got his Packard. I'll give you a lift if you want."

On the way to Jake's rooming house, Elsa casually mentioned, "I'd sure like to see that new talking movie showing downtown."

"Let's go then. It'll be my treat. I've got nothing else to do this evening, that's for sure."

After the show, Elsa and Jake strolled down the brick paved Main Street south of the Tarrant County Court House.

"I know a little restaurant that stays open late, mostly for the after-theater crowd. They've got a speakeasy window in the back, so we can have a drink if we want."

When they stopped to wait for a streetcar to pass, Elsa took Jake's arm. Jake thought she had lost her balance in her high-heel shoes, but she continued to hold on to him as they crossed the street and went into the Worth Bar & Grill.

As they entered, one of the waiters offered to seat them at a table by the window looking onto the sidewalk.

"I'd prefer to sit in one of the booths toward the back, please," Elsa said to the waiter.

Jake had one drink and Elsa had a couple as they sat and talked. When they went to get Elsa's car, she handed Jake the keys.

"Why don't you drive, Jake? I'm a little tipsy."

Going north out Main Street across the Trinity River Bridge from downtown, Elsa slid across the seat to sit close to Jake.

"Where do you live, Elsa?"

"Not far from here. You want to see my place?"

Jake was not ready to go back to his lonely room at the boarding house where he was staying and especially on a Friday night.

"Yeah, let's go to your place," but then Elsa's boyfriend, Dutch, crossed Jake's mind. "You sure it's alright?"

Elsa nodded yes and smiled.

"That's my street up there, take a right."

Jake parked the car out in front of a two-story, brick apartment house and went up the stairs with Elsa to the small, one bedroom flat where she lived.

Elsa searched in her purse for the door key and finally came up with it. She handed it to Jake.

He unlocked the door and followed Elsa into the apartment.

"Welcome to my humble abode."

Elsa threw her purse and gloves on the couch.

"It's a little cool in here. Turn on some heat, would you, Jake?"

Elsa went into the bedroom.

Jake found the wall heater and turned it on. He sat on the couch wondering what Elsa was doing in the bedroom.

"Everything all right in there?" Jake asked.

"I'm fine. You come on in here."

Elsa had taken off her dress and was placing it on a hanger as Jake entered the bedroom. The light bulb in the small lamp on the nightstand gave off only a dim yellow glow in the dark room.

Elsa stood near the window, clad only in a silk camisole and a slip that hung low on her hips.

"Why don't you get out of those old clothes before you come to bed," Elsa asked softly. "You are, spending the night, aren't you?"

Darn right he was! He had admired Elsa for too long from afar not to stick around tonight.

"Yes, ma'am! I mean Elsa, but excuse me for a minute. I'll be right back."

Jake went into the kitchen and found three empty milk bottles. He placed them pyramid style four inches inside of the apartment door. If Dutch came through that door in the middle of the night, he wanted to know about it!

Jake returned to the bedroom and fumbled awkwardly to remove his shoes and shirt. Elsa came over to help him loosen his belt and step out of his trousers. Jake lay down on the bed and propped himself up with his arm behind a pillow to watch Elsa.

Elsa crossed in front of the small lamp and its dim glow outlined the curves of her hips. The light shown through the slip and illuminated her shapely legs.

Jake did not move for fear of spoiling the moment.

Elsa's slip fell to the floor around her ankles. She stepped out of the slip, pulled the camisole slowly off over her head and lay down beside Jake.

Jake's heart rate went well past the red line and he felt like his cylinder head pressure would blow a gasket any second.

He had never had sex with a woman like Elsa and only a couple of times with girls his own age. He had sex with a rather athletic young girl he met at the Gainesville County Fair. She had let him make love to her in a hay wagon behind the exhibits building. The brief less than passionate encounter was over so quick he was still not real certain what sex was all about.

He would never have to wonder about that sort of thing again. On that night, in the early morning hours in her apartment, Elsa Bowles taught Jake Martin everything he would ever need to know about sex for the rest of his life.

Deep Ellum

Jake returned home two weeks before Sarah left for college at the University of Texas at Austin. Sarah had been in St. Louis most of the summer visiting her mother's sister, her Aunt Jane.

Sarah and Jake spent every evening of the two weeks together and they even talked about making love a couple of times. When Jake seemed willing, Sarah was not.

The night before Sarah left for Austin, they parked the Phaeton on the hill overlooking the old tree house by the creek and sat talking.

"If you tell me not to go, Jake, I'll stay home!"

"I won't do that, Sarah. Your folks have planned on you going to college for a long time and it's a real opportunity for you."

"What are you going to do while I'm away? Are you going to stay here and work the ranch?"

"Don't think so. I plan to go to Dallas and try to get a job flying. You'll be home from time to time and I'll come up when you're here. I'll even try to get a plane and fly down to Austin sometime."

"I know I'm going to miss you something terrible. It's been lonely enough this last year with you away at flying school. I don't want to go, Jake! I want to stay here with you."

"Listen Sarah, I'm sure we'll get married one of these days, but things are just the way they are for right now."

They sat quietly for a time and then Sarah said, "It would be alright with me, if you want to now."

"What do you mean?" Jake asked.

"We can make love if you want to."

"You don't even know how. You've never made love to anyone before."

"I know, but I'm sure you can show me how."

"Why would you say a thing like that?"

"Because I have never made love before and because I don't want to lose you."

"No, if we are going to get married, then it's best we wait. Besides, you'd regret it in the morning."

"Maybe," Sarah said wistfully, "maybe so."

***

The evening after Sarah left for college, Jake sat on the couch in the living room looking through some of his old flying magazines by the fading light as the sunset filtered through the windows.

Big Jake sat in his favorite overstuffed easy chair across from Jake reading the newspaper. He liked to read the newspaper every night after supper so he would pick up a copy of the paper at the drug store on his way home. That way he did not have to wait for the postman to deliver it the next day as he claimed the news would be old by then.

Flo finished in the kitchen and came into the living room. She turned on the dry-cell battery radio she and Big Jake listen to of an evening.

"It's already getting dark early now, have you noticed," Flo commented as she lit several of the coal-oil lamps around the room.

Jake never cared for the lamps. He did not like the smell or the flickering shadows they cast. Since being in the city, he had gotten accustomed to electric lights.

"Pottsburg has been wired with electricity for several years now and we have poles now what with the lines being run out here to the house for Mom's new crank telephone. You know, Dad, they could probably use the same poles to run the electricity."

Big Jake listened as his son talked, but did not look up from his paper.

"I'm sure you're right, Son, but I haven't gotten around to looking into it. Besides your mom mentioned several times she might be interested in moving to town, so she'd have some of the more modern conveniences."

Flo sat quietly crocheting on a white doily and listening to the exchange between her husband and son, but then she spoke up.

"No, not anymore. I've thought on it for a spell and I think we'll stay put here on the place."

"Well, there you have it. Never try to out guess a woman," Big Jake said good-naturedly. "I'll talk to the electric company people first chance I get and see what's involved."

Jake thought this might be a good time to have a talk with his folks.

"Mom, Dad. You know I'm not much of a rancher. I'm a little better oilman, but not much."

"I think you underestimate yourself, Jacob. Why do you say that?"

"Because this ranch is you and Dad's life and I respect you for all you've accomplished here, but it's not what I want to do."

Big Jake laid the paper on his lap and took off his reading glasses.

"Are you trying to say you've given up on the idea of going to college?"

Jake shook his head yes. "Well that and some other things too!"

"Can't say that comes as any great surprise, Son."

"Dad, did you know there are whole new industries being devoted to aviation? New airlines are starting up all over the country. Aircraft builders are producing newer and better planes. I'd like to be a part of all that. I'd like to go to Dallas and live on my own for a while. If things don't work out, well then…"

"I've always known you wanted to be a flyer. Matter of fact, I know a couple of ranchers up Amarillo way who have bought their own planes. That being said, Lord only knows, you've tried hard to do everything we've ever asked of you around here."

"Except maybe go on to college, huh Dad?"

Big Jake let his son's last comment pass. Deep down, he did not feel college was all that important. He had not gone to college and had done reasonably well for himself.

"Maybe you ought to pursue your own dreams. Your grandfather had a dream when he started the Flying M and look what came of it."

Big Jake laid the newspaper on the floor beside his chair and placed his reading glasses on the smoking stand beside him. He got up and went over to get a file folder out of his tattered, old brown leather briefcase.

Jake smiled to himself as he remembered his mom had tried to get him to part with the old briefcase on several occasions, but Big Jake liked his old one. Flo bought him a brand new one several Christmas' ago, but the new briefcase was still in the box in an upstairs closet.

Big Jake sat back down in his chair.

"Wilcox came by the office the day before yesterday and we discussed some things you might be interested in."

Big Jake opened the folder and thumbed through several of the pages.

"They've changed a lot of the tax laws up there in Congress. They got a lot of new laws coming up on the books. One of them's called a War Tax. They're wanting to build up the military and the Navy again. Guess they think somebody might be going to attack us."

"Dad, they've got to. Do you have any idea what devastation airpower can do now days? An Air Corps Captain and cross country racing pilot by the name of Billy Mitchell proved that when he demonstrated he could sink a battleship with his airplane."

"I'm sure you're right. Anyhow, what's at the bottom of all these new regulations is just another tax. Give you an example. That ol' Lincoln I didn't trade in on the new one, if I sell it, the money would be taxable income. So what's the point, just as well keep it."

Jake never concerned himself with money matters. His needs were simple and what money he needed for a new saddle or his tuition to American Flyers was always there.

"I understand that, but why do these new taxes have anything to do with me?"

Big Jake handed the folder to his son.

"You take a look at these papers, read them over. I'm sure you're smart enough to comprehend them, maybe even better than I do. Wilcox has got it all worked out."

Jake took the folder and looked in it. The heading on the first sheet read Trust Fund.

"The simple explanation is your mother and I have got more money coming in than we can spend the rest of our lives. The new oil well equipment company in Gainesville is even showing a profit now. The crash of '29 didn't hurt us since we raise beef. People still gotta eat. The wildcatters keep drilling new oil wells on the place. You know ol' Will Rogers claimed that we Americans would be the first generation in history to drive to the poor house in an automobile. So I guess everyone's gonna need gasoline to do that, too."

Jake closed the folder he had been thumbing through and stood up.

"I'll read over these tonight and I guess we can talk about it in the morning. Goodnight Mom, goodnight Dad."

Jake went upstairs to his room with the folder under his arm. That night he fell asleep reading the documents, but before he did, he read enough to understand what they were all about. Jake had also read an article in the newspaper about Henry Ford setting up something similar to this for his son, Edsel and for Edsel's children.

***

The following morning, Jake brought the folder downstairs with him and handed it to his dad.

"Sir, I read them over like you asked and it all makes sense to me. Don't guess there's much to talk over after all. If this is what you want to do, it's fine with me. I've signed all the places needing my signature."

Big Jake prepared to leave for his office in town. He took the folder and placed it in his briefcase.

"Makes sense to me too, Son."

Jake offered to carry his dad's briefcase and then walked with him to the car.

"I'll be going back and forth between here and Dallas quite a bit from now on and I've been looking to buy one of those new Ford Model B coupes. The new '32s have modern lines like the more expensive coachbuilt automobiles. What do you think, Dad?"

Big Jake took the briefcase from Jake, threw it in the front seat and got behind the wheel of his new Model K Lincoln sedan.

"Thought you might want the Phaeton to drive. You always liked the ol' car and I sure don't drive it anymore, just sits there."

Jake leaned his arm on the roof of his dad's car to talk through the rolled down window.

"Yeah, it's a neat car, but don't much want people to think I'm some kind of society guy. Besides, that car's worth four times what a new Ford would cost me."

"Might as well take it, this one ain't gonna cost you nothing. If you're embarrassed about driving it, just tell everyone your rich uncle gave it to you."

Jake laughed, as he knew his dad referred to Uncle Sam.

"Gee, that's swell. Thanks, Dad!"

Jake stepped back from the car.

"You still planning on going down to Dallas?"

"Yes, sir. Think I'll head on down that way this afternoon."

"Give your mom a call and let her know where you'll be staying so she won't worry."

Big Jake gave a Texas Wave to his son as he pulled away. A Texas Wave, a casual rise of the right hand with a slight turn of the wrist. Often used as a greeting when passing someone on the road, it only meant everything is fine with me and I wish you the same.

***

Jake needed nothing, but had always wanted his own airplane. He had in mind one of the new Monocoupe airplanes built by a startup company at Lambert Field in Robertson, Missouri near St. Louis. Lindbergh owned one of the first production models and Jake wanted one like it. Sometime back, he had checked with the company and none were available, so he would either have to wait for delivery or settle for some other type airplane.

Red told Jake about a fellow in Dallas who had a Fairchild model 24 for sale. The F24w high-wing monoplane carried three passengers with a reputation of being a very stable airplane. This one had the 145 horsepower Warner engine called the Super-Scarab. Jake preferred this version to the one with the inverted Ranger R-690 engine.

Jake arrived in Dallas a little before noon in his newly acquired Lincoln Phaeton. Dallas was only about a two-hour drive from the Flying M if he would have kicked the Phaeton up to a mile-a-minute, but Jake took it slow and easy enjoying the drive across the North Texas flatlands.

He picked up Red at his folk's house near White Rock Lake in east Dallas and drove over to Love Field to meet the man selling the Fairchild. The plane was fairly new, but had a lot of flying hours on it and patches where some minor hail damage to the fabric covering had been repaired.

"Looks to me like she's been rode hard and put up wet," Jake commented after looking over the plane.

The pilot showing him the Fairchild laughed.

"May be, but I think she's a pretty good airplane. Owner bought a new Lockheed Vega and left the Fairchild here for me to sell. You might feel better about the plane if we took her out for a test flight."

"Great idea. Let's go!" Jake replied enthusiastically.

Red climbed in the back. The pilot took the left seat and Jake got in the right.

"I'll do the takeoff," the pilot said to Jake, "and then you can take her around the pattern a couple of times."

When they returned, Jake admitted, "I like the plane pretty well."

Red seated himself uncomfortably on some aircraft parts boxes and waited as Jake went over the Fairchild again.

"What do you think, Red?" Jake finally asked.

Red had been hawking every local airport, charter operation and airline office since they left flight school trying to get a job as a pilot. He was well acquainted with the local airstrips and the aircraft on them.

"Jake, I've checked out every airplane for sale at every airstrip in the area. Irving, Garland, North Dallas, Meacham Field, South Fort Worth, Haltom City and Mangham. This is the best deal I've found."

Jake paced back and forth for a bit.

"Hell Jake, your mind's already made up. Just pay the man and let's go get something to eat."

Thus, Jake became the proud owner of a bright yellow Fairchild model 24 and his new trust fund bank account decreased by two thousand, three hundred dollars.

In 1917, Love Field had been an Army training station for the war in Europe and operated in conjunction with Camp Dick, the Army post at Fair Park. More recently, Love Field had become the center of aviation activities for Dallas. On the northeast side of Love Field, next to the hangar where Jake bought the Fairchild were two more large wooden hangars.

One of the hangars served as home base for an aircraft operation called Texas Air Service. The owner of TAS had some extra aircraft storage space in the hangar, which he rented out to private aircraft owners. The operator, a man named Toots Warlick, allowed the pilots to work on their own airplanes in the hangar. Because of this, Jake arranged to hangar his newly acquired Fairchild at the TAS facility.

Jake rented an apartment on Mockingbird Lane a short ways from Love Field. He worked almost every day going completely through the Fairchild, overhauling the engine and repairing the damage to the fabric covering.

Jake removed all of the gages and indicators and took them to be calibrated at Eric Johnson's Texas instrument repair shop also located in the TAS hangar. Jake and Eric often got into long theoretical discussions about the future of air navigation or some new article in Popular Mechanics magazine.

Charley Armstrong, a pilot and mechanic at TAS, built racing planes in his spare time. He helped Jake restore the Fairchild to factory new condition.

Jake ordered a lot of parts for rebuilding the Fairchild and so he had his mail delivered to the hangar. A couple of letters a week arrived from Sarah in Austin and he wrote back to her on a regular basis.

With the Fairchild reassembled and flyable, but not completely finished, Jake took the plane on a test flight over to Meacham Field and stopped in at American Flyers to visit with Allen and Ted. When he saw Tinker out in the hangar, he asked about Elsa.

"Not sure, Jake," Tinker sighed and scratched his head. "She just didn't show up for work one day. Somebody said she took off to Mexico with that bootlegger boyfriend of hers."

After the test flight, Charley helped Jake paint the Fairchild a solid light gray. Then they added a gold lightening bolt down both sides of the plane starting at the engine cowl and running all the way to the tail. For a finishing touch, a silver winged letter M was superimposed on the gold stripe midway down the fuselage on both sides. Black pin striping accented the gold lightening stripe and the flying M logo.

The Fairchild was ready for cross-country flying by late fall and Jake flew it home to the ranch for Thanksgiving. He put some permanent iron tie-down stakes in the ground over by the oak trees in what he now jokingly referred to as Waldo Airfield.

Late Thanksgiving afternoon, a blue-norther rolled in and Jake wanted to get his plane back to Dallas before he got weathered-in.

***

With the Fairchild fully restored, Jake decided the Lincoln Phaeton also needed a paint job, anything except the ever-popular black the color of choice on most coachbuilt cars of the era. Using the paint shop at the hangar, he and Charley painted the body battleship gray and the fenders a contrasting midnight blue.

The Phaeton went next to a custom saddle-maker's shop where two skilled Mexican craftsmen installed soft hand-tooled, tan leather upholstery on the seats and a new tan canvas top. The finishing touch was the mounting of six new General wide whitewall tires on the car. All of which made the large car even more strikingly impressive.

Jake drove the Phaeton home for Christmas, as the weather was too bad for flying. Big Jake and Flo were always glad to have Jake spend some time at home. He only saw Sarah one day before she left with her family to go visit kinfolk in Oklahoma City. Big Jake had told Travis he needed to take some time off from the ranch and Sarah's mother finally convinced him.

When Jake came home on visits, Flo would ask him to tell her all about all the things he had been doing.

"The doings in Dallas," she called them.

Mostly, Jake told her flying stories he had heard around the hangar about one shenanigan or another some dumb pilot had pulled. Flo loved to laugh and was always amused at Jake's long-winded stories.

Big Jake carried a small notebook with a tooled, brown leather cover and a Parker fountain pen in his shirt pocket. Throughout the year, he made notes as to who he had advanced a few bucks cash against next year's crop or who he had staked to a couple of sacks of seed. In the same book, he also kept a list of who had been widowed and who in town had come on hard times. From this second list, Big Jake made up his annual Christmas list.

When Jake was younger, he had always looked forward to going with his dad on the annual Christmas run, but for the last several years, he had not gone along.

After breakfast on Christmas Eve morning, Big Jake left the house to go get one of the ranch trucks. When he drove past the front of the house on his way to Sittler's General Store, Jake came out the front door and flagged him down. Jake knew without asking where his dad was headed and jumped in the truck with him.

At the store, Mr. Sittler had saved back some boxes for Big Jake. With his notebook in hand, Big Jake took each box and walked around the store adding certain items to the boxes. When Big Jake finished with a box and sat it down, Mr. Sittler knew to add a can of shortening, a large bag of beans, two slabs of salt pork, baking powder and some hard candies.

Jake loaded the boxes and a dozen large print sacks of flour into the truck.

Big Jake shook Sittler's hand as they were leaving.

"I want to wish you and your family a Merry Christmas. Have a wonderful holiday and thanks again for the help."

"Well, we made it through another year. That's something. Merry Christmas to you and Flo! You too, Little Jake, good to see you again."

Sittler stood in the open front door of the store and waved as they drove off down Main Street.

Their first stops were in the poorer part of town. Some called it colored town and others called it shantytown. Jake and his father never referred to that part of town in those terms. They dropped off boxes at widows' houses, an old black man's house, an injured worker's house and a home where a Mexican lady had taken in three orphan children.

Jake lost count as they made their calls, one by one, until Big Jake's list for that part of town was done. Then they headed out to the countryside making a couple of stops along the way and finally turning onto the road to the Washington's place. Judging from what remained in the truck, Jake figured this would be their last stop.

Zack's dad had not had a good year. The weather had been dry at the beginning of cotton planting and had rained when the cotton bolled ready to pick. Nearly the whole cotton crop had been lost.

When they pulled up in front of the Washington's place, Jake took one of the last two boxes out of the truck and carried it to the house. Big Jake reached for a smaller box Flo had sent along containing two pies, a cake and some other goodies she had baked especially for the Washingtons.

Mrs. Washington opened the door and invited them into the house. Jake sat the box on the kitchen table in the main living area of the small house while Big Jake and Zack's dad visited about last year's crop.

"Not to worry, Benjamin," Big Jake reassured the old Negro farmer. "There'll be cottonseed for you to start over again this spring. I'll see to it."

Zack went with Jake back out to the truck to get the remaining box and a large sack of flour. Zack hoisted the sack of flour over his shoulder.

"Mama is gonna like the calico print on this here flour sack. She'll make a Sunday dress out of it for sure."

Zack steadied himself as he and Jake walked together up to the porch. Jake sat his box down on the porch and helped Zack lower the heavy sack of flour. The two then sat down on the porch steps.

"You know, Jake, I've been thinkin' about joinin' the Navy and I sure does need your advice on the matter."

"There ain't much opportunity for a black guy around these parts and I've been hearin' lots of good stuff about the Navy. They'll take young fellas like me to serve as stewards onboard some of those bigger ships."

"Zack, I don't know much about the Navy except what I've read, but one of my flight instructors served in the Navy and he seemed to like it alright."

"They sure does make it look good. Them recruiting posters say 'Join the Navy and See the World' and shows a picture of a beautiful tropical island in the background."

"You got that right," Jake said to Zack, but thinking more about his own ambitions.

"Kinda been thinkin' I might get a better deal of the cards in the Navy. What does you think, Jake?"

Jake pondered Zack's question for a moment.

"Don't sound like too bad an idea to me neither, specially when all you got to look forward to here is a lifetime of choppin' cotton. I feel the same way you do, but I don't guess a battleship is the life for me."

Big Jake came out the door with Mrs. Washington.

"Bless you, Mr. Martin. We appreciates all you and Mrs. Flo does, thinkin' of us this time of year and all."

Jake got up to leave with his dad.

"See you, Zack."

Zack lifted the flour sack on his shoulder to carry it in the house.

"See ya, Jake."

***

Toots Warlick contracted with several of the banks in Dallas for Texas Air Service to fly canceled checks to surrounding cities like Little Rock and San Antonio. This had proved cost effective for the banks because the faster they processed the checks through the clearinghouses, the better their cash flow. TAS also had a contract to carry some of the overflow airmail to outlying small towns.

Warlick purchased two single-engine Alphas from TWA to meet the terms of the contracts. The Alpha was the open cockpit version of a powerful low-wing monoplane built in 1928 by Northrop. TWA was replacing these Alpha models with the newer Northrop Gamma models, which had enclosed canopies. A Northrop model similar to the ones TAS acquired, pioneered the first all-weather coast-to-coast airmail flights.

The Alpha had a large enclosed cargo area centered over the wing. Because of this, the cockpit had been positioned midway between the wing and the tail. The Alpha's conventional landing gear and large seven-hundred horsepower Wright Cyclone radial engine made it impossible to see forward over the nose during ground handling and also made the Alpha extremely hard to land.

TAS had two regular full time pilots, Tommy Harding and Charley who flew the airfreight routes at night. Tommy was a relatively low time pilot like Jake and Red.

Warlick needed extra pilots to fill in from time to time, so Jake and Red both got checked out in the Alphas and flew them part-time. Warlick paid Red a meager salary. Jake had his pay applied to the Fairchild's hangar rent. Red and Jake mainly took the flights to build their total flying time and to gain flight experience in high performance aircraft.

Charley, Jake's pilot-mechanic friend, started work on building a new speed racer using the plans from a Crosby Buchaneer. Charley had helped Jake rebuild the Fairchild and in turn, Jake was helping with the Buchaneer.

Jake had gone home to the ranch for a long weekend and the morning he arrived back at the TAS hangar, he found everyone in a solemn mood. Something was wrong.

Red, who had just returned from the night Tulsa run, met Jake as he came in.

"It's Tommy Harding. His return flight from Texarkana last night didn't make it back. They found the wreckage of his airplane early this morning over near Caddo Lake."

"What happened? Tommy was an excellent pilot. Was the weather bad?" Jake asked.

"No, the weather was fine all night. I didn't see a cloud in the sky coming back from Oklahoma. No one knows for sure what happened, but suspicions are he fell asleep. He'd been working a lot of hours to make some extra money. You know his wife just had a new baby?"

Jake shook his head no. "Damn!" he mumbled and stood looking down at the floor. After a moment, Jake turned and went over to the half-built Buchaneer, opened his toolbox and went to work.

Red thought he saw Jake wipe his eyes with a shop rag, but could not be certain.

***

Sarah stayed in the girl's dormitory on the campus at the University of Texas, but had pledged a sorority. Weekend activities, including a formal dance, were planned for the new pledges and Sarah wrote Jake a letter asking him to be her escort.

Jake was honored Sarah asked him and agreed to go down for the weekend. He flew the Fairchild to Austin and got a ride from the airport to the campus where Sarah had arranged for him to be a guest at the Sigma Chi house.

The evening Jake and Sarah attended the formal dance sponsored by the sororities, Jake felt out of place and uncomfortable. He did not identify with Sarah's new lifestyle and did not care for her new circle of college friends, but he made the best of the situation.

Jake was to attend church with Sarah on Sunday morning and attend another function that afternoon. Instead, early that morning Jake took a taxicab to the airport and departed in the Fairchild before sunrise.

He left Sarah a note apologizing for his leaving early and wrote to her later saying he would probably not be visiting her at the university again. He would try to get home to see her when she came home on holidays and wished her all the best at college.

Sarah did not write to Jake as often after that weekend. She lived a different lifestyle and ran in a different social set than Jake. Whenever Sarah did go out on a date to a dance or a social event, she would write and explain to Jake that she was not dating anyone on a regular basis.

Flo thought of Sarah like a daughter and always assumed she and Jake would marry someday. Flo and Sarah occasionally exchanged letters. Flo received a letter from Sarah after the weekend incident saying she continued to hold out hope she and Jake might eventually get together, but for now it seemed like yet another obstacle had come between her and Jake.

Jake always answered Sarah's letters, but his were shorter and less informative. Sarah involved with her schoolwork and sorority, Jake with flying and his new life in Dallas. Neither Sarah nor Jake intended for them to drift apart, but they were.

Jake called Sarah one night at college and they agreed they were not going steady, but someday they might become engaged. Sarah was not pleased she had to talk to Jake about the matter on the pay phone in the dorm lobby with her friends listening.

The last letter Jake received from Sarah was delivered along with another letter postmarked San Diego. Zack wrote to let Jake know he had joined the Navy and would write again after he was assigned to one of the ships in the Pacific Fleet.

Jake tried dating other girls. He went out with a couple of different waitresses, but nothing ever came of the relationships. A nurse he met and dated was great in bed, but Jake thought she had a personality like an icicle and soon lost interest in her.

***

Lawrence Wilcox, the son of the Martin Company's attorney, attended law school at Southern Methodist University in Dallas. Jake looked him up and they became friends. Lawrence went by Larry to his friends and liked to pal around with Jake and Red on weekends. The trio fancied themselves the Three Musketeers, but might better have been characterized as the Marx Brothers based on their antics.

The trio frequented a string of upscale bars along Lemmon Avenue, but their favorite hangout was down on East Elm Street. The locals referred to this wide-open section of downtown full of second-hand stores, pawnshops and saloons as Deep Ellum.

The patrons of the bars in the area were mostly blue-collar workers, hard working and hard drinking men and women. They worked at the railroad yards, the Ford factory and out at the limestone quarry on Chalk Hill.

Modern times had left the bars along Deep Ellum frozen in time. Some of the old rundown bars were right out of a western movie complete with wooden plank floors, mahogany liquor cabinets and large mirrors on the wall behind the bar.

There was never a shortage of excitement down on Deep Ellum, especially on a Saturday night. Larry and Red liked to go to a cut-n-shoot old bar called the Buckhorn Tavern. The place had a large dance floor and a western swing band played there on weekends.

A fellow named George Blessie owned the Buckhorn, but for obvious reasons, everyone called him Buck. Girls in full skirts and high-heel shoes with ribbons tied around their ankles frequented the Buckhorn. The girls were shills who worked on commission. Buck did not allow any freelance hookers in the place. Seldom did nice girls come into the Buckhorn, except for an occasional small group of co-eds who were slumming and they never stayed very long.

The shills would flirt with the men in order to get them to buy another drink and order a whiskey or champagne for the girl. The drinks served to the gentlemen's temporary companion were not liquor at all, but ice tea or a watered-down Coke. Buck paid the girls off at half the price of girl's drinks at the end of the night. Any tips the girls received were theirs to keep.

Larry and Red always managed to drink a little too much on these outings. Jake, not being much of a drinker, always did the driving and saw that his two pals got home safely. Red and Larry were in no danger of getting rolled, as neither carried much money and Jake usually picked up the bar tab at the end of the evening anyway.

Most evenings, Jake usually nursed one beer for several rounds. He liked to sit where he could watch the bar patrons and girls at a table in the corner with an old fellow by the name of Dean Earhart. Dean took a liking to Jake and asked him a lot of questions about flying.

Dean ran a loan shark operation out of his wallet. He always sat at the same table at the saloon, called it his office. Ol' Dean had been a dogface pony soldier with General Pershing's cavalry and his best stories were of his days on the Mexican boarder.

"Me and a couple hundred other horse soldiers chased that bastard Pancho Villa all over south Texas and half of Mexico," Dean began. "We would ride into a town and ask the peons, which way did he go? They'd all point in one direction. We, of course, would take off in the opposite direction because we knew they would all lie through their teeth for ol' Pancho."

So it went on any average Saturday night down at the Buckhorn Tavern on Deep Ellum until along about two in the morning when Buck paid off the girls and ran the rest of the drunks out of the place, which usually included Jake, Larry and Red.

***

On a late winter morning in early 1933, Jake returned from a fight to Abilene where he delivered some parts for a broke down oilrig. The flight had been a rough one with bad weather enroute most of the way.

Earlier that week he had blown a tire landing in the Fairchild and busted a wheel bearing. The Fairchild was down awaiting replacement parts.

Charley had been having problems with the fuel system on the Buchaneer and Jake was helping him fix it when someone yelled out into the hangar for him.

"Jake, you got a phone call in the office."

Jake went to take the call.

"Jacob, I'm sorry to have to call you at work. It's about your dog."

"I know, Mom. Ol' Prince is nearly deaf now. Is he sick or something?"

"It's worse than that, Jacob. He wondered onto the railroad tracks during the night and got hit by the train. I doubt he ever heard it coming."

Jake visited with his mother for a few more minutes, thanked her for calling and hung up the phone. He went back to work helping Charley and cut one of his hands pretty bad on a piece of jagged aluminum.

"Son of a..." Jake howled and threw the tin-snips clear across the hangar. Jake wrapped his bleeding hand up with his handkerchief, gathered up his tools and threw them in the toolbox.

"Charley, I'm beat. I'll give you a hand later in the week, but I'm out of here for now."

"Sure, I understand. I've had a few days like that myself. Take it easy, Jake. See you when you're feeling better."

Usually, Jake did not go down to Deep Ellum during the week, but this afternoon he intended to make an exception.

When he got there, he ordered a beer from the bar. The girls did not bother Jake about drinks. He was a regular and had a reputation for leaving a nice tip when he left.

Jake went over to sit with Dean seated at his usual table. Jake sat quietly watching as Dean made a couple of twenty dollar loans, carefully explaining to each of his clients that they had thirty days to pay back twice the amount they borrowed.

"Most people come by to pay on the weekends when they get paid," Dean explained making casual conversation as he could tell Jake was upset about something. "Pretty dead around here during the week, huh Jake?"

Jake slumped over the table tearing at the label on the longneck beer bottle with his thumbnail.

"Yep."

Dean inserted a brown After The Acts cigarette into a holder and lit up.

Jake rocked back against the wall in his chair and the old wooden chair creaked.

"Who's the new girl working the bar? Never seen her in here before."

Dean finished writing down something in a small notebook as he held the cigarette holder between his teeth and cocked his head to keep the smoke out of his eyes.

"Oh, her. Buck's been letting her work days since she came on hard times after her husband got killed. Think her name's Julie. Has a kid that one of the night girls keeps for her during the day."

In a while, Julie came over and laid five one-dollar bills and some change on the table.

"You'll have to take this. It's all I can come up with for now."

Dean looked at the money.

"Honey, I advanced you fifty dollars. I can give you a little more time, but you got to do better than this."

Julie forced back her tears.

"I can't make what the night girls do and I can't work nights. You know, the kid. I have to take care of my little boy at night. Ever since Tommy got killed, things have been real rough, Mr. Earhart."

Jake looked directly at Dean and when he caught Dean's eye, he very casually shook his head no.

Dean looked past Julie at Jake with a questioning stare and then nodded casually indicating he understood Jake had a problem with what was going on.

"Tell you what Julie, we'll talk about it later."

"Thank you Mr. Earhart," and she turned away to go back to work.

"Was Julie married to Tommy Harding, the guy that got killed in a plane crash?" Jake asked.

"Yeah, I guess so. Her married name is Harding and her husband got killed a while back, but I hadn't heard how."

Red came through the door and came over to the table where Dean and Jake were sitting.

"Been looking all over for you, Jake. You never come down here during the week. What's going on?"

"Aw, nothing much, Red, just having a bad day."

Jake stood up from the table.

"Wait here for me, Red, will ya? I may need you to do me a favor in a little bit."

Red pulled a chair up to Dean's table and sat down.

Jake went to the end of the long bar where Julie stood waiting for her next mark. He took her by the arm and walked her over to the far side of the empty dance hall where no one could hear them as they spoke.

Red and Dean watched from across the room.

In a few minutes, Julie started to cry.

"What the hell's he doing to that girl?" Dean said.

Red shrugged his shoulders.

"Never known Jake to ever be rude to a woman?"

Suddenly, Julie's face lit up with a big smile and she shook her head yes several times. She leaped at Jake and gave him a big hug around the neck.

Jake came back to Dean's table and sat down beside Red. He reached in his hip pocket and took out his wallet.

"How much does she owe you, Dean?"

Being a little worldlier than his young guest seated at the table, Dean had already figured it out as he watched Jake and Julie from across the room.

"She owes a hundred, but I've already marked it off as a bad debt. If you're gonna pay it for her, the fifty she originally borrowed will be fine."

Jake counted out the fifty and laid it on the table.

"Thanks, the next couple dozen rounds are on me."

Jake handed the keys to the Phaeton to Red.

"Use my car and take Julie to get her kid and her things, then take her to the bus station downtown. She says her folks in Louisiana will take her in, but she hasn't been able to raise enough money to get home. Put her on the next bus to Baton Rouge, but stay with her till she gets on then give her this money."

Jake handed Red some folded up bills.

"Could you do that for me, Red?"

Red looked at the keys and the money.

"Sure Jake, glad to, but why don't you take her? I mean I don't mind, but what are you going to do?"

"Tell you what I'm going to do my fine red-headed friend," Jake said turning towards the bar. "I'm going to get stumbling, falling down, pie-eyed drunk and you can come back and get me when Buck closes up tonight."

***

A few weeks went by. Jake was under the Buchaneer helping Charley re-route the brake cables from the cockpit. Charley had test flown the plane the day before and the brakes were grabbing. The two talked as they worked.

"I kid you not, Jake. On the last flight, I hit an indicated airspeed of two-eighty or more in level flight and I wasn't even at full throttle yet."

"Yeah, aviation technology is really advancing fast."

"Only war has ever advanced aviation faster then air racing!"

Warlick came over to the Buchaneer with two men.

"Jake, you need to come out from under there. A couple of pilot friends of mine would like to see you."

Jake crawled out from under the Buchaneer and wiped his hands on a shop rag to shake hands with the two men. Jake had never seen them before, but he recognized their airline uniforms.

"Glad to meet anyone ol' Toots calls friend. What'd you want to see me about?"

"These fellows have got something they want to give you," Warlick said introducing Jake to the two pilots and stepped aside.

The younger of the two pilots pinned a small lapel button on Jake's shirt collar.

"Let's just say it has something to do with the Harding girl," the older pilot said to Jake.

Jake looked down at the small pin with the initials QB on it.

Both of the pilots congratulated Jake.

"Good to have you with us, we'll be in touch," the older pilot said and the two turned and left.

Charley and Warlick had stood quietly watching the proceedings. Charley smiled, "You don't even know what it is, do you?"

Jake looked questioningly at Charley and shook his head no.

"Stands for Quiet Birdmen. Pilots taking care of their own, that kind of thing. You may not know it, but the QB is a real honor. Don't think I ever heard of them giving it to anyone as young as you before."

***

Bob Wills and the Texas Playboys were playing at the Trianon Ballroom down on Industrial Boulevard. This guaranteed the joint would be jumping and was the intended destination of the trio on this particular Saturday night.

They stopped for an early supper at Sammy's Diner on Turtle Creek Road where the best Hot Shot, an open face hot roast beef sandwich with mashed potatoes and brown gravy, in town was served.

Red, intent on promoting an idea he had, explained, "Sure, we'll get to the Trianon before the night's over, but I'm telling you, we need to go see about these hookers this guy told me about."

"I'm staying out of this discussion," Larry said.

"I know this guy who told me they're movie star look-a-likes and play the role for you. I've never been with a prostitute before and I'd sure like to try."

"Just where are we supposed to find these professional working girls?" Jake asked, speaking with his mouth full.

"Over at the Stoneleigh Hotel or at least that's what this guy told me."

"I'm not sure that's an altogether good idea, Red."

"Come on, Jake, let's at least go check it out."

Jake seriously considered it for a few minutes.

"Nah, that's trouble waiting to happen. Let's go on down to the Trianon like we planned."

"Maybe you're right, Jake. Life is, after all, only a series of good and bad decisions, isn't it?"

"Yeah, you never know when you make a good decision," Larry added, "but you sure as hell know when you've made a bad one!"

The three sat for a while in their booth at the diner and played can-you-top-this, each telling the funniest story or the latest joke they had heard recently.

***

The last hurrah of the three young men in Dallas came on the weekend before Larry graduated from law school. Jake and Red picked Larry up at SMU for their usual Saturday night on the town.

Red had a new plan for the night's entertainment. Just across the Trinity River Bridge on Highway 80, on the main road between Fort Worth and Dallas, was an upscale nightclub. The club and casino, an illegal gambling establishment, had operated for years in a wooded site near the river in Oak Cliff.

The trio arrived at the casino and parked the Phaeton in the middle of the crowded gravel parking lot. As they entered the club, a fella about the size of a tree and who talked out of the side of his mouth, greeted them at the door.

"Diz's a gentlemen's club. Yous can't go in without a dress tie on."

Properly attired in neckties furnished by the hatcheck girl, the trio was admitted to the casino. Larry and Red headed for the bar, but Jake wanted to try his hand at the crap table. He had a long held theory about doubling his bet when he won and staying when he lost.

Red went straight for a tough looking bleached blonde in a short white cocktail dress perched on a bar stool with her legs crossed. He soon engaged her in conversation.

Larry got involved in a lengthy discussion with a couple of well-known local attorneys he recognized.

The casino and club operated for years with Dallas law officers looking the other way, but that era was about to come to an end. Dallas County had recently elected a tough new sheriff, Bill Decker. He was a Thompson sub-machinegun-toting gangbusters-kind-of-a-cop cut from the same mold as a modern G-man.

Prohibition had been repealed and Decker had already shut down most of the illegal booze operations. He now intended to do the same to the illegal gambling joints in the county.

Jake was still at the crap table when all the houselights came on full bright. Several women screamed as a couple of dozen Dallas County deputy sheriffs came busting through the front, back and side doors. Patrons ran for the exits, but were promptly ushered back into the casino by more uniformed officers.

One by one, each of the club patrons were asked for their identification. The trio stood quietly against a hallway wall waiting their turn to be hassled.

"Did you see that? The coppers showed several of those people to the side door and let them leave."

"You mean escorted, don't you, Red?" Larry whispered sarcastically. "I recognized that one guy. He's a Dallas city councilman and I'll bet that young bimbo with him isn't his wife either."

Decker came over to Jake. "Let's see some identification, young man." He looked at Jake's ID and looked Jake straight in the eye. "Jacob Teel Martin it says here. That you?"

Jake nodded his head yes.

"I know a Big Jake Martin. He's a rancher up north of here, fine gentleman."

Jake hesitantly replied, "Yes, sir, that's my dad."

Decker held Jake's ID up in front of Jake's face, looked sternly into Jake's eyes and handed it back to him between two fingers.

"So you're Big Jake's son. Little young to be in a gambling establishment, aren't you?"

Jake took his ID from Sheriff Decker.

"I'll be twenty-one in July, sir."

Decker glanced at Red and Larry, then back at Jake.

"These two, they friends of yours?"

"Yes, sir, they're my best friends. We came here together tonight."

Decker walked away without saying anything else.

In a couple of minutes, two deputies grabbed Jake, Larry and Red by the arms and ushered them to a side door. The two large deputies gave the three a good hard shove and pushed them out the door.

The door slammed behind them and they found themselves standing outside the casino. There sat Jake's Phaeton right where they left it in the middle of the now nearly empty parking lot. The three looked at each other and no one needed to yell run!

Jake loosened his borrowed tie, pulled it off over his head and threw it high in the air as he ran. Larry, right on Jake's heels, followed suit but dropped his tie casually on the ground as he ran. The top was down on the Phaeton. Jake jumped behind the wheel and Larry went into the shotgun seat. Neither bothered to use the car doors. Red did a swan dive into the backseat.

Jake looked over his shoulder to back out of the parking lot and saw Red folding his borrowed tie neatly.

"What ya want that tie for?"

Red stood up to stick the tie in his pocket.

"It's now officially my lucky tie. Besides, I kinda like it."

Jake shifted from reverse into low forward gear and pitched Red down into the back seat as he tore out of the parking lot and onto Highway 80, throwing gravel and raising a cloud of dust all the way to the pavement.

As he drove off into the night, Jake recalled something he had read in Shakespeare. 'Oh what a tangled web we weave when first we practice to deceive' and then he wondered where this winding road of life was about to lead him next.

Century of Progress

On Sunday afternoon, the day after the casino incident, Jake sat in his apartment reflecting back on recent events. Larry was engaged to a girl back in Wichita Falls. He would be getting married soon and joining his father's law firm. Red was about to be hired as a full time pilot for one of the new startup airlines.

Based on the recent episode at the Oak Cliff Casino and the night he had almost gotten himself talked into going to a hotel of ill repute, it might be wiser to approach life with a more serious agenda. He was not quite ready to head back to the ranch. There were a couple of things he planned on doing and now seemed as good a time as any.

Jake let his landlord know he was leaving, loaded what personal belongings he had into the Phaeton and drove over to the Texas Air Service hangar. Everyone had left for the day. Jake pushed the Fairchild out of the hangar onto the ramp, drove the Phaeton into the hangar and parked it in the spot normally reserved for the Fairchild.

The beautiful starlit evening lit up the summer sky as he went about topping off the fuel tanks with gas, checking the oil and giving the plane a thorough preflight inspection. He got his suitcases out of the back seat of the Phaeton and carried them out to the plane.

Jake took his flight case, charts and some navigation tools out of the plane and went into the TAS office. He cleared off one of the desktops and spent the next several hours going over charts as he planned his first solo cross-country flight into the Midwestern U.S. He fell asleep at the desk in the early morning hours.

The city of Chicago, founded in 1833, was in the process of celebrating its 100th anniversary with a yearlong celebration and world's fair called the Century of Progress Exposition. Jake had heard about the Exposition and wanted to go to Chicago to see the event. He had also planned to take a long cross-country flight in the Fairchild and flying to the Expo would achieve both of those goals.

Chicago was over a thousand miles from Dallas and would be the farthest flight he had undertaken so far in his flying career. Flying such a distance cross-country over unfamiliar landmarks would not be easy. There were few navigation aids and weather information would be sketchy due to the great distances between reporting stations.

Only three years earlier the first woman, one Laura Ingall, had flown solo coast to coast in a Moth biplane from Roosevelt Field in New York to Glendale in California. The flight took her thirty hours and she made nine re-fueling stops on the way. Amelia Earhart became the first woman to fly across the Atlantic solo only last year. Long distance flying still posed many risks to plane and pilot.

***

Just before dawn, Jake rolled down the Love Field runway in his Fairchild, turned northeast and set a course for eastern Oklahoma. Three hours later, he landed at the Tulsa Municipal airport and taxied up to the fueling tank. Jake cut the engine and climbed out of the Fairchild. With the sun up, the day was growing warmer. Jake took off his leather jacket and threw it in the back seat.

He still had fuel remaining in the Fairchild, but two cups of coffee and an orange juice mandated a short stop. Besides, if he ran into bad weather, he did not want to run short on fuel.

Jake was familiar with the route so far as he had flown into the Tulsa airport in the Northrop Alpha several times and had even gotten to know the base operator.

The gas boy came over to the Fairchild.

"Not flying the Alpha today, huh Jake? Fill'er up?"

"No, this one's my own plane. She and I decided to take a little vacation. Sure, top off both tanks, but don't check the oil. I'll do that myself."

Just across the fueling pad sat a sleek, shiny new all aluminum cabin monoplane being checked out by the pilot. Jake went over to admire the plane.

"Good morning, I'm Jake Martin. Nice looking airplane you got here."

"Yes sir, good morning to you, too. I'm the test pilot for Spartan Aircraft Company across the runway."

"Quite a sleek design and all metal, too. What is it?"

"It's our newest prototype, still in the experimental stage. Go ahead, you're welcome to look her over."

Jake ran his hand along the leading edge of the wing and bent down to look at the undercarriage.

"Retractable landing gear," Jake commented. "When do you expect to get this model into production?"

The test pilot finished fastening the engine cowl on the Spartan and replied, "Looks like it will be at least a year minimum. We're always looking for prospective buyers though. Better get your order in soon if you want one of the early models."

The gas boy finished fueling the Fairchild and removed the stepladder. Jake paid for the fuel and checked the engine oil. The engine burned very little oil and Jake was pleased with that.

Jake taxied to the east-west Tulsa runway. Holding slight brake while he taxied, he did a quick mag check and made a rolling takeoff as he turned onto the runway.

Climbing out, Jake set a course for Springfield, Illinois. Today he had one of those rare phenomena called a tail wind. The Fairchild droned on performing its required duties without the slightest whimper making its way steadily along above the moving landscape far below.

That afternoon, Jake landed at the Capital City Airport north of Springfield. He could have made it on to Chicago by dark with no problem, but he wanted to arrive over Chicago during daylight hours.

The Springfield airport terminal had a small café so Jake enjoyed a good meal served up by a rather pleasant and talkative older lady. Jake hiked back to his plane tied down out on the grass field with some other airplanes.

Tonight he would sleep under the stars. He got his bedroll out of the plane and bedded down under the wing of the Fairchild. In the morning, he planned to fly over Meigs Island and along the Chicago lakefront where the Century of Progress celebration was being held. The trip would be his own personal air tour of the event. He fell asleep counting the shooting stars.

***

Airborne the following morning and a short two-hour flight late, Jake's excitement grew as he came in over the sprawling city of Chicago. He circled out over Lake Michigan and flew down the shoreline to Meigs Island. He saw several seaplanes along the lakeshore, the Sky Ride entrance across the yacht basin and had a bird's-eye view of a giant dirigible airship moored to a tower.

From there, Jake flew back over the city to the Chicago Municipal Airport about ten miles from Meigs Island. He landed and made arrangements to park the Fairchild there for several days.

Ben O. Howard was building airplanes on the ground floor of an old apartment building across the street from the main Chicago airport. Howard had been very successful with his two planes, the Ike and the Mike, in the National Air Races.

Jake was considering placing an order for one of Howard's new planes and Charley had suggested he look Ben up. Jake corresponded by mail earlier with Ben and he was pleased Jake stopped by to see him.

Ben showed Jake the plans and the beginnings of the new airframe, a large high-wing cabin monoplane. Ben intended to call it the Mr. Mulligan and enter it in the 1935 Bendix Trophy Air Races. Jake particularly liked the powerful five hundred horsepower Wasp engine intended for use in the plane.

Jake caught a bus from the airport to the main downtown entrance to the Century of Progress Exposition on Meigs Island. He headed straight for the Hall of Science pavilion and was so impressed he spent the rest of the day at the one exhibit. The concept demonstrating a new broadcast media called television fascinated him.

The Expo continued into the evening, but Jake was tired and needed a shower. He took a taxicab to the Palmer House Hotel where he intended to book a room, but went into the Harvey House restaurant at the main railway station to have dinner first.

Jake finished dinner and had ordered a coffee when he heard a very distinctive and familiar sounding laugh coming from nearby. He knew that laugh, but here in Chicago?

Curiosity got the best of him. He stood up and looked around the dining room. There sat Elsa Bowles at a table with two other girls.

Jake went over to the table.

"What in the world are you doing in Chicago, Elsa?"

Elsa was so surprised for a moment she could not speak. Then she jumped up and hugged Jake's neck.

"I was born here, you cad! The question is what are you doing here?"

"Looking for you," Jake replied jokingly.

"You silver-tongued phony," Elsa said and hugged Jake's neck again.

Elsa always wore a lot of costume jewelry and her necklace got caught on Jake's sweater. They laughed as Jake untangled them.

Elsa turned to her friends seated at the table.

"Look what the cat drug in," and she introduced Jake to her friends.

Elsa and her two friends invited Jake to join them as he hoped they would. Typically the lone-eagle, Jake was still pleased to find a familiar face in the crowd.

Casual conversation ensued over another round of coffees. In a short while, Elsa's friends politely excused themselves saying they needed to get on to the YWCA where they were staying before curfew. Jake insisted on picking up the two working girls' check and they let him. They thanked him as they left and Jake sat back down with Elsa.

"What happened to Dutch? Tinker told me he heard you two had lit out for Mexico."

Elsa laughed.

"New Mexico, Jake, New Mexico! Oh, we split the sheets in Albuquerque and I came home to Chicago. Probably for the best, Dutch was trouble waiting to happen anyway."

Elsa, with her elbows on the table and her face in her hands, stared admiringly at Jake as they talked.

"You're a sight for sore eyes, Jake Martin. How long are you going to be here and where are you staying?"

Jake watched Elsa's lips as she talked. She had the prettiest shaped lips of any woman he had ever known.

"I'm bumming around the country in a plane I bought. I planned on trying the Palmer, but I'll bet they're booked solid with the expo in town."

"I was hoping for something like that. Of course, you'll stay with me. My apartment's only a short walk from here. Let's go!"

Elsa's ankle strap high-heel shoes and Jake's long stride caused her to hold onto Jake's arm as they walked. She was a very attractive lady and Jake had thought about Elsa a hundred times since the night they spent together back in Fort Worth.

"You don't mind being seen with an older woman, do you Jake?"

Jake looked down into Elsa's smiling face.

"Don't guess I know how old you are, Elsa. You always seemed like the youngest one in the room to me, the life of the party."

Elsa skipped a couple of steps when Jake said that and she held onto Jake's arm even tighter.

"Let's just say I'm pushing twenty-nine real hard. Anyway, how old are you Jake?"

Jake thought for a moment. "Let's see. What is today?"

"The twenty-eighth. Why?"

"Dad-gum, now that you mention it, I turned twenty-one on the flight up here. How about that?"

"At least now I can't be accused of robbing the cradle!" Elsa remarked smugly. "Here, this is my place," and she pointed to a stairway entrance door.

Elsa's upstairs apartment had been converted from the second floor of a dry goods store. The place was spacious and well furnished, although nothing seemed to match.

She delighted in showing Jake around.

"I decorated it myself, call it early depression. Things don't have to match. If I like them, I just buy them. I get a lot of stuff from secondhand stores and estate sales. How do you like it?"

Jake settled into an overstuffed couch with oriental upholstery and looked around.

"Fine, real nice."

"I'll fix us something to drink. What would you like?"

"Coke, if you got one."

"One Coke on ice coming up. See what you can get on the radio, some good music maybe."

Jake turned on the large, wooden cabinet model console radio and tuned it around looking for a good station.

"Listen to this. It's New Orleans coming in all the way up here in Chicago."

As Elsa returned from the kitchen, the announcer on the radio said, "You're listening to WWL Loyola University, voice of the south, a clear channel station," and the station returned to playing music.

Elsa took off her shoes and curled up on the other end of the couch folding her legs under her.

"I'll take a few days off work from my job at the insurance agency so we can go to the Exposition together."

"You can do that?" Jake asked.

"Sure. You think I what to miss a once in a lifetime chance to see the Expo and be with you at the same time?"

"Won't you lose your job for missing work?"

"No way, dearie!" Elsa giggled, "That old bald-headed boss of mine has had the hots for me ever since I went to work at that five-'n-dime insurance outfit. I won't get fired!"

"Yeah and if I know you, you're probably running the place by now anyway."

The two talked until the wee hours of the morning, laughing and recalling things that happened back at the flying school in Fort Worth and finally went to bed about two in the morning.

***

The Chicago city fathers conceived the Century of Progress Exposition to help people look to the future and hopefully put the depression era behind them.

The first airplane flights from Chicago originated from Grant Park. The water-soaked marshland on the lakeshore across from the downtown city park had been filled and transformed into an island for the world's fair. Meigs Island would be converted into an airport for the city after the event.

The Exposition's architecture emphasized the utilization of light for effect. A heavy emphasis was placed on energy as the salvation to mankind's future and a popular new art deco theme prevailed in design of the buildings throughout the fairgrounds.

Jake and Elsa had slept in most of the morning, but finally arrived at the yacht basin entrance to the Century of Progress around eleven and stood in line waiting for their turn to board the giant Sky Ride to the island.

A wide walk-bridge to enter the expo was located at the west end of the island. Jake had entered that way the day before, but Elsa insisted on riding the Sky Ride. Cables connected the Sky Ride between two 628-foot high suspension towers that dominated the landscape.

While they waited in line, a boy was selling souvenir brochures for seventy-five cents. Jake had given him a dollar for one and was reading it aloud. "It is the largest man-made structure west of New York City. Passengers are propelled high above the water in streamlined cable cars to the entrance of the park."

Jake had spent many hours in the air, but was a little uncomfortable in the cable car. He had a sudden sensation of height that he did not like and thought it odd he had never experienced acrophobia when flying in a plane.

Elsa, on the other hand, was absolutely thrilled with the breathtaking view of Chicago from the cabin window of the Sky Ride cable car.

Exiting the Sky Ride, they entered the park and strolled down the Esplanade of Flags. Behind the rows of giant red flags lay the Pavilions of Commerce.

Elsa turned and pointed upward.

"Look, Jake, an airship just lifted off. It's going to come right over the top of us."

Jake watched as the large craft floated overhead. Except for the muffled sound of its diesel engines, the craft moved silently across the sky above the exhibits.

"The Hall of Science is at the end of the Esplanade, but I spent all day there yesterday." Jake said.

"I'll make quick work of it because I'm anxious to see Chinatown," Elsa said hurrying on ahead.

Exiting the back of the Hall of Science, they went through the Oriental Pavilion and into the Chinese Temple.

"Look at the red pillars and the oriental murals surrounding the Buddha," Elsa exclaimed.

Jake handed Elsa a coin to place in the altar box in front of the massive statue of Buddha.

"Did you ask Buddha to grant you a wish?"

"Yes, but it won't come true!"

"What did you wish for?"

"Never mind. Maybe I'll tell you later."

"Oh," Jake said and he began to read to Elsa again from the brochure as they walked. "The building was completely constructed without any nails. The carvings are assembled from 28,000 small pieces of wood."

"When do we eat?" Elsa asked.

"You hungry?"

Elsa was always hungry and ate twice what Jake did, but she never seemed to gain a pound.

"Of course I'm hungry. We didn't have any breakfast. Where should we eat?"

Jake flagged down one of the people-haulers that moved up and down the wide streets between exhibits.

Jake asked the driver, "Where's a good place to have lunch?"

"The Pabst Blue Ribbon Café would be my choice, mate," the driver replied. "I go right by it."

Out front of the large Pabst's beer sign, they jumped off and went into the Café. They enjoyed a delightful lunch of authentic German food. Jake had a beer and Elsa had two.

They spent the rest of the day strolling around the park, stopping to look at whatever happened to draw their attention.

During their second day at the Expo, Jake booked a ride in a twin-engine Sikorsky SK-38 seaplane operated out of a dock on the lake. Pal-Waukee Aviation sold passenger rides in their *Carnauba Clipper* NC-6V and it would be Jake's first experience with a flying boat.

"It's an airplane ride and a speedboat ride all in one," Elsa exclaimed.

"Elsa, you're right! That's exactly what it's like."

That night, they stayed late at the Exposition and marveled at the mercury columns of neon bulbs towering hundreds of feet into the air and constantly changed colors like the Aurora Borealis.

***

Over the next several days, Jake and Elsa wandered through the many exhibits like the Firestone Building and strolled the stained glass hallways of the large Christian Science Monitor structure.

They enjoyed lunch in a café overlooking the beach on Lake Michigan. Jake tipped the maitre d' to get a window table overlooking the shoreline.

Parades of people in costumes roamed the boulevards. The Pavilion of Countries housed exhibits from Ancient Egypt to the Ukraine and the Great Wall of China.

When they visited the Travel and Transportation exhibit, Jake wanted to stay longer, but Elsa prodded him to hurry up so they could have dinner at the Cafe de la Paix on the Rotunda.

Elsa rested on a park bench while Jake went through the new Budd stainless steel, streamliner passenger train. He also toured the shiny, new silver aluminum Zephyr, which used a powerful diesel engine and ran faster and more efficiently than the massive old Baldwin steam locomotives Jake admired so much as a young boy.

They saved their final day at the Exposition for the World of a Million Years Ago, which featured roaring, hissing, giant mechanical dinosaurs. They rode all the rides twice and went through their favorite exhibits more than once.

Like most who attended the Century of Progress Exposition that year, their minds were boggled with thoughts of a world to come.

On the evenings they did not stay late at the Expo, Jake took Elsa to the best nightclubs in Chicago. Elsa had never been to most of them, but she knew where to find them all.

***

The night before Jake planned to leave, they returned to Elsa's apartment and Jake took Elsa in his arms.

"I know!" Elsa said, before Jake began to speak.

"I'm going to be heading back to Texas tomorrow. Weather looks good in that direction."

"That's what I pretty much expected. Going to make me a single woman again, huh Jake? I never could keep a man anyway," Elsa said trying to make a joke, but she did so with a certain sadness in her voice.

Elsa pulled away from Jake.

"Oh Jake! I never held out any real hope for a lasting relationship for us. Mostly, I only wanted to enjoy the time we had together, but somehow, I hoped it wouldn't be over this soon."

"Is that what you wished for at the Buddha?"

"Yes," she whimpered and used the sleeve of her white silk blouse to stop a tear from rolling down her cheek.

There might not be two people who got along better or enjoyed one another's company more than Jake and Elsa, but what were they to do? Not only were there ten or more years' difference in their ages, but also both knew they were not in love and more than likely never would be.

"Do you think you'll ever leave Chicago, maybe come back to Texas?" Jake asked.

She wiped the lipstick from Jake's lips with her thumb where she had kissed him.

"Nah, Chicago is my kind of town!" Elsa said and forced a smile.

Jake laughed and then Elsa laughed, too.

That night Jake could not sleep and neither could Elsa. Jake took Elsa in his arms and held her most of the night. The first rays of daylight shown on the windowsill under the faded yellow shades by the time Elsa finally went to sleep, but Jake never did.

As Jake prepared to leave, Elsa got up and walked to the door with him. They said goodbye at the top of the apartment stairs.

Elsa looked up at Jake and caressed his face.

"So long cowboy. See you around."

Jake would not have taken being called cowboy from anyone except Elsa.

He went down the stairs a few steps and paused to look back at Elsa standing in her lace rayon nightgown in the open apartment doorway. He raised his hand and half-heartedly waved goodbye.

"See ya, Elsa."

He turned to leave and did not look back again.

***

Jake took off from the Chicago airport, circled out over Lake Michigan to gain altitude and then came back over Chicago for one last look at the city down below. He set a course south by southeast for Dayton, Ohio, his next stop.

Dale Harkins, a student with Jake at American Flyers, was now in the Signal Corps and stationed at an airfield near Dayton. Jake contacted Dale before he left Chicago and obtained a clearance to land at the airfield to pay Dale a visit and tour the base.

To the west of the hill where the Wright brothers made their first glider tests was an Army Air Corps airfield. The Testing Division of the Army Corps of Engineers from old McCook Field had been relocated to there in 1927. The facility, appropriately named Wright Field, lay in a valley near the Miami River basin called Huffman Prairie. A new large dam near there now kept the city of Dayton from flooding and nearly washing away as it had in 1913.

The sunshine glistened off of the streams and water ponds of the Ohio farmlands as Jake flew south. He could have found the airfield by dead reckoning, but he used his radio direction finder to home in on WING radio, one of Dayton's regular AM broadcast stations.

Coming in over the airfield in the Fairchild, Jake set up a circling pattern. The tower flashed a green light, indicating he had clearance to land.

The Fairchild taxied up in front of three large hangars where a dozen Army Air Corps men were working on airplanes. Near the base of the control tower, a man in Army officer's summer khakis waved instructions where to park the Fairchild. The officer was Jake's friend and flight line duty officer for the day, Second Lieutenant Dale Harkins. He had been watching for Jake to arrive.

Jake climbed out of his plane and greeted Dale.

An Army lineman tied the Fairchild down with some ropes to some steel cleats on the concrete ramp.

Dale explained, "Army regulations require that I escort you while you're here on the base."

"Great," Jake said, "that will give us a chance to ~~out lie each other~~ talk over old times."

As they walked from the flight line, Dale pointed to an Army biplane trainer climbing out in the distance.

"See the plane there. We still have an active pilot training school here at Wright Field. Famous pioneer aviators like airmail pilot Hap Arnold and Flight Officer Roy Brown graduated from the Wright Flying School in the early days."

"Brown, he was the flyer credited with downing the notorious Red Baron wasn't he?"

"That's right. The original flying school was over on Huffman Prairie back in those days."

"I saw some old rundown hangars over that way on my approach. Things are growing a little since ol' Billy Mitchell woke 'em up."

"Yeah, but it's still a fight between the old time Army officers and the new Air Corps crowd, but things are getting better. Our flight schools here and at Vandalia are scheduled for relocation to San Antonio in the near future. They're moving them to Texas because of the better year round flying weather."

"Would there be any chance of my getting to meet Mr. Wright while I'm here?"

"Wilber died eight years after their first flight, but I guess you knew that. Orville still lives here, but he prefers not to be bothered by visitors."

"I understand. Where is Huffman Hill where they tested the gliders before their powered flights at Kitty Hawk?"

"I thought that might be something you'd want to see. It's on the other side of the base from here. I've arranged for a vehicle and driver to take you. When you're done, he'll deliver you downtown to a hotel. See you tomorrow when I'm off duty."

Dale walked with Jake over to the waiting car.

"Hey Dale, thanks for setting all this up for me. See you tomorrow."

Out Route 4 towards Fairfield and up a hill was the historic site. Jake got out of the car and walked a couple hundred yards over to the crest of the hill. He stood quietly gazing out over Huffman Prairie and down the hillside now overgrown with trees and high grass.

He tried to imagine what it must have been like to succeed at what so many men dreamed and so many had failed since time began, to lose the bonds of earth and fly free in the sky.

***

The next day Jake met Dale for lunch at the officer's mess on the airbase. They talked mostly about their shared experiences at American Flyers.

"Is there any chance I can see the new Research Center? I'd sure like to see the new aerodynamics wind tunnel."

"I asked the ol' man for permission this morning," Dale said referring to his commanding officer, Major Patterson. "Don't think it'll be a problem. I'll take you over there myself if the ol' man approves it."

"That'll be swell. Before I forget, I'm staying at the Van Cleve Hotel again tonight. Why don't you and Peg join me for dinner at the hotel? It'll be my treat. I understand the Mayfair Room is one of the best."

"You ready?" Dale said, standing up and placing his uniform cap under his arm.

"Yes," and Jake stood to leave with Dale.

"What'a ya say about tonight?"

"Peg would really enjoy that, but her girlfriend, Helen Corbett is in town for a visit and is staying with us. She and Peg grew up together back in Oklahoma."

Dale stopped at a table to introduce Jake to his C.O., Major Patterson.

"Your Fairchild, how do you like it, Martin?"

"Great little plane, sir. I enjoy flying her," and Jake visited with Patterson for a few minutes about flying.

"Enjoy your visit," Patterson said. "Understand Harkins is giving you the tour this afternoon. Let us know what you think of our new R&D facilities."

"Well, I guess you just got the permission you were looking for," Dale said as he and Jake left the mess hall. "Let's head on over there."

"What's she like, this girlfriend of Peg's?"

"She's got a great personality, lots of fun."

"You mean she plays the piano well. Right?"

"You got it," Dale said grinning and Jake laughed.

"Well then, bring ol' Helen along, if she'll come."

***

That evening at the Van Cleve Hotel, Jake changed into his dinner clothes and went to the hotel lounge to have a drink while he waited for his friends.

Dale had changed out of his uniform into a civilian suit and arrived with Peg and Helen. They joined Jake at the bar and Dale made the introductions.

Peg, who had not seen Jake since the boys' flight school days in Fort Worth, gave Jake a polite hug.

Helen Corbett, a small pleasingly plump young lady, was talkative and entertaining. At dinner, she kept the conversation going.

"My great ambition," she explained, "is to become an author. I think I'll try my hand at writing cookbooks. What the heck, I love to cook and I love to write."

After dinner, the foursome discussed what they might do for the rest of the evening's entertainment over a round of Irish coffees.

"Lets all go over to the Strand Theater on Third and Main Street and see a vaudeville show," Dale said.

"Why don't we go to the Idlewild Club instead?" Peg suggested. "I think Jake and Helen would enjoy hearing the band that's playing there."

Dale raised his coffee cup.

"I'll drink to that. Peg's right, there's a great band playing there and they know all the latest tunes."

The group piled into Dale's beat-up ol' Chevy sedan.

"All aboard for the Dixie Highway," Dale said.

The club's marquee identified it as the Idlewild and advertised the Dickson Talbott Orchestra in large letters. A triangle standup sign at the front entrance with the singer's picture read "Tonight! Jennie Herman Singing All Your Favorite Songs."

Dale let Jake and the ladies out at the entrance to the club and went to park the car.

"Get us a table down front," Peg prodded Jake.

Jake negotiated with the headwaiter by placing a fiver in his hand and they were shown to a table right in front of the bandstand.

Dale came in, as they were being seated and worked his way through the tables to join them. He saw a fellow he knew across the room tablehopping and motioned for the fellow to join them.

"Milt, over here. Come have a drink with us."

The fellow came over to their table.

"Milt, you know Peg. Helen and Jake, I'd like you to meet my friend, Milton Caniff. He's a syndicated journalist of some renown."

"Pleased to meet you, Mr. Caniff," Jake said, standing up. Jake understood Dale's humor. "I'm a real fan of *Terry and the Pirates*. I read it whenever I can get my hands on a newspaper that carries your strip."

Milt pulled a chair up to the table and sat down.

"I'm getting wider circulation lately. More papers are starting to carry Pirates. Very well, now its been established that I draw comics for a living and I know ol' Dale here is a soldier boy. What do you do for a living, Jake?"

"I'm more or less a rogue pilot. I can't claim to do much of anything to make an honest living."

"Don't listen to that nonsense," Dale said, "he and his dad own half of North Texas."

"Oh, you're a rancher are you Jake," Milt said making polite conversation. "What do you call the ranch?"

"Downtown Dallas," Dale said and everyone laughed.

"It's the Flying M. Our spread's up along the Red River near the Texas-Oklahoma border," and Jake felt just a touch of homesickness as he spoke those words.

Peg was trying to listen to the music.

"Hush, you guys. The band is playing 'Smoke Gets in Your Eyes' and I want to hear this song."

When the music ended, the bandleader, Dickson Talbott, stepped to the microphone.

"Most of you probably recognized that song from the new movie *Roberta*. Well folks, that's the end of our first set this evening. We'll take a short break and be back with Jennie singing some of your all time favorite hits."

Dickson stepped down from the bandstand.

"Dick, over here," Milton called out. "I want you to meet some fans of yours."

Dickson came to the table and introduced himself.

"You all don't really hang out with this joker, do you?" Dickson said referring to Milton.

He took a seat at the table, held up two fingers for the waiter to see and lit a Chesterfield cigarette.

Peg noticed his ring.

"Is that a lion's head on your ring?"

The waiter sat Dickson's usual on the table in front of him, a draft beer with a bourbon chaser.

Dickson held out his hand so Peg and Helen, who had been trying to look at the ring, could see it better.

"It's a tiger or at least that's what it's supposed to be. There are only ten of them in existence."

Peg observed Milton also wore an identical ring.

"I couldn't help noticing you are both wearing the same tiger rings. Is there a story behind them?" Peg asked.

"You explain it, Dick," Milton said.

"Ten of us went to high school at Stivers and we made up this private club, called ourselves the Ten Tigers."

"Did it have something to do with your music, Dickson, and your art, Milton? The rings, I mean."

Milton was sketching a cartoon on a large white paper napkin. He laughed, but did not look up.

"Nah," Dickson said. "We played sports and hung around together. That's about the gist of it except we all still stay in touch."

Dickson lit another Chesterfield.

"I grew up playing the saxophone. Now, ol' Milt there, I don't know where he learned to doodle like he does."

"You and your band are really good," Helen said. "Where did you play before you came to the Idlewild?"

Dickson took a couple of sips from his boilermaker and then another drag from his cigarette.

"Over on third Street, but this place is a heck of a lot better than the last joint we played. Some mob guys shot it out there. Me and the band had to crawl out of the place on our hands and knees with bullets flying."

The musicians came back onto the bandstand.

"Thanks for coming folks. Time to go back to work. Come again and tell your friends about us."

Helen tugged at Dickson's white jacket sleeve as he stood up.

"Will you play Herman Hupfeld's 1931 hit for me? Its one of my favorites."

Jake, seated next to Milton, watched as he sketched on the napkin. Milton finished the cartoon and handed it to Jake to look at.

Milton had drawn a picture of his cartoon character Terry with a captain's hat cocked back on his head waving from an open cockpit airplane.

The caption underneath the sketch read "In Case of Emergency." The words in the cartoon bubble from Terry's mouth were "Grab your coat and get your hat, leave your troubles on the doorstep. Just direct your feet to the sunny side of the street!"

"What're you going to do with this sketch?" Jake asked.

"Would you like to have it?"

"Yes, I would."

Milton wrote "To Jake," on the drawing, signed it "Milton Caniff," and handed it to him.

"Thanks!" Jake replied and carefully folded the napkin with the signed cartoon on it and put it in his inside vest pocket.

Everyone applauded as Dickson returned center stage.

He fastened the lanyard around his neck to his tenor saxophone as he intended to play lead on the next song.

Stepping to the microphone, he said, "Now ladies and gentlemen a request by the lovely lady seated down front here. We would like to play our rendition of 'As Time Goes By' for your listening pleasure."

Around two in the morning, Dale and the ladies dropped Jake off at his hotel.

***

Mid morning the following day, Jake arrived back at Wright Field by taxicab and went over to flight operations to check the weather to the west. Stations were reporting only scattered clouds at Indianapolis and St. Louis.

Dale walked out to the Fairchild with Jake.

"I plan to make it as far as Robertson, Missouri before nightfall," Jake told to Dale. "If the winds will co-operate."

"Write if you get honest work," Dale said.

"Wilco," Jake replied and climbed in the cockpit. "See you in the funny papers, Dale."

Wilco being pilot slang, short for will-comply.

Flying west, following Highway 40 to Indianapolis, Jake set a course for St. Louis. He intended to land at Lambert Field and spend the night there and visit the Monocoupe factory the next day.

Jake also knew that Sarah was in St. Louis staying with her aunt for the summer and she had given Jake her aunt's phone number. He was to call her, if he came through.

The flight to Robertson was routine, although a little bumpy from the afternoon heat thermals.

Jake arrived at Lambert Field an hour before sunset, too late to contact anyone over at Monocoupe. An airport employee getting off work gave Jake a lift to a nearby tourist court, the Blue Bonnet Inn.

Jake booked a room for the night and used the telephone in the office several times to try to call Sarah, but no one answered.

After dark, Jake walked to a nearby grocery store, bought some soda crackers, a chunk of bologna and an RC Cola. That was his dinner and he went to bed.

Jake had not reached Sarah because he had written down one of the digits in the phone number incorrectly. What change of course might the lives of both Sarah and Jake have taken, had they met and talked that night?

***

The following morning at the Blue Bonnet Inn tourist court, Jake checked out and took a taxicab to the Monocoupe factory. He went directly to the sales office and waited for it to open.

When the factory salesman arrived, Jake introduced himself as an interested buyer. The sales representative showed him around the factory and then took him for a demo flight in one of the new models.

The short flight proved well worth Jake's time. The Monocoupe seemed cramped, not nearly as stable as the Fairchild, but a little more responsive to the control inputs. He had gotten used to the size and comfort of the larger Fairchild and quickly concluded the Monocoupe was not the airplane he was looking for to replace the Fairchild.

"What do you think of our new Monocoupe now that you have seen and flown in it?" the salesman asked Jake.

"I need some time to think it over. I'll contact you if I decide to purchase one," Jake replied politely and he thanked the salesman for the demo.

Jake returned to the ramp where he parked the Fairchild the night before. While he waited for his plane to be refueled, he tried to call Sarah one more time. There was still no answer.

Departing Lambert Field he took up a southwesterly heading. The mid-day clouds grew thicker and before too long, Jake found himself over the top of a heavy overcast cloud layer. There appeared to be no breaks in the clouds up ahead. He barely had enough fuel to turn around and go back to St. Louis, but it grew even darker and more ominous back the way he had come. The weather would likely close in rapidly behind him and get worse.

According to his dead reckoning navigation, he figured to be about a hundred miles east-northeast of Joplin. Easing the power off, he started a slow descent into the cloud layer, hoping the ceiling below the clouds was sufficiently high enough to level out before flying into one of the higher points along the Ozark Mountain range.

Keeping his plane in level flight was not an easy trick with minimum instruments and no navigation aids.

Descending into the clouds, he became suddenly and totally engulfed in a gray sphere where dimensions in space and distance no longer existed.

Jake's inner ear told him he was flying straight and level, but he knew by the sound of the engine and the stress on the airframe this was not the case. He had entered the deadly and dreaded suicide spiral, the classic piloting error and the cardinal sin of instrument flying. What was worse, he had done it to himself.

Time to start flying with his brain and disengage the seat of his pants. Jake knew the Fairchild to be a very stable airplane. He neutralized the rudder pedals and the yoke and held them in that position. Fortunately, he had not adjusted the trim tabs since entering the clouds. With every ounce of courage Jake could muster, he eased the throttle back slightly and let go of the controls.

The Fairchild rocked back and forth in the clouds. The truth being, Jake could not have pointed to up if his life depended on it and it did. The sky above him grew darker and below him became increasingly brighter. The altimeter was winding down a little too fast, so Jake added back a little power to slow the descent. He did not touch the controls.

Jake pondered what flight altitude the Fairchild would be in when he did break out of the clouds and would he have time to recover the aircraft. He wondered how low the overcast was and whether or not the last thing he would ever see would be a pile of rocks coming at him.

The gray shrouded windshield suddenly became a green mountain pasture and a grove of trees some five hundred feet below him.

The Fairchild was in the clear and only slightly wing low and nose down. He had successfully descended through the clouds, no thanks to his flying ability. The Fairchild's stability and Jake's having the good sense to let go of the controls, avoided a circling nose-down two hundred mile an hour power dive into the ground.

Jake flew for the next three hours at low altitude under the clouds and about dark, the lights of Dallas appeared on the horizon.

This isolated experience on this day's flight, unrealized by Jake at that moment, would set him on a personal quest to find, fund and develop better flight navigation systems for private and commercial aviation aircraft.

Elizabeth

Jake returned home to the Flying M ranch feeling a bit like the Prodigal Son. No one asked him much about living in Dallas, except Flo. She would, from time to time, coax him into telling her some of the stories about the troubles he had gotten into. He would oblige her, but omit a few of the more incriminating details.

Flo had hired Zack's younger sister, Violet, as a full time live-in housekeeper. She and Flo were always working on some kind of project around the house like canning or quilting. Nothing pleased Big Jake and Flo more than to have their son home. Big Jake put no pressure on him to go back to work.

Maybe by choice, force of habit or for need of something to do Jake fell into the ranch life routine after a week or so. Soon it seemed like he had never been away. Hanging around the house and cowboyin' never had any great appeal to Jake, so he started reporting to work on a regular basis at the Gainesville factory.

The facility had recently been enlarged and the Martin drilling equipment company was now called M&H Manufacturing. The initials of the new company stood for Martin and Hughes.

In the corner of the development and testing area of the factory, Jake cabbaged onto a beat-up, old wooden desk and hooked up a phone for a makeshift place to work. He kept busy troubleshooting equipment breakdowns and chasing supply shortages.

On a day when everything was going wrong all at the same time, the head driller and district superintendent for Phillips Oil came in to complain.

"Every time we drill through a layer of hard rock and hit clay, the drill head clogs up and the equipment bogs down. When that happens, we're generally gonna bust something. Then we spend the whole next day pulling drill pipe to change the bit."

"I know. I've heard this complaint before," Jake said.

"Well?" the driller asked impatiently.

"Well, what?"

"Well, you're the engineer here, so fix it! Design something that will work."

"I'm not an engineer."

"The others that work here said you were! Told me to come see you. You were the smartest one around."

"They were either being kind to me or having fun with you," Jake said kidding the driller, "but tell you what, I'll look into the problem and see if I can come up with something."

Jake pondered the driller's problem over the next several days, but nothing really came to him.

On Sunday afternoon, Jake was in the front yard with Flo. She was cleaning out some flowerbeds using a garden hose and laid the hose down on the ground to pull some weeds. When she returned to pick up the hose, it had bored a hole into the ground and the hose was moving down into the hole.

"Will you look at this?" Flo complained to Jake as she tugged at the hose to pull it out of the hole.

Jake looked at where Flo was pointing.

"That's called hydrodynamic pressure. It does that naturally."

"I have no idea what you just said, Jacob. Where in the world did you learn all those fancy words anyway?"

Jake pulled the hose out and stood staring down at the hole in the ground the hose had dug.

"Mom, you're an absolute genius!" Jake yelled. "That's the answer to the drilling problem."

"What drilling problem?"

"If water is forced down through the drill pipe and out through the turning heads of the drill bits, it will push the clay out and keep the heads from clogging. Not only that, it will cool the drill head when they're drilling through hard rock."

"Land O' Goshen, Jacob, I still have no earthly idea what you're talking about, but I guess that's a good thing. Is that right?"

Jake picked his mom up off the ground and spun her around.

"Yes, that's a really good thing, Mom. It's the answer to a problem we're having at work and you found it!"

"Put me down this minute, young man!" Flo screamed laughing.

He put her down and took off for the house to get a pencil and some paper to draw out what he wanted the machine shop to start working on Monday morning.

***

Over the next several days, Jake and a couple of machinists went to work building a prototype of the new hydrodynamic drill head. Jake was explaining something to one of the machinist when the telephone rang and he went to answer the phone.

"Martin here, it's your nickel. Go ahead."

"What're you going to do with this ol' Fairchild parked down here, just keep paying the hangar rent?" the voice on the other end of the line asked.

"Red! How in the heck are you?"

"I'm good, Jake."

"I do intend to come down and get the ol' bird one of these days, just been busy. There's an airport here at Gainesville where I intent to keep it."

"Got a suggestion. I've been working with this doctor who bought a Beechcraft stagger-wing cabin model biplane. He's not a very experienced pilot and I've been flying with him to get him proficient. What do you say I bring the Fairchild up to you this weekend? I'll have ol' Doc follow me up and fly back to Dallas with him."

"Sounds like a great idea, Red, thanks. Be nice to have the Fairchild here. Kind of miss going flying."

***

That weekend, Red telephoned to say he was at Love Field and ready to leave for Gainesville with the Fairchild.

Jake left the ranch house to meet Red at the airport and was waiting when Red circled the field and landed.

"Great ol' plane you got there," Red declared as he climbed out of the Fairchild's cockpit, "flies real nice. How you been country boy?"

"Fair to midlin'. How's yourself, Red?"

They both looked up at the sound from the bright red Beechcraft coming in over the field. The doctor piloting the plane was a little hot on final approach and bounced three times on landing before slowing to a full stop.

Jake and Red watched the doctor's landing and both grinned at each other.

"First couple of landings weren't that good, but the third one was decent enough. Wouldn't you agree, Jake?"

"Oh no, I liked all three," Jake commented sarcastically and they both laughed.

The Beechcraft taxied up beside the Fairchild and shutdown. Red introduced Jake to the doctor and they spent some time looking over the Beechcraft stagger-wing model 17A.

"Men don't grow up, the price of their toys only get more expensive," the doctor commented, as he showed off his new plane.

The three visited for a short while about flying until Jake looked at the sky off to the northwest.

"It appears we've got a rainstorm moving in."

"Yeah, I saw the tops of those thunder-bumpers on the way up here. Think we'll head on back and try to outrun it."

The Beechcraft taxied out and rolled down the runway for takeoff. Jake stood quietly and watched as the bright red plane headed south and disappeared out of sight.

***

Jake spent his spare time at the airport fooling with the Fairchild and enjoying once again flying on a regular basis. He worked longer hours at the Gainesville factory and even though he still lived at home, he spent less time at the ranch. When he came in late at night, he tried to be as quiet as possible so as not to wake his folks.

On one of the weekends that Jake knew Sarah was home from college, he called her house.

Sarah answered the phone.

"Hello," she paused and waited. "Hello?"

Jake said nothing.

"Jake, is that you?"

Sarah's sixth sense had told her that it might be Jake on the other end of the phone. She held for the longest time waiting, but still no response.

Jake carefully hung up the receiver without saying anything. Jake did not want to talk to Sarah so much as to hear her voice or know that she was all right. Nobody understood less than Jake why he had done that.

The only other thing of any consequence Jake had done in the last couple of months was to finally part with the old Lincoln Phaeton. He traded it off for one of the new '34 model Roadsters, which Ford introduced in late 1933.

On most Saturday nights, the National Guard Armory at Ardmore held a dance. The first weekend after he bought the new Ford, a popular western swing band had been booked into the Armory. Jake decided to drive up to the nearby Oklahoma town and put a few miles on his new Ford.

Tickets at the door were fifty cents for singles and seventy-five cents for couples. Soft drinks, fruit punch and cookies were on sale at the concession stand, alcoholic was not. Liquor was not legal in the state. The Baptists and the bootleggers voted together in every election to see that the state remained dry.

If someone wanted liquor, there was always a bootlegger handy to sell them a fifth of whiskey out of one of his four vest suit pockets. Jake had given up drinking hard liquor since he left Dallas and would pass when a bootlegger approached him to make a sale.

The western two-fiddle band was a big hit with the crowd. Jake ran into several of his old high school friends and visited with others he knew. Most were married now and had come to the dance with their wife or husband.

A girl from Jake's high school class, Jolene Skinner, came to the dance with her brother and his wife. She was a nice looking, well-mannered young girl who had reached a point in her life were she began to fear she might become an old maid.

"Dance with me, Jake," she said.

"I will, Jolene, but let's wait for a slow one."

Jolene waited patiently beside Jake with her arms folded. The next song was a slow tune and Jake escorted her to the dance floor.

"Jake, it would be alright with my brother, if you wanted to take me home after the dance."

"We'll see, Jolene,"

When the song ended, Jake returned her to the table where her brother and some others were seated. He went to stand against the wall with some other single guys to watch the crowd and listen to the music.

A rugged looking fellow in a black cowboy hat came through the door with two young ladies in tow. Obviously, the redhead was with the cowboy, but the tall, slender one with dark brunette hair appeared to be a third party.

Jake could not take his eyes off her as she made her way smoothly and gracefully across the room. She was more like a woman than the girls Jake was used to being around. She was head and shoulders far more attractive than any other girl in the room. The rest of the room faded into a blur as Jake watched her take a seat at a table on the far side of the dancehall.

A young fellow who worked with Jake at the factory walked by and Jake asked him, "Do you know who that tall brunette is over there with the cowboy and the redhead?"

The fellow turned to look in the direction Jake indicated.

"Oh her? Her name's Elizabeth Rivers. She graduated the year before I did at Gainesville High. She was homecoming queen her senior year. Last I heard, she tied the knot with some football player."

"Thanks," Jake said.

He hesitated for a moment to work up his nerve and then made his way over to their table.

Elizabeth looked up at him with a sultry smile. "Yes?" she said.

"Hi Elizabeth, I'm Jake Martin. Would you like to dance?"

"Of course I would. That's what I came for. Thank you for asking."

She took Jake's extended hand and went to the dance floor with him.

"Jake. I like that name. Everyone calls me Liz so you can drop the Elizabeth stuff. How did you know my name anyway?"

"Well, I didn't 'til a few minutes ago." Jake nodded over towards the far wall. "That fellow over there in the blue shirt told me when I asked him."

The dance ended and Jake just stood there holding Liz around her waist.

"Come on over and sit with us," Liz said when the next song started.

Having a one-sided conversation with a rodeo cowboy and his girlfriend at the table was not Jake's idea of an interesting evening, but he tried for a song and a half, then asked Liz to dance again.

Jake did not care much for dancing, but Liz seemed to love to dance and holding her close to him on the dance floor was a whole lot more fun. The thin low-necked, black-lace dress she was wearing did not leave much to his imagination and they danced the rest of the evening.

"I think the band's fixing to quit for the night. Maybe I could take you home, Liz?"

"That would be nice. I think my friends would just as soon be rid of me this evening anyway," and she went to tell them Jake was taking her home.

Liz directed Jake to an older part of Gainesville.

Jake was unfamiliar with that part of town, but had always heard it referred to as the wrong-side-of-the-tracks.

The Roadster pulled up in front of a small frame house with no lights on.

"This is my folk's house. I'm staying here with them temporarily."

Jake cut off the engine, rested his right arm on the seat back and turned to face Liz.

"What does your father do?"

Actually, Jake did not care what her father did he was only trying to make polite conversation.

Liz leaned back with her long, dark hair resting on the top of the car's seat.

"He works for the railroad, but I think his main occupation is getting drunk every night. I dread going in the house until after he's asleep."

"That's fine. We'll sit here and talk for a while."

"What would you like to talk about?"

"You, I'd like to talk about you."

"Rather boring subject, don't you think?" Liz smiled, "but I'm flattered you think that I'm interesting. What would you like to know about me?"

"I know you went to high school here in Gainesville, but there's something I don't understand."

"What would that be?"

"It's the way you speak. Your grammar is perfect and your pronunciation of every word is so exacting. Folks around here don't talk the way you do."

"If you had known me a few years ago, you would not say that. I talked like a hick. People make judgments about you from the way you speak, so for the last two years, I have concentrated on teaching myself to speak properly. I even sent away for a mail-order course titled 'Speaking English Correctly' and I listened to those seventy-eight RPM records over and over again."

Jake stared at Liz's slender, shapely figure in the dim light and made no pretext of hiding it from her. He had decided he liked what he saw.

"So you see, Jake, what you see and hear may not be what it appears to be."

Jake did not seem to care or try to understand what she was trying to tell him.

"I'd like to see you again, Liz."

"I best go in the house now. Thank you for bringing me home and for a nice evening."

"Can I see you next weekend? Maybe we could go to a movie or something."

Liz got out and shut the car door quietly. She looked at Jake with a coy smile that implied yes.

"I'm sorry no, but thank you for asking. Right now, I'm involved."

Jake wanted to ask what she meant by involved, but he did not and he watched her as she went into the darkened house. He started the Roadster and pulled away slowly so as not to wake up anyone.

***

The following Saturday night, Jake went back to the dance at the Armory. He hoped Liz might show up and stayed most of the evening, but she never made an appearance.

The next day, Jake decided to take an afternoon drive. He had no intention of going anywhere specific, at least that was what he had convinced himself, until he pulled up out front of the small frame house where he had taken Liz the Saturday night a week ago.

A rough looking old man in work overalls sat in a rocking chair on the small front porch of the house. Jake got out of the car and paused before entering the yard.

"Does Elizabeth Rivers live here?"

"You must mean my daughter. Don't know about her living here, but she's stayin' here for now."

Jake went through the gate and approached the porch.

"Who are you?" the man asked.

"Jake Martin's the name," and he stepped up onto the porch and offered to shake hands with the man.

The old man ignored him and looked away toward the railroad tracks to watch as a long fright train passed.

Liz came to the screen door.

"Jake! What are you doing here?"

Liz opened the screen door and invited him into the living room. A large woman seated in the center of a well-worn couch that sagged in the middle from her weight, smiled at Jake.

Liz introduced Jake to her mother.

Liz's mother was not only large, but a quite unattractive woman and it caused Jake to wonder for a moment how a beautiful girl like Liz could have come from such a mother.

"Pleased to meet you, ma'am," Jake responded and turned to Liz. "It's a pretty afternoon, I thought you might like to go for a ride."

Liz did not hesitate.

"Just let me grab a sweater."

Jake drove around town for a while and then pulled up in front of the city park.

They sat watching as some small Mexican boys took turns rolling a barrel hoop with a stick and running along behind it down the dirt road beside the park.

The sounds of a baseball game being played on the far side of the park could be heard in the distance.

Jake looked at Liz.

"Tell me more about yourself. I mean tell me what you meant the other night when you said you were involved."

"What do you want me to tell you, what I think you would like to hear or do you want the truth?"

Her response surprised Jake, as he had not considered the possibility Liz might make things up about herself.

"I guess I'll take the truth."

Liz jerked herself around in the car seat to face Jake directly and with a stern look she began.

"Make yourself comfortable. This may take a while."

Liz sighed and took a deep breath.

"I'd rather you think I'm something I'm not, but you asked for it, so here goes," and with that, Liz dropped the perfect pronunciation of every one of her words.

"My senior year in high school, I dated our school's star football player. After a few months of dating him, I thought I was pregnant. I didn't tell the dimwit, but that's the reason I agreed to marry him when he asked. I wasn't in love with him! He was a real asshole. Turns out I wasn't pregnant after all. Isn't that a laugh?"

Liz's stern look turned slowly to sadness and it became apparent to Jake that Liz's reflecting back on her past experience was not pleasant for her.

"Why don't we get out of the car and walk in the park for a while," Jake suggested.

As they walked, Liz continued, "Last fall, my loving husband received an offer for a football scholarship at the University of Oklahoma. I'm sure he never told the college he was married. He told me I was holding him back and one day he up and took off without me. I filed for a divorce two months ago."

"Oh," Jake said.

"Yes, oh! And that's the reason I can't go out with you. My lawyer would throw a hissie if he found out I was dating anyone before the divorce finalized."

The fellow at the dance had told Jake that Liz might have been married before, but this was more than he had expected to hear and certainly a darn sight more than he wanted to hear.

"There you are. I've been as honest as I can be with you. I'm sure you don't want secondhand good or to deal with my problems, so you best take me back to the house now."

"I'll take you home, but I want to see you again."

Liz still refused even though Jake tried to convince her they could be discreet. They walked back to Jake's Roadster and Jake took her home.

***

Jake received a letter from Zack postmarked Honolulu. He wrote to say that he was now a stewards mate third class and had been assigned to the USS Arizona.

Red was flying full-time for Southern Airways in the new all-metal, twin-engine Lockheed Electra airliners. He called Jake from Dallas once in awhile to keep Jake up to date on what was going on with the airlines.

The last time Red called, Jake told him, "I think I've decided to sell the Fairchild. I'm thinking about buying a more powerful aircraft, something along the lines of a Howard or a Spartan."

Summer turned to fall and Jake continued to work at the Gainesville factory. His social life was nonexistent.

On occasion, Larry would invite Jake over to his house in Wichita Falls. Larry's new bride, Jenny Lou, would prepare one of her home-cooked meals for him when he visited. Jake liked Jenny Lou, but no one could help liking her. She was a pretty, blonde-haired young girl with one of those bubbly personalities.

Larry and Jake often went out for a beer to talk business after one of Jenny Lou's dinners and on this most recent visit, Larry had just finished preparing the paperwork to apply for a patent on the new hydrodynamic drill head and wanted to discuss it with Jake.

"How do you want me to register the patent?"

"In the company name, of course, not mine."

After they talked for a while, Larry brought up what was really concerning him.

"My father is getting up in years and would like to cut back on his workload. He has asked me to take over the Flying M and the Martin companies legal business. Before I take the proposal to Big Jake, I'd like to know how you feel about it."

"Fine with me, Larry. If Dad agrees, I see nothing wrong with it."

***

Late on a Friday afternoon about a month after Jake last saw Liz, he was wrapping up his workday at the factory when the phone on his desk rang. Jake started not to go back to answer it, but he figured it might be some driller with a broke down rig, so he answered the phone.

"Martin here, go ahead."

The woman's soft, low-pitched voice on the other end of the line sounded familiar.

"Jake, how've you been?"

"Fine, how's yourself?"

"This is Liz. Just thought I'd give you a call. I've got some good news and some bad news."

"Go on."

"The bad news is my mom died about a month ago and I haven't seen my father since the funeral or maybe that last part is some of the good news."

Jake wondered why Liz had called to tell him about her mother as he had only met her briefly that one time.

"Sorry to hear that, Liz. Where are you living now?"

"I'm staying with a girlfriend in Sherman. You may remember her. She was the redhead who was with me the first night we met. Anyway, the good news is my divorce was final yesterday. If you would like to come and get me, we can go out and celebrate."

"Give me the address and the directions. I'll be there as soon as I can."

Jake arrived at the address well after dark.

Liz stood watching out the window for him and when Jake pulled up, she came running out and jumped in the car.

Jake suggested they go to a picture show.

Liz readily agreed. Anything to do was better than another evening sitting around her girlfriend's house.

After the movie, Jake drove out in the country a ways and parked near a moonlit open pasture. He reached for Liz and she moved closer to him.

They kissed passionately several times, but when Jake started to lay her down in the seat, Liz held him back for a moment.

"It's been a while since I was with anyone like this and I probably want you more than you want me right now."

Jake had nothing to say. He had long since lost any control over his passion and desire for Liz.

"Let's get one thing straight, Jake. I won't be a one night stand."

Jake drew her near.

"It's your call. It's whatever you want it to be."

What took place that night in the front seat of Jake's 1934 Ford Roadster was not love making, but pure unadulterated physical passion fueled by loneliness, insecurity and sexual desperation.

What took place next could only have been described as unbridled sex between two people who wanted and maybe even needed to be with someone more than anything else in the world at that moment in their lives.

***

Jake spent all his spare time with Liz. He rented Liz a small apartment in Gainesville and moved her out of where she had been staying with her girlfriend. Anything she wanted for herself or for the apartment, Jake got it for her. In his own way, he tried to make up for the bad breaks he felt Liz had been dealt so far in life.

On a couple of Saturday nights, Jake took Liz up to the dance at the Armory where they had first met, but they eventually stopped going.

Liz was one of those women who seemed to invite men's stares wherever she went. She did not do it intentionally, but it happened fairly regularly without any effort on her part. Liz tried hard not to look back when a man stared at her because she knew it bothered Jake.

On a cool, clear winter Sunday afternoon, Jake asked Liz if she would like to go flying in the Fairchild. She had never been in an airplane before, but agreed to go even though she seemed apprehensive about flying.

Shortly after takeoff, Liz became terrified and began to plead with Jake to land the airplane. Jake did not understand her sudden fear and tried to calm her down unsuccessfully. He returned to the airfield and landed the airplane as soon as he could.

After they were on the ground, she tried to get out of the plane before it stopped and he grabbed her arm to hold her in the cockpit. When he finally got stopped and let go of her, she ran from the plane.

He ran after her. When he caught up with her, he held onto her and felt her whole body trembling.

"I will never!" she gasped, "I will never get in an airplane again! Please, please Jake, don't ask me to!"

"Just calm down and stop worrying about it, alright!"

Jake had never seen anyone react with such a sudden overwhelming fear of flying as Liz had done and he wondered whether Liz would ever be able to overcome her fear.

***

Jake slept in late at the ranch on a holiday morning. The factory was closed for Washington's Birthday. He went down to the kitchen where his mom was puttering around and poured himself a cup of coffee from the pot on the stove where Flo had been keeping it warm for him. He sat down at the table.

"Mom," he began and he told her about the flying incident with Liz.

"All I can tell you, Jacob, is that one man's meat and taters is another man's poison."

Flo would have normally said potatoes, but she was trying to amuse her son who seemed to be in an overly serious mood that morning.

"What you're trying to tell me is that one person's paradise is another person's hell. Is that it, Mom?"

"That's pretty much the size of it. There are three things that keep a man and woman together. The first is a common interest and those can be anything from a business to children. The second is when both people not only love, but like and respect each other."

"What's the third one, Mom?"

"Well, there's always the ever popular sex!"

Jake laughed at the way his mom had worded it.

"If you find any two of those qualities in a couple, then they're a good match. If you find all three, it would be an exceptionally good match."

"Like you and Dad, huh Mom?"

"Yes, like your father and I," and she smiled.

Jake accepted what Flo told him as a valid explanation to his dilemma and decided he would not ask Liz to go up in his airplane again. He would let the matter pass.

Their talk reminded him of the Carnauba flight from Lake Michigan and how excited Elsa had been the day they had flown in the seaplane. He told his mom about his experience in the flying boat in Chicago.

"You know Mom, what I'd really like to do one of these days is get my hands on a big airplane like one of those new flying boats. One of those China Clippers like they use to take passengers across the Pacific."

"Can they do that now, Jacob? Can they actually fly all the way to China in an airplane?"

"Well to Hawaii anyway, but someday soon all the way to China. You can't imagine what it's like, lifting off from the water in one of those planes."

"Oh, I can imagine it, but that's all I want to do."

"Mom, I haven't told Dad about this yet, so maybe you ought to tell him for me."

"Tell him what?"

"Red and I both have applied with some of the larger airlines to go to work as full time pilots. Nothing seems to have come of it though. We haven't heard back from any of them."

Flo had a saying for nearly everything and replied, "A watched pot never boils."

"So I should just go on with my life and not worry about it. Is that what you're saying?"

"You'll have to be the judge of that, Jacob."

"Come to think of it, you've never gone flying with me. When would you like me to take you up?"

Flo raised both hands in the air.

"Not me. You're not going to get me up in one of those things. No-sir-re-bob, no way I'm going to go gallivanting around the sky in one of those flying contraptions."

"I took Dad up awhile back. He enjoyed it, but said he didn't think flying was the sort of thing he'd want to do all the time."

Violet had finished her housework and came into the kitchen.

"Mrs. Flo, yous ready for me to get started cleaning all those empty Ball jars and gets them ready for canning?"

"Yes Violet, I'll be there to help you in a minute." Flo turned to her son and said, "Don't you have something better to do than hang around here and be underfoot all day?"

"Sure Mom, I'll get out from under foot. See you later."

***

Jake went to put his work clothes on and left to drive out to the airport. He spent his day off changing the oil and making some minor repairs to the Fairchild.

Jake had been going with Liz for about three months and that evening after he finished working on the Fairchild, he went over to Liz's apartment.

Liz had been waiting for him as she had something important to tell him.

"I've missed one period and I've been having morning sickness for a week now," she told Jake. "I'm not making this up like the last time. I'm pretty sure I'm pregnant."

Jake accepted what Liz had just told him in a matter-of-fact sort of way.

"We'll get married right away. I won't have any kid of mine running around without a last name."

"You really mean that?"

"I'll make the arrangements for us to get married this weekend."

Jake and Liz would be married at the Lutheran church in Nocona Park where Big Jake and Flo had been members for a long time.

Liz told Jake before the wedding, "I hope if my father shows up, he will at least be sober."

Her father did not come to the ceremony and although Liz did not say anything more about it, Jake thought that deep down Liz was disappointed.

Larry stood up with Jake. Liz's girlfriend, the redhead from Sherman, was her bridesmaid and Big Jake gave the bride away.

Jake felt that his dad sincerely liked Liz, but then again Big Jake seemed to see something good in everyone. Will Rogers always said, "I never met a man I didn't like," and that was pretty much the same credo Big Jake lived by.

Jake suspected his dad thought Liz might be trouble for him even though Big Jake never said exactly that, but things he had mentioned in passing several times lead Jake to believe his dad had some concerns.

Jacob Martin, Jr. and Elizabeth Rivers were married in a simple ceremony followed by a reception and barbecue dinner at the church.

***

Years ago, Big Jake had a summerhouse built for Flo on the edge of the ranch near a grove of trees on the road into Pottsburg. The summers were cooler in the bottomland down by the creek bridge.

Jake could remember spending half a dozen summers there as a young boy. Flo eventually got to where she would rather not go through the hassle of moving to the second home each year and they quit going. Flo simply liked having all of her things in one place.

Big Jake had electricity run to the main house, as Jake had suggested. With ceiling fans and a swamp cooler installed, the main ranch house was now quite comfortable in the summers. Flo and Big Jake gave the summer place to Liz and Jake as a wedding present.

The house was a single story, rambling brick and rough cedar structure with a high pitch tin roof. The place had been added onto in stages and grown into a rambling ranch house with one room connecting to another. Unlike the classic structure of the main ranch house, the summerhouse had low wood-beamed ceiling and was more akin to a mountain lodge then a town home.

During the months that followed their wedding, Jake with the part-time help of some of the ranch hands, enlarged and remodeled the summer place adding electricity and indoor plumbing. Even though it had become an impressive year-round home, everyone still referred to the place as the summer ranch house.

Liz was very happy having her own home and waited patiently for their child to be born. Jake continued to keep busy with his work at the Gainesville factory and occasionally went flying by himself in the Fairchild.

***

In the spring of 1935, Sarah came home from college for Easter vacation. With Liz's baby almost due, Sarah and Flo planned a baby shower for her. Jake suggested they have the shower as a surprise at their house.

Several dozen ladies attended the baby shower. During the shower, Jake stayed out of the way by hiding out in a backroom, which he had converted into a combination workshop and study. When he went to the kitchen to get a cup of coffee and maybe sneak a piece of cake, Sarah was there.

"Hi gal, understand you graduate from UT in May."

Sarah looked up from slicing a white coconut cake.

"Sure do. It's been a long haul. I want you to know I'm happy for you and Liz. You're a really lucky guy, beautiful wife and expecting a new baby and all."

"I know you are Sarah. I wouldn't expect you to feel any other way. It's the kind of person you are."

Sarah laid the cake-knife down on the counter.

"I've been waiting for an opportunity to tell you something, Jake. I would like you to know before everyone else."

Jake leaned back against the kitchen counter.

"What's that, Sarah?"

"Until you married Liz, I never gave up hope for things working out for us."

Jake looked away.

"Please look at me, Jake. I've been dating Hank Donaldson for a while now. He's working at the Flying M trying to save enough money to go to veterinary school."

"I know all that, Sarah."

"Hank has asked me to marry him and I've accepted. He wanted us to wait until he finished veterinary school, but I told him I didn't want to wait. I'll get a job and help him go to school, if that's what it takes. We're getting married in June."

"Best wishes, Sarah. Tell Hank congratulations for me," Jake said graciously, but with a less than a sincere tone to his voice. He picked up his coffee cup and started out of the kitchen.

"Well you did first!" Sarah yelled after him, almost in tears. "Damn your hide anyway Jake Martin!"

Jake paused in his steps. He did not look back at Sarah or say anything. He stood there for a moment before returning to his study.

Jake and Liz did not make it to Sarah's wedding. Lora, their first child, was born that very day. Lora was a darling, little blue-eyed, sandy-haired girl who stole Jake's heart from the very first moment he held her in his arms.

Texas Air Service

At the Bendix Air Races of 1935, Ben Howard was injured in a crash in the Mr. Mulligan cabin racer. Due to this, all of the Howard models scheduled for production were delayed and thus Jake would not be able to get one of the new models for some time.

Even Wiley Post, who had set world's records in his strutless, high-wing Lockheed Vega, planned to order one of the new Howard monoplanes. Unfortunately, Post died that same year in a floatplane crash in Alaska on August 15th along with his friend Will Rogers, a sad day for Big Jake, as he knew Wiley personally having met him years ago in Oklahoma. Big Jake was also a fan of Will Rogers and often quoted the popular humorist.

With the Howard models back-ordered, Jake decided not to wait for delivery and settled on purchasing one of the new Spartan low-wing cabin models like he had first seen on his flight to Chicago. He flew the Fairchild up to Tulsa to the Spartan factory where he signed a contract and placed an order for a new Spartan monoplane.

The new airplane was scheduled for completion in about a month. In the meantime, Jake called Toots and Red to ask them to put the word out around Love Field that Jake's Fairchild was for sale.

Jake received a call from a gentleman in Dallas who heard the Fairchild was in immaculate condition and wanted to see it. Jake flew to Love Field, demonstrated the plane and sold it the same day.

That night, Jake called Liz to tell her he was staying over in Dallas for a few days to conduct some business. Liz did not like Jake being away. She was pregnant with their second child and had her hands full with eight-month-old Lora. He promised to be home by the weekend and told her she could reach him at the TAS hanger or at the Melrose Hotel where he would be staying.

The new hydro-drill heads had gone into full production and Jake managed to slowly phase himself out of the Gainesville factory operations. Jake's business in Dallas was airplane business, the only business he was interested in at this time. He did not know exactly where or how, but he intended to become part of that business.

Red was flying as a copilot for Southern Airlines in the new Lockheed Electras on the Houston and New Orleans run. The new airline planned to open a Dallas, Texarkana to Little Rock route and Red was in line for a promotion to captain. The chief pilot left a message for Red that he wanted to meet with him.

The next morning around nine o'clock, Red picked Jake up at the Melrose Hotel on Oak Lawn in a beat up old Plymouth coupe he had purchased. The Southern Airways offices where they were headed were only a short five-mile drive away, but when Jake got in the old Plymouth, he could not resist kidding Red about his car.

"Think we'll make it by noon?"

"Beats walking," Red replied.

At the chief pilot's office, Red introduced Jake as his friend and fellow pilot.

"We can promote you to captain," the chief pilot informed Red, "and give you a pay raise if, and the operative word here being if, you'll go back on the Ford Trimotors."

"You mean make the Dallas to Lawton to Oklahoma City milk run?"

"That's it. It'll be awhile before we have any new openings for captains on the Electra. We've just finished promoting most of our senior Trimotor pilots to captain on the Electra."

Red did not hesitate.

"Sounds fair to me. I prefer flying pilot-in-command. Don't care what the crate is, I'll take the offer."

"Thought you might," and turning to Jake, the chief pilot asked, "Don't I know you from somewhere, Jake?"

Jake recognized the man as one of the pilots who gave him the Quiet Birdmen pin.

"Yes sir, I believe you do."

"That's right, you're the young pilot we awarded the QB to. What're you doing these days, still flying the mail for ol' Toots?"

"No sir, as you know, TAS lost the contract to Southern and there's not much charter work anymore. I was wondering if Southern had an opening for a copilot. If so, I'd like to apply."

"You went to flight school over at American Flyers, same as Red didn't you?"

"Yes sir, same class."

"If you're half as good a pilot as ol' Red here and if you can fly those Alphas without killing yourself, I guess we ought to hire you. Would Allen give you a good recommendation?"

"I believe he will."

"He will!" Red interjected. "I'm sure of that."

"You're both right. I was talking with Allen the other day and your name came up, Jake."

"What did ol' Allen say about Jake's flying?" Red asked.

"Allen said he could not only fly our airplanes, but that he could…"

Red finished the chief pilot's sentence for him, "…fly the box they came in!"

All three men laughed.

"Listen Jake, we don't have any full-time pilot positions open right now, but we could sure use you part-time, if you're interested."

"Part-time is fine with me."

Jake and Red prepared to leave.

"Thanks for the promotion, Chief," Red said.

"Don't thank me. You guys more than earn your pay in those ol' Trimotors. Red, you know the drill so take Jake here around and show him the ropes."

"Thanks," Jake said to the chief pilot. "I appreciate the opportunity to fly for you all."

"You're welcome, Jake. Give your particulars to the scheduling clerk on your way out. You'll need to get checked out in the Trimotor, so tell the clerk to put you down as copilot on Red's next flight. He can check you out enroute, no need for us to waste air time on an experienced pilot like yourself."

As they left the chief pilot's office, Red joked, "Last year this time you couldn't spell 'airline transport pilot.' Now you are one!"

The part-time pilot's salary was about enough to buy Jake's new airline uniform, but not enough to cover his travel expenses from home. The extra expense of staying over in Dallas would be his.

Jake did not want another apartment even though it might have been cheaper. He would stay at the Melrose whenever staying over in Dallas. Hopefully, flying part-time would work out to where he would not have to be away from Liz for long periods of time.

***

That evening, Jake and Red stopped by the TAS hangar to visit Toots.

"Sold both of the Lockheed Alphas," Toots explained. "We're using a couple of Stinson Voyagers now for charter flights. They're cheaper to operate."

"Yeah, I saw one of them in the hangar when we came in. How's business otherwise?" Jake asked.

"Maintenance end of the business has picked up and Eric's business is good, too. Southern is welcome to those airmail contracts and good riddance."

"I'm glad you feel that way, Toots, cause Red and I are both flying for them now."

"Congratulations, Jake. So they found another pilot as dumb as Red to fly those old crates," and Toots laughed.

Toots was a heavyset fellow and his belly shook when he laughed hard. Jake and Red laughed harder at the way Toots was laughing than at what he said.

Red and Toots continued their conversation while Jake went to see Eric at the Texas instrument shop.

Eric was seated at a workbench with the parts to a new type of radio automatic direction finder. He looked up when Jake came in.

"Just the man I've been wanting to see," Eric mused. "I need a pilot with too much time on his hands."

"You may have found him. What've you got going?"

"I need an aircraft to use as a flight-test bed for our new system and I can't afford to buy a plane and hire a pilot."

Jake looked over the parts strung out on the bench.

"This the new stuff here?"

"That's it. A new blind flying system I've designed that will integrate with the navigation equipment," and Eric gave Jake a run through on how the new system worked.

"I'm suitably impressed. Tell you what Eric, as soon as I pick up my new Spartan at Tulsa, I'll fly it straight here. It's going to need some radios anyway. We'll use it as a flight-test airplane for the new equipment."

"Good of you to offer, Jake, but I can't afford an expensive airplane like that. Besides, if this design is successful, we're going to need more shop space and employees in order to go into production."

Jake thought for a moment.

"I believe in what you're doing here, Eric, and I'd like to be a part of it. If you will incorporate your business, I'll foot all the aircraft flight-test costs and my attorney will even do all the paperwork for you."

"You'd do that, Jake?"

"Of course, I'll do most of the flying myself. Red can help out when he's off work. As to expanding, I'll advance you thirty thousand in funds to expand your facility once we get the new design working. You think you'd want to do that?"

Eric smiled and then laughed as he asked, "Are a genie out of a bottle or something? Not only yes, but hell yes!"

"My dad always said money is like manure, it don't help anything grow if you don't spread it around."

"What's the catch?"

"No catch, but it won't be free. I want twenty percent of the original stock issue. You make it work and we'll both make a lot of money. We might even save some lives if we make flying a little safer."

"Boy, have you got a deal!" Eric bellowed and shook Jake's hand real hard.

***

The Texas instrument repair shop went into full development mode on the new blind flying system. Eric worked night and day to build the prototype system so it would be ready when Jake's new plane arrived.

Jake delivered his new Spartan monoplane from Tulsa directly to Dallas for Eric to begin installing the experimental system.

Jake had not given his old Fairchild a name, only the large winged M logo on the sides of the fuselage, it being the practice of the times to name one's airplane the same way boat owners named their sea-going crafts. Lindbergh called his plane the *Spirit of St. Louis* and Wiley Post named his record setting Vega, the *Winnie Mae*.

The new Spartan, with its all aluminum airframe and highly polished finish, shined like chrome in the sunlight. Jake painted a red stripe down the side of the plane, bordered top and bottom by a narrow black pin stripe. On the Spartan's engine cowl where the stripe originated, he painted a flying red horse inside a circle.

The new Spartan low-wing monoplane was christened at an evening beer party in the hangar. Jake hosted the party or at least he purchased the keg of beer and announced that his new plane was to be named the *Pegasus*. Red made it official by pouring a mug of beer over the engine cowling.

Jake tried not to be away from home more than two nights in a row because Liz would get too lonely and would be upset with him when he finally came home. He evenly divided his time between the ranch and Dallas. When Eric did not need the *Pegasus*, Jake would fly it home to Gainesville and leave it in the hangar at the airport. Liz would drive over in their Ford Roadster to pick him up.

Before long, Eric was ready to install the full system in the *Pegasus* and the plane would be down for an indefinite period of time. Jake thought it an opportune time to go home and enjoy some quality time with his wife and new daughter.

One of the prettiest flying days God ever created was the day Red flew Jake home to the ranch in the *Pegasus*. They landed in the cow pasture where the old Jenny first landed. Everyone now referred to the landing spot as Waldo Field because Jake had called it that for years.

Jake opened the cabin door, climbed out on the wing and jumped to the ground. Red had not yet shut down the engine and the prop wash blew Jake's hair as he walked away from the plane.

Red taxied back down to the far end of the grass strip to takeoff and return the plane back to Eric in Dallas.

The powerful Pegasus engine roared to life as it rolled forward. The tail rose in the air and the plane lifted off, raising a cloud of dust in its wake.

As the *Pegasus* passed low over Jake head, he waved.

Red rocked the wings twice in reply and the engine sound faded in the distance.

The day was warm and pleasant as Jake walked the three miles to the summer ranch house down the old dusty dirt road he had walked so many times before as a young boy.

***

Several times a week, when Jake was home, he would go down to his dad's bank after business hours to review the Martin Company's business investments. Big Jake liked to get his son's opinion on their backing of new ventures, as he felt Jake kept up on the latest trends.

At home, Jake busied himself working in his rose garden or fixing up the place. On a morning when Jake was on his way into town for supplies, he saw Sarah coming toward him in her car and they stopped in the middle of the road to visit through open car windows.

"You know you leave Liz alone too much, Jake. She told me she has asked you to move her to Dallas."

"Yes she did, but that wouldn't work either because most of the time I'm in Dallas, I'm flying or working on my plane between flights. She'd be more alone there than she is here. At least here, she's got Mom and Violet to visit with and to help out with Lora."

"All I'm telling you is she's not a lone eagle like you, Jake. She's insecure and hates to be alone at night."

"Well, why don't you help me out here, Sarah. Maybe be a friend to her. I'm sure a good friend might ease the problem."

"Dang your hide anyway, Jake Martin. Sometimes you ask too much of me. Even if I would do it, Hank and I are moving to Lubbock next week. He starts school at Texas Tech and I've taken a job at the animal research center there."

Jake and Sarah said goodbye wishing each other well and went on their way.

They could not have known it at the time, but this casual meeting would be the last time their paths would cross again for almost six years.

***

When bad weather rolled in, Southern Airways preferred to have two pilots onboard and Jake often flew as copilot with Red in the Trimotor when needed.

When the weather was nice, severe-clear as Jake and Red jokingly referred to it, only one pilot was assigned to the shorter routes. From time to time, Jake picked up an extra run as pilot-in-command when one of the regular pilots was out sick or delayed on another run. He learned a new term they had for it, temporary captain.

The Southern Airways Trimotor flights seldom carried a full load of passengers, but the Kelly Airmail Act paid them two dollars per pound, per mile. This helped subsidize the airline enough to make the flights marginally profitable.

The Waters Act of 1926, revised in 1930, gave the Postmaster General additional powers to subsidize fledgling airlines. Before long, the large airlines and airline consortiums aggressively competed for these lucrative airmail routes. Some of the smaller airlines were bought up for their contracts alone.

Pilots like Red and Jake put their lives and the lives of their passengers on the line everyday. Making it through to the next destination in bad weather solely depended on their skills at the controls. Deep down many of the pilots wondered, but seldom admitted aloud, when they might get reliable navigation aids.

Leaving Dallas on a March morning in 1936, Jake was flying copilot for Red in the Trimotor. A strong cold front moved into Lawton from the northwest. Texans call these storms blue-northers as they actually appear on the horizon as dark blue in color.

Snow and icing conditions were likely for most of Oklahoma, but they hoped to be able to make their landing in Lawton and fly on to Oklahoma City before the storm hit. They would then wait the storm out and make the return flight to Dallas the following day as scheduled.

Unfortunately, the front moved in faster than they anticipated and about forty miles south of Lawton, flying at five thousand feet, the Trimotor started picking up ice on the leading edges of the wings.

"Let's descend to a lower altitude," Jake suggested, "and see if we can get into some warmer air."

Red agreed and started the descent. At a thousand feet above the ground, they began encountering snow. Their forward visibility was a complete white out. They could see the ground down and backwards in the direction of the blowing snow, but not forward.

"We'll have to be careful not to overshoot the airport," Jake reminded Red. "There's a line of high ridges north of Fort Sill over by Medicine Park."

As they approached Lawton, they could not see the airport up ahead. Red watched out the side window to position the aircraft downwind and waited until the landing strip passed under the left wing. He and Jake were well aware that when they turned into the wind, all they would be able to see would be a wall of white snow.

The turbulent air bounced the Trimotor around like a freight wagon on a bad road. Red fought to keep the plane level. Jake monitored the flight instruments and adjusted the power to maintain their altitude and airspeed.

As Red turned into the wind, both pilots swung their heads to look out the side windows trying to judge their height above the ground. They knew their altimeter reading was no longer valid because with the passing of the storm front, the barometric pressure would have changed.

"Watch your rate of descent, we're not there yet!" Jake coached Red.

"I'm trying! Give me a little more power."

Jake complied.

Red held ten mile an hour above the normal approach speed in case he had to go around and stayed about two-hundred feet above the ground, enough to clear any tall trees until the road and a wire fence at the boundary to the airport passed under the plane.

Red hollered, "Now!"

Jake pulled the power full off. Both had seen the same thing at the same time, the airport beacon light flashing faintly up ahead through the falling snow.

Red eased back on the wheel and held the Trimotor in a three-point attitude waiting to feel the ground under the landing gear.

"Thump, thump, rumble," came the familiar sound of the wheels touching down.

Jake reached over and slapped Red on the shoulder.

"You had such a headwind, we didn't' even use half the runway. I'll bet we weren't even doing thirty mile an hour over the ground when we finally touched down."

"Nothing to it. See, even a blind pilot can land an airplane," Red joked.

Red turned the Trimotor onto the taxiway to the airport terminal.

Jake looked back into the cabin to check on their six passengers.

"Everyone okay back there?"

Four of the passengers sat with rather blank looks on their faces and a heavyset businessman had slept through the whole thing.

A little old lady in a seat nearest the cockpit replied, "We're all fine, but I got to tell you something, sonny. I think the train rides a whole lot smoother than this here airplane does."

"Yes ma'am," Jake said and looked around at Red who was laughing.

The storm had only dusted the airfield with a half-inch of snow as the front moved rapidly to the southeast. Rays of late evening sunlight broke through the overcast sky.

The fast moving storm front passed over Lawton in a few hours and the air temperature dropped below the freezing point. This was good because the air upstairs would be even colder and there would be very little chance of picking up ice on the wings.

Loaded with three new passengers, minus two that got off in Lawton, the Southern Airways flight proceeded on to Oklahoma City where they deplaned their passengers.

The second and worse part of the late winter storm hit Oklahoma City early that evening shortly after Red and Jake landed. The roads into town quickly became un-passable. Jake curled up on a couch in the flight service station and went to sleep.

The next morning, Jake woke up and peered out the frost-covered window to see two feet of snow covering the runway and their plane. He looked around for Red and found him curled up on a pile of full mail sacks over in the corner by a potbellied stove still sound asleep.

Jake woke him up. After a couple of cups of coffee brewed by the flight service station attendant, Jake and Red agreed that one thing appeared certain. The Southern Airways flight to Dallas via Lawton was not going anywhere today. They could not even taxi let alone takeoff.

Jake tried to call Liz at home, but there was no answer so he called the main ranch house.

Flo answered the phone.

"Yes, Liz is here with us. You might be interested to know you are the father of a new eight-pound baby boy. Doc Winens came out from town last night on horseback in the storm to make the delivery."

"Is Liz okay?"

"Yes, Jacob, mother and son are doing fine. Liz wants me to ask you if it's alright to name the boy Michael?"

Jake was surprised as he thought Liz was not due for a couple more weeks.

"Jacob, you there?"

"Oh yeah, Mom, sure. Michael is fine with me. Was she thinking of the archangel when she picked the name?"

"No, I don't think so. She just said she thought the name had a nice sound to it."

"Listen Mom, tell Liz I'll be home as soon as this storm lets up and we can get out of Oklahoma City."

Michael Teel Martin was three days old before his father returned home and saw him for the first time.

***

When Jake laid over in Dallas to fly for Southern Airways, he spent his standby time at the TAS hangar tinkering with the *Pegasus* and the new radio instrument navigation system.

Eric's concept was to develop a gyro stabilization platform that would interface with the radio navigation. This integration would be the prototype for what Eric called the AFDS or Automatic Flight Direction System.

The most significant problem was the equipment's large size and weight. The heat generated from the circuit also caused components to burn out. Eric worked continually on ways to use lower voltages, but this was hard to accomplish and still achieve the required outputs.

Eric with his design work and Charley building the racing airplane had taught Jake more about electronics and aeronautics than he could have learned at the finest university in the world. These new technologies were not yet even assimilated into the academic curriculum. Jake had literally earned a Ph.D. in these fields without any formal acknowledgment.

Jake flew the *Pegasus* up to Wichita, Kansas early on a Friday morning. He wanted to flight-test the system on a long cross-country and also to show the new system to Walter Beech. He would then fly to the ranch and spend the weekend at home before returning to Dallas on Monday.

Late that afternoon, cruising at an altitude of ten thousand feet enroute to Gainesville, Jake smelled smoke in the cockpit and it appeared to be originating in one of the new radio panels. He cut off all of the electrical power to the radios, but something continued to smolder in one of the equipment boxes. Jake reached for a small soda fire extinguisher to keep it handy in case the panel burst into flames.

Crossing the state border of southern Kansas into northern Oklahoma, Jake knew he was not far from Enid Army Air Base in case he needed to make an emergency landing, but he could easily make the Stillwater airport by the time he played off his altitude and airspeed.

Reducing engine power, he applied twenty degrees of flaps and started his descent for an approach to landing at Payne County Airport near Stillwater. He already knew the wind direction by observing the smoke from some burning trash north of town.

He used extra care in looking for other planes in the traffic pattern, as he did not intend to use a standard circling approach to a landing. On final, he checked the tetrahedron to confirm the wind direction and landed straight in on the active runway.

The smoldering in the equipment had stopped by the time he taxied the *Pegasus* up to the main hangar. Jake went into the airport service shop and found the owner operator, a man by the name of Paul Silvers.

"Do you have an electrical or radio shop repairman here?" Jake inquired.

"No, we send most of our work to Oklahoma City to be fixed," Silvers replied. "What's the problem?"

"Don't know for sure. If we can bring my plane into the hangar out of the wind, I'd like to take a look at it myself."

Silvers hollered at his helper to open the hangar door and the three men pushed Jake's aircraft into the hangar out of the strong Oklahoma wind.

"I do have one suggestion," Silvers told Jake. "Some of the engineering students over at Oklahoma A&M have done some work for us on occasion. One or two of them are pretty sharp on electrical stuff."

"How would I get a hold of one of these guys?"

"Call over to the A&M campus and see if they can recommend someone. You're welcome to use the phone in my office."

Jake made the call and got some lady on the phone.

"I need to know if you can put me in touch with one of your electrical engineering students that might be able to do some repair work for me."

"Do you need your house re-wired or something like that, mister?" the lady asked.

"No, the radios in my airplane went out and I need someone to help me repair them."

"Oh, why didn't you say so in the first place?" The lady's voice brightened. "That would be Earl Mason. He went to school at Coyne in Chicago before he got married and transferred back here. He is the only one around here knows anything about that sort of stuff. You can call him at home. His phone number is Melrose 051."

Jake thanked the lady at the university, hung up and dialed Earl's number.

A young lady answered the phone.

"Hello, is Earl Mason there?" Jake asked.

"No, this is Lola, his wife. What do you need Earl for?"

Jake explained his problem to Lola.

"I'm sure Earl can handle that," Lola assured Jake. "I expect him home any minute now and I'll send him right on out to the airport."

Jake called Liz next to tell her he was stranded in Stillwater and as he expected, Liz was upset.

"Look Liz, I'm sorry," he explained. "Things like this happen. I'm dealing with the situation as best I can. With any luck, I should be home sometime in the morning."

With the *Pegasus* in the hangar and the doors closed against the fierce prairie wind, Jake climbed in the cockpit and began removing access panels from the equipment.

In about a half an hour, the young fellow came through the hangar side door with his own toolbox in hand.

At first, Jake was reluctant to let Earl work on his airplane's circuitry as he looked to be no more than sixteen years old. As it turned out, Earl was actually in his early twenties and was just young looking.

Earl began by looking over the schematic Eric had drawn and had luckily left a copy of in the back seat of the *Pegasus*. Earl seemed to understand how the equipment operated. He systematically rewired some of the circuitry. As Jake watched, he realized the young fellow knew what he was doing.

Jake worked along with Earl well into the night. Silvers and his helper had long since gone home. About three o'clock in the morning, Earl finished the repair and using a battery charger unit in the hangar, they fired up the system. The equipment all worked and to Jake's astonishment, the circuit drew less amperage and ran cooler than before.

"Earl, how'd you do that?"

"First, I built a Wheatstone bridge circuit to distribute the load better. It's old technology, but it works. Then I changed out some of the resistors to better balance the load and…"

Jake interrupted, "Do you want a job? Eric's outfit in Dallas could really use a smart young fellow like you."

"Thanks, but no," Earl replied without hesitation. "I'm trying to finish my degree here at A&M and my wife Lola is expecting our first child in July. I'm sure we don't want to move to Dallas right now. Actually, I'm hoping to go to work for Beech or Boeing aircraft, maybe even for the Air Corps in Wichita after I graduate."

Over the last two cups of coffee in the pot, Jake listened as Earl explained how he modified the equipment to improve the performance.

Earl had seen Eric's name on the schematic.

"You need to tell your man, Eric Johnson that he needs to design a thing I call a transition resistor. The more you can miniaturize that part of the circuit, the less current will be required. Those vacuum tube diodes are where most of the heat comes from and are what caused the resistors to burn out and smoke so bad."

Jake gave Earl his business card and wrote the phone number of Texas instruments in Dallas on the back.

"In case you ever change your mind about a job, here is the number to call." Jake handed Earl the card. "We could use a good mind like yours, but I'll tell Eric everything you said because it sounds to me like it's the same problems Eric has been trying to overcome."

Jake paid Earl what he asked for his time with an extra hundred-dollar bill folded inside it.

"I can't take all that," Earl said politely.

"Sure you can, put it toward your college. Besides, you earned it coming out here and working all night."

"Thanks, but Lola ain't going to believe this one!"

Jake left a note on Silver's office desk along with a business card and the address where Silvers could bill him for the use of the service hangar and shop.

Jake spent what remained of Friday night, actually Saturday morning, propped up asleep in a desk chair in the hangar office.

At first light, Jake pulled the *Pegasus* out of the hangar and closed the hangar doors. The wind was calm and a beautiful spring morning dawned on the horizon as Jake and the *Pegasus* rolled down the runway headed for Gainesville.

The re-wired electrical system worked great and Jake was anxious to show the redesigned circuit to Eric the following week.

What Earl had suggested as the design Eric should look into was a micro transducer. Jake had no way of knowing at the time that Earl's design concept was the pre-cursor to the transistor, a device that would revolutionize the entire electronic industry in coming decades.

***

Southern Airways announced its merger with Universal Aviation and Standard Air Lines to form a new airline consortium called American Airlines. The airline pilots that started with the two older airlines had a formal seniority system and in the negotiations, their managements insisted on keeping all of their pilots.

The result of those negotiations meant Red and Jake would lose their jobs at Southern Airways along with some other good pilots. Jake welcomed the layoff, as he had been feeling a little guilty about not spending more time at home with Lora and his new son Michael.

Red corresponded with Juan Trippe at Pan Am about a job flying for Trippe's airline. Pan Am required all of their pilots to have a college degree. Red had two years of college before going to flight school at American Flyers and finished his bachelor's degree part-time while flying for Southern Airways.

Trippe insisted on interviewing all new hire Pan Am pilots personally, so Red now planned to go to New York to meet with Trippe in an effort to get hired by Pan Am. Red conveniently forgot to mention to Jake that Pan Am required its pilots to have a college degree. He asked Jake to go to New York with him, but no matter about the degree requirement, as Jake declined to go anyway.

MANHATTAN

On a spring morning in 1936, Jake was home with Liz, Lora and baby Michael at their house on the Flying M ranch. He had gotten up early and was wandering around the front yard with a cup of freshly brewed coffee in his hand. Liz and the kids were still in bed asleep.

The morning dew had dampened his house slippers as he walked through the grass. He stopped to stare for a while at the garden patch, thinking about setting out some tomato plants or maybe he would finish outlining the garden patch with rose bushes this year.

Jake looked up when he heard the sound of a vehicle off in the distance crossing the creek bridge. A plume of dust rose from the dirt road, too small for a car and too fast for a horse so it had to be the Sittler boy on that old war surplus Harley Davidson motorcycle of his. The two-cylinder engine on the Harley backed down as the rider turned into the gate and headed up to the house.

Jake waited patiently as the Sittler boy dismounted and came over to him.

"Mornin' Mr. Martin, got a telegram here for ya. Looks like it might be from New Yoke City."

Jake sat his coffee cup down on a large rock.

"Suppose you've already read it. What's it about?"

Jake fished in his pocket for two bits to give to the boy whose part-time job was to deliver telegrams and handed the tip to him.

"Thank you, Mr. Martin."

The Sittler boy looked down at the ground and kicked some dirt with his boot.

"Well?" Jake said and waited holding the telegram in his hand.

"Something about a flying job, I think."

The boy mounted his motorcycle and gave the engine crank a kick-start. He waved as he took off back out the gate and turned onto the dirt road back to town.

Jake opened the envelope and read the telegram. Pan Am airline hiring. Stop. Both may have jobs. Stop. Staying at Plaza Hotel. Stop. Red.

Jake looked off in the distance, folded the telegram up and stuffed it in his pocket. He picked up his cup of coffee that had gotten cold and went in the house.

Liz was just getting up and not in a very good mood. She had been up most of the night with the baby.

"What was all the commotion outside?"

"Good morning, honey. Oh, just the Sittler boy on that old motorcycle of his."

Jake dressed and left for work. He went first to the bank to visit with Big Jake and discussed investing some of the Martin trust funds in one or more of the emerging aviation businesses. They talked about Pam Am briefly.

At the factory, Jake thought about the telegram and Red's suggestion during most of the workday.   Along about five o'clock that afternoon, an hour later in New York, Jake called Red at the Plaza Hotel from the factory. Jake wanted to get the details from Red first hand.

"Robert Allen at American Flyers has recommended us for positions as copilots with Pan Am airlines here in New York," Red explained. "I think we can both get on with them. How soon can you get up here?"

"I don't know Red. I'll get back to you tomorrow and let you know."

That evening after dinner, Jake waited until things quieted down. After Liz put Michael and Lora to bed, she positioned herself comfortably on the sofa and was thumbing through a *Town and Country* magazine, which came in the mail that morning. He seated himself in a chair across from her.

"What would you think about me going to work flying for Pan Am airlines in New York?"

"What brought this on, out of the blue?"

Jake handed her the folded up telegram he had been carrying in his pocket all day.

"Seems they might have an opening for me and Red with their airline."

Liz read the telegram and sat quietly for a moment.

"Actually, Jake, it sounds like the kind of offer you have been hoping for."

"It's not really an offer, only a possibility."

"I've been really bored out here in the country. Would I be able to go to New York with you?"

Jake stood up and paced the floor for a bit. He had a family now he needed to consider. Life was after all only a series of choices, he thought, some good, some bad.

"Sure, don't see why not, but if you do, we'll keep the place here to come back to when we can. I've lived in the big city before and after awhile it gets on your nerves."

"Might not get on mine, I'd really like to see New York. I've read and heard so much about it."

"Okay, tell you what let's do. I'll go up to New York and make sure the job offer is solid. Then you can come up. Mom and Violet can take care of Lora and Michael for a while until we can get settled. Violet's a good nanny."

"Oh Jake, I'm getting excited just thinking about living in New York City. Think of all the exciting things there are to do."

Liz rattled on for a while with Jake only half listening. He pondered whether this would be the right thing for Liz, as unstable she could be at times, but Jake too was bored with the country life. He longed to return to flying and even more so to be part of a new worldwide airway system.

***

Pan Am airways got its start when its founder, Juan Trippe, a young Yale graduate, obtained a U.S. Airmail Service contract to fly the airmail to Havana in 1927. The young man was a flyer himself and like Jake, he held a strong fascination with aviation.

Trippe came from a wealthy family and never hesitated to use his family's influence to further his business interests. Jake and Trippe were kindred spirits of a sort.

By the time Trippe acquired the airmail contract, he had already failed at two previous attempts to start an air service. Undaunted by prior failures, he negotiated for the exclusive landing rights in Cuba with President Gerardo Machado. The young aviation pioneer also convinced two other small airlines to join him and contribute funds to the new venture.

There was one minor problem. The new airline had no airplanes. The aircraft selected to make the ninety-mile over the water flights, a Fokker FK-7, could not be delivered in time to meet the contract deadline. Even worse, the new airfield at Key West was not ready.

By leasing a single-engine FC-2 floatplane from West Indian Express in the Dominican Republic, Trippe's new air service met the deadline and a new airline was born.

The small seaplanes departed for Havana from Key West because of their limited range. The airmail actually covered more miles on the Flagler railway line than it did airborne. Due to this somewhat odd beginning, Key West City laid claim to being home to the first U.S. international airmail service. Trippe soon acquired longer range, three-motor Fokkers for the new flying boat company, then called Island Air Service and moved the operation to Miami.

In the early 1920s, two Americans living in Mexico established CMT airline. Company Mexican de Transportation serviced the booming oil fields around Tapioca. In 1929, the U.S. Post Office asked for bids on an airmail contract from the U.S. to Mexico City route. Trippe bought CMT and successfully bid on the airmail contracts. The airline later became known as Mexicana.

Because of his given name, his dark hair and his many business ventures south of the border, most people assumed Juan Trippe to be a Latino. He was not. In fact, he did not even speak Spanish very well. If on occasion, the misconception assisted in a South American negotiation, he made little or no effort to correct the impression.

In the early days of the flying boats, Trippe's friend Igor Sikorsky designed and built the Model SK-38 flying boats for the airline. Larger flying boats were soon needed and Sikorsky provided Pan Am with the Model SK-42 Clipper.

Captain Edwin Musick and his crew flew the new SK-42 Clipper non-stop from San Francisco to Hawaii in April of 1935. The flight took over twenty hours and the excessive fuel required greatly reduced the Clipper's payload.

The flight returned to San Francisco with thousands of letters, which made it an historic first delivery of airmail across the Pacific. The flight proved to be an excellent publicity stunt on the part of Trippe, but the SK-42 teetered on the maximum edge of its performance capability when it made the flight.

A longer-range SK-42B model, delivered to Pan Am in mid 1935, would make the same flight to Hawaii. Trippe hired Charles Lindbergh to make the flight without passengers to determine if the 42B would be able to handle the new route. Lindbergh's report was favorable.

The following year, a giant new flying boat based on the wing design of the Army's largest bomber and the hull design of the Navy's largest seaplane was proposed by famous airplane designer Glen Luther Martin. Glen was no relation to Jake.

The new and longest-range yet flying boat, the GLM-130 Clipper, would soon be ready to conquer both the Pacific and the Atlantic Ocean routes.

***

Jake flew the *Pegasus* to Floyd Bennett Field where he landed and arranged to hangar the aircraft while in New York. Trippe was expected to return from Miami after a visit to the Pan Am seaplane base at Dinner Key. Jake and Red had an appointment to meet with Trippe at his office the day following Jake's arrival.

Jake arrived on time at the Pan Am New York offices. Red was running late so Jake went ahead and introduced himself to the secretary.

"Please have a seat, Mr. Martin," she said. "Mr. Trippe is engaged at the moment, but he is expecting you. I believe we are also expecting a Mr. Elliott Henderson?"

"Yes ma'am, he should be along any minute."

Jake looked around for a place to wait and took a seat in the outer office. He picked up a *New Yorker* magazine from the small table next to his chair.

The elevator doors opened and Red rushed over and sat down beside Jake.

"Is he here, are we expected?"

"Yes," Jake said without looking up from the magazine he was looking through.

"Boy, this New York City traffic is something else!"

Jake finally looked over at Red and noticed how he was dressed.

"You've got that dang tie on!"

Red looked down and brushed the tie with his hand.

"Of course, I told you it's my lucky tie. Besides, I kinda like it."

In talking with a pilot at Floyd Bennett Field, Jake had found out about Tripp's policy of only hiring pilots with college degrees. This would not be an obstacle for Red, but it would be for Jake. No matter, he wanted to discuss a stock purchase with Trippe and would stick it out to support Red's effort in applying for a pilot's job.

"Red, you did finish college, didn't you? I mean graduate and get a degree."

"Oh sure, I graduated the semester after we got laid off flying for Southern. Hung my diploma on the wall at home right beside my flight school graduation certificate."

"That's about all they're good for," Jake mumbled.

"Huh, what'd you say?"

"Never mind. I'll go into the interview with you, but there's no way in heck an uppity Yankee outfit like this is going to hire some uneducated Texas flatlander like me."

"Aw Jake, don't talk like that, you're the smartest guy I know."

Red paused when the door to Tripp's office opened.

Juan Trippe emerged from his office and looked toward Jake and Red.

Through the open door, Jake could see a tall, slender middle-aged fellow sitting across from the large executive office desk in the center of the room. Jake recognized the man as Charles Lindbergh.

Trippe invited Jake and Red into his office. Lindbergh stood as they entered and Trippe introduced them.

Jake and Red had followed Lindbergh's flying exploits with great interest over the past few years. This was quite a personal thrill for the both of them.

Lindbergh excused himself and left the office. Trippe offered his two new guests a seat.

"What is it we're supposed to talk about today, gentlemen?" Trippe asked as he returned to his chair behind the large desk.

Red moved to the edge of his chair.

"About flying for Pan Am, Mr. Trippe! In your correspondence you said…"

Trippe smile, as he was only putting Red on.

"Of course, Mr. Henderson. They call you Red don't they?"

"Yes sir."

"You come to me highly recommended by Bob Allen. If he says you're good enough to fly for Pan Am, that's good enough for me."

Red tried unsuccessfully to get Trippe's attention to ask a question, but Trippe proceeded to fill out some kind of form on his desk and ignored him.

Trippe signed the form at the bottom and reached across the desk to hand the form to Red.

Red jumped to his feet and took the paper from Trippe.

"Report to the Pan Am hangar out on Long Island tomorrow morning about eight o'clock," Trippe said.

Red took the paper and shook Trippe's hand.

"I'd like to go on out there now and get familiar with things, if that's okay."

"That'll be fine. Give that hire slip to Captain Steve Nelson, our chief pilot. He'll get you set up to start checking out in one of our flying boats."

Red held the pilot hire slip in his hand and smiled like he had just placed first at the Cleveland Air Races.

"Thank you, Mr. Trippe, you'll never regret this!"

"Sure hope not. Good luck to you, Red, and welcome aboard."

The intercom on Trippe's desk buzzed.

"Yes, what is it?" Trippe asked.

"It's long distance. The operations manager at Dinner Key in Miami is holding on the phone for you, sir," was the reply from the secretary's voice over the intercom.

"Good to meet you, Mr. Trippe," Jake said as he got up to leave with Red. "Maybe we can visit another time when it's more convenient."

"No it's fine Martin, stay for now," and Trippe motioned for Jake to return to his chair. "Tell him I'll call him back and hold the rest of my calls for now," Trippe told his secretary on the intercom.

"I'll wait for you outside in the lobby, Jake," Red said and left closing the office door behind him.

Jake nodded okay and sat back down.

"Understand you've got some questions on a corporate level you'd like to ask about our airline. Is that right, Martin?"

"Just call me Jake, everyone else does."

"Very well then, Jake it is. If you're comfortable with it, you're welcome to call me Juan."

"The Martin Trust is looking into several different growth companies as investments. I've read most of the prospectus on Pan Am and your airline is a good candidate."

Trippe leaned back in his chair.

"No better time than the present to invest in this airline. We're expanding faster than we can buy equipment to service the routes. We're presently flying to two-dozen countries that cover twenty thousand flying miles of air routes. A couple of years ago, we bought out O'Neill's airline."

The airline Trippe referred to was the New York, Rio and Buenos Aires Airline, also known as the NYRBA. He reached for a cigar in a box on his desk and motioned for Jake to take one.

Jake shook his head no.

As he talked, Trippe waved his hands wildly and would occasionally use the unlit Cuban cigar in his hand to make a point, but he never bothered to light the cigar.

"The Sikorsky SK-38 helped us get started and we've upgraded to the Model SK-42B now. It's not common knowledge, but Lindbergh whom you just met, made a test run from the west coast to Hawaii for us. It's his opinion that even Igor's new 42B that Andre Priestler redesigned for us won't do the job in the Pacific either. Not enough payload, range, all those things."

"If the Sikorsky won't do the job, then what are you going to use in the Pacific?"

"We're working on it," Trippe said and went on to explain a myriad of his new ideas for Pan Am.

Jake listened intently to everything Trippe said, but at the first opportunity, Jake brought up the need for a new Clipper again.

"I think your answer might be the new GLM-130, but if Boeing Aircraft ever builds the model 314 they have on the drawing board, it'll be even better. In my opinion, those are the types of aircraft you'll need to operate safely in the Pacific."

"You're up on your aircraft designs, Jake, but like you say, the 314 is still only an idea on the drawing board," and Trippe smiled.

From Trippe's comment and his sly smile, Jake deduced Pan Am probably already had placed an order for one or more of the new GLM-130s.

"What are you and Big Jake prepared to offer?"

Jake was a little caught off guard when Trippe called his father by his familiar name, but he quickly decided Juan Trippe had not become successful in business by not knowing whom he was dealing with.

"We've authorized our company attorney, Larry Wilcox, to invest two million immediately. Our pockets are deeper than that if the debenture you offer is attractive enough and the new aircraft can be used as collateral."

Trippe stood up and came around to the front of his desk. He extended his hand to Jake.

"I assure you the offer will be that attractive. One thing about dealing with a Texan, they don't beat around the bush. Tell Big Jake 'hello' for me when you call him and say that it sounds like we might have a deal."

Jake and Trippe shook hands.

"Looking forward to doing business with you… Juan. There is one thing I would like to request. That is, if we're going to be investing in Pan Am."

"What's that?" Trippe asked, returning to his chair behind the large desk.

"Authorization to visit your engineering department from time to time in order to stay abreast of things. I've got a bit of experience in development and I might even be of some help to your company in that regard."

Trippe leaned over his desk to fill out and sign two authorization forms. He handed the forms to Jake.

Jake did not look at the forms as he assumed them to be his permission to inspect the Pan Am operations and for access to the facilities. He thanked Trippe and started to leave.

"Do you know how to get to the hangar and how to locate Captain Nelson?" Trippe asked.

"I'm not sure I understand exactly what you mean."

Trippe smiled.

"That first piece of paper authorizes you access to our engineering departments. The second piece of paper is your employment hire sheet. Give it to Nelson when you and Red finally figure out how to get out there."

Jake looked at the papers in his hand.

"I thought you only hired college graduates."

Trippe stood and buttoned his light tan, double-breasted business suit.

"We've got some good pilots, but we need some great pilots to make this thing in the Pacific work. I made the rule. I can break it if I want. Welcome aboard, Jake."

"Thank you, Juan, thank you very much," Jake said and could not help but beam with a wide smile as he shook Trippe's hand.

Thus was the beginning of a lifelong friendship between two men who shared a common bond, a vision and a passion for aviation.

***

That evening, Jake called home from his hotel to tell Liz all that had transpired.

"How are the kiddos and how are you doing with me being gone?"

"I want to know how long it will be before I can come to New York!" Liz asked.

"I will be starting my training in the flying boats soon and you can come up sometime after that's completed. I'll start looking for a place for us to stay."

Liz asked excitedly, "Can I take the train to come up to New York?"

"Don't be silly. It's faster to fly. As my wife you can fly for free, if they have seats available."

Liz continued to plead with Jake.

"Okay, you can take the train, but when you make the arrangements, book a Pullman. It's a long ride. I'll let you know the date, but it shouldn't be more than a few weeks."

***

Jake and Red reported daily to Captain Nelson at the Port Washington seaplane dock where the Pan Am training flights were conducted.

Nelson was a middle-aged fellow of medium height and build. He had a slight touch of gray at the temples of his dark brown hair. His navy blue uniform was well tailored and immaculately pressed. His white uniform cap with patent-leather black bill shined in the sunlight.

Nelson appeared rather stern with a Dick Tracy look to his unsmiling profile, but Jake took a liking to him right off. Nelson had logged thousands of flying hours, which included one around-the-world flight in a Navy P2Y Consolidated Aircraft flying boat in 1933.

Jake, Red and four other new-hires began their flight training with Nelson and another instructor pilot. As part of their lengthy cockpit checkout, trainee pilots were blindfolded and required to touch each control, switch or lever when the instructor called out its name. This verified the pilot could fly the Clipper in total darkness if the lighting failed.

A smaller SK-38A seaplane, retired from one of the routes due to its limited payload capability, was being used as a primary flight trainer for the new pilots.

Once airborne, the flying boat flew like any other land-based aircraft, but considerable orientation was required to train the new pilots in water handling. Docking instead of taxiing and parking an airplane required newfound skills. Experience in marine craft handling was helpful, but not required. Jake was fortunate in that regard, never having been further out on the water than the middle of a catfish pond.

The pilots sharpened their takeoff, low altitude flying and water landing skills in the bays and inlets along the northern Long Island coastline. The hardest thing to learn for new pilots was judging their altitude above the water. Landing near the shore where the pilot could judge his altitude based on the relative size of distant objects was easier than the more difficult task of landing on the water where there were no references except the horizon.

Jake began thinking about an instrument Eric could design capable of measuring the length of a radio wave between the aircraft and the ocean's surface, which would measure the aircraft's height above the water. Jake was on the right track, but bouncing a radio wave off of the water would eventually prove to be the design that worked.

Land based planes most often landed nose high and power off. The new pilots had to master power on touchdowns and not letting the nose of the flying boat pitch forward on touchdown. Otherwise, there was a danger of performing a fatal maneuver known as the submarine.

The seaplane pilot trainees also had to learn to maintain a wing level attitude to prevent one of the outrigger pontoons contacting the water before the hull could slow the seaplane. If the outrigger touched first the aircraft might veer hard to one side and this too could possibly be fatal.

Jake was amazed at how fast a touchdown on the water would rapidly decelerate the seaplane versus the long rollouts of a land-based airplane on a landing strip.

Two types of water takeoffs were practiced over and over. The rough water takeoff required agile operation of the flight controls to prevent the nose of the flying boat or one of the propellers contacting a wave.

The smooth water takeoff, usually encountered in bay areas, caused the hull of the aircraft to be suctioned onto the water preventing liftoff. A wide, high speed circling taxi run was executed to create an artificial wake on the smooth water. Then the pilot would come back across the wake into the wind. This would break the hull suction allowing the craft to gain airspeed.

The fourth week of training included crew position instruction in the larger SK-42 aircraft. The newly hired junior flight officers trained only in the copilot's position. Senior Pam Am flight officers transitioning to captain were used in these training scenarios and flew in the pilot's crew position. These master pilots, as they were known, would become the commanders in charge of the soon to be expanded Pacific Flying Clipper fleet.

Needless to point out, Jake exceeded all the other new pilots in his skill at handling the two different models of flying boats and in performing every maneuver.

All of the new hire pilots were assigned as junior flight officers. Most were sent to man the expanding South American air routes, but Jake, Red and Chuck Stine were retained in New York.

Jake and some of the other pilots had Stine pegged as irresponsible. They had all seen him do some unsafe things, but he always seemed to get by with them. Jake considered reporting Stine for one incident of negligence, but decided against it at the time.

***

On the morning of May 7th, Jake's phone rang. He woke and fumbled to reach for the phone and answered it.

"Jake, this is Red. She's due to arrive from Germany this afternoon. Get yourself out of bed and pick me up so we can drive over to Lakehurst, New Jersey. We can get there in plenty of time to see her land, if we get a move on."

Jake was not completely awake yet as he sat on the edge of the bed rubbing his eyes.

"See her, who, what land?" he asked.

"The dirigible *Hindenburg*, you know Jake, the German Zeppelin."

When Jake and Red arrived at Lakehurst, the sky was high overcast and a light rain shower was passing over the Navy airfield. The *Hindenburg* had arrived earlier, but circled and left so as not to get caught attempting to moor during the rainsquall.

The *Hindenburg* returned around seven in the evening and circled the airfield again. A light rain shower still lingered over the far edge of the airfield and there seemed to be a reluctance on the part of the airship's commander to make a commitment to a landing.

Speculation by the onlookers centered on the surrounding air being so disturbed that a static discharge might occur when the airship contacted the mooring tower.

The *Hindenburg* was one of the largest dirigibles ever built and yet relegated to using hydrogen for buoyancy. Adequate supplies of Helium only occurred naturally in the United States. The only supplies of any quantity came from wells near Amarillo, Texas and the U.S. government would not permit the Kelly Company to sell helium to Germany.

The clouds became more ominous as the *Hindenburg* made a sharp turn and committed to its final approach. Two ropes dropped from the bow of the airship. Dozens of sailors on the ground ran to grab hold of them and guide the airship to the tower.

"Did you see that?" Red exclaimed.

"See what?" Jake asked.

"I swear I saw a flash of static lightning right behind the airship's tail stabilizers."

"Guess I didn't see it," Jake said.

Red turned to ask the people standing nearby, "Did you see a flash?"

One lady said she had, but most everyone else said they had not.

Suddenly, a ball of blue-white fire moved forward along the top and side of the dirigible's upper tail fin and grew larger. In seconds, flames engulfed the airship.

Jake observed the strangest phenomena as the airship began to fall to earth. The flames all moved upward. Only small amounts of debris, pieces of the structure and the burnt fabric covering floated to the ground.

Bright yellow flames from what appeared to be a fuel fire emanated from the engine area. Jake recognized a petroleum-based fire coming from the diesel fuel supply for the engines. As it turned out, those exposed to the burning fuel and not the hydrogen were the most seriously injured.

Jake actually observed dozens of people walking right out of the hydrogen flames, appearing like ghostly figures emerging from a fog. At the very worst, only their hair and eyebrows were singed.

One or two people hurt themselves as they jumped from the airship's cabin windows and limped as they struggled to escape from under the collapsing airship's airframe.

The monster of the sky was no longer buoyant and the doomed airship's massive structure settled to the ground like a giant floundering whale.

Red ran to help a lady who stumbled and fell as she ran from the crash. Jake took off running behind Red. He wrestled one of the German flight officers to the ground and rolled him to smother the flames on his uniform.

Navy firemen arrived quickly on the scene extinguishing the remnants of the diesel fires. Navy medical corpsman began taking care of the injured. The whole thing was over so fast, Jake looked around and could find no one else that needed assistance.

The only fatalities and persons seriously burned appeared to have come from the area near the diesel fuel storage tanks. Hydrogen proved to be a far less lethal killer than ordinary petroleum fuel. Jake wondered if history would take note of this fact or would it be the other way around.

"I glanced at my watch," Red said, "and from the time the flames erupted until the airship started crashing to the ground, only thirty-two seconds elapsed."

Jake and Red hung around the airfield for the rest of the evening and after dark. There was nothing to do except stand around like everyone else and discuss what had happened.

The crash of the *Hindenburg* was filmed by a newsreel cameraman and remained an awesome and fearful sight, but amazingly, much less of a disaster than it would continue to be reported.

***

Chuck Stine hung out at the Manhattan Jazz Club on 42nd Street and often sat in to play piano with the band. Chuck seemed to have a new girl every night. The young, good-looking pilot and jazz master of the ivory 88s had no trouble attracting the ladies.

Jake not only thought Stine's piloting skills were lacking, but for some reason he just plain did not like the fellow.

Red, on the other hand, seemed to get along fine with Chuck and befriended him. Red began hanging out at the Jazz Club and took up with a cute little black-haired Italian girl, seeing her on a regular basis.

Attractive young ladies were easy pick-ups for the young handsome pilots in their airline uniforms and the musicians who frequented the club. Jake went to the Jazz Club a couple of times with Red, but resisted the temptation to get involved with any of the girls even though several of them made a good run at him. Jake put his love life on hold until Liz came to New York.

The Friday before Liz arrived in New York on Sunday, Jake took delivery on a new two-tone, tan and brown Dusenburg Cabriolet from the Manhattan Coach Salon.

He drove it to the Jazz Club that Saturday night and took Red out to have a look at his new automobile. Red could not resist the opportunity for a good pun.

"Wow, that's a real doozy!" he exclaimed.

***

On Sunday, Jake went to Grand Central Station to meet Liz when her train pulled in and to surprise her with the new Dusenburg Cabriolet he bought for them.

Jake had rented a small one room flat near the LaGuardia Marine Air Terminal when he first came to New York, but for Liz's arrival he reserved a room at the Plaza Hotel across from Central Park. They would stay there for Liz's first week in New York, as Jake wanted to show her around Manhattan.

They ate out at a different restaurant every night and Liz became more impressed with the city each passing day. On one occasion, they stopped by the Manhattan Jazz Club to have a drink with Red and his girlfriend. Chuck was playing the piano with the band that night and Liz was a little too overly impressed with Chuck to suit Jake.

Liz liked all the nightspots. She loved the air of excitement and the people. She got Jake to take her out every chance she could and they frequented the Latin Quarter and the El Morocco among others.

Red liked the Cotton Club in Harlem and tried to get Jake and Liz to go with him and his girlfriend when he could. Jake did not care for the place, but Red never had any problem convincing Liz to go and drag Jake along with her. She loved to dance the Charleston and what better place to do so than at the Cotton Club.

Liz entertained herself shopping and going to the movies when Jake was away flying. Occasionally, she went to a stage play on Broadway, but only to matinees, as Jake did not like her being out at night alone.

Jake wanted to rent a house out on Long Island, a place where they could bring the children before long. He planned on purchasing a small Egg Harbor cabin boat, with the idea of exploring the nearby coastline inlets he had seen from the air.

Liz, on the other hand, loved Manhattan and continued to put Jake off about moving out of the city. She found an apartment a few blocks off Central Park and told Jake she would prefer to live there. Jake gave in to her and they moved into the upscale apartment building sublet from a couple who departed on a world cruise and were not expected to return for almost a year.

The apartment was a high-rise with a fantastic view of the Manhattan skyline. The owners left the apartment fully decorated and furnished in an Art Deco motif. Jake had to admit, compared to their ranch house this was quite a plush place to live.

Jake commuted to work at the LaGuardia Marine Air Terminal where his flights originated and left the Dusenburg parked at the airport as his flights returned all hours of the day and night.

*** *** ***

Liz soon returned to her behavior of getting upset when Jake was away too long on flights. Most of the time he managed to pacify her upon his return home by taking her out to all her favorite places for dining and dancing around Manhattan.

On one such occasion at dinner, Liz asked Jake, "Would you stop flying if I asked you to?"

"Why would you want me to?"

"As much as I love being here in New York, I would go back to Texas with you, if you would stop flying and stay home with me all the time."

Jake questioned her further and discovered the underlying cause of Liz's most recent request. She had gone to see the movie *Ceiling Zero* while he was away on his last flight. In the movie, James Cagney played the part of a hard driving pilot who took too many chances trying to get his plane through in bad flying weather and was killed.

"Oh, that's only a movie," Jake reassured Liz. "Real flying is much safer. It's not like that at all."

He was intent on soothing over Liz's concerns, as he did not want her to worry. Truth be known, Jake had taken many of the same or even worse chances than Cagney's character in the Hollywood movie.

Whenever possible, Jake would swap his longer Rio flights with an eager, unmarried junior pilot for shorter flights like the Bermuda Island run. His flights were more frequent, but he did not have to be away so long at a time. He did this for Liz and it worked out well, except on the rare occasion when he had to fly stand-by on a long overseas run for a pilot who had called in sick.

Cab Calloway and his band played at the Cotton Club on Saturday nights. On the first weekend Jake had off, Liz asked him to take her to the Cotton Club. Jake and Liz arrived early. Red and his girlfriend soon came in with Chuck Stine and some others.

During the course of the evening, Liz drank too much and danced provocatively in the center of the dance floor. Her skirt flew high in the air several times exposing her panties.

Jake noticed Stine seated at another table watching Liz intently as she danced. Jake finally had enough. He grabbed Liz off the dance floor, waved goodbye to Red and escorted her out to the car.

Liz pouted all the way home, but it made no difference to Jake how long she pouted, he was not going to stand for that kind of behavior from his wife.

Jake resigned himself to the probability Liz would not speak to him for the next couple of days, but Liz busied herself around the apartment the next morning acting like nothing ever happened.

***

After his second day off on standby, Jake got a call to report for duty as first officer on the *American Clipper*. One of the copilots called in sick and he would have to make the New York, Azores to Lisbon flight. Jake did not know it at the time, but the copilot who had been assigned to the flight and called in sick was Chuck Stine.

Leaving LaGuardia with a full load of passengers, cargo and fuel, the *American Clipper* set course for the Azores where they would refuel before flying on to Lisbon. The weather ahead loomed bleak and ominous, SOP, standard operating procedure, over the Atlantic that time of year.

A little less than two hours into the flight, one of the four engines began losing power. Jake thought he had heard the engine misfiring earlier and had been watching out his cockpit window for traces of oil over the leading edge of the wing.

Sure enough, the number-four engine manifold pressure fell off and began throwing oil. They had blown a cylinder head or jug as they were often called, a fairly common occurrence on these radial engines. However, to continue running an engine leaking oil could start a fire.

"Go ahead and shut it down," the plane commander ordered Jake when he reported the problem, then he turning to the navigator he said, "I need our exact position."

"Aye, aye sir," Jake replied as he and the flight engineer went through the shutdown procedure on the bad engine. "Captain, we're not even close to the no return point. Don't you think we should return to LaGuardia?"

"I agree, Jake," the plane commander replied. "We know the weather's good behind us. We'll return to LaGuardia."

The navigator wrote down their position in longitude and latitude and passed to the radioman who transmitted it back to Pam Am operations on the low radio.

"Be advised, *American Clipper* with single engine failure returning to point of departure. Present position…"

The winds aloft were favorable and a short two hours later, the Lisbon flight was on its return approach back to LaGuardia on three engines. Close into New York, the crew jettisoned the remaining un-needed fuel before making the night water landing.

Another aircraft with a fresh crew was waiting to re- board the passengers and depart.

Jake filed the necessary reports with maintenance and talked with the chief mechanic about the engine. He called home from the maintenance office, but there was no answer.

***

Driving home Jake became increasingly concerned. Liz almost never went out at night alone. When he arrived at the apartment, he found it empty and Liz's purse was gone.

Jake drove over to the Manhattan Jazz Club. He found Red seated in a large round booth in the corner of the crowded club with his girlfriend and several other couples. Jake half expected to find Liz nearby, but Liz did not appear to be there.

Red looked up with a surprise on his face when he saw Jake standing there looking out over the dance floor and around the room.

"Thought you were on the Lisbon flight tonight." Red asked as he stood up and faced Jake.

"I was. We blew an engine about two hours out and had to return. Liz wasn't home when I got there and I'm worried about her. Do you have any idea where she might be?"

An odd expression came over Red's face.

"Oh shit, I was afraid that was what you were going to ask me."

Jake grew angry and displayed negative body language as he stood waiting for Red's explanation.

"Spit it out, Red. What are you not telling me?"

Red took Jake lightly by the arm to lead him away from the table where others were listening to their conversation.

"Come on, I want to save you some embarrassment, if I can. I've been trying to get up nerve enough to tell you ever since I found out about this a couple of days ago. One of Chuck Stine's old girlfriends told me Liz agreed to see him when she knew you would be out of town."

Jake grabbed Red by the shirt.

"Just when in the hell were you gonna tell me?" and he let go of Red. "Never mind, where does this bastard live?"

Red straightened his shirt and adjusted his shoulders.

"Just a couple blocks over. Leave your car here and I'll walk over there with you."

Red led Jake to a second story apartment where they stood quietly in the hallway listening outside of Stine's apartment door. Music from a phonograph record could be heard playing and Jake could occasionally hear Liz's laughter along with some muffled conversation.

Jake let go with one good swift kick at the doorknob and busted the latch. He had not bothered to try the door, which might not even have been locked. The door flew wide open slamming against the wall with a loud crash, nearly busting the flimsy wood door off its hinges.

Liz and Chuck stood in the middle of the room. Liz held a drink in her hand. She gasped and dropped it when the door flew open. The glass shattered when it struck the hard wood floor.

The two possibly might have been dancing as Chuck was only holding Liz by the waste. He let go as Jake came bursting into the room.

Liz stood shuddering, clad only in her bra and skirt. Her blouse was on an armchair by her purse. Her hose and shoes lay on the floor beside the chair where she had obviously taken them off.

Jake went straight for Chuck grabbing him by the throat and dragging him to the floor. The two went sliding across the room on an oval throw rug, crashed through an end table and into the wall knocking over a lamp. The lamp bulb flickered and went out as Jake drug Chuck to his feet. The only other dim lamp across the room cast long shadows of the two struggling men on the far wall.

"Take it easy, Jake!" Red yelled. "You're going to kill the guy over nothing."

Red's use of the word "nothing" caused Jake to pause and gave Red time to pull him off of Chuck.

Jake stood glaring at Chuck.

Chuck held his neck gasping for air.

"Whoa, Tex. What the hell do you think you're doing barging in my apartment like this? She's here of her own free will. Nobody made her come here."

Jake started for Chuck again and Red held onto him.

"Don't call me Tex, you asshole. Do I look like a State to you?"

Jake paused for a moment and thought to himself, what a stupid thing to say. He pushed free of Red and got right in Chuck's face.

"If you value what's hanging between your legs, you'll never go near my wife again or any other pilot's wife for that matter. We castrate horny young bulls like you where I come from. We call them steers and that's what you're going to be the next time I catch you around anything that belongs to me."

The mental picture Jake painted caused Chuck to place one of his hands over his crotch. He held out his other hand in self-defense as he backed away.

"Okay, okay. You made your point. Just get the hell out of here!"

Jake grabbed Liz by the arm and drug her barefoot down the stairs and onto the sidewalk. She managed to grab only her blouse and purse on the way out of the apartment.

Liz clutched her purse and blouse in front of her to cover herself. Jake took the purse from her hand and let go of her long enough to allow her to put on her blouse.

Red caught up to them. He had Liz's shoes and offered her one to put on. She hopped on one foot to put on the shoe, but before she could reach for the other shoe, Jake began dragging her along behind him again. Limping with only one shoe on, Liz finally screamed and kicked the shoe off as she ran to keep up with his long strides.

"Anything that belongs to you?" Liz yelled at Jake. "What does that mean? Do you think you own me?"

"Sorry, I did think you belonged to me! I must have been mistaken," Jake replied with a resolute sadness.

"Oh Jake, I wasn't doing anything wrong," Liz pleaded.

"Yet!" Jake replied sarcastically.

"I get so lonely when you're gone. I needed a friend. Someone to pay attention to me!"

"How lonely can you get? I hadn't even been gone a few hours. Besides, I don't think friendship was exactly what 'your friend' had on his mind!"

Liz continued to make excuses for her conduct the long two blocks back to the car. Jake opened the car door for Liz and she got in. He threw her purse in after her and slammed the door hard.

Red stood at the curb as Jake pulled away like a bat-out-of-hell. Red with one of Liz's shoes in each hand threw both arms up pitching Liz's shoes into the air. He shook his head in disgust and turned to walk back towards the Jazz Club.

Liz said nothing on the drive home. Jake pulled the Dusenburg up in front of their apartment. Liz got out and went on upstairs.

"Leave the car here. Don't park it," Jake told the doorman. "I'll be going out again soon."

Jake entered the apartment, went into the bedroom and threw two suitcases on the bed. He began piling things from Liz's closet and dresser into the suitcases.

Liz stood watching him with her arms folded.

"Get out of those clothes," he ordered her, "and get dressed in something decent."

"Why? Where are we going?" Liz demanded as she tried to find something to put on.

Jake went to the closet for another armload of her clothes.

"What are you doing?" she screamed, but Jake ignored her.

"Jake! We were only dancing. That's why I had my shoes off. I was hot. I was sweating. I took my blouse off so I wouldn't stain it with perspiration."

Jake stopped and looked straight at Liz.

"And your hose, too?"

"Listen to me, Jake! Please tell me why you're packing my things?"

"You're going back to Texas on the next flight out."

All of Liz's arguments faded at that moment and the fear of flying gripped her. She began to plead with Jake.

"You know I can't fly. Please don't make me!"

In a very solemn tone of voice, the one Liz had learned meant don't-give-an-inch, Jake said, "That's tough! There's an eight o'clock flight to Oklahoma City and you're going to be on it if I have to physically carry you onto the airplane and strap you in the seat myself."

Liz went to change her clothes. Afterwards she came over to Jake who was standing at the bedroom dresser looking at a framed picture of them taken on their wedding day. He looked at her, then back at the picture and threw it across the room. Crashed against the wall, it fell to the floor in pieces.

Liz turned away seemingly resigned to her fate now and finished packing the suitcases.

"I'm ready to go now," she said.

***

At the LaGuardia air terminal, Jake and Liz sat quietly as the sunrise shown through the large plate glass windows. The American Airlines flight to Oklahoma City was preparing to board. Jake walked Liz to the foot of the boarding stairs.

"Just go home and take care of the kids. We'll work things out, I promise. I'll call Travis and have him send someone from the ranch to pick you up at the airport."

Liz had a strange and distant look on her face, a look of one condemned or resigned. Jake could not tell.

Jake wondered if it might be the shame she felt or maybe the possibility that she no longer felt any love in her heart for him. Jake did not know what to make of it. He stepped back to watch her go.

Liz looked back at him as she started up the boarding stairs and said only, "Goodbye, Jake!"

RIO TO FRISCO

Jake did not think of himself as a religious man, but years ago he had gotten into the habit of quietly saying a short prayer before takeoff. "God Almighty, grant us safe passage," Jake would say quietly as he pushed the throttles forward on takeoff.

He did this whether he was flying alone or carrying passengers. He might even be more likely to say a longer prayer with someone else at the controls, maybe due to arrogant self-confidence or maybe only because he had a little extra time.

Experienced Pan Am pilots, those having the greater number of flying hours, were soon promoted to first officer positions. Most were former military flyers, but Jake and Red also quickly advanced to first officer positions on the SK-42 Clippers and were assigned to the New York, Miami to Havana flights.

The less experienced pilots received assignments to South America to fly the feeder routes to Rio. Still others like Chuck Stine were retained in New York as junior flight officers. In that position, a pilot normally served only as a relief pilot on long distance flights.

Jake made the scheduled flight from New York to Havana on a regular basis, but on occasion he laid over in Havana to fly the round robin to Rio de Janeiro. The long flight to Rio tested the aircraft and the physical endurance of the men who flew them.

Within walking distance of the Rio seaplane port was the Hotel Carnival where the flight crews stayed on layovers. Jake often went down the street to a local bar called Pepito's to have a couple of beers and listen to the Latin music. Jake had always been a loner, but more so since being separated from Liz.

Jake practiced his Tex-Mex on any of the locals that would listen and he could usually find more than one attentive listener for the price of a cerveza or two. His pronunciation did not improve in light of the fact they spoke Portuguese in Brazil and not Espanol.

The peóns sat sipping their free drinks and pretended to understand Jake's Tex-Mex. They laughed in all the right places. They laughed when he laughed. Jake knew this, but he did not care because it was better than drinking alone.

***

When in New York, Jake spent his time out at the Port Washington engineering facility working in the development hangar. Radio expert, Hugo Leuteritz, worked to improve the Adcock navigation and on designing a new super heterodyne communication system for use in the Pacific.

Hugo worked closely with RCA and Gables Engineering to build the new gear and based on Jake's recommendation, Hugo also contacted Eric at the Texas instrument shop to fabricate some of the circuits.

Jake felt his holdings might be considered a conflict of interest and so he called Trippe to tell him the Martin Company held stock in the Texas instrument company.

"I don't care who owns the company," Trippe told Jake. "If Hugo says that's the best place to get the parts we need, that's who we'll do business with!"

Jake often worked all night along side the technicians building the new radio systems to be installed in the GLM-130 Clippers when they arrived. The Cokes from the cooler box at the hangar were five cents with a two-cent deposit on the bottle.

"When I was a kid, a Coke only cost three cents," Jake would tell anyone willing to listen. "Why, the price of a Coke has almost doubled in the past few years!"

Jake's fellow workers at the hangar might listen politely to Jake's complaining, but it made little difference as Jake usually bought the Cokes for everyone working late anyway.

When they finally got the new short wave radios working, it turned out to be a good night for wave skip. They listened to radio Berlin and were able to talk to the Pan Am base radio operators at Havana and Rio. Their signals came in loud and clear over the airwaves, a form of long distance radio contacting known as DX'ing.

***

Occasionally, Jake would go to a picture show. All the latest Hollywood movies were showing down on Broadway and a new movie China Clipper was playing. Several of the pilots had been talking about the movie so Jake, Red and two other pilots went to see it. They were nearly thrown out of the theater twice for all their hooting and making fun.

Leaving the theater, Jake commented, "I really liked that new actor Humphrey Bogart, but someone should have at least shown the poor guy how to pretend like he was flying an airplane the size of a Clipper. If a pilot over-controlled a Clipper like that, he'd do a barrel roll."

"That phony Hollywood set cockpit was too much!" one of the other pilots said laughing.

"The Pat O'Brien character's part was my favorite," Red said. "I'll bet that's exactly what ol' Trippe is really like."

The following day, Jake went to lunch with Trippe and a couple of the Pan Am board members at the Stork Club. Big Jake and Larry had concurred with Jake on his plan to invest in Pan Am and authorized Jake to finalize the deal, which would allow Pan Am to purchase three of the giant new flying boats they needed.

During lunch, just to be ornery, Jake mentioned to Trippe, "Some of us pilots went to see the new Bogart film *China Clipper* the other night. Have you had a chance to go see it?"

"I don't want to talk about it," Trippe replied.

"Okay, then I guess we won't talk about it, Juan," but Jake suspected he had seen the movie.

"I didn't care for the movie."

"Oh, you didn't?" Jake asked smiling.

Trippe ignored Jake pretending to be reading the menu and then blurted out, "That Pat O'Brien fellow, he'll never make it as an actor, that's for sure!"

Jake did everything he could to keep from laughing aloud and nearly choked when he tried to take a drink from his water glass.

***

The first GLM-130 flying boat came ready for delivery at the Boston factory. Captain Nelson requested Jake to go with him to pick up the prototype aircraft and fly it to the Pan Am Port Washington base for the company engineers to conduct extensive testing of the new aircraft.

Nelson had Jake pulled off regular flight status and assigned to help test the new Clipper. The Pan Am engineers wanted to know how well the new Clipper performed. Jake spent the next two months flight-testing the new GLM-130 and working with the Pan Am engineers.

The flight characteristics of the new GLM-130 amazed its pilots. The new Clipper could lift more than its own weight. Only two other transports, the Douglas DC-3 and the Boeing 247, being produced could do this and they were both land-based aircraft.

The Navy's P2M-1 patrol planes built by Consolidated Aircraft were considered the most successful flying boat design 'til now. GLM used their experience gained modifying the P2M to design the all-new model 130 Clipper. The new larger Clipper incorporated sea-wings, called sponsons, which doubled as fuel tanks. The Clipper's four Pratt & Whitney R-1830 radial engines, with double-rows of cylinders, developed 830 horsepower each.

The new Clippers were luxuriously appointed and equipped to provide full course meal dining in flight. A smoking lounge and sleeping compartments were also available for the up-scale clientele who typically booked these flights.

***

Pan Am began promoting a new flight service called Sky Cruises. They were like a tour on a luxury cruise ship, except these cruises flew between the West Indies islands in a flying boat instead of sailing.

Winter approached and it would soon be high season on the Caribbean and South America routes until after Carnival. Pan Am Ops reassigned Jake as a first officer on the New York to Havana to Rio flights. There were benefits to flying the southern routes in the wintertime, as winter in New York was summer in Rio.

A late winter ice storm struck the east coast of the United States in early spring of 1938. Jake was flying as first officer on a return flight from Rio in the *Brazilian Clipper* NC-823M. After a fuel stop in Miami, the flight encountered heavy icing and severe turbulence. The commander made the decision to land the Clipper at the Navy base in Norfolk, Virginia and wait out the storm.

Fourteen hours overdue, the *Brazilian Clipper* delivered its passengers and cargo to LaGuardia Marine Air Terminal. When Jake checked in, Gloria the Flight Ops secretary handed him a message to call the airport operator at Floyd Bennett Field. Jake made the call.

"Mr. Martin," the voice on the other end of the line explained, "I hate to tell you this, but the large wooden hangar where your airplane is stored, well sir, last night a heavy buildup of ice caused the roof to collapse. Several aircraft in the hangar were damaged and unfortunately the *Pegasus* suffered the worst damage of all the planes."

Jake drove out to Floyd Bennett Field to survey the damage. The young mechanic who had done some work on the *Pegasus* met Jake as he drove up. Jake sorted through the rubble inspecting the Spartan. A strong cold wind blew snow flurries across the airfield that accumulated on the debris. The mechanic followed Jake around assisting as Jake dug through the wreckage.

"Sir, I really like that Spartan. It's the neatest airplane I have ever seen. I'll do a lot of the rebuilding work when I'm off and won't charge you for my time."

"You got a pocket knife I can borrow?" Jake asked as he listened to the young mechanic.

The mechanic opened a small, bone-handled pocketknife and handed it to Jake.

Jake reached through the broken windshield and carefully peeled a yellow and red decal off the *Pegasus* instrument panel. He folded the borrowed pocketknife up and returned it to the mechanic. Jake held the decal up in his black, calfskin-leather gloved hand.

The mechanic tilted his head slightly to read it and smiled.

Jake stuffed the decal in his dark blue regulation Pan Am airline uniform trench coat pocket.

"Where are you going to get the parts if I have you rebuild her?"

"I can make a lot of them myself from sheet metal."

Jake felt the young man overly optimistic about the labor-intensive project and knew he did not have the time or the inclination to rebuild the aircraft himself. Jake removed his right-hand, leather glove and reached in his inside vest coat pocket for a small notepad and pen.

"How much money you got on you right now kid?"

The young mechanic fumbled through his pockets with a questioning look on his face and finally came up with a couple of bills and some change. He held it out to Jake.

"Two dollars and thirty-four cents, sir. Why?"

Jake scribbled on the notepad, tore the sheet from the pad and handed it to the young mechanic. The paper read "Bill of Sale. Sold to the bearer, one Spartan airplane NC-1410 for the good and valuable consideration of $1.00 U.S." signed "J.T. Martin, Jr."

Who better to give the *Pegasus* to than this young fellow who appreciated it and might even restore the Spartan. Jake handed the paper to the young mechanic and took one of the dollar bills from the mechanic's hand.

The young mechanic was so overwhelmed at owning such an airplane he could not collect his thoughts enough to thank Jake.

The sight of the startled young mechanic standing in the midst of all the damage, holding the bill of sale in his hand, amused Jake and he laughed.

"Maybe you ought to rename it the Phoenix when you get her rebuilt."

"What? Oh yeah," and then it sank in that Jake had just given him an airplane! "Thank you, Mr. Martin, thank you very much. I'll fix her up good as new," the young mechanic hollered after him.

Jake doubted the young mechanic ever would, as he walked back to where he parked the Dusenburg.

"You're welcome," Jake replied and waved goodbye and never looked back.

***

To date, the Pan Am Clippers had enjoyed an amazing flight safety record, but suddenly everything began to go wrong. The *Samoa Clipper* enroute to Pango-Pango crashed between Guam and Manila in January. A fuel leak caused the crew to attempt to jettison the excess fuel and the Clipper burst into flames in mid-air. All nine crewmen and six passengers were killed in the crash.

The famous Captain Musick who made the first Hawaii flight died in the crash. The newspaper headlines read "Pango-Pango Disaster." Jake knew of Captain Musick and regretted that he never had an opportunity to meet him in person before he died.

Jake was still assigned to the Rio and Havana flights when the disaster happened. When the flight crews got together to discuss the crash, conversation always turned to the public's fear of flying.

"Statistically," Jake always pointed out, "flying is safer, mile for mile, than any other means of transportation, but let an aircraft crash anywhere in the world and it's headline news."

A new World's Fair would soon be held in New York City, but Jake was out of the country more than at the Pan Am base in New York. He volunteered for more of the longer flights with layovers out of the country, the flights he had avoided while Liz had been in New York.

When Jake laid over in New York, he called Liz to check on her and the kids. Liz would tell him things like, "Lora is growing like a weed," and about Michael doing this or that, but she never talked about herself. She always professed to be, "Just fine," when he inquired.

Lora was talking now and Liz would let her get on the phone when Jake called. "Hi, Daddy," she would say and then excitedly try to tell him about something that had happened to her. He would listen and smile as Lora talked.

The self-imposed separation between Jake and Liz had gone on for almost a year now, but he had made the choice.

To Jake, it had not seemed that long. Time passed quickly with all his new flying duties. He could have flown back to Texas anytime he was off for a few days, but Liz never asked him to and he had not offered.

The last time Jake talked to Liz on the phone, he told her, "It looks like I'm going to be promoted to captain and it's likely I'll be assigned to San Francisco. Maybe you and the kids can go to California with me and we'll try to make a fresh start."

"Sure, that will be fine," Liz said.

Her less than enthusiastic monotone reply gave Jake pause to wonder, but he continued to hope time would heal the wounds between them and began making plans for them to be together as a family when he was reassigned.

***

Having flown as first officer with Captain Nelson flight-testing the prototype GLM-130 Clipper, Jake was promoted to captain. He was assigned to the New York, West Indies run or the island-hopper as most of the pilots called it. Pan Am still maintained a large fleet of the older Sikorsky SK-42s, which were used on those routes and not the new GLM-130s. Jake did not care. He was just pleased to be flying as pilot-in-command.

On his first flight as commander, Jake was scheduled to fly *Bermuda Clipper* NC-16736 on the island-hopper route. He had not bothered to review the names on his crew manifest. When he reported for the flight, he discovered the copilot assigned to the flight was his old nemesis, Chuck Stine.

Chuck reported for duty early that morning and began the pre-flight on the Clipper. When Jake arrived, Chuck greeted him and said, "Captain, I want to apologize for the problem I caused. I mean, the thing with your wife. I wasn't even thinking about her being married and..."

"Look, jerk! Just do your job and we'll get along fine," Jake snapped, letting some of his pent-up anger at Chuck get the best of him and speaking out without thinking.

With the aircraft loaded and ready for departure, Jake boarded the *Bermuda Clipper* and climbed into the pilot's seat.

Chuck, seated in the copilot's position, prepared to run through the pre-takeoff checklist.

"Captain Martin, I know you don't have much use for me and you've probably got a damn good reason for feeling the way you do."

Jake began having second thoughts about his earlier adverse reaction to Chuck.

"Listen Stine, no hard feelings. The thing with Liz was probably more my fault than yours. I knew better than to leave her alone so much. Nothing more needs to be said. Let's just stick to flying. Okay?"

Chuck strapped into the copilot's seat and picked up the checklist.

"There is one thing I need to tell you, sir."

"Okay, make it quick. What is it?"

"You know, the German Luftwaffe helped Franco by bombing Guernica, Spain last April. Well, the British seem to feel that war with Germany is imminent and they're looking for experienced pilots to fly their Supermarine Hurricane fighters while they train new pilots for the Spitfires."

"That's all very interesting, Stine, but what's that got to do with us?"

"The short version is you won't have to be annoyed by me hanging around anymore. I applied with the Royal Air Force and received my letter of acceptance a couple of days ago. I'll be leaving for England the end of the month."

"Good, maybe you'll go kill some Huns now, instead of me and a plane load of Pan Am passengers," Jake mumbled making a joke.

Chuck smiled and raised the checklist to eyelevel.

"Right, sir. All electrical switches on, master switch on, ready to crank number one."

Jake looked out the side cockpit window and reached for the toggle switches on the overhead console.

"Clear on the left, starting number one."

***

Exactly one week before Thanksgiving, Jake had gotten in late from a Havana flight and was sleeping in at the small apartment he rented near LaGuardia when the telephone rang.

"This is Gloria over at operations, Captain Martin. Sorry if I woke you. I needed to let you know your transfer to San Francisco came through on the telex this morning. You and Captain Nelson are to report to the Pan Am seaplane base at Alameda in San Francisco two weeks from today."

"What about my flight this Friday?"

"You've been taken off the active flight status schedule at LaGuardia, so I assume you're on your own."

"Thanks, Gloria,"

Jake hung up the phone and stumbled around the apartment to get dressed trying to organize his thinking. This will work out great, he would go to Texas to spend Thanksgiving and the extra time would give him a chance to work things out with Liz before reporting to California.

After Jake gathered his thoughts, he placed a call to Liz back in Texas. He let the phone ring for a long time in case she was outside, but no one answered.

Jake called his mom's house.

"Mom, is Liz over there?"

"No, Jacob, she's not, but I'm glad you called. Your dad needs to talk to you. He's been trying to get a hold of you for a couple of days."

"I've been out of the country, Mom. I'll call him at the office right away. Love you."

As he hung up the phone, he thought he heard Lora's voice in the background say, "I want to talk to my daddy!"

Jake called his dad at the bank.

"Dad, do you know where Liz and the kids are this morning? There's no answer at the house."

After a short silence on the line, Big Jake asked, "You doing all right, Son?"

Jake knew his father well enough to tell by the tone of his voice something was wrong.

"Yeah, I'm fine. What's going on?"

"Just fixin' to try to call you again. The kids are okay, Son. They're with your mom and Violet."

"Where's Liz? Is she okay?"

"Seems she's up and left."

"What do you mean, left?"

"Ran off, I guess. She went to the Wilcox Law Offices and left some instructions. Wilcox can fill you in, but I think the best thing you can do for right now would be to come on home for a spell. Your kids are gonna need you here with their mama up and leaving."

Jake packed his personal belongings and tossed his bags in the back of the Dusenburg. He drove to the Manhattan Coach dealership downtown and accepted the best cash offer the dealer would make him on the Cabriolet.

Jake signed the sales agreement and the dealer had a driver deliver Jake to the airport in the Dusenburg. Jake got out of the car with his suitcases at the terminal building. He mumbled under his breath, "Dang Dusenburg, never liked the thing anyway!" and kicked the passenger car door closed with his foot.

At the LaGuardia terminal, Jake visited with the Pan Am employees at Flight Ops and then went to clean out his locker in the pilot's lounge. He stopped at Gloria's desk to turn in his keys. Captain Nelson had come in to do the same thing.

"Where you headed, Jake?" Nelson asked.

"Home to Texas for a couple of weeks. How about you, Steve?"

"Going to catch a ride to Miami and then head down to Key West City for some serious deep sea fishing. See you in about two weeks in Alameda. Here's the telephone number where I'll be staying in San Francisco if you need anything when you get there."

"Enjoy your time off, Steve."

"You too, Jake," Nelson replied.

"Don't let these fly-boys put anything over on you, Gloria," Jake said as he dropped his keys on her desk.

"No danger of that, Captain Martin. Good luck to you."

Jake boarded one of American Airlines' new DC-3 Skyliners, the afternoon flight to St. Louis. The plane was full so Jake rode the small jump seat behind the pilot. At St. Louis, he changed to a nearly empty Boeing 247D flight to Oklahoma City and slept most of the way, arriving in OKC late that night.

Travis was waiting for Jake at the terminal.

"Big Jake told me to drive his Model K sedan to come up and get you, Little Jake. Said it'd be too fur and too uncomfortable a ride in my old ranch truck."

"Thank goodness for small favors, huh Travis?" Jake said throwing his suitcases in the backseat of the large black sedan. "You drive, okay?"

"Thought I would," Travis replied.

During the two-hour drive home to the ranch, both men avoided talking about Liz having left. They passed the time conversing about the ranch, how many heifers might calve in the spring and things of that sort.

Travis dropped Jake off at the main ranch house around midnight.

Violet met Jake at the door in her night robe.

"Mister and Ma'am is already in bed asleep, Master Jake. Your room is made-up waitin' and they says to tells ya they'll sees you in the mon'in."

"Thank you Violet," Jake whispered as he sat his suitcases down inside the door. "Where are the kids?"

Violet pointed to the guest bedroom on the opposite end of Jake's upstairs bedroom.

Jake went to the bedroom to check on Lora and Michael. They were both sound asleep. Jake covered them up and stood at the doorway admiring them as they slept.

"I wonder what in the world the future holds for us next, little ones?" he said quietly.

***

Morning always came early on the ranch and Flo's old rooster started crowing at the first crack of dawn. Jake smelled the coffee brewing on the stove. He got dressed and went down to the kitchen.

The back door opened and Big Jake came in from the corral.

"Mornin' Son. How was your trip?"

"Ouch," Jake muttered, as he burned his lip on the cup of hot coffee he had just poured. "Good as to be expected, I guess. How you been, Dad?"

Big Jake poured a cup of coffee from the blue metal pot on the stove and sat down at the kitchen table with Jake.

"After you visit with your mom and the kids for a while, come on down to the office. Lawrence, I guess you call him Larry, is driving over from Wichita Falls. Said he'd be over around noon."

"I'm not sure I understand how Larry figures into this. On the phone, you mentioned Liz had left some instructions with him. What kind of instructions?"

"Liz went to his office before she ran off and signed some papers, but best let him explain it all to you."

Big Jake's voice had taken on a somber, more serious tone and so Jake reconciled himself to wait a while longer for the details.

"Sure, okay, but what the heck happened? Did she just up and leave or what?"

Big Jake did not look his son in the eye.

"Rumor is, she'd been seen with another man, some evangelist preacher passing through. Lord only knows what took place. I sure don't."

Big Jake paused when he heard footsteps in the hall on the hardwood floor. He smiled like the proud grandfather he was and got up to go get dressed for work.

Jake turned in his chair to the hall doorway where Flo stood with her hands on the shoulders of Lora and Michael still in their pajamas.

"Yes, there's your dad. Go say hello to him," Flo said as she gave both of the children a little nudge towards their father.

Lora, being more familiar with her father, went right to Jake and climbed onto his lap. Michael stood looking at his father and then went over and stood beside Lora.

Violet came into the kitchen to help with breakfast. Big Jake left for the bank right after he ate and Jake spent the rest of the morning visiting with his mom and paying attention to his two kids.

Around eleven o'clock, Jake asked Travis to run him over to the summer ranch house. Jake went to the detached shed they used as a garage and swung open the double doors. His '34 Ford Roadster was still there with the key still in the steering-column lock.

Jake got in and turned on the switch. The battery was up. He pulled the choke full out, pumped the accelerator a couple of times and hit the starter button. The Ford Roadster fired off, idled a little rough, then smoothed out as Jake eased the choke off and he backed the car out of the garage.

"I'm good here," he hollered and waved to Travis who had waited to see if the car would start. "You can go on back to the ranch now. Thanks for the ride."

Travis waved back and pulled away in the ranch truck.

Jake got out of the car, shut the doors to the shed and left for town. He did not go into the house.

The noon bell in the Town Hall tower sounded as Jake pulled up in front of the bank. Larry's car, a black Buick sedan, was parked at the curb near the brown sandstone bank building. He went into Big Jake's office through the private side entrance.

Big Jake was at his desk with Larry seated in one of the guest chairs across from him discussing another business matter as Jake came through the door.

Larry stood up and greeted Jake.

"It's been too long, Jake. You need to come home more often." Noticing the solemn look on Jake's face he added, "But maybe not under these circumstances."

"Good to see you again too, Larry."

Jake pulled up a chair and Larry began to explain the situation.

"I received a call from Elizabeth about three days ago. She told me she wanted a divorce and that she did not wish to place any claim against you or the Martin estate. She wanted to give you full custody of the children because she thought you could take better care of them. There may have been other reasons, but she didn't say so. I thought I heard a man's voice in the background telling her to say she didn't want the kids."

Jake was visibly upset.

"Why didn't you call me right away?"

Larry remained calm in hopes of calming Jake.

"Actually, your dad tried and I tried several times myself. I even called the Pan Am flight operations people. They told me you were on a flight out of the country."

"Yeah, I guess that's right. They gave me the message when I got in. Just go on!"

Jake was trying hard to control his emotions. He looked down, noticed his hands were shaking and put them in his pockets.

"Look, I know how you must feel. You don't want to hear this and I don't want to be the one sitting here telling you. It's part of the dirty job of being your attorney and it comes with the territory."

"No, Larry, you don't know how rotten I feel, but I thank you for caring and trying to help anyway."

Jake got up and paced the floor.

Larry glanced over at Big Jake who nodded for Larry to continue explaining what happened.

"She seemed determined to leave right away. If she lit out and we couldn't locate her..."

"I know," Jake said, "it'd be a big legal mess."

"Pretty much. So I told her to come to my office and sign some release papers for the kids and a petition for divorce, but that I wouldn't do anything with the papers until I talked to you first. She came within an hour and signed all the necessary papers."

"Where were the kids during all of this?" Jake asked, looking at his dad. "No, you don't need to answer that. She dropped them off at Mom's house for the day, didn't she?"

Big Jake nodded yes, but said nothing.

"She must have been ready to leave town then," Larry continued, "cause when she left the law office, I watched out the window to see where she went. A man waited for her by a car parked at the curb downstairs. She got in the car on the passenger's side and they drove off."

Jake punched the wall a couple of times with his fist, but not hard enough to bust anything. He sat back down in the chair.

The three men sat in silence for quite a spell.

Then Jake said, "It takes a long time to let go of something you care about, but twice is one too many times."

Jake stood up and looked straight at Larry.

"Just do it!" Jake paused and then said, "Just tell me what I've got to sign and let's get it done."

After the meeting, Jake drove back to the summer ranch house to look around. Flo and Violet had collected most of the kids' things earlier. Most of Liz's personal belongings and all the suitcases were gone, so Jake assumed her leaving had not been a hasty decision. She must have been planning it for some time.

Jake boxed up the everyday usable items from the kitchen and did the same with his personal things from the house. As he looked through the house, he paused in each room to reflect back on things that had taken place.

He stacked the boxes by the door in the living room and looked around one more time before shutting the house up and locking the door. He took some tools from the shed to drain the water pipes and shut off the natural gas. He cut the electricity off at the circuit-breaker box and the muted humming of the water well pump stopped.

***

The quitting time whistle blew as Jake parked his car out front of the factory at Gainesville. The roar of the big machinery fell quiet as the factory shut down for the evening. A handful of people were coming to work on the swing shift as Jake went in to visit with some of the employees he worked with.

A quality inspector was using Jake's old desk now and had left for the day. Jake sat down and propped his feet up. He sat quietly for a long time attempting to deal with the reality of the last few days. At first, he felt angry with Liz for leaving. Then he began to blame himself. Finally, he decided things were the way they were and maybe even the way they were supposed to be.

The evening had been dark for a couple of hours by the time Jake left the factory and not a fit night for driving. The sky was overcast and a light fog hung in the air. Jake drove way too fast for the road conditions and visibility. Worse yet, his mind was not on his driving. He turned off the main road onto the three-mile dirt road leading to the Flying M ranch house.

In the darkness up ahead, he glimpsed something on the road. An instant later, a Black Angus cow loomed in the headlights. Jake locked up the brakes on the Ford and swerved, scarcely missing the cow by inches.

The Roadster fishtailed, but he got it under control. That was until the second cow came into view and he let up on the four-wheel drift he was holding just enough to miss the second cow, but paid a dear price. The Roadster careened into the bar ditch, through a barbed wire fence and came to rest against a large oak tree.

The engine stalled on impact and the only sound in the quiet night was the spewing of hot water from the busted radiator. As the water contacted the even hotter engine block, a large plume of white steam rose upward from under the hood, illuminated in the ghostly light of the only headlamp that still worked.

Shaken up badly, but otherwise unhurt, Jake cut the ignition off and got out to look over the damage. The right front axle was broken and the wheel twisted under the frame. The grille was busted and the right front fender smashed.

The cows that had been lying on the road got up and stood motionless watching Jake.

"Damn black cows," he mumbled, raised both hands in the air and yelled, "Yah, get!"

The spooked cows ran off.

Not our cows, Jake thought to himself, we don't even raise Angus. Must be a break in somebody else's fence around here.

Jake pondered for a moment that there must have been some skill involved in his missing both cows, but shuddered when he considered what might have happened if he had hit one of them at the speed he was traveling.

"Thank you, Lord!" Jake uttered and his voice cracked the stillness of the dark night.

He reached in the car, turned off the lights and started walking the two miles home to the main house.

As he hiked down the road, he kicked an occasional rock down the dark road ahead of him, an old trick he learned at an early age so as not to surprise a rattler and step on it.

***

The next day, Jake located ol' Mick by phone at the pump station and told him what happened with the cows on the road the night before.

"Did I not tell you," Mick said, "them cows will sleep on the road at night when they gets out. Nearly hit one myself a couple times."

"Indeed you did, Mick, many times. Could you bring over the oil well pipe truck? It's the only one with a hoist on the back and we'll go get my Roadster."

"Happy to, Little Jake, I'll be over there shortly."

Mick picked up Jake and they went to get the Roadster. Jake tied a log chain to the rear of the Roadster to pull it away from the tree and lifted the front-end off the ground with the hoist. Mick pulled the Ford back onto the road and went back to help Jake repair the fence.

Arriving at the summer ranch house with the Roadster in tow, Jake got out of the truck and opened the shed doors. Mick backed the Roadster into the shed. Jake engaged the hoist and lowered the Roadster onto the dirt floor. He covered the Roadster with a large paraffin-coated canvas tarp, closed and bolted the doors to the shed.

Mick helped Jake load the boxes from the house into the back of the truck and they hauled them back to the main house. Jake and Mick visited for a bit and then Jake carried the last box containing some of his clothes and boots upstairs to his old bedroom to store them.

That evening, Jake told Lora and Michael that their mother had gone away for a while. He avoided giving them any false hopes by promising she would return anytime soon.

"Did she die, Daddy?" Lora asked.

"No, Lora, She didn't die," Jake said and looked away.

"Don't cry, Daddy. Everything is going to be all right. We still got you."

Jake held onto the two of them for the longest time. Michael finally squirmed down and went off to play with something, but Lora sat quietly by his side.

***

Over the next several days, Jake devoted all his spare time to paying attention to Lora and Michael. On the Sunday afternoon before Jake had to make a decision about going on to California, he and Big Jake were out by the corral.

Lora entertained herself nearby and Michael hung over the corral fence trying to get the attention of one of the horses. Lora was not fond of horses, but young Michael loved animals.

"I swear," Big Jake chuckled, "I think that boy would walk up to an elephant and try to pet it if one came around. You know, there's something about that boy that reminds me of your granddad. Must be something in the genes."

"You mean in the blue jeans, don't you, Dad?" and they both laughed.

Jake went to get a gelding, one of the more gentle saddle horses out of the corral. He bridle and saddled the horse and lifted young Michael up onto the mount.

"Grab hold of the saddle horn," Jake told Michael. "Here we go, cowboy," but Jake held onto the bridle.

Lora took her father's hand as they walked Michael on the horse around the ranch house yard.

"Giddy-up horse," Michael yelled several times.

Lora laughed at her little brother, but remained quite content to hold her daddy's hand and walk along beside him.

Flo stepped out on the back porch and snapped a picture of them with her brownie box camera.

After a while, Jake walked the saddle horse back to the corral and lifted Michael to the ground.

Travis came over to help unsaddle the horse and put the tack away.

"How are Sarah and Hank doing?" Jake asked Travis. "Haven't heard much about them. Do they have any kids yet?"

"No, they thought they'd wait 'til Hank finished veterinary school before starting a family."

Jake looked around to see what Michael might be into, but Big Jake had a hold of him.

"Be sure to tell them hello for me when you see them."

"Sure will, Little Jake. Good to have you back on the place. You need to come home more often."

Jake, with Michael and Lora in tow, walked back to the house with his dad.

"I guess you'll be heading on to San Francisco now or have you changed your plans, Son?"

Jake picked Michael up and sat him on his shoulders as they walked.

"I don't want to stop flying, Dad. It's about the only thing I really enjoy doing."

When they reached the house, Jake and his dad sat down on the wooden steps of the back porch.

"Do you think it would be okay if I went on to Frisco and left Lora and Michael here with you all and Violet for a while?"

"It's the career you chose, Son. Don't see how you can do anything else, at least for right now. Your mom and I already discussed it and we're in agreement the kids should stay in familiar surroundings until you know where you're gonna settle."

Father and grandfather watched as Michael ran after Lora who tried to keep him from catching her.

"Son, I'd like you to do something on your way out to San Francisco for me."

Jake hollered to Lora, "He caught you fair and square, now you have to catch him," and turning his attention back to Big Jake he asked, "What's that, Dad?"

"Dan will be managing the new oil well equipment manufacturing company we're building near Culver City. He's been out there some time now supervising its construction."

"Yes, I know, go on," Jake said.

"I been thinking it'd be a good idea if you stopped by to see how things are going. See if there're any problems we need to take care of from this end. Of course, knowing Dan, he wouldn't complain even if he had a problem. He'd try to handle it himself."

Jake understood how his dad always encouraged him to take more of an active role in the family businesses.

"Sure, I'd be glad to go see Dan. In fact, I would like to see the new facility for myself, but I'll have to leave a day early to make a stopover in L.A."

Daniel Parker, Jake's cousin, was Flo's sister's boy. He was eight years older than Jake, but they had been friends growing up. Dan went to work for the Martin Company right after he graduated from Southwestern College and married a girl named Ida from Pottsburg. They met when both started work at the Gainesville factory.

***

Jake needed a new car for the drive to California, so he called ol' Harley Willis, the local Lincoln dealer over at Wichita Falls. Harley sold Big Jake a new Lincoln every two or three years.

"Harley, this is Jake Martin. No, not Big Jake, this is his son. And yes, I know I sound like my pa on the phone. Wanted to check with you and see if you have any of those new streamlined model Lincolns in stock."

"I've got a brand new Zephyr three-window business coupe, Mr. Martin. It just came in. We unloaded it at the railway depot yesterday."

Jake had read several articles about the new lightweight Zephyr and he particularly liked the art deco styling used in the car's interior. The car Harley described was exactly what Jake had been looking to buy.

Harley, on the other end of the phone, continued to oversell the deal.

"These new flat-head V-12 engines are really impressive performers, yes-siree-bob. Good gas mileage. This one has the Columbia two-speed rear axle overdrive on it," and Harley went on about the car.

Jake smiled as he listened to Harley and finally he got a word in.

"Harley, Harley, that's fine. I'll take the car. Deliver it out here to the ranch along with any paperwork I need to sign and pick up a check. Oh, and Harley, that was a great sales pitch... No, no need to thank me. You did a fine job of selling me on the car."

Jake was still smiling when he hung up the telephone.

Harley delivered the new Zephyr late that afternoon.

That evening, Jake explained to Lora and Michael that he would be going away to return to his flying job.

"You two stayed here with grandma and grandpa on the ranch when I was away in New York. It won't be any different this time. I'll be back again before too long."

Of course, Michael was too young to fully understand.

"Will Violet still be here to take care of us like before, Daddy?" Lora asked.

"Yes she will. It's part of her job to take care of you two."

"Violet said that I could call her mammy if I wanted, is that okay?"

"Yes, Lora, that's fine if you want to do that."

***

Jake was ready to leave early the following morning. He decided not to wake the kids to say goodbye.

"Just tell them that I love them," he told his mom.

Jake took the old Childress Highway west past Wichita Falls. As he drove, he recalled how the bluebonnets filled the hillsides along this stretch of the road with blankets of deep blue in the spring and summer, but they were not in bloom this time of year. At Amarillo, he intersected U.S. Route 66, the main road to California out of Chicago.

Jake made good time in the new Zephyr and by two o'clock in the afternoon he came into Santa Rosa where he stopped for lunch at Ron Chavez's Club Cafe. He arrived in Albuquerque in the early evening and spent the night at the Casa Grande Hotel on Central Avenue.

Jake rose early the next morning for huevos rancheros at the hotel restaurant and washed it all down with several cups of strong coffee.

By sunup, he drove west out of Albuquerque on Central Avenue and crossed the Rio Grande. Outside of town near the railroad trestle bridge, a large sign read "700 Miles of Desert Straight Ahead - Last Chance for Water Bags and Thermos."

The Zephyr slowed a little climbing Nine-Mile Hill, until the Columbia rearend shifted down and the old V-12 engine wound-up. At the top of the grade, the rearend shifted into high. The Zephyr picked up speed and headed for the open highway that stretched across the vast miles of tan terra firma like a black arrow, sixty miles to the blue horizon ahead.

Jake stopped in Seligman, a railway changeover point in the middle of Arizona, for gas and a cold drink. He figured he could make Needles, California before nightfall. He had been running ninety most of the day and made Barstow along about dark where he pulled over and took a short catnap.

Coming out of the Sierra Madres through Apple Valley into San Bernardino well past midnight Jake was not sleepy, so he decided to keep on driving. More than once he had been on flight duty for seventy-two hours straight with only a couple of hours sleep.

Around three o'clock in the morning, Jake pulled the Zephyr onto Santa Monica Pier where he parked and fell asleep sitting up in the front seat listening to the ocean waves come ashore.

He awoke to sunlight shining in the car window and the squawking of seagulls fighting over some scraps of food. Jake drove over to Lincoln Boulevard and had breakfast at the diner on the corner.

***

After breakfast, he took Venice Boulevard to the west side of Culver City to the site where the new Martin Company factory was under construction.

At the construction field office, Jake located Dan who had been expecting him.

"You got here early. Wasn't looking for you until tomorrow," Dan said greeting Jake. "Welcome to our humble diggings."

"Just decided to drive straight through, wasn't tired enough to stay over anywhere. How are things going?"

Jake drew some water from the large drinking can and washed his face.

Dan handed Jake a clean shop towel to dry with.

"Good as to be expected, I suppose, specially with all these contractors running around."

"Dad asked me to stop by, but I guess you knew that. He wanted me to see if you were having any problems."

"Nothing I can't handle," Dan smiled, "but let me show you around as long as you're here."

"Dad said that's what you'd say."

"How are your mom and dad, anyway?" Dan had heard about Liz leaving, but figured Jake would talk about it in his own good time.

"Dad's his same ol' self and Mom's sassy as ever. They're fine," Jake replied as he and Dan began their walking tour of the construction site.

"You will stay with us, won't you, Jake? Ida's cooking dinner for us tonight."

"Planned on it, but I'll need to leave early in the morning. It'll be good to see Ida and your two kids."

"Teenage kids, Jake! There's a difference. You'll find out one of these days."

The size of the new factory as well as its progress impressed Jake. He also noticed the new factory site adjoined the Culver City Municipal Airport and was only separated by a railway spur line that passed between the two properties.

"What is the possibility of expanding the factory across the railroad tracks to connect it with the airport?"

"I'll check into it, Jake, but why do you ask?"

"Just an idea I was mulling around about building another facility. It's not important."

Back at the temporary construction office, Jake went over to the new bright red hand-crank Coke machine a vending company had recently installed. He fumbled in his pocket for some change, deposited a nickel and pulled the hand-crank leaver. Nothing happened. He had not bothered to read the large white "6¢" above the words *Coca-Cola The Pause That Refreshes*.

"You need another penny," Dan said taking one out of his pocket and offering it to Jake.

"What happened to five cent Cokes? Why, when we were kids, an RC or a Coke was only…"

"Yeah, I know Jake, only three cents and one-cent deposit on the bottle. I always preferred Grapette myself," Dan said plugging the extra penny in the machine and turned the handle for Jake. Dan went over to a large table and laid out the blueprints for the new factory for Jake to look over.

Jake asked a few questions and after a while he rolled the blueprints back up.

"Don't see any reason Big Jake or the management back at Gainesville won't be more than pleased with how well things are going here."

"Jake, are you thinking about coming out here to work with us?"

"Nope. Looks to me like you got things well in hand here. I'm headed for the Pacific, always wanted to see that part of the world!"

The China Clipper

The Pan Am Clipper that made the first trans-Pacific passenger flight originated from San Francisco and flew non-stop to Honolulu, Hawaii. The aircraft, Sikorsky flying boat NC-716, bore the name China Clipper on its bow. Subsequently, the public and the press referred to all of the Clippers leaving San Francisco after that, as a China Clipper, regardless of the aircraft's name on the bow.

The flights from Frisco to Hawaii were an over-the-water distance of twenty-four hundred miles and were the longest commercial air routes being flown at the time.

The non-pressurized cabins resulted in the flying boats having to cruise at altitudes below twelve thousand feet and an optimum flight level for maximum fuel efficiency was even lower. Flying at those altitudes exposed the passengers and crew to turbulent air and all kinds of rough weather conditions.

Trippe's goal was to provide air service to Manila in the Philippines and eventually to Hong Kong. He also wanted to establish a route to New Zealand. To do so, he pursued a draconian plan to build layover stations with hotel facilities on the islands of Midway, Wake and Guam. These small volcanic islands became the steppingstones needed to bring the Orient into range of the Pan Am Clippers.

Midway Island was part of the Hawaiian chain, but Wake Island was a tiny atoll some two thousand miles west of Honolulu. Wake Island was first claimed by the United States in 1898, but largely neglected until 1930 when jurisdiction over the island passed to the U.S. Navy Department. Guam was an even more distant island in the Mariana chain.

In early 1935, Trippe dispatched engineers and a work force of eighty men on the supply ship New Haven to the islands to begin building facilities to service the Pan Am Clippers and passengers. All of the supplies to fabricate the new bases on the islands needed to be shipped in, as there were no raw materials on the islands.

Adcock radio navigation stations were a major factor in establishing these island bases. The station's signal was essential for the Clipper's crew to be able to locate the tiny islands in the middle of the Pacific.

When the island bases were completed, Pan Am would be able to provide commercial air service to Manila, a distance of over eight thousand miles by air from San Francisco.

Captain Musick and his crew made the first Pan Am Clipper flight to Manila departing Alameda seaplane base on November 22, 1935. The Clipper's gross takeoff weight exceeded twenty-six tons. Arriving in Manila on the 29th, the *China Clipper* delivered forty-one passengers and the first U.S. airmail to the Philippines. Captain Musick's photo appeared on the cover of *Time Magazine*.

The following year, Pam Am began regular passenger service to the Philippines and in October, Captain Tilton and his crew were scheduled and actually flew one of the Pan Am Clippers through to Hong Kong, thereby finally living up to their namesake of *China Clipper*.

The total flying time from San Francisco to the China coast averaged sixty hours. The new Hong Kong air service flights departed Frisco once a week. The journey took five days to complete and included four overnight island stays.

Jake was still assigned to New York when the first Pacific Clipper tragedy occurred. Jake and his crew were airborne on a return flight from Havana when their radio operator received a message that saddened all of the crew.

"*Hawaii Clipper* overdue arrival Manila from Guam. Position of aircraft and status of those onboard, unknown."

Speculation was that Japanese agents hijacked the airplane. Very little conversation took place on the flight deck over the next few hours. Jake's radioman made several attempts to contact other aircraft by Morse code for more details, but no additional information was forthcoming.

Upon landing, their worst fears were confirmed. The terrorist had shot all onboard the *Hawaii Clipper* and destroyed the aircraft. The incident happened on July 28th, 1938, Jake's twenty-seventh birthday. Under the circumstances, Jake decided not to mention the coincidence to anyone.

Red and Jake were too young to be pioneer Pacific Clipper pilots, but they and those who followed them were destined to be the captains who would change the airborne crossing of the Pacific from a daredevil stunt into safe, dependable transoceanic air travel.

***

For Jake, 1939 loomed as a new year and a new adventure. He was about to follow in the footsteps of the men who conquered the Pacific by air.

The morning Jake left Dan's house in Los Angeles, he picked up Highway 101 and headed north out of Santa Monica. He spent the day driving up the coast. North of San Luis Obispo, he saw the Hearst Castle high on a hilltop overlooking the Pacific Ocean and thought to himself what a magnificent view they must have from up there.

That evening south of Oakland, a rainstorm moved in and Jake drove the rest of the way in the rain. He turned on the AM radio. There was a little static from the local rain showers, but not bad. Playing on the radio was the *Hour of Charm Orchestra featuring Evelyn and Her Magic Violin*. The vacuum windshield wipers seemed to slap in tempo with the music as he drove.

Later that evening, Jake listened to radio news commentator H.B. Kaltenborn comment on Orson Welles' *Mercury Theater* radio show. Welles had caused a panic with his *War of the Worlds* radio broadcast. Some people mistook the broadcast for an actual news program, panicked and prepared to fight off the invading Martians. Jake was out of the country at the time and missed the whole thing.

The commentator's topic switched to the latest news about rumors of war in Europe. Jake turned the radio off, preferring to drive in the quiet for the next fifty miles into the City-by-the-Bay.

Arriving in Oakland, Jake stopped to use a pay phone. He called Captain Nelson who gave him directions and the name of the landlady who rented apartments in Alameda near the seaplane base.

***

The following day, Jake reported to Pan Am operations at Alameda. He did not have to wait long for his next assignment. His name was listed on the flight-crew status board as assigned to *Honolulu Clipper* NC-18601 due to depart for Hawaii the following day.

The Pan Am Pacific fleet now operated the new Boeing 314 flying boats called the Yankee Clipper and Jake looked forward to flying them with great anticipation. They were largest American made flying boats ever built. First proposed three years earlier, the 314 incorporated the wing design of Boeing's XB-15 heavy bomber.

Each of the four Boeing 314 Wright Cyclone engines had 14-cylinders in double rows and burned the new high-test 100 octane rated fuel. Counting the fuel in the sponsons, the ship could carry 4,525 gallons of fuel. The aircraft had a wingspan of 152 feet, was 106 feet long, stood 27 feet high and weighed forty tons.

The new passenger cabins could accommodate seventy-seven day-coach or forty night-sleeper passengers depending on the configuration. The new 314s doubled the carrying capacity and range of the older GLM-130 Clippers. The new greater carrying capacity made trans-Pacific flights more affordable and available to those other than the few privileged passengers who made these flights before.

The first two Boeing 314s to be put into service crossing the Pacific were the *Honolulu Clipper* NC-18601 and the *California Clipper* NC-18602. Pan Am soon placed more orders for new Boeing 314 flying boats.

The third Boeing flying boat NC-18603 was actually named the *Yankee Clipper* for its drawing board namesake. This Clipper, along with the new *Atlantic Clipper* NC18604, were both delivered to Pan Am back east to fly the new trans-Atlantic routes. One would fly the northern route over Nova Scotia to Europe and the other would make the Azores to Portugal run.

***

The morning of Jake's first Pacific crossing flight, he arrived at the seaplane base before sunrise to look over the large new airplane the crew would be flying. The flight was scheduled to depart at noon and the rest of the flight crew assembled around nine o'clock.

Captain Hudson, plane commander for the flight, introduced himself to Jake and assembled the crew.

"Fellows, I'd like you to meet Jake Martin. He just transferred in from New York and he'll be with us on the Hawaii flight today. Come to think of it, Jake, you don't talk much like a New Yorker."

"No sir, I'm not. I was born and raised in Texas," Jake replied as he shook hands with the other crewmen.

"You've been assigned to the third officer's position for today's flight," Captain Hudson told Jake.

"Yes sir, I saw that on the flight status board."

"This'll give you a chance to get familiar with the way we operate out here in the Pacific. With your experience, I'm sure you'll be moved on up to a first officer's slot real soon."

The flight would be carrying nine crewmen. In addition to Jake and the commander, the crew consisted of a first officer, a second officer, a pilot/navigator, a radioman, a flight engineer and two stewards.

Jake followed the other Pan Am crewmen into the flight planning room and the two stewards left to go inventory the stores on board the Clipper. As soon as fueling was completed, Jake and the first officer made a pre-flight inspection of the aircraft.

The passengers began arriving at the dock and porters loaded their luggage onto the Clipper. The stationmaster began boarding passengers at eleven that morning.

At ten minutes after noon the giant Boeing 314 flying boat was airborne. Tradition dictated making a wide circling turn out over San Francisco Bay to give the passengers a view of the newly completed Golden Gate Bridge and the under construction Oakland Bay Bridge.

The *Honolulu Clipper* climbed steadily west, leveled off at its cruising altitude and picked up airspeed. The air was smooth and cooler at altitude. The flight would take eighteen to twenty hours depending on the winds.

The first steward moved about the cabin making the passengers comfortable and taking orders for cocktails. The second steward announced early seating for dinner would begin at five o'clock and began setting the tables.

A half-hour into the flight the Pacific coast faded on the distant horizon behind them. Up front on the flight deck, the crewmen settled in for the long haul. Several of the crew loosened their neckties and the radioman put on a pair of house slippers.

An hour later, the commander and first officer were still at the controls. Jake had taken the flight engineer's seat shortly after takeoff and had been observing the two pilot's cockpit protocol.

The first officer, flying copilot, made some notes on a clipboard in his lap. When he turned to hand the paperwork back to the flight engineer, he noticed Jake observing over his shoulder.

"Looks like we're going to get lucky on this flight. According to reports from Pearl, the weather should be good all the way," the first officer commented.

Captain Hudson slid his seat back and indicated for Jake to take the pilot's position as he climbed out.

"It's all yours, Jake," Captain Hudson said and pointed out the forward cockpit window. "Honolulu, two thousand miles, that-a-way."

The commander had made a joke, as *they-went-that-a-way* was a popular line in cowboy movies of the time.

Jake took the kidding good-naturedly. He moved into the pilot's position and adjusted the seat, as he was a little taller than the commander.

"The panel layout is about the same as the GLM-130s we flew back in New York," Jake remarked to the first officer, "but this cockpit sure has a lot more room."

Jake took the controls.

"You got it," the first officer said releasing his grip on the control wheel and leaning back in his seat.

After four hours, the second officer relieved Jake at the controls and the pilot/navigator relieved the first officer in the copilot's position.

Jake moved to the rear of the flight deck and passed by the commander who had retired to the captain's chair in a little alcove behind the radio operator's station.

"Plot a dead reckoning navigation course from our present position based on the last wind drift check the navigator made," the commander requested of Jake, "and let me have a look at your calculations when you're finished."

"Aye, aye sir," Jake replied.

Jake's response being the only correct reply to a nautical order. He sat down at the navigation table across from the radioman and went to work. When Jake finished the plot, he handed his work to Captain Hudson who compared Jake's to one he had requested earlier from the second officer.

"Looks like you both got the same answer. Wonder if it's because that's roughly the heading we've been flying for the last several hours," Captain Hudson joked.

Jake smiled because he knew he had actually worked the plot from scratch, as did the commander.

"We'll take a couple of star sightings tonight to confirm our position and wind drift. Okay, now give me your best guess for our ETA. Write it down with your name on a piece of paper and put it with a dollar in the hat."

The commander pointed to his upside-down hat on the nav-table containing several small folded up slips and some one-dollar bills.

"Make your best guess and put it in the hat. Closest one to the minute wins the pot."

The commander got up to leave the flight deck and addressed crew. "I'll fly the mid-watch tonight so I'm going to go sack out for a couple of hours. You guys think you can keep her straight and level while I'm taking a nap?" he said with a smile.

After the commander left, the radioman cocked one earphone up on the side of his head and said to Jake, "Captain Hudson likes to be on course, cuts the total flight time down a little. I usually wait until I'm able to pick up the Adcock radio beacon out of Honolulu before I put my guess in the hat."

"You sure that's fair?" Jake replied kidding the radioman.

"Aw, you new crackerjack pilots always beat me anyway," referring to Jake and the other relatively new second officer on the flight. "Whoever is at the controls on final approach can always fudge a little."

The crew continued to rotate flight positions, taking their meal breaks and sack time in turn to relieve the fatigue of the long flight. Jake relieved the flight engineer while he caught some sleep.

Along about midnight, Jake went aft to the bunkroom. The overhead was lower there and he stooped slightly to walk. He found a bunk and stretched out. Near the wing root the ride was smoother and the luggage in the cargo hold muffled the aircraft sounds. The steady low-pitched drone of the four engines soon lulled Jake off to sleep.

***

Shortly after three-thirty in the morning, Jake was awakened by the sound of the pilot at the controls adjusting the power settings. He could tell they were climbing to a higher altitude.

"Most of the passengers are asleep so the thinner air shouldn't bother them," Jake heard the flight engineer say as he returned to the flight deck.

"Everyone on deck check the pink of your fingernails often," the pilot said. "If they start to turn blue, holler up and we'll go on back down a little."

Jake did not have to ask why they were climbing to a higher altitude. According to the recent wind drift report lying on the navigator's table their flight path was about to cross the edge of a Pacific high-pressure area. At eleven thousand feet they would have a slight tail wind.

Jake sat leaning against the bulkhead and gazed out the port side window. The starry sky engulfed the ship like a giant black ball. A dull glow still remained on the northwest horizon where the moon set a few minutes earlier.

Out past the yellow flames shooting out of the engine exhaust stacks like a blowtorch, was nothing except a vast dark-blue ocean as far as the eye could see. Jake turned to look aft between the wing and the sponson and it reminded him for a moment of the day he looked out between the wings of the old Jenny biplane.

When his eyes focused in the distance, he could see the outline of the eastern horizon and the sky turning a faint yellowish-blue. Ten hours before, the setting sun had sank into the horizon ahead of them. He watched as the sun rose slowly behind them and would catch up to them before this day's flight concluded. Jake recalled his mother's words, "The heavens are God's tabernacle."

That afternoon, the island of Oahu appeared in the distance and Captain Hudson took his seat in the pilot's position. One by one, the crewmen shaved and put their neckties back on as they prepared to dress in full uniform for touchdown and docking.

Captain Hudson descended and flew parallel to Waikiki Beach giving the portside passengers an island view. Over Diamond Head, he circled and returned giving the starboard passengers the island view, a tradition observed by all Pan Am Clippers upon arrival in Hawaii.

The *Honolulu Clipper* touched down on the water and made a high-speed taxi run over to the steamship pier near the Aloha Tower where the Clipper docked to deplane its passengers. Captain Hudson and several of the crewmen formed a reception line to greet and thank the passengers for flying with Pan Am as they went ashore.

After unloading, the crew ferried the *Honolulu Clipper* over to the seaplane dock at Pearl Harbor for service and maintenance. The Clipper would remain tied up there until departing the day after tomorrow. The harbor provided calm anchorage and excellent protection from overnight rainsqualls, which passed across the island and sometimes caused high waves to come ashore.

***

Jake was invited to join the rest of the crew for the evening at a restaurant on Waikiki Beach for dinner. Captain Hudson's wife and a couple of the other officer's wives lived in Honolulu part of the year and joined them for dinner.

Jake enjoyed the dinner, but was a bit uncomfortable around married couples. He never had been very good at social activities with people he did not know well and excused himself early.

Jake walked around Waikiki for a while finally ending up at the bar on the large patio behind the Royal Hawaiian Hotel overlooking the beach. He ordered a drink and sat listening to a local band play as three tan-skinned native girls in grass skirts sang and swayed to the music. One of the girls reminded him of Delores.

Jake sat deep in thought for the longest time staring out over the dark blue ocean. He watched as the waves came ashore and burst with a sparkling silver glow. The band had quit and the waiters were clearing the tables when Jake finally paid his check and left.

The crewmen were permitted to sleep in after the long Pacific crossings, but reported to the operations base at Pearl mid-morning to complete maintenance paperwork and flight planning for the next day's return flight to the mainland. The facility at Pearl was equipped to handle any needed repairs on the Pan Am Clippers.

When Jake reported for duty, Captain Hudson told him, "You've been reassigned to the *California Clipper*. We've got two extra pilots returning with us to the States and the Manila flight is short a relief pilot."

Jake had observed the *California Clipper* NC-18602 tied up at the next pier over when he arrived.

"Fine with me, sir. I've kind of been wanting to see the Philippines anyway. Should I report over there now, sir?"

"Good attitude, Martin. You're going to fit right in. Yes, see Captain Ford. He's expecting you."

Jake reported to Captain Ford and joined the rest of the crew preparing the *California Clipper* for the next leg of its long flight to Manila Bay. Jake and his new crew would cross six thousand more air miles of ocean in the next three days.

The Clipper's flight crew and its elite group of travelers would spend the next night on the island of Midway. They would cross the International Date Line and jump one whole day ahead in time. The following two nights would be spent on Wake Island and the Island of Guam, finally reaching Manila on the fourth day.

∗∗∗

Trippe committed Pan Am to purchasing a fleet of SK-43 Baby Clippers to expand the feeder routes in Brazil and to service the new Seattle to Alaska route. The expenses incurred by the rapid expansion of Pan Am combined with the public's resistance to fly the airline after several major crashes resulted in financial problems.

All of which culminated in the stockholders asking Trippe to submit his resignation. Jake and all of the Pan Am employees were shocked when they heard Trippe had stepped down as president. Jake had instructed Larry to vote against the board's move to relieve Trippe by using the Martin Company's proxy, but they were in the minority.

The chief shareholder of Pan Am, Sonny Whitney, replaced Trippe as managing head of Pan Am. The management shakeup proved short lived. In January of 1940, the directors voted to return Juan Trippe to the post of president of Pan Am. Once again, Trippe returned to the helm of his beloved airline and its growth was again full-speed ahead.

Red had been promoted to captain shortly after Jake left New York and assigned to Washington State to fly the shorter range SK-43 Clippers between Seattle and Alaska. Bad weather and heavy fog often plagued these routes.

The *American Clipper* NC-18606 soon entered service with the Pacific flights and demand for experienced flying boat pilots increased. Jake succeeded in recommending Red for a first officer's position on the new Clippers and got him transferred to San Francisco.

***

Eighteen months after Jake had been assigned to the Pacific fleet, he was promoted to commander on the Boeing 314 flying boats. He more often than not volunteered for the Hong Kong runs and as a result spent more time in the Asian Pacific than he did in San Francisco.

The seaplane base in San Francisco was relocated from Alameda to Treasure Island and a powerful new searchlight was installed on Yerba Buena Island. The light located at the Port of Trade Winds could be seen from a hundred miles away on a clear night.

The once dangerous and hazardous air crossings over the vast Pacific Ocean had become routine. Jake made many flights through to Hong Kong and several to New Zealand. These mighty aluminum flying boats and the men of steel who flew them made the world a smaller place.

The stationmaster at the seaplane base hired a slender, attractive twenty-one year old blonde named Margo as his new secretary. Margo was not only pretty she was also smart. To phrase it the way one of the other pilots had, "Margo could charm the balls off a brass monkey!"

Jake claimed, "The first time Red came through operations and saw Margo, he went to point like an old birddog."

Red wasted no time getting to know Margo and they became inseparable from their first date. No matter what time of the day or night Red came in from a flight, Margo would be waiting in her car in the parking lot for him. Red was ready to get married and apparently so was Margo as they were married exactly six weeks to the day from when they first met.

Since being assigned to San Francisco, Jake returned only twice to the ranch in Texas to spend time with Lora and Michael. He flew home commercial both times.

Jake borrowed a small, single-engine plane from a pilot he knew and flew into the Culver City airport to visit Dan and Ida over one of his weekends off.

In Honolulu, Jake dated an attractive young girl by the name of Lonnie, a bathing suit beauty contestant. Her social activities and Jake's absences soon separated them.

The only lady Jake dated stateside was Rita, a fun loving, Gypsy-looking girl who reminded him of a dark-haired Elsa. He picked her up in a bar one night or maybe it happened the other way around. When they first met, she had shown Jake a picture of a Merchant Marine she said was her boyfriend, but Jake suspected the photo was of Rita's husband from the suntan ring mark on her left hand.

***

Pan Am engineers wanted more speed and range out of the 314 Clipper and Boeing proposed modifying the flying boat's empennage. *Pacific Clipper* NC-18600 was returned to the Boeing factory for modification.

Nelson and Jake were scheduled to flight-test and return the modified Clipper when the Clipper was ready. They were the logical choice, having done the preliminary flight-testing on the GLM-130 back in Boston.

Captain Nelson, Jake and a flight engineer named Benny Weston caught a ride with a deadhead SK-42 *Alaska Clipper* flight and were dropped off at the Boeing seaplane port.

The Boeing engineers had extensively redesigned the Clipper's tri-tail configuration, installing a larger single tail. The new design promised a twenty-knot increase in cruise speed and better fuel economy.

After a full day of ground and high-speed taxi tests at the Boeing seaplane facility, the ferry flight crew of three departed late afternoon for San Francisco. The return flight was uneventful and the newly modified Boeing 314 performed as promised.

The aircraft was not loaded to gross weight and did not have anywhere near the full fuel load required for a Pacific crossing. This out of CG configuration differed from the previously delivered Clippers and may have been a factor in the fateful series of events that followed.

The *Pacific Clipper* and its three-man crew arrived north of San Francisco after dark inbound for Treasure Island. The city lights sparkled through a light fog hanging over the bay. As Jake and Nelson started their descent, suddenly without warning, there was an explosion in the number four engine.

"Captain, I can see flames in the cowl flaps on number four," Jake reported from the copilot's position.

Nelson was holding full left rudder pedal and still losing directional control. The Clipper's airspeed slowed.

"Full throttle on number four, Jake. Let's try and blow the flames out."

Jake applied full power to the bad engine.

Benny was watching out the side window and hollered forward, "There appears to be fuel feeding the fire, sir!"

Jake scanned the engine gages on the instrument panel and reported, "Losing manifold pressure, RPM falling off. She's not responding, Captain!"

Jake reached for the engine fuel-cutoff switch and mixture simultaneously with Nelson telling him to do so.

"Cut off the fuel feed to the engine!" Nelson ordered.

Jake knew the only option remaining was to try and feather the engine to decrease the drag. He reached for the number four engine controls and looked at Nelson.

Nelson nodded yes to go ahead and Jake pulled the throttle lever and attempted to feather the prop.

"The blades aren't rotating! The prop's still spinning. I'm sure the fire melted an oil line and that's why the prop won't feather," Benny speculated.

"Damn! If the engine seizes, that prop's coming off," Jake mumbled and kept trying to get the prop to feather.

The fire receded a little, but had already melted holes in the aluminum cowling.

The failure of the prop to feather meant the prop blades remained flat against the air stream causing excessive drag on the starboard side of the aircraft.

Jake moved forward to place both feet on the rudders.

"You need me to help stand on the rudders?"

"I'm okay," Nelson said calmly. "I'm holding her as straight as I can with the ailerons, but crank in max rudder trim."

Every time Nelson attempted to level out, the aircraft tried to stall. He had no choice except to keep descending and hope they did not run out of altitude before they reached the Bay.

"I think it's the new tail section," Benny said. "Not enough control in the yaw axis when you lose an engine."

"That's probably some of it, Benny," Nelson responded, "but she's behaving like she's also out of CG."

Jake adjusted his seat forward to help Nelson if needed, tightened his seat belt and hollered back to Benny, "Better get buckled up. Looks like we're going in!"

Benny made a final radio call to Treasure Island stating their position and situation. He shut down all non-essential electrical systems and strapped himself into his seat.

Jake strained upward in his seat to see over the nose.

"Captain, I can see the lights along Embarcadero. The beacon at Yerba Buena must be in the fog bank."

"I see them, Jake," Nelson replied glancing out his side window. "Treasure Island and the Oakland Bay Bridge are socked in solid. I'm going to plan our touchdown south of the bridge in Alameda Bay."

Nelson held a steady rate of descent to keep the airspeed up and maintain directional control. He wanted as smooth a water as possible, but needed to be high enough to clear the bridge's upper structure.

They passed over Yerba Buena Island at about fifteen hundred feet and entered the fog layer. Forward visibility and the harbor lights disappeared completely. At five hundred feet per minute rate of descent, they were going to hit something in three minutes or less.

Nelson referenced the attitude gyro to keep the airplane as level as possible.

"Flaps twenty and give me altitude readouts starting now!"

Jake lowered the flaps to twenty degrees. There was a good chance their altimeter was not exact, but all they had to go by. Jake began the altitude read outs.

"Three hundred. Two hundred. One hundred. Fifty!"

Jake and Benny braced themselves.

Nelson hauled the nose of the Clipper up, anticipating contact with the water any second. When he did, the right wing stalled and dropped an instant before touchdown.

"I'm sorry, Jake! I can't…"

The Clipper's number four prop and starboard sponson struck the water at the same time. The giant seaplane veered hard to the right and plowed sideways as the bow wave came up over the windshield.

Jake had placed his hand on the all-kill panel and managed to throw the switches an instant before being slammed hard against the right bulkhead, preventing any electrical or fuel fire on impact.

Nelson, or for that matter no pilot, could have held that Clipper any straighter. Had the giant bird stalled twenty feet higher in the air, it would have cart wheeled and broken into a thousand pieces.

There are times in the lives of men when only God may choose if they will live or they will die. This was one of those times.

Muffled crunching noises and one terrible crack, like a large tree limb snapping, echoed through the airframe. Then horrendous unidentifiable sounds, which the brain manages to tune out in circumstances like these, were followed by a deafening silence.

The fuselage of the aircraft had cracked open at the wing root and water was pouring into the cargo hold. At best, it would be only a matter of minutes before the water started filling the flight deck and flooding the cockpit.

Jake was experiencing a lot of pain in his right leg, which was pinned between the right rudder pedal and the bulkhead. He struggled and finally managed to pull his leg free. In the darkness, Jake could make out that Nelson was still in his seat.

"Captain!" Jake raised his voice, "Captain?"

There was no answer.

"Benny, you okay back there?" Jake yelled aft.

"I'm okay," Benny hollered back as he unbuckled his seatbelt to come forward.

Nelson was slumped over the controls with a bad gash on the side of his head. Blood was running down his chin and he was unconscious. Benny unbuckled Nelson and Jake helped Benny pull him out of the pilot's seat.

The water was ankle deep on the cockpit floor. Based on the amount of water in the cockpit, Jake figured the Clipper was sinking rapidly.

"Probably the only thing keeping us afloat is the buoyancy of our nearly empty fuel tanks," Jake speculated.

Benny opened the overhead hatch and climbed out. He lay on his belly and reached down to help Jake lift Nelson out through the hatch.

Jake held Nelson up by his underarms. He tried hard to lift Nelson up to Benny, but Nelson's two hundred pounds and the pain in his leg was too much for Jake.

Under his breath, Jake uttered, "The Lord is my strength," and with one final effort, he raised his captain high enough for Benny to get a hold of Nelson's shirt collar and together they lifted the injured pilot out and onto the top of the floating aircraft.

Benny laid Nelson down easy on the wing.

Jake stepped on the copilot's seatback with his good leg and pulled himself through the hatch. He glanced back into the darkened cockpit and could see the seawater had already flooded over half of the flight deck.

"I expect this thing will sink any minute now," Benny speculated as he leaned down through the open cockpit hatch to fish out some floating seat cushions and handed them up to Jake, who was holding onto the still unconscious Nelson.

The water from the bay had quenched the engine flames. What was left of the engine glowed a deep orange in the pitch-black darkness. The Clipper settled into the water, but stopped short of sinking. The top of the wings and the upper fuselage remained above water. The large vertical stabilizer protruded out of the water in the darkness behind them, like a giant shark's dorsal fin.

The lights along the distant shoreline shown through the fog causing it to glow a dull gray in the pitch-black darkness that surrounded the Clipper. Water slapping softly against the Clippers hollow airframe and the faint wailing of a foghorn were the only sounds in the still night air.

A short time passed and a small boat at engine idle bumped the far end of the wing tip of the mostly submerged *Pacific Clipper*.

"Ahoy, anyone there?" a voice from the fog called out.

Jake was lying propped up on the wing with his right leg extended. He sat up and yelled back, "Over here!"

A six-passenger wooden Chris Craft speedboat pulled alongside the cockpit. The person steering the boat backed the stern of the craft skillfully up to the leading edge of the wing between the cockpit and the inboard engine.

Two middle-aged men were onboard. They were gentlemen fishermen caught offshore when the fog had rolled in and were making their way slowly ashore when the Clipper crashed in the water nearby.

"Where are the others," one of the men asked?

"We're it," Jake replied. "There are no passengers. We were on a test flight."

Jake and Benny lowered Nelson's limp body down to the two men in the boat who laid him gently onto the teak wood top deck of the speedboat.

When Jake stepped off the wing into the boat, he fell forward, gripping his right leg in pain. The simple fracture, of which Jake was not aware, had just become a compound fracture. His lower right leg bone protruded through a bloody mass of flesh just below his knee.

The older of the two men helped Jake up onto a seat.

"I'm a doctor. Better let me look at that."

Jake was in pain, but pointed to Nelson.

"No, take care of him first. I'll be okay for now."

The doctor ignored Jake and bent down for a closer look at Jake's broken leg. With a small pocketknife, he cut Jake's pant leg and tore the cloth to above the knee.

"Get a hold of something, this is going to hurt," the doctor warned Jake, as he straightened the leg and pulled the bone back inside the flesh.

Jake nearly passed out, but he held on. Once again, Jake pointed to Nelson and pleaded, "Look, if you're a doctor, take care of him! Would you, please?"

The doctor replied softly, "I've already had a look at him. I'm sorry young man, but your friend didn't make it. He was not alive when we lifted him into our boat."

***

Two days passed since the *Pacific Clipper* crash. Bright rays of sunlight shown through the windows of the sterile, sparsely filled, hospital ward. Jake lay in steel-frame hospital bed with a large cast on his right leg suspended by cables, weights and pulleys. He was already bored.

From down the hallway, Jake could hear the voice of a young nurse scolding someone. "I don't care who you are, you can't go in there with a lit cigar!" The double-doors at the far end of the ward flew open and Juan Trippe entered, followed by two nurses fussing at him.

"It's okay, ma'am. I don't mind the cigar," Jake told the nurses. "Besides, you'll lose the argument with this guy anyway."

The two young nurses left in a huff.

"Hi ya, Jake. Laying down on the job, I see."

"Well hello, Juan! How is it I rate a visit from our esteemed airline president? Now let me see if I can guess."

Trippe pulled up a chair without being asked.

"What do you mean guess? You know darn right well why I'm here." Then realizing he might be overheard, Trippe lowered his voice. "You crazy China pilots dumped one of my brand new airplanes in the bay. That's why I'm here!"

Jake tried to raise up enough in bed to see Trippe as he talked.

"Don't blame me. Those damn Boeing engineers… Well, we're just lucky we didn't lose a planeload of passengers!"

Trippe re-lit his cigar, which had gone out.

"I know. That's what we need to talk about. You knew Steve Nelson pretty well, didn't you?"

Jake struggled to make eye contact with Trippe who had seated himself below Jake's line of sight.

"About as well as you can know a fellow, I guess. Don't start trying to blame the crash on him though. Pilots don't come any better than Steve Nelson."

Trippe scooted his chair closer to the hospital bed.

"Nah, that's not where I'm going. I mean he never talked about his family, did he?"

Jake hesitated a bit before he replied.

"Come to think of it, he didn't. Why?"

Trippe leaned forward in his chair.

"Well that's the point, he doesn't have any. He grew up in an orphanage and learned to fly in the Navy. Never married or had any kids as far as I can find out."

Jake was puzzled.

"Okay, Juan, spit it out. What's the deal?"

Trippe sat back in the chair and gave a slight gesture into the air with both hands.

"We're gonna hush the whole thing up. Boeing is going to stand behind the aircraft and build us a new one with the same side number, NC-18600. On paper they're going to re-build the *Pacific Clipper*, but not really. We'll get a brand new airplane without those fool modifications. Besides, our insurance underwriters wouldn't pay a claim on a ship with an untested experimental tail section anyway."

Jake tried to roll over to look at Trippe, but flinched from the pain.

"Ouch!" Jake complained. "Don't give me that bologna. The press will have a field day with a fiasco like that."

Trippe stood up, moved close to Jake and spoke softly.

"Did you see anything in the papers about it?"

"No," Jake agreed, "and I've been reading them, too."

"And you won't. I kid you not, for some reason the press didn't find out about it. We were able to get a barge and a crane out to the *Pacific Clipper* while she was still afloat and before the fog cleared on shore. A tug tied onto the Clipper and towed it out of the bay and further up the coast. They ran her aground on a sand bar close into shore and a ship salvage crew cut her into four sections. The salvage crews loaded the sections onto three barges and by nightfall were on their way up the coast to Seattle before anyone found out about the incident. Nobody planned it this way, it just worked out like that."

Jake rested his head back down on the bed pillow.

"Where does that leave Nelson?"

"We're gonna log the incident in the company records as a training accident without reporting the crash. No fault, no blame. In other words, it never happened."

Trippe stood up and started to pace the floor.

Jake said nothing. He turned away and stared up at the high ceiling in the hospital ward.

Jake thought to himself, what a sad ending to a great pilot's career. He wondered what he might have done to change the inevitable outcome of the crash. He wanted to blame himself for what happened, but he knew there was nothing he could have done. Fate was the hunter here, and like it or not, they had been the prey!

Trippe paced for a few more minutes and then returned to Jake's bedside.

"Come on now, ol' fella. What's done is done. Nothing is going to bring Steve back and it isn't going to accomplish anything to chastise some Boeing engineer who screwed up and miscalculated on the design."

Jake still did not answer. He wasn't ignoring Trippe, he was only lost in thought.

Trippe shut up talking, went over to the window and looked out for a while.

Jake was thinking back to a cool sunny day when he and Steve had made a flight together out over Long Island. The air was smooth as silk and from Jake's vantage place in the sky, he remembered feeling like God was in His heaven and all was right with the world. Life seemed simpler then.

Possibly it may have been the pills they were giving Jake for pain or maybe he was just in a melancholy mood. Whichever the case, Jake's thoughts drifted a thousand miles away to Sarah. For the first time, he seriously wondered how different his life might have been now, if he had married her instead of Liz and stayed on the Flying M.

Trippe stood at the window watching some kids play baseball in the park across the street. The kids were playing with an old tattered softball and using a broomstick for a bat.

"Somebody ought to get those kids some decent equipment to play ball with," Trippe mumbled.

"What did you say, Juan?"

"Nothing, just thinking out loud," Trippe replied and walked back over to Jake's bedside.

Jake's attention returned to the problem at hand.

"The engineers screwed up, miscalculated you say?" Jake looked at Trippe who nodded his head yes. "I can identify with that," Jake said, "Done it a few times myself. I guess worse things happen." Jake was referring more to his personal life being screwed-up than he was to the crash of the Clipper or his flying career.

When Jake spoke the words *worse things happen*, neither he nor Trippe could have any idea of the coming war in the Pacific when tens of thousands of young men and women would go off to serve their countries, never to come home again.

Trippe had come in person because he knew the decision was going to be a hard one for Jake.

"Well what's it gonna be? It's your call, Jake."

Jake turned to look directly at Trippe.

"It'll be the way you said, Juan."

Trippe slapped the painted-white steel bedpost.

"That's the spirit ol' man. As soon as you can get your ass up out of this bed, go back to Texas and take a month off. Spend some time with those two boys of yours."

Jake groaned as Trippe shook the bed and smirked as he corrected Trippe.

"Its a boy and a girl!"

The sound of distant footsteps echoed from the hallway and Trippe looked towards the ward door as though someone might be coming for him.

"Right, spend some time with your two girls. Then I've got a job for you."

"And, what might that be, Juan?"

"The pilots and crews at Treasure Island don't like taking their orders from the non-flying station managers. I plan to solve the problem by assigning you as the new Flight Operations Manager as soon you're ready to take over. It'll be the best way to keep you busy until you can return to flight status."

"Yeah okay, but only until my leg heals. Then I'm going back to flying!"

Trippe turned his head to the commotion down the hall.

"Got that figured out, too! As soon as we get enough new Clippers in service, I'm going to send you on a goodwill tour of the Orient. It'll be a good publicity builder and maybe open up some new air routes."

Trippe stood up just in time to meet the two younger nurses who tried to evict him earlier. They had returned with the head nurse who came along this time to see that the hospital rules were strictly enforced.

Jake laughed as Trippe, flanked by three starch-collared nurses, was escorted out of the ward. Jake hollered after him, "See ya, boss!"

VIEW FROM SAN SIMEON

The night the Pacific Clipper crashed in the Bay, Red and his crew were inbound on a return flight when Benny's last radio message was transmitted to Treasure Island operations. Red and Margo were waiting at the hospital when Jake arrived. They waited well into the night as the doctors operated on Jake's leg and stayed with him all the next day.

Jake called his mom and dad on the telephone the following day from the hospital. "Look folks," Jake explained, "it's only a broken leg. I'm fine and there's no need for anyone to come out here."

Flo sent their love and get well wishes in a note attached to some roses delivered by a local florist. She knew roses were Jake's favorite.

Red and Margo were Jake's only visitors the first week of his stay in the hospital, besides Trippe. The second week Jake was hospitalized, a Civil Aeronautics inspector showed up unannounced. Jake knew the inspector as he had once taken a check ride with the man. The inspector came to visit under the pretext of paying Jake a social call, but grilled him repeatedly as to how he had broken his leg.

Jake stonewalled it. He never lied, but avoided volunteering any information that might have implied any association with his job or a plane crash.

On the Sunday afternoon a week after Trippe came to see Jake, Red and Margo were there and the three got into a long-winded discussion, which started when Red remarked to Margo, "You know, ol' Jake here nearly bought it out there in the Bay the other night."

"Of course you understand," Jake added for Margo's benefit, "officially I didn't."

"I wonder if there really is a heaven." Margo asked. "What do you think, Jake?"

"I think there probably is a heaven, but I suspect it's nothing like a lot of people believe."

"What do you mean?"

"For one thing, I don't think we'll be sitting around on puffs of clouds and I hope we won't be playing harps and singing hymns all day."

"If there is a heaven and you end up there, what would you want God to say to you?" Red asked.

"Don't know? Maybe if I killed myself in a plane crash, God would say 'Screwed up again, huh Jake?' What would you want God to say to you, Red?"

"The way I've got it figured, God would have to have a good sense of humor for Him to let me in anyway, so I'd probably expect Him to come over to me and say 'Did you hear the one about the priest and the rabbi that went into a bar?' or something like

The three of them laughed and Jake laughed the hardest. His leg hurt when he laughed, but he did anyway. Red could always cheer Jake up when nobody else could.

"Jake, we got to go now," Margo bemoaned. "Red has an errand to run before it gets dark,"

"What errand's that, Margo?"

"You explain it to him, Red."

"Oddest thing, a couple days ago I went to my mail slot at Flight Ops and there was a memo from the Pam Am offices in New York. The letter contained a check and a list of baseball equipment I was supposed to buy and give out to the kids at the park across the street from here."

"So the stuff is all in our car," Margo explained, "and we have to go do that now."

"Why that ol' hypocrite!" Jake exclaimed smiling. "Has a soft spot in that ol' heart of stone after all."

"Who's that, Jake?" Red asked.

"Oh, a fellow I thought I knew better than I really did… You all better get going while all the kids are still out there in the park!"

After Red and Margo left, Jake began to think about what Trippe had done. This became the second most profound epiphany in Jake's life. All those years of his dad's annual Christmas rounds and now this baseball thing with Trippe, suddenly he realized how little it took to do the right thing when the opportunity presented itself. More importantly, to do it without needing to be thanked.

That was why he knew without being told to help Tommy's young widow at the Buckhorn. Why the Quiet Birdmen had come to pay him a visit and what ol' Charley Armstrong had meant that day back at the TAS hangar when he had asked him "You don't even know what it's all about, do you Jake?"

He was no saint and had no intentions of living his life like one, but for some reason God had spared his life in that crash. So from this moment forward, whenever someone needed help and he was able to help them, he was going do so without expecting any thanks in return.

***

Jake had been in the hospital for two weeks driving the nurses crazy with his crankiness. The doctor finally agreed to release him and taped a rubber bumper to the bottom of Jake's leg cast so he could get around on crutches. Jake pondered what to do when he left the hospital and had decided he would not go back to Texas while he waited for the leg to heal.

The evening before Jake was due to be released from the hospital, Benny Weston came to visit. He had just returned from a round-robin flight on the *Hong Kong Clipper*. Benny still had his uniform on when he walked in.

"Hi there, Captain, how's tricks?"

"Boy, am I glad to see you, Benny! I had it figured they'd sent you off in the wild blue yonder somewhere."

Benny stood with his white uniform cap in hand.

"Sorry I haven't been by to see you sooner, but think somebody wanted me out of the country. They assigned me to the next morning's flight out after the crash."

"You mean the one that never happened?" Jake added with a smirk of his face.

"Yeah, that one!" Benny chuckled. "I've got the next week off and I wanted to come by and see you before I headed home. The nurse at the desk said they're gonna let you out of this place tomorrow."

"If they don't, I'm leaving anyway. I've been getting around pretty good on these walking sticks."

Jake gestured towards the crutches leaning against the wall beside the bed.

Benny looked over at the crutches and continued to look around for a place to lay his hat. Finally, he gave up and sat down in a stiff-backed chrome metal chair, the only chair around, and held his officer's cap in his lap.

Pilots and crews trust one another everyday with their very lives. Even more so, mutual experiences in war or a catastrophe will often bond men together for a lifetime. Jake and Benny shared such a bond after their years of flying together.

"Benny, I sure could use a favor."

"Whatever you need, Captain, you name it."

"I guess my Zephyr is still over in the company parking lot isn't it?"

"Sure is. I saw it there when I came in."

"The keys are in the left glove box of the Zephyr behind the steering wheel. I need you to take my car, go over to my apartment and pack me some clothes and things."

"You mean all of your belongings?" Benny asked.

"No, just some stuff for a month or so," Jake replied as he struggled to sit up on the edge of the bed. "Hand me one of those crutches over there to lean on."

Benny stood up, laid his hat in the chair and helped Jake up. He placed one of the crutches under Jake's arm.

"Where you going? I mean where are we going? You sure aren't driving your car with a bunged up leg like that."

"Need you to drive me down to Los Angeles. Can't quite handle going back to Texas right now so thought I'd spend some time on the beach. I've arranged to rent a house at a place called Paradise Cove. It's just north of Santa Monica. I'll hole up there till the leg heals."

"Sounds like a good plan to me. I'll catch a ride back to Frisco with the flight that brings the international mail up from L.A."

"Thought you might," Jake said.

The two talked about flying and a little about the crash, Benny being one of the few people Jake could talk with about the crash.

Jake told Benny about Trippe coming to see him.

"He wants me to take a desk job managing flight operations for the Clippers here."

"You flying a desk?" Benny laughed. "That might last a couple of months." Benny stood up to leave. "Got to run home, kiss the wife and see the kids. Pick you up in the morning, Captain."

***

The furnished beach house Jake rented was nestled in a protected cove only a stone's throw from the water's edge at high tide. The beach was an ideal place for Jake to recuperate. Dan and Ida came out from town to visit and to help him get settled.

Jake spent a lot of quiet time on the beach reading and sitting in the warm sun. Each day his leg got a little stronger and after a few weeks, he was getting around on only one crutch.

When the time for Jake's leg to heal lapsed, he went to see the doctor referred to him by the hospital back in San Francisco. He was anxious to have the cast removed. The x-rays revealed Jake's leg bone structure had not knitted properly and the leg bone was not as straight as the doctor hoped.

"You did a lot of damage to that leg before the bone was properly set," the doctor told Jake. "More than likely you will have a slight limp the rest of your life."

The doctor applied a smaller cast to Jake's leg so he was able to get around with only the slight assistance of a cane to walk.

The doctor's prognosis was difficult for Jake to accept, but he never complained to anyone.

***

Mid-summer, on a Sunday afternoon, Dan and Ida arrived at the beach house unannounced.

"We're taking you out to dinner at the restaurant on the fishing pier just down the road," Ida told Jake. "You mentioned on our previous visit you'd like to find a good place nearby that served fresh seafood."

At dinner, Ida asked Jake, "Why don't you call Flo and have her and your dad bring the kids out for a visit while you've got some time off?"

Jake looked over the steaming hot seafood platter the waiter had just placed in front of him and anticipated his first taste.

"Mom won't fly and Dad doesn't need to be driving that far," Jake said dismissing Ida's suggestion. "They're too much home bodies to be away very long anyway."

Ida placed her hand on Jake's forearm as he lifted his fork to take a bite of crab-stuffed grilled flounder.

"They could take the train. Get a Pullman sleeper. That'd be comfortable enough for your folks, wouldn't it?"

Ida let go of Jake's arm.

"Might be," Jake agreed, as he finished taking the bite of seafood.

"In fact," Ida continued, "Flo said she could even bring Violet along to help with the children… Oops!"

Jake looked at Ida and laughed when he saw the funny expression on her face.

"I think that's what Mom used to call, letting-the-cat-out-of-the-bag," Jake said smiling.

As Jake suspected, Ida and Flo had talked on the phone earlier about their coming to California to visit Jake.

Flo's grandmotherly instinct to get Lora and Michael together with their father far outweighed any apprehension she might have had about making the long journey to L.A.

"Okay, okay, I get the message. You and Mom already got this visit all planned out, don't you? Well why not? Dad's wanted to come out and see the new factory ever since its been finished. They can all stay with me and Dad can use my car to get around."

With that, Dan chimed in, "Now you're talking, Jake. It'll be good for all of you to get together."

A week later, Dan picked up Big Jake, Flo, Violet, Lora and Michael at the downtown train station when they arrived from Texas. Dan took them on a scenic drive around Los Angeles giving them a tour of the city on the way out to Jake's beach house at Paradise Cove.

***

Big Jake was anxious to see the new oil well equipment factory in full operation and so on Monday morning Jake accompanied his dad into the new Culver City factory.

When they pulled up at the factory, Dan stood waiting for them out front. A man in an Army Air Corps officer's uniform was standing with Dan waiting to greet them. When Jake got out of the car, Dan placed his hand on the officer's shoulder.

"Jake, I think you know this fellow here!"

Jake immediately recognized Dale Harkins.

"Of course, I do. I'd recognize that ugly puss anywhere, but I don't know any Army Air Corps majors."

"Well, you know one now," Dale laughed. "The Air Corps has just recruited a hundred thousand new men and us old timers got kicked up the ranks fast."

Jake laughed and they shook hands.

"Dad, this here toy soldier and I went through flyin' school together back in Fort Worth."

"Pleased to meet you young man," Big Jake said. "I think we might have even heard a few stories about you."

"Not all bad, I hope. Good to meet you too, sir."

The four men went into the factory. Dan had scheduled a meeting for Big Jake to talk with all of the managers.

Jake showed Dale around the facility. Out back of the factory, they found a place in the shade to sit, visit and enjoy the rare Mediterranean California morning.

The sun glistened on the yellow weeds in the open field behind the factory. As they talked, they watched a couple of light planes, a Curtis Robin and a Piper Cub practiced touch and go landings, playing ring-around in the traffic pattern at the airport across the way.

"I see you're walking with a cane. How'd you hurt your leg, Jake?"

"Broke it in a freak accident, but it's healing fast," Jake changed the subject. "Say, how are Peg and the kids? You haven't mentioned anything about them."

"Peg's sassy as ever and the kids are growing like weeds. You know, all the usual stuff."

"Whatever happened to that friend of Peg's? What was her name? You know, that pleasant girl who went out with us in Dayton that time."

"Oh, you mean Helen. She married a cattle rancher from Tulsa. They've got a nice spread over by Okmulgee. She has three boys and is expecting another according to the last Christmas card we got from her."

Jake and Dale discussed the U.S. military buildup and the possibility of war. They talked about the effect of an oil blockade on Japan and why the Japanese would not let Pan Am fly its Clippers into their country.

When Jake and Dale arrived back at the factory office, Big Jake and Dan were waiting on them to go to lunch. Dan suggested they have lunch over at a delicatessen on Sepulveda.

"You'll like this place," Dan confided. "They make a great corned beef sandwich, but out here they call it a New York Reuben for some reason."

Over lunch, conversation turned to the possibility of the U.S. entering the war in Europe. A few nights before, President Roosevelt had given one of his Fireside Chats on the radio. He explained a new policy he called, "Lend Lease," saying, "If your neighbor's house was on fire, would you refuse to loan them your garden hose?"

Jake suspected Dale's visit to California might have something to do with the new policy.

"What brings you out to this neck of the woods, anyway?" Jake asked.

"Had some business over at Douglas Aircraft. Air Corps is buying some more C-47 Skytrains. DC-3s to you, but everyone I know calls them Gooney Birds."

"I've also heard them called Gooneys. Guess it's because they're so clumsy on the ground and fly so well in the air."

"We flew out here in one. Good plane, but they say there're only two kinds of DC-3 pilots, those who've ground looped one and those who are going to. Navy's designation is R4D and the Canucks call them a Dakota."

"You guys buying for the RCAF now too?"

Dale leaned forward into the table.

"Off the record, you understand, I won't say exactly buying. About a month ago, a bunch of us ferried a couple dozen C-47s up to an abandoned airfield north of Montreal. Our orders were to park the planes and leave the keys in the ignition, so to speak. We all flew back to Wright Field in a couple of chase planes. One of the pilots from the second delivery group told me a bunch of RAF pilots came and picked up all of the planes we'd left parked there. I guess that's what ol' FDR meant by Lend Lease."

After lunch, Jake and his dad drove Dale over to the airstrip at the Douglas Aircraft factory where Dale met up with his flight crew and some procurement officers who were all returning to Wright Field that evening.

After they dropped Dale off to meet his crew, Big Jake said, "I'd like to stop by the airport terminal at Mines Field and make an airline reservation to fly back to Texas tomorrow. Got some business to attend to, but your mom, Violet and the kids can stay till they're ready and come home on the train."

***

Jake drove his dad to the airport the following day to see him off. This was the first time Jake had driven since the accident. He was getting around much better now.

Lora and Michael loved the beach and like most kids, they adapted quickly to their newfound lifestyle. The visit had been a fun time for everyone and had given Lora and Michael a chance to get reacquainted with their father.

"Lands, the washin's easy here!" Violet told Jake and Flo. "All I has to do is rinse out the wet swimmin' suits."

Violet was enjoying her vacation as much as the rest of the family, but soon after Big Jake left, Flo mentioned several times that it would sure be good to get back home to Texas and to the ranch.

The morning after Big Jake had been gone for about a week, Flo said to Jake, "Your father is starting to miss me. Even though he didn't say so, I could hear it in his voice last night when I talked with him on the telephone. I think it's time we head home, Jacob. Would you make the arrangements with the railway people for us?"

"Sure Mom, I'll take care of it."

"You know Violet is engaged and we wouldn't wanna let that nice young feller get away," Flo said to Jake knowing Violet was listening from the kitchen. "Would we Violet?"

"No, ma'am, we sure doesn't," Violet hollered back and giggled. "No-sir-ree sure wouldn't wanna do that."

***

A few days after Flo and the kids left for Texas, Jake began to think about returning to San Francisco. He still would not be able to return to flight duty, but he could at least be involved in the day-to-day operations at Treasure Island if he took the manager's job Trippe had suggested.

Jake was taking an early afternoon nap when the telephone rang.

"Tired of laying around yet, ol' fella?"

"You must have read my mind, Juan. Yeah, I am getting a little restless and was thinking about calling you."

"Good. Betty and I are flying into L.A. tonight. William Randolph Hearst has invited us up to his place at the Casa Grande at San Simeon."

"Sounds interesting. Folks around here call the place the Hearst Castle. I understand it's really something. I've seen it from the coast highway, but never been up there."

"Well, you're invited to come along with us, Jake. Hearst requested I bring one of my key people along. Wants to discuss business, I suspect."

"And since when did I become one of your key people?"

"You're not. Don't have any key people, except me."

Jake understood Trippe's humor and laughed.

"Only kidding, ol' man. Hearst is a shareholder in Pan Am and I need you to help me soften him up. You'll be my out-of-town expert, China

Clipper pilot and all that sort of glamour bullshit. Meet us at the L.A. airport tomorrow morning. Hearst's private DC-3 will be waiting to take us to San Simeon."

Jake started to say okay and goodbye, but Trippe had already hung up.

***

Early the next morning, Jake arrived at Mines Field and located the Hearst Publishing Company's DC-3 on the ramp at the private terminal. He introduced himself to the pilot and they visited for a while about the Douglas DC-3 and how long the pilot had been flying for Hearst.

"Do you make a passenger run to San Simeon every day?" Jake asked.

"We make the flight most every day, but depends on if The Chief or Miss Davies are having a get-together whether we carry passengers. For large events, they charter a train from the Glendale station and park the railcars on a siding until time to return."

Jake walked with the pilot around the Skyliner and they watched as the copilot did his preflight inspection.

"Looks like our passengers are here now," the pilot commented and pointed to some arriving cars. "Glad to have you along today, Captain Martin. Enjoy your visit."

The VIPs for the flight started arriving and Jake recognized several of them as major motion picture stars. The rest of the group consisted of aspiring starlets and film company executives.

When Trippe and his wife Betty arrived, the aircraft was loaded and readied for departure. The copilot closed the airstair door and went forward.

Jake took a seat in the cabin across from Trippe.

After takeoff, the copilot came to the rear of the cabin where Jake was seated.

"The captain asks if you would like to go forward and ride the second seat for a while."

Jake started to pass on the offer out of courtesy to the young copilot, then asked, "You sure you don't mind?"

"No problem, sir. I make this flight everyday. You're more than welcome to go forward."

Jake had been hoping for an opportunity to get more familiar with the Three and had even been trying to rationalize buying one ever since Donald Douglas had introduced the plane.

"Thanks, I would like to."

Jake went forward to the cockpit and climbed in the copilot's seat. During the flight, Jake and the pilot discussed the DC-3 and the pilot asked a lot about Jake's experiences flying the Pan Am Clippers in the Pacific.

The Hearst pilot flew the Douglas at a low altitude just off the coast of San Luis Obispo and then cut across Marro Bay. Flying that route gave the passengers a wonderful view of the scenic California coastline.

Passengers on the right side of the plane spotted sea lions feeding along the shore while passengers on the left side watched out the windows for migrating whales.

Arriving at the foothills of the Piedra Blanca Mountains, the copilot came forward to the cockpit for their approach to a landing.

Jake returned to the cabin to sit facing Trippe in the club seating.

"Is there anything special I should know about these meetings we're going to have with Hearst?" Jake asked.

The cabin *No Smoking* sign lit up and Trippe put out the cigar he had been smoking.

"The Chief, as they call him, is going to pump us about the airline's growth potential. We in turn, are going to try to get him to invest more money with Pan Am. As you know, I'm planning to expand our Pacific routes. We're going to need more planes and people to do that. Keep an upbeat tone to whatever he wants to discuss."

"I can handle that," Jake replied with a smile.

"There is one other thing you should be aware of," Trippe added as an afterthought, "That actress, Marion Davies, she and Hearst are real tight. Best avoid anything except polite conversation with her and try not to get caught alone with her, if you know what I mean."

"Juan Trippe! Shame on you," Betty quipped and smacked her husband on the shoulder for what he had just said.

The three of them laughed.

"I thoroughly understand, Boss."

Jake turned to look out the window. The pilot was starting his approach to land in a large open field not far from the ocean shore.

***

The DC-3 landed in a valley at the foothills of a ridge of mountains. As the passengers deplaned, they were treated to a spectacular view of the Hearst Castle perched atop a high peak several miles away.

Three coachbuilt sedans and a Woody station wagon were waiting to take the guests up a winding road leading to the main entrance onto the estate grounds.

A young starlet Jake had politely spoken to when he boarded the plane in Los Angeles had been shown to the station wagon. She climbed back out, came over to the LeBaron sedan and squeezed into the back seat next to Jake. He noted the pleasant fragrance of her Channel No.5 perfume, his favorite.

"I'm Miss Claudette Parsons," she whispered to Jake. "Its not my real name. Maybe I'll tell you my real name later, but while we're here, just call me Claudette."

"I'm Jake, Jake Martin. Pleased to make your acquaintance, Claudette."

On the way up the winding road to the castle, the guests passed herds of cattle and African wildlife grazing on the hillsides. The driver of the sedan rambled on, informatively pointing out things of interest as he drove.

"Over there is a herd of Spanish cows, a special breed raised here on the ranch. Down the hillside there, you can see some gazelle grazing."

"How did Mr. Hearst's father make all his money and how big is this ranch anyway?" Claudette asked the driver.

"Lead and silver mining mostly, ma'am," the driver replied looking at her in his rearview mirror to answer her question. "The ranch covered over three hundred square miles when The Chief's father owned it, but it's a little smaller than that now."

"Oh look!" Claudette called out.

"That's our zoo, ma'am. Hopefully, you'll have a chance to see our animals up close while you're here."

Lunch awaited the arriving guests on the terrace. Jake was introduced to Greta Garbo, Cary Grant and Irene Dunne, along with a covey of starlets and executives from Hearst's Cosmopolitan Productions. Jake was seated at the table between Claudette and Julia Morgan, the architect.

"I understand you designed much of Casa Grande and other buildings on the estate, Miss Morgan."

"Of course," she replied tactfully, "with a great amount of helpful input from Mr. Hearst. We are mostly doing remodeling work now."

"I'm simply fascinated with the whole estate," Claudette sighed. "I can't wait to write to my mother and tell her about this place, but she'll never believe me!"

Miss Davies rose to address the group and clinked her crystal water glass with a small silver spoon.

"Some business matters came up Mr. Hearst needed to attend to, but I assure you he'll be with us this evening for dinner so may I welcome you to our humble surroundings," Miss Davies paused, which was everyone's cue to politely laugh, "and we hope you have a pleasant stay."

A butler escorted Jake to a bungalow across the courtyard from the Neptune Pool and down a Grecian style staircase. In the bedroom, his luggage had already been unpacked and his things placed neatly in drawers or hung in the closet. A courtesy bathing suit and bathrobe were neatly laid out on the bed.

Jake crossed the spacious bungalow to the large picture window with a westerly view. The window framed a panoramic sight of the Pacific Ocean overlooking San Simeon Bay a thousand feet below.

Jake changed into the out-of-fashion, two-piece black swimsuit and went up to the Neptune Pool for a welcome dip in the sparkling water. Several of the guests, already at the pool, engaged Jake in polite casual conversation.

The afternoon sun sank low out over the western ocean and Jake returned to his bungalow for a shower and a nap before the evening meal.

***

Jake almost overslept and hurried to get dressed in his Pan Am captain's uniform. Trippe had asked Jake to wear his uniform at least one evening for dinner to make an impression. Jake never gave it a second thought. He was quite comfortable in uniform. After all, he had almost lived in one for the last five years.

The cocktail hour was already in progress in the main hall below the twin bell towers when Jake arrived at the La Casa Grande only a short walk from his bungalow.

Trippe was visiting with the actor Errol Flynn who obviously had gotten a head start on the drinks before arriving at the reception. When Jake came up, Trippe introduced him to Flynn and several of the other guests standing nearby.

"Grab a cocktail quick when the waiter comes by," Trippe prodded Jake. "Hearst only allows the waiters to serve drinks twice around the room before dinner."

Jake took one of the only remaining drinks, a whisky-sour, from the waiter's tray as he passed by. He took one sip and sat the small drink on a nearby end table. If Jake was going to have a drink, he preferred bourbon and water, but he was out of luck for right now.

Jake joined the small group gathered around Flynn as he told about a scene he filmed in his last pirate movie.

"I did all of my own stunts in that film," Flynn bragged and laughed. He took a drink of his martini and added, "Whether I did them or not!"

Trippe gave a raised eyebrow and smirked. He found Flynn a rather arrogant and braggart sort of fellow. To the contrary, Jake took a liking to Flynn right off and even found him entertaining to talk with.

Trippe leaned over to Jake and whispered, "It's about time for him, Hearst that is, to make his appearance. I've seen this performance before. Watch that panel in the wall over there. Actually it's a door. Hearst will open it slightly to enter the room and seem to suddenly appear among his guests. It's one of his favorite tricks."

As Trippe predicted, Hearst appeared among his guests as if having been in the room the whole time.

Dinner was announced and the guests ushered to their seats in the main dining hall. The hall reminded Jake of something out of a Robin Hood or King Arthur movie.

Jake was seated with Claudette on his left slightly down from the center of the table. Betty Trippe was on Jake's right with Juan next to her. Hearst and Miss Davies were seated directly across the table from Juan and Betty Trippe.

"Boy, are we lucky!" Claudette whispered to Jake. "Rumor is the further you're seated away from the center of the table, the sooner you're expected to end your stay."

"Don't think it's all luck," Jake replied with a grin.

After dinner, Miss Davies invited all of the ladies to join her in the parlor. The men retired to the billiards room where they were offered cigars and a round of cognac or sherry. Here in the smoke filled billiards room was where the conversation would oscillate between joking and matters of business and state.

Few guests were as well versed on current events as Hearst. Having already reviewed all of the newspapers flown in that morning, he was well prepared to discuss any topic.

Trippe had been known to talk for hours to someone whose conversation interested him and Hearst shared that same characteristic with Trippe.

"Will you be riding with us tomorrow, Martin," Hearst asked, "or are you one of those city folks who doesn't ride?"

Jake seemed caught off guard by Hearst's directness.

"Well sir, I was thinking about wimping out on the horseback riding. I still have a little discomfort in my leg, I mean sitting a saddle..." but then Jake, unaccustomed to making excuses, just shut up and went back to watching the billiard game. Under his breath Jake unintelligibly muttered, "Aw hell, never mind."

"What's this?" Hearst asked directing his next comment at Trippe. "I tell you to bring one of your best men, and you bring along a gimp pilot that doesn't even ride? My horses can't be any rougher riding than those flying Clipper airplanes of yours," Hearst joked. "Why, I flew to Hawaii in one of them and we bounced all the way there. Considered taking a ship home."

Trippe reached out and took one more drink from the tray of the last waiter leaving the room.

"Don't be too rough on 'ol Jake," Trippe scoffed. "He was raised on a ranch and probably sat a saddle before he could walk."

Hearst was pleased to hear that and his face lit up.

"Oh, is that so? Where's your ranch located, Martin?"

Jake turned back from watching the last billiard shot.

"North Texas. It's just a small place compared to this one. Only twenty sections instead of the three hundred plus you've got out here, Mr. Hearst."

"Texas huh, everything out there in Texas as big as they say it is?"

Chuckles echoed across the room from the men playing billiards who were also listening to Hearst and Jake talk.

"Well," Jake responded, "There was this ol' boy back home who claimed to have a ranch that took all day to drive across. 'That's a pretty big ranch,' I said to him. 'No, just a sorry pickup truck,' he replied."

Jake's story was followed by laughter from around the room and Jake heard one of the men at the billiards table say, "Looks like we've got someone willing to take on The Chief." The other gentleman at the table who was about to take his next shot, retorted, "Many have tried, many have failed!" He took his billiard shot and the two men chuckled privately.

"I did notice you seem to favor your right limb a mite. How'd you hurt your leg?" Hearst asked Jake.

Jake decided to have some fun with Trippe for getting him into this conversation.

"In the crash," Jake replied and cut his eyes over to watch the reaction on Trippe's face who had almost choked on his last swallow of cognac.

Hearst glanced at Trippe and then looked back at Jake. Hearst took the bait and asked, "What crash was that?"

Jake paused painfully long before continuing.

"The crash of '29, of course. The same one everyone else got hurt in."

Trippe gave a sigh of relief and tried, not very successfully, to laugh along with the others.

"No, just stepped down on it wrong," Jake said. "I'm fine, I'll be ready to ride with you all in the morning."

Two of the group of gentlemen excused themselves to retire for the evening, as did Errol Flynn. While at the Neptune Pool earlier that day, Jake had observed Flynn openly flirting with an actress of some minor renown. Jake suspected Flynn intended to retire to her bedroom for the evening rather than his own.

"I assure you Pan Am is in solid financial condition," Trippe explained continuing his conversation with Hearst. "With the new Pacific air routes we are opening, we may soon be the largest air carrier in the world."

"What about the Japanese Empire?" Hearst asked Trippe.

"Closed society. Haven't made any inroads into Japan."

"Oh," Hearst said thoughtfully.

Trippe came up with an idea he wanted to run by Hearst. He had explained it briefly to Jake earlier and Jake was amused. Obviously Trippe felt like this might be a good a time to bring the matter up.

"I know your people out here in the movie business are always looking for good ideas. Well, I've got one for them. It's a motion picture about two couples traveling the world in an airliner."

Hearst did not appear to be very interested. "That wouldn't be, like say maybe, in one of those China Clippers of yours would it, Juan?"

Trippe looked a little like the proverbial cat that had just been caught with the canary in its mouth.

"Could be, but we wouldn't go so far as to have girls dancing on the wings like they did in that movie *Flying Down to Rio*. Why, you could even use Miss Davies in the leading role."

"We'll see, Juan, we'll see," and Hearst turned his attention back to Jake. "You never answered me about why your airplanes ride so bumpy."

"The only solution to the problem is higher and faster airplanes," Jake replied. "Maybe we'll get them someday, but until we can get up and over the tops of the weather, there's not much we can do to eliminate the rough rides."

"No, I mean what are you going to do about the problem right now?" Hearst asked, putting Jake on the spot and pressing him for a better answer.

Jake had given Hearst an aeronautically correct answer to his question and a mistake on Jake's part. Since that had not worked, he would try another tact.

"Our immediate plan is to color code the air pockets so the pilots can drive around the bumps. Kind of like missing the potholes in a road."

Hearst realized Jake was now having some fun at his expense and smiled to himself. He often used the same tactic and decided to play along.

"What colors would you use to code the air pockets?"

Jake paused thoughtfully for a moment.

"Maybe blue for smooth air and red for hot air."

"I think there's a lot of that red coded stuff floating around the room here tonight," Hearst retorted, which brought another round of laughter from those remaining in the room.

Miss Davies entered the doorway accompanied by several of the lady guests.

"Goodnight all. We are going to retire for our beauty rest now."

All except Jake, Trippe and Hearst excused themselves for the evening.

"Juan, how'd you come to get interested in airplanes anyway?" Hearst asked.

"When I was a young boy growing up in Manhattan, my father took me to see Wilbur Wright and Glenn Curtiss race around the Statue of Liberty. I've been fascinated with airplanes ever since."

"Then you're a pilot too, are you?"

"Yes, I joined the Navy with some of my classmates from Yale. We learned to fly and they shipped us out to France, but the war was over by the time we arrived."

"No chance to become a hero, like your great uncle, huh Juan?"

"No, he was awarded the Medal of Honor fighting the Barbary pirates in Tripoli, but I guess you knew that being a newspaper man and all."

"Yes I did, but I thought you were Venezuelan. I mean the dark hair, your name being Juan and all?"

"Nope, my people are mostly Irish. They came to America from England in the sixteen hundreds. I got the name Juan from my aunt Juanita." Trippe smiled. "Now, she did marry a sugar baron and moved to Venezuela."

"You do speak Spanish, don't you?" Hearst asked. "I mean all those South American air routes you've acquired. You had to negotiate with somebody!"

"Don't speak Spanish, at least not very well. Money talks louder than words in that part of the world. The name Juan didn't hurt anything either."

"Juan, you silver tongued, son-of-a-gun. I'll bet you could sell ice water to the Eskimos," Hearst joked.

Along about midnight, Trippe also gave up on the conversation and headed off to bed.

Jake and Hearst traded stories about ranching and flying well into the morning hours. The two men had a lot in common, having both been born and raised on a ranch.

Hearst told Jake how he came up with the idea to build La Casa Grande.

"The site here is where we used to come camping in the summers when I was a young boy. We called this place Camp Hill back then. That was before my mother, Phoebe, God rest her soul, took me to Europe. I didn't realize it at the time, but there in Europe is where I first conceived many of my ideas for building Casa Grande."

Jake knew Hearst harbored a long-standing interest in dirigibles, which dated back to the 1920s. He told Hearst about being at Lakehurst when the Hindenburg crashed.

"The most amazing thing was that when this spectacular fiery crash settled to the ground, only thirty-two of ninety-seven souls onboard actually lost their lives."

"Amazing, I know. We carried the films of the crash in our newsreels," Hearst reflected stiffening his lips.

Both men sat quietly as though sharing a moment of silence for those who had perished.

"I understand you helped the Graf Company finance their dirigible's around the world flight."

With that, Mr. William Randolph Hearst began a long dissertation on the subject of airships.

"Yes, I followed all the early dirigible flights. You were just a pup when the *Shenandoah* crashed in 1925 and after that I thought the days of the dirigible were over."

Jake picked up the story, "I do remember reading about it, though. As I recall, they were caught in a storm over Ohio. In fact, I flew over the very spot in my old Fairchild years ago. As I recall, the rigger yelled down for a farmer to tie the lead lines to a tree stump. Then one of the crewmen climbed down, borrowed the farmer's shotgun and fired several times into the remaining helium bags to bring her to the ground."

"Not real high state-of-the-art technology, huh Jake?" Hearst laughed. "Oh yes, I had grand hopes for the *Graf Zeppelin*. Sent two of my best reporters with the airship on its around the world flight to cover the story for my newspapers."

To which Jake commented, "You know the Navy didn't retire the dirigible *City of Los Angeles* until 1932. She made eighty-one ocean crossings and never crashed."

"Good point," Hearst commented and with that, both men were talked out and the two called it a night.

***

At sunrise the next morning, the horseback riders started up the mountain trail with Hearst and Jake in the lead. Shortly before lunch, the trail riders returned with Hearst and Jake way out front.

The rest of the tenderfoots straggled in slumped low in their saddles complaining about their sore backsides all the way to the stables.

Rain clouds from offshore rolled in over the Piedra Blanca hills and lightening strikes hit the ground several times in the distance. Those guests enjoying the Neptune Pool left to go to the opulent indoor Roman Reflector Pool located below the tennis courts.

Jake joined Claudette and the rest of the guests as they continued their afternoon swim and socializing on the gilded tile floor. The light coming through the windows glistened on the surface of the water in sharp contrast to the deep, dark blue colors in the Reflector Pool.

Jake had been swimming laps to excursive and strengthen his leg. Although he had not complained like the others, it had been a while since he had sit a saddle and his backside was also sore.

By late afternoon, the pool area was devoid of swimmers, except for Jake and Claudette.

Claudette splashed her legs in the water at the edge of the pool next to where Jake was swimming. She smiled as she slipped into the water nearby, swam over to him in the water and held onto the edge of the pool beside him.

"Pretty fancy swimming hole," Jake remarked.

Claudette was well aware of the fact that she was a very attractive young woman. She was a tall slender blonde whose body language reminded Jake so much of Liz he imagined her for a moment as Liz with blonde hair.

Jake was a little bit overwhelmed by Claudette. Women like her had always been his weakness, but for once in his life, he was going to avoid making a pass at the lady.

The two lone occupants of the Roman Reflector Pool engaged in small talk, but lowered their voices to a whisper as every word they spoke echoed like they were in a canyon.

As they talked, Claudette became chilled and moved close to Jake for him to keep her warm.

Jake was growing a little tense when the tower bells chimed five o'clock.

The two left the pool to return to their separate guest quarters, dress for dinner and participate in another boring evening with their fellow guests.

The latest of Miss Davies' movies and some newsreels arrived on the morning plane and after dinner, all of the guests were invited to preview them in Casa Grande's small private theater. Attendance seemed to Jake not to be optional.

***

At breakfast the following morning, several suitcases were placed by the front door of La Casa Grande and a chauffeur-driven sedan was waiting out front. Jake seated himself at the table and noticed the place card for Mr. Errol Flynn had been removed.

When Flynn arrived for breakfast, he was escorted by one of the butlers through the front door to the opened rear door of the waiting sedan. Two butlers carrying his luggage followed him out.

"What's going on?" Jake asked Claudette seated at the table beside him.

Claudette leaned over to Jake and whispered, "Seems he was observed coming out of someone else's bedroom last night and that's a no-no. I also understand Mr. Hearst did not care for his excessive drinking."

Jake sighed. "Too bad. I kind of enjoyed visiting with the ol' fella. Guess the only sin around here is getting caught."

Claudette covered her mouth with her linen napkin as she giggled.

As the guests left the breakfast table, Trippe motioned for Jake to come over.

"We accomplished what we came for. Hearst has agreed to invest more money in Pan Am. The pilots will soon be getting those new Boeing

Clippers they have been wanting and when the revenue from those new babies starts rolling in, our stock will double in value. I think a lot of what we accomplished was because of the way Hearst identified with you. Thanks, Jake. Oh, and Hearst said to tell you that you're welcome to stay as long as you like."

"Great, glad it all worked out the way you wanted, but I need to talk to you about going back on flight status."

Trippe had hoped to avoid this discussion.

"Listen Jake, Betty and I are leaving to go back to New York. Got some irons in the fire I need to take care of. Report back to San Francisco and get that mess cleaned up. Reorganize the Treasure Island operation and we'll talk again in a few months. Is that acceptable to you?"

"Yeah, I knew you were counting on me for that," Jake reluctantly conceded. "I can handle the pilots and I'll straighten out the management situation."

When Trippe and Betty were ready to leave, Jake rode in the car with them down to the airstrip to see them off.

When he returned to Casa Grande, Jake took a long walk in the flower gardens and kept to himself most of the rest of the day. He even skipped dinner, as there was some amateur theater thing planned for the evening and the guests were expected to participate.

That night, Jake turned in early at the bungalow where he was staying. He had just switched off the small lamp beside the bed and rolled over to go to sleep when the door to the bungalow opened slowly.

At first, he assumed one of the servants was dropping of some fresh towels. Then he saw the silhouette of a shapely woman's figure in the doorway.

She paused at the open door to lean back against the doorframe with her hands behind her back. In the pale glow of the garden lights, Jake could see she was wearing a sky blue negligee. The lady's long blonde hair fell across her slender shoulders. There was no longer any doubt as to who was about to enter his bedroom.

Jake propped himself up with one of the large bed pillows and watch as Claudette shut the door, crossed the room and slid into bed next to him. Her warm body felt very nice in the cool night mountain air.

"I hope you don't think I do this sort of thing all the time." Claudette whispered softly.

I am not so sure about that, I'll bet she does, Jake thought to himself, but offered no response. Silence seemed to be the wisdom of the moment. Besides a gift was a gift and the way this package was wrapped, no complaints were in order.

***

The following morning, Jake went to breakfast early and requested to be put on the list for the DC-3 flight back to Los Angeles.

Jake returned to the Paradise Cove beach house, packed his belongings and drove back to San Francisco. Late that night, he settled back into his apartment and prepared to report to work at Pan Am operations.

The following morning, Jake walked into the seaplane base at Treasure Island and called everyone together.

"I'll be in charge here until further notice!" Jake announced to the assembled group. "If you've got any complaints, bring them straight to me. In the meantime, I plan to get this operation running smoothly if it hair-lips J. Edgar Hoover!"

A few cheers followed muffled laughter from some of the pilots and a round of applause from the rest of the employees, most already knew Jake. Many of the crewmen had flown with him in the past.

Jake involved himself in every aspect of reorganizing the flight crews and the schedules. Time passed quickly. Weeks turned into months and the months soon turned into a year. When Christmas came, Jake caught a commercial flight home to Texas to spend Christmas and New Year's 1940-41 on the ranch with his family as he promised he would.

Jake traded his Zephyr Coupe in on a new Lincoln Continental Cabriolet. His new canary yellow Continental was a strikingly impressive automobile with its tan canvas top and saddle brown leather interior, but with the salt sea air and Jake never taking time to clean the car up, it began to show its age fairly rapidly.

Jake religiously practiced walking as straight as possible, disguising the slight limp he had unwillingly developed.

Red kidded him saying, "Aw, you're just trying to imitate walking like that cowboy actor, John Wayne."

On two occasions, Jake assigned himself to the Hawaii, Manila to Hong Kong flights as an observer on the manifest, but not being at the controls just was not same as being the flight commander.

JOURNEY TO RANGOON

By the first week in September of 1941, Jake was fed up with flying a desk and ready to return to full time flight status. Over the last several days, he had placed numerous long distance calls to Trippe in New York, but his calls went unreturned.

Late on a Friday afternoon just before leaving the operations office for the day, the private line rang. Margo had left for the day so Jake picked up the phone.

"Jake my friend, what's going on?" Tripp's unmistakable voice inquired from the other end of the line.

"Well, for one thing, I've been trying to reach you for over a week now by telephone. I've flown this damn desk so long I think I'm going to shut down all four drawers and ditch this desk in the drink."

Trippe laughed. "If you wanted to go back on flight status, why didn't you just let me know?"

"Dang it, Juan, you know very well..." Jake paused and took a deep breath, he knew Trippe was only wisecracking. "Look, I've got the place running smooth like you wanted and I'm fixing to reassign myself to a flight crew. You best get whoever you want to take over managing this place out here ASAP."

Trippe had already arranged to send a replacement, but of course he had not bothered to apprise Jake of the fact.

"Your new operations manager will arrive from Miami on Monday. You got any new Boeing 314 Clippers coming in?"

Jake propped his feet up on his desk and leaned back in his chair anticipating this might be one of those lengthy conversation.

"Matter of fact, the new one came in yesterday, but of course you knew that."

"Yes, I did. I'd like you to assign the new Clipper to the route that the highest time Clipper is now flying," Trippe went on to explain in a more pleasant tone of voice.

"That would be the Manila run. We're using the *Pacific Clipper* on that route now. You, however, might prefer to refer to her as the *Pacific Clipper Two*!"

Trippe laughed.

"Good one, Jake. Okay, you take the *Pacific Clipper* out of service and fly it to Burma on a goodwill tour. You can handpick your flight crew, but hold it to yourself and five other crewmen. Tell them to expect to be gone a couple of months."

"What goodwill tour? I was talking about going back to flying one of the mainline routes."

"I'll telex you a ports-of-call itinerary and the names of some local government officials to contact along the route. Plan to layover in Honolulu a few extra days outbound. Take some time off. Go to the beach."

Jake sensed there might be more to this assignment then Trippe was telling him.

"Take some time off? That don't sound like the Juan Trippe I know."

"Yeah, okay. The Navy at Pearl Harbor wants to install some new equipment in one of our Clippers."

"Not going to mess with the tail are they?" Jake asked sarcastically.

"You're a barrel of laughs today, aren't you? No, its some new type of electronics equipment the Navy wants to flight-test. They'll be sending along a couple extra crewmen with you to operate it."

Jake took his feet off the desk and leaned forward to speak clearly into the phone.

"Okay, Juan, spit it out. What are you setting me up for this time?"

In a would-I-do-a-thing-like-that-to-you tone to his voice, Trippe replied, "You remember, what we talked about at San Simeon. I want you to see about opening some new routes to the Orient and in particular one into Rangoon."

"And who am I suppose to contact in Pearl when I get there about this new equipment?"

"See a Navy admiral by the name of Halsey. I think everyone calls him Bull. He'll fill you in on the details. And Jake, relax, have a little fun on this flight."

"Fill me in on what details?" Jake asked, but of course, the other end of the phone line was dead. As usual, Trippe had already hung up.

The new Boeing 314, *Anzac Clipper* NC-18611, was ready for service. Over the weekend Jake completed all of the paperwork to put the new Clipper in service and to pull the *Pacific Clipper* off of its regular passenger route.

The longest in-service Boeing 314 as a matter of record was NC-18600, the first one delivered to the San Francisco base. However, it actually had about the same total airframe time as the other Clippers, it being the replacement aircraft for the one that had crashed.

For better or worse, the *Pacific Clipper* or *Pacific Clipper Two*, as Jake had jokingly referred to it when talking with Trippe, was going to be the flying boat he and his crew would be taking on their Official Pan Am Public Relations Goodwill Tour of the Orient.

***

Jake's replacement arrived from Miami on Monday to take over as the new operations manager at Treasure Island. Jake introduced him around and showed him to the manager's office.

Jake picked his well-worn flight case up off the floor and set the opened case on top of the desk. He went through the desk drawers throwing one or two things from each drawer into the briefcase.

"You've got a great crew here," Jake said to his replacement as he cleaned out his desk. "Make yourself at home. Coffeepot is down the hall. For what its worth, nobody will care how you ran things back east, so save yourself the trouble of trying to tell them. Run things the way they've been running and you'll be fine."

"I was wondering..." the new manager said starting to ask a question.

"Got any questions, ask Margo. Oh, and get your own coffee, don't ask her to."

Jake picked up his briefcase by the handle, hung his leather flight jacket over his left arm and extended his right arm to shake hands.

"That's it?" the new manager asked.

"That's it! And for what it's worth, it's more than I got. Welcome aboard and best of luck."

Jake planned to spend the next couple of days getting ready and needed to select his flight crew, but there was one thing he wanted to take care of first. Jake had an idea for changing the *Pacific Clipper's* image. He recruited the assistance of a couple of aircraft handlers and personally delivered the Clipper to the maintenance facility hangar.

"Go through her from stem to stern," Jake told the maintenance supervisor. "I want this ship in top shape and looking good. Have the metal shop touch up the chipped places on her paint and while they're at it, tell them to change the name on the bow from the *Pacific Clipper* to the *China Clipper* and let me know when she's ready to go."

Jake started out of the hangar to go back to Ops when the maintenance supervisor hollered out to him, "We ain't had a *China Clipper* around here since the old Sikorsky days," and several of the workers laughed.

Jake replied loud enough for everyone in the hangar to hear. "Yeah, I know and this one might even make it all the way to China. Nice touch, don't you think?"

When Jake returned to the Ops office, Margo stopped him and said, "Captain, we're sure going to miss you around here. How long are you going to be gone?"

"Couple of months, Margo."

"Well, I'll be off on leave by the time you get back. Expecting again, you know."

Red and Margo had been married two years now and already had a one-year-old little boy.

"Yes, Red told me. Seems like you've been that way ever since you and Red met, Mrs. Henderson!" Jake said smiling.

Margo laughed. "Seems that way to me too, Jake."

"When Red gets in from his flight this afternoon have him come and see me. I'll be in the flight planning room."

***

When Red arrived late that afternoon, he went to find Jake in the flight planning room where he was going over some China, Burma and India maps, referred to by navigators as CBI charts.

"Margo said you wanted to see me, Jake. What's up?"

Jake had one of those serious looks on his face that Red knew all too well.

"Trippe's asked me to make a goodwill tour of the Orient. It's tied in with some kind of cockamamie flight–test mission out of Pearl Harbor and I'm supposed to pick my own crew."

Red was tired from his recent flight and was trying to be patient with Jake.

"Are you asking me if I want to go or are you telling me I'm going?"

"Red, you know you're my first choice of pilots anytime, but with Margo expecting, I don't think it's a good idea for you to be away right now. We'll be gone at least two months, maybe longer."

From the confused look on Red's face, Jake realized he should have come straight to the point.

"I'm telling you you're not going."

"Well, I'm both relieved and disappointed." Red replied, "Disappointed I'm not going with you, but I knew something was up when our new operations manager introduced himself to me and addressed me as Commander Henderson. What's that all about?"

"As you know I listed myself as chief pilot when Captain Hudson retired and Captain Gray transferred back to New York. When I took my name off and made up the new crew manifests, I just put you down as chief pilot. That's all." Jake said trying to play it down.

Red knew that chief pilot also meant an automatic promotion to commander and a pay increase. He tried to thank Jake for the promotion.

"Jake, I…"

"You earned it, Red," Jake said interrupting him. "There're a few pilots around here with more gray hair than you, but nobody more qualified."

"Well, thanks anyway," Red said.

"Best part is you'll be making up the flight schedules each month and you can work it out to be home when Margo bingos. We'll likely cross paths in Guam or Manila between now and Christmas. I'll stay in touch. If it's another boy, don't name him after me."

"Don't worry about that, Captain Jacob Teel Martin. Good luck and God grant you safe passage, my friend."

"You also, Red!"

Both men had gone their separate ways several times in their flying careers, but this time, they seemed to sense a feeling that there was something a little more final about their parting.

***

The following day, Jake spent the morning running errands and did not arrive at Ops until mid-day. He had also stopped by the bank and purchased a thousand dollars worth of twenty-dollar gold pieces.

Jake was in the flight planning room with stuff from his briefcase strung out all over the chart table when Benny Weston came in.

"You wanted to see me, Captain?" Benny asked.

Benny was a slightly overweight family man with five kids ranging in age from a three year old to a teenager. He would as soon be out flying as hanging around the house and was Jake's choice for a communications officer on the tour.

Benny could fill any of the crew positions and had flown with Jake many times as well as having been with he and Nelson that fateful night they crashed in the Bay.

Jake explained the mission to Benny.

"Count me in, Captain." Benny said and was fiddling with the cloth money sack of coins as he and Jake talked. "What's in the sack?"

"Life preservers," Jake replied jokingly.

"Little heavy for the candy kind, too small for a May West," Benny said picking up the sack and looking in it. He placed the sack back on the table and smiled. "Yeah, it's hard to get those Chinamen to take paper money sometimes, isn't it?"

"That it is, Benny. Listen, you take the rest of the week off. Spend some time at home with your wife and kids. We're gonna be gone quite a while."

Benny gave a casual salute as he left. "See you early Saturday morning, Captain."

Jake interviewed several low time copilots and decided on a young second officer named Herbert Solomon who was anxious to make the flight for the experience. Herb was a first generation Jewish American, well educated and a good pilot. Herb would fly copilot with Jake.

Jake selected as his first officer a pilot named Philip Perkins. Phil was about the same age as Jake, but had a little less flying experience. He was a serious and responsible flyer who was clearly on a career path to captain. Phil would fly as PIC when Jake was off the flight deck. Since they would not be carrying passengers, they would not need as many crewmen, but they would each have to spend longer periods of time at the controls.

For flight engineer, Jake's choice was a man everyone called Chief. He was the best engineer mechanic on base. Chief retired from the Navy after twenty years as a chief petty officer with an AP designation for airplane pilot. He had logged lots of hours in seaplanes and would fly as copilot when Phil was PIC.

When Jake assigned him to the crew, he asked, "I know your last name is Tuddle. I've listed you on the crew manifests many times, but we've always called you Chief. What the heck is your given name?"

"You really don't want to know, do you, Captain? Well maybe you do. It's Marion, sir."

Jake kept a poker face.

"Your right, Chief, I didn't want to know."

Navigation would be critical to the success of their venture into new airspace. Crossing the Pacific, they would have the Adcock stations to home in on, but once into Southern Asia, they were on their own. Jake assigned an old hand by the name of Elmer Garinzola to round out the officer crew as navigator.

Pilots that flew with Elmer bragged, you could blindfold him, spin him around three times, put him in the middle of the Pacific and inside of a minute he would tell you where he was. Not only that, but he would give you the course and distance to the nearest Pan Am base.

Elmer was also a qualified radio operator and could relieve Benny on the long flights. Jake selected these men because he determined them to be the most qualified crewmen for the task at hand. He also liked and respected each of them for their dedication to duty.

Trippe had authorized only six crewmen, but Jake intended to make one more addition to the crew manifest, a steward by the name of Wilford Maltbey. Jake had no intention on eating Campbell's canned soups and cold Van Camp's pork-n-beans for the next two months.

Wilford, affectionately called Willie by everyone who knew him, would be the seventh crewmember. Willie was an older English bachelor gentleman with a thick British accent. He attended the French Cordon Bleu cooking school as a young man and had served for a while as an English manor butler before coming to America and signing on with Pan Am. He had made many Pacific crossings as a steward.

When Jake approached Willie about joining the crew, he asked Willie, "Whatever made you want to take a job bouncing around in these Clipper ships?"

Willie just shrugged and said, "I always wanted to see the world and this is the best way I found to do that and get paid for it, too."

"If you come with us on the flight, you'll likely see some ports you haven't visited before."

"Sounds exciting, sir."

"I'll tell you why I want you to come with us even though I'm only taking a small crew and no passengers. Your job will be to keep the Clipper neat and orderly. I want you to prepare all those fancy meals you know how to cook. Anytime we're in port, you buy whatever you need to fix the best meals you can create. I'll cover the expense. I read one time that Napoleon said 'An army travels on its stomach.' Well, so do flyers. A full belly produces a happy mind and I'm going to be counting on you to keep these guys happy. Okay, Willie?"

Standing proudly as though he had been honored to be asked, Willie straightened his crisp white steward's jacket and replied, "Consider the matter taken care of, Captain Martin."

***

Jake and his assembled crew departed for Hawaii in the newly renamed *China Clipper* mid-day on Saturday. Jake was at the controls. He positioned the flying boat into the wind and eased the throttles forward. Under his breath, he uttered his usual short and specific prayer, "God Almighty, grant us safe passage."

Phil in the copilot's position was monitoring the power settings and replied, "Say again, Captain."

"Nothing, just mumbling," Jake replied as he added more backpressure to the yoke to rotate and lift off the water. "Leave it at full power after liftoff, Phil. I'm going to make a tight turn out to the west. I think our crew has seen the Bay Bridge a couple of times by now!"

The giant ship shuddered crossing the last shallow wake in the Bay and eased slowly into the air. A small vortex of water spun from each of the sponsons and glistened in the morning sun as the Clipper gained airspeed.

"Flaps up."

"Flaps coming up," Phil replied and followed standard cockpit procedure by placing his left hand behind the throttles at the climb power-setting mark, this so that the pilot did not have to look back into the cockpit to set the climb power.

Jake adjusted the throttles and elevator trim after his turn out, which was as close to a Chandelle as the ol' large Clipper was capable of performing.

Chief had been leaning forward to check the engine gauges and laughed as he got a hold of the handrail.

Phil made a minor prop and mixture setting adjustment and confirmed, "Eighty percent power, flaps are up."

Jake held the Clipper's nose in a shallow climb attitude to pick up airspeed. They were heavy on fuel, but were not carrying any cargo or passengers so the Clipper climbed well in the cool morning air.

Herb monitored every movement in the cockpit and would make this his personal responsibility to do so anytime he was on the flight deck for the rest of the journey.

Benny, from the radio operator's station announced, "Ah, yes! Defied death and gravity one more time."

Elmer from the navigation table added, "Yeah, hours and hours of utter boredom, occasionally interrupted by intermittent terror and panic."

"You guys in the cheap seats, hold it down back there," Chief said razzing them back.

The crew was in high spirits, off on a new adventure, something a little different for a change.

***

In late September, the weather over the Pacific could be beautiful or turn stormy in a matter of hours, but their luck held. The crew of the *China Clipper* was able to navigate a course between two weather fronts moving across the South Pacific and found smooth clear air most of the way to Hawaii.

On final approach into Honolulu, Jake did not make the traditional loop around Diamond Head, nor was it necessary to dock first at the Aloha Towers steamship pier, as they had no passengers to deplane. Benny obtained a clearance for a straight-in approach to Pearl Harbor.

After touchdown, the Clipper docked at the Navy's seaplane port across from Ford Island. As the large flying boat was being tied securely up to the pier, Jake stepped onto the dock and was met by a young Navy lieutenant.

"Captain Martin, I presume," the lieutenant said. "I've been assigned to handle the modifications on your aircraft. While you're here, I've arranged for you and your crew to be housed at the Bachelor Officer's Quarters."

Jake looked around for someone other than the young lieutenant.

"I think I'm supposed to meet some admiral here by the name of Halsey. Can you tell me where to find him?"

"Yes sir, I can. Admiral Halsey is out to sea with the carrier group. They're running war game exercises."

Another Trippe operation, situation normal, all fouled up Jake thought to himself.

"Very well. Tell us what you need, Lieutenant."

Jake motioned for Phil to come over to listen.

"We'll need your crew's assistance installing the new equipment and for a couple of your men to attend some training sessions."

"This is your man right here, First Officer Perkins," Jake said motioning Phil front and center.

"At your service, Lieutenant," Phil said.

"Phil here will see that your Navy guys get whatever help they need," Jake told the lieutenant and addressing Phil he said, "But don't let them make any modifications to the Clipper that Chief doesn't approve first."

"Aye, aye Captain."

Jake handed Phil a business card with some writing on the back.

"I'm not staying on base. Here's where you can reach me in town. If it's an emergency! Otherwise, I'll see you in two or three days."

***

Jake liked to stay at a small, rather inconspicuous hotel near Waikiki Beach he discovered on one of his earlier visits to Honolulu. The Beachcomber Hotel was only a short walk from the beach and not far from the prestigious Royal Hawaiian where he often went for a drink along about sunset. Several of Jake's favorite restaurants that he frequented were also nearby.

Jake needed the R&R bad. It would be a chance to unwind after the past months of twenty-four-hour-a-day pressure and responsibility of operational management.

Jake had his little black notebook of addresses and phone numbers in his pocket. If the young ladies' phone numbers were still good and they had not recently married, he hoped to renew some old relationships.

The following three days of Jake's absence from his crew and routine aviation lifestyle, flung him headlong into an unusual episode of mystery and intrigue. Through a female acquaintance, Jake became involve in a series of events, which lead to the exposure of a Japanese spy ring in Honolulu.

Jake never discussed the incident with anyone until years later when he related the story to a young writer who wrote a fictional novel based on the incident. The episode eventually became the basis for the relatively unknown author to sell the novel as a screenplay entitled *"Flight to Waikiki."*

***

Flying was Jake's first love and once again he was back doing what he enjoyed most. He returned to the Navy dock at Pearl on their third day in

Honolulu. The *China Clipper* had been fitted with an odd shaped antenna that protruded from the nose and another strange looking antenna just under the right wing beam.

The Navy called the new electronic device a Radio Direction and Ranging transceiver. Jake had heard of experiments with these new types of radio waves, but did not know that there were actual working versions of them in existence, until now.

Benny met Jake as be boarded the Clipper and showed him around. Sections of seats had been removed and replaced with racks of electronic equipment. Much of the new equipment had been enclosed behind false bulkheads to make the Clipper still appear to be a passenger airliner to dignitaries and guests that might board the aircraft. The tables where passengers were once served elegant dinners were now covered with charts and control consoles.

Benny introduced Jake to the Navy men working on the Clipper as they went through the aircraft.

"Captain, this is Tony Romano. He works for Hal, who's around here somewhere. They're going to be doing the actual testing of the new electronics gear and will be going with us. Tony has been explaining to me how this stuff all works and it's amazing what this new equipment can do."

"Glad to meet you, Tony. Can do what? Give me an example of what it can do," Jake said.

Tony was a short in stature, cheerful sort of young fellow who spoke with a thick New Jersey accent.

"For example," Tony began, "this gadget here can locate a ship in the ocean a hundred miles away from ten thousand feet in the day or night time and provide the contact's bearing and range from your position."

Tony showed Jake a few more things and then went back to finish setting up his workstation in the cabin.

Jake continued his walk through inspection of the Clipper and watched as some last minute equipment was fastened into place.

When Jake returned to the dock, the young lieutenant approached with a man in a Navy khaki uniform. There were several Navy petty officers working around the Clipper, but the man with the lieutenant had no rank or identification insignias on his khaki uniform.

"Hal Smith is the name," the man said introducing himself to Jake.

Hal was a middle-aged, Mr. America take-charge looking kind of guy. He reminded Jake of Johnny Weismiller who played Tarzan in the movies.

Jake suspected Hal was an Office of Secret Service agent or some type of civilian Naval Intelligence operative. Smith, Jake thought to himself. At least he could have come up with a more original name.

"Exactly what is it that you and Tony are going to be doing onboard my aircraft, Mr. Smith?"

Hal looked around as though to make sure no one was standing close enough to listen.

"I intended to discuss this with you after we were airborne, but basically Washington would like to know where and what the Japanese fleet might be up to. Don't expect you to go out of your way, but it would be nice if we happened to run across them."

Jake, having missed his navigation points more than once, advised Hal from the voice of experience.

"You cloak and dagger electronics types may not know it, but the Pacific is a really big pond to go looking for something in."

"Yes sir, I do understand that, but it's our job to at least try. Oh, and we'll need an extra days layover in Manila to go see The General."

"Whoever the hell 'The General' is," Jake mumbled. "For what it's worth, you guys are sure a lot more anxious to run across the Japanese Navy than I am."

Tony had walked up as they were talking and he laughed at Jake's last comment. That was until Hal glared at Tony and he wiped the smile off his face.

After several hours of orientation and briefings on the new equipment installed in the aircraft, Jake prepared to flight-test the Clipper. He wanted to be sure the modifications would have no adverse effect on the aircraft's flight characteristics.

Airborne from the harbor with only himself, Phil and Chief onboard, Jake put the aircraft into several unusual flight attitudes followed by power-on and power-off stalls. He pulled the power off on each engine, one engine at a time with the Clipper in slow flight.

Jake satisfied himself and Chief that the new antenna array had no noticeable effect on the flight handling characteristics of the Clipper.

After docking and refueling at Pearl, Jake told the crew, "Make preparations to depart early in the morning. I want to be airborne when the sun comes up."

The outboard right engine on the *China Clipper* had been throwing oil and Jake asked the base mechanics to wash it down and work with Chief to run a compression check on the cylinders. The check indicated there was no problem with the engine.

***

At first light, the *China Clipper* skipped across the waters of Pearl Harbor and lifted off headed for Midway. A little before sunset that evening they approached the Pan Am seaplane base on Midway Island.

The *American Clipper* had departed eastbound earlier that morning with a load of passengers before the *China Clipper* arrived. There were no Pan Am passengers on the Island, so some of the crew took advantage and went to sleep in the guest quarters. The passenger hotel facilities were a little nicer than the crew quarters.

Jake, however, intended to spend the night on the beach. There were several hammocks strung between some palm trees and the cool breeze coming in from off the ocean would keep the insects away. Benny, Elmer and Tony also went along to spend the night on the beach.

The absence of an evening moon made the Pacific sky even blacker and the stars shown so bright it seemed like one could almost reach out and touch them.

Tony grew up in New Jersey and during his recent stay in Hawaii it had rained most of the time, so he had never seen the heavens as clear as the sky was that night.

Jake and his navigator, Elmer, were taking turns identifying constellations and pointing them out as they lay in their hammocks gazing up at the stars.

Tony listened for a while and then joined in the conversation.

"Look at that long white streak across the sky. Seems funny there would still be smoke and pollution way out here?"

"That's not pollution," Elmer said. "That's the Milky Way. You're looking edgewise across our galaxy into the faint glow of billions of distant stars."

There was a period of silence, save for the lapping of the waves on the shoreline and the rustle of palm branches in the breeze. Then Tony asked, "What exactly is a galaxy?"

Elmer and Benny chuckled quietly.

"Go to sleep, Tony!" Jake said and smiled to himself in the darkness.

***

After overnight stops on Wake Island and Guam, the *China Clipper* arrived at Manila Bay where Hal had requested they stay over for a couple of days. Hal had a prearranged meeting with General MacArthur, the military attaché to the President of the Philippine Republic.

MacArthur occupied a suite of rooms on the top floor of the swank Manila Hotel on Roxas Boulevard not far from the steamship piers.

The rest of Jake's flight crew went into town to carouse for the day and probably well into the night.

Jake went with Hal for his meeting with MacArthur at the hotel and was briefly introduced to the General when they arrived.

"We appreciate all you and your airline are doing for us," MacArthur said to Jake.

"My pleasure, General. Always glad to help out when we can," but Jake did not have a clue as to what MacArthur had been referring to when he thanked him.

Hal left to go upstairs with the General and some other military officers. Jake was excluded from the meeting. Being familiar with the Manila Hotel as he had been there before on prior flights, Jake made his way to the hotel bar to wait for Hal.

To Jake's delight he spotted Gus, an old Aussie seaman and first mate on the cargo vessel *Southern Cross*. Jake and Gus had run into each other before during Jake's earlier flights into Manila.

Gus was seated on his usual barstool in the sparsely occupied Polynesian style bar and restaurant. Gus always came to the bar at the Manila Hotel when he was in port. He had told Jake one time, "It's quiet here, not rowdy like those harbor bars downtown and the place's got a little bit of class."

Jake approached Gus and slapped him on the back. The two wayfarers were always glad to run into each other and trade stories over a few drinks. Jake insisted on buying the next round.

"Off to Hong Kong or headed back to the States, Captain?"

"On my way to Rangoon this time, Gus."

"Dangerous place that Rangoon, not far from all the fighting up north between the Chinese and the Japs. We off-loaded some P-40 Tomahawks with the wings detached last time I made port in Rangoon. Was the third shipment of those fighter planes we'd dropped off in the last year."

Jake's interest peaked as he suspected the P-40s Gus referred to were part of the AVG, the infamous American Volunteer Group he had heard so much about.

"Go on, Gus. What else did you see?"

"Odd part about it, there weren't any gooks there to receive them, only an Army Air Corps officer who accepted the shipments at the dock. The officer had the planes loaded onto what looked like a U.S. Army truck with a Republic of China Star insignia painted on the door."

"Its all over the papers and the newsreels about the Chinese fighting the Japs ever since they invaded the coastlands of China a year or so ago. I don't think the Chinese even have an air force and if they do, it's only some old out-of-date biplanes. Do you think we're selling brand new P-40s to the Chinese?"

The old seaman shook his head no and then said, "Well, maybe in a roundabout way, I guess they might be. The bill of lading was addressed to the Central Aircraft Manufacturing Company, but I think those planes were headed for that outfit the locals call the Flying Tigers."

Jake was like-minded and ordered another round of drinks.

"I've heard of them, a bunch of rogue soldier of fortune pilots who fly on contract for the Republic of China government."

Gus raised his fresh glass to toast Jake.

"To your good health, mate," and he took a long drink.

"FDR embargoed Japan's fuel imports. That should have slowed their war machine down a little bit."

"That embargo didn't slow them up much. They steal fuel anywhere they can find it. We sails way to the south now when we're headin' into the waters west of here. Those little slant-eyed bastards'll board your vessel, take your fuel and anything else they can off-load. Then leave you adrift at sea. And I've heard stories of worse, I have."

In a couple of hours, Hal came downstairs from his meeting with MacArthur and had a couple drinks at the bar with Jake and Gus. Along about nightfall, the three men went to a table and ordered dinner. After dinner, Jake and Hal bid Gus so long and went back to the seaplane port in the Navy jeep Hal had borrowed.

***

Leaving Manila the next day, the *China Clipper* and its nine-man crew departed for Singapore. The British flew air routes into Singapore, but no Pan Am Clipper had ventured this far west into the Asian Pacific until now.

Arriving at Singapore, Jake circled the city and the harbor several times. By the time the Clipper touched down in the bay, a large crowd had gathered on the docks and along the shore. The crewmen were hailed as heroes because the people thought that the Americans were honoring them by inaugurating a new Pan Am air service to their country, but their celebrating was premature.

The *China Clipper* remained in Singapore for the better part of a week. Jake met several times with the government officials who regulated aeronautics and trade. In a meeting with the Director of Commerce, the director seemed very interested in Pan Am establishing a new air route into Singapore. After the meeting, the director's secretary stopped Jake in the Bureau of Commerce building hallway.

"It would be necessary for a certain amount of money to be deposited to the director's foreign bank account," the secretary explained. "This to insure that the proper paperwork is filed and processed. You do understand, Captain, this is the way things are done in Singapore."

"Financial matters of that type are handled out of our New York office," and while Jake was assuring the secretary the matter could be worked out, he was thinking to himself this guy and his boss are a couple of jerks. "Possibly, your director would enjoy an all expense paid vacation to New York to work out the details for your new air service?"

The secretary placed his hands together in the fashion of a prayer and bowed politely.

"Thank you for your generous acceptance of our ways. I will communicate this information to my superior. Please to enjoy your stay in Singapore, Captain Martin."

Willie used the Singapore layover as an opportunity to do some shopping in the local fresh food markets.

Jake assigned Phil and Herb to giving several short sightseeing flights out over the city of Singapore in the *China Clipper* to various government officials and their families.

Hal and Tony went along on the flights pretending to be part of the regular flight crew and completed some aerial photography and map updating of the harbor area.

"I think I can hear a roughness in one of the engines," Chief told Jake when they returned from their last flight. "I'm relatively sure it's the right outboard engine. The same one that's been throwing oil."

"Damn," Jake inarticulate when Chief told him about the engine. "Well, better have another look at it again before we leave tomorrow."

Chief checked out the engines one more time and did routine maintenance on the Clipper. Benny gave Chief a hand, but once again, they could not find anything wrong with the number four engine.

***

The next morning the *China Clipper* departed Singapore for Rangoon. There were rainsqualls all around the area, but the weather was forecast to be better to the west. Sure enough, about a hundred miles out of Singapore, they encountered blue skies and smooth dry air.

By late afternoon, their position was approximately fifty miles southeast of the city of Rangoon, Burma. Jake climbed into the pilot's seat to relieve Phil and to make the descent for their approach into Rangoon. Herb was still flying in the copilot's seat.

The outboard right engine backfired twice and then began running rough. Jake went to full-rich mixture on the engine and eased the throttle back slightly. Traces of engine oil appeared on the sides of the nacelle and trailed over the leading edge of the wing.

The night he and Nelson ditched in San Francisco Bay flashed through Jake's mind that instant. The engine was the same one they had lost on the old *Pacific Clipper* and before painting the name *China Clipper* on this Clipper's bow, it also bore the name *Pacific Clipper*.

A sudden fear gripped Jake for a moment and without realizing it, he responded to his apparitions aloud!

"Bullshit! There's no way this is going to happen again, so cut out the superstitious crap. I flight-tested this airplane myself back at Pearl. This airplane is more stable with an engine out than that old *Pacific Clipper* even if the prop won't feather."

"Amen to that, Captain," Benny who was seated at the flight engineers station behind Herb, said.

With Benny's response, Jake realized he had spoken aloud and then he laughed.

"What was that all about?" Herb leaned back and asked Benny.

"Maybe I'll explained it to you one of these days," but Benny never really ever intended to.

"It's decision time, Chief!" Jake hollered aft. "What's your thinking?"

"I suspect it's a cracked cylinder head. Let's shut it down before we really tear up something. Most of our fuel is burned off and we're relatively light for landing. We really don't need that engine to make it into Rangoon."

"I agree," Jake said. "Herb, normal engine-out procedure on number four."

"Aye, aye sir," Herb replied, beginning full-feather and engine shut down on number four.

Chief came forward and watched over Benny's shoulder to make sure the wrong engine was not inadvertently selected for shut down. The prop blades rotated normally and the vibration stopped.

"Full-feather and shut down complete, Captain."

"Thank you, Herb," Jake said as he concentrated on resetting the trim tabs.

Except for a fifteen mile-an-hour drop off in airspeed, the Clipper flew straight and level. They proceeded into Rangoon on the remaining three good engines.

Jake showed no outward emotion, but Benny knew better than anyone else onboard how relieved Jake was that the engine's prop blades had rotated properly.

They had left Singapore early enough that morning for it to still be daylight when they approached the harbor at Rangoon. The ancient city of Rangoon lay at the junction of two rivers, which formed a bay that opened onto the open sea. British Sunderland flying boats landed in the Bago River on their weekly flights to Rangoon from India.

There was no designated area for seaplane traffic in the Rangoon harbor. Because of this, flying boat pilots had to be careful not to collide with a sampan or run over one of the many small fishing boats. Standard procedure for seaplane arrival in unmarked harbors was to make a low pass indicating the aircraft's intended path and circle back for touchdown.

The *China Clipper* approached the harbor at dusk. Jake did not intend to make a go around on three engines and return for a night touchdown, unless absolutely necessary. He set up a straight-in final approach to the harbor.

There was a reasonably clear path ahead in the center of the main waterway. Jake turned the Clipper directly into the prevailing wind, which he had judged from the ripples on the water. Fortunately, that was also up current.

A large sampan quickly changed course when its crew saw the Clipper headed in their direction. Jake held an extra ten knots over the normal approach speed for safety and they touched down without incident.

"A textbook engine-out approach in every respect," Benny said complimenting Jake.

"Thank you, Benny. At least we didn't have to make an engine-out, night approach into an unlighted harbor."

Jake brought the *China Clipper* alongside a dock not far from an armada of tied up fishing boats. A small crowd gathered on the dock where the fishermen came to sell their catch each day. The onlookers watched as the giant flying boat tied-up.

As Jake stepped onto the dock, a man in a light tan uniform moved through the crowd and approached Jake. The man bowed slightly.

"Good afternoon flying officer, sir. May I introduce myself? I am Harbor Master Kim Jong. Welcome to Rangoon."

Jong spoke the King's English with only a slight trace of an Oriental accent.

Jake bowed slightly in return.

"Thank you. I'm Captain Martin with Pan Am airways. Looks like we'll be staying here for an indefinite period of time. We experienced engine trouble on the way here and we'll be needing to make some repairs."

Jong motioned for Jake to come with him.

"Yes, I noticed that one of your propellers was not turning as you approached the dock. I thought you might have had a problem. Please come to my office, Captain Martin and we will fill out the necessary paperwork."

Jake picked his way through the crowd along with Jong to his second story office on the pier.

"Where can we safely park our aircraft so we can work on it?" Jake inquired.

"There is a concrete pier where the cargo ships unload. Your large flying boat will be most safe there and you can be moored to the side of the pier where you will be able to work on the engine from the dock. There is also a covered storage area near there, which will provide your crew a spot of shade from the afternoon heat. I will arrange for the man who leases the docks to meet you there in the morning. We are not expecting any high winds, so you are welcome to remain here for the night. However, if a storm were coming, this wooden dock would not hold your large aircraft."

In a short while, Jake returned to the Clipper.

"We're not going anywhere and there's nothing to be accomplish tonight, so just relax and enjoy the evening." Jake finished explaining the plan for in the morning.

After one of Willie's excellently prepared meals, the crew sat around on the wooden dock beside the moored Clipper discussing the day's flight and the engine failure.

Jake had certainly been correct about enjoying the evening. A light breeze came in from off the water and Venus shown like a beacon in the easterly starlit night.

The old wooden dock creaked in the stillness of the evening from the lapping of the water or when someone walked across its wooden planks.

Chief was smoking a pipe as they talked.

"I hope it's only a blown jug or a burnt valve. I brought a spare cylinder and valves along. We can repair it in a couple of days, if that's all it is."

Benny, sitting just out of the light of the small Coleman lantern, spoke up from the darkness.

"I guess we can only hope for the best at this point."

"Where're we going to get fuel, Captain?" Elmer asked.

"Ah Elmer, you're always worrying about running short of fuel," Benny commented.

"And you should be too, Benny," Elmer retorted. "You know my motto, save a few gallons for mom and the kids!"

"Where are we going to get fuel, Captain?" Herb asked.

"There's a fuel supply someplace around here where the Brits get gas for their Sunderland flying boats. I've also heard rumors about some high-powered fighter aircraft near here." Jake was referring to the Curtis P-40s Gus had told him about. "They use the same high-octane fuel we need. As soon as we determine our engine situation, I'll go scouting around and see what I can scare up."

Off in the distance, hundreds of small houseboats were tied one to the other. They bobbed on the water in the darkness and the light from small lanterns sparkled through the bamboo woven walls of the boats. The smell of fish and rice being cooked on open fires floated on the evening breeze.

A dozen or so small children squatted in the shadows watching and listening to the flyers. They would giggle sometime at what one of the crew did or said. One by one, the crewmen gave up the evening and retired for the night to one of the bunks onboard the Clipper.

***

Shortly after sunrise the next morning, Jake and his crew moved the *China Clipper* to the cargo pier. There were half-a-dozen coolies waiting on the dock to assist as the Clipper came alongside. Several of the coolies were standing by with rubber tires tied to the end of a rope for cushioning the hull against the concrete pier. As the Clipper closed on the dock, the head coolie motioned to where the Clipper could tie-up.

Shutting down the remaining right engine, Jake skillfully floated the giant flying boat up to the pier with its right wing positioned out over the dock.

Chief tossed the bowline to one of the coolies.

Benny stepped out onto the sponson and by means of a series of hand motions, managed to get the coolies to position a couple of the rubber tires between the sponson and the concrete pier before it bumped.

Chief went onto the dock to see that the craft was properly secured. When he was satisfied, he gave Jake a thumbs-up. Jake shut down the two port engines, which he had been using to hold the Clipper against the pier.

The rest of the crew came ashore.

Jake paid the cargo dock master his fee for the mooring space and he left with his coolie helpers. About five hundred yards down to the end of the pier, there was access to a city street with traffic going by. Jake walked aft of the Clipper a ways down the pier to check out their location and was comfortable with the security.

Toolboxes and gear were unloaded in preparation for having a look at the problem engine and determining how bad the damaged was. To do this, they first needed to get to the engine by removing the cowling. The whole crew pitched in to help drag some wooden shipping crates over under the wing and position them under the nacelle for use as a makeshift work stand.

Chief walked out across the top of the wing and laid down on his belly above the engine to unfasten the top of the cowling. Benny and Tony climbed up on the wooden shipping crates and handed down the cowling sections to Phil and Herb on the dock as each one was removed. Chief only took a couple of minutes to determine which one of the cylinders was busted, but it took him another half hour to get the jug unbolted and complete his inspection.

Jake was standing on the dock waiting for the verdict as Chief came down off the wing wiping his hands on an oil soaked hand towel.

The rest of the crew gathered around and waited as Chief approached Jake to give his report.

"I don't think I like the look on your face, Chief."

"It's a blown cylinder alright, Captain, but that's not the worst of it. The engine case is also cracked. We're gonna need a whole new engine. Do you think Pearl or Manila might have one?"

Jake shook his head no. "I'm pretty sure they won't."

"I agree," Chief said. "Most likely, Frisco or Seattle will be our only hope of finding a replacement and I suspect we're looking at a month or more to get one out here by cargo ship."

"Get cleaned up and put your dress uniform on," Jake told Benny. "I need you to go into town with me." Jake turned back to Chief. "The proverbial 'Slow Boat to China,' huh Chief?"

Chief smiled at Jake's corny cliché from a currently popular song.

"You got that right, Captain."

"I'll go into town and telegraph Frisco to see what they can do for us in the way of locating an engine," Jake told his crew. "You all hang around here and help Chief build a better scaffolding. When Benny and I get back, I'll fill everyone in on where we stand."

Benny returned from washing up and had changed into a clean uniform. Jake and Benny walked down to the end of the pier and hailed a taxicab from the street.

Jake told the driver, "To the telegraph office, please," as they climbed into the small English made taxicab and the cab pulled away for downtown Rangoon.

They were lucky the driver spoke a bit of English and he was very helpful. He told them what parts of town it would be wise for them to avoid.

"The Silver Monkey Bar and Grill is good, you go! Many Englishmen flyer like you guys hang out there when come town," the driver told them when he dropped Jake and Benny off at the telegraph office.

Stranded in Rangoon, they would be forced to wait for a replacement engine for the *China Clipper*. They remained hopeful that there might be a spare engine in Hawaii, but until they heard back from the maintenance center at Treasure Island, they would not know for sure.

SUZETTE

As they left the telegraph office, Benny said, "I could sure use a cold beer in this heat. How about we find that bar the driver told us about, the Silver Monkey. He indicated the bar was just the other side of the market."

"Suits me," Jake replied. "We'll check back with the telegraph office in a few hours."

They crossed the street and entered the marketplace headed for the Silver Monkey. Jake and Benny strolled through the narrow aisles of the market, stopping once or twice to look at some of the odd assortment of goods for sale.

Down one of the aisles, Jake caught a glimpse of a strikingly beautiful young woman carrying a small shopping basket under her arm and browsing casually.

Her stature attracted Jake's attention, as she was tall for an Asian woman. The lady's coal black hair was cut in a pageboy an inch or so above her shoulders. She wore a full-length, Mandarin high-collar, black silk dress with slits on the sides of the skirt. An embroidered golden dragon crossed the front of the dress and circled down around her left hip to the ankle length hem.

Jake paused to watch her from a distance as she moved slowly through the market selecting some fruits and vegetables. He got a better look at her when she stopped to pay the vendor for the items she had placed in her basket.

Benny walked a few steps ahead and turned to see where he had lost Jake. He looked back and followed Jake's line of sight to the young woman.

"Careful there Captain, the Dragon Lady looks like trouble to me!"

Jake realized he had been caught staring and smiled. He continued on with Benny to the edge of the market where he paused.

"Benny, you go on, I want to look around the market for a while. I'll be there in a little bit."

Benny did not have to ask, he knew Jake well enough to know what was on his mind.

"Sure Captain, I'll save you a beer."

Jake worked his way back through the crowded market to where he had last seen the tall Asian lady, the one Benny had referred to as the Dragon Lady, but she had vanished from sight. Jake continued to search the aisles of vendors, picking his way through the throng of local people until he finally gave up and left for the Silver Monkey to meet Benny.

On his way to the bar, Jake passed a small European-style hotel with a cobblestone patio that faced onto a tropical garden. He paused and looked in for a moment and then went on to the Silver Monkey.

Entering the bar, Jake found Benny seated at a table with an Army Air Corps pilot and a couple of young British flying officers. Benny introduced Jake to his newly acquired friends seated around the table.

The American pilot was an Army Air Corps first lieutenant by the name of Roy Briggs, assigned to the American Volunteer Group in Burma.

"My job title is Liaison Officer," Roy told Jake as they were introduced, "but it turned into my being the supply officer for ol' Claire Chennault and his men."

"You mean the commander of the AVG?" Jake asked.

"Yes," Roy replied. "It's been a fulltime job keeping them supplied with new planes and equipment."

As Lieutenant Roy spoke, he referred to the AVG as the Jing Bow several times.

"Who or what are the Jing Bow?" Jake asked.

"That's what the local people call the AVG. Means Always Alert." Roy confirmed what Gus had told Jake back in Manila. "Chennault's pilots are on contract to the government of China fighting the Japanese. I'm on loan to CAMCO, the Central Aircraft Manufacturing Company, an American outfit that's the prime contractor on this job."

Jake and Roy hit it off right away. They had a lot in common. Roy had been a flight instructor at Enid Airbase back in Oklahoma before being assigned to Burma. The two men reminisced about a place in the Kiamichi Mountains where they had both gone deer hunting as boys.

A few beers, an hour or so and a dozen flying stories later, Roy got up to leave.

"I need to go check on a couple of P-40 Hawks being assembled out at Mingladon Airfield for shipment up north."

"I've only ever seen one P-40," Jake said indicating his continued interest in the plane. "The fighter was parked on the ramp at Hickham Field in Hawaii. The Army pilot was with the 49th Fighter Squadron over at Wheeler and he claimed the plane was really great to fly."

"The two new P-40s we recently received are the Super Hawk models. The AVG has about a hundred of the older Tomahawks, but these two new ones have all the features of the new Warhawks, which Curtiss is supplying to the Army Air Corps. These new models have a more powerful engine and climb a lot faster than the earlier Hawks. I understand someone back at the Curtiss factory nicknamed the last few of these limited-run P-40s, the Tigershark. You'd enjoy flying one of the new models, Jake."

"Yeah, I'd like to fly one."

"I'll see what I can do."

As Roy left the bar, one of the British airmen called out to him, "Tally ho, ol' man. Give 'em hell for us!"

The British airman was referring to the efforts of the AVG in holding off the Japanese air forces up north.

***

Late that afternoon, early morning back in the States, Jake and Benny walked back to the telegraph office to see if there had been a reply from San Francisco.

They had received a reply. The only available engine was in Seattle and would be shipped immediately to Hawaii, but off-loaded there. The cargo line out of Seattle would no longer enter the western waters of the South Pacific due to the conflict between Japan and China.

Thinking of his old seaman friend Gus, Jake sent a return wire to San Francisco suggesting they contact the Southern Cross Shipping Lines about picking the engine up in Hawaii and getting it through to them in Rangoon.

Jake and Benny took a taxicab back to the cargo pier. The crew went to meet the cab as it pulled onto the dock and gathered around Jake as he got out and paid the driver.

"The situation is this," Jake explained to the crew, "it looks like we are stuck here for at least a month," and he went on to give them the rest of the details about getting the replacement engine shipped.

The irritated crewmen began grumbling about their situation.

"Hey guys," Jake said, "there's a lot worse places we could be stuck. Most of the locals here are friendly, some even speak a little English and the prices are cheap. By rotating our duty schedule, everyone should have plenty of time off. Go to the beach, go fishing, consider this a paid vacation. That's what I'm going to do."

"Wall-cum to Wong-goon!" Phil remarked sarcastically, which lightened the tension some and everyone laughed.

After Jake's pep talk and Phil's remark, the crew resigned themselves to making the best of their extended visit to South Burma.

Onboard the Clipper, there were sleeping births, which would serve as the crew's quarters for their coming weeks stay in Rangoon. The crewmembers started the following day to build a scaffold and rig a hoist on a tripod for dismounting the damaged engine.

Jake planned to have the aircraft ready to install the new engine as soon as it arrived. They would also take the opportunity to do other minor repairs and routine maintenance on the Clipper. Jake knew that keeping the men busy would be the best thing for them.

September in that part of the world was summer and the days were extremely hot and humid. Chief suggested the crew work on the aircraft in two shifts, an early morning shift and a late afternoon shift to avoid the mid-day heat.

Jake mandated the *China Clipper* be guarded around the clock. He worked up a schedule for one man to be awake and on guard duty at all times.

Phil and Herb both pressed him as to why all the precautions and Jake related some of the stories he had heard at the Silver Monkey to them.

"From what I've heard, the Japanese army has moved far enough south to have airfields within striking distance of Rangoon. So far, the threat of the AVG intercepting them has detoured the Jap bombers from raiding this far south and on the city here. That doesn't mean our luck will hold forever and there's always the possibility of unfriendly locals or plain ol' banditos."

The rest of the crew gathered around to listen.

"In case our luck runs out, here's the plan. I'll purchase a bunch of those matchstick bamboo mats. The stuff must be cheap enough. They use it for everything around here. We'll position the mats on poles around the plane dockside and I've got another idea for the outboard side. On the outside chance we were caught in an air raid, this might help to camouflage the Clipper."

***

Each afternoon for the next three days, Jake lingered for a long time in the market place before checking at the telegraph office for messages and going over to the Silver Monkey. He kidded himself that he was looking around to become more familiar with the local culture, but he knew he was only hoping for the opportunity of a chance meeting with the Dragon Lady.

On the fourth day, Jake was about to abandon his daily quest when he suddenly spotted her across the market purchasing something from one of the vendors.

He casually worked his way closer to her. When they made eye contact, he attempted to speak to her, but she quickly looked away. Jake pretended to be looking at some of the fresh fruit behind where she was standing and in an act of desperation, he resorted to a dirty trick to get her attention. He intentionally bumped her basket, spilling part of the contents on the ground.

She said something in a harsh tone of voice to him in the local dialect. Then realizing he was obviously a foreigner, she repeated her irritation in French.

Jake only guessed, but he thought she might have said something about how clumsy he was and he jumped at the opportunity to make an apology.

"I'm sorry, I don't speak French, but please excuse my clumsiness."

Jake gazed into the young lady's flawlessly beautiful face and saw such gentleness in her deep dark eyes.

She forced back a smile, but said nothing.

Jake struggled for something further to say to her as he wanted to keep the conversation going, but with the language barrier, how was he going to talk with her. He spoke clearly and slowly.

"My name, Jake. What your name?"

The Dragon Lady could no longer keep from smiling.

"My name Suzette," she said and paused. "However, Mr. Jake, I must tell you, that while you do not speak French, you also do not speak English very well either."

Jake laughed at himself for sounding so silly as he bent down to pick up the contents of Suzette's spilled shopping basket.

"When you replied in French, I just assumed you wouldn't understand my English. I guess the laugh's on me."

Jake offered to carry Suzette's shopping basket after he replaced the contents he had spilled. They continued down the aisles of vendors. Suzette stopped several times to add one or two items to her basket and paid for them. Jake offered to pay for the items.

"No," Suzette told him, "you will give them too much and the next time, they will also expect me to pay more."

When they reached the end of one of the long aisles, an Oriental man with a large press-type camera snapped a flash picture of Jake and Suzette. The photographer assumed they were together as a couple and bowed as he handed Jake a claim ticket for the photo.

Jake took the claim ticket, nodded politely and placed it in his pocket.

"Could I interest you in sharing afternoon tea with me?" he asked turning to Suzette.

Suzette looked down and shook her head no, but Jake continued to insist.

"There's a really nice little tearoom just around the corner."

"Yes, I know the place, however, you may find it a little expensive. They only serve traditional British high tea this time of afternoon."

"I'd consider it an honor if you'd let me make it up to you for spilling your basket."

Finally, Suzette reluctantly accepted Jake's invitation and as they left the market, she said, "Thank you for asking me to tea, Mr. Jake, but I am beginning to suspect now that your spilling my shopping basket was not altogether an accident."

"Guilty as charged," Jake replied smiling.

They walked the short distance to the patio tearoom off the dining room of the hotel Jake often passed on the way to the Silver Monkey.

Seated on the patio, the two struggled to exchange casual conversation and Jake nervously asked way too many questions all in a row.

"What is your full name Suzette? Are you a native of Rangoon and how is it that you speak American English and not the King's English like the others around here?"

"You see, I know you are a Pan Am airline pilot as I recognize the uniform. A captain I believe, but I need you to tell me your full name as it is not proper for me to continue addressing you as Jake."

"Yes of course, my family name is Martin."

"Very well, Captain Martin, there is one other thing I'd like to ask."

"Anything you'd like. Go ahead."

"I was aware that you and your friend were watching me from a distance in the marketplace the other day. I would like to know what was being said about me."

"Wow!" Jake gasped thinking he had sure walked right into that one. "Honest?" he asked.

"Honest!" Suzette replied.

"We referred to you as the Dragon Lady. We weren't being rude, of course, but you do remember the dress you were wearing?"

"Yes. Very well then, I think I will consider that a compliment. Now I will try to answer all of my gracious host's questions. I was born Suzette LeBourget. My father is French and my husband's name is Chen Laun, so on official documents I use my full name Suzette LeBourget-Laun."

"Your husband!" Jake's voice went up almost an octave. Composing himself he said, "I mean your husband. Where is your husband now?"

"He was sent north with the men in his regiment almost two months ago to join the fighting."

Jake took note of her appearance as she spoke. She was a mature woman and yet there was a certain child-like quality about her. He was curious as to her age.

"I had no idea such a beautiful young lady like yourself would be married. When I asked you to join me, I hadn't considered that possibility."

"Yes, I assumed that," Suzette replied pleasantly.

Suzette clearly understood Jake was surprised and by the use of his word "young," she also guessed that he might be asking how old she was.

"I was born in China in 1920. Let me see, that makes me twenty-one, doesn't it. My husband is an officer in the Army of Burma. We were married six months ago in a marriage arranged by our parents. Are these not the answers to your questions, Captain Martin? One you asked and one you did not," she said smiling pleasantly at Jake.

Her father was French and her husband Burmese, so that was why she spoke both French and the local dialect, Jake thought to himself, but where did her fluent English with an American accent come from? He decided the better part of wisdom would be to just let Suzette talk, as she seemed more at ease with him now.

Even if she was married, he enjoyed her company so much that he would be content to sit and talk with her for the rest of the afternoon, if she would only stay. Jake, well aware of his own loneliness, also sensed a certain loneliness in Suzette.

"My father, Jean Claude, is presently an attaché with the French Embassy here in Burma. As a young diplomat, he was stationed at the embassy in Beijing. He met and married my mother there. She was Chinese."

"Was?" Jake asked.

"Yes, she died when I was a small child. My father is Catholic, so I was raised in the Catholic faith. I grew up on my father's family estate in the North of France. My aunt raised me until I was fourteen. Then I was sent to a girl's finishing school in Boston. I attended two years of college at UCLA before coming to Burma to join my father."

"That certainly explains the accent or lack thereof. Where is your father now?"

Suzette's expression appeared to indicate concern when Jake asked about her father.

"He was ordered to Algiers shortly after the Germans invaded Poland. I have only heard from him once since he left." Suzette's face brightened and she said, "But enough about me. Tell me about the illustrious Captain Martin who flirts with married ladies in the marketplace."

"What would you like to know about me?"

"I know you're an American, but where are you from in the United States? You seem to have a slight southern accent and yet it sounds different to me."

Jake explained he was from Texas, that he had grown up on his father's ranch, and willingly answered a dozen other questions she asked. He was absolutely fascinated with Suzette and when she spoke, he listened intently.

"I am sure you are curious as to why a married woman is sitting here having tea with a man she has only just met. It is not really very complicated. I live alone in an apartment not far from here. My husband and father are both away and it is somewhat of a treat that I am allowing myself to visit with a handsome young American flyer. One can discuss personal things with a total stranger, knowing that their paths will never meet again."

Jake started to say something and Suzette interrupted, "Besides, it is giving me a chance to use my Yankee English, which I have not been able to do this past year."

Jake wanted to keep the conversation light as possible, as it seemed clear to him Suzette had not enjoyed much happiness in recent months.

"You've been hanging around the Brits and Frogs too long when you call me a Yank!" Jake said jokingly.

Suzette laughed.

"Thank you, Captain Martin, it has been a while since I allowed myself the luxury of laughter."

"Okay, let's stop this Captain Martin stuff, right now. If you will call me Jake, I promise not to call you the Dragon Lady!"

"Very well, Jake it is. I have heard how fiercely independent you Texans are. Tell me, do you consider yourself a Southerner or a Westerner?"

They both laughed and continued to talk until the afternoon grew late.

Suzette had made it clear she had no intention of ever meeting with him again or telling him where she lived.

When she excused herself to leave, Jake accepted the situation. He hoped, but stopped short of praying, that maybe someday he would see her again. If this were not to be, then it would not be.

***

Over the coming days, Phil, Herb, Chief, Benny, Elmer and Jake took turns working on the Clipper, standing watch and going ashore. Jake took the third watch. He was on duty before sunup each morning and was up when Willie started the morning coffee. Jake had excused Willie from guard duty, as he spent a lot of time cooking for the crew.

Hal explained to Jake that he and Tony would be over at the American Embassy working during the day if Jake needed to get a hold of them. Hal wanted to check on what the embassy people were hearing about Japanese army movements from refugees when they were debriefed. Hal and Tony returned each evening to take their turn on watch.

The Clipper's crewmen rotated off guard duty every fourth night and were at liberty to spend the night ashore, if they chose to do so. The rest of the time, the crew slept in the Clipper berths.

The bunk beds were comfortable enough, but the cabin compartments were hot at night and difficult to sleep. The late afternoon rains cooled things off for a while, but made the nights even more humid. Chief rigged a battery-powered fan that moved some air through the compartments and it helped a little.

Several days after Jake had met Suzette, he woke up sweating in the middle of the night and lay bunk for a while thinking about her. He had tried hard to forget her, but in his half-awake, half-asleep thoughts he dreamed of her.

Jake climbed out of his bunk and went out onto the dock to get some fresh air. Benny was on guard duty. Elmer could not sleep either and he was sitting out on the dock shooting the bull with Benny to pass the time.

Jake went over to sit with them for a spell. Benny lit up a cigarette and Jake bummed one of Benny's cigarettes.

"Benny, do you remember that pretty young lady we saw in the marketplace?"

Benny gave Jake a light from his Zippo lighter and it clinked in the quiet darkness when he snapped it close.

"Sure, you mean the Dragon Lady. Why do you ask, Captain?"

Jake took a drag from the cigarette and coughed.

"I finally met her the other day and we spent the afternoon talking. Damn it, anyway. Would you believe she's married?"

"Well," Benny said, "that's the breaks."

"I still can't get her off of my mind," Jake said and sat quietly for a while.

The three men watched as a sliver of a silver moon rose against the black starlit eastern horizon.

Jake took another drag of the bummed cigarette, looked at it and flipped it into the harbor water.

"How in the world do you guys stand to smoke these things?" Jake asked as he left to go back into the Clipper to shave and get dressed, as he was due to relieve Benny on guard duty shortly.

Later that morning, after one of Willie's finely prepared breakfasts on board the Clipper, Jake walked over to the fishing boat docks. The rumors of a possible air raid on Rangoon still worried him. He talked with several of the sampan owners and offered to pay them to pull their boats along side the Clipper. Jake thought this would help hide the Clipper and prevent it being spotted from the air.

At first, the boatmen refused for fear of possible damage to their own boats, but Jake made two of the larger sampan owners a lucrative offer and they agreed. With that, some of the smaller boat owners also offered to tie-up along side the Clipper for a lesser fee. Jake hired the dozen or so who agreed.

Jake returned to the far end of the cargo pier near the street and hailed a taxicab to town. He convinced himself he was on his way to the Silver Monkey, but asked the driver to let him out at the marketplace.

In his pocket, Jake had the dog-eared claim ticket for the photograph taken of him with Suzette in the market the day they met. He figured the photo shop must be close to the marketplace somewhere. The shop was nearby and he located it easily.

When he entered the shop, an Oriental man came out from the back room through a pair of black curtains to wait on him, the same man who had taken the photograph.

Jake handed the man the claim ticket.

"I would like to pick up this photograph, please."

The photographer bowed slightly as he took the ticket from Jake's hand.

"Ah so, remember you and lovely lady." He spoke in broken English with a slight British accent. "Do not have print of this photograph. Believe was delivered to lady's apartment. Happy to print another copy from negative, still have, if you wish order one?"

"Yes, I would like to order one."

Jake handed the man a large bill, much more than the copy of the photograph would cost.

"Very sorry," the photographer explained, "but cannot change large bill."

Suddenly, it dawned on Jake what the man had said a moment or two before that.

"Where did you deliver the photograph?" Jake asked anxiously.

The photographer went to a small file box and thumbed through some index cards. He wrote down the address on a slip of paper and handed it to Jake, bowing politely.

Jake looked at the paper with the address on it.

"Can you give me directions?"

"Not far, very near here," the photographer said and gave Jake detailed instructions to the address.

Jake pushed the bill across the counter to the man.

"Don't need any change. I'll pick the photo up later and thank you, you've been very helpful."

Rushing out the door of the shop, Jake followed the photographer's directions to Suzette's nearby upstairs apartment and climbed the stairs. As he approached the apartment door, he could faintly hear a woman crying. Jake stopped to listen for a moment and then knocked softly on the door. The door was not latched and it pushed open.

Suzette was seated across the room near the balcony window, her hair tattered, her cheeks red and tear-stained. She looked up at Jake through swollen eyes as he entered. She did not speak, but looked back down at the floor.

Jake crossed the room to where Suzette was sitting and sat down on a small wicker chair facing her. Then he noticed Suzette clutching a crumpled piece of stationary in her hand. Jake could see that the letter was not in English, but neatly printed in what Jake could identify only as the same style of writing he had seen on the store signs around Rangoon.

Jake knew something was terribly wrong, but had not yet figured out what.

"Suzette, is it your father?"

"No," she muttered and began crying again.

A young girl in her late teens came and stood in the open doorway. She started to say something to Suzette in the local dialect, but seeing Jake there with Suzette she spoke in English, which she had learned at a British missionary school and Suzette had helped her with.

"Suzette, are you all right? Can I do anything for you?" the girl asked.

Suzette did not respond.

Jake carefully pried Suzette's hand open and took the crumpled piece of paper from her. He went over to the doorway where the young woman was standing.

"My name is Maelee," she said. "I live in the apartment below with my parents. I sometimes stay up here with Suzette to have some quiet time. My parent's apartment is so crowded and she enjoys my company."

"Can you read this letter to me?" Jake asked holding the letter out to Maelee.

Maelee took the letter.

"It is more of a military dispatch than a letter," Maelee commented and began to read the letter aloud. "Burmese Army Headquarters, Nineteen September 1941. Dear Mrs. Laun, We regret to inform you that your husband, Lieutenant Chen Laun was killed in action yesterday. He died bravely with his men while defending our country."

Maelee handed the letter back to Jake and added, "It is signed by some general in our Army."

"Thank you Maelee. I'm a friend of Suzette's and I will stay with her for a while."

Maelee closed the door behind her as she left.

Jake returned to the seat across from Suzette.

On the small end table to the left of Suzette's chair was a picture in a silver metal frame, a photograph of a nice looking young man with a pencil thin Clark Gable mustache in an Army officer's uniform. Suzette reached for the picture and handed it to Jake.

Jake took the photo in the silver frame and studied it for a moment. He placed the dispatch with the picture and handed them back to Suzette.

"I understand," he said.

Suzette clutched them to her bosom and looked at Jake with tears running down her face.

"Why?" she asked pleadingly.

"I don't know why," Jake replied sadly.

Suzette tried several times to talk to Jake about her husband, but was unable to do so without starting to cry again.

Jake sat quietly with her well into the evening hours and finally suggested that she should get some rest.

She agreed and went to lie down.

He placed a small electric fan on a stand near her, turned the fan on low and left saying that he would check on her in the morning.

***

The following day, Jake returned to Suzette's apartment were he was met at the door by the young girl, Maelee, who had read him the dispatch the day before.

"Suzette extends her apologies to you, Captain Martin, but she wishes not to see you."

"What do you mean, doesn't want to see me?"

"I believe she wishes you not to try to contact her ever again."

Maelee closed the door slowly until it latched.

Jake stood for a moment outside the apartment door and then reluctantly left. He tried on several occasions after that to see Suzette, but each time he was unsuccessful. If nothing else, he would have at least liked to have known why Suzette refused to see him.

***

A week passed and mid-morning on a hot sunny Saturday, Jake was seated on a small wooden shipping crate in the shade of the Clipper's wing. He was tinkering with a piece of radio gear from the aircraft.

A young boy in a messenger's uniform approached Jake and asked, "Captain Martin?"

Jake assumed the boy was delivering a message from Pan Am operations back home, but the message was not a telegram. He took the envelope from the boy and handed him some coins from his pocket.

The pink envelope that the boy handed him carried a faint scent of perfume. Jake opened the envelope. The note inside read "Dear Captain Martin, Mrs. Suzette LeBourget-Laun requests the pleasure of your company at tea this afternoon. Same time, same place."

Jake jumped straight up, bumping the workbench and scattering the radio parts. He let out a yell like a cowboy riding a bronc and went into the Clipper to shave, clean up and put on his best uniform.

***

When Jake arrived at the hotel tearoom that afternoon, Suzette was already waiting at the same table on the patio where they had first sat and talked. Gone was the Oriental attire. She was dressed in traditional European style clothes, a black suit jacket with matching knee length skirt and open-toe high-heel shoes with narrow straps at the heel. Her silk hose, with seams up the back, exactly matched the tone of her pale tan skin.

Suzette was seated sideways at the table with her legs crossed. Her black hair curved around her face accenting her dark eyes and ruby red lips. She watched Jake as he entered the tearoom, turning her head to follow him as he approached the table.

To Jake, she looked as though she had just come from posing for a layout in one of those Paris fashion design magazines. Jake had not intended to be smiling. He wanted to appear distinguished, but he was grinning like a foolish schoolboy.

Suzette uncrossed her legs and turned to face Jake as he took a seat across the table from her.

"I wasn't sure you would come. I mean because of the way, the way I refused to see you when you came to call on me," she said with a great amount of trepidation.

Suzette moved her hand across the table to Jake.

He took her hand and held onto it.

"I was just worried about you. You weren't in very good shape the last time I saw you!"

"Yes, I know…"

Jake changed the subject so that there would be no need for Suzette to explain further until she was ready.

"How are you doing? Have you heard from your father?"

"Yes, thank you for asking. I am doing much better now. And yes, I received a letter from my father. He is still in Algiers."

Suzette spoke nervously at first, but Jake managed to put her at ease and cheer her up as they talked.

Jake listened as she told him about the letter from her father. He could not take his eyes off her and watched her perfectly shaped lips as she spoke.

If Jake had not known he was in Burma, he might have thought he was meeting a young lady at any street cafe back in California. He wondered who was this strange young woman he had run into on the other side of the world. She was charming, intelligent and witty, not to mention the fact that she was very beautiful.

"You were so kind to sit with me that night. I could not let you leave Rangoon, without thanking you personally. What I'm going to say next is the corniest line I will ever speak, but here goes… Jake, from the first moment we met in the marketplace, I felt like I had known you all of my life, like I had recognized your soul."

Suzette spoke the words aloud, but Jake had sensed the same thing. Jake recalled when he was a boy and how he daydreamed of far off lands, wondering about the people who lived there. That was it! He felt as though he had known Suzette all of his life.

She embodied every quality he ever hoped to find in a woman. Here she was seated across the table from him in this godforsaken far-off corner of the world, all of which was far too heavy to understand or contemplate further.

"Tell me, ma'am, what might there be to do in this here hick town by way of an evening's entertainment?" Jake said jokingly in a thick Texas drawl.

Suzette smiled and giggled like a schoolgirl.

"The British built an Opera House here in Rangoon many years ago. It is a beautiful structure. You should go see it while you are here. I understand the Opera Das Rheingold by Wagner is tonight's performance."

Jake would welcome any opportunity to spend some time with Suzette if she would go with him.

"It's a good thing they picked a German opera, I hate Italian opera. Would you go with me?"

Suzette smiled, but did not reply to the invitation.

"Before I give you my answer, you must tell me a secret, something you seldom if ever tell anyone else."

"Well, there is one thing," Jake said and indeed there was one thing he seldom shared with his lady friends.

"Tell me, tell me! What is it?" Suzette asked anxiously.

"My real name is not Jake, it's Jacob Teel."

Suzette smiled, but her smile soon faded into a very serious expression. She had a reason for asking him to share a secret first.

"My dear Jacob, the man that turned my head the very first moment I saw him, there is something now that I must tell you!"

From the tone of her voice, Jake dreaded what Suzette might be about to say next. If Jake could have looked into her soul at that instant, he would have known why she expressed herself in that way. Suzette was convinced that what she was about to tell Jake would drive him away from her forever.

"Go on?" Jake said with some apprehension.

Suzette looked down and fumbled with her teacup. She could not bring herself to look directly at Jake.

"As you know, my husband left for the front lines and the fighting a month or so before I first met you in the marketplace. On the day before that, 'my time of the month' I believe is how you Americans say it, is when I first realized I might be carrying my husband's child!" Suzette's voice cracked and she paused.

"It's okay," Jake said softly. "Just go on."

"Then, last week, the same day I received that horrible dispatch… Oh Jake, I am so sorry for us," she said shaking her head sadly. "I am two months now with child."

Suzette raised her head and looked directly into Jake's steel blue eyes. She watched his face intently for any reaction, but Jake sat quietly, his hands folded in front of him, looking at her. His poker face expression gave no clue as to what raced through his mind.

Suzette spoke again before Jake could say anything. In the bravest voice, she could muster, she said, "I guess you know, it took every ounce of courage in my body to come here and tell you this. Now would be a good time for a gentleman to get up and leave."

Again, Jake did not react. Then he said, "With child, hmm? Children are a good thing, nothing to be sorry for. I have two of my own and I love them very much."

Suzette looked at Jake with the most endearing look he had ever seen on anyone's face in his whole life.

Slowly, he leaned over the small table close to Suzette. He looked past her, not directly at her and whispered, "I guess I'm not much of a gentleman. I choose the Dragon Lady, with or without child."

Suzette smiled with a joy she could no longer contain.

"Very well, Jacob Martin'san, you are the one who has chosen the dragon. She has not proved to be very lucky for the men who have known her so far. I hope you do not get singed by her flames."

Jake stood, tossed some bills on the table to pay the waiter and extended his hand to Suzette.

"Where are all these out-of-the-way restaurants that serve all this great local food you told me about and what time does this opera start?"

***

Late that evening, they took a taxicab back to Suzette's apartment.

Jake walked up the stairs with Suzette and she invited him in. When Jake thought he had stayed about the proper length of time, he stood up and prepared to leave.

"I'll take my leave now, lovely lady," Jake said. "Thank you for a wonderful evening."

Suzette stood and moved very close to him.

"Please don't go, I don't want to be alone with my thoughts anymore."

Jake stayed the night, all day the next day and the night, too. For the next three weeks, the two were rarely apart. When Jake went to check on the Clipper and his men down at the dock, Suzette would accompany him. She would wait patiently on the dock or sit in the passenger cabin while he tended to matters of the day.

Jake would occasionally walk down to the Silver Monkey bar for a short while to visit with some of the flyers, but he was never gone very long. There was no telephone at Suzette's apartment, so the crew would leave messages for Jake at the Silver Monkey when they needed him for something.

Two people, as different as the two worlds they had come from, met and fell in love. The only mercy God had granted them was, not knowing. Not knowing that their world, the whole world as they knew it, was about to come crashing down around them. This was the calm before the storm.

Flying Tigers

The morning sunlight seeped through the cracks in the louvers of the apartment balcony window that Suzette had decorated for Christmas.

A bonsai tree on the table was adorned with earrings tied on for ornaments and beside the tree a small slate chalkboard on which was written *Only 21 Days Until Christmas*. Suzette updated it everyday.

Jake had only been up for a few minutes when Suzette was awakened by the honking of a car horn in the narrow street below where a 1931 model English made, Austin taxicab waited.

This was the morning Jake had agreed to ferry one of the P-40s with Roy to an airfield up north. Jake arranged the day before for the taxicab driver to pick him up at this early hour.

Suzette sat up in bed.

"Where are you going?"

Jake pulled up his trousers and slid the tightly woven cotton uniform belt-end through the metal buckle.

"To take one of the fighters up to the airfield at Mangwe. You remember, I told you about it last week. I'll be back late tomorrow night on the train."

Suzette made no attempt to hide her fear. She lost her husband to a war she knew or cared nothing about and now she must deal with the possibility that she could also lose the man she had just fallen in love with.

"Why are you doing this? It's not your job! Let them deliver their own planes. Please don't get involved."

Jake picked up a small duffel bag and his leather flight jacket. He bent over, kissed her and said, "Flying airplanes is what I do. Don't worry your pretty head about it, just go back to sleep."

Suzette grabbed hold of Jake and pulled him to her.

"I love you so much, Jake! Please be careful."

"I love you, too!" Jake said smiling. "I'll be fine, see you tomorrow night."

As Jake left, shutting the apartment door quietly behind him, Suzette sighed. She tried, but had not gotten her way. Like Jake had always told her, flying was what he did and one way or another she would just have to learn to accept that.

She punched at the bed pillow and squirmed a couple of times in the bed to find her place, rolled over and went back to sleep.

***

Mingladon Airfield, where the AVG's Curtiss P-40s were re-assembled, was twelve miles north of town. The old taxicab arrived at the airfield in about twenty minutes.

The two single-seated pursuit planes to be ferried had arrived by cargo ship and were delivered overland by truck to Mingladon. These two aircraft were the latest of the Curtis Hawk series 81A-3. Nicknamed the Tigershark, they would be the last of the Curtiss built P-40s exported to the Nationalist Chinese air force via CAMCO.

When the original order for P-40 Tomahawks came into Curtis from CAMCO, the first fifty had been pulled out of an order destined for the Royal Air Force. They were hybrid models with some features of the newer Warhawks, but used the older style fuel tanks, which the British had refused to accept delivery on.

Their newer sister ships, the Kittyhawks, were being put into service with the U.S. Army Air Corps, which was gearing up for possible involvement in the war in Europe.

When Jake arrived at the airfield, both planes were waiting on the ramp.

The twelve-pointed white sunburst on a blue field, the international insignia of the Nationalist Chinese, had not yet been painted on the wings. Neither plane yet had the famous red and white shark's mouth painted on the nose, the markings that would readily identify these Curtiss P-40s as part of the Fei Hou, which translated meant "the tiger that flies." These last two planes were destined for the Panda Bear, Adam and Eve, or Hell's Angels squadrons collectively known to the world as the Flying Tigers.

Lieutenant Roy was already there and talking with his mechanic who had just finished fueling and pre-flighting the two aircraft to be ferried north.

"Beautiful day for flying," Jake said to Roy as he joined the two men.

Roy turned and greeted Jake, "Well, good morning to you, too."

"You do know I have never flown one of these models before, don't you?" Jake asked.

"You got beaucoup flying hours, don't you? I don't suppose Pan Am would let you drive those ol' water monsters for them if you couldn't fly."

Jake put on his leather flight jacket and took the cap with goggles the mechanic handed him.

"Thanks. Name's Jake, and you're?"

"Billy Latimer, sir."

"You sound like a Texan to me. Where you from, Billy?"

"Amarillo, sir."

"That's what I thought. Not far from my ol home town," Jake said. Then he turned to ask Roy, "What's the stall speed and VNE on one of these babies?"

When Jake asked about the VNE, he was referring to the Velocity Never Exceed speed that overstresses the plane's airframe and above which would cause structural failure.

"When she won't fly anymore and when she comes apart. And maybe not necessarily in that order," Roy wisecracked.

Billy helped Jake on with his parachute.

"Here," Billy said, handing Jake an oxygen mask. He commented to Roy, "That's the last new one we've got, sir."

"Take the mask with you," Roy said to Jake. "They may need it up at Mangwe, but you won't need it today. We're not crossing the Pegu Yoma Mountains. We'll fly down the valley and have the Irrawaddy River in sight all the way."

Roy pointed north with his open hand.

"Jake, it's good to have another Texan in this here fight with us," Billy said. "And you have a good flight too, Lieutenant. Both them planes are in good shape. Try to keep 'em that way for a day or two, okay sir?"

Roy smiled and replied, "You bet, Billy."

Billy half-waved and half-saluted as he headed back to the hangar.

"What will be our heading?" Jake asked Roy.

"Fly about three-five-zero after takeoff. If you lose sight of me, the airfield is just off to the right side of the river about 200 miles up. The HF radio only has one channel, but no need to call, they can tell us Yanks from the Japs. Besides, they're expecting us."

Roy had picked up the habit of referring to Americans as Yanks from the British airmen. He took a pack of cigarettes out of his shirt pocket and offered one to Jake as he lit up.

"Thanks," Jake said, shaking his head no.

Roy took a long drag from his cigarette.

"The only thing I'd ever flown before I flew a single-seated fighter was a couple of trainers," Roy said. "You know the old joke about flying a single seat plane don't you, Jake? You climb into the cockpit, if the throttle is in your right hand and the stick is in your left, you're facing the wrong way. Stand up, turn around and sit back down as though you had intended to do that. Then place all the shiny switches in the opposite position and leave the rusty and painted ones alone. The aircraft should start!"

Jake smiled.

"Finally," Roy said, "got a smile out of the stoic Captain Martin."

Then Jake laughed.

"Ever land a tandem job from the backseat and the nose seemed too high?" Roy asked.

"Sure," Jake replied.

"It's about the same. You can't see over the nose to taxi, so you have to kick the rudders and zigzag to see forward. A full stall landing is easier than a wheel landing. Seriously though, a P-40 dives better than it climbs."

Jake was listening to Roy as he talked, but for just a moment, his thoughts drifted off to Suzette who had scolded him for volunteering to make this flight.

Roy continued, "Keep the nose down 'til you've got plenty of airspeed. We're almost at sea level here, so she'll jump into the air. Stay on the rudders when you first put the power to her. Watch the torque. Don't sock the power to her when she's nose high and slow or she'll crank over on her back."

"Got ya, sounds about like those old use Northrop Alpha's I flew on the airmail routes."

"If you've flown an Alpha, a P-40 will seem like a pussycat to you."

"What if we run into some Japs?"

"Not likely. They haven't been raiding this far south, but if we do, run like hell! The guns on these two aren't loaded. We shipped the last of our ammo north by truck last week."

Jake reached for the handhold slot on the side of the fuselage, climbed onto the wing and into the cockpit.

The other P-40 was waiting with its canopy open. Roy waved with the back of his hand as he went to his plane.

A young woman in a brown summer RAF uniform exited the Quonset hut near the hangar. She ran after Roy to hand him a large manila envelope and said something to him.

Roy pitched his cigarette, took the envelope and smiled as he said something back to her.

Jake could not hear what was said, but the envelope obviously contained a dispatch for the unit at Mangwe.

Roy's plane was first to crank. The P-40 coughed a couple of times as the engine turned over and then the un-muffled sound of the eleven hundred horsepower Allison engine filled the air with a deafening noise.

Jake's engine roared to life and droned in unison with the other P-40.

The sun was well above the horizon now and there was a light breeze out of the northwest, but already it promised to be another sweltering hot day.

The two planes taxied slowly toward the open airstrip and turned into the wind. Jake was riding the brakes to rev the engine as he switched first to the left mag, then to the right and back to both.

The sound from Roy's plane indicated he was doing neither. Instead, he was already adding takeoff power. Jake did the same to keep up with him. Both planes lifted off about the same time and started a slow climb to the north.

Jake eased back on the throttle, adjusted the prop setting to establish a good rate of climb and turned the elevator trim to take the backpressure off the control stick. At eighty percent power, the fighter climbed like a homesick angel. Jake positioned his aircraft just off Roy's right wing where he knew Roy could keep him in sight.

The bright sun shown in through the Plexiglas canopy heating the cockpit and Jake adjusted the two small outside air vents to his face. He fumbled in his shirt pocket for his sunglasses and put them on. Heat thermals were already starting to build and the fighter's wings rocked gently until reaching cooler air.

At about nine thousand feet, Roy leveled out and powered back to cruise speed. With the nose down in level flight, there was a beautiful panoramic view on the horizon. The river below wound like a giant snake up the lush mountain valley.

About twenty minutes into the flight, Roy looked back over his right shoulder at Jake and made a downward pointing motion with his index finger.

The lead P-40 nosed forward into a shallow cruising descent and Jake followed. The rate instrument indicated a four hundred foot a minute descent. This told Jake they were about ten minutes out from the airfield.

Just up ahead, off to the right of the river was Mangwe airfield and Jake followed Roy on a long straight-in approach for landing.

"GUMP," Jake said to himself aloud, the universal verbal pre-landing checklist that works for most airplanes. This reminds the pilot to check the Gas, Undercarriage, Mixture and Prop. The main landing gear locked into place as Jake went full forward on the prop, selected twenty degrees of flaps and reduced the throttle setting.

Both fighters touched down side by side at about the same time with Jake's plane slightly behind Roy's.

Jake had not quite pulled off all the power and had kept a little extra throttle in for better control. His plane skipped one time and settled into a three-point landing after he pulled the rest of the power off. Not too bad for my first P-40 landing, he thought to himself.

The two fighters caused a cloud of dust as they taxied across a patch of dirt where dozens of coolies were working on the airstrip carrying baskets of earth on their backs. The prop-wash blew the hats off several of the workers as the P-40s taxied by and their hats hung from the tie strings around their necks.

An impressive line-up of Tomahawks with the under-part of the nose painted with red and white trademark shark's mouths were parked all in a row.

From a distance, some of the aircraft appeared a little worse for wear at first glance. As Jake taxied closer he could see the shabby ones were not real P-40s at all. They were decoys to fool the Jap recognizance aircraft into thinking the Flying Tigers had a lot more airplanes than they really did. The decoys were constructed of bamboo and canvas.

Roy held right brake and added power to swing his aircraft into the lineup. Jake followed and pulled into the line beside him.

Several of the squadron members came out onto the ramp to stand and watch as the two new fighters arrived.

Both pilots revved their engines slightly and pulled the mixture control full off. As the engines died, five of the Tiger pilots and two of the mechanics walked toward Jake and Roy's planes.

The lead mechanic, Mac, approached Roy as he was climbing out of the cockpit.

"How's she running, Lieutenant?"

Roy removed his cap and goggles. He placed his leather gloves inside the cap.

"Like a top. These new models are a real joy to fly."

"Are they armed," Mac asked, "or do we need to load the guns when we top them off?"

"They're not armed. We forgot to take some ammo off the last truckload headed up here before it left Mingladon. Oh, and the weapon-arm switch is still safety-wired, per regulation."

"That thin copper wire stuff, we don't even bother to put it on anymore," Mac said as he and Roy walked over to Jake's aircraft.

Jake had gotten out of his aircraft without unbuckling his seat-pack parachute instead of leaving it in the aircraft seat. Standing now on the ground, he took it off and was trying to decide whether or not to return it to the cockpit.

"How about yours, sir, she running okay?" Mac asked Jake.

"As far as I could tell, she's running great. An amazing machine compared to those ruptured ducks I lumber around the sky in."

Mac offered to take the parachute from Jake.

"There's fresh coffee in the ready room if you guys are interested," Mac commented as he went to throw Jake's parachute in a nearby shed.

Roy exchanged greetings with the pilots who had come out to meet them and introduced Jake around.

"Jake here, is a pilot for Pan Am and volunteered to fly the other P-40 up here with me today and this is the squadron's Executive Officer. Just call him Pappy, every one else does."

Jake shook hands with Pappy and the others. The small group engaged in casual conversation as they sauntered from the flight line.

Roy handed Pappy the sealed envelope he had been given back at Mingladon.

"This is for The General. I was told to get it to him as soon as we arrived."

Pappy stuck the package under his arm.

"Thanks, Roy. Good to meet you Jake," Pappy said and departed for General Chennault's temporary office.

Jake followed Roy and the other pilots over to a small shack under some banyan trees with a long wire antenna running from it.

As they approached the shack, one of the pilots said to Jake, "This is what we jokingly refer to as our Ready Room, but it does have a coffee pot and a good short-wave radio receiver. At night, when the airwaves clear up, we can listen to Tokyo Rose. She's a big bag of wind, but plays some good tunes. You know, back home stuff."

***

An hour or so went by and word was passed for everyone to assemble on the grassy area outside of the operations building. General Chennault came out of the building with some papers in his hand to address the group.

"Well men, it seems the U.S. Pacific Fleet has been put on alert for a possible attack by Japanese forces. The message doesn't seem to say anything about when or where the attack might take place."

There were some muffled comments among the group.

"I guess there's nothing secret about this top secret dispatch in view of the fact that we've been getting our ass kicked around the sky for some time now by these Japs."

One of the men yelled out, "Sir, we've been doing a little kicking ass of our own," and everyone laughed.

Chennault acknowledged the remark with a nod

"At any rate, it looks like we might be getting some company from the American forces and some more help from the Brits in the near future. That's about it, now you guys know as much as I do about what's going on."

Pappy stepped forward.

"Okay, pilots to standby and the rest of you go on back to work."

The advance squadron at Mangwe was down to seven aircraft. They lost one P-40 in air combat, but not the pilot. He bailed out and walked some thirty miles all the way back to Mangwe carrying his parachute. The other aircraft had been shot up on the ground, but the squadron was still a pilot short because one of the men was down with malaria and in the hospital.

The two new fighters Roy and Jake brought up from Rangoon would bring the squadron strength back up to nine aircraft. A replacement for the ailing pilot was being transferred over from Kunming and would arrive sometime in the next few days.

Jake went to catch up with Pappy.

"I understand there is a morning train to Rangoon and I was wondering if I could arrange for some transportation to the train station."

Pappy slowed up to walk with Jake.

"Sure, no problem, we'll get you there. The train doesn't depart 'til ten a.m. and it's never on time anyway. Why don't you just bunk here for tonight? One of the men will show you where. I assure you, the quarters here are better than one of those flea-bitten flophouses in town."

"Thanks, Pappy, for your hospitality. I'll check with you in the morning."

"No thanks required. We appreciate you pitching in to help out."

***

Incoming enemy aircraft never surprised the Flying Tigers. In the beginning days of the conflict, General Chennault organized an early warning system comprised of lookout posts throughout the countryside. Local volunteers manned these posts around the clock. This elaborate spy and lookout network reported every movement of the Japanese air force. Rumor had it that Chennault was told when the enemy opened their hangar doors.

When a call came in from one of the lookout posts, a first alert lantern was run up a flagpole. When incoming enemy planes were confirmed, a second lantern went up the pole. Finally, an order to scramble was given and a siren was sounded for the pilots to man their aircraft.

Under the shade of the nearby banyan trees, the pilots assembled in a collection of wicker chairs and wooden lounges. The heat was sweltering, but there was a light breeze coming across the airfield. The hot, dry air reminded Jake of August in Texas.

Jake borrowed one of the lounge chairs following the lead of several of the other pilots and settled in for an afternoon nap.

About three o'clock that afternoon, the air raid warning siren woke Jake. As he struggled to get fully awake, the pilots and ground crew were running to the fighter line.

"What's going on? Is there anything I can do?" Jake hollered trying to get the attention of those running by.

"Better head for the bomb shelter! It's over by the cook tent," one of the men running past yelled back at him.

Jake stood watching as each of the pilots manned their planes and cranked the engines. As they pulled out zigzagging to taxi, Roy ran to jump in the same plane he had ferried in earlier that day and Jake wondered why an Army guy was flying with the Tigers.

Chennault and Pappy had left earlier that afternoon for a meeting somewhere and were not back yet. Jake looked to his right and then to the left to see if he could find someone in authority to get permission to take up the remaining Tigershark, which sat unmanned on the empty flight line ramp with its canopy open.

Rule twenty-three seemed to apply to this situation, Jake thought to himself. Rule twenty-three was a longstanding joke among pilots, which maintained that it was easier to obtain forgiveness than it is to obtain permission.

The lone Tigershark stood out like a whore in a red dress at a Sunday school picnic parked among the tattered bamboo fighter decoys.

Danged if I'm going to let some Jap shoot up a brand new P-40, Jake thought, especially the one I just went to all the trouble to ferry up here. Finally realizing he was only arguing with himself, he took off running for the only remaining flyable aircraft left on the field.

From out of nowhere, Mac was running along beside him with the seat-pack parachute he had taken from Jake and thrown in the shed earlier.

"You might need this," Mac said as he climbed onto the wing of the P-40 ahead of Jake and threw the chute into the bucket seat.

Jake was right behind him.

"Are the guns loaded in this plane?"

"Yes sir, did it myself right after you landed!"

Jake climbed into the cockpit pulling the shoulder harness on. Mac fastened Jake's parachute and shoulder harness as Jake went through the start sequence and the engine fired off.

Mac plugged the oxygen mask hose in and dropped the mask in Jake's lap.

"You're going to need this, too. Give 'em hell for me, Captain!" he said and jumped off the back of the wing.

Mac turned his back to the prop blast as Jake started his takeoff roll from where the fighter was parked.

The rest of the squadron had already lifted off and were climbing out in the distance. They were headed northwest to meet an oncoming Japanese Sentai bomber squadron from Rahena, Thailand.

Jake tried to catch up with the Tiger formation, but at best, he would only be able to keep them in sight as they climbed for altitude to be above the incoming bombers and their escorts as they approached.

Chennault trained his pilots to attack using a high-speed dive through the enemy formation. This tactic proved so effective that the Flying Tigers had shot down nearly a hundred enemy aircraft to date, while losing only a very few of their own in the air.

Once the Flying Tiger P-40s expended their altitude in the initial diving attack, they climbed again in order to make a second attack on the bombers. On these subsequent passes the fighters were much more vulnerable to the gunners onboard the bombers.

The Jap fighters escorting the bombers would now engage the Flying Tigers and British fighters that had joined in the attack. The pilots had been warned by Chennault not to try to turn inside the lighter weight Jap fighters, but to use the Hawk's superior speed to their advantage.

Jake snapped on his oxygen mask and turned the tank valve to the mixed position. He would not need a hundred percent until he reached a much higher altitude. He was gaining on the squadron up ahead of him as his aircraft was performing slightly better than the others and he was also using a higher climb power setting.

Jake easily identified Roy's aircraft from a distance, because like his P-40, it still did not have the shark's mouth painted on the nose. He pulled alongside Roy's plane.

Roy looked over and gave Jake a thumbs-up and Jake returned the signal. Roy then signaled Jake by making a diving motion with his right hand and patting himself on the head. Next, he held up his microphone for Jake to see and shook his head no.

Jake clearly understood the signals. He was to maintain radio silence and to follow Roy in as his wingman when they made their initial diving attack on the bombers. Jake shook his head pronouncedly yes to confirm that he understood.

The squadron pilots throttled back at twenty thousand feet to save on fuel. They didn't have to wait long before the Japanese bombers passed under them. The seven Tigers, plus Roy and Jake, were about to attack fifty Jap Sentai and Takashita aircraft below.

The thought crossed Jake's mind that these were not particularly good odds. He wondered if more Japanese fighter escorts might be lurking at another altitude. The Jap fighters could come in high above them and make the same diving attack on the P-40s after they traded their altitude for airspeed attacking the bombers.

No sooner had the thought crossed Jake's mind than the squadron peeled off toward the bombers below. Each P-40 selected a bomber to attack. Jake was right on Roy's wing and headed for the bomber in formation next to the one Roy's P-40 was apparently diving on.

Jake armed his guns by breaking the brass safety wire on the red switch cover and threw the switch. He was ready to squeeze the trigger on the control stick, but he waited.

Roy had not yet fired and Jake had always heard that combat pilots learned to hold off firing until almost on top of the target and then to only fire in quick short bursts to save precious rounds of ammunition, considering a fighter's guns held only three short precious minutes in total continuous firepower.

Roy's gun muzzles flashed and Jake pulled the trigger on his guns. Jake was so close to the bomber when he fired the bomber completely filled his windshield. Smoke poured from the bomber Roy had attacked, but Jake clean missed the one he had fired on.

Not realizing how much airspeed he had gained in the dive, Jake's aircraft was going well over four hundred miles an hour. He had fallen victim to target fixation and barely missed colliding with the bomber when he went screaming past.

Jake took too long to pull out of the dive and discovered that the rest of the aircraft were all well above him. The Jap fighter escorts and the Tiger P-40s were scattered all over the sky. Jake started a full power climb back to altitude and at the same time made a wide turn to come in behind the bomber formation.

Over his headset, Jake heard one of the Tiger pilots report, "Heads up you guys. There's a squadron of RAF Buffaloes joining us at nine o'clock high. Don't go shooting down any of the wrong fighters."

Jake approached the last bomber in the formation. This was how his grandfather had taught him to hunt ducks, to pick off the duck in the back of the formation so as not to alert the whole flock.

Squeezing the gun trigger, Jake fired a short blast from his guns and watched as his rounds fell way short of the target. He quickly realized why Roy had waited so long to fire before. He was going to need to be a whole lot closer to hit his target. He also remembered one of the Tiger pilots explaining that an effective kill could only be made inside of fifty yards.

This time, Jake moved in closer and lined the bomber up in his gun sight. The tail gunner in the bomber was firing back, but the gunner's bullets were also falling short. Jake moved still closer preparing to fire and that was when he heard several thuds like someone banging on the side of the cockpit with a ball-peen hammer. Two holes appeared in the canopy, one where a bullet came in and another where the bullet went out, just above his head.

That technique was not going to work, so he backed off the throttle to put some distance between him and the bomber until out of the tail gunner's range.

On the next try, he added power and came in high on the bomber. He was betting he could maneuver the P-40 faster than the Jap tail gunner could swing his heavy machinegun, aim and fire.

Jake rocked the control stick causing the P-40 to swing left and right. Each time the bomber came across his gun sight, he fired a short burst. Every burst was a direct hit and one of the tracer bullets struck the fuel tank in the bomber's right wing.

Jake pulled up hard to the right to miss pieces of flying debris. As he overtook the bomber, he came close enough to see the face of the now limp tail gunner in the rear-facing seat. A sight that would be burned into Jake's memory and that he would always regret having seen. The bomber's wing exploded and folded upward as it fell out of the sky in flames.

In a hard climbing turn to the right, Jake found himself looking directly at the under belly of another bomber passing over the top of him. Jake squeezed the gun trigger and large yellow flames burst from the bomber's underside.

The Jap bomber's bomb bay was loaded with incendiary bombs and one of Jake's bullets ignited them. For only an instant, Jake was pleased with himself as he thought of the lives he may have saved on the ground.

Looking back over his shoulder, Jake continued the climbing turn to avoid the burning bomber until his P-40 approached a full power-on stall.

The plane fell rearward and entered an inverted flat spin. Plummeting earthward totally out of control, he pushed the stick forward. Nothing happened except the horizon continued to rotate rapidly in front of the nose.

Jake pulled the power off, kicked the rudders and flopped the ailerons until the nose pointed down. He eased the throttle forward again and five thousand feet later, he finally got the fighter back under control.

Alone and disorientated, Jake was trying to get his bearings when tracer bullets went flying past the side of his cockpit.

"Where the hell did that come from?" he yelled aloud.

Out of the corner of his eye, he caught a glimpse of a Japanese fighter right on his tail and turning with him. This one was a radial engine model, painted dark green, with a red rising sun meatball on the side. For whatever reason, Jake thought what an ugly paint job.

Applying full military power, he pulled up hard to the left. Jake knew this was his only option, as the Jap fighter could turn tighter to the right than he could.

He continued to pull up hard until he was upside down. The Jap fighter was no match for the Tigershark in a climb. When Jake looked up through the top of the cockpit, which was really down and over his shoulder, he could see the Jap fighter falling away.

Jake chopped the power and rolled into a slow spiral lining up the now doomed fighter in his gun sight just below him. He fired once and the Nakajima fighter, with its wooden construction, burst into flames.

Jake rolled his P-40 over on its back and into a screaming power dive, a basic aerobatic maneuver known as a split-S. Coming out the bottom of the dive, Jake banked left and then right to insure there were no more fighters on his tail.

Almost out of sight now on the distant southern horizon, he could still see the bombers. Several were smoking and one had dropped out of formation going down. He could spot none of the other P-40s. They were probably as low on fuel as his aircraft and had already broken off their attack to return to Mangwe.

Jake continued to climb, but at a low power setting to save on fuel. He knew Mangwe airfield was off to the east, but had no idea exactly where he was. After years of flying, he preferred not to think of it as being lost, more like he was only temporarily disorientated. Leveling off at eighteen thousand, he took up a southeasterly heading.

Out of nowhere, another group of tracer bullets went trailing past the side of his cockpit.

"Oh shit, not again!" he moaned as he looked into the small panel mounted rearview mirror. Two of those rising-sun-bastards were on his tail this time, but these were painted battleship gray, not green like the fighter he had encountered earlier. A sudden and sickening realization hit him. These two were late model Mitsubishi A6M Zeros.

Jake knew his plane would not perform well at this altitude. In a tight maneuver, the P-40 would stall-out in the thinner air rolling over on its back and making him an easy target for the Zeros.

Instinctively, he pulled the power full off, reached for the flap lever and placed it in the full down position. If you can't outrun 'em, out-slow 'em, Jake mumbled to himself. The sudden added lift from the flaps caused the P-40 to lunge upward and nose over, jerking him forward in the cockpit like he had flown into an invisible barrier.

Such a stunt might have ripped the flaps off the fighter's wings at a lower altitude, but up here in the thinner air, the plane held together.

Because of the excessive speed the two Zeros had built-up diving on Jake's P-40, both fighters passed under him and came out in front of him. Jake was literally looking down his gun sight at both aircraft. He kicked the rudder pedals and fired short blast to spread his rounds across the aircraft on the right and the one on the left.

With his free hand, he raised the flaps and added power to stay up with the two enemy fighters. Both planes started to pour smoke from their engines. Why they did not break off in opposite directions Jake would never know, but the lighter weight Zero had no cockpit armor plating like most American built fighters, so possibly one or both of the pilots had been wounded or killed.

Jake fired two more short bursts at each plane. Parts began coming off of the Zeros with each successive hit and flying past Jake's plane. He continued to pull the trigger until his guns went silent.

Out of ammunition and low on fuel, Jake wanted no more of this. If he had to bail out, it would be a first in his flying career and he was not very fond of the idea. He took a guess at the heading back to the Mangwe airfield and set up a nine hundred foot a minute rate of descent.

The descent kept his airspeed up and he held his course for roughly ten minutes, but when low on fuel, ten minutes can seem like an eternity. Ever present on his mind was his empty gun magazines. He intended to put as much distance as possible between him and anymore Jap fighters.

The Irrawaddy River appeared on the horizon and just beyond lay Mangwe airfield. As Jake approached for a landing, he saw that the other eight Flying Tiger aircraft had already returned. He touched down and taxied his P-40 towards the ramp where the other fighters were parked. His engine cut out twice and let go one last cough before quitting completely. He was out of gas.

The group of Tiger pilots and ground crew who had gathered for Jake's late return all walked out to his plane. Laughing and joking, they pitched in to push his out of gas P-40 the last hundred yards to its parking spot.

Jake climbed out of the cockpit to cheers and stepped onto the ground greeted by congratulations.

"That was a hell of a piece of flying for anyone's first time in combat, two Takashita bombers and a Nakajima fighter to your credit. Not a bad days work," Roy said.

Jake smiled as several of the pilots slapped him on the back, but the celebration stopped when Jake said, "Make that plus two A6M Zeros."

The pilots looked at one another questioning Jake's last comment.

"Zeros?" Roy asked as the group walked towards the squadron office. "I didn't see any Zeros up there today. You're lucky you didn't have to go up against a Zero, Jake. Those old NK2 George fighters, like the one you shot down, can't climb with a P-40, but a A6M Zero can!"

"No, I'm not kidding you," Jake insisted. "After you guys ran off and left me, I was jumped by two Zeros."

"What color were they?" Roy asked.

The other pilots waited silently for Jake's reply.

"Gray, these two were gray, not green like the ones escorting the bombers. I got lucky and hit both of them when they overshot their dive."

That statement by Jake brought some jeers and was followed by a round of heavy kidding from the pilots.

"Gray is the color we usually see on the Zeros, at least the ones I've seen," Roy said backing up Jake's story to some extent. But all the pilots knew that anyway.

A pilot named Walker, whom everyone called Duke because he claimed to have played football for two years at Duke University in his home state of North Carolina, was not buying any of Jake's story.

"Yeah, but two in one pass? I'll tell you, 'Captain Marvel,' we'll just put that one in the book with all the rest of the tall tales these pilots come back with around here. Three guys will all hit the same plane and claim three kills."

"Baloney," another pilot said. "Who you talking about anyway, Duke, Yourself?"

Pappy greeted the pilots as they entered the squadron office. Several clerks waited to fill out debriefing reports on the pilot's combat results.

Jake decided not to mention the two downed Zero fighters again. The reports were generally good with the pilots claiming eight downed and no losses for the day.

Pappy asked, "Which way were the bombers headed?" and all of the pilots agreed they were headed due south.

"That's strange," Pappy commented, "why would they be headed towards Rangoon? They've never ventured that far south before."

When the de-briefing concluded, Pappy asked for everyone's attention.

"Gentlemen, you are invited to a dinner in honor of Generalissimo Chiang Kai-shek who will be traveling quite a distance to pay us a visit. It will be held over at the Aussie's plantation house tomorrow evening.

Attendance is not, I repeat is not, optional. The General and Madam Kai-shek will be our guests so be ready to get picked up at six o'clock for cocktails in the best uniform you can scrounge up for the evening."

Jake was only half listening, as it did not involve him, he was headed back to Rangoon tomorrow. His thoughts were of Suzette and how worried she must be about him right now.

The Burma Road

The following morning, after bivouacking with the squadron, Jake went to Pappy's office to arrange for a ride into town to catch the train back to Rangoon.

Pappy sat reviewing some dispatches and looked up from his desk as Jake came in.

"Bad news, Jake. Based on the morning reports, one of the main railway bridges between here and Rangoon was hit by the Jap bombers during yesterday's raid. The trains won't be running for several days now, maybe longer."

"Did they bomb Rangoon?"

"Preliminary reports indicate yes, but no details."

Jake plopped down in a bamboo chair across from Pappy.

"Where does that leave me?"

"You can stay here with us. We can always use another good pilot," Pappy joked.

"Under other circumstances, I just might take you up on that, but I've got an airplane crew and some unfinished business waiting on me back in Rangoon."

Pappy smiled.

"And from what Roy tells me, your unfinished business is a real knockout."

"Well, actually I was referring to my Clipper," Jake replied laughing, "but that, too."

"The Dragon Lady, I believed Roy called her."

"Yes, and yes she is. By the way, did anyone ever tell you guys you're a bunch of old lady gossips?"

Jake's good-natured retort amused Pappy.

"Tell you what, Jake, I'm sending Mac in one of our supply trucks to Rangoon over the Burma Road tomorrow. There are still some spare parts we need stored in the hangar at Mingladon airfield. He's leaving early in the morning and you're welcome to ride along."

Jake slapped the arms of the chair with both hands and stood up.

"Thanks, Pappy, you're a lifesaver."

Jake walked over to the ready room shack, got a cup of coffee and sat down with the pilots on standby alert. The pilots were discussing the possibility that the Jap bombers might have hit Rangoon for the first time yesterday.

Jake began to worry about the *China Clipper* crew and about Suzette, but there was no confirmation or any details about the raid. The morning passed and no alerts sounded.

"It appears the Japs might be going to give us the day off," one of the pilots remarked.

Jake was sitting quietly, lost in thought, when a clerk from the squadron office tapped him on the shoulder.

"General Chennault requests your presence for lunch at noon today, Captain Martin," the clerk said.

"What's this all about?" Jake asked,

"I'm sorry sir," the clerk replied politely, "the General doesn't always confide in me."

"Thanks, I'll be there," Jake replied realizing he had asked a stupid question.

Jake wondered if the invitation had anything to do with his taking the P-40 without permission yesterday and if the Flying Tigers had something like a military courts martial, which might apply in these circumstances.

After thinking it over, Jake concluded whatever resulted from his actions would have to be. He would offer no defense for what he had done and accept whatever the General had to dish out.

Around noon, Jake went to Chennault's temporary office behind the Ops building and waited on a covered patio out back. Centered on the thatched-roof covered patio was a large round, linen-covered table with six oversized wicker chairs. Several Burmese servants were setting the table with crystal and fine china.

Jake took a seat on an old wooden bench at the edge of the patio and watched as a man worked in the tropical tree-shaded garden area that enclosed the patio yard.

Indistinguishable sounds of several men talking emanated from the General's office window.

The office doors opened onto the patio and General Chennault entered with an American Army Air Corps colonel and two Nationalist Chinese officers. Chennault introduced Jake to his other guests.

"Be seated gentlemen. Our cook, Wong, has prepared some fresh fish from the river for lunch today. These fish are similar to our catfish back home."

The guests took their seats.

"I think you'll enjoy them the way Wong has prepared them. Wong is an excellent cook and the only cook I have. Two Wong's don't make a right, you know," Chennault joked.

Polite laughter followed the General's pun.

A discussion about what would happen to the Flying Tigers if America entered the war occupied most of the luncheon conversation.

"I didn't get a chance to thank you for delivering our new P-40 up from Rangoon," Chennault said to Jake. "As always, we're short-handed around here and appreciate you volunteering."

"You're more than welcome. I enjoyed having the chance to fly one of your fighters. They're real nice planes."

"There is, however, one thing I don't understand."

"What is that, General?"

"How is it a brand new P-40 has two holes in the cockpit and a couple in the fuselage?"

Jake suspected Chennault had shared his clandestine flight in the P-40 yesterday with the others at the table and was having a little fun at his expense.

"Ventilation, I believe, sir," Jake replied. "I think Curtiss may be experimenting with better cockpit vents. You know how hot those cockpits are in the afternoon sun and even hotter with some Jap fighter on your tail."

Chennault glanced at his other guests and laughed.

"Good answer, Jake. Ventilation, huh? Yes, I suppose you're right. That's kind of what I was thinking, too."

Jake understood Chennault could not have approved his unauthorized flight in the Tigershark. This was Chennault's way of dismissing the incident and Jake's use of the P-40 would not be mentioned again.

"They say a doctor buries his mistakes, but a pilot gets buried with his," the Army colonel remarked.

"You got that right, Colonel!" Jake replied.

Chennault motioned for one of the houseboys to bring over a box of cigars and each of his guests were offered one. Jake passed on the cigars. Chennault lit up a Camel cigarette and got up from the table.

"If you'll excuse us gentlemen, I need to discuss something with Captain Martin."

"I'll be returning to Rangoon tomorrow. It's been a pleasure meeting you all," Jake said as he stood up and excused himself to the others at the table.

Chennault and Jake walked to the edge of the patio.

"I understand you and your Clipper crew will be returning to the States from Rangoon."

"That's correct, sir."

"There's something you can do for me. A young lady by the name of Kim Wong will be at the American Embassy. If you could see that she gets to Hawaii, I'd consider it a personal favor," the General said offering to pay the fare.

Jake refused the airfare money Chennault offered. He also figured the details of the General's request were none of his business and didn't ask.

"You got it, General. I'll take care of it."

Jake returned to the spot outside the ready room shack he had staked out earlier under the banyan trees and took a short nap.

Roy and Jake passed the rest of the afternoon critiquing yesterday's air combat. Around four o'clock, Jake heard the drone of a twin-engine aircraft in the distance, but no air raid warning sounded.

Roy also looked up to scan the horizon.

"I hear it, too, but I assure you, if there's no alert sounding it's a friendly."

Off in the distance, Jake's eyes focused on a lone twin-engine C-46 Curtiss Commando transport escorted by two Flying Tiger aircraft from another squadron. The three airplanes approached the airfield and landed.

The brown over gray transport taxied up in front of the P-40 lineup and the two escorts pulled into the row of fighters. When the engines shutdown, the cargo door swung open and a uniformed Chinese soldier dropped the boarding ladder and attached it to the deck.

Generalissimo and Madam Kai-shek appeared in the doorway accompanied by their military staff. General Chennault, Pappy and the three officers from lunch greeted the Generalissimo and Madam. They all loaded into several vehicles and promptly drove away.

"Most likely off to that fancy plantation owned by an Australian gentleman," Roy commented.

The two fighter escorts were Flying Tigers from the Teddy Bear squadron out of Kunming. The pilots came over to the ready room area to a hearty welcome by several of the pilots who had flown with them before.

***

Early that evening, along with the whole Flying Tigers squadron members, Jake piled into the few drivable vehicles available. Jake climbed onto a flatbed truck with a dozen others and road standing up behind the cab.

The driver made his way down the dark dirt road leading up to the plantation house nestled in a grove of giant trees. The Aussie farmer's large white, two-story house resembled a stately Southern American antebellum mansion. The place reminded Jake of something right out of Margaret Mitchell's Gone With The Wind.

The airmen and crew gathered on the veranda as they waited in a reception line to be introduced to Generalissimo and Madam Kai-shek. Each of the men spoke briefly to their honored guests who thanked them for their brave and valiant service to the Nation of China.

After the formal greeting, the men were shown into the main living area of the house and served cocktails by native houseboys in white jackets. The men swapped good-natured barbs about the small size of the cocktail glasses in which the drinks were served.

Pappy entered the room and gave a slight cough to get the men's attention.

"When the reports from yesterday sorties by our outposts came in late this afternoon, several of the observers reported seeing two Jap Zeros go down in flames and crash on the west side of the Pegu Yoma mountains. I've checked with the commander over at the British Brewster squadron and they're not claiming them."

Some muffled questioning went across the room.

"So, which one of you clowns failed to report downing a couple of Zeros," Pappy asked, "or have we got somebody in the area competing with us to shoot down Jap planes?"

Laughter followed Pappy's remark and then the room suddenly went dead silent. Duke and a couple of the other pilots looked straight at Jake.

Jake casually took a sip from his small cocktail glass and said, "I told you they were gray."

Silent surprise turned to congratulations from the men and Duke Walker exclaimed, "Laws'ee, Captain Marvel, maybe your long-winded tale had some truth to it after all."

"Or maybe those two Jap pilots committed hara-kiri when they saw you coming," one of the other pilots joked.

"If they're yours, Martin," another one of the pilots commented, "you can lay claim to being an Ace."

"Credit one of the pilots that'll get paid a bonus for it," Jake told Pappy. "I wasn't up that day, remember?"

"Too bad you're headed back. We need a replacement for Ol' George Boyington. He got crosswise with Chennault and took a commercial flight home through India," Roy said.

The pilot Roy referred to, a former Marine officer, was able to get his Marine commission back and returned to fly against the Japs in the Pacific as the CO of an F4U Corsair squadron that became known as the Black Sheep.

"Yeah, we could use a pilot like you, particularly after five kills in one day."

Jake looked away, avoiding eye contact with Roy.

"That's the problem."

"What's that, Jake?"

"The word you just used, kill!"

Jake's remark caught Roy off guard and he asked quietly, "What do we have here, a closet conscientious objector?"

"No, I just never liked to kill living things. Goes against my nature."

"Well, when you do start liking it, that's when we'll worry about you," Roy reassured him.

Chennault entered the room to join the group.

"Gentlemen, I guess now is as good a time as any to discuss something off the record with you. The Army Air Corps has approached the Generalissimo about taking over the Flying Tigers."

Negative remarks and a few hisses from the group followed Chennault's announcement.

"If this happens, I want to know if you will consider going off contract and signing up with the Army Air Corps. You would all be commissioned as reserve officer pilots in the Army."

Duke replied the loudest.

"No way! We've been doing their dirty work for the last two years and I for one am not about to go under the command of some straight-laced, drill-happy Army commander. I'll go home first."

Most of the other pilots echoed Duke's comment.

To which Chennault angrily replied, "Maybe we need to pass out some white feathers!"

The comment surprised even Pappy who had served with Chennault for some time now. The men had never heard Chennault make a derogatory comment like that before and a few cuss words drifted across the room.

Pappy faced Chennault with his back to the men.

"Sir, I don't believe that remark was called for."

Chennault realized he had spoken out of his annoyance with the men's outward defiance and the tension of the moment. He paused before he spoke again.

"I was out of line. You guys are the bravest men I've ever had the privilege to command. Mr. Walker, gentlemen, I sincerely apologize for the uncalled for remark I just made," Chennault said and left the room.

At dinner, Jake found himself seated next to Madam Kai-shek. Her English was less than precise, but she was well able to hold a conversation with Jake and the pilots seated around her.

"I asked our host to seat me with you young flyers as I get so tired of listening to those blow-hard generals and politicians," she said smiling.

Her comment proved to be a good icebreaker and the men laughed politely.

"Tell me, Captain Martin, why is your uniform different from the other Flying Tiger pilots? I don't seem to recognize it. Are you a Naval officer instead of an Army officer, perhaps?"

"Of a sort, ma'am," Jake replied politely. "I'm a Clipper pilot for Pan Am."

"Of course, I should have recognized the uniform. I've flown your airline, but that was several years ago out of Hong Kong. Oh my, that seems a lifetime ago. Before all this evil began in our country. Before the revolt in the north and before being invaded by the Kami Zen."

"I don't believe I'm familiar with the term 'Kami Zen,' ma'am." Jake replied curiously.

"It refers to those who desire to rule the world by force," Madam Kai-shek explained. "They call themselves Kamikaze, which means Divine Wind."

***

Early the next morning, Jake was awakened by the sound of a P-40 engine being test run by one of the mechanics. Today was December the 7th and he reflected that the date was still only Saturday December 6th back in Hawaii on the other side of the international dateline.

Jake lay in his cot for a few minutes wondering if the Clipper would be ready when he returned. He would go by and pick up Suzette tomorrow evening and in a couple of days, they would be sunning themselves on the beach at Waikiki.

Jake dressed quickly and went to meet Mac who had just finished gassing up the large flatbed truck.

A couple of crewmen were helping Mac load a Browning .30 Caliber M1917A1 machinegun and some ammunition canisters onto the truck. There was a gun mounting post behind the passenger seat of the canvas-top truck cab where the Browning could be mounted.

"You believe in going prepared don't you, Mac?" Jake said as he walked up.

"Always," Mac replied, "but I hope we don't need to use it. If you're ready, let's hit the road. We can make Rangoon by late afternoon if we push hard."

Jake climbed in the passenger seat and Mac headed the truck out across the open countryside and down a cart trail until they intersected the Burma Road and headed south.

Soon after pulling onto the road, they began passing long lines of refugees fleeing the Japanese army invading from the north. Many were burdened with large bundles of personal belongings. A few, with their extended families, walked behind two-wheeled, ox-drawn carts piled with all their worldly possessions.

The people on the road kept well to the side and Mac was running about forty-five miles an hour. The road was rough and tossed them around in the cab.

From time to time, they came upon small rag-tag groups of wounded Burmese soldiers or a slow moving vehicle carrying the more seriously wounded.

Jake and Mac passed the time by talking.

"I've always like history," Mac told Jake. "Think I'll become a teacher and coach when I go stateside," and Mac went on to tell Jake about the girl he left back home and how he planned to marry her when he got back. "Where are you and your crew headed when you all leave Rangoon?"

"With all that's going on in this part of the world, we'll return to Honolulu. I considered going on around the world to India, on to Mombassa and across the African continent. Always wanted to see the Serengeti, but after Lake Victoria, there's no water. Well, there is the Congo River too, but don't know where we'd get any avgas. If we had trouble over West Africa, we might be the first Clipper to make a sand landing instead of the first commercial airliner to circumnavigate the globe."

"Could your Clipper fly from Africa back to the States?" Mac asked.

"No, but that's the easy part. The narrowest route across the Atlantic is from the west coast of Africa to Brazil. From there, we'd go north up through the Caribbean. That's a route I've flown many times before."

***

After about four hours on the road, they began passing units of Burmese regulars and British commandos moving south in long single-file columns. They were still making good time until they came upon a convoy of British lorries, which slowed them to a crawl. Mac managed to pass a couple of the vehicles, but most of the time the winding mountain road was too narrow to permit passing.

Jake heard the sound of an engine in the distance over the sound of the vehicles on the road with them. He knew the sound of an airplane's radial engine all too well and the high pitch indicated the sound was coming towards them.

As they rounded the next curve on the narrow mountain road that looked north out over a chasmal valley, Jake's worst fears were confirmed. A flight of two single-engine Jap fighters cleared the far peak and nosed over to dive on the rag-tag column of soldiers and refugees.

An instant later, all hell broke loose. Foot soldiers ran for the ditches. Bullets flew across the ground kicking up small billows of dirt in a straight line in front of the truck as the shadow of the first plane passed over them. Jake recognized the fighter as a Japanese A6M Zero.

"Should we abandoned the truck and go for the ditch?" Mac asked. "What's our best chance?"

"Up here on this ridge with the angle they've got on us, we're sitting ducks anywhere we go! Can you get us past that truck up ahead? We'd be better off moving. A moving target's harder to hit and around that next curve we might be out of their line of fire."

No sooner than Jake spoke the words, the abandoned vehicle in front of them exploded. Mac could not get by, so he edged up to the rear of the burning lorrie and pushed it over the cliff. The road was clear for about the next twenty yards. Mac gunned the truck and took off, but they were still in the open.

The second Zero commenced its dive as the first Zero circled back to make another strafing run.

Jake climbed over the truck seatback and lifted the Browning machinegun onto its mount. Frantically, Jake unsnapped the metal ammo box and latched the bullet link belt into the gun's chamber.

Jake nearly fell off the truck when Mac slammed on the brakes, managed to hold onto the gun handle until he got his footing. Two disabled trucks were blocking the road ahead. They weren't going anywhere.

Jake cocked the gun and waited until the second Zero came right at him. He fired, but the Zero went by too fast for him to swing the gun and keep up with it. The Burmese riflemen were also firing at the plane from their hiding places along the ridge. Neither Jake nor the soldiers hit the aircraft and Jake knew why, they were firing at the aircraft instead of leading it.

On that dive, the second Zero hit a British command vehicle just behind them, but missed their truck. The first fighter commenced its second strafing run and Jake realized this was going to be a slaughter.

Mac gave up on moving the truck and jumped in the back to untangle and feed the ammo belt to the machinegun.

Jake lifted the Browning off its mount and grabbed the gun by the barrel. The barrel proved too hot to hold and burned his hand. He reached for his flight jacket in the truck seat and wrapped the leather jacket around the barrel in order to hold onto it.

As the Zero came in, Jake took careful aim and repeatedly fired in front of the fighter. The Zero passed directly overhead, its engine boiling black smoke, and crashed into the side of the cliff a hundred or so yards away in a gigantic fireball. So close, Jake could feel the heat from the blast on his face.

"Damn! That was spectacular," Mac yelled. "I've never been that close to one that blew up before."

Just about the time Jake began to think they might have a chance the one remaining Zero was joined by two more Zeros coming in from a higher altitude.

The lead Zero approached. Jake aimed and pulled the trigger, but the Browning jammed. He could hear the whine of the other two Zeros starting their dive as he struggled to un-jam the weapon.

The lead Zero pulled up and burst into flames and Jake yelled, "I didn't even fire! Someone back up the road must be shooting at them!"

Mac pointed skyward, "No, look!"

Nine Flying Tiger P-40s, with their shark's teeth noses gleaming in the sunlight, appeared over the mountaintop with their gun muzzles blazing. The remaining two Zeros peeled off from their power-dive and attempted to make a run for it, but both were hit repeatedly.

One blew up in mid-air and the other careened earthward smoking all the way in. The explosion from the crash echoed through the mountain pass.

Three of the Tiger aircraft circled back and passed low overhead rocking their wings. Jake recognized the one with no tiger's teeth yet painted on the nose and waved his jacket in the air at Roy as they passed over.

The roar of their engines thumped the air with a pounding Doppler effect as they went by. The soldiers ran into the open from their hiding places, raised their arms and cheered as each of the Tiger's fighters flew passed.

Zoom. Zoom. Zoom.

To the north, more Jap planes were headed toward the easy prey along the Burma Road and the Flying Tigers climbed out to meet them head-to-head in air combat.

Jake and Mac solicited the help of the soldiers in pushing the two burned-out vehicles off the cliff to clear the road. As they pulled away in the truck, the British infantrymen formed up into a column and spontaneously broke into song. "It's a Long, Long Way to Tipperary," they sang.

Back on the road and moving again, Mac asked, "I wonder if as a pilot you can count the planes you shoot down from the ground?"

"Why is that, Mac?"

"You know," Mac shrugged his shoulders, "towards becoming an Ace."

Jake smiled and asked, "They give you some kind of medal for being an Ace?"

"Don't think so."

"Well, if they do, I'll bet its inscribed on the back 'To Those Who Saved Their Own Ass Five Times.'"

Mac laughed.

"Never thought of it that way. Tell me something, Jake, do you think the history books will record anything of this conflict?"

"Seriously Mac, I suspect this struggle will go down as just another forgotten war. The Army and the Navy sure wouldn't want anyone to know a handful of fighter jockeys turned back the whole Japanese army."

Unbeknownst to Jake and everyone else on the road that day, the main Japanese ground force had already started moving down the northern part of the Burma Road.

During the ensuing days, the three squadrons of the Flying Tigers would destroy the bridges in the mountain passes and repeatedly attacked the Japanese military convoys until their movement south was stalled and the Jap Army was forced to retreat.

Thus, the history books would eventually record that the Flying Tigers almost single-handedly had turned back the Japanese invasion of southern Burma.

***

Mac and Jake reached the outskirts of Rangoon in the late afternoon and drove to the section of town where Suzette's apartment was located. As they approached the neighborhood, they saw many of the buildings had been severely damaged by bombs.

Jake began to have a bad feeling about the situation when he saw the last narrow street leading to Suzette's was not passable. He got out of the truck and made his way through the rubble to what remained of Suzette's apartment building.

Mac stayed with the truck to prevent any vandalism or looting by people roaming the streets rummaging through the debris and carrying off anything of value.

Jake approached the building and found the apartment totally destroyed. He recognized part of the balcony from Suzette's second-story window in the collapsed rubble.

Jake climbed to the top of the debris pile where he thought he recognized something. He bent down and picked up a small slate chalkboard on which was written "Only 19 Days Until Christmas."

Jake's hand trembled as he picked the slate up and read it. First he felt anger and then his whole body went numb. He made his way through the wreckage over to where an old man, two women and a boy were trying to salvage what little they could of their belongings.

"The girl, the young woman," Jake asked with great apprehension pointing upward to the shell of what was left of Suzette's apartment, "do you know where she is?"

One of the women replied in the local dialect.

The teenage boy spoke up, "They no speakee English."

Jake tried again to ask about Suzette, but the boy did not understand his question. Jake removed the photograph of him and Suzette taken in the market from his wallet. He pointed to Suzette in the picture. The two women and the old man talked among themselves.

Jake listened and tried to get the drift of what they were saying, but he could not.

"I tell you what they say, mister. The girl-lady who live there," the boy pointed to the photo of Suzette in Jake's hand, "she killed when bomb hit building. They take her with rest people killed."

The boy waved his hand and pointed towards downtown.

Jake grabbed the boy by the shirt and screamed, "Who took her? Where did they take her?"

The startled boy tried to pull away from Jake.

"City building, center town. They call it morgue. Closed now, you go tomorrow, find lady!"

Jake realized he was scaring the boy. He let go of the boy's shirt and placed his hand on the boy's shoulder.

"I'm sorry. Thank you for your help."

Tears swelled in Jake's eyes and clouded his vision. He fumbled in his pocket for some money and offered a large wad of bills to the boy for his assistance.

"Very sorry for you lady, mister," the boy said refusing to take the money from Jake.

Jake forced the bills into the boy's hand.

"You need this worse than I do, but you better spend it quick. In a few days in might not be worth much."

The boy had no idea what Jake was talking about, but he bowed politely and said, "Thank you, mister."

Jake stumbled back down the debris pile and leaned back against a section of wall that was still standing in order to steady himself. He slid slowly down the wall until he came to rest seated on the ground.

"My God, my God how can this be," Jake cried out. "It should have been me, not her!"

Jake sat trying to understand how life and all his plans could change so much in a few short days.

A brief time passed and finally Jake composed himself. He rose to his feet and walked back to where Mac waited in the truck and climbed in.

"Will you drive me out to the shipping docks before going out to Mingladon?" Jake asked.

Jake had talked with Mac about Suzette back on the Burma Road and could only guess at the outcome of Jake's quest by his somber mood.

Mac put the truck in gear and pulled away.

"You okay, Jake?"

Jake shook his head no.

"I'll try the morgue tomorrow and see if I can find anything out there and then I'll go to the French Embassy. Maybe they'll know something."

***

When the truck pulled onto the cargo pier where the *China Clipper* was tied up, piles of luggage and people, mostly Caucasian, were crowding the dock.

The crew had removed the scaffolding from the now replaced engine nacelle and was in the process of removing the bamboo coverings shrouding the Clipper. The old damaged engine lay on the dock amidst a puddle of its own oil. The new engine installation had only been completed an hour earlier. The engine was still warm from Phil and Chief having made a test-run. The *China Clipper* was ready to fly.

Benny saw Jake get out of the truck and ran to meet him, "Captain, where in the hell have you been?"

"It's a long story, Benny."

"I even went over to the Dragon Lady's apartment looking for you. Listen, Captain, we're all real sorry about your friend."

"I guess it hasn't fully sunk in on me yet!"

"You told me you were going north with Roy for a day, but I was about ready to give you up for…"

"I know, Benny. I thought the same thing myself a couple of times these last few days."

Mac had gotten out of the truck and was standing with Jake and Benny as they talked.

"What are all these people doing here?" Mac asked.

Benny did not know Mac, but he recognized the Flying Tiger insignia on his shirt.

"They're from the American Embassy to be evacuated," Benny said answering Mac's question. "Have you guys been on another planet or something?"

"On the Burma Road most of the day. I guess that's about the same thing," Jake said sarcastically.

"Why?" Mac asked.

"You guys don't know, do you? You haven't heard yet. We're at war!" Benny said with a look of amazement.

"Sure Benny, we know that," Jake replied with a puzzled look. "The Chinese have been fighting the Japs up north of here for years now. Mac here and I even got shot at today on the road down here from Mangwe."

"No, I mean we're in a bloody world war. You really haven't heard. The Japs bombed Pearl Harbor this morning. Hit us from aircraft carriers at sea and sank most of our battleships in the harbor."

Jake looked at Mac who was as equally shocked.

"The bastards hit us on Monday, December the eighth," Mac remarked. "I'll bet this is a date that will go down as a black day in American history."

"No," Benny replied, "its still Sunday the seventh back in Hawaii. The attack began at seven fifty-five in the morning, their time. Caught most of our guys sleeping."

"They may have only awakened a sleeping giant!" Jake said displaying both anger and sadness.

"Time will tell," Benny said. "Time will tell."

"Gotta get going," Mac said preparing to leave. "Need to get those spare parts at Mingladon loaded and back up to Mangwe."

"Okay Benny, let me get Mac on his way and you can fill me in on what's going on here." Turning to Mac, Jake said, "There's no way you're going to make it back up that road we just came down!"

"The General must have anticipated something like this," Mac said. "He said he'd try to get a C-46 down here if the Burma Road became impassable."

Jake was not an outwardly emotional man, but he hugged Mac and slapped him on the back.

"Good luck to you, Mac, and thanks for the ride."

"See you in the funny papers, Captain," Mac said climbing in the truck and waved as he pulled away.

In Jake's mind, he could still see the Zeros diving on them with their guns flashing. Jake had shared a life and death experience with Roy. On parting, he had felt that he and Roy's path might never cross again. Jake had that same feeling as Mac drove away.

***

Jake stood motionless on the dock at the water's edge and watched as the drama unfolded. The chaos reminded him of a movie he had seen in 1937. The turmoil and chaos was right out of the opening scene of that Ronald Coleman movie *Lost Horizons*.

The noise of the crowd faded into a dull distant roar and for a moment Jake could almost feel Suzette's presence. He recalled her smiling face as he wrestled with his feelings, torn between duty and emotion. What would be gained by his staying behind to search for Suzette's body? The boy said the two women witnessed her being taken away and he had seen the destroyed apartment with his own eyes.

If these people were the last of the American Embassy evacuees, then surely the French Embassy had also evacuated all their people by now. His responsibility was to his crew and to these people right here, right now. Duty, honor and country called and he must rise to the occasion!

Jake looked out across the mob of people and the baggage piled up on the dock. He and Benny worked their way through the crowd gathered around the Clipper.

"The replacement engine arrived the day you left and we went to work getting it installed," Benny explained as they moved through the throng. "Then when word came this morning of the attack on Pearl, all foreigners were advised to leave Rangoon by tonight. Most of these folks showed up at the American Embassy and then came here."

"Coming through," Benny yelled out as they made their way to where Phil, Herb and Elmer were keeping the people on the dock and back away from the Clipper.

"Man! Am I glad to see you, Captain! This guy here," Phil said pointing to a gentleman in a formal black suit, "says he's from the American Embassy and a lot of these people have visas to depart on the first available U.S. transportation out of Rangoon," Phil laughed, "but I think we're the only U.S. transportation out of here. So what do we do now?"

Jake acknowledged the Embassy man with a nod.

"Looks like you got the situation well in hand, Phil. You guys just keep holding these folks off the ship awhile longer 'til I can figure out the best way to handle this."

Several people from the crowd tried to get Jake's attention yelling, "Captain! Captain!"

Jake ignored their efforts.

"Benny, you go bolt the boarding door over the sponson and position yourself there. No one boards the Clipper for now except one of our crew 'til I say so. Got it?"

"Right, Captain, I mean aye, aye, sir."

"Willie, you go on aboard now."

Benny and Willie took off running to the Clipper.

"Oh and Willie, if it ain't drinkable or edible, throw it overboard in the bay," Jake hollered after them.

"The china and the silver too?" Willie asked.

"That too! Don't leave in on the dock. The coolies will just fight over it and someone'll get killed." Jake turned to Elmer, "You work with this Embassy fellow to get us a head count of the people who have a visa or can prove they're American citizens. Don't think we're gonna get all of them on board, but we'll see what we can do."

"Thank you, Captain Martin," the Embassy man said and left with Elmer to go set up a makeshift check-in counter on a nearby shipping crate. Elmer motioned for the people to form a line in front of the temporary check-in counter.

"Phil, you go to the cockpit and get the Clipper ready to depart. Watch for any signal I might give you to start the two bayside engines."

"Watch for your signal. Got it, Captain," Phil took off running to catch up with Benny and Willie.

"Chief, did we ever get any fuel?" Jake asked suddenly realizing he was not sure they had.

"Yes sir, Captain, she's full up. That Sunderland crew came over yesterday and topped her off. The fuel truck driver said he didn't think any of his planes would be coming back. Left without asking to be paid."

"I guess even a blind hog finds an acorn once in a while. Don't they, Chief?"

"You got that right, Captain. What do you want me and Herb to do?" Chief asked.

"Just what you've been doing. Get the rest of those bamboo mats clear of the props. Then start moving those small boats and those two big sampans out of the way."

"Get ready to get underway, Captain?" Herb asked.

"That's right, Herb, get ready to get underway." Jake replied and asked, "Where's Hal?"

"Right behind you, sir," Hal responded. "You're going to be short two crewmen on the return. That'll give you a couple extra seats. Tony and I are headed up river on that junk I've hired," Hal said pointing to a large sampan tied up further down the pier. "We'll join up with the British and some American intelligence officers near Waylu."

Jake looked at Hal and Tony and shook his head.

"You guys got more guts than brains to stay here in a hotbed of trouble like this. Gonna miss you guys. Kinda gotten used to you two jerks being around."

"We love you, too!" Hal replied sarcastically. "Before we leave, we'll help you try to get some of these sampans moved out of the way so you can takeoff."

Elmer returned to where Jake was standing.

"The head count is sixty-one, plus two babes-in-arm, plus the crew, of course. It's going to be rough carrying that many, our Clipper being an executive version with berths and all. There won't be near enough seats."

"I know, but I think we can carry the weight if we don't have any cargo or baggage. Listen, Elmer, is there a female in that bunch by the name of Kim Wong?"

"Yes, I remember her, a young woman in her twenties. She's the third woman with a small child, but she is Burmese and doesn't have a visa."

Jake looked out over the crowd on the dock to see if he could spot her.

"She's the one in the far back," Elmer said pointing to the young girl in a gold dress holding a baby.

"Well that makes one more passenger, Elmer. Tell that Embassy fellow to give her a visa unless he wants to stay here and hold her hand."

Elmer started to leave to tend to it.

"And Elmer, you make sure she and her child are onboard when we leave."

"Aye, sir!"

Jake walked to the front of the waiting crowd and climbed atop the large wooden shipping crate, which had contained the replacement engine.

"Your attention, please!" Jake said in the sternest and most authoritative voice he could muster.

The noise level was still too high. Jake yelled out, "Hey!" and then some of the crowd began to help quiet the others down so all could hear.

"Only those with American passports or visas from the U.S. Embassy will be allowed aboard," Jake announced. "If we can take all of you, we will."

The crowd let out a cheer.

"However," the crowd was still too noisy and Jake raised his voice. "However!"

The crowd grew quiet.

Jake began again, "No baggage will be permitted onboard. We're going to be lucky to get the passengers on. If you have any jewelry, money or small personal keepsakes, get them out of your suitcases and trunks. Now! Put whatever valuables you can carry on your person. The women may carry a small handbag or purse. The luggage, footlockers, baggage of any kind stays on the dock where it sits. No exceptions. If you don't want to leave it, you can stay here with it!"

Jake stepped down from atop the shipping crate.

Elmer and the Embassy gentleman began allowing the checked passengers, one by one, onto the gangplank that went down onto the Clipper's sponson.

Benny had understood Jake's instructions clearly and he double-checked each passenger before allowing them to board the Clipper.

A tall dark Oriental man in a silk suit approached Jake and said, "I am not an American citizen and I have no visa, but I will give you ten thousand American dollars if you will take me onboard your airplane."

Jake knew enough of the local social order to understand the man was an opium dealer.

"Sorry, just sold the last ticket a few minutes ago," Jake replied with a smirk on his face. He turned his back on the man and walked away.

"Twenty thousand!" the man called out to Jake.

Hal yelled for Jake from the edge of the pier at the bow of the clipper, "Better come here. We've got a problem with these sampan people. They're still tied up and won't cast off."

Tony struggled to hold back a dozen angry boatmen that Hal had been arguing with and said, "Yeah, Captain, they're demanding payment for the service they say they provided."

"They're right. I promised to pay them if they would help hide the Clipper."

Hal was holding a large stack of Burmese bills in his hand and replied, "I know! I tried to pay them with this, but they refused the paper money. The boat owners contend that if the Japanese occupy Rangoon, the Burmese money won't be any good and they're demanding payment in silver or gold."

"They're probably right," Jake said. He turned to Tony and spoke in a subdued voice, "There's a moneybag full of coins in my briefcase stashed in the Clipper cockpit. Run and get it while I try to calm this bunch down."

Hal and Jake continued to assure the boatmen they would be paid and shortly Tony returned in a dead run with the moneybag and handed it to Jake.

Jake did a quick head count and gave each of the boatmen the same amount of coins. Two of the boatmen demanded more.

"What I gave you was more than I agreed to pay originally. That's all there is, Take it or leave it!" Jake said and threw the empty money sack on the ground.

The boatmen took their payment in gold coins and slowly began returning to their sampans.

Tony and Hal began working with the boatpeople to get them to move their boats out of the way, but the two boatmen who thought they should have been paid more remained defiant and still blocked the Clipper.

Jake raised his right arm high in the air and made a circling motion with his pointed index finger.

Phil was watching from the cockpit for Jake's signal and fired off the outboard engine. The prop blast nearly swamped a couple of the smaller boats and the two blocking the Clipper quickly commenced to move out.

The large junk Hal hired remained tied up further down the pier and not in the way of the Clipper.

"That's our ride, the one I made a deal with to take us up river. Good luck to you, Jake."

Hal and Tony took off running for the junk.

Tony stopped a short distance away, turned and hollered back, "So long, Captain. Thanks for the memories... Ah, I got a million of 'em." He gave a wide salute, more like a wave goodbye than a salute, smiled and took off running to catch up with Hal.

Tony was quoting a new song recently made popular by Bob Hope followed by a rather poor impersonation of one of Jimmy Durante's famous lines.

Jake laughed, waved back and muttered, "So long. So long you ancient warriors. I hope America's got a lot more like you cause it looks like we're gonna need them!"

Long Way Home

The last passenger crossed the gangplank followed by Jake. Chief released the stern rope and Herb let the bow rope drop free. Benny pushed the gangway off the sponson. The wooden plank splashed into the water and bobbed like an abandoned raft as the Clipper drifted away from the dock.

Engines one and two were already running. Jake reached the cockpit and climbed into the pilot's seat to take the controls as the Clipper moved away from the pier.

Phil fired off the number three and four engines and Jake added just enough throttle to hold the Clipper against the swirling harbor current.

In the early evening darkness, Jake could still make out Hal and Tony watching them from the deck of the junk through his open cockpit window. The junk crew had also cast off and they were headed for the mouth of the river.

Jake glanced aft in the cockpit. Most of the crew were smiling and Chief gave him a thumbs-up. He applied power and began a high-speed taxi run for the open harbor bay.

Air raid sirens began to wail throughout the city of Rangoon as Jake positioned the Clipper into the wind. Fighting the current on the Bago River, he eased the throttles forward to full power and quietly uttered his usual prayer aloud, "God grant us safe passage."

Phil did not ask what Jake had said this time.

The China Clipper made an exceptionally long takeoff run, barely lifting off the water with its heavy load of passengers and fuel. Jake tried to keep her in the air, but she settled back onto the water and skipped one more time before finally lumbering into the sky.

As the Clipper climbed slowly into the evening sky, flashes from the exploding bombs to the north of Rangoon city could be seen. The flashes appeared to be near Mingladon airfield and Jake thought of Mac.

Off to the far south, a coal black steamer was exiting the mouth of the bay and headed for open sea. The large ship was difficult to spot except for its white deck on the dark water. The old LaFrance steamer was running with its lights out, obviously hoping to slip away from the Japanese attack under the cover of darkness.

The Clipper climbed slowly, but steadily on a southeasterly heading into the night.

"Hold this heading and stay well out over water," Jake instructed Phil. "I doubt the fighters will venture out over the water this far. We'll turn east for the coast of Siam in a while and fly directly across French Indo China."

Chief came forward to relieve Jake.

"Should we try to radio for air space clearance?" Chief asked Jake as he climbed into the pilot's seat.

"To hell with airspace permission, all rules are off now. Besides radio silence might be our safest bet."

Jake stopped at the navigation table to confirm their position with Elmer. Then he asked Benny, "You got those frequencies and codes Hal gave us for Honolulu?"

"That's affirmative," Benny replied.

"Okay, no radio transmissions. Monitor any LF stations you can triangulate and cross check them with Elmer."

"Right, Captain."

"Elmer, we'll use dead reckoning. Looks like a good clear night ahead so take star shots as often as you can. Use your best guess on winds aloft to plot a course and calculate our fuel to Manila for me."

Jake turned to Herb who was nodding off to sleep and said, "You hit the sack and get some rest, then relieve Chief at the controls in four hours. I'm going back to the cabin and see how ol' Willie's getting along handling our ex-patriot guests."

The *China Clipper* lumbered along into a clear dark starlit sky enroute to the Philippine Islands.

Jake elected not to fly into the city of Manila and early that morning he gave the order to turn south for Lucena on the southern part of the main Philippine Island.

Hal had told Jake of General MacArthur's Filipino volunteers who had a base there. Jake figured that if the Japanese were to attack the Philippines, it would be at Manila. Their best chance of getting avgas would be to try to make contact with part of the U.S. Pacific Fleet.

***

Herb was flying copilot with Jake when they began their decent for Lucena Bay shortly after sunrise. As they approached one of the offshore islands about two miles out from touchdown, Herb said, "Captain, there's a squadron of PT boats off our starboard heading right for us!"

Jake leaned forward, banked the right wing slightly to see past Herb and looked out through the copilot's window.

"Those are U.S. Navy PT boats. That's what I was gambling on! Those Allison engines burn the same kind a fuel we do. Sure hope they have some to spare."

"Yeah, and I hope they don't shoot first and ask questions later. Landing check list complete," Herb said and continued to glance out the cockpit window as the PT boats approached and the Clipper settled onto the water.

"You got it, Herb. Cut all the engines as soon as we're still in the water," Jake said as he climbed out of the pilot's seat. "I'm going forward to the bow hatch. Everyone stay put until I talk to these guys."

Phil climbed in the pilot's seat as the Clipper coasted to a stop in the smooth harbor water and helped Herb complete the shutdown checklist.

Five PT boats surrounded the Clipper. The noise from their engines at fast idle was deafening and each of their turret gunners had their .50 caliber guns leveled right at the Clipper.

The lead PT boat bobbed in the water about fifteen feet away. A young slender Navy officer in a wrinkled summer khaki uniform with the pant legs cut off stood on the bow. The crewman beside him, a sailor in blue dungarees with no shirt, held an automatic weapon at rest. He had a boatswain's mate insignia tattooed on his arm and his white seaman's cap was cocked back on his head.

Jake opened the bow-hatch very slowly with one hand and raised his other hand in the air.

"Take it easy! We're Americans. I'm Captain Martin with Pan Am. I've got a planeload of passengers bound for Honolulu and we need fuel!"

The PT boat came alongside the Clipper and tied on.

"You got any documentation?" the officer asked.

Jake turned around and bumped into Benny who, of course, had not remained put as he had been told.

"This what you need, Captain?" Benny said and handed Jake the packet containing a letter signed by the Chief of Naval Operation Pacific Fleet.

Jake handed the letter across to the PT boat commander and noticed the single silver bar on his lapel.

"What's your name, Lieutenant?"

"Kennedy, sir," he replied as he read the letter that instructed any U.S. Navy or Marine forces coming in contact with the *China Clipper* to render any assistance as might be requested. A notation at the bottom of the letter read "Destroy this letter in the event of hostile engagement."

"We'll have to come aboard and check out your passengers and cargo."

"Come on aboard, Mr. Kennedy."

Jake lowered himself down out of the open hatch and bumped into Benny again.

After the boarding inspection, Kennedy explained, "You're in luck. We've got more fuel on shore than we can use. We keep our boats topped off because we never know when we might have to pull out. I have orders to set fire to the fuel dump if we have to evacuate and judging from the radio traffic we're hearing that might be sooner than later. We'll give you a tow ashore and fill'er up."

"Great, but the draft on our hull will beach us on that sandy shoreline like a stranded whale."

"No problem, Captain Martin. We'll only beach the nose and passengers who want to wade ashore can. When you're loaded, we'll pull you back off with one of our boats. They have more than enough power to do that."

The Clipper, its passengers and crew were only on the island for a few hours, but time enough to take on fresh water and for Willie and some helpers to stock-up on some island fruits. He was going to have to feed these people something for the next four days.

Chief enlisted all the help they could muster to unbolt most of the special electronic equipment and unneeded interior parts. The parts were loaded onto waiting PT boats, carried out to deep water and dumped overboard.

"So much for that stuff. No more of those questionable over-gross takeoffs! Right, Captain?"

Jake replied simply, "What stuff is that, Chief?"

***

By the following morning, the *China Clipper* had made its way to Guam. The crew found the Pan Am seaplane base abandoned when they tied up to the dock.

On the adjoining dock, a partially submerged East Indies Airways Short Empire flying boat sat on the shallow bottom. Not far away, a damaged yacht bobbed in the water alongside an old model Sikorsky seaplane that most likely had not been flyable even before its recent damage.

Chief and Herb ran to check the fuel dump and found ample fuel in the storage tanks. Chief started up one of the ground power generators and they were in luck the fuel pumps still worked. The fueling would have taken the better part of the day to load the needed 5000-gallons by hand.

The crew went to work filling the Clipper's tanks.

Jake did not allow any of the passengers except the Embassy man to deplane, as he intended to depart on a moment's notice if there was another attack on the base.

As Jake stood on the dock looking around, he caught sight of a dozen or so dark skinned natives watching them from some distant trees. He and Benny went over to talk to them. Between their broken English and Jake's Tex-Mex, he gleaned enough information out of the natives to piece together what had happened.

When Jake returned to the dock, Phil and the others were waiting to hear what he had found out. The Embassy man listened with the crew and it would be his job to apprize the passengers of what he had found out.

"As best I can make out," Jake explained to his crew, "the Japs attacked here by air about the same time as they hit Pearl. All of our planes were enroute so none of them were caught in the attack."

"My guess is, they were radioed to turn back when the attack started," Phil said.

"Probably. The people here think the Japs will be back. There are seventeen U.S. Army soldiers along with a contingency of Guam National Guardsmen holed up in town at Susanna Plaza. They plan to make a stand there if and when the Japanese land ground troops."

Nothing else was said after Jake finished talking and the crew went back to fueling the plane, checking the engine oil and preparing to depart for Wake Island.

Phil and Benny walked past with five-gallon oilcans and Jake grabbed Phil by the arm.

"Here, I'll take those to Chief. You and Benny go up to the transmitter building and destroy that Adkins navigation equipment!"

"Right, Captain," Phil said. "You're thinking the same thing I was. The Jap planes probably used the Adkins station here to home-in on the island."

"Yeah," Benny said. "I know the station's still transmitting because I picked up the signal coming in!"

"Don't set fire to it!" Jake ordered. "That might attract unwanted attention. Just smash the equipment 'til it's unusable."

Phil and Benny took off running for the radio shack.

Five anxious minutes passed and Chief approached Jake to report, "Ships fueled and ready, Captain."

"Thanks. As soon as Phil and Benny get back we'll depart," Jake replied and looked up to see them both running for the Clipper. "Okay Chief, crank-her-up."

***

By the wide-ranging Japanese attacks across the Pacific, it had become clear that the China Clipper and its crew were caught in the center of a massive preplanned invasion. Jake and his crew had greatly underestimated the Japanese imperialistic ambitions, as had the America Navy.

Airborne enroute to Wake Island, Jake addressed the crew on the flight deck, saying, "Wake may not be our best option, but right now it's our only option."

The crew discussed it for a bit and then Jake said, "We might have been better off heading for the port at New Caledonia in New Zealand, but who could have figured that the attack on Pearl was anything more than an isolated incident on the outer limits of the Jap's capability?"

On the Clipper's approach to Wake Island, a long trail of black smoke drifted for miles out over the ocean and could be seen before the island came into sight. The view of the harbor from the cockpit shocked all of the crewmen.

As they taxied to the now destroyed Pan Am base, they passed a damaged GLM flying boat washed ashore and a Boeing Clipper burned to the waterline still at the dock.

In an air attack on the island the day before yesterday, the Japanese had destroyed the operations office and the hotel. The bombed out maintenance hangar was still smoldering from an oil fire.

The *China Clipper* pulled into the passenger dock and two men in civilian clothes came out to meet them and helped secure the Clipper.

Jake exited the ship first and recognized the men as Pan Am station-keepers who worked at the seaplane base. The older man's name was Oscar and his younger helper was Kenny, but Jake did not recall their last names.

"Greetings, Captain Martin," Oscar said. "Good to see you back. We heard you lost an engine in Rangoon."

"Yes, but it looks to me like you got worse problems here. Why no uniforms?"

"We didn't want to be mistaken for military combatants in the event the Jap forces landed on the island, so we changed out them," Kenny explained. "The Japs have been bombing us almost every day now since they hit Pearl."

"What happened to all our contract people?"

"Those that are still here are down at the south end of the island with the Marine detachment helping build fortifications," Oscar said. "It's a wonder those trigger happy coastal artillerymen didn't shoot at you coming in."

"That's the reason we came in low and from the north. Didn't know what to expect. Marines? When did we get Marines on Wake Island?"

"They arrived a couple months ago. Shortly after you came through the last time. The ship that brought the Marines took the civilians, mostly women and children, back with them."

"In that case, we need to get fueled and get going. We won't even deplane the passengers."

"There's still fuel in one of the fuel dump storage tanks, but the pumps were damaged in the attack. There's no power either."

"You got a hand crank pump around here?"

"Yes sir, and there should still be fuel in the that flying boat," Kenny said pointing to the beached Clipper, "but we'll have to wade out there to drain the fuel."

With that Jake turned to the Chief and said, "Tell that Embassy fellow to deplane the passengers. Looks Like we're going to be here for a while. If the Jap planes come back, our Clipper will be a prime target. Everyone will be safer onshore."

"Captain, if we're going to be transferring fuel by hand, I'm going to grab every able-bodied man and woman I can find to give us a hand."

"Right Chief, that's what I was fixing to suggest. Elmer, you get binoculars and go stand watch out on the far end of the dock. Holler up if you hear or spot any planes."

"You mean like those two over there!" Elmer said pointing offshore.

Jake turned quickly to see two radial engine fighters going south about twenty miles off the coast.

"Not to worry," Oscar said, "those are Marine Wildcats. That's ol' Captain Elrod with VF-211. He and the few planes he's got left, go out on patrol regularly looking for the Jap fleet."

The crew with the help of the able-bodied passengers and the two station-keepers worked to siphon the fuel out of the storage tanks. Two dozen of the passengers volunteered to set up a bucket brigade in the water to hand-off the fuel drained from the tanks of the swamped flying boat.

Can by can, hour by hour the fuel was carried to the *China Clipper* and her tanks were slowly filled.

Inland a ways from the shore, several of the women passengers helped Willie to prepare some food over an open fire. This would be their first hot meal since the night they flew out of Rangoon. The less able-bodied passengers, children and mothers with babes rested along the shore content to just not be moving for a while.

Along about noon, a jeep with a driver, two armed guards and a Marine Corps major drove up. The major, a wiry little guy with what was left of his hair short cropped, stepped out of the jeep and asked, "Who's in charge here?"

Benny pointed to Jake. "Him, sir."

"I'm James Devereux, the commanding officer of the Marine detachment. My fighter patrol reported seeing you docked here this morning."

Jake returned the introduction and explained their situation, "Yes, sir, we saw them go over. As soon as we're fueled, we'll be departing for Midway and Pearl."

"Good idea. The Navy is sending a task force out here to defend Wake. Only question is, can we hold out 'til they get here? I've been told they're starting to call us the 'Alamo of the Pacific' back at Pearl."

One of the armed Marine guards, a sergeant, commented to Benny, "Yeah, and we all know what happened to the Alamo, don't we?"

"What's that you say, sergeant?" the major asked.

"Nothing important, sir," the sergeant replied.

"We're full up on passengers, but is there anything else we can do for you?" Jake asked.

"Yes, there is," and the driver handed the major a large overstuffed envelope. "These are letters home from the men. I'd be much obliged if you'd carry them with you."

"It'd be an honor, Major," Jake said accepting the package.

The major saluted with the handle of the swagger stick he carried. He and the armed guards climbed back in the jeep and drove off, disappearing over a nearby sandy hill.

As they worked, Oscar and Kenny gave Jake and his crew a detailed description of the attack.

"The *Philippine Clipper* got airborne during a lull in the attack," Oscar said. "All our employees, except for us and the seven that were killed, flew out onboard her."

"They almost didn't get off," Kenny went on to explain. "The Clipper settled back onto the water twice and I didn't think they were going to make it. I swear, that ol' Clipper must have had a hundred bullet holes in it and she still got airborne!"

"My young friend and I elected to stay here and I'm glad we did. I wonder if they made it to Hawaii?" and the old man added wistfully, "I really wonder?"

"And the seven that were killed, where are they?" Jake asked.

"We buried them on that hill," Kenny pointed to a small sandy hill with seven small wooden crosses a hundred yards away. "I'm afraid they didn't have much of a decent burial. We didn't know what to say over them."

Jake thought of Red, who had been flying this route.

"By any chance, was there a pilot by the name of Henderson here when the attack occurred?" Jake asked Oscar.

"Ol' Red? Sure, he got out on the *Philippine Clipper* with the others, but a shell hit close to him when he ran for the ship. I saw it from a distance and I think he was hit. I don't know how bad he was injured. Two of the other crewmen helped him onboard."

Phil approached Jake and said, "Captain, I think you better come and see this."

Phil took Jake to where he and Chief had found two badly burned bodies, which the station-keepers had overlooked. There were enough of their Pan Am uniforms left to identify them as employees.

"We found them when we moved this large pile of debris looking for more cases of oil," Phil explained. "It's no wonder the station-keepers didn't find them."

Oscar shook his head sadly. "We thought those two made it out on the *Philippine Clipper* with the rest!"

Jake suggested that they be wrapped in some nearby canvas tarps and asked for volunteers to carry them to the top of the hill where the other seven were buried.

"Herb, you get a couple of the younger men passengers to help you and go dig two more graves."

Jake remembered Kenny saying the other victims had not had much said over them when they were buried. He went to get a red-leatherette Gideon Bible out of his flight case. The pocket size Bible only contained Psalms and the New Testament. Jake did not know why he carried the small Bible, he never read it, but always carried it with him.

Late that afternoon, Jake went with his crew and a few of the passengers to the top of the hill where Herb and the men helping him had just finished closing the two new graves. A small wooden cross was placed on each of the freshly filled graves. A group of about twenty gathered around and the men removed their caps.

Jake took the Bible from his pocket. He opened the pages to a Psalm and began to read from exactly where his eyes first fell. He read, maybe not too accurately as he was tired and his eyesight blurred, but what he read seemed to fit the occasion.

"The earth is the Lord's and all that is therein. For, He hath founded it upon the sea and the land. Whoever shall ascend into that which is the Lord's, dwells in a holy place and shall receive His blessing and salvation."

Chief and several others crossed themselves.

Herb tossed two small stones on each grave and prayed, "God grant these we have buried here, peace."

Jake returned the Bible to his pocket and placed his dirty and tattered white uniform cap back on his head.

"You passengers get on back and get boarded. Tell everyone we'll be departing momentarily."

At the edge of the dock, Jake paused and called his crew together.

"The rest of this flight is going to be pretty much of a crap shoot. Nothing except luck and the grace of God will get us past the Japanese patrol aircraft or keep us from accidentally running across part of their fleet. You're all aware we can't make it from Wake to Hawaii without refueling, so we have no choice except to try for Midway."

He paused and waited. None of the crew said anything.

"Okay then, let's get going."

The *China Clipper* lifted off in the early evening heading eastward into a dark blue cloud-covered sky. Wake Island faded on the horizon behind them and the setting sun turned from a deep magenta to a dark red.

From his crew station on the flight deck, Benny quoted an old seafarer's saying, "Red sky in the morning, sailor's warning. Red sky at night, sailor's delight."

***

By sunrise the following morning, they were about seventy miles out from the Island of Midway. Phil had been flying the last four hours. He spotted the fighters first and pointed to them.

Herb who was flying copilot yelled out, "Fighters at ten o'clock high and coming in fast."

Jake was seated behind him in the flight engineers seat and had been nodding off to sleep. He came quickly awake and strained to look up through the windshield.

"They're ours! Navy F4Fs, I believe."

"I hope they recognize our markings!" Herb said.

Both fighters passed by with a closing rate on the Clipper in excess of five hundred miles an hour.

Herb turned his head as the two Navy fighters passed by the right side of the Clipper.

"Wow, that was close! At least they didn't open fire."

"Hold your course and altitude," Jake told Phil, "they'll be back."

Within a couple of minutes, one dark blue Navy Wildcat appeared off of the left wing and the other came up under the right wing of the Clipper. The two fighters were so close Jake could see the pilot's faces.

"Gentlemen, I think we have an escort to Midway," Jake said smiling widely.

The *China Clipper* set down at Midway and much to Jake and his crew's surprise, they found the island's Marine Corps defenders still holding Midway. The fuel dump at Pan Am was empty, but plenty of avgas was available at the port end of the island and a Navy PBY came alongside the Clipper to help with the fueling.

The Marine Corps officer in charge greeted Jake and his crew on arrival and suggested, "You best get going for Honolulu ASAP. We could be jumped at anytime."

"So you do know when the Japs are coming," Jake asked.

"Not exactly sure. Our patrol planes have been out searching night and day for their fleet. They must be out of our range, but we'll find the bastards! That is, if they don't find us first."

A gunny sergeant standing near by, smiled and said, "Here kitty-kitty," and everyone laughed.

Benny gave the Marine communications tech the info Hal had provided.

"Donald Duck is the code name the intelligence officer told us to use. He said to identify our aircraft with that call sign on approach to Pearl."

"I'll advise Pacific Fleet in Hawaii in a coded message that the *China Clipper* will be inbound to Honolulu sometime tomorrow," the Marine tech told Benny.

With the fueling completed, the Clipper was airborne for Hawaii in less than an hour.

***

The evening of their forth day out of Rangoon, the westerly most island of the Hawaiian chain appeared in the distance.

Benny made contact with the Navy base at Pearl Harbor.

"This is Donald Duck, one-hundred miles north-northwest of Honolulu requesting landing permission at Pearl Harbor. Seventy-two souls onboard."

"Welcome to Honolulu, Donald Duck," came the reply over the radio. "We've been expecting you. Proceed directly to Pearl Harbor. Winds are westerly and calm. Cleared for the approach, advise when you have the harbor in sight."

The Clipper crew had now gained back the day they lost crossing the international dateline last September. The date was Thursday, December 11th. With Jake at the controls, the *China Clipper* approached Ford Island and prepared to set down just beyond Battleship Row.

Flying down the channel into the harbor, the Clipper passed over the *USS Nevada* run aground in shallow water.

Before being torpedoed, the Nevada backed clear of her berth and began to steam out of the channel. The slow moving battleship became a target of opportunity for the Jap dive-bombers. She was hit repeatedly, opening up her forecastle deck and starting a fire in the superstructure. In serious trouble, the Nevada twisted around until facing back up the harbor. With the help of tugs, the Nevada was backed across the harbor and grounded stern first to keep her from blocking the channel. Many of the ship's crew lost their lives in a valiant attempt to put to sea.

Jake made a wide banking turn out over the dry-dock area. Benny leaned against the window taking photos with his 35mm German Leica camera.

Flying over the floating dry-dock, the destroyer USS Shaw with its bow blown off, sat at an angle in the water.

The torpedoed cruiser USS Helena was already under repair in the Number Two dry-dock. The Number One dry-dock held the relatively undamaged battleship USS Pennsylvania. The wrecked destroyer USS Cassin and the capsized destroyer USS Downes were outside the dock.

A large black oil slick floated on the water around the ships and along the shoreline.

The Clipper's descent flight path crossed over Ford Island and directly down Battleship Row on the south side of the island. The sunken *USS California* rested stern up with a cluster of small vessels all around working on her.

The flagship of the battle force, the California took torpedo hits fore and aft in the early minutes of the raid. In spite of the damage she prepared to get underway. In the second attack, the California took another hit from a bomb. The order to abandoned ship was given. By the time the crew returned onboard, it became impossible to control her flooding and she slowly settled to the bottom of the harbor, coming fully to rest only yesterday, December 10th.

Next in the row of battleships were the only slightly damaged USS Maryland and the capsized USS Oklahoma.

The Maryland had been moored inboard of the Oklahoma and protected from torpedoes, but nine torpedoes struck the Oklahoma, an older ship with much less protection against underwater damage. Her hull's port side was opened at the forward gun turret all the way back to the third turret, a distance of 250 feet. She had listed quickly and the port bilge struck the harbor bottom as she rolled on her side, coming to rest only twenty minutes after first being hit.

The starboard propeller of the USS Oklahoma rose above the water line and a large work barge continued to support the rescue efforts alongside. Near the end of Battleship Row was the sunken USS Arizona. She had sustained the worse damage of any of the battleships.

The Arizona's hull had been shattered by a freak direct bomb hit into the ship's magazine forward of the two gun turrets setting off a horrendous secondary explosion.

The China Clipper settled gently onto the calm water of Pearl Harbor and taxied to the Navy pier. Several seamen were waiting to tie the Clipper up at the dock. As Jake stepped onto the dock, the same Navy lieutenant who had sent Hal and Tony off with Jake greeted him.

"Welcome back, Captain Martin. I hope you took good care of our experimental equipment. We're anxious to get our hands back on it."

Jake stretched long and hard.

"I guess if you call securely stored at the bottom of Lucena Bay taken care of, I would say that your equipment is well taken care of."

The lieutenant was visibly upset.

"What do you mean bottom of a bay? We needed that equipment back."

"There's your equipment, lieutenant!" Jake said pointing to the women and children coming off the Clipper.

An ONI officer arrived with some Navy supply personnel who came to look over the Clipper. He approached Jake.

"Captain Martin, you might be interested in a message we received from Smith and Romano yesterday."

"Oh, you mean Hal and Tony?"

"Yes sir, they said to tell Donald Duck that the Silver Monkey suffered a direct hit from a Jap bomb and that they send their regrets. I'm not sure exactly what that means. Some kind of code, I suppose."

Jake laughed long and hard. He was so tired and happy they had made it back to Hawaii, he was almost giddy.

"No, just a private joke. It's their way of letting me know they're okay and that everything is running in greased grooves or about normal back in Rangoon."

Then the officer smiled politely. "Sir, after you've had a chance to rest up, Admiral Halsey would like to meet with you for a personal debriefing. For now, your car is here." The officer motioned towards the Navy gray four-door Ford sedan waiting at the end of the dock. "I believe you radioed ahead requesting transportation to the Naval hospital."

***

When Jake arrived at the base hospital, he inquired at the nurse's desk about Red's condition, as he had feared the worst. He was pleased to find out the doctors expected Red to fully recover and be returned to his flying duties.

Jake burst into Red's room exclaiming, "Boy! If this isn't a sorry way to finagle some time off."

Until this morning, when one of Red's crew brought him the news that Jake was inbound, he had not known whether Jake was alive or dead. Red's face broke into a wide smile.

"Yeah, got so much lead in my ass from that Jap shell, I'd a sunk if I'd a fell in the water."

"How'd you let this happen to you?"

"Don't know how, but I sure know why," Red replied with a straight face. "I didn't have my lucky tie on!"

Jake wondered what Red was talking about for a moment and then he remembered the tie and both men laughed.

"You still got that darn thing?"

"No, lost it. Left the old tie in a locker somewhere. Help me out of this bed. I can't take laying here anymore."

Jake helped Red get out of bed and on with a hospital-issue light blue terry-cloth robe. He walked Red over to a chair and pulled up another chair for Red to prop one leg on.

The two long-time friends visited for most of the afternoon. Jake told Red about losing the engine going into Rangoon and having a chance to fly with Chennault's Tigers. Jake did not mention Suzette to Red, as he had not fully dealt with the loss himself.

Red told Jake about the attack on Wake Island, how they barely got off in the *Philippine Clipper* and asked, "What can you tell me about the rest of our Wake Island folks that didn't make it out with us?"

"Oscar, Kenny and the contract workers are still there with the Marines. The other Clipper crew was hit before they cranked the first engine. We found two more bodies in the hanger wreckage and buried them on the hill with the others. There were nine crosses in all when we departed."

"That's about what we all thought," Red said sadly.

"What do you know about the other Clippers?"

"The Hong Kong Clipper came under attack in port about the same time the Japs hit Pearl. Word is that the ship was docked at Kowloon, fueled and ready to depart for Manila when the Clipper was strafed. A tracer round hit the fuel tank and she burned to the waterline."

"Dang it, anyway! Good ship, too. I've flown her several times. Did the crew get out?"

"I think so. Oh, and I heard that Captain Ford was enroute from New Caledonia to Auckland in the *California Clipper*. When they got word of the attack, he headed west. The last anyone heard from them, they radioed they were enroute to India."

"Think they headed home the other way around?"

Red chuckled and mused, "Yep! Can you imagine LaGuardia tower's surprise when they get a call from a Pacific based Clipper requesting an approach clearance?"

"Considered the idea for a while myself back in Rangoon. Hope they make it."

The two old friends sat quietly for a while, both recalling the recent events and then Red spoke up.

"The *Philippine Clipper* that we came back in has already been assigned a U.S. Navy Bureau of Ships Number. I'll bet your Clipper... What is it now? Oh yeah, the *China Clipper* or do you prefer to call it the Donald Duck," Red grinned. "Anyway, I'll bet she's already been commandeered by the Navy!"

"You know it's the old *Pacific Clipper*! I just had the name painted over," Jake retorted with a smile, "but I'll bet you're right, there were some Navy supply officers at the dock eyeing her like a couple of hungry vultures."

"Yes-sir-ree-bob, they'll have her in the repair shop being modified into a cargo flying boat and painted Navy blue before you can say Jack Robinson."

"Who's going to fly all these boats, anyway?"

"So far, two hundred Pan Am pilots and crewmen have volunteered to work on contract for the Navy. I guess we will be flying everything from troops to supplies."

"What's this 'we' stuff? Did you sign up, too?"

"Yeah, I'm staying. I'm gonna see this thing through to the end. No damn Jap Navy fleet is going to take my flying job away from me."

Jake knew it was more than Red's job he was talking about. He knew Red had his own personal score to settle with the Japs.

"Well, I'm not. I'm going home. I checked with the Pan Am stationmaster on the way over here and he's already assigned me to the Monday flight back to San Francisco. I guess there are so many of you guys staying here they're short pilots on the return flights to the States."

Jake looked up as a hospital orderly entered the room.

The orderly had a clipboard in his hand and addressed Jake, "I understand you're the one inquiring about a sailor by the name of Zechariah Washington?"

Jake stood and faced the orderly.

"Yes, do you have word as to where he might be? Was he injured or transferred off the *USS Oklahoma*?"

"Stewards Mate Washington was not transferred, sir. Unfortunately, the news is not good. He died with a large number of his fellow seaman still onboard the Oklahoma when she capsized."

"Whoa!" Jake said and sat back down in the chair.

"I'm sorry, sir," the orderly said.

Jake thanked the orderly who left the room as a Navy nurse entered.

"Captain Henderson, you've been up a little too long. You need to rest now."

Jake and the nurse helped Red back to his bed.

"Well, at least some of us made it out of this mess alive," Jake took Red's hand and held onto it. "I'll come by to see you again before I fly back to the states. You rest and get healed up so you can get back to flying."

"I plan on doing just that, Jake. You'll tell Margo I'm okay and not to worry about me, won't you?"

"Sure, I'll tell her, but it won't do any good."

"Oh, by the way, when I left Treasure Island, that ol' yellow Continental of yours was still parked right where you left it. The wind pulled the tarp loose, so I tied it down a little better."

Dealing with the difficulty of his friend in pain, Jake tried to remain cheerful as he prepared to leave.

"Thanks pal," Jake said forcing a smile. "As usual, always looking out for me. Bet the battery's gone dead on the ol' beast by now."

Jake paused at the door and looked back.

"You know they don't give out those Purple Heart medals unless you're wearing the right uniform."

"That's okay. I'll remember to duck next time."

***

On Friday morning, a Navy driver arrived at the base quarters where Jake had spent the night. The driver was to take him to Admiral Halsey's office. Jake had sent his only uniform to be cleaned and was wearing a Hawaiian shirt with borrowed Navy blue dungarees.

On the way, Jake asked the driver, "Why do they call Admiral Halsey by the nickname Bull?"

"Don't know," the driver replied. "Close to Bill for William, I guess. Name suits him though, but I wouldn't call him that to his face."

At the Admiral's office, a yeoman asked Jake to have a seat and wait. A meeting of Navy and Marine brass was just breaking up. They filed past Jake and nodded politely on their way out. The Admiral came out behind them.

"I appreciate you coming, Martin. Let's walk," Halsey said and motioned to a side door leading outside.

The two men walked slowly across a green grass covered field that bordered the harbor across the bay from Ford Island. Battleship Row, with hundreds of men and equipment repairing the damage ships loomed in the distance.

"How bad do you think this attack is going to hurt us?" Jake asked Halsey.

"Fortunately, the Japanese Navy had as their main objective damaging our fleet. Turns out this may have been a major strategic blunder on their part."

A little surprised at Halsey's answer, Jake paused and looked directly at the Admiral.

"I'm not sure why you'd say fortunately, sir?"

Halsey's expression brightened as he explained, "They dealt us a devastating blow to our immediate readiness, but their limited resources for conducting a long distance attack were limited at best. Pearl Harbor's industrial and logistical capabilities are essentially intact. It'll take awhile to get all our ships repaired and back up to fighting strength, but this is only round one in a ten round fight."

"Stepped on the tiger's tail, huh, Admiral?"

Without cracking a smile, Halsey replied, "No, more like kicked the tiger in the balls. But they woke him up from his nap and now they've made him mad!"

Jake laughed and then asked, "Admiral, exactly what did you want to talk to me about?"

"Mostly, I'd like you to give me some kind of feel for what you saw in Burma and what you think we might be up against fighting the Japs."

Jake told Halsey about his experience with the Flying Tigers and on the Burma Road. He told him some of the experiences related to him by the British soldiers and airmen fighting the Japanese.

"So you think they've spread themselves too thin. Is that what you're saying, Jake?

"Yes sir. Back in Texas we'd probably say they bit off more-n they can chew."

"I agree. You know, I'm still amazed that you and your crew managed to slip past the Jap fleet and never even ran into so much as one of their patrol planes."

"Plain dumb luck I suppose! It's a big ocean out there. Say Admiral, I've been wondering, I noticed you're wearing gold Navy aviator wings. Did you go through flight training at Pensacola to be a Navy pilot? I'm only asking because I'm thinking about enlisting as a fighter pilot when I get back to the States."

"Funny you should ask about that, Jake. No, I never went to flight school. I started flying myself after the general staff assigned me a plane and I ended up logging more hours than some of my pilots. One day, some of the guys got together and gave me the gold wings and a yeoman entered it in my service record. You know, we got a bunch of old Navy chief APs who earned their wings the same way."

"Bet some of those guys date back to the dirigibles."

"Yes, they do. Okay, my turn to ask something off the record. You've done a lot of over water flying. What's your opinion on the Amelia Earhart disappearance?"

"I've thought on it a few times and basically it's easier to determine your longitude than it is to get a good fix on your latitude. You're a pilot, you know how we navigate over water when we're out of the range of a radio nav-aid. The way most pilots find one of these little specks of an island in this big pond is to come in north or south of it by determining the longitude, then turn toward the island. I believe was nothing more than a wind miscalculation. Earhart and her navigator simply turned north instead of south and flew away from their intended destination. By the time they realized their error, they didn't have enough fuel left to backtrack."

Halsey paused, removed his tan cap with gold braid on the bill and wiped his forehead with his handkerchief.

"Your thinking is the same as mine, but there has been a lot of speculation about the possibility that she and her navigator were shot down by a Japanese patrol aircraft. Maybe she came across their fleet by chance and the Japs didn't want their position and strength known?"

The two men continued to exchange thoughts as they returned to the Admiral's office and Halsey thanked Jake for coming.

From there, Jake went to locate some of Zack's shipmates. One of the sailors from the Oklahoma, who served with Zack, had managed to recover some photos and a few of Zack's personal effects. He gave them to Jake to take to Zack's folks.

That evening, Jake went to visit Red in the hospital one more time before leaving for the States in the morning.

***

Phil, Herb and Chief had told Jake they would be remaining in Hawaii. Like Red, they intended to sign up to fly the Clippers for Pan Am under contract to the Navy.

On Monday morning, Jake arrived early at the Aloha Tower in downtown where the *Honolulu Clipper* would depart.

Jake was pleasantly surprised when he found out that Benny, Elmer and Willie were assigned to the same flight.

The passengers were mostly dependent women and children returning to the States. Their husbands and fathers would man the ships and aircraft that would soon put to sea to meet the oncoming Japanese threat.

Fourteen hours later, Jake, along with three of his original crewmembers, arrived at Treasure Island where they deplaned their passengers and secured the Clipper.

Jake went to the operations office to see Margo. He knew she would be anxious to hear first-hand about Red and he assured her that Red was going to be fine.

Next, Jake went to visit with some of the people he had worked with the past couple of years at the seaplane base. Several of the station employees inquired about Red and the other crewmen. Jake answered all he could.

As Jake was leaving, the head mechanic used the opportunity to kid Jake and hollered across the hangar, "*Honolulu Clipper*? That's not the one you left here with. Where'd you lose our ol' *China Clipper*, Captain?"

Jake smiled and replied, "The Navy didn't like your lousy paint job. They're fixing to repaint that Clipper Navy blue and change up her décor a little."

Jake went to his old office to use the telephone.

"Get me the Pan Am home office in New York, person to person to Juan Trippe," Jake told the Bell Telephone long distance operator and he gave her the number.

Jake waited as the Pan Am office receptionist accepted the call and came on the line.

"Mr. Trippe is in a meeting now. Can I take a message?"

"I don't care what he's doing. Tell him Jake Martin is on the phone and I just flew halfway around the world to get to a telephone that works. I want to talk to him and I want to talk to him now!"

SARAH

In a few minutes, Trippe came on the line. "Jake ol' fellow, we gave you up for dead at least a couple of times. Good to hear your voice."

"Thanks. I guess none of those Japs drew my number. Listen, I know the past week's been hell on everybody including you, so I'll make this as short as possible. I'm officially tendering my resignation as of now."

"Jake, we're shorthanded now with all the pilots going to the Pacific to fly cargo and others are leaving to join the service. I sure need you to reconsider."

"I know you do, but you've got a dozen captains who can fill my shoes and might even do a better job. Been fun working for you, but during the last couple months, I've come to realized life is too short and I need to set some things right."

Trippe understood by the tone of Jake's voice that Jake had no intention of changing his mind.

"I heard about Suzette and I want you to know I feel real bad for you, Jake."

"Juan! I swear I don't know where you get your information. Is there anything that goes on that you don't know about?"

"I'll level with you. I think this Pacific war is the beginning of the end of the flying boats. These new long-range, land-based transports are going to take over trans-ocean flights. I'm going to sell the Navy every Clipper they will buy to use in this war. Then Pan Am will be in a position to buy all new aircraft when this thing is over."

"It's an ill-wind that doesn't blow somebody some good. What would we do without you, Juan?"

315

"You remember ol' Hap Arnold, don't you? He's one of the new top dog generals now and they're going to put him in charge of the Army Air Corps. He called me the other day and offered me a commission as a brigadier general in the Air Corps. What do you think of that?"

"I think that's great, Juan, but knowing you I suspect you told him where to stick it. You're more used to giving orders than you are taking them."

Trippe chuckled, "Right as always, my friend. Best of luck to you and let me hear from you once in awhile."

Jake heard a dial tone and looked at the telephone receiver in his hand. As usual, Trippe hung up before Jake could say goodbye.

Jake walked out to the parking lot behind the seaplane base hangar to his parked Continental Convertible. He shook the layer of soot off the tarp, rolled the weathered tarp up and placed it in the trunk.

Jake questioned if the battery was up enough to start the car as he climbed in behind the wheel, unlocked the steering column and turned the ignition switch on. He pulled the choke full out, pumped the accelerator a couple of times and pushed the starter button. The V-12 turned over slowly and fired right off.

"Good girl!" Jake said aloud and patted the dashboard. "Small wonders will never cease."

Jake drove to his apartment in Oakland where he soon discovered the landlady had rented his apartment to another tenant and stored his belongings in the garage.

"Someone told me they thought you had been killed in the attack on Pearl Harbor," the landlady explained.

"Now I know how Samuel Clemens must have felt," Jake said as he walked with the landlady to the garage where he loaded some personal belongings into the Continental.

The landlady stood with her arms folded watching.

"Mr. Martin, you know I'm really sorry about the mistake, thinking you were dead and renting the apartment."

"It's not a problem, ma'am. No need to worry about it. Can I use your phone to make a local call?" Jake asked as he finished loading the things he wanted.

From the landlady's apartment telephone, Jake called Benny at home. "Benny, this is Jake. I know you're glad to be home with your family and I hate to bother you, but there is a bunch of my junk stored in a garage out here at my old apartment. When you get time, come over here and take anything you can use. Give the rest to whoever."

Jake listened to Benny for a moment then said, "Yeah, I know there's some nice stuff here, but I won't be back this way anytime soon. And yes, you're welcome. Listen Benny, take care of yourself."

Jake hung up the telephone. He turned to the landlady and asked, "Do I owe you any back rent?"

"No, actually I owe you. You were paid ahead when you left and again, I'm sorry about the misunderstanding."

"Think nothing of it, ma'am, an honest mistake. Let's call the rent even for you storing my stuff. My friend will be by in a few days to pick up what's left."

***

Jake pointed the Continental south down the Pacific Coast Highway for Los Angeles. At San Luis Obispo, he stopped at a small diner to use the pay phone to call Dan and Ida. He asked if it would be okay to spend the night before returning to Texas.

Jake's yellow Convertible pulled up in front of Dan's house late that evening. Ida had waited dinner and the three visited until after midnight. Dan and Ida were anxious to hear first-hand about what Jake had seen at Pearl Harbor as it had been in the news so much. This was fine with Jake because the last thing he wanted to talk about was Rangoon.

"What are your plans for the future?" Dan asked. "You know we could use your help out here. Orders are coming in faster than we can meet the demand. In fact, we're going to have to start hiring women in the shop."

"I've got to go home for awhile. I need to see my kids and I need some time to think things over."

"Well, when you're ready, you come out here and run Martin Company and we'll go back to Texas and ranch."

"Big Jake would never let you off the hook that easy, Dan, you know that. There is no way we could replace you. You are Martin Company, California."

"I'll take that as a compliment, but one of these days I'm going to retire and raise cows and grandkids, maybe not this year though. Say, I made a trip to Hughes Tool in Houston and flew there in one of those new Boeing 307s Pan Am has put in service. There're bigger than a Douglas DC-3 and have a pressurized cabin. You flown one yet?"

"No, but I've seen them. They can fly well above ten thousand feet and have a high cruise speed."

"Ida, how about we make a pot of coffee?"

Dan slapped his leg and stood up from the overstuffed chair where he had been sitting and went to the kitchen with Ida.

Dan's comments about the new Stratoliners gave Jake an idea.

"Can I use the telephone?" Jake asked.

"There's a phone on the hallway table. Help yourself, Jake," Ida hollered back from the kitchen.

Jake called a couple of the local Pan Am master pilots he knew who were currently flying regular runs out of L.A. in the new, land-based Boeing 307 Stratoliner.

Sure enough, one of the pilots Jake called was on a flight that would refuel in Dallas tomorrow and told Jake he was welcome to come along and ride the jump seat. Jake went into the kitchen to tell Dan and Ida his plans.

"We sure would've liked you to stay a little longer, but I understand you need to get on home," Ida said.

"You can leave that ol' yeller machine of yours in my garage," Dan said. "It'll be fine there. I'll have one of the company drivers take you over to the passenger terminal at Mines Field in the morning."

The three sat around the kitchen table drinking coffee and visited for a couple more hours before calling it a night. Jake would head home to Texas tomorrow.

***

The following evening, Jake arrived in the Pan Am Stratoliner at the Dallas Love Field terminal on Lemmon Avenue. The flight was scheduled on to Miami as soon as the plane was refueled. He thanked the two pilots he hitched the ride with and got off.

As Jake exited the airliner, he felt a slight twinge of melancholy as he stepped off the airstair and looked up at the Pan Am logo on the nose of the Stratoliner. The winged globe Pan Am insignia had represented a major portion of his life these last seven years.

Jake turned when he heard a familiar voice to see Flo and Big Jake waiting by the gate at the end of the chain link fence outside the old tan brick terminal building.

Flo waved excitedly.

Dan had called and told them Jake was on his way home and they had driven down earlier that day from the ranch.

Big Jake greeted his son and shook his hand.

"You know your mom. She loves to shop at Neiman-Marcus when she can talk someone into driving her down to Dallas, so we've been here most of the day."

Jake gave his mom a big hug.

"The kids are at home with Violet," Flo said. "They're anxious to see you, so I told them they could wait up for you tonight."

***

With Jake's return to the ranch old memories, both good and bad, came crashing back on him as though they had only happened yesterday. The last seven years seemed a lifetime ago and he began to unwind, forgetting about Asia and Suzette sometimes for an hour or so at a time.

After Jake had been home a few days, he decided after supper one evening to tell his mom and dad about Suzette and what had happened in Rangoon.

His folks listened quietly as he told them of meeting her and about the day he left her alone.

"I blame myself for what happened to her,"

"She sounds like a very lovely young girl. Were you in love with her, Jacob?"

"More than I could have imagined ever caring about anyone. And yes, Mom, I would have married her and brought her home to meet you."

"I'm sorry things happened the way they did for you, Son. Sometimes life doesn't always work out the way we think they should. Sometimes God has other plans for us."

Since Jake seemed to want to talk, Flo and Big Jake took turns asking him about his experiences in the Pacific. Jake answered their questions, but decided not to tell them about flying in combat against the Japanese. To the contrary, he always played down any danger he might have been exposed to so as not to cause his mom extra worry.

From the time Jake came home, Lora seldom left his side. She rose early every morning and ran to Jake's room to see if he was still there.

"I wanted to make sure you hadn't left me again, Daddy," she would say when Jake would wake up and see her standing beside his bed looking at him.

Michael took longer to warm up to his dad than Lora, but eventually Michael started to come around.

***

On the Sunday after Jake had been home for over a week, he finally got up enough courage to go see Mr. and Mrs. Washington. He knew they would be home, as they did not work on the Sabbath.

"I'm going to run over to the Washington place and pay Zack's folks a visit," Jake told his mom.

Lora heard him and came running.

"I want to go too, Daddy. Molly has a new baby boy and I want to see him."

Jake went to get the photos and personal effects he had been given in Hawaii to deliver to Zack's family. Michael did not want to go. Jake, Lora and the cow dog puppy she named Panda piled into one of the ranch trucks and off they went.

Jake stayed for several hours at the Washington's visiting with Zack's parents. He told them everything he could think of about the attack on Pearl Harbor, what he saw of the sunken battleships and some of the things Zack's shipmates had told him.

Mrs. Washington said to Jake, "Even though you and Zack went your separate ways, you grew up together. You two seemed more like brothers than friends. Nothing will ever take that away from us."

Mr. Washington added, "Amen," and Jake repeated the Amen.

***

Jake had been wearing his old Pan Am uniform shirt and slacks for the past couple of weeks. He lived in a uniform for so many years he had grown comfortable in them, but for better or worse, he would now leave that part of his life behind. He went to Sittler's General Store and bought some khaki pants and a couple of plaid shirts.

The next morning, he put on his new clothes along with a pair of old cowboy boots he found stored in the upstairs closet. He discarded the uniform, but kept his old cracked-leather flight jacket. After all the wear and tear it had been through, the jacket was too comfortable to get rid of. Besides, the ol' jacket was kind of a keepsake.

More than once, Jake started to go over to the old summer ranch house where he and Elizabeth lived when they were first married, but he did not want to deal with the memories and so he continued to procrastinate, attending to other matters instead.

Flo had mentioned the old summer ranch house several times since Jake had been home, but he avoided discussing the matter until his mom brought it up one morning at breakfast.

"Your dad and I considered renting the place. Hank, Sarah's husband, asked about leasing the house on a couple of occasions, but we didn't know what you might want to do with it, so it has just sat there. The place is starting to get a little rundown now, I'm afraid."

Flo had not spoken her mind directly, but Jake clearly understood she and Big Jake continued to hold out hope he might one day remarry and return to the ranch.

The holidays came and went. Jake renewed his relationships with his parents and his two children. He spent his new found leisure time playing with Michael and Lora. The two stayed nearby when he was tinkering with things like trying to get an old Fordson tractor running. Jake kept busy mostly to shut out the recent past.

Like most Americans in 1942, he and his folks listened to the radio every evening to get any news of the war.

To have something to drive around, Jake adopted an old dark green International-Harvester pickup truck that had been on the ranch for years and had probably not been washed since being put into service.

He started the cleanup job by turning the garden hose on the truck, inside and out. Lora and Michael looked on as he saddle-soaped the seats, replaced the spark plugs, changed the oil and tuned up the carburetor.

Cleaning up the old truck only further exposed where a bull had charged the truck a couple of times and the rusty scratches in the paint from the mesquite thorns the old truck had been driven through.

When Jake finished with the truck, he stepped back to admire his work and said to Michael and Lora, "See there, she's good as new,"

"Well, not quite new," Lora said.

"Beauty is in the eye of the beholder, dear daughter."

"What's that mean, Daddy?"

"It's kind of hard to explain, but one of these days it'll make sense to you, I imagine."

Jake concluded he had reached an all time low when he took up smoking roll-your-owns. Travis had loaned him a pack of Bull-Durham when he and some of the wranglers were out tracking down stray calves.

"Maybe cigarettes aren't all that habit forming when you have to roll them in a Texas wind before you can smoke'em," Jake commented to Travis.

Jake often drove the ol' green IH pickup truck to town to sit with the old timers at the café and drink coffee. Sometimes in the afternoons, he went over to the bank and spent a few hours at Big Jake's office familiarizing himself with the Martin Company's business enterprises.

He also drove over to the Gainesville plant to renew some of his old friendships. Lora, Michael and the cow dog tagged along with Jake most everywhere he went. Things seemed once again to be running reasonably smooth, but there was an empty place in Jake's heart, a place Suzette had once so abundantly filled.

***

Early on a spring-like March morning, Jake was going into Sittler's General Store when he bumped into a woman nearly knocking her down. Jake grabbed hold of the lady to keep her from falling.

"I'm so sorry, ma'am!"

Looking into the young lady's face, Jake realized person he had almost knocked down was Sarah. He had not seen her since returning home.

Sarah found herself holding onto Jake's arm and laughing.

"We're a little too old for you to be tackling me like when we were kids, Jake Martin!"

Jake took a good look at Sarah and realized she had matured into a very attractive woman.

"Sarah, is that you?" Jake stammered. "You're doing your hair different. I almost didn't recognize you."

Sarah got her balance and let go of Jake's arm. She tossed her long, flowing reddish brunette hair back off her face. Sarah had taken up ironing her hair to straighten it.

"Nope, the same ol' me. My goodness, my hair's a mess, I didn't expect to run into anyone I knew today."

"You look great, Sarah. You're a sight for sore eyes."

She smiled, but did not acknowledge the compliment.

"I heard you were home. For a while, I thought you might at least come by to say hello."

Jake began to make excuses as to why he had not stopped by to see her and pay his respects, but he knew why he had not called or gone by to see her. He was not ready to accept Sarah being a married woman.

Sarah understood this, but felt time would eventually take care of the problem.

"I guess you heard about Zack?" Jake asked.

"Yes and I went to pay a visit to Zack's family when I heard the news."

"Mom said Hank enlisted in the Marine Corps?"

"He's in training to be a medic, but he hasn't given up on becoming a veterinarian and plans to go back to school as soon as this war is over."

Jake was stammering for the right words to make conversation when Sarah said abruptly, "Jake, it's good to see you again. I've got to get on home now," and she left Jake standing on the sidewalk out front of Sittler's store.

Jake suddenly felt very alone as he watched Sarah leave and hollered after her, "Take care, Sarah. See ya."

Sarah smiled and waved through her car windshield as she backed out of her parking spot at the curb in front of Sittler's and drove off.

Jake stood there for a moment, turned and started into the store, but he had forgotten what he came for.

***

A few days after running into Sarah, Jake took Michael, Lora and the cow dog for an afternoon ride in the pickup truck.

"Where we going, Daddy?"

"For a ride, Lora. We're just going for a ride."

Jake drove around for a while before he pulled up in front of the small frame house Sarah rented on an acreage not far outside of town.

"Oh, I know who lives here. This is Aunt Sarah's house. She's my very favorite," Lora said excitedly.

"Who told you she was your aunt?"

"She did."

Sarah saw Jake and the kids pull up out front. She came to the door and hollered out to them, "You all coming in or you just going to sit out there?"

"No, grab a jacket and come with us," Jake hollered back.

Sarah had just returned from taking her horse, Blackie, for a long ride that morning and was still dressed in blue jeans, a chambray shirt and her riding boots. She stepped back in the house to get her buckskin jacket and ran to get in the pickup.

Michael promptly climbed in her lap.

"Where we going?"

"We don't know, Aunt Sarah. Daddy says we're just going for a ride," Lora answered as Michael did not talk all that much.

To which Jake added, "It's a surprise."

When Jake slowed up to turn off the old town road into the long front drive leading up to the summer ranch house, it quickly became apparent where they were all going.

"Looks pretty run down from here," Jake said.

"Yes, we had some bad storms last year. Hank really wanted to take on the place and fix it up, but now with the war on and all…"

"I know, Sarah, these times are hard on everyone."

Sarah sighed. "Tell me Jake, do you think you'll ever come home to stay?"

Jake did not answer Sarah's question. He parked the pickup and went around to open the door for her and the kids. The inside door handle on that side was broken.

The members of this anomalous family outing spent the next few hours at the place. Sarah picked things up a little. Jake got some tools from the pickup and boarded up a broken window.

"I don't believe I could ever live here again. Maybe I should rent the place out like you and Mom suggest."

"If you're not gonna use it, that'd be best, cause its sure getting run down sitting here empty."

"I'd rather sell the house and some of the acreage around it, but you know Big Jake. His dad, Old John, told him never to sell any of the land, so I guess that's the way it'll always be."

While the kids played in the yard with the dog, Jake and Sarah stood in the kitchen talking. Mostly they reminisced about happier times.

Out of nowhere Jake said, "What a fool I was not to marry you, Sarah!"

Sarah's expression of surprise indicated she expected to hear almost anything from Jake except that.

"Where in the world did that come from? I had no idea you still felt that way about us."

Jake moved toward Sarah and reached out to hold her. She was ready to cry as he kissed her and she kissed him back. Jake was no stranger to Sarah. Then she did cry. He held onto her not wanting to let go and she made no effort to pull away from him.

Neither seemed to know exactly what to do about what they were feeling at the moment. They continued to hold each other for a few more minutes. Then Sarah pulled away and wiped the tears from her eyes.

Jake went to the door and hollered to the kids, "Time to go you guys."

Lora made Michael put down a horny toad he had caught and wanted to take home with them.

Jake closed up the house and the four piled into the pickup.

Not much was said as Jake drove back to Sarah's house. The kids were tired from playing all day. Sarah seemed distant and Jake was lost in his thoughts.

Out front of her house, Sarah said, "Bye, Jake," but she did not look at him. Sarah gave Lora and Michael a hug and walked towards the house.

As the pickup pulled away, Lora was looking out the rear window and waved goodbye to Sarah.

***

At breakfast the following morning, Flo said, "Lora told me you all went to see Sarah yesterday. How is she coping with Hank being away and all?"

"Oh, she's fine, Mom," Jake answered offhandedly.

"You know, Jacob, the Tenth Commandment might not be the worst one to break, but I for one, would try not to break any more of them than I could help."

Jake knew very well his mother was referring to coveting someone else's wife and he should stop short of violating the Seventh Commandment. He also knew he should listen to his mother, but in his present state of confusion, her advice fell on deaf ears.

The answer to what he should do with his life seemed glaringly obvious to the most basic of fools. There was a family business here that needed to be run and he was the heir to that business. There were two children here that desperately wanted a full time mother and Sarah was clearly their uncontested choice for the role.

There was one problem that was difficult to ignore. Sarah already had a husband. Someone was going to get hurt if Jake pursued Sarah. In one instant, Jake would think this was not fair to Hank and the next instant, he would say to hell with fair.

Sarah was the one person who always seemed to understand him, maybe even the only one who did. She was his closest friend. Why did he let his life get so screwed up and why had he made the choices he had? He should have just stayed home and married Sarah.

After going over and over the dilemma in his mind, Jake called Sarah and asked her to take a drive with him.

When he showed up, Sarah asked, "Where are the kids?"

"I didn't bring them this time. I want you to take a ride with me out to our place."

Sarah did not have to ask where "our place" was. She knew where Jake was asking her to go with him and she climbed in the pickup.

At the old wooden bridge, Jake pulled off the road and parked the pickup on the small rise overlooking The Creek and the Red River Valley.

They got out and walked a ways towards the tree house that Zack, Sarah and Jake had built. They gazed up at the giant old cottonwood and could see only a couple of rotten boards dangling by some rusty nails, all that remained of the dream house they once built as children.

"Sarah, I want you to go away with me for a few days. We'll drive up to Oklahoma to a lodge I know in the Kiamichi Mountains and spend some time together. Maybe we can work this thing out."

Sarah offered no argument against Jake's less than honorable proposal. She had been wrestling with the problem the same as Jake. Sarah looked down into her clasped hands folded in front of her plain print dress and pale pink knit sweater jacket.

"Okay," she said and looked up at Jake, "but I won't be able to leave until tomorrow."

Jake feared Sarah would change her mind if she had time to think it over and pleaded, "Leave with me right now or as soon as you can pack some things."

"No, I said I will go with you tomorrow. And I will!"

***

When the telephone rang at the ranch house the next morning, Jake was waiting near the phone so he would be able to pick it up before Violet or Lora could.

Sarah explained, "I'm going to park my car at the summer ranch house and you can pick me up there at noon. I don't want anyone seeing us leave town together. I lied and told my folks I was going to go visit some friends for a couple of days."

After Jake hung up the telephone, he went to find Flo.

"I'm going to be away for a few days, Mom. Going to run up to Oklahoma."

Lora overheard Jake and ran to him. She pulled her father down to her eye level and with tears running down her cheeks, she said, "Daddy, don't go away. Please don't go away again."

Jake dried her tears with his hand.

"I'm only going to be gone a few days. One day, we're going to have our own home and be together all the time."

"You promise?"

"I promise, Little One, I promise."

Jake held her in his lap until she tired of sitting there and squirmed down to go do something else.

When Jake arrived at the old summer ranch house, Sarah was waiting in her black 1938 Ford convertible coupe. She stepped out of the car as Jake pulled up. Sarah was dressed in a fashionable lady's suit and wearing high-heel shoes. Her long hair was rolled under at the neckline, a currently popular hairstyle in the movies.

Sarah put one hand on her hip as she stood looking at Jake's beat-up old ranch truck and asked sarcastically, "We're not going to try to make it to Oklahoma and back in that pathetic old thing, are we?"

"What's wrong with my truck? It runs fine. It'll get us there and back okay," Jake proclaimed as he climbed out of the old green IH pickup truck and slammed the door hard, as it often did not shut.

Sarah held out her car keys to Jake.

"Come on, we'll take my car. You can drive."

Jake got his old leather jacket and a small bag out of the pickup and threw them in Sarah's Ford.

As they pulled away, Sarah said, "Take the old dirt road by the railroad tracks out of town. You may not be planning on living here the rest of your life, but I am."

"I was going to," Jake mumbled.

Sarah had been reading a book she brought with her and the two rode quietly until they were well past the little Oklahoma town of Durant and headed toward Muskogee. She grew tired of the silence and closed her book.

"Sarah and Jake. Has a rather nice ring to it, don't you think?"

Jake had been waiting for Sarah's mood to brighten.

"Definitely better than Jake and Hank, I suppose."

Sarah tried not to laugh, but she did anyway.

"Don't joke about a thing like that!" and Sarah changed the subject. "Jake, do you remember on my ninth birthday when you boxed up a garden snake?"

They talked for the next fifty miles, the two of them taking turns recalling old stories finishing each other's sentences and laughing.

Sarah likely felt the same as Jake, what a wonderful thing to share the same memories.

They pulled into the Kiamichi Lodge about dark and Jake went into the office to register.

"I'd like one of the cabins towards the back," Jake said to the lodge owner. "You know the ones near the mountain ridge with a view of the valley from the back porch."

"Sure, Mr. Martin," the lodge owner responded looking at the name on the registration. "You can about have your pick of cabins this time of year, too late for hunting season and too early for tourists. You been here before?"

"Yes, hunting with friends a couple of times."

Looking out the window at Sarah seated in the car, the lodge owner said, "Honeymoon this time, it looks like?" as he handed Jake the key to the cabin.

"Yeah, more or less," Jake replied as he left.

Sarah and Jake settled into their cabin and got ready for bed. They lay across the large double bed talking for an hour or so, until Sarah reached over and turned out the lamp on the knotty pine bedside table.

The room glowed brightly with blue cast shadows from a nearly full moon shining in the cabin windows.

Jake held Sarah close to him for a while and thought how nice it felt to hold someone he really cared about, someone he had shared so much of his life with. He had been with a dozen different women over the last few years and would be hard pressed to recall their faces, let alone remember all their names.

Sarah loved Jake ever since she could remember. She always imagined they would marry and often wondered what their first night together would be like.

She had put on a brave face all day, but now she felt a little guilty. Not because she was here, heaven only knew her years of devotion to Jake earned her the right to be with him. She was here, more than any other reason, because she wondered what might have been.

Sarah whispered quietly, "Well, if we're going to do it, lets do it."

***

Jake woke to the bright morning sunlight streaming across the white bed sheet and the sounds of a dozen different kinds of birds chirping in the pine trees.

Sarah had been up and dressed for some time. She was sitting on the back porch of the cabin looking off into the distant rolling hills, rocked back in an old wooden porch chair. She had finished the book she brought along to read.

Jake hollered out to Sarah, "You hungry yet?"

"Well maybe," Sarah answered as she came in from the porch and crawled back into bed next to Jake.

A half-hour later Jake re-worded his question.

"How about we go find someplace to eat breakfast," Jake said, as he got up to get dressed.

"Great," Sarah said and laughed as she beat Jake to the bathroom and latched the door behind her.

"Well then, I won't shave."

"What'd you say?"

"Nothing. There's a little town about ten miles from here on the Talimena Pike Road that used to have a good cafe. If it's still there, they've got an ol' Cherokee Indian squaw that cooks up a fine breakfast."

They drove into town and found the café. The old Indian woman's daughter was cooking for the café now.

After breakfast, Jake stopped at a small grocery store so Sarah could get some things to fix supper for them at the cabin that night.

The wild flowers were already starting to bloom on this warm early spring day in the Oklahoma hill country. Jake put the top down on Sarah's Ford and they took the long road around the mountain back to the cabin for the scenic drive.

That afternoon they climbed the mountain peak near the cabins and went for a long walk along the ridge. At Lookout Point, they stopped to rest and talked for a while.

Sarah raised the question she had struggled with ever since having agreed to come away with Jake.

"If you want to marry me, how can I possibly tell Hank I am divorcing him to marry you?"

"I'm as sorry about the circumstances as you are, but it's a necessary part of what has to be done. Besides, you were my girl long before you ever met Hank."

"Let's not go into that!" Sarah said sarcastically. "Tell me about all the things you've done and the places you've seen since you left home."

Jake began and Sarah listened with great enthusiasm.

When they returned to the cabin, they went to sit on the porch. As the sun set in the blue mist of the hills, Sarah said, "We've talked about everything that has happened to us during the years we've been apart, but every time you mention Rangoon, there seems to be something missing from the story."

Jake would not look Sarah in the eye, he only stared down at the floor.

Sarah knew he was keeping something from her.

"I know you well enough to know something happened to you about that time. You're different now. Something changed you, something more than the Japanese attack. Tell me what really happened in Rangoon."

"I should have leveled with you from the first and now's as good a time as any to fess up. You're right. I met a young widow lady in Rangoon, a Eurasian girl. Her name was Suzette. I never met anyone like her in my life and probably never will again."

From then until after dark, Jake told Sarah everything about the three months he had spent with Suzette and what had happened when he went north.

When Jake finished and Sarah had heard the sadness in his voice and felt his pain, she cried, not for herself and not for the girl that had died, she cried for Jake.

***

Jake and Sarah spent that night, the next day and one more night together at the cabin in the mountains. On the morning after their third night together, Sarah was up at sunrise.

Jake was still sound asleep when Sarah woke him, "Get up! Get up, we need to talk."

Jake washed his face in cold water, slipped on his trousers and went to sit down across the small kitchenette table from Sarah.

"Okay, what is it?"

Sarah took a deep breath and said, "I've reached a decision and it's going to have some effect on both of our lives. You want the long version or the short version?"

"The short version, for now!" Jake said still trying to fully wake up.

Sarah straightened her shoulders and looked at Jake.

"I will not leave Hank to marry you."

"Oh yeah, well good morning to you too, Sarah, I didn't sleep very well last night either."

Jake stood up and stumbled around the small kitchen area of the cabin as though looking for something.

"Could we, maybe, make some coffee?"

Sarah jumped to her feet.

"Sure, coming right up."

"How in blazes can you be so darn cheerful this early in the morning," Jake said and went to sit on the porch.

Jake sat looking out over the low-lying morning fog in the valley below, lost in thought.

Sarah came out on the porch with two coffees in large blue metal cups and handed one to Jake. She sat down on the porch chair beside him.

"Careful, the cup is hot."

Jake burned his lip anyway, "Ouch!"

"Well, I told you the cup was hot!"

Quiet filled the still morning air as they sat for a while engaged in small talk like an old married couple. Then Jake said, "Okay, now the long version."

Sarah began, "Okay." She paused as though trying to put her thoughts in order and began again. "Okay, here it is. Where were you when I needed you? Where were you when Elizabeth needed you? Off flying somewhere in one of those gosh-darn airplanes you love so much or off to some god-forsaken country whose name I can't even pronounce, let alone spell."

"Okay, what's your point?" Jake said staring off in the distance.

"Jake, look at me. I have loved you all my life. More, than one person should love another. You just think you need me right now, but you don't care about what I would have to go through to be with you! You didn't care enough about Elizabeth to try and understand her! All you've ever cared about was your next adventure and finding out what was over the next horizon!"

Sarah stopped. She was ashamed of herself for saying aloud in anger what she felt and what she had kept bundled up inside all these years.

"Just calm down," Jake said softly and tried to hold her, but she would not let him.

"I'm okay. Just give me a minute."

He waited patiently for Sarah to compose herself and then said, "I don't think it's fair for you to say I don't care. I do care about you, my family and my friends."

"I didn't mean you don't care. I mean you don't care enough to make the sacrifices those relationships require. Let me put it this way. We said a lot of things in the moonlight the other night we probably didn't mean. More to the point, we said some things we can't live up to. I always thought I'd marry you, we'd have children, live out our lives and grow old together."

"But we chose differently," Jake said.

"You chose differently! And I learned to accept the fact that some things are not meant to be. Possibly the only woman you may have ever loved was that China Doll you told me about. I'm sorry that she died, but that wasn't my fault or your fault! Sometimes my dear, dear Jacob, sometimes things don't always work out the way we'd like!"

"Where does that leave us," Jake asked.

"My dad always told me 'you dance with the one who brung you.' When your dad was rough on you and made you work summers on the ranch, I remember Zack telling you that 'yous plays the cards yous dealt.' Hank was there when I needed him, you weren't. I made a promise to him and I broke that promise this week with you. I never intend to break it again. I'm going to be there for Hank when he comes home. I'm going to dance with the one who brung me and play the cards I was dealt."

Sarah was calmer now. She said her piece and now she only wanted Jake to try to understand.

Jake sat staring into his cold and empty blue metal coffee cup. He didn't say anything. He just sat there.

Sarah stood up. "So, when you're ready we'll go."

Jake knew Sarah was right. He smiled at her as Sarah was very dear to him whether she married him or not.

"That was definitely the long version, I'll give you that. Is there anything I can do to change your mind?"

"Nope," Sarah said and smiled tenderly back at him.

"Well, at least one of us seems to have the good sense to know the right thing to do."

The morning was cool so Jake put on his jacket and went to the cabin door.

"Be back shortly, I'll walk up to the lodge and settle our bill."

The lodge owner was just opening as Jake walked up. They exchanged the usual small talk about it being a nice day and if Jake and his wife had enjoyed their stay.

Jake paid the bill and asked, "Could I use your phone to make a long distance call? I'll reverse the charges."

"Sure," and the owner pointed to the telephone behind the desk. "You'll have to come around here."

Jake figured it a little early for Big Jake to be at his office, so he called the house and Violet answered.

"I need to talk to Dad," he said and held on.

Big Jake came on the line, "Son, you all right? Where you calling from?"

"Yes Dad, I'm fine. Oklahoma. I wanted to let you know I'm going to stop by the Army Air Corps recruiters at Sheppard Airbase before heading home, so it might be a couple more days before I get back. Don't say anything about this to Mom or Lora, at least for right now."

"You sure about this, Son?"

"I've thought it over and I'm sure. I need you to take care of something for me. I'd like you to arrange to rent the old summer ranch house to Sarah so she will be living there when Hank comes home from the Marines. Find out how much rent she's been paying at her place and rent it to her for the same amount. Oh and Dad, put some acreage with it. She'll need a place to keep Blackie."

Big Jake could tell by the tone of his son's voice, what he had asked was important to him.

"Sure, I'll take care of it, if that's what you want to do with the place, but why don't you want to handle it?"

"That's the problem, Sarah can't know I had anything to do with this, so please don't indicate in anyway that I did. I'll explain later and thanks, Dad."

Jake walked back to the cabin where Sarah was waiting out front in the car.

"I've loaded our stuff."

Jake climbed behind the wheel and drove off down the mountain road.

They stopped at a little café in McAlester. Jake asked to see a breakfast menu, but the waitress told him they were too late. They both ordered the Blue Plate Special and talked while they waited for their lunch to be served.

"If you're not in a real big hurry to get home, Sarah, I'd like you to drop me in Wichita Falls at the airbase."

"Sure, that's not far out of our way, but why?"

Jake leaned back resting his arm on the back of the booth as the waitress served their food.

"I've been thinking about enlisting in the Army Air Corps as a fighter pilot."

Sarah, clearly caught off guard, sighed, "Oh Jake, not that I wouldn't expect you to do something like that. I mean, my gosh! Just because things aren't working out between us…"

"No, no," Jake said interrupting her. "I've been thinking about this ever since Pearl Harbor. With my flying experience, they'll probably ship me off to Europe where I can get into the fight right away."

"Jake," Sarah pleaded, "you don't have to do this."

"Yeah, but I want to. These are crazy times and I think it's something I could do to contribute to the war effort."

Late that afternoon, they pulled up in front of the main guard gate at Sheppard Airbase. Jake got out of the car, reached in the back seat for his old leather jacket and shut the door.

Sarah slid over under the steering wheel. She looked up at Jake and he was staring at her as though he might be trying to memorize her face.

"You know I do love you, Sarah. I guess I always have."

"True or not true, it pleases me to hear you say the words. I love you too, Jake, and I suppose I always will."

Jake stood looking at Sarah with his hand resting on the open window of the driver's door. There was nothing left to be said. He stood with his hand resting on the door as though he did not want to let go. After a moment or two, he looked at Sarah one last time, forced a smile, turned and walked towards the guard gate.

At the gate, the uniformed military policeman asked him, "Can I help you, sir?"

Jake turned to watch as Sarah pulled away. He watched until her car disappeared into the evening dusk.

Turning back to the MP, Jake said, "Yes, I suppose you can. I'm here to enlist."

Santa Fe Chief

Jake signed in at the airbase and spent the night in the recruit's barracks. He slept in his underwear as he forgot and left his small bag in Sarah's car. Today he would take the tests required for acceptance as an Air Corps flying officer candidate.

A little before sunrise, Jake and a couple dozen other candidates in the barracks were rousted out of bed, given five minutes to dress and escorted to the testing area.

After several hours of written and oral tests, the recruits were ushered to the medical building for a physical examination. The men lined up for a group medical exam. Afterwards, they waited for a male nurse to call them in to discuss their eligibility with the flight surgeon.

Jake's name was called and he entered the surgeon's office. The doctor had the silver oak leafs of a lieutenant colonel on his lapel.

"Good morning, Colonel," Jake said.

"What the hell you doing here?" the surgeon asked.

"What do you mean? I'm signing up to fly for the Air Corps. I thought the Army needed good pilots to fight the war in Europe."

"We do, but in the remarks section of your application you have written 'will only accept active duty as a combat fighter pilot.' I've reviewed your flying experience and I certainly agree you are well qualified as a pilot, Mr. Martin, but you're thirty years old. We don't accept new fighter pilots for combat duty after the age of twenty-six. You only got this far because someone thought you were signing up to be a flight training instructor."

Jake attempted to argue with the flight surgeon, but the surgeon held firm.

"Look, there's one thing we really need and that's experienced pilots for our new training command up at Enid. Old hands like yourself can be a great help to the war effort by training new pilots."

Jake had never thought of himself as an old anything, at least not until today.

He shook his head no, "That's not for me."

The surgeon tried again.

"I'm even willing to bend the regulations a little for you. You conceal that limp in your right leg pretty well, but fact is, you're probably not physically qualified by Army standards to go through basic combat training, so you've got two choices."

"What are they?"

"I can check the 4F block on this form and that's the end of it... Or I can fill in the remarks section with an endorsement, passed for stateside special assignment only," and the surgeon looked at Jake. "What's it going to be?"

Jake sat quietly for a moment. Choices, there that monster was again! The one that had stalked he all his life and it had raised its ugly head one more time.

"I wonder if the Navy has any openings for an old, gimp legged pilot," Jake wisecracked.

The flight surgeon put a check mark in the 4F block, closed the manila file folder and called out, "Next."

***

Jake got dressed and left the infirmary. He walked out the main gate and sat down on a bench at the bus stop. According to the bus stop sign it would be about twenty minutes before the next city bus was due. While he waited, Jake pondered how to best make use of his time before returning to the ranch.

One thing he would like to do would be go to L.A. and pick up his car, but right now he did not feel like flying. Maybe for the first time in his life, Jake Martin was not in the mood to go anywhere fast. He needed some time to be alone and think things through.

The city bus pulled up and he took it to the downtown Greyhound Bus Station where he went to the ticket counter.

"When does the next bus depart for Oklahoma City?"

"In about two hours," the ticket agent answered.

Jake took out his wallet to pay the agent.

"Give me a one-way ticket to Ok-City, please."

Jake left the bus station in search of a place to eat, somewhere that served something besides hot dogs. Walking down one of the side streets, he came upon a small white frame house with a flower garden in the front yard. The sign on the porch read Chatterbox Tea Room. Jake went in and found the tearoom full of nicely dressed ladies out for an afternoon luncheon.

The hostess approached Jake and asked, "Would you like to wait on a table by yourself or would you mind sharing a table with some of the ladies."

"I'll sit with those two ladies over there, if they don't mind," Jake said and he gestured toward a table for four with two elderly ladies in black dresses with starched white lace collars.

The hostess knew the two ladies personally. She also knew they would welcome a gentleman's company and seated Jake at their table.

Jake introduced himself and the ladies reciprocated.

During lunch, the two wanted to know all about Jake, if he was married, did he have children and what did he do for a living. Jake enjoyed the conversation and the lunch. The break proved to be a welcome diversion from his current state of uncertainty.

After finishing his homemade apple cobbler dessert, Jake thanked the ladies for sharing their table and excused himself. As he left, he overheard one of the ladies say to the other, "What a fine young man. Such a shame he doesn't have a nice wife to take care of him."

Jake paid the hostess for his check and that of the two elderly ladies he had sat with.

Jake walked the few blocks back to the bus station and waited for his bus to Oklahoma City to depart. When the bus loaded, there were only a few passengers. Jake took a window seat by himself.

As the bus pulled out of the station and headed north out of town, Jake observed storm clouds moving in from the west. The day grew bleaker as the bus traveled on to Lawton. He watched the farmlands pass by through the droplets of rain trailing across the window.

Jake leaned back in his seat and began to mull over the past several days. Odd, how things turned out with Sarah and the Air Corps both not wanting him. Wow, talk about rejection, he thought to himself. Did he have the character and personal fortitude to handle all of this rejection?

Strange, he should be mad as hell, but he felt no anger. In fact, he felt almost relieved, like a giant weight had been lifted from his shoulders.

Jake closed his eyes and tried to sleep, but inevitably his thoughts would return to Rangoon and his memories of Suzette, but a single small voice drowned out all his other thoughts. The voice was that of Lora's saying, "Please don't leave us again, Daddy."

***

The bus pulled into the downtown Oklahoma City bus station on Reno Street and Jake got off. He slipped on his leather jacket and pulled the collar up tight around his neck. The streetlights glowed eerily in the misty rain and early evening darkness as he walked to the red brick train station on the overpass a few blocks away.

The Santa Fe Chief connecting to Los Angeles was due into the station in a couple of hours. Jake purchased a private compartment with a sleeping berth. At the newsstand, he picked up a copy of the Daily Oklahoman and took a seat on one of the hard, wooden, church pew-style benches in the station waiting room.

Like most of the American public, Jake was well aware the war news being reported as having happened a day or two before had likely taken place weeks ago. The War Department censored anything that might give the slightest clue as to U.S. troop movements.

Jake had not seen a newspaper in several days, so for the next hour or so, he read the entire newspaper from the front page to the want ads. Three stories interested Jake more then the others.

The first article reported that on March 4th, two Japanese flying boats made a bombing run on Pearl Harbor. No great damage was reported and Jake assumed that the attacking aircraft had gotten away without being shot down because there was no mention of it in the article.

The second was an article in the business section describing how the automobile manufacturing companies were converting over to wartime production. The early 1942 model cars would be the last new models produced for an indefinite period of time and some of these were being shipped missing chrome parts, as the metal was needed for the war effort.

The third article was a rather lengthy story about General MacArthur in the Philippines.

"All aboard for the Atchison, Topeka and Santa Fe connecting with the Chicago Limited and points west," came the garbled announcement over the public address system.

Jake folded the newspaper up and laid it on the bench beside him. He now considered himself caught up on current events.

Walking forward on the train station platform before boarding, Jake went to admire the new diesel powered Santa Fe Super Chief streamliner's engine, but the old Baldwin steam engines he had loved since a boy were still his favorite.

The Santa Fe Chief departed the Oklahoma City station a little before midnight. Jake's sleeping berth was already made up when he entered the compartment.

He took off his damp leather jacket and placed it on a hanger to dry. Tired from the long bus ride and the waiting, he kicked off his boots and without removing his clothes, stretched out across the berth and fell asleep.

***

In the darkness of the early morning hours, the train stopping at some dimly lit railway station in the middle of nowhere awakened Jake. He guessed the place might be Tucumcari, suspecting they had already passed Amarillo.

Thinking there might be some fresh coffee available, he left his compartment to find the club car. He passed through the Pullman car with curtains drawn on berths of sleeping passengers and entered the coach car.

An old Navajo Indian man and an attractive young woman had boarded at the last stop and were getting seated. Jake stopped to help the young lady put her suitcase in the overhead rack.

"Thank you. My name's Norma Jean. What's yours?"

"Everyone calls me Jake."

The young lady seemed friendly enough. Wide-awake now and in the mood to talk with someone, Jake sat down in the club seat beside the Navajo man, across from Norma Jean to visit for a while.

Norma Jean was fair-skinned with mousy brown hair and had a pleasant smile. She fidgeted a lot as though she was never quite comfortable where she was sitting. The train pulled slowly away from the station and Norma Jean commenced to tell Jake all about herself.

"I'm twenty-one years old," she began.

Jake could not help but notice her full bosoms that strained to escape her low cut blouse and her somewhat shapely figure. He was not buying the twenty-one though, he figured her to be about eighteen or nineteen, if that.

Something about her fascinated Jake. He smiled as she talked expressing herself with unique body language. She had a certain indefinable quality. Jake noticed others watching her. She was the type of woman that easily turned people's heads.

"My full name is Norma Jean Morten. Actually, I guess its Norma Jean something else since I got married again. Oh well," she sighed, "I'm thinking about changing it anyway. I was married in Las Vegas a couple of days ago, but I left the jerk. He told me tonight he was enlisting in the Navy. Said being married without kids he'd be drafted into the Army if he didn't sign up."

The elderly Navajo man seated beside Jake said nothing, but he listened as Norma Jean talked and stared out the window into the darkness.

Norma Jean's voice had a soft pleasant tone to it, but with no other conversations going on, everyone seated around them, who were still awake, listened as she talked.

The more she talked, the more Jake realized this young lady was no dummy. Her word pronunciation was exacting and once she stopped doing the poor-little-ol'-me act she did so very well, she seemed quite intelligent.

Norma Jean paused to rummage through her purse for a compact and some makeup.

"Where is your husband now, Norma Jean?" Jake asked.

"I don't know exactly where we were. We were staying in some flea-bitten motel along Route 66 not far from where I got on the train."

"You mean you left him there?"

Norma Jean touched up her makeup, straightened her hair and adjusted her blouse.

"Yes, we stopped there for the night. He'd been drinking and after he fell asleep, I hitched a ride to the train station. And here I am!"

She put her compact and makeup away.

By looking at her clothes, Jake was fairly certain the girl was not overly blessed with financial assets. But who was he to judge seated there in wrinkled clothes and a tattered old leather jacket.

Out of curiosity, Jake asked, "What kind of work do you do, Norma Jean?"

"I'm a model, I'll show you. I've got one of my photo shots in my bag here. I was the Miss Automotive cover girl for their 1942 garage calendar."

Norma Jean fumbled through a large bag she carried in addition to her purse and the suitcase. She produced a dog-eared calendar with a full color print of her on the front.

"Here, look."

Jake took the calendar and tried not to act surprised when Norma Jean handed him a completely nude color photo of herself lying on her side across a velvet sheet.

"What do you think?"

Jake actually thought this pretty girl with childlike qualities appeared to be physically very much a woman, but he did not say so. Jake handed the calendar back to Norma Jean hoping she would put the print away.

Instead, she passed the calendar around to anyone who showed an interest in looking at it within several rows of her seat. Each person took a look at the calendar and passed it on until it eventually came back to her.

"I'm headed to Los Angeles to find work. I'd like to get a job as a movie actress, but I don't know exactly how to get started. Could you help me, Jake?"

"I'm not sure exactly how I could?"

"That's okay, I'll figure it out."

The sky brightened and morning daylight shown in through the coach car windows.

"The dining car might be open by now," Jake suggested. "Would you care to be my guest for breakfast?"

"Of course I would. I'd be honored to join you."

The Navajo man, who had been half dozing and half listening to their conversation for the last few hours, spoke up for the first time.

"Kind of you, mister. Doubt the girl's got a penny to her name. Had to loan her two dollars to buy her ticket back there at the train station."

Jake offered to repay the two dollars to the old man for Norma Jean, but the old man declined.

"Heavens no, mister. You all's conversation alone has been well worth the two bucks."

Jake laughed as they stood up.

Norma Jean was a little embarrassed, but smiled politely. Clearly she had planned on meeting someone like Jake who would pick up the check for a meal or two along the way.

Jake could care less. He agreed with the old Navajo man, Norma Jean's company was well worth a few bucks.

Over breakfast, Norma Jean continued to amuse Jake with her stories. She had an entertaining manner about her and a keen sense of humor.

Jake thoroughly enjoyed passing the time with Norma Jean and she helped him forget about all his recent rejection. Life seemed to be running in smooth grooves once again.

***

The train pulled into the old adobe, red-tile roofed train station in downtown Albuquerque. Three mariachis were playing guitars on the train platform as Jake and Norma Jean got off to stretch their legs with the other passengers.

Norma Jean spotted a group of Indian ladies selling jewelry and ran to look at the items they had for sale. By the time Jake meandered up, she had already put on a silver bracelet and was admiring the matching necklace.

Jake took some bills from his pocket to pay the heavyset Pueblo Indian lady for the jewelry.

"You no want argue over price, white man?" the Indian lady asked in a deep gravelly voice.

"I may not look like it to you, ma'am, but my great grandfather, on my mother's side, was a full blood Apache." Jake said and handed the lady her asking price for the jewelry. "And no, I no want argue over price."

The Indian lady took the money. She smiled and said, "Yah-ta-hay, mister."

"Yah-ta-hay," Jake replied.

Norma Jean jumped with joy. She screamed, threw her arms around him and gave him a great big hug. Jake was a little embarrassed when the people around them laughed.

The train whistle blew twice, indicating time for the passengers to board the Chicago Limited for California.

"Let's go to my compartment," Jake suggested. "It'll be a little less embarrassing visiting without spectators."

"Oh, I don't mind people watching me. I'm used to it," but she offered no objection to going to his compartment.

Jake's new compartment sleeping berth was in the day configuration with two club-seat couches. Norma Jean sat curled up on the couch opposite Jake. She admired her new jewelry for a while and then fell asleep.

Jake watched her as she slept and wondered what life might have in store for young Norma Jean. He gazed out the train window at the stark western New Mexico desert. The barren scenery moved past the window as though projected there like on a motion picture screen.

Evening approached and night came. The porter went down the corridor announcing, "Last call. Last call for dinner in the dining car."

"Norma Jean," he said waking her, "you might like to freshen up before we go to supper. I'll go on ahead and get us a table. Come whenever you're ready."

Jake stopped in the noisy connecting passage between the train cars. He stood for a while looking out the open top half of the boarding door listening to the click-ety-clack of the wheels on the rails. The sounds and the wind blowing in his face reminded him for a moment of his days flying the old open cockpit biplanes.

Jake was seated in the dining car when Norma Jean entered wearing a tan skirt, white blouse and matching tan cardigan sweater over her shoulders that she had changed into. She had on black, horn-rimmed glasses and took them off after she sat down at the table.

At dinner, Norma Jean commented, "I don't like the color of my hair," and she asked Jake, "What do you think I should do with it?"

Jake seldom offered women his honest opinion about anything, but with Norma Jean, he thought what the heck.

"You seem to have many of the same qualities of Jean Harlow. Maybe you should consider platinum blonde."

But, Norma Jean had already made up her mind. "No, I think a natural blonde color would be best. Jake, when we get to Los Angeles where are you staying?"

"Don't guess I know just yet."

As young as she was, apparently Norma Jean was accustomed to getting what she needed from men and was obviously looking for a place to stay when she got to Los Angeles. She was probably even looking for someone to keep her, at least for a while.

Jake certainly did not mind helping a girl out or for that matter, keeping a woman. He just did not need those kinds of problems right now.

Norma Jean sensed Jake's mind was on other things and when they finished eating, she said, "Let me show you something. This may amuse you."

She took her cardigan sweater from the back of her chair, put the sweater on and buttoned it at the neck. Next, she took her glasses, which she had used to read the dinner menu from her purse and put them on.

"Excuse me, I'm going to the little girl's room, but watch me as I leave."

Norma Jean walked quickly down the center aisle of the dining car and no one paid her the slightest attention.

She returned to the table.

"Okay now, you wait here and leave after I do, but watch them this time. I'm going to do her."

Norma Jean removed her sweater, unbuttoned the top button on her white blouse and returned her glasses to her purse. She shook her head to fluff her hair and tossed the sweater over one shoulder as she stood up.

Jake did not know exactly what Norma Jean meant by "do her," but he was willing to play along and find out.

"Sure, I'll be right along."

Norma Jean strolled slowly, with a provocative motion in her hips as she walked down the center aisle of the dining car. She puckered her lips just so and paused ever so briefly a couple of times to look coyly back over her shoulder.

Conversation in the dining car came to a halt. Men and women both turned their heads to watch as she passed.

Jake mused quietly, "I'll be darn, and to think it's the same woman."

Norma Jean waited for Jake in the next car and walked back to his compartment with him.

Jake opened the door and stepped back into the passageway to allow Norma Jean to enter.

"Aren't you coming in?"

"No, you can have the berth tonight. I've got some thinking to do. I'll take your seat in coach."

"Oh, no need to do that. There's plenty of room in that big berth for both of us."

"Really, I'll be fine," Jake insisted. "Get a good night's rest. I'll see you in the morning when the train gets into L.A."

Norma Jean seemed surprised Jake turned down what was obviously her offer to spend the night with him.

"Okay. Goodnight Jake, but if you change your mind..."

"I'll be fine, goodnight," Jake said, as he pulled the door closed to the compartment.

***

Jake walked down the long corridor like a drunken sailor from the swaying motion of the train, which was now running at close to its maximum speed across the flat Arizona country.

He went to the club car and ordered a bourbon and water. There was a trio playing some popular Glenn Miller tunes and Jake sat listening for a while. Returning to the coach car, he found the old Navajo man leaning against the window asleep.

Jake took the seat across from him, got comfortable and stared out the window into the darkness. The train occasionally passed the lights of a small settlement off in the distance steadily moving westward and droning on into the night.

He reflected for a while about his experience with the Air Corps flight surgeon. He could call Trippe and get him to call his buddy Hap Arnold to pull some strings. There was still the Air Navy, he had not tried them yet and Admiral Hulsey might even help out there.

No! Not only no, but hell no. He had offered to serve the best way he knew how and they turned him down. If he could not accomplish this on his own, then to heck with it. Besides, he mused, he would probably get his ass blown out of the sky by some German fighter ace first day up and what the heck good would that do anybody?

At that point, Jake considered it might be the bourbon talking and maybe not the way he really felt, so he turned his thoughts to more constructive things. He began to think of ways he might contribute to the war effort other then becoming a fighter pilot.

According to newspaper reports, General Motors had already converted some of their facilities over to building tanks. Ford was building jeeps and was constructing a whole new plant at Willow Run to assemble four-engine B-24 Liberator bombers.

Ever since his days at TAS, Jake always thought one day he might like to build airplanes. What if he converted part of the Martin Company California facility into an aircraft manufacturing plant? The machine shop at Martin Company had begun making components for North American and Douglas aircraft companies months ago.

Jake's mind raced wildly as he began to formulate a plan, but no way the government would allow Martin Company to discontinue production of the badly needed oil field equipment they currently manufactured. Petroleum was a critical component of the war effort.

What about the vacant land across the railroad tracks from the factory adjoining the airport? The existing Martin Company facilities could be expanded to join the airport. This would be a perfect site for building a new medium range twin-engine bomber he envisioned.

Jake reached the sobering conclusion his days as a lone eagle were over and he had a plan now. This time he was going to make the right choice. He was going to face up to what life expected of him. Sarah, by her strength and her example had helped him to see that.

Jake's mind quieted and he started to doze off, but once again he recalled Lora's voice pleading with him not to leave her. California and a steady job was the answer. What better place to build airplanes and make a fresh start with his kids. No more chasing off on unknown adventures.

The train stopped at Needles and a porter woke the old Navajo man.

"This is your stop, sir."

The old man took his carpetbag from the rack.

"Best of luck to you, mister."

"You too," Jake said to the old man.

He watched out the window as the old man stepped off and the train took on a couple of new passengers before pulling out again.

The Santa Fe Chief sped ever westward on the endless steel rails that glistened in the new moonlight across the Mojave climbing into the San Bernardino Mountains.

Jake was pleased with the decisions he had made this night. He fell asleep to the rhythmic sound of the wheels and the gentle rocking of the coach car.

***

That night as the Santa Fe Chief sped into the night, far across the Atlantic the war in Europe raged on.

In a small French village, a Nazi tank and some armored vehicles rolled down a narrow cobblestone street. Two blocks ahead of the German armored column a dozen or so French Freedom Fighters crouched in waiting.

The column passed a small stone house where a young woman lay on a bed in an upstairs room. She was in pain and struggled not to cry out loud. In the shadows of the darkened room, an older woman and a doctor were at her bedside. She was in labor and her baby was coming.

The sound of two rapid explosions followed by small arms fire drowned out the new mother's screams. Several German army vehicles burst into flames only a short distance away from where the child was born, a healthy new baby boy had entered the world.

***

Early that morning, the Chicago Limited pulled into the Los Angeles station.

Norma Jean walked with Jake as he carried her suitcase through the train station. Outside the main entrance to the station, he sat her suitcase down and flagged a taxicab.

Jake used the back of his train ticket envelope to write down two names with phone numbers.

"Here are a couple of managers names at aircraft factories here in the area," Jake said handing the envelope to Norma Jean. "I don't know how successful you're going to be finding a job as an actress, but I do know they're hiring women to work in the bomber plants. If you find you need work, call one of these guys and tell him Jake Martin said to give you a job."

"I guess this means I won't be seeing you again?"

"More or less."

Norma Jean smiled and took the envelope.

The taxi driver got out and held the backseat door open.

Jake handed the driver a twenty and instructed him, "Give the lady the change."

"Yes sir," the taxi driver said, taking the lady's luggage to place it in the trunk of the taxicab.

"Tell the driver where you want to go Norma Jean."

She gave Jake a hug and kissed him on the cheek. "You're a good man, Jake Martin. Thank you for everything. You're a giver, not a taker like so many others I've met."

"Good luck to you, kid. I wish you all the success in the world."

***

Jake went back into the train station to find a telephone booth and called Dan at the Martin Company.

"Dan this is Jake. I'm at the L.A. train station, just got in. Could you send a car to pick me up? I want to tell you about an idea I've got."

Dan sent one of the young engineers to pick up Jake and the two visited about how things were going at the factory on the drive over to Culver City.

Arriving at Martin Company, the driver let Jake out in front of the administrative offices. Dan saw the car pull up from his office window and went to meet him in the lobby.

"What's this big idea you came all the way out here to tell me about?" Dan said grinning suspiciously.

"Didn't exactly come out here to tell you about the idea. I kinda thought it up on the way here."

"Can't wait to hear all about it. Let's go to my office."

In Dan's office, Jake explained the details of his concept for starting an aircraft factory.

Dan listened carefully and when Jake was through, Dan leaned back in his chair.

"Suits me fine, Jake. This means you're taking over as president and general manager like we talked about before, right?"

Jake had not anticipated exactly that response to his proposal. Actually, he expected Dan to be against the idea.

"No, of course not. I figured you'd keep on running the Martin Company drilling equipment products division like you always have. I'll take some corny title like executive vice-president of the Aircraft Division."

"You're right, sounds corny. But if that's what you want. You know Big Jake is still chairman of the board of the corporation. Have you cleared any of this with him?"

Obviously, Jake had not thought it necessary and said simply, "No!"

Dan shrugged his shoulders.

"Oh well, come to think of it, don't know why he'd object. He's been trying to get you involved in the family business for as long as I can remember. Guess we shouldn't look a gift horse in the mouth."

Jake's mind was on another matter, "I've got one major concern and I'm almost afraid to ask."

"What's that, Jake?"

"Who owns or controls the rights to the property between us and the airport? Is it going to cost us an arm and a leg to get hold of the property?"

Dan assumed Jake had already checked it out and answered with a questioning look, "No, I remember you asking about that property the first time you came to see the facility. After you raised the question, I thought it might be a good idea to put an option on the place, so I did."

"Dan, you're an absolute genius! What would we do without you?"

"Based on our current conversation, it doesn't appear any of us are going to get a chance to find that out anytime soon," Dan joked.

"You got that right." Jake jumped to his feet. "I'm anxious to get started. Where's an office I can use? I'll need somewhere to work."

"Take this one."

"No, you're the company president. If I need to impress somebody in a meeting or something, I'll borrow your office. For now, I only need somewhere big enough for a drafting table and a couch. What else you got?"

"Upstairs there's an office, which I hesitate to mention. It's presently being used by some government bean counters. They're doing an audit for the war department."

"Don't like bureaucrats and bean counters are the worst of the litter. We'll put them out on the factory floor where it's plenty noisy and maybe they'll finish their audit quicker."

"This'll be interesting, I'll just watch," Dan commented smiling broadly.

"Oh, and one other thing. I'm going to need a secretary, really more of an administrative assistant."

Dan thought for a minute going over some of the recent new hires in his head.

"I recall one of the new girls, a rather pretty young lady fresh out of Business College. She might work out well for you."

Jake made a sour face shaking his head no, "No, what I need is a mature, experienced and efficient ol' gal. One who gets a little testy when someone crosses her."

Dan grinned like a Cheshire cat.

"Boy, have I got an assistant for you. Her name is Gertrude Beatrice. Gertrude's worked here ever since the factory opened. I've placed her in every department and every one of them wanted her transferred out within a few weeks. One thing's for sure, she knows where all the skeletons are buried."

"Sounds like what I need."

"I can't do that to you!" Dan confessed. "The best way to describe Gertrude is she'd be well suited to play the twin-sister to the wicked witch in *The Wizard of Oz*."

Jake laughed, "Perfect! She's the one I want. Have her report to my new office, wherever that is, as soon as you can get her there."

"It's upstairs, halfway down the hall on the right."

As Jake left Dan went over to his secretary and said, "Locate Gertrude and have her report to me in my office."

Gertrude Beatrice, a middle-aged spinster, was a true lady in the old style of the professional workingwoman. A tall, slender woman who always worn her dark, slightly graying, brunette hair neatly in a bun on the back of her head. She usually dressed in black and fastened her blouses at the neck. She demanded respect from everyone she came in contact with and if she did not get it, they were likely to experience a bit of her wrath.

"Yes, Mr. Parker," she said, reporting to Dan.

"Okay, Gertrude. This is not another transfer. This time, I'm promoting you to a higher position within the company. You have been requested to fill a position as administrative assistant to the EVP of our new Aircraft Division, Mr. Martin. Get a steno pad and a pen and report to his new office immediately."

Gertrude started to leave and then paused.

"Pardon me, sir. Exactly where is our new EVP's office located?"

"It's the old auditor's room. Oh, and Gertrude, make this one work! I don't have a whole lot more places I can transfer you to."

***

Jake took a stroll through the manufacturing area and then went outside behind the factory. He crossed the railway spur-line and walked onto the vacant land between the existing Martin factory and the Culver City airport.

Jake did not see a stone-covered field grown up in weeds. He envisioned an aircraft assembly line with shiny, new silver twin-engine airplanes rolling out onto the ramp ready for flight-testing and delivery.

If Jake could pull this off, it would be a dream made into a reality. He remembered Juan Trippe predicting that with the strides being made in aviation, when the war was over, the airplane would unite the world like never before.

Jake returned to the factory to locate the room Dan suggested he might use for his new office. As he started up the stairs, the young engineer who had picked Jake up at the train station yelled, "Mr. Martin," and ran to hand Jake his old leather flight jacket. "Here, you left this in the company car."

"Thanks," Jake said taking the jacket and continued up the stairs.

Entering the office, Jake found Gertrude standing with her arms folded and five angry government auditors waiting. He looked around for somewhere to put his flight jacket, went over to an old wooden hall tree in the corner and hung it on the rear hook.

The auditors stood glaring at Jake.

"Okay, don't just stand there," Jake said in his most authoritative voice he could manage. "Get your stuff packed up. You're being relocated."

"Oh yeah, and by what authority?" one of the disgruntled auditors asked.

So as not to let them see him smile, Jake turned away.

"These spaces are needed for a high priority national defense project. Sorry, it's all top secret!"

To which the bean counters began a half-hearted effort to pack up and remove their stuff to their new workspace out in the factory.

Gertrude followed Jake around the room with steno pad and pen in hand. So far, she had not spoken a word.

Jake turned to face her and said, "Okay, Gertie…"

She interrupted him, "I don't care for that name, sir. Please address me as Gertrude or as Miss Beatrice."

Jake intended to establish who was boss from the beginning and he ignored her objection.

"Look, Gertie, I talk, you listen and write. Start numbering with one. See that the bean counters and their stuff are cleared out of our office by quitting time. Order some office furniture for me like a desk and some chairs, the usual stuff. I also want a large comfortable couch, one big enough to take a nap on."

Gertie started writing.

Jake pointed to the large wooden drafting table in the corner and said, "The drafting table stays and that old wooden hall tree stays. Everything else goes."

Gertie continued to make notes as she followed Jake to the outer office doorway.

Jake noticed Gertie staring at his right cheek. He wiped his unshaven chin with his hand and looked at the lipstick on his fingers. He grinned as he remembered Norma Jean's kiss and realized he had been walking around all morning like that.

He wiped his chin and fingers on his handkerchief and said with a smile, "It's not what you're thinking."

"Of course not, Mr. Martin. Should I write that down too, sir?" she said pretending to be nonjudgmental.

Jake laughed, at least Gertie had a sense of humor. He looked out in the hall and asked, "That room adjoining this one. What's it used for?"

Gertie looked where Jake was pointing.

"It's a large storage room and janitor's closet."

"Good. Have the room emptied and a door cut through between this office and that room. It'll be your office. Add whatever furniture you need to my order and get us some phones hooked up with one private line that doesn't go through the switch board."

"I'm not sure I can get a private phone line with the war on and all, Mr. Martin."

"No excuses, Gertie. Do you know why I asked for you?"

"No, sir, I really don't. I was wondering about that?" Gertie replied with a questioning look.

"Because they told me you know how to get things done!"

Gertie swelled with pride from what she considered to be the ultimate compliment and it came from her new boss. She almost smiled, but forced it back.

"Yes, Mr. Martin. Will there be anything else?"

From that day forward Jake never called Gertrude Beatrice anything except Gertie and she never address him any other way except as Mr. Martin.

***

The day had been a long one for Jake. The factory whistle blew signaling quitting time for the day shift and the beginning of the night shift. Jake went to Dan's office where Dan was preparing to leave for the day. Jake plopped down in one of the leather office chairs.

"You're staying with us until you find a place of your own aren't you, Jake?"

"Thanks, no. I had Gertie call and book me a room at the Hollywood Roosevelt, but I would like a ride over to your place to pick up my car though."

"Was wondering if you might be wanting the old beast?"

"Dan, there is one thing I'd like you to do for me. Would you ask Ida if she'd look for a woman who can keep house and who would be a good nanny for Lora and Michael?"

"Sounds like a good plan to me. I'm sure she'd love to do that for you. Come and go to dinner with us and you can ask her yourself. We're going out to eat at Musso and Frank's. I'll call Ida and tell her to drive your car over and she can ride home with me."

"Come to think of it, except for a Baby Ruth candy bar I haven't eaten since yesterday on the train and that seems like a week ago, but I need to make one phone call before we go."

Dan finished placing some folders in his briefcase, closed it up and hung his suit jacket over his arm.

"Use my phone. I'll wait for you in the lobby."

Jake called his folks at the ranch and Flo answered.

"Hi, Mom. How's everything?"

Flo spoke loudly, as she thought she needed to yell over a telephone when talking on a long distance call.

"Everyone's fine here, Jacob. We're all wondering when you'll be home. Your dad said you had some other matters to tend to."

Not wanting to get into a lengthy conversation at this time, Jake said, "Yes, Mom. Could I talk to Lora for a minute, please."

Flo handed the phone to Lora.

"Where are you, Daddy?"

In a very gentle voice, Jake said to her, "I'm in California, sweetheart."

Lora sighed, "But I don't want you in California, I want you here."

"How would you like to come to California?"

Lora turned to her grandmother and excitedly said, "Daddy's in California and I'm going out there. You want to come too, grandma?"

Flo took the phone from Lora.

"What in the world are you telling this child?"

"Well, Mom, it's like this. You and Dad been wanting me to take an interest in our business holdings for some time now, so I'm going to do just that. I'm planning to expand the California factory to build airplanes for the war effort."

Flo turned to Big Jake, "He intends to build airplanes in California! Did you know about this?"

"Well, not 'til this afternoon when I talked to Dan," Big Jake replied and chuckled to himself at Flo's reaction to it all.

"Listen Mom, you all can talk this over after I hang up. I'm going to live out here now and make a home for the kids here."

Flo dropped the receiver to her side and turned to Violet who was standing nearby listening.

"Catch me, I'm going to faint!" Flo said joking.

"Mom, Mom! Listen to me. I want you to start thinking about you and Violet bringing Michael and Lora out here before too long. I'll let you know as soon as I can find a place for us to live."

"Who'll take care of the kids after we leave?"

"Ida is looking for a woman to keep house and be a nanny. I'm sure she'll find someone dependable. Got to go now, I'll call again in a couple of days. Love you."

Jake hung up the phone and went to meet Dan.

He had a lot to do in the morning, mainly purchase some new clothes. This ragtag half ex-pilot, half-rancher look of his was most likely not going to go over real big out here in California. He had come to play in the big league now and the least he could do was be prepared to look the part in the morning.

Tired from his long day, but finally feeling good about what he was going to be doing again. Than and only then, he suddenly realized he had managed to go almost one whole day without thinking of Suzette.

MARTIN AERO

Seated at the desk in his new upstairs office at Martin Company, Jake ceased to daydream about the past and returned to the reality of the present...

Jake laid several of the old black and white photographs he had been looking through on the desk in front of him and placed the rest back in the large brown accordion folder.

He thought for a moment and then went over to his old leather flight jacket hanging on the wooden coat tree in the corner, removed a couple of souvenirs from the pockets and returned to his desk to add them to the photos he had selected.

"Gertie, would you come in here please," Jake called out.

"Yes, Mr. Martin," she said entering his office with steno pad and pen in hand.

"There," he said pointing to the photos and the items from his jacket on the desk, "These are the things I'd like you to have mounted and framed. I want to hang them on the wall over the credenza."

"Yes sir," she said picking the items up.

"Gertie, I understand you've worked in about every department around here. Is that correct?"

"Just about. Well, not the machine-shop, of course."

"Tell you what I want you to do. Go to the various departments and gather up any information related to aircraft work this company has done. Also, get copies of any orders we have filled for aircraft manufacturers."

"What if one of the managers or someone objects?"

"Tell them to see me."

"Yes, sir!" Gertie said, almost smiling.

She was pleased, as apparently she was working for the big boss now. Better than that, he sounded like the type of man who would back her up.

***

Jake had considered approaching Sunderland, the British flying boat company, for the rights to build a U.S. military flying boat version for the Navy. But according to Trippe, long-range, land-based airplanes would soon render the flying boats obsolete.

There were also rumors of Howard Hughes and Henry Kaiser entering into a joint venture to build a new flying boat even larger than the Boeing 314.

Because of these two factors, Jake ruled out going into production on any other aircraft design except a high-speed, high-altitude, pressurized twin-engine aircraft. Before he did, he wanted to know what the current state of the aviation industry was in California. The best way to do this was to go find out first-hand.

For openers, Jake already knew that in addition to making oil well drilling equipment, the shop was producing landing gear parts for Douglas and Northrop. Over the next couple of weeks, Jake familiarized himself with the machine shop's capability to fabricate parts. He also instructed marketing and the contracts department to refer all further aircraft related inquiries directly to him.

As it turned out, the shop had recently received an inquiry from Hughes Aircraft for bids on parts for a new experimental airplane on which Howard Hughes was personally overseeing the design. The majority of the rest of the orders came from Douglas Aircraft Company.

Under the pretext of reviewing some of the work orders for the Martin Company machine shop, Jake personally paid a visit to the Douglas factory. While he was there, he asked if he might be able to see Mr. Donald Douglas.

Mr. Douglas knew of Jake from his past association with Juan Trippe at Pan Am and sent one of the secretaries to escort Jake to his office. The two men shared many common aviation interests and visited for quite a while.

"I've been wondering why your company hasn't looked into a pressurized version of the DC-3 for the airlines?" Jake asked and went on to tell Douglas about flying in one of the Pan Am Boeing Stratoliners.

"We considered it, but my engineers told me that we might as well start from scratch as to try to pressurize the Three. With the current engines available to us, we can't get enough payload out of a twin-engine aircraft, which is why we think the answer is to use the newer DC-4. We have a pressurized DC-6 on the drawing board now."

"Makes sense to me when you think about it, I guess a four-engine job might be better. I wonder why the Air Corps stuck with the B-17 design if there's a better way to go?"

"That's an easy one, Jake. It's a proven design and was already in production. They didn't have time to get a new design tested and approved. Boeing can't keep up with the demand now. We have the same problems and that's why we rely on companies like yours. The Army has asked us to start up production on the 17s here and Lockheed over at Burbank may also produce some. Their old Vega factory on the Empire of China site is being expanded as we talk."

"I assume all the new DC-3s and C-47s are currently going straight to the Army or the RAF."

"Yes, taking them as fast as we can make 'em."

"I haven't owned my own plane in several years, but ever since I had a chance to fly Hearst's DC-3, I wished I'd bought one when I had the chance."

"Maybe we could find you a used executive model or there is one bird I could hook you up with. We've got a like new 1939 model Dragon. It's similar to the DB-2 model we proposed to the Army as the XB-23 bomber. The plane is based on the DC-3, even utilizes the DC-3 wing."

"Sounds interesting."

"This aircraft is a UC-67, in other words a transport version, a DB-2 without a bomb bay. This particular plane has been here at the factory since new so it doesn't have a lot of flying hours on it."

"Here?"

"Sure, it's out in the hangar."

"Great, I'd like to take a look at it."

"It has a real nice twelve-passenger interior, but the paint job, well now, that might need a little explaining. You see we custom modified this particular airplane for a rather eccentric fellow. He wanted this real elaborate paint job, but never took delivery on the plane."

"Let me guess, Howard Hughes."

Douglas smiled.

"You're pretty sharp on the uptake, Jake. You are welcome to go have a look at it. Fly her if you want and let me know what you think."

Douglas buzzed his chief pilot, Jim Craiton, over the intercom and asked, "That Model 67 Dragon we've got, is it available for a test flight?"

"You mean that flying Oriental house of ill repute, our favorite hangar queen. That the one you're referring to, boss?" the voice over the intercom came back.

Jake laughed.

"Yes Jim, that's the one. And I think it's worth mentioning you're on the intercom speaker and the prospective buyer is here in my office."

"I believe you're referring to the aircraft with the custom interior and rather artistic paint job. She's been recently gone through and in top shape ready to fly," Jim said over the intercom in a more serious voice.

"The fellow's name is Jake Martin. He's an old Pan Am pilot. Go with him if he wants to test fly the plane."

"Yes sir. Tell Mr. Martin we're expecting him."

"Jim will meet you on the flight line, Jake."

"Thanks, Mr. Douglas."

Jake started out of the office.

"Don't you even want to know the price?"

Jake stopped and stepped back into the office.

"Of course, excuse me. How much are you asking?"

"We sold thirty-seven of them to the Army for one hundred-thirty-three thousand each, but this one's got a few hours on it. How does a hundred even sound to you?"

"Sounds more than fair to me," Jake said and recalling Douglas had referred to the C-67 as the Dragon, he asked, "For reasons I won't try to explain, I'm partial to the nickname 'Dragon.' Tell me about the name."

"Not sure it's such a great name for a plane. Sales on that model weren't overly successful for us."

"Then you won't care if I use the name for a new aircraft design that's still on the drawing board?"

"What's in a name?" Douglas said quoting Shakespeare. "You can't copyright a name anyway and we won't be naming any of our new models that. It's yours for the taking."

"Thanks, just thought I'd ask."

"You did know that North American might also be going to use the name Dragon for their new XB-28, didn't you?"

"No, didn't until now," Jake replied and shrugged. "That's okay. I'm going to bid against them on the high-altitude medium bomber contract, and we'll win."

Douglas seemed amused at Jake's overconfidence.

"Good luck then. It's been real interesting talking with you, Jake. If you want the C-67, let us know."

***

Jim Craiton, Douglas Aircraft's chief pilot, met Jake on the ramp where the large twin-engine cabin model plane had been pulled out of the hangar, chocked and parked ready for flight.

Donald Douglas' description of the plane's paint job as artistic had been a gross understatement. The C-67 sported a glossy, dark blue paint job with a yellowish-orange, fire-breathing dragon going down both sides of the fuselage and up the vertical stabilizer fin.

"Wow!" Jake exclaimed when he first laid eyes on the plane. "Now that's an impressive paint job."

After a brief exchange of introductions, the two flyers began their walk around of the plane and Jim pointed out some of the features of the C-67 executive transport.

"This model has the Wright R-2600 engines which develop about 1,600 horsepower each. Has a maximum takeoff weight of 32,000 pounds, cruises easily at 190 knots and has a range of about 1,400 miles."

"What kind of time is on this aircraft?" Jake asked.

"Exceptionally low for one of these models! Eight hundred total flying hours, which is barely broken-in for one of these birds and both engines have had recent top overhauls. We custom outfitted this one for this eccentric rich fellow..." and Jim stopped mid-sentence realizing he was not exactly sure of Jake's background.

"No," Jake said smiling. "I'm not one of those really rich guys, but I might be getting a little eccentric. I'm buying a plane for our company and I've admired the Gooney Bird ever since Douglas started making them."

Jake's comment set Jim more at ease.

"If you like the DC-3, you'll love the C-67. With the smaller fuselage, it's more streamlined and thus faster, but she still has all the stability of the Three."

Jim waited while Jake checked out the landing gear and then continued giving Jake a tour of the airplane.

"You'll notice this model has the new speed-fairings that completely cover the wheel wells and also the new streamline oil coolers being used on the latest airline versions of the DC-3. These two modifications alone give the plane an increase of ten knots in airspeed."

Jake climbed the chrome-railed airstair and boarded the C-67 Dragon. The passenger cabin was lavishly carpeted with a burnt-orange thick pile. The swivel, reclining cabin chairs, upholstered in spotted tiger-skin cloth, each had mahogany armrest consoles with drink holder and ashtray. Between the zebra skin upholstered center club seats was a foldout mahogany card table and the table's top was inlaid with a MacArthur Projection map of the world.

Jake paused for a moment before going forward to the cockpit, reflecting that General MacArthur had always advocated a Pacific ocean-centered world map.

Jim followed Jake onboard and a ground crewman closed the airstair behind him. Jake slid into the pilot's seat and began to familiarize himself with the cockpit.

"We've got ground power now," Jim said climbing in the copilots seat. "You can turn on the master switch."

Jake turned the aircraft power on, checked the fuel gages and looked over the instrument panel layout.

After a brief run through of switch locations and radio equipment, Jim took Jake through the start-up procedure.

Jake looked down at the fuel selectors between the pilot's seats labeled *Right Motor* and *Left Motor* and chuckled.

"Hadn't seen that since my Ford Trimotor flying days."

Jim looked to see what Jake had referred to.

"Yeah, that's a holdover from the early transports. Called them motors instead of engines. All the later models and military versions are labeled left and right engine."

As they taxied out, Jim explained the new wartime procedures required of all civilian flights.

"We have to notify the tower and military controllers of our flight intentions."

"I heard that a few weeks after Pearl Harbor the coastal artillery here fired fifteen hundred rounds and never once confirmed an enemy sighting," Jake commented.

"That's true," Jim replied. "What do you want me to tell the tower is our intended route of flight?"

"We'll head out over the harbor towards Santa Catalina and put her through the paces over the water. Then we'll go back for a couple of touch and go landings at the Culver City airport. If that's all right with you?"

Jim nodded that he understood and keyed his microphone to call the tower and advised them of the Dragon's intended route and destination.

Rolling down the runway, the powerful lightly loaded, large plane lifted off easily. Jake set up a five hundred foot a minute climb on a steady heading to the west. Once out over the water, he leveled off at six thousand feet.

Jake systematically put the hybrid, modified-bomber transport through a series of single-engine turns and power-off stalls.

"I see you're no stranger to flight-testing aircraft," Jim commented as he observed Jake's flying technique.

Jake, pleased with the aircraft's handling, grinned and replied, "Actually, that was the first job I was assigned to when I went to work at Pan Am in New York."

Jake turned the plane towards Culver City.

Jim advised the military controller of their intentions and enroute he gave Jake a few pointers on the ship's handling characteristics.

Jake made a smooth power-on wheels landing with partial flaps for his first landing at the Culver City airport.

"Hardly felt the wheels touch on that one!" Jim commented.

Applying full power, Jake took the Dragon off again and flew the traffic pattern. On the next approach, Jake used full flaps and did a full-stall, power-off three-point landing. He taxied the Dragon to the terminal building and shut down.

Jake and Jim got out and went into the small airport terminal building lobby where Jake took two Cokes from the cooler and opened them. He handed one to Jim and asked the airport counter attendant, "How much for the Cokes?"

"Cokes are eight cents, mister," the attendant replied. "That's unless you want to take the bottles with you, then that'll be two cents extra."

Jake laid two bits on the counter. Motioning at the telephone, he asked. "You want to throw in a phone call for that price?"

"Local call?" the attendant asked,

"About a quarter mile over there to that factory," Jake said pointing out the window. "That local enough?"

"You work over there, mister?"

"Kind of. Name's Martin, I own the place," Jake said, reaching over the counter to shake hands with the man.

Jim laughed out loud at the look on the man's face when he said, "Yes, sir, you go right ahead, Mr. Martin."

Jake dialed the phone and got Gertie on the line, "Send a car and driver over to the airport terminal behind our factory. I have a passenger to go to the Douglas plant," and turning to Jim, he asked, "That okay with you?"

"Sure, Jake, I assumed you were buying the ol' girl sometime between 'wow' and the takeoff roll."

Jim smiled and took the last drink from his Coke.

Jake hung up the phone and walked Jim out to where the car would pick him up.

"Tell Mr. Douglas I'll send someone with certified funds tomorrow to pay for the plane and Jim, thanks for the check-out."

***

Jake went back into the terminal building, located the airport manager's office and barged in unannounced.

"I'm Jake Martin, your neighbor from the wrong side of the tracks."

The manager stood up from his desk and shook hands.

"I heard your company is planning on building airplanes over there. By the way, you're a much younger man than I expected you to be, Mr. Martin."

"You're thinking of Glen L. Martin. I'm used to it. It's a common mistake, but ol' Old Glen has built some fine airplanes over the years and I've flown a lot of them. However, we're no relation."

"I see. Please have a seat Mr. Martin. What can I do for you?"

"I want to lease some hangar space."

"If that large plane you flew in is what you're wanting to hangar, we don't have any hangars big enough."

"Yes, I know. That's why I want to lease the airport's ramp space adjacent to our factory land."

"I'm not sure…" The airport manager said, seeming cool to Jake's proposal.

"We'll need to build two new large hangars on the airport property. The first hangar will be used for operational flight-testing and it needs to be completed as soon as possible. We'll also store our company plane, the *Dragon One*, in that hangar."

The manager walked to the window and looked out at the plane parked on the ramp. He smiled and remarked, "I can see why you might want to keep that one in a hangar."

Jake was pleased to discover the airport manager at least possessed a sense of humor.

"Yes, it's a very impressive paint job, isn't it?" and Jake continued his list of requests. "The second hangar will need to be larger. It'll be used for post production delivery make-ready of the new bombers for acceptance by the Army Air Corps."

When the airport manager heard all of Jake's plans, he became much more enthusiastic.

"How soon are you going to be needing all this? There's a war on, you know."

Jake had grown really weary of hearing people use this for an excuse and had developed a standard reply. As he prepared to leave, he said with a serious look, "Top national defense priority, you know!"

***

After Douglas Aircraft, the next company on Jake's contact list was Hughes Aircraft. This time, he skipped the pretense of making a call on behalf of the Martin Company machine shop. He went directly to the main office and asked to see Howard Hughes in person.

Hughes' assistant told Jake, "Mr. Hughes is busy working with some engineers in the design department and I can't disturb him at this time."

Jake had heard the rumors of Hughes' perfectionist tendencies and how he always involved himself hands-on with his projects, which might have accounted for the reason so many of Hughes' projects came in behind schedule and over budget. Jake played his ace card.

"Very well, please tell Mr. Hughes Jake Martin was here and because you were unable to let me talk with him, the parts for his HX-2 project might be delayed until we can get additional technical information."

Jake pretended he was about to leave.

"Just a moment, Mr. Martin. If you'll come with me?"

Jake followed the assistant who asked him to wait in the hallway outside of a large engineering design room full of engineers working at drafting tables.

Jake could see the assistant talking to Hughes through the glass divider wall. The assistant pointed to Jake and Hughes motioned for Jake to come through the door.

Hughes, dressed in a wrinkled, gray business suit, sat perched on a stool in front of a drafting table. Several engineers in starched white shirts, dark men's slacks and conservative dark ties flanked Hughes on both sides.

Several drawings of an ultra-modern, twin-tail-boom aircraft lay partially obscured on the drafting board. The title on one of the drawings read XP-73.

Jake made a mental note of the plane's designation.

Hughes greeted Jake without standing.

"That's what I call service! Only this morning I asked when to expect an estimate on our machine parts order. Maybe we ought to do more business with Martin Company."

"Well, for the most part, you do. Our drilling equipment factory in Gainesville, M&H Manufacturing, is a joint venture with Hughes Tool Company."

Hughes rolled up the drawing he had been looking over and handed it to one of the engineers.

"Give me a set of detailed drawings for this," Hughes told the engineers and dismissed them. "Noah Dietrich handles the oil part of our business. I do remember my dad talking about the Martin family, ranchers up in North Texas. You're a younger man than I had you figured for."

"Your thinking of my dad, Big Jake Martin. I was only eleven at the time, but I met your father when he came to my grandfather John's funeral."

"Is that right?" Hughes said as he unrolled a landing gear drawing on the drafting board and pointed to the strut. "Should this part be strengthened?"

"I don't know, but when I get back to the factory, I'll find out and have you an answer by tomorrow."

Jake listened as Hughes described some of the other design problems they had encountered and then Hughes uncovered the three-view drawing of the XP-73 on the drafting table Jake had noticed earlier.

"What do you think of this design?"

Jake studied the drawing and remarked, "Good concept."

"Are you familiar with the de Havilland Mosquito?"

"Yes, it's one of the fastest planes in the RAF. I've never flown one, but know of them."

"The Mosquito has an all wooden airframe, laminated wood, but nevertheless wood. That's what gives the plane its excellent weight-to-power ratio and makes the damn thing so fast. This plane," Howard pointed to the drawing of the XP-73, "will also have an all wooden airframe and I expect it to exceed the Mosquito's top speeds."

In the course of their conversation, Jake referred several times to the Pan Am Clippers and to his experience with the Boeing 314 flying boats in the Pacific.

Hughes was impressed.

"Can I call on you from time to time regarding another design project I'm working on? I think I've got a solution to the German U-boat threat."

Jake agreed, as he was certain the project Hughes referred to was the HK-1 flying boat. What Jake did not know at the time was that Hughes planned on building the largest plane in the world. Whether it would be the largest and whether it would ever fly, remained an unknown.

***

When Jake arrived back at the Martin Company factory, Dan was waiting to talk to him. A sign painter in white coveralls with a large wooden tray of enamels and brushes was also waiting.

"This painter fellow says Gertie called him. You may want to tend to him first," Dan said.

Jake took a folded up piece of paper from his pocket.

"That large airplane parked across the way…"

"You mean that golden dragon with an airplane on it? I saw it from the street when I drove in."

"Everyone's a comedian!" Jake smirked and handed the painter the paper. "Paint *Dragon One* on the nose. This sketch will give you the lettering style and dimensions."

"You got it, sir," the painter said and left.

Jake turned to Dan and asked, "Now what have I done?"

"I know you want to move fast on those aircraft parts, but we're already running behind on the drilling equipment parts and you're giving the shop too many rush orders."

"Okay Dan, you handle it, would you? You tell the shop to see you if there's a conflict and you designate what work gets done first. Fair enough?"

"Sure. Maybe we'll add a third shift?"

"Jake, you know you're quite capable of handling this whole operation. Why do you want me hanging around? When my mother died she left Flo one section of land, but she also left Ida and me the other two sections. It's all rolled into the Flying M ranch right now and Big Jake looks after it. Why don't we head on home and you run things here?"

"Listen, Dan, I've got a whole new factory to build and an aircraft company to start from scratch. There's no way I can do all that and manage the drilling equipment business, too. Bottom line is, I need you here right now!"

Dan stood up and stomped around the room. He was choked up and cleared his throat to speak.

"Dang your hide, anyway! Last night I had myself all talked into going back to Texas. Then you come up with this I need you crap. You could've said almost anything except that. You could've said I'm the best man for the job or some bullshit thing like that and I'd have been out of here. You had to go and say, 'I need you...' Well, if you need me, Jake, I'm here for you!"

"Listen Dan, even I sometimes miss the slow pace and quiet life on the ranch," and then making a joke, Jake said, "But the feeling wears off in a few minutes."

Dan laughed half-heartedly.

"It's not all me, it's what's coming at us. Apparently, when you ran those bean counters out of your office, one of them went squealing to somebody up at the War Department."

"And?"

"And you've probably never heard of a man by the name of William Knudsen."

"Yes I have, he's a bigwig executive-type up at General Motors."

"Not anymore. Now he heads up a government agency called the National Defense Commission. President Roosevelt appointed Knudsen to coordinate all defense work."

"So how does that affect us?"

"We were suppose to have checked with his office before starting any new projects. His office got wind of your plans to develop a new bomber. He and some Army Air Corps brass are coming out here from Washington DC."

Jake pounded the table with his fist.

"Damn it! That's all I need is to have to deal with a covey of bureaucrats right now."

"Welcome to the big league, country boy!"

***

In a couple of days Knudsen, accompanied by an Army full colonel, a secretary and two civilians with briefcases arrived at the factory.

Knudsen asked where the president's office was and proceeded to go there and set himself up at Dan's desk.

This really chapped Jake, but he remained polite and on his best behavior. Little good it did him, as Knudsen had clearly arrived with the predetermined notion of shutting Jake's aircraft development project down.

For about an hour Knudsen read Jake and Dan the riot act with the Army colonel adding his criticisms to that of Knudsen's from time to time.

"Don't you know there's a war on, Mr. Martin?"

Was Jake ever-getting sick and tired of hearing that.

"Who do you think you are, Martin? You may design and build an airplane, but where do you think you're going to get the engines. My agency has the authority to divert engines to manufacturers on a priority basis. Who's going to approve the flight-testing on your aircraft if the Air Corps decide they need a different design?"

Jake seldom considered the possibility of failure at anything he pursued. He kept his mouth shut as long as he could, but finally, he had all the criticism he could take.

"You mean divert the engines like you did the Hughes photo reconnaissance aircraft? You mean cancel the program on a design that's twenty years ahead of its time like the Northrop flying wing, simply because you won't approve the funding for the research on advanced flight controls?"

Knudsen, clearly caught off guard by Jake's remarks, snapped back, "How do you know about the Hughes engine situation?"

"Let's just say I know," Jake said and leaned over Dan's desk to get right in Knudsen's face.

"You and your people get your brownie points by making the defense establishment efficient. Like those little blue E for efficiency pins you want all the factory workers to wear. Oh, and those blue E pennants you like to see flying on the factory flagpoles under Old Glory."

"That's not all we do!"

"Maybe, but you just told me what you're going to do to stop my company from helping this country's war effort. That's the difference between you and me. I'm an American first and a businessman second."

Jake's last statement was a blatant insult, but it took a minute for those in the room to realize he had just implied Knudsen was placing his own personal interest above the best interests of the country. The room fell eerily silent. Knudsen's staff had never seen anyone stand up to the man like Jake had just done. Knudsen said nothing.

Jake paced for a minute to regain his composure.

"Here's what I can do for the war effort. I can double the production of the drilling equipment machine shop by building an aircraft machine shop next door to produce landing gear parts needed right now on three different aircraft. And for what it's worth, I could tell you where there's a giant oilfield in Texas that has never been tapped before. There's enough oil under the ground there to supply the Air Corps with fuel for years to come."

The phone on Dan's desk rang. Knudsen was still seated at Dan's desk, so Jake sat down on the front edge of the desk to answer the phone.

"Annie, I thought you were told we'd be in a meeting and weren't to be disturbed. Who is it, anyway?"

"It's Mr. Juan Trippe. Remember, Mr. Martin, you told me to always put his calls through."

"You got me there, Annie. Put him on."

Jake held for a moment as everyone stared at Jake and waited while he took the call.

"Juan, good to hear from you. Sure, I'd like to come up to Palm Springs and see you guys while you're here, but you really called at a bad time. I'm in a meeting with this Knudsen bunch from Washington..." Jake listened. "No, but thanks anyway. I appreciate it, but I don't need..."

Jake looked at the receiver and placed the phone back on the cradle. Trippe had hung up.

Knudsen commenced his bureaucratic tap dance on Jake's plans by saying, "You see, Mr. Martin, you haven't filed the proper paperwork and thus we can not allocate you a wartime priority for the construction of your buildings."

"And that's only the beginning of your problems," the Air Corps colonel interjected. "How do you know we even want the medium bomber you're proposing?"

Jake looked at the colonel.

"Because I'm a pilot and I've flown in combat. I've seen how the best of them fly, like Chennault's pilots. You're crews aren't going in high enough with the B-17s to get above the anti-aircraft guns and then they're missing their targets from that altitude. With a pressurized bomber, they can fly enroute high above the enemy's ability to shoot them down and then drop down for a high-speed, low-level bomb run. That's the answer to keeping our crews from getting their brains kicked in on every mission."

The colonel was a ground-pounder and had never flown a combat mission, but he knew Jake was right. He offered no response.

Dan and Gertie had been standing in the doorway to the outer office listening to the exchange when the telephone rang on the secretary's desk.

Dan's secretary answered the phone and motioned for Gertie to come and take the call.

"Yes, General Arnold," Gertie said over the phone. "I'll see if there's a colonel here by that name," but she knew there was.

Gertie entered Dan's office and asked, "Is there a Colonel Polaski here?"

The colonel who had been addressing Jake earlier, spoke up, "I'm Colonel Polaski."

"There's an urgent phone call for you. If you prefer, you can take it in the outer office," Gertie said so politely that sugar would not have melted in her mouth!

Knudsen frowned as the Air Corps colonel stepped into the outer office and picked up the phone.

"Colonel Polaski, here."

The group in Dan's office grew silent as everyone listened to the phone conversation in the outer office.

"Yes sir… Yes sir," the colonel said. "Yes sir, I'll see that it's taken care of," and he hung up.

The colonel went directly over to Knudsen, who was irritated because of the interruption, and leaned forward to whisper to Knudsen.

"Hap Arnold says to give Martin whatever he needs to get the job done!"

Jake was standing near enough to hear what the colonel whispered and he smiled.

Knudsen, still seated at Dan's desk, sat silently for a moment. Then he took a deep breath, reached for his briefcase and opened it. He removed several folders, as though in slow motion, from the briefcase and laid them on the desk in front of him. Meticulously, he took a fountain pen from his shirt pocket, unscrewed the cap and held the pen firmly in his hand ready to write.

"Maybe we can shorten this process a little after all. What will be the official name of your aircraft company, Mr. Martin?"

Jake, recalling that day in 1923 when his dad had referred to the old Jenny as an aero-plane, without hesitation answered, "Martin Aero."

Jake looked across the room at Dan who mouthed the words, "Where did that come from?"

"You see, Mr. Knudsen, we call the factory here in California the Drilling Products Division," and mostly for Dan's benefit, Jake added, "So it only follows that the airplane manufacturing part of our business would be called the Aero Products Division of Martin Company."

With Jake's last remark, Dan and Gertie left the room to keep from laughing out loud in front of everybody. They had won. They had beaten Knudsen at his own game.

"I don't know how he did it, but Jake pulled it off," Dan said to Gertie after they were out in the hall.

Knudsen continued filling out the paperwork.

"Exactly what type of aircraft is it again you plan to build, a pressurized twin-engine medium bomber?"

"That's correct, based loosely on the GLM B-26. We intend to call the plane the Dragon Bomber."

"You are aware North American has a bomber on the drawing board by the name Dragon, are you not?"

"Our company plane, the *Dragon One*, was the last of the C-67 Dragons built and Donald Douglas said we were welcome to the name. As to North American, I believe the Air Corps will cancel the contract for the B-28. North American can't keep up with the demand for their P-51 fighters and B-25 bombers now."

"We haven't canceled it yet," Knudsen said tartly.

"I think Mr. Martin may be correct," Colonel Polaski said. "Command pilots, like Doolittle, favor the B-25 Mitchell bomber and are demanding more of them. And North American's proposed XB-28 production facility in Omaha will more than likely be used to produce the new B-29 Superfortress along with Boeing."

"Very well, Mr. Martin, it seems your sources are better than mine. However, contrary to your information, we are continuing with the XB-35 Flying Wing project. The GLM Baltimore facility will be building them as Northrop can't meet their current production schedule." He skeptically added, "That is, if they ever get that weird thing to fly."

Jake waited patiently while Knudsen, with the help of his secretary, filled out the rest of the forms. Finally, Knudsen stood and handed Jake copies of the paperwork.

"Here's your priority authorization for building the new plant and certification for two new aircraft proposals. Your Dragon Bomber will be designated the XB-27."

Jake looked at the forms in his hand and asked, "You said 'two' new airplane designs?"

"Yes, those forms also authorize you to develop a new fighter designated the XP-74."

"As of right now, at least, we have no plans for developing a fighter aircraft."

To Jake's surprise, Knudsen actually smiled for the first time and offered to shake hands with Jake.

"From what I've learned about you today, Mr. Martin, nothing would surprise me. You're obviously already aware, Hughes' new fighter design is the XP-73 and GM Fisher has requested the designation XP-75 for their new fighter. Turns out, we skipped a number. Who better to assign that designation to, than you? Good day and good luck."

As Knudsen and his staff prepared to leave, his secretary approached Jake with her steno pad in hand prepared to write something down.

"Mr. Martin, I believe you mentioned earlier that you know of some undeveloped oil resources in your home state of Texas. If you would care to give me the exact locations, I will make a note of them."

"No need to, missy," Jake said. "My father leased those oilfields to Phillips three weeks ago. They'll be pumping oil for the war effort inside of a few months."

The secretary's jaw dropped, "Then you were bluffing?"

"Not exactly, ma'am. I believe I said I would tell you where there are some oilfields that have never been tapped. The fact that my dad had already advised the War Resources Agency of their location is only a minor technicality."

Jake smiled and excused himself to go to his office.

Dan and Gertie accompanied Knudsen and his group out of the building and returned to Jake's office.

Jake handed the government documents to Gertie.

"Here, when you get a chance you might want to read these over and then file them somewhere safe."

"Should I stamp the file folder PI like they do in Washington, Mr. Martin?"

"What does 'PI' mean?"

"Political Influence." Gertie replied and gave a little giggle at her joke.

Dan was more amused at her giggle than her joke.

"Say Jake, that reminds me. What in the world caused Hap Arnold to call here when he did?"

"You haven't figured that one out yet?" Jake said with a wide smile.

"I did," Gertie said. "Didn't you associate the call from Mr. Trippe with the call from General Arnold?"

Dan shook his head and smiled.

"You ol' hound dog. You always got a bone hidden somewhere," Dan said. As he started to leave to return to his own office, he added, "Oh, by the way, Ida found what she thinks is a real good housekeeper and nanny for the kids. Give her a call."

Jake went over to the drafting table in the corner of his office and stood looking over some of the many sketches strung out across the board. He picked up a pencil to markup one of the design drawings. Then he sat down on the drafting stool and started a new drawing of some of the features he wanted to incorporate into the XB-27.

Jake did not even hear Gertie when she stuck her head into his office and said, "Goodnight, Mr. Martin."

Jake worked well into the early hours of the morning that night. When he finished, he knew exactly what they were going to build and what the new Aero Dragon Bomber would look like.

The Dragon Bomber

Jake had forgotten to call Ida, so the next morning when Gertie came in to work, he said to her, "Get Ida Parker on the phone for me, please."

Jake sat down at his desk and picked up the phone.

"Hello Ida."

"Jake, I've found this great Hispanic woman, a widow lady. Her name is Lydia Gomez and she's just what you're looking for to keep house and take care of the kids."

"Is she willing to live-in?"

"Actually, her circumstances are a little depressing. Her Merchant Marine husband was lost at sea in the North Atlantic when a U-boat sank his ship. She has one son, a teenage boy who joined the Marines and she lives alone now in a rented house in Long Beach. She said she would be willing to relocate, but would require private quarters."

"You're a jewel, Ida. Tell her she's hired and we'll be getting back with her as soon as I find a house. In fact, tell her she's on the payroll as of today."

"Jake, I'm not going to let you procrastinate any longer on this house thing. I've found you a place. A friend of mine from church is selling her beautiful home in Santa Monica. The place overlooks the ocean a block off the beach on the east side of the Pacific Coast Highway at the corner of Adelaide and Ocean Avenue. I think it's just what you need and it has maid's quarters in the back."

"Okay, I'll go look at it when I get a chance."

"Can you go look at it today? My friend's husband is a National Guard officer and his unit has been activated. She's going home to North Carolina to live with her folks until he returns from overseas and she wants to list the house with a realtor right away if you're not interested."

"I can't get away. I'll look at it this weekend."

"Look here, Jake Martin. You're paying for a hotel room and Gertie tells me half the time you spend the night on that old office couch in your office."

"Okay, Ida…"

"And the kids aren't coming out here until we find you a house."

"Okay, I know when I'm outclassed in an argument. Have the lady or her agent bring the paperwork to my office and pick up a check."

"You should take a look at it first."

"Ida, it's okay, really. If it's good enough by your standards, its good enough for me and my kids."

***

Lydia Gomez insisted on meeting Jake before she would take the position. Ida arranged for Lydia and Jake to come to dinner at her and Dan's home.

Jake showed Lydia pictures of Lora and Michael. After visiting for a bit, both agreed the arrangement would work out. Jake thought Lydia was endowed with many of the same qualities and attitudes as his own mother.

Lydia moved to the new Ocean Avenue residence and settled into her separate quarters a week before Jake moved into the main house. She brought everything she owned from the little frame house she rented for years in Long Beach.

Jake borrowed an old army cot from Dan's garage to use for a couple of nights. The following Sunday afternoon, he stopped at a yard sale and purchased a bunch of used furniture, which barely began to fill the large house.

Flo and Violet arrived by train with Lora and Michael. Ida and Dan went with Jake to meet the train. The kids ran for Jake nearly knocking him down when they got off the train and hung onto him for the longest time.

"Mom, you and Violet are staying over at Ida and Dan's tonight. We don't have much furniture yet. The kids and I will camp out on the living room floor at the new house."

Lora and Michael cheered.

"Ida will bring you over tomorrow to meet Lydia."

***

Jake left for work early the next morning. When Ida arrived at the new house with Flo and Violet, they found Lydia seated on the floor playing the card game Fish with the kids. The breakfast dishes were still on the rickety old folding table being used as their kitchen dinette.

After the women visited for a while, Ida announced, "We're going shopping ladies. I'll drive and you buy!"

Michael did not want to go so they left him at home with Lydia. The foursome spent the day buying everything needed to run a house. Eight-year-old Lora insisted on picking out everything for her own room. Flo also made a point of asking Lora's opinion on most of the other furnishings. All that remained when they were through shopping was to wait for the furnishings to be delivered.

By the end of the following day, the five women had Jake's household furnished and running ship shape.

The children had taken a liking to Lydia right off and Flo soon decided she was ready to return home.

On the morning Flo and Violet left for Texas, Jake and the kids drove them to the train station. There was a lot of hugging, crying and more than one final goodbye scene.

Jake stood on the train platform holding Lora and Michael by the hand. The three watched as the train pulled out of the station. For better or worse, Jake and his two kids were on their own for the first time.

***

American wartime morale was lifted somewhat by the April 18th Doolittle raid on Tokyo in 1942, followed by the surrender of the Vichy French army to the American and British forces in North Africa.

Summer and fall passed quickly with Jake pushing hard to get the new aircraft assembly and machine shop buildings completed.

A temporary structure was put up on the factory parking lot to house the engineering group working on the new XB-27 design and production drawings. Jake divided his time equally between aircraft design meetings and following the construction progress of the new facilities.

The War Department hired movie studio people to make suggestions on how to camouflage defense plant buildings. Painted fake foliage and streets decorated the roof of the new Martin factory. From the air, the west wall and the roof of the main building appeared to have a road going right up over the top of the building.

The new operations hangar, the first new building completed, was built and ready for use in sixty days. The new machine shop was completed shortly thereafter. All component parts being manufactured under contract for other aircraft companies were transferred to the new machine shop from the drilling equipment machine shop. XB-27 parts production increased rapidly with the new aircraft machine shop in full operation.

The assembly building where the airframes would be joined would be finished in a matter of days. The new engineering design loft and the administrative offices would be located on the second floor of this building.

Interior glass windows overlooked the factory assembly line where the XB-27s would soon be built. The buildings had no exterior windows. Jake's interior office wall looked onto the assembly line where materials to build the first XB-27 were already being stacked.

Jake and Gertie moved into their new offices in the yet unfinished aircraft assembly building and the design department would be relocated there the following weekend.

***

When the Martin factory was originally located at the site in California, a banker and real estate investor by the name of Percy Mulholland had been involved in the land acquisition and issued ten percent of the common voting stock in the Martin California Corporation in return for services rendered. He turned out to be a rather shady businessman the Martin family regretted having associated themselves with.

An additional five percent of the stock had also been issued to several other minor investors as part of the land deal. Other than this outstanding fifteen percent, the Martin and Parker families owned all the remaining shares of stock.

When Jake began expanding the operation into the aircraft business, Percy threatened to bring a minority stockholder's suit against Jake and the Martin Company. Percy contended a substantial amount of the profits from the drilling equipment division were being squandered on the new aircraft enterprise.

Jake responded to the threat by saying, "Don't you know there's a war on?"

Which in fact, was the only reason Percy and his cronies were not able to proceed with a suit to stop the construction of the new bomber plant.

Jake had personally interviewed every engineer and manufacturing supervisor hired. Thus, the exceptionally well-qualified aeronautical design staff accelerated the early stages of the project and moved the XB-27 production start date ahead by months.

Informal design meetings, held right at the drafting tables over multiple cups of coffee, often lasted well into the evening hours.

For the Chief of Flight Line Maintenance, Jake hired an experienced senior airline mechanic, a middle-aged fellow by the name of Gene Wooley. Gene usually wore a dark-blue pair of jumpsuit-style coveralls. A wily ol' round-faced fellow with a pleasant attitude, he was a natural born mechanic and could fix anything.

Jake hired two flight-test pilots. Both were excellent pilots, but too old to be accepted into the military. The senior pilot, Raymond Sharpe, served with the American Expeditionary Force in Europe during the First World War as a member of the Hat-in-the-Ring squadron and flew with Captain Eddie Rickenbacker.

The other pilot, Harry Hammond, was a little younger and had been a bush pilot for years in Alaska and the Yukon. He had recently returned to the States when the war broke out.

Jake personally checked out the new flight-test pilots in the *Dragon One*, running them through the paces in the company airplane before hiring them.

After one such flight, Dan met Jake's returning flight to talk over a matter, which had come up earlier that morning. When Dan left to go back to the main building, Harry walked along with him.

"Jake's one heck of a good pilot," Harry commented. "Where'd he learn to fly like that?"

"I've always suspected it's somewhere in the soul. Some folks are born with it, and some aren't."

"I'm sure your right. You know, there is one thing that strikes me a little odd?"

"What's that, Harry?"

"Seems to me Jake walks with a slight limp. Did you ever notice that?"

"No, never noticed," Dan replied and smiled politely.

***

In February, before Jake arrived in L.A., a lone Japanese submarine surfaced off the coast of Santa Barbara and shelled an oil storage depot.

Very little damage had been done, but ever since the one isolated incident the general-public reported everything from shoreline rocks to whales as an enemy submarine.

Things got worse. Two days after the sub incident, in the early morning hours, the radar station on Palos Verdes reported sighting multiple flying objects a hundred miles out to sea. Air raid sirens sounded and the city went to blackout.

Eyewitnesses in Long Beach reported seeing fast-flying objects caught in the searchlight beams, but no bombs fell. During the fifty-five minute alert, Coastal Artillery batteries fired hundreds of rounds into the air. The only damage resulted from the anti-aircraft shells falling back onto buildings.

The government made some single-engine Fairchild model 24 reconnaissance airplanes available to Civil Air Patrol squadrons. The local CAP received two of the badly needed planes for patrol service.

The planes offered by the government were similar to Jake's first plane, the *Flying M*. The exception being these two had the inverted in-line Ranger engine instead of the Warner radial engine as on his old model 24W.

Financial sponsors for the planes as well as volunteer pilots to fly night patrols along the Los Angeles area coast were needed. Jake volunteered to do both.

When the two government-supplied Fairchild Rangers arrived, Jake sent the two planes to the Ops hangar for a thorough going through and inspection by Gene's crew of mechanics.

The two planes, with silver painted fabric and anti-glare black on the nose cowling, already had the traditional large red, white and blue three-propeller CAP logo painted on both sides of their fuselage.

A new and hastily organized CAP squadron met every weekend at the Culver City airport terminal building. The members asked Jake to be the Squadron Commander, but he declined in favor of having Ray Sharpe, Martin Aero's new chief test pilot, take on the job. Jake took his turn one night a week flying night patrols with an observer the same as the rest of the pilots in the squadron.

***

The B-25 Mitchell medium bomber distinguished itself as a low-altitude attack aircraft in early combat, but Jake based his fuselage design on the B-26 because of the barrel-like monocock construction of the

Marauder. He felt it was better suited for pressurization than the Mitchell's rectangular shaped fuselage. GLM Aircraft allowed Martin Aero to copy a B-26 fuselage jig for use in building the first XB-27 airframe tooling.

A special longer wing, using a Clark-Y bucket at the root and a Laminar flow bucket outboard, had been designed. The Clark airfoil would provide the new bomber with greater lift during climb and the Laminar airfoil would increase the bombers speed at cruise altitudes. The longer wing would also increase the bombers payload capability.

To give the Dragon even longer range, wing mounted drop-tanks like those used by the P-51 could be mounted under each wing. The B-27 was truly a unique design incorporating all of the best features of the most recent fighter and bomber designs into one aircraft.

The new design eliminated the rear-facing tail-gunner's crew position. The top-turret gun would be fired from a forward remote position like on the B-29 and synchronized so as not to shoot the plane's vertical stabilizer off when firing rearward.

Aircrewmen often claimed that the tail-gunner on most high altitude bombers often literally froze his tail off. This updated design grouped all of the crew into the smaller pressurized area of the main fuselage, a concept used on British and German aircraft. The greater crew comfort would reduce crew fatigue resulting in smarter, more alert thinking which was a real asset when making the split second decisions required in air-to-air combat.

The flight engineer would man the top-turret from an overhead Plexiglas bubble and the gun would be fired by remote control similar to the guns on the new B-29.

Unlike the heavily armed B-17 Flying Fortress, the Dragon Bomber would not have a full 360-degree defensive firing coverage. The prevailing thinking was that a pursuit plane could not climb fast enough to intercept a B-27.

Jake's short tour with Chennault's Flying Tigers had also convinced him most attacks would come from fighters already at altitude and laying in wait for the bombers.

The rest of the Dragon Bomber's armament consisted of four .50 caliber machineguns fix-mounted in saddle pods, two on each side of the nose providing the bomber with a lethal low-altitude air-to-ground firepower capability.

The side-mounted guns would allow the Dragon Bomber to retain its Plexiglas nose for the bombardier-navigator's station to be equipped with the newest, very accurate Norton bombsight. Thus, the Dragon Bomber would be fully operational with only a four-man crew, exposing fewer airmen to the danger of being killed or captured.

The key to the XB-27's speed and performance proved to be one of Jake's best kept secrets. Ford Motor Company refused to produce the Rolls-Royce Supermarine engines for the British prior to the U.S. entering the war. However, on their own, Ford engineers had designed a liquid cooled V12 engine with a turbo-exhaust driven supercharger that developed two thousand horsepower.

The engines never made it into a fighter aircraft design and so far, had only been manufactured in small numbers. This engine was Jake's first choice and the B-27 Dragon Bombers would all use these new engines.

This traditional fighter aircraft-type engine with its low-profile nacelle would give the operational B-27s even more speed due to its streamlined aerodynamics.

Allocations for these engines had been easily obtained, as Ford could not produce them in large enough quantities for use on a high production-run fighter while also putting a maximum effort towards mass producing tanks, jeeps and the B-24 Liberators.

***

To the best of Jake's knowledge, Gertie had never been up in an airplane and had never shown the slightest interest in flying in one. Whenever Jake prepared to make a flying trip, he would always use the opportunity to needle her a little about going flying.

"Gertie, we'll be needing you on this next trip to Boeing. Got a lot of paperwork to do, so stand by to go. Oh yeah, better go check out a flight suit in your size. Wouldn't want you to get one of your pretty black dresses soiled."

Usually Jake would tell her late on a Friday afternoon to plan for a flight on Monday so she would worry about it over the weekend.

Gertie never knew for sure if Jake was serious or not. The first time or two Jake pulled this prank on her she did go check out a flight suit and came to work with a small overnight bag packed.

Jake would wait until the day of his departure and then tell her, "Gertie, turns out we won't need you after all, so you don't have to go on this flight."

He never intended to have her go anyway. He needed her to stay in the office to look after things in his absence. Jake was always quick to tell everyone Gertie ran the place, but still he seldom ever missed a good opportunity to ruffle her feathers.

Gertie finally resolved her dilemma by checking out a flight suit in her size and keeping it in her desk drawer.

Jake scheduled a meeting with the Boeing designers working on the B-29 in Wichita. After pulling his usual dirty trick on Gertie and not taking her along on the flight, Jake and several of the engineers flew up to Boeing's B-29 factory in the *Dragon One*.

At the Boeing factory, Jake's engineers saw first hand how the airframe on the B-29 Super Fortress was sealed for pressurization and tested underwater.

Boeing engineers puncture-tested an airframe in a decompression chamber. When bullets passed through the airframe, contrary to popular myth, they discovered the airframe did not explode and come apart. The pressure only started to leak. For years, the Army Air Corps had resisted pressurized high-altitude aircraft without good cause.

Another thing Jake noticed about the XB-29, the indicator dials on all the instruments at the engineer's station all pointed to the same clock position when reading normal. This relieved the flight engineer from having to read each individual instrument one at a time and thus, the flight engineer could tell at a glance when any one of the instruments indicated a problem.

During their visit to Boeing, Jake and each of his team members test fired one of the new remote control gun turrets. This was the turret that would be supplied to Martin Aero for use on the XB-27. They would come from the same sub-contractor currently supplying Boeing with these top-secret devices.

***

The new assembly building at Martin Aero had only been completed a month when the first two XB-27 fuselages were mated to their wings. Aircraft #1 would be the prototype and aircraft #2 would be the first production bomber. Things were starting to take shape.

Nine aircraft would be built on the first production run and the prototype aircraft's assembly accelerated for use in initial flight-testing.

Jake came to trust and value the opinion of his lead design engineer, a middle-aged fellow by the name of Albert Swartz, a rather small, soft-spoken Jewish fellow whom everyone called Al. He was the smartest theoretical mathematician and aerodynamicist Jake ever met. Jake considered it a stroke of luck that Martin Aero had been able to hire him.

On any typical early morning, prior to the assembly line starting up and before most of the administrative staff arrived, Jake often met with Al down on the assembly floor to review the work in progress. Jake liked to hear Al's opinion on various problems.

Jake and Al finished their usual walking tour of the production line and being a particularly pleasant summer morning, they walked out to the flight-test hangar. On their way, Jake watched as an Army Air Corps C-45 Twin Beech circled the airport for a landing.

"Got some Air Corps brass and civilian VIPs flying in this morning. That's probably them now," Jake said. "We'll go meet them and I'll introduce you."

Al and Jake waited on the ramp for the plane to land.

"It's a beautiful day and we're going to be tied up in meetings all day. I think I'd rather go flying."

"I guess that's the difference between me and a man like you, Jake. I want to know if the plane will fly and you want to fly it."

"You might be on to something there, Al."

Momentarily, the C-45 taxied up to the Ops hangar.

Jake greeted the small group as they came off the plane.

"This is Al Swartz, our lead design engineer."

Ray and Harry had also came out to meet the plane.

"And these two fellows here are the best two flight-test pilots in the business. These three gentlemen will give you a tour of our production line and the engineering department. We'll meet back in the conference room at ten and I'll see you then."

The group left for the factory and Jake remained behind to check on some things at the OP hangar where the C-67 company plane and the two CAP aircraft were housed.

A flight Ops office and pilot's lounge adjoined the new hangar. Transit aircraft and military VIPs having business at the Martin facilities often used the lounge.

Jake stopped by the hangar to tell the crew chief to expect a transit Army plane to RON, a term used to indicate the aircraft would remain overnight.

As he left the hangar, he noticed two young ladies in Women Army Air Corps uniforms under the wing of the C-45 looking at the landing gear. Curiosity got the best of him and he went over to see what they were doing.

Even at a distance, he could see the tall one was a real looker. He walked across the ramp towards them and as he drew closer he saw both of the young women were wearing pilot's wings.

The larger of the two WAAC pilots bore a striking resemblance to the movie actress Jane Russell, except she was a blonde instead of a brunette. The other WAAC pilot was a petite, very pretty young lady with short-cropped black hair.

Jake chuckled to himself, as the two ladies reminded him of female versions of the cartoon characters Mutt and Jeff.

"Good morning, ladies. Welcome to Culver City. Can I be of any assistance to you?"

Jake could not take his eyes off the tall one. She carried herself with a femininity that transcended the drab Army tan, knee-length uniform skirt and tight fitting two-pocket blouse she wore.

"Good morning, sir," both girls replied in unison.

Jake noticed their uniforms were fitted a little too tight, the short skirts and tailored blouses being the current style of ladies attire.

"Do you ladies always fly in those tight skirts?"

The smaller WAAC pilot smiled as she spoke up.

"No, we used your facilities over in the Ops office to change out of our flight suits. Hope you don't mind."

"No. I mean sure, that's what it's there for. You're welcome to make use of it anytime."

The smaller WAAC was more outgoing and obviously did most of the talking for the pair.

"I'm Second Lieutenant Judy Modisett, the copilot on this flight and this is Lieutenant Margaret Jones or Maggie as she likes to be called. We just flew you in a fresh supply of Army brass."

"Thanks. You couldn't have managed to get lost instead, could you?"

"Sorry," Judy replied with a smile.

Jake continued to be captivated, almost mesmerized by Maggie's size and beauty. He did not mean to be impolite, but he was staring at her.

Maggie, in low-cut heels, appeared about an inch taller than Jake and almost equal to him in weight. The lady did not have an ounce of body fat on her anywhere. Maggie was just a big girl.

The words Amazon Beauty flashed through Jake's mind because if there ever was one, she was standing in front of him right now.

"You always wear those stuffy old business suits?" Maggie said finally speaking up and returning Jake's barb about their tight uniforms.

Jake could not think of a good comeback, so he smiled politely.

Maggie wanted to make sure Jake knew she was only kidding, so she said, "I thought guys in California wore Hawaiian shirts and walked around offering girls cool drinks with little umbrellas in them."

Not aware of Maggie's dry sense of humor, it took a moment for her wisecrack to sink-in and then Jake laughed.

"Don't have any cool drinks on me, but I'm good for dinner down on Hollywood Boulevard any night you're up for it. That is, if you ladies are interested."

Gene, the chief mechanic walked up.

"Understand there's a landing gear problem on your airplane, ma'am."

"It's only a low oleo strut on the right landing gear," Maggie explained.

Gene went over to look at the strut.

"No problem. I'll be right back with some compressed air to pump her up."

Maggie glared at him and Gene looked away.

"I mean pump up the strut," Gene said, revising his wording.

This extracted a small giggle from Judy.

Jake started back to the hangar with Gene and Judy hollered out to him, "Say, just how would a couple of fly-girls go about connecting with that dinner invitation?"

"I've got to meet with the brass you gals flew in for us," Jake said, turning around to walk backwards as he left. "Come to Gertie's office about quitting time."

"Gertie, who's Gertie?" Judy hollered back.

"She runs the place. Just ask anyone for directions to her office!"

Jake turned back to walk with Gene to the hangar.

"I didn't know we had women pilots flying on a regular basis with the Army now."

Gene looked over his shoulder at the two lady pilots waiting by the nose of their Twin Beech.

"Oh yeah, I've seen those two in here before. They used to be ferry pilots, but the Army recently assigned a bunch of them to the new air transport unit they formed to free up pilots for combat. The Amazon's a pretty good looker, isn't she?"

Jake laughed because Gene had just said what he had been thinking to himself a little earlier.

"You can say that again!"

***

Late that afternoon, Jake finished his meetings with the Air Corps procurement people and returned to his office.

Maggie and Judy were seated in guest chairs in Gertie's office maintaining their best behavior.

"These two officers, pilots, ladies... Whatever. Claim they have an appointment with you, Mr. Martin."

Jake stopped in his tracks. He forgot all about offering to take them out to dinner.

Both girls looked up and smiled at Jake as he came in.

He laughed as he thought to himself they looked like two young girls who had been sent to the principal's office and Gertie the school principal.

His two guests for dinner stood up ready to leave.

"Where's this fancy chow place that you're taking us tonight?" Judy asked.

Jake laid some papers on Gertie's desk.

"Goodnight Gertie, see you tomorrow. Oh, call Lydia and tell her I won't be home for dinner."

As they were leaving, Maggie asked, "Lydia, is that your wife? She can come too, we don't mind."

"No, that's my kids' nanny, she's their boss. You've already met my boss," Jake said gesturing back towards Gertie, but Jake knew why Maggie asked.

"Have a nice evening, Mr. Martin," Gertie said with a slightly sarcastic tone to her voice.

Jake and his two adopted WAAC pilots went out to the parking lot where Jake opened the passenger door of his dirty, faded yellow, three year old Continental Cabriolet.

Judy, seeing Jake's car was a convertible, stopped before getting in and said, "Put the top down!"

Jake, tired from a long day of meetings, protested, "Nah, its too much trouble. I'm hungry, let's go eat."

"Aw come on, Jake," Maggie said. "Put the top down. This is Hollywood, isn't it?"

Jake gave in and put the top down, but did not fool with snapping the boot on. The now happy duo piled in the front seat with Jake. He drove out of the factory main gate and turned north onto Centinela Avenue.

During dinner at the Brown Derby, Jake found out everything he might have ever wanted to know about the two lady pilots and a few things he would have just as soon they not bothered to share with him.

Maggie's father had operated a small airport not far from Minneapolis for thirty years before he died a few years ago. Her father taught her to fly as a teenager.

Both women volunteered for service with the Army Air Corps Ferry Command when the U.S. first entered the war and had only recently been assigned to transport Air Corps procurement people around.

Judy, now more talkative than ever, rattled on.

"I learned to fly from my first boyfriend. He was a pilot in a flying circus before the war and did the drunk-farmer act in air shows. For a short while, I was a wing-walker."

"You're kidding!" Jake said.

"Nope," Judy said and raised her drink glass in the air. "That's what I did. I sure did."

Maggie remained reserved at first, but talked more as the evening wore on.

"I'm never getting married. I'm not the least bit interested in getting married. I dated the same fellow all through high school, a strapping farm boy by the name of Bo. The summer after we graduated, I thought I had gotten myself pregnant and he said he'd marry me, but I wasn't and he didn't."

After two Daiquiris and a Pina Colada, Judy became increasingly melancholy.

"My boyfriend is a pilot in a B-29 squadron," she said miserably, almost ready to cry. "He's going to be sent overseas. Somewhere in Asia, I think."

Maggie, who was a couple of sheets to the wind herself, said, "Shush, loose lips, sink ships!"

"Oh yeah?" Judy replied sniffing back tears. "I'm sure I won't get to see him before his squadron leaves. What if he gets killed and I never see him again?"

Judy continued to repeat the same sentence with slight variations in the wording several more times.

"Just ignore her when she gets like that," Maggie told Jake. "Bo, my ex boyfriend, is a tank driver with the Minnesota National Guard. When the war broke out he got shipped to North Africa with his armored unit. Best I can tell from the news, he's serving under General Patton."

Judy put her index finger to her lips.

"Shhhh, shame on you! Loose hips slinks slips... Hmm, I wonder what else loose hips do?" she said and giggled.

Typical of Jake, he mostly listened and nursed a couple of drinks all evening. The hour was late when he delivered his two dinner companions to their government provided hotel room near the Douglas factory.

Jake escorted them to the door.

"Goodnight ladies, I'm going to leave you now."

"Thank you, kind sir, for dinner and a charming evening," Maggie replied.

Judy, now having a little difficulty standing up, looked Jake up close in the face and said, "Isn't he cute?"

"You've had too much to drink," Maggie said sternly to Judy catching her under one arm as she weaved. "Put a lid on it."

"Stop by and be my guests anytime you're in town."

"Don't make any offers you don't intend to keep!" Maggie replied with a coy smile.

Maggie

The prototype XB-27 rolled off the assembly line in the fall of 1942 and moved to the Ops hangar where it was made ready for preliminary flight-testing.

Martin Aero's chief test pilot Ray Sharp and copilot Harry Hammond prepared to make the Dragon Bomber's maiden flight. Gene Wooley, Martin Aero's chief mechanic would fly as flight engineer on the inaugural flight.

Jake would have preferred to make the first flight himself, but being the principle-operating officer of the manufacturer prevented him from doing so. The Army Air Corps procurement department had a strict policy against this.

The day came when the bright, shiny silver new XB-27, not yet painted in the Army's olive drab color, was ceremoniously rolled out. The aircraft's serial number 296165 had been stenciled in black letters on the tail.

Colonel Polaski had been transferred from D.C. to California to serve as the Air Corps procurement officer for Lockheed and Martin Aero. His wife did the honors of christening the new bomber.

The crowd moved back for Ray to start the engines. The invited guests, VIPs and employees watched as the XB-27 taxied to the end of the runway. The power came up and the nose wheel strut rose as the Dragon Bomber rolled forward. Ray applied full throttle and used up most of the runway on the takeoff for safety in case he had to abort.

Ray made a wide circling turn and brought the Dragon Bomber in low. He buzzed the field at high speed and pulled up to return for his approach to a landing. The Dragon Bomber taxied back to the hangar and the engines were shutdown. The waiting crowd cheered and applauded.

The first flight had been a success. Extensive testing, including high-altitude performance, would be conducted on another day. This day's flight had only demonstrated the plane would fly.

Ray reported to Jake and Al, "The XB-27 performed in every respect as anticipated or better." Harry and Gene both concurred.

A cocktail party and luncheon in the operations hangar for those attending the ceremony followed the flight. Jake circulated for a while, taking congratulations and mixing with the guests.

After the initial excitement, Jake needed some time to reflect on today's flight and savor what Martin Aero Products Division had accomplished in so short a time.

He slipped out the back door of the hangar and once outside where no one could see him, he yelled, "Yes!" and jumped in the air swinging his arms like an umpire who had called the last strikeout in an extra inning ballgame.

Jake returned to his office. Gertie was at her desk having a piece of cake and some punch from the luncheon.

"You've got company," she said as Jake walked past.

Jake entered his office to find Maggie seated in his desk chair dressed fashionably in a pair of beige slacks and a white blouse. Her long legs were crossed with her high-heel shoes propped up on Jake's desk.

"Hi ya, sailor. Want a date for the evening?"

Jake laughed and went over to sit on the couch.

"When did you get here? Didn't see you at the rollout."

Maggie swung her feet off of Jake's desk and stood up. She moved gracefully across the room and sat down on the couch beside Jake.

"I flew some of the brass in earlier this morning. I was there, but you were too busy to notice me."

"Sure is good to see you again, Maggie."

Jake's admiring look did not escape Maggie's notice.

"Clean up pretty good, don't I?" and she laughed.

Jake stood up from the couch and extended his hand.

"Let's get the heck out of here."

Maggie rose slowly and moved very close to Jake.

"Where we going?" she asked in a deep sexy voice.

He could smell the pleasant scent of her hair. Not a perfume, but the scent of a woman.

"To a beach house in Malibu."

Maggie's breasts gently touched Jake's chest and she looked straight into his eyes.

"Okay, you little shit."

Maggie smiled and turned away to leave with Jake.

Jake's over six feet and two hundred pounds had never exposed him to being addressed in that manner before. He sure hoped that was not going to be Maggie's pet name for him. Unfortunately, he was wrong about that.

***

Driving along the Pacific Coast Highway, Jake asked Maggie, "Why'd you call me sailor back there?"

"You don't know?"

"I can pretty much guess. I'd say you found out I'm an old flying boat captain, didn't you?"

"That's not all I found out about you, Cowboy."

"You've been doing your homework. Can't play the big shot with you anymore, you know all about me now."

"Not all, I suspect, but it's a start. The night you took Judy and I out, we did all the talking and you did all the listening. That's the reason you know all about us, but I had to do all the finding out about you on my own."

Jake stopped at a small store for some groceries and a bottle of wine. When he got back in the car Maggie asked, "Whose beach house is this we're going to?"

Jake pulled back onto the Pacific Coast Highway.

"It's not exactly anyone's beach house right now. The place is empty. A builder is trying to sell me a house on the beach and he loaned me the key to have a look at this one. The kids are at home and you know how that is."

"Well no, I really don't, but I can imagine. I'm an only child and I suppose my dad spoiled me."

Maggie let her long blonde hair down to flutter in the breeze from the open car window. Jake alternately glanced at the road ahead and over at Maggie. The fading afternoon sunlight reflecting off of the ocean water silhouetted her profile emphasizing her natural beauty.

"Oh yes, your kids. I forgot that you have two children. Where's their mother?"

Jake would have preferred not to answer, but to be polite he replied simply, but honestly, "I don't know."

Maggie did not go there again with her questions, as it seemed to her Jake did not wish to talk about his family right then. She sat quietly enjoying the ride.

After a few miles of silence, Jake said, "My kid's names are Lora and Michael. You'll like them when you get a chance to meet them. They have a way of charming strangers, so be on your guard."

"Okay," Maggie said.

"You see I'm not real pleased with the old two-story house where we're living now so I've been looking around for something out of the city. The kids used to live on the ranch with my folks and they might like to be back out in the country. They're building some modern houses out in Malibu and I thought I would check them out."

Jake pulled the Continental into the driveway of the beach house just off the PCH. The garden lights and a few lights in the house were on.

"Hey, we're in luck. Looks like the utilities are on and judging from what I can see through the front window, the place appears to be furnished. Come to think of it, the builder did say they were using this one as a show house."

Jake unlocked the front door, carried the sack of groceries into the beach house and put them in the kitchen.

Maggie went to the patio window and stared out across the shimmering ocean waters into the evening darkness. The lights of several ships off in the distance moved slowly on the horizon making their way up the coastline.

"Water looks inviting. How about a swim?"

"You bring a bathing suit?" Jake asked.

"No, but I have a decent set of panties and bra on under this outfit," Maggie replied with a smile.

Maggie's candor amused Jake.

"Okay by me, so long as you don't mind seeing me in my Fruit of the Looms."

She opened the patio door, stepped out onto the wooden deck and slipped off her high-heel shoes. She was not wearing hose, as silk stockings were hard to come by with the war on. After removing her blouse and slacks, she folded them neatly and placed them on the patio table.

Maggie stood statuesque for a moment in her silk panties and well-filled bra before descending the patio steps and walked slowly across the darkened sandy beach.

Jake stripped down to his jockey under shorts, left his clothes in a pile on the patio deck where he took them off and ran after her.

The starlight lit the glow of the phosphorus in the surf coming ashore, clearly outlining the water's edge as Maggie waded into the surf and Jake stopped to watch her standing knee deep in the water with the ocean foam swirling around her long shapely legs. When Maggie turned to look back at Jake, a small wave knocked her down and she screamed as she fell into the cold water.

Jake laughed and did a belly flop dive into the surf beside her. He came up with her in his arms, both choking from the salt water and laughing. The two stood together holding their warm bodies next to each other.

Maggie leaned way back to gaze up into the starry night sky as Jake held onto her.

They kissed passionately and stood in the almost waist high surf for a few more minutes, but the water was way too cold and they waded ashore holding hands.

Maggie broke and ran with Jake right behind her to the patio grabbing their clothes as they went past them and scrambled into the house.

Jake watched as Maggie lowered the strap on her bra from her shoulder.

"Turn around, would you, please?"

He turned away and took the opportunity to slip out of his wet shorts. As he looked up, he could see Maggie in the large mirror over the mantle above the fireplace.

Maggie removed her wet things even though she had seen the mirror and knew Jake was watching her. She smiled at him in the mirror as she reached for an Indian blanket thrown over the back of the couch for decoration and wrapped the blanket around her.

Jake pulled his trousers on quickly and built a fire in the fireplace.

Maggie went to get the groceries out of the sack and spread the food out picnic style on the carpet in front of the fire. She opened the wine Jake had purchased at the grocery store and poured it into a couple of coffee cups she had found in the kitchen.

At first their conversation seemed a little strained, but soon the two curious strangers babbled on like a couple of teenage school kids. Besides a strong physical attraction, they shared nothing in common except their mutual love of flying. They passed the time trading flying stories and laughing.

Maggie told of her and Judy's favorite trick.

"After we've thoroughly checked out the airplane, we'd wait out of sight until the aircraft is loaded with our all male passengers, usually pilots or aircrewmen. Then we board and leisurely stroll down the center aisle watching the faces of the men as it slowly dawns on them that two women are going to be piloting their plane."

Jake was laughing at one of Maggie's stories when he made eye contact with her and the smiles slowly faded from their faces. Carnal temptation could no longer be resisted.

The Indian blanket slid from Maggie's shoulder as she allowed herself to fall gently into Jake's arms and he lowered her slowly onto the spread out blanket.

Jake and Maggie made love on the living room floor and fell asleep in each other's arms.

Just before Maggie dropped off to sleep she whispered in Jake's ear, "You little shit, now you made me care about you."

Jake did not hear her. He had already fallen asleep.

***

Maggie was up and dressed before Jake that morning. She found some coffee in the kitchen and made a fresh pot. When Jake woke up, she was making an effort to clean up some of the mess they had made the night before.

On their drive back to Culver City, Maggie mentioned casually, "Now you've made me late for work the first day on my new job."

"Did you miss a flight or what?"

"No, I'm late for work at the factory. I forgot to tell you the Army has assigned me as liaison officer to the aircraft acceptance unit at Martin Aero effective today."

Jake smiled.

"I guess this means we'll be seeing a lot of each other from now on."

Maggie smiled back.

"Yeah, I guess that's what it means."

***

That afternoon, the Malibu homebuilder came by Jake's office to pick up the keys to the show house.

"How'd you like the place on the beach, Mr. Martin? Is it what you're looking for?"

"Not exactly, little too small. I drove the area and saw a new house up on a bluff with your sign. I think a larger house more along those lines is what I need."

Jake shuffled through the mess of papers on his desk for the house keys to return to the builder.

"Oh yes, those are nice lots," the builder said. "Not right on the water, but they do overlook the ocean and have access to the beach," indicating he was pleased Jake was showing an interest in the more expensive home sites.

"Is the one that's under construction sold?"

"Yes, but the lot next door is available. That one has an even larger backyard with a wooden stairway on the back of the property, which goes down to the beach."

"I know, I walked over there and actually, I like that lot much better," Jake said still looking for the keys to return to the builder. "Gertie!" Jake hollered.

Gertie entered the office and went over to the coat rack where Jake hung his suit jacket. She took the keys from his jacket pocket and placed the keys on his desk as she passed by returning to her office.

Jake looked at the keys and gave Gertie one of those looks as she exited with a smug expression on her face.

"Let's talk about the lot that is available. I've made a list of things I'd like in a new house. I'd like to see what you can come up with to build on that lot."

"Would be glad to, but with building materials and labor in such short supply, it might be as much as a year before we could finish the job," the builder explained.

"Okay, tell you what I'll do. I'll keep the house I'm in for now, but if we can make a deal I'll lease the beach house, furnishings and all, until the new house is finished. I need a place for guests and a place where the kids and I can get away on the weekends."

"Boy, have you got a deal, Mr. Martin!" the builder said jumping up to shake Jake's hand. "Oh and you might as well keep those keys for now."

"Fair enough. I'll rough out some plans for the house I've got in mind and have them sent over to your office. Come on, I'll walk out with you."

"I'll have my architect look them over as soon as we get them."

"Along the back of the house I want large picture windows that look onto the backyard. The yard will be landscaped with the grass running all the way out to the edge of the small cliff that overlooks the ocean."

The two men went down the stairs to the main lobby and Jake continued to enthusiastically explain all of the ideas he wanted to incorporate into the house.

"Those palm trees that frame the view of the setting sun in the western sky, don't let anyone touch them. Those palms will make a picture postcard view of the ocean from the back patio. I'll also need a small bungalow adjoining the main house for Lydia."

"And who is Lydia, your mother-in-law?"

"No, she's my kid's nanny. I want her to feel like she has her own place. As for the library and study, well… You can tell more when you look over the plans."

***

Maggie and Jake began seeing each other on a regular basis, spending an occasional evening together at the Roosevelt Hotel. Jake took Maggie home with him to the Santa Monica house to visit from time to time, but she never stayed over. Weekends or at least Sundays were spent at the beach house.

Maggie and the kids got along fine. She enjoyed playing with Michael and would talk with Lora for as long as Lora wanted to talk, but she never developed any real motherly instincts towards the children. The kids regarded Maggie more as a houseguest than one of the family.

Maggie was self-assured and did not seem to be out to prove something, as did so many women who took on traditional men's jobs. With Jake and Maggie it was always clear who was to navigate and who was to steer.

Jake continued to be fascinated with Maggie's beauty and charm and Maggie cared very much about Jake, but their relationship was more like close friends than lovers.

The sex was good and the subject of marriage never came up. Based on Jake's past experience with women, he often thought that if he did re-marry, a friend might be a better choice of a partner than a lover.

From time to time, Maggie would get a letter from Bo in North Africa and she would read the letter to Jake. Bo's letters were not very personal, but reading between the lines, one could tell Bo still cared for Maggie.

***

Ray and Henry commenced high altitude flight-testing on the XB-27. Al Swartz, the senior design engineer had contended from early on in development that the plane would require more aerodynamic lift at high altitudes. Sure enough, the results of the initial high altitude flight-tests bore this out.

Ray reported, "At twenty-seven thousand feet, she would not climb at more than two hundred feet a minute and the climb rate fell off rapidly above that altitude."

As a result, the Dragon Bomber prototype underwent modification to have twenty inches added to each wing section just beyond the outboard prop line.

Subsequent high altitude flight-tests proved the XB-27 capable of still climbing steadily at thirty thousand feet. A side benefit of the wing extension was that a larger fuel tank bladder could be installed, thereby increasing the aircraft's range.

Al had also predicted the longer wingspan would increase the cruise speed at higher altitudes and once again, he was right.

***

Late on a Friday afternoon, Jake was in his office when Maggie burst through the door with Judy in tow.

"Guess who just flew in on her broom stick!"

Judy, with a wide smile on her face, was waving a piece of paper in her hand.

"Look what I've got, a forty-eight hour pass. Let's party!"

Judy had not been around for a couple of months and she always livened up the place.

Jake was glad to see her.

"What's your pleasure, Miss?"

Judy plopped down on the brown leather office couch.

"There's only one thing I want to do, that's go see my lieutenant in Wichita. He's shipping out next week, but I can't make it there and back on a bus and the airlines are booked solid with VIP types."

Gertie had entered with the two girls and was standing in the office doorway with her arms folded, listening.

"Don't we have some unfinished business at Boeing?" Jake asked Gertie without looking directly at her.

Gertie clearly understood Jake's flippant remarks.

"Gobs and gobs I suspect, Mr. Martin." she replied in her usual straight-faced manor.

Jake picked up the phone and dialed Gene's extension at the flight operations office.

"Gene, what's the status of the company plane?"

Gene on the other end of the phone replied, "Fueled and rarin' to go, as always, sir."

Judy's face lit up and she ran to hug Jake nearly knocking the phone out of his hand.

"Okay Gene, have the ol' bird pulled out and ready. We'll be departing in about a half hour."

Judy turned to Maggie and asked, "Who is this amazing guy you hang out with anyway?"

Never missing a good opportunity, Jake said to Gertie, "We're going to fly over to Wichita. Want to go with us?"

"No, but thank you just the same, Mr. Martin. Maybe some other time," Gertie replied and went back to her desk.

"Jake Martin, you ought to be ashamed. Quit aggravating that woman," Maggie said.

***

Enroute to Wichita, Jake remembered he would need special permission to land at the Boeing facility, but when he radioed for clearance, he discovered air control was already expecting his aircraft.

Maggie was in the copilot's seat and Judy was riding in the jump seat between them.

He turned to the two girls and said, "Of course, I should have known Gertie would get on the phone as soon as we left and obtain the proper clearances."

Jake keyed his mike, "McConnell Field, this is Douglas November zero-zero-one for landing."

A wise cracking, young male voice from the tower replied, "Roger, *Dragon One*. We'd know that paint job anywhere! Your traffic is a B-29 on short final. Follow him for landing and you're cleared to the Boeing ramp."

Maggie unsuccessfully forced back a smile at the controller's remark. Jake mumbled, "Wise ass."

Then Maggie and Judy both laughed out loud.

Judy's tall handsome young B-29 pilot lieutenant stood waiting for her out front of the main hangar. Jake pulled the *Dragon One* onto a parking spot and had not even cut the engines before Judy was out the door. She ran to jump into her boyfriend's arms and wrapped her legs around his waist.

Maggie looked at Jake and remarked, "Well, we won't be seeing those two for the next twenty-four hours. I guess we're on our own."

There was a thundershower rolling in from the west. Jake got the control locks out of the luggage compartment and inserted the locks into the ailerons and rudder.

While he and Maggie waited for someone to put the plane in the hangar, several dozen of the workers came out to look over the Douglas C-67 and admire the paint job.

Jake turned to Maggie and said jokingly, "Well Dorothy, maybe we're not in Kansas after all! Where'd all the Munchkins come from?"

The ground handlers finally came and hooked a tow bar up to Jake's plane and a tug pulled it into the hangar for safe storage from the approaching storm.

"Captain Pegasus, is that you?" called out a vaguely familiar voice from behind Jake.

Turning to the sound of the voice, Jake instantly recognized Earl Mason, the young fellow who had helped him with the avionics on his old Spartan monoplane back in Stillwater years ago.

"Earl! What in the world are you doing here? No, don't answer that. I remember you telling me you planned to go to work for the government. Looks like you did."

Earl walked Jake and Maggie to the flight line office.

"Been up all night trying to get that stuff to work," Earl said motioning back across the ramp to an array of large antennas mounted atop some olive drab Army trailers.

Jake did not have to ask. He knew Earl was referring to a Top Secret project currently underway there at Boeing.

"Looking at putting H2S systems in the 29s, huh Earl?" Jake commented. H2S being the British code name for RADAR.

"How'd you know about that?"

"Actually, I flew one of the first airborne systems on a Clipper a couple years ago in the Pacific. Turned out the Navy wasn't all that happy with my test results."

"The Germans have a countermeasure system called Liechtenstein, but where these planes are going it won't be a problem."

From Earl's reply, Jake guessed this group of RADAR equipped B-29s were headed for Asia and the CBI theatre to fly a route over the mountains the pilots call The Hump.

Having flown all night. Maggie was tired and hungry.

"Earl, where's a good place to get some breakfast in this aircraft factory boomtown of yours?" she asked.

Earl pointed to his light blue 1940 Nash Ambassador in the parking lot.

"My house, of course. I'm sure Lola will fix us up something. Oh, she'll fuss because I didn't call ahead to let her know I was bringing company, but don't pay any attention, she'll be fine. Besides, you'll get to meet my son, Marvin. He should be about the same age as your boy. What's your boy's name again? Sorry, I forgot."

"Michael," Jake said as they piled into Earl's car with the A-card gas sticker in the corner of the window and the woven, paper-mat seat covers.

"Neat car, Earl. Don't see many of these around."

"You know how it is, got to keep these ol' cars running nowadays. I do all my own mechanic work."

Jake and Maggie spent the morning visiting with Earl and Lola. Lola had grown up in Beggs, a small Oklahoma town south of Tulsa, and she knew of Jake's family. An old timer named Chisum was a friend of Lola's dad and he used to herd cattle with Jake's grandfather, John Martin.

Earl and Lola's crowded apartment was too small for guests, so that afternoon Earl drove Jake and Maggie to a nearby tourist court to spend the night.

"I'll pick you two up in the morning around eight."

Maggie came wide-awake late that evening and punched Jake to wake up.

"Let's walk over to Gracie's, that little steakhouse across the street next to a bowling alley."

After dinner, she challenged Jake to go bowling. They had a couple of beers and did not bother to keep score.

***

The following morning at the main gate, a civilian police sergeant was on guard.

"Where's the young fellow who is usually on guard duty this time of day?" Earl asked.

"He's off today, sir."

Earl produced an Air Corps Special Services ID card with the rank of major and showed it to the gate guard.

"Oh, I recognize you now. You're the man working on the classified project out on the runway, but I'll need to see some identification for your other two passengers."

Earl, assuming the guard would recognize Jake Martin, made the mistake of pointing to Jake with his thumb and saying, "Him? Oh he's okay, he's just one of our local German espionage agents."

Unfortunately, the guard did not seem to understand Earl's dry Oklahoma wit or think his remark was funny. The guard stepped back, drew his .45 automatic and cocked the action with a click-click sound.

"He holding a gun on you?" the guard asked excitedly.

"No!" Earl replied. "This situation has gotten way out of hand! I was only kidding. Call the Boeing Corporate office and they'll vouch for Mr. Martin."

"You all stay right where you are," the guard ordered and stepped back into the guard shack to dial the phone.

Within minutes, a large black sedan roared up to the guard gate and the VP of engineering at Boeing stepped out.

Seeing Jake sitting sheepishly in Earl's car, the VP declared, "Who are these people anyway?"

"Oh very funny, Chris. Specially when you're dealing with a Keystone Cop with no sense of humor," Jake emphasized glaring at the gate guard.

"Hello Martin!" the VP said laughing. "Heard you were flying in. What's the problem?"

"Good to see you too, Chris," Jake said. "Earl here's an old friend of mine."

"I know Earl. Everybody around here knows Earl."

"Gate guard didn't!" Jake mumbled.

"Who's the lovely lady accompanying you?"

"Lieutenant Jones. She's one of the Army liaison officers assigned to Martin Aero."

Maggie handed her military ID card to the Boeing VP.

He looked at Maggie's ID and handed it back to her.

"Picture doesn't do you justice."

"Thank you," Maggie replied.

Jake thanked Earl for the lift and his hospitality.

After signing the guard's logbook, Jake and Maggie were issued visitor's passes and Chris gave them a lift over to the factory.

Maggie accompanied Jake to design meetings in the engineering department the rest of the day. Jake explained several of the problems with the turret gun interrupt switch and one of the Boeing engineers gave Jake a schematic with a recommended fix to take back with him.

Early that evening, Judy returned to the Boeing factory and rendezvoused with Jake and Maggie. The trio flew back to Los Angeles with one extremely happy and pleased young lady on board.

***

Many months later, Jake heard the story of the B-29 squadron, which had made the first bombing raid on the Japanese occupied coast of China over the mountains from the west. The raid was successful, but at a high cost. Many of the B-29 crews had not made it back through the bad weather and over the high mountain ranges. Judy's boyfriend was one of them.

***

On Christmas Eve of 1942, Maggie spent the holiday weekend with Jake and his family at the house in Santa Monica. Lydia's son was home on leave from the Marine Corps and also staying with them. He expected to be shipped out to the South Pacific in the next few days.

Lydia fixed a large dinner. Lora and Michael enjoyed the day even though most of their gifts were things like storybooks and punch-out cardboard toys. Metal toys were a thing of the past with the war on. Jake managed to find an antique gold locket for Lora she was thrilled with and six pre-war lead toy soldiers Michael had been wanting for his collection.

After the household had gone to bed, Jake fixed a couple of eggnogs for he and Maggie. They went into the living room to sit on the couch in front of the large, ornate marble fireplace.

The fire was dying a little and Jake stoked the embers to get it going. Then he handed Maggie a small jewelry box tied with a Christmas bow.

She hesitated before opening it and asked, "What's this?"

From her reaction, Jake suddenly realized Maggie must have thought the gift an engagement ring.

"Oh no, it's not what you're thinking. I'm sorry. Go ahead and open it. You'll like them, I'm sure."

Maggie opened the box, pulled back her hair and held one of the blue-diamond earrings up to her earlobe.

"Yes, you're right. I like them very much. Thank you."

Maggie laid her head on his shoulder and kissed him on the neck. The two sat quietly illuminated in the darkness by the flickering fire and the glowing coals.

"Would you marry me if I asked you to, Jake?"

"I suppose I would. Are you asking?"

"No, I just wondered if you would."

Maggie sat next to him with her hands folded in her lap holding the box her Christmas gift came in.

"I think I could be a good mother to Lora and Michael, but I'm sure you could find better. Look, Jake, I'm a poor Minnesota country girl. My dad barely eked a living out of his small airport operation and a few dairy cows."

"Whoa there, country girl. I've read a few books by a coal-oil lamp myself. Used an outhouse and froze my tail off in a winter storm, too. You gonna hold it against me that my dad owned more cows than your dad?"

"You know that's not what I meant. I know you grew up on a ranch, but you live a rich man's life now. That old lifestyle ended when you left home just like mine did."

Maggie smiled and took Jake's hand.

"I love flying like you do. In a lot of ways we're very much alike. We both have a need to see what's over the next horizon. I've already done more in my life than I ever dreamed. I wonder sometimes when the clock will strike twelve and the carriage will turn back into a pumpkin."

"So let's just get married."

"No," she said not looking him in the eye.

"What's the problem then?"

"Jake, you're one of the neatest guys I've ever met. Sometimes I love you so very much it hurts!"

"Uh-oh, here comes the but."

Maggie looked directly at Jake.

"But… I'm not 'in love' with you and if you were honest, you're not in love with me. Oh, I could be a mother to your kids, but I'd never be the wife you want or the wife you really need."

"Okay, we'll just go on like we've been."

Maggie placed her cheek next to his and whispered, "That's all right with me, you little shit!" and she kissed him on the lips to keep him from saying anymore.

***

There were a couple of things Maggie had not told Jake, as she wanted to wait until after the holidays before telling him.

She had not received a letter from Bo in over two months and feared he was either dead or had been captured. She had seen a recent Warner-Pathe Newsreel that worried her. The report depicted an armored battle in North Africa against Field Marshal Rommel, the Desert Fox, and she was relatively sure Bo's unit had been in the battle.

The first B-27s were now scheduled for delivery in a couple of months and Maggie had received orders transferring her back to active duty status as a ferry pilot. She would soon be reassigned to make the Atlantic crossings delivering C-47 and C-46 transport aircraft to the Army Air Forces in England.

Dancing at the Savoy

By April of 1943, the first nine B-27 Dragon Bombers were close to being ready for delivery to the Air Corps in Europe. The Army made a decision the new aircraft would not be shipped partly disassembled onboard cargo ships across the Atlantic.

Two reasons for the decision were that the Allies were losing a large number of Merchant Marine vessels to German submarine wolf packs and the bombers were needed for a special top-secret mission, a planned raid on the V-2 launch sites at Peenemunde.

The planes would be ferried to Europe by installing fifty-five gallon fuel drums in the bomb bay as auxiliary long-range fuel tanks. This would permit the B-27s to make one fuel stop in the Midwest and one final fuel stop in Nova Scotia enroute to England.

On a cool, damp cloudy morning at the Culver City airport, Colonel Polaski officially signed the acceptance receipt for the delivery of the first nine B-27s. Each Dragon Bombers sat fueled and ready on the Martin Aero ramp awaiting its crew.

The flight crews consisted of pilots and flight engineers from the Ferry Command, a dozen contract pilots, three WAAC pilots and several pilots from the newly formed Women's Army Service Pilots unit, called WASPs.

There were no qualified gunners among the ferry crews and thus no ammunition had been loaded onboard the bombers. The decision had been made to arm the bombers in theater, which also had the added benefit of saving weight.

The crews crowded into the hangar operations office in preparation for departure. An Air Corps major briefed them on their route of flight. Most of the crews sported dark blue ball caps with an embossed golden-winged dragon patch on them. The caps were souvenir gifts from Martin Aero. Jake had designed the logo and Gertie had ordered the caps made up especially for the flight.

Maggie was one of the assigned pilots and had flown in early that morning with a group of pilots from Hamilton Field, headquarters for the Army Air Corps Ferry Command.

She was surprised when the major conducting the briefing announced, "Civilian contract pilot Jake Martin will be pilot-in-command on this flight. He will be flying the lead aircraft and his call sign is Dragon Leader."

The lieutenant assisting the major commenced roll call, "Mr. Martin?"

"Here," Jake answered from the far back of the room.

The officer continued, "Copilot lead aircraft, Lieutenant Margaret Jones?"

Maggie was looking around the room for Jake and her attention snapped quickly forward.

"Okay! I mean here, sir."

Maggie turned again to look for Jake and spotted him standing with Gene their flight engineer and Gertie who had come to see them all off.

Jake smiled and tipped his Dragon Bomber ball cap.

***

Crossing the flight line to their assigned aircraft, the damp wind cut through the crew's thin summer flight suits. Maggie ran to catch up with Jake walking briskly towards their aircraft with Gene and Gertie.

The Air Corps lieutenant, who had assisted the major who conducted the briefing, ran up beside Jake.

"Sir, sir! I see your name on the roll as the pilot assigned to the lead aircraft, but I don't have a service file on you. Do you have some type of written orders assigning you to this flight?"

"Not with me," Jake answered and kept walking.

"Then you will be unable to depart until I get them."

"So file a complaint."

"In fact," the lieutenant said, "that's exactly what I'll have to do. I'll have to file a formal complaint with the aircraft company."

Maggie caught up with them. She had one arm in her flight jacket and was juggling some navigation charts as she struggled to get her other arm in the jacket.

"Just hand it to him, Lieutenant," Maggie said.

"Beg your pardon, ma'am?"

"You're talking to the man who owns the company."

Gertie stood clutching her white blouse and black suit jacket at the neck as she braced herself against the wind.

"If you'd like me to, Lieutenant, I could try to get General Arnold on the phone and possibly he could clear the matter up for you?"

The lieutenant saw Colonel Polaski waiting by Jake's assigned aircraft and obviously decided that discretion was the better part of valor.

"Thank you, sir. Have a good flight," he said and turned to leave.

As Jake approached his aircraft, the colonel extended his hand to Jake.

"I came out to wish you and your crew good luck, Martin. I would have bet money your company would never have met the delivery schedule, but you did. You're a tough man to bet against. Godspeed."

"Thanks, Colonel. Give my regards to your wife. She did a good job christening our first aircraft," Jake said and turned to Gertie. "Sure you don't want to go?"

Gertie just smiled.

"Okay then, take care of things while I'm gone."

"Yes, I will. Please be careful," Gertie said almost ready to cry.

"By the way, since when did you and Hap Arnold get so friendly that you can call him on the phone?"

"Why, I talk to the General nearly every day, Mr. Martin. Did you need me to tell him something for you?"

"You know what ol' Fats Waller says about that?"

"Yes, I know, 'It's a sin to tell a lie.' I know!"

"What's this?" Maggie lamented. "The infamous Jake Martin's corny dry-wit has rubbed off on Gertie?"

"Goodbye," Gertie said and took off running, as lady-like as she could against the strong wind in her tight black skirt, back to the Ops hangar.

Jake handed his flight case up to Gene who had climbed aboard the aircraft. With a big wide grin on his face, Jake motioned to the boarding ladder extending down from the open nose-wheel bay doors and said, "After you, Copilot Lieutenant Jones."

With the flight crews aboard their assigned aircraft, the engines began to crank and fire off. First one, then three, then seven, until all eighteen powerful engines droned in unison. The bombers taxied out single file with Jake's aircraft in the lead, one by one into takeoff position and rolled down the runway.

The bombers climbed slowly overhead until all were airborne. As the flight of nine bombers formed up, they turned to an easterly heading staying below the thick gray overcast at about three thousand feet AGL.

The ceiling was higher as they passed over San Bernardino and the aircraft moved into three well-defined V-shaped formations of three bombers each with Jake's plane in the point formation.

Jake would have preferred to get the flight up above twenty thousand feet where the engines would perform more efficiently and conserve fuel, but due to the high overcast, the bombers climbed only high enough to clear the Sierra Nevada mountain range.

The flight of nine Dragon Bombers were somewhere over northeastern Arizona before the ceiling went broken and allowed them to climb out to twenty-five thousand feet and still stay formed up. At cruise and with a strong high altitude tail wind, their ground speed approached four hundred miles per hour.

The long flight provided plenty of time for casual conversation. Gene, seated in the jump seat between Maggie and Jake, had been doing most of the talking.

Somewhere over Missouri, Gene tired of the small talk, logged one more scan of the engine instruments on his clipboard and went to the rear of the pressurized cabin. Using a parachute pack for a pillow, Gene stretched out on the floor below the top turret gun and took a nap.

"Jake, I've been wondering about something," Maggie said. "I haven't flown with you all that much, but I've noticed when we takeoff, you mumble something to yourself. I always thought you were going over the takeoff checklist in your head, but today... I finally realized you were saying a prayer!"

Jake answered her in a matter of fact way, "Oh yeah, I always do that, except once in a while I forget."

"What exactly do you say when you pray?"

"I usually say something simple like, God grant us safe passage, and then Amen, of course."

Maggie looked questioningly at Jake.

"I don't get it? Never thought of you as religious."

Jake scanned the flight instruments, looked out the side windows to check the formation and then looked back over at Maggie.

"Me and ol' flyin' buddy of mine named Red used to have some good discussions on the subject of religion, but I guess you and I never got around to talking about it."

"Then you are religious!"

"Aren't you?"

"Sort of. I guess everybody is a little. I used to go to Sunday school when I was a kid back home. Does that count?"

"Seems like it ought to count for something," Jake replied and continued to scan the instrument panel and check the formation.

"The way I see it, you don't have to be a Bible pounding, sack cloth wearing religious fanatic to believe in God. He created this world and I think He pretty much runs the place by His own rules and not ours."

"I'm amazed! I thought I knew everything about you, but I never thought of you in that way."

"What way is that, Maggie?"

"I mean you spend money like a drunken sailor. Your life is in shambles most of the time. You can't stay with one woman more than a few years and I don't remember you ever going into a church as long as I've known you."

"I suppose, you're right, but about the church part, I feel closer to God up here in His heaven than I ever have in any church. The prayers on takeoff… Well, they're mostly habit. I started it a long time ago and it still feels right. Helps me stay humble by reminding me I'm not always as much in control of things as I think I am."

Maggie leaned back in the copilots seat.

"I'll be darned! You're a man of many surprises. Maybe that's what has always fascinated me about you."

The formation of nine bombers landed at Willow Run airfield near Detroit for refueling and the crews remained overnight. The second leg of the flight took them to Saint John, Newfoundland, where the B-27s landed at a Royal Canadian Air Force base. A hot meal was provided and bunks in the transit barracks were available for the crews to catch six hours sleep before a pre-dawn takeoff.

***

By sunrise the following morning, the flight of nine bombers passed east of the Avalon Peninsula, southwest of Cape Farwell, Greenland.

Jake had been staring down at the North Atlantic Ocean waters far below for the longest time.

"You know, if we ditched in the drink out here, we'd only survive for about three minutes in these waters before freezing to death."

"Oh my!" Maggie sighed. "You're just a barrel of laughs. Thanks for all the cheerful information."

The weather over the Atlantic had been one of those rare, clear blue sunshiny days. The air was smooth at their altitude except for an occasional buffet from the Jet Stream winds and the Dragon Bombers were on autopilot.

The new autopilot on the B-27 was only a single axis gyro system, which sent inputs to the plane's ailerons. Most pilots referred to them as a wing leveler, but the device did quite a good job of easing the pilot's workload.

The crossing time passed quickly and the flight of nine bombers was about an hour's flying time off the southwest coast of Ireland. Jake was nodding off to sleep and Maggie was reading a well-worn pulp magazine she had purchased to read on the trip.

Gene had just finished logging the engine readings when he caught a glimpse of something in the distance.

"There's something on the horizon at about our same altitude," Gene cried out. "Looks like several aircraft."

Jake snapped awake and Maggie's magazine dropped to the floor. The three small dark specks in the distance grew rapidly larger.

"What the hell could be up here at this altitude and way out here?" Jake exclaimed, but he only had to wait a couple of seconds more for the answer.

Three Arado 196s were headed straight at them with their gun muzzles flashing. The two flights of opposing aircraft were closing on one another at a speed in excess of eight hundred miles an hour.

The fraction of a second that the bombers were in gun range may have been the only saving grace that kept the German fighter's from firing more accurately.

Jake put his plane into a hard left turn pulling about three-G's and pushed the nose forward out the bottom of the formation.

"Get on the controls, Maggie! Hold her there till we do a full one-eighty." Picking up his mike, Jake came up on the guard-frequency. "This is Dragon leader. All aircraft follow me! Maintain my heading and altitude!"

The bomber's airframes creaked and shuttered as their flight instruments bounced off the top of the pegs.

Gene did not have his seatbelt on and he floated up off of the jump seat and braced himself against the cockpit ceiling with both hands.

The B-27 Dragon Bombers plummeted out of the sky at a three thousand foot per minute rate of descent.

Maggie held the turn with all of her might as Jake got back on the controls to help her.

"Weren't we supposed to maintain radio silence?"

Jake grinned.

Don't you think the Jerrys know where we are by now?" he asked as he rolled the Dragon Bomber out on the reciprocal heading and eased their rate of descent.

The evasive maneuver had exceeded the B-27's design VNE, a real testament to the Dragon Bombers superior structural integrity.

The surprised Luftwaffe pilots, not aware they were attacking unarmed bombers, now had to maneuver rapidly to mount a second attack on the fleeing bombers. Their prey had failed to hold its course and altitude as bomber formations normally did. Instead, they had turned and ran.

Jake figured the fighters could barely match the speed of the B-27s at altitude and the German fighters had apparently intercepted their flight much further out from land than anticipated. Heading into the jet stream, the fighters would soon be on the outside limit of their fuel range with no choice except to turn back.

The bombers had used far less fuel than expected due to flying with the jet stream and Jake knew his planes had more than enough fuel to run from the fighters for some time and still proceed on to England.

The fighters attempted to make one more attack coming in behind the Dragon Bombers, but the bullets fell short of their mark as the bombers slowly increased their distance from the fighters.

One B-27 had been hit and its damaged right engine was smoking badly. The pilot of that aircraft had been slower than the rest of the bombers to make his turn to a descent when Jake had given the order.

After the second attempted attack, the fighters fell away like tired lions finally giving up chasing a gazelle and headed back to the mainland.

"All aircraft," Jake broadcasted over the guard radio frequency. "This is Dragon leader. Maintain this altitude and stay with our crippled friend. We'll fly our present heading and altitude for now. When you see me turn, follow me back to our original course. Return to radio silence. Dragon leader out."

"I want to put some distance between us and those fighters before turning back," Jake commented to Gene and Maggie.

"How do you suppose they located us?" Gene asked.

"My guess is a German U-boat spotted us and reported our position to the Luftwaffe for interception."

"Let's hope there's not another bunch laying in wait for us closer in," Maggie said pensively.

Nine bombers, including the one bomber flying on a single-engine, arrived at their destination and landed at the RAF airfield at Northampton, near London. The damaged bomber was given priority clearance for landing and the other eight circled in behind.

Jake's bomber landed second and parked. He exited the aircraft with Gene and Maggie right behind him and ran over to the damaged bomber as its three crewmen climbed out.

"Is anyone hurt?" Jake asked.

The plane commander of the crippled Dragon Bomber replied, "Only our pride!"

A reception party of 8th Air Force personnel and RAF airmen welcomed the twenty-seven exhausted aircrewmen to England. A feeling of relief permeated the rest of the aircrews as they gathered around the damaged bomber.

Everyone personally inspecting the shot-out engine and milling around discussing exactly what had happened took up the next hour.

The RAF had a military intelligence and photoreconnaissance Mosquito aircraft unit at the Northampton airbase. Jake was invited to meet with the unit to be debriefed about the attack by the three patrol aircraft on their nine bombers.

A stenographer took down Jake's description of their encounter and how they had managed to evade the fighters.

Jake thumbed through an aircraft identification book, stopped on one of the pages and pounded the photo with his index finger exclaiming, "That's them!"

Rex Green, the squadron commander in charge of the intelligence unit was looking over Jake's shoulder.

"Arado 196s. We've had a few sightings of those, but normally they don't range that far out."

"They may have used drop-tanks," Jake added, "but they didn't have them when they jumped us."

When the interview concluded, Rex said, "I'm sure you don't remember me, Captain Martin. My wife and I were passengers on a flight to Hawaii several years ago when you were flying as captain on the Pan Am Clippers."

"Sorry, I don't. I met so many passengers during those years, but thanks for returning the hospitality today, Commander."

***

In a few days, the military personnel would be assigned to a new B-27 squadron being formed at a base here in England. The ferry pilots and crews would be flown back to the States on an as-space-available basis in deadheading C-54 cargo planes.

Jake went to arrange for feeding and housing the B-27 aircrews and Maggie tagged along with Jake on his errands. After he finished at the RAF quartermaster's, he turned to Maggie who stepped back and took a good look at Jake.

"Do I look as bad as you do?" she asked jokingly.

They both stood laughing at each other and then Jake said, "I'm going to London and spend a few days at the Savoy Hotel. You coming?"

"I'm right behind you, dearie. I don't know which sounds best, a square meal, a hot shower or a soft bed," Maggie glanced at the sly grin on Jake's face. "Oh, I know what you've got on your mind. That'll just have to wait!"

Jake was pondering exactly how they might get to downtown London when an Air Corps staff driver approached.

"Mr. Martin, sir, I'm Corporal Brown. General Patterson over at 8th Air Force command sends his regards and apologies for being unable to meet your flight. The general said to tell you his car is at your disposal."

"General Patterson? Oh, that's Ol' Major Patterson. He was Dale's boss back at Wright Field in Dayton," Jake said and slapped the driver on the shoulder. "That's great! You're timing is admirable, Corporal Brown. You can deliver me and this lovely lady to the Savoy Hotel."

On the ride into London, they passed through parts of the city severely damaged by bombs and other parts of the city ironically untouched by wartime damage.

The car turned onto the thoroughfare, which ran along the north side of the Thames River. On the way to the Savoy Hotel, they passed by the main railway station gutted by a direct hit from a thousand pound bomb. The railway bridge over the Thames into the station had also been bombed and collapsed in the river.

The staff car pulled up in front of the Savoy. A bellboy opened the rear car door for Maggie, took their canvas bags and escorted them into the lobby.

Jake signed the register J. M. Jones, USA.

Maggie looked over Jake's shoulder and saw how he signed them in. She chuckled to herself and chalked it up to Jake's usual defiance of any kind of authority.

"If you would show Mr. And Mrs. Jones to their room please," the desk clerk said handing the room key to the bellboy who promptly picked up the two bags and headed to the elevator with Jake and Maggie in hot pursuit.

After Jake left the check-in desk, the manager handed the desk clerk a copy of a cablegram. The clerk read the cable and on the register underneath Mr. & Mrs. Jones he wrote, CEO Martin Aero, Mr. J. Martin, et ux.

The manager had recognized Jake and Maggie the instant they walked into the Savoy Hotel lobby. Gertie had advised the hotel manager earlier by cable that the head of Martin Aero would be staying with them and would likely be traveling incognito with an attractive WAAC lieutenant.

Exiting the elevator, the bellboy set the bags down and opened the door to the room. Maggie went through the door and spun around admiring the room.

"First dibs on the shower," Maggie yelled throwing her flight jacket on the bed and unzipping her jump suit.

Jake stopped the bellboy short of entering the room as Maggie clothes dropped on the floor and she crossed the room headed to the bath. Jake tipped the bellboy, picked up the two bags and kicked the door closed with his foot.

"Thank you, Mr. Jones. Enjoy your stay," the bellboy left standing in the hall hollered.

"I'm sure we will," Jake hollered back through the door and dropped the bags in the middle of the floor as he headed for the shower with Maggie.

The only other sound in the room besides the running of the water was Maggie yelling, "Quit it. Don't! Stop it," and then she laughed.

***

Jake and Maggie slept most of the following day and that evening Jake went to wait in the American Bar for Maggie to come down to dinner.

As he crossed the lobby, mixed contingents of allied military officers with their spouses along with assorted political muckety-mucks milled about in the hotel lobby and outside the ballroom.

The Savoy's American Bar was known as a hangout for famous American celebrities like Frank Sinatra. Vera Lynn once sang there. Jake ordered a Glenlivet Scotch and struck up a conversation with two RAF officers at the bar. When he saw Maggie in the doorway of the bar, he left to join her and they went into the dining room.

Perusing the menu, Jake asked the waiter, "Are there no meats available? I was kind of in the mood for a thick juicy steak and there's none on the menu."

The waiter smiled politely.

"Sounds wonderful to me too, sir, but no, we haven't had any beefsteak for quite some time now. Would the gentleman care to select one of the entrées on the menu?"

The English were not known for their culinary arts, but at least Maggie enjoyed their meal.

Music emanated from the nearby ballroom where a small band played some pop tunes. After dinner, Jake and Maggie joined those dancing in the ballroom. This was the first and possibly the only time Jake and Maggie ever danced together, a romantic evening Maggie would hold as a fond memory for the rest of her life.

For Jake and Maggie, the rigors of meeting the wartime aircraft delivery schedules had taken its toll on both of them. Their stay in London proved a chance to kick back, unwind and enjoy one another's company for a few days.

They visited the British Museum, Trafalgar Square and other famous London landmarks. They had fish and chips at the Shakespeare Pub, took long chilly walks alone the banks of the Thames River and enjoyed afternoon tea at a small café on the main thoroughfare.

Their hotel room was warmly furnished and cozy. The windows of the room were blacked out with heavy dark drapes to prevent light leaks during nighttime air raids.

Jake and Maggie stayed in of an evening. Maggie liked to read in bed. Jake had accumulated a large number of scribbled notes on the B-27's flight characteristics during their recent Atlantic crossing and spent several hours each evening compiling them into something he could make sense of once he returned home.

***

Early in the morning on their fourth day's stay at the Savoy, the telephone rang. The voice on the phone inquired, "I have a call from someone at 8th Air Force flight operations. The party is asking for a Mr. Martin and gave this room number. Is he by chance there?"

The desk clerk was continuing Jake's little charade of signing in as Mr. Jones and Jake had forgotten for a moment how he had signed the hotel register.

"Oh yeah, I'll take the call."

Maggie could not hear what was being said on the other end of the phone, but she heard Jake reply, "That's great. I'll be there as soon as I can get there. And thanks."

When he hung up the phone, Maggie asked, "What was that all about?"

"I guess I didn't tell you," Jake said, pretending he had forgotten to mention it. "I asked to go along as a technical representative on one of the B-17 raids over Germany. The executive officer needed to clear the request with the Boeing people first and its been approved. If I want to go on the mission scheduled for the day after tomorrow, I need to meet with the squadron C.O. and the plane commander. That means I have to go on out to the airbase at Huntington today."

Maggie shook her head.

"Always having to stick your neck out and see what's over the next horizon." Her voice cracked a little with emotion. "You know damn right well you didn't tell me because you knew I'd want to go along."

"Maggie, there was no need to ask. They wouldn't have approved your request. In the air raids over the last few months its been estimated that our bombers have killed twenty thousand German civilians. If an American flyer has to bail out and the locals get to him on the street before the Gestapo, it's likely he'd be beaten to death. Lord only knows what they'd do to a woman flyer!"

Maggie sat waiting patiently in a chair for Jake to get ready to leave and walked him to the door.

"I'll be fine here. Love you, be careful," she said and she kissed him on the cheek.

Jake went to the lobby and took a cab to Kings Cross Station where he caught the train to Huntington.

At the 8th Air Force airbase at Huntington, Jake met with the people required to clear his flight. He sat in on an aircrew briefing and went through a grueling four-hour orientation on the B-17 emergency procedures and bailout training. That evening when Jake finished the training, he ate dinner at the chow hall with another Boeing rep and some of the crewmen he trained with that day.

Jake was more than tired he was beat. He found a telephone in the ready room and called the base operator.

"I need to place a call to the Savoy Hotel in London," and after several minutes, the hotel operator came on the line. "Ring Mrs. Jones's room for me, please."

Maggie picked up the phone in the room.

"Jake, are you all right? I expected you back earlier this evening. We need to talk."

"I'm okay, Maggie, but I'm dog tired. I'm not coming back into London tonight if that's all right with you. There're some bunks here in the ready room and I'm going to sack out here. I'll see you first thing in the morning."

Maggie was understanding as always.

"Sure, I've been there myself. I was just getting worried. Thanks for calling, I'll see you in the morning."

***

Jake arrived at the Savoy the next morning and as he passed through the lobby, the desk clerk nodded politely and said, "Good morning, Mr. Jones. I believe Mrs. Jones is in the dining room."

Jake went into where Maggie, in full dress uniform, was seated at a white linen covered table. She had just finished having breakfast and smiled when she saw Jake.

The waiter approached as Jake seated himself at the table with Maggie.

"Just coffee for now."

"Tell me, Jake, does a five cent cup of Java back home taste better or worse than this black market, two-dollar a cup stuff they serve here?"

"Better I suppose, but only because it's back home," Jake replied with a smile. "How'd you sleep?"

"Not good…" Maggie said and started to say something else, but hesitated.

"Me neither."

He knew from Maggie's attire something was up and had also noticed the packed bag beside her chair.

"What's going on, Maggie? You said last night you needed to talk to me about something."

Maggie's mood saddened and she started to cry. Jake had never seen Maggie cry before, so he knew something was bad wrong. Maggie forced a smile.

"No, I won't let you remember me this way, I mean see me this way."

"What is it, Maggie?"

"I checked in with headquarters yesterday while you were away and my orders have come down. I'm flying out to the States tonight."

"Where're you being assigned?"

"To the Willow Run plant. I'll be delivering B-24 Liberators," Maggie replied attempting to be cheerful, but Jake knew she was faking it. "The pilots call the B-24s built by Ford the Widow Maker. I wonder if a female pilot crashed one, would they call it the Widower Maker?"

Jake smiled at Maggie's little joke and said, "There's more isn't there."

"I hate to leave you, but orders are orders."

"Not a problem. I can get the orders changed."

"I know you could, but I don't want you to. There is something more. When I checked in, there was a personal message for me about Bo. He was wounded and is onboard a hospital ship headed for home."

"That's tough. How bad is he injured?"

"I'm not sure, but my flight will beat him back to the States and I'm going to be there when his ship arrives."

They sat for a while. Jake ordered breakfast and around ten o'clock, he asked, "What time's your flight?"

"Not until late tonight, but I need to head on out to the airfield in time to check-in."

Jake sat looking into Maggie's beautiful sky blue eyes, realizing he might never see her again. She had never seemed more beautiful or more appealing than she did at that very moment with the sad little girl look on her face.

"Are we still checked into our room, Mrs. Jones?"

"Yes, Mr. Jones, but I just got all dressed up to travel and even went to a lot of trouble to put my makeup on just right," but she knew what Jake was thinking.

They sat looking at each other. Maggie smiled first.

"Oh, what the hell!" she said as she stood up. She threw her napkin on the table, picked up her bag and started for the elevator. She paused and looked back over her shoulder, "You coming, sailor?" and Jake ran to catch up with her.

***

In their room, they made love one last time. More than an act of passionate sex, their being together served as a reason for two very special friends, not really lovers, to hold each other close one more time before saying goodbye.

Afterwards, they lay together on the bed. Maggie pulled the sheet up and held it with her hand to cover her large breasts. Jake laid facedown beside her holding a pillow to prop himself up and they talked until time for Maggie to go.

As she dressed, Maggie said, "You know, Jake, our paths might never cross again. If they don't, then every once in awhile when your thoughts drift off to all the strange and far off lands you've been to and all the women you've known, once in awhile I want you to think of me and I'll do the same for you."

Jake carried Maggie's bag and walked with her to the lobby. Near the front entrance, they kissed goodbye.

Maggie held Jake real tight and whispered in his ear, "Maybe one of these days you'll find another little China doll like the one you lost and live happily ever after."

"I know Maggie, I know. You're the second woman in my life that has told me the same thing."

"You mean Sarah, of course," Maggie said smiling and she picked up her bag to leave.

Jake smiled and nodded yes.

"Well that's what you get for making a friend out of your lover and telling her all the stories about your old girlfriends."

Maggie went out the door to the waiting staff car. The driver saluted the WAAC lieutenant, took the bag from her hand and opened the rear passenger door for her.

Jake stood in the open hotel doorway and called out to her, "You know, Maggie, I really do care for you."

Maggie paused before getting in the car. "Yeah, I know. I love you, too," and then she mouthed the words, "You little shit!"

Jake smiled and waved back. He knew exactly what she had said. He heard her loud and clear.

Maggie seated herself in the car and the driver shut the door. She waved goodbye to Jake through the window.

Jake waved back. "Boy! Am I going to miss that lady," he mumbled to himself as he watched Maggie's car drive away.

THE ANNABELLE LEE

Jake advised the desk clerk he would be leaving early in the morning and settled his bill. That evening Jake ordered dinner sent up to his room and retired early.

An Army staff car picked Jake up at the hotel the next morning to deliver him to the 8th Air Force airfield north of London. The airfield at Huntington was only about fifty miles from London, but the heavy fog and early morning darkness caused the drive to take almost two hours.

Jake leaned back in the corner of the rear seat of the sedan and slept most of the way. In his Pacific crossing days flying the old China Clippers, Jake had long ago mastered the art of sleeping sitting up.

Jake arrived at the airbase and checked in with the operations officer.

"You Jake Martin, the Boeing rep?" the officer asked.

"Yes sir, that's me."

"You've been assigned to B-17 side number 14614. That's the *Annabelle Lee*. They're short a bombardier, so give them a hand as best you can."

From there, the officer sent Jake to checkout his high-altitude flight gear, a sheepskin lined brown leather flight suit with plug-in electrical heating coils, oxygen mask and a parachute.

Reporting to the crew ready room, Jake located Captain Arnett, the plane commander for the B-17 he had met two days earlier.

When Jake entered the ready room, no one needed to explain the tension. These were the aviators who had been part of the October 14th raid, now referred to by the airmen as Black Tuesday. On that, the first raid on the heavily defended ball-bearing factories at Schweinfurt two weeks

419

earlier, this bomber group lost nearly half of its two hundred B-17s. Many were lost to the deadly German high altitude anti-aircraft fire called flack and the rest were repeatedly jumped by Luftwaffe fighters' enroute.

"Guess I'm with your crew on today's mission," Jake said reporting in.

Twenty-six year old Captain Arnett, or Arnie as his crew called him, was an old man in the bomber business by current criteria. Before the war he managed a Western Auto Supply store in a small town in Pennsylvania.

"This is your lucky day, Jake. We drew the Tuskegee Airmen for fighter escorts. They're the best P-51 pilots around. We're a lot safer when they're along."

One by one, Arnie introduced Jake to each of the aircraft crewmembers as they gathered to await the preflight briefing.

The B-17 crews were like a superstitious bunch of baseball players not wanting to do anything to change their luck. Some of the crew wore the same shirt, scarf or lucky charm on every mission. So far, the *Annabelle Lee* always returned them safely from every bombing raid. Any change was considered a bad omen and Jake was unaware that his presence represented a change in the crew.

Arnie introduced Jake to a twenty-one year old lieutenant, a former engineering student at MIT.

"This is our squadron maintenance officer and my copilot. He's the best B-17 engine expert in the 8th Air Force."

"Understand you'll be flying in our bombardier's position today. There used to be a Norton bombsight in the nose of every plane, but they've cannibalized ours to use in another aircraft. We've lost so many aircraft and crewman we're short of bombardiers," the young copilot explained to Jake.

"That's encouraging!" Jake replied with a smirk.

"Ol' Mr. Whitney will be flying in the lead B-17 ahead of us. He's the best bombardier and navigator in the squadron. We call him The Professor because he taught astronomy at the University of Indiana before joining the Air Corps. All you have to do is watch for the lead plane to open their bomb bay doors and when they dump, you drop."

A tall lanky young Oklahoma boy walked up.

"Here's Okie now," Arnie said. "He's our flight engineer. In addition to monitoring and transferring the fuel, he's also our top turret gunner. Okie will check you out on what you need to do. If you need anything and I'm busy, ask this fellow."

"Ever fire a .50 caliber before?" Okie asked.

"Some," Jake replied, referring to, but not explaining the incident on the Burma Road. "And a couple of times from wing mounted guns on a fighter."

"Same idea, I guess. Point and fire, but we're not as fast as one of those single-engine pursuit planes you might have flown, so you'll have to lead the Jerry fighters quite a bit with your gun sight."

"Kind of like shooting at a running deer," Jake commented, remembering a day twenty years ago hunting with his grandfather when he intentionally missed an easy shot.

"Yeah, kind of like that, but these running deer shoot back! I'll go forward with you when we board the *Annabelle Lee* and check you out on the bomb release procedure. When we're on the IP, that's the Initial Point of the bomb run, I'll go to the bomb bay to cock and arm the bomb racks so listen for me over the ICS."

"We know we got the best equipment for the job," Arnie interjected, "because a captured German fighter pilot told us attacking a heavily armed B-17 formation was like trying to make love to a porcupine!"

"Good to have you along, Jake," Okie said and he went over to talk to a flight engineer on another B-17.

The tail gunner, the belly gunner and the two waist gunners arrived and introduced themselves to Jake. They were polite, but not overly friendly. Most had lost one or more friends the last couple of months, which made it difficult for these men to make new acquaintances. Each man seemed preoccupied with the impending mission.

Jake went to the ready room window and cupped his hands around his face to peer out into the pitch-black morning sky and all he saw was the heavy fog. When he turned around, Arnie had been looking over his shoulder.

"They say it's going to burn off at sunrise. Maybe it'll at least lift enough for us to takeoff."

"I suppose flying a ten man weapons system is a little different than delivering a load of quail to a Caribbean resort hotel," Jake said, referring to his days of flying passengers on holiday with Pan Am.

"I suppose it is… Maybe it won't be long before this thing is over and I can get one of those cushy, high paying jobs myself."

Jake went to sit down on the floor between the crew's navigator and radio operator. He leaned back against the wall and tried to relax for a while having gotten up in the middle of the night to arrive at the airfield. To stay awake Jake struck up a conversation with the navigator, a nineteen-year old youngster, who had been talking nonstop to those around him.

"I'd like to return to school at Ohio State and become a math teacher when this thing's over. But you see, they need me here right now. My job is to keep the aircraft on track and know our exact position at all times. That's our best bet for making it back. It's not uncommon for the bombers to become separated if we run into bad weather and then we have to use dead reckoning to get back to base."

Jake suspected the navigator's energetic and nervous conversation was the young man's way of dealing with his apprehension over the coming mission.

"The RAF has less accurate bombsights than our Norton and the RAF bomber can't fly at the necessary high altitudes," the navigator went on, "so some agreement was negotiated between the brass relegating the RAF to the night bombing runs. So now the U.S. 8th Air Force is responsible for all daylight bombing raids over Germany."

The radio operator, a rather quiet young fellow, had been a HAM radio buff since his early teens. Arnie mentioned earlier their radioman could read Morse code faster than any radioman in the squadron.

"How bad are the fighter attacks?" Jake asked the radioman who was holding onto a steel helmet by the strap with the rest of his gear.

"Bad, but seems like we're beginning to encounter a little less opposition from the Luftwaffe now. I think our fighters are starting to gain some air superiority. The flack is the worst though. I got this piece of sheet metal I put between my seat and the bulkhead. I leave it in the plane and I tote this helmet around to put on when the flack starts. When we go for the big ones like Schweinfurt, they throw everything they got at us. Worse part is, they seem to know when we're coming."

"Why wouldn't they?" the navigator said. "We leave a contrail twenty miles long in the sky behind us."

"It's more than that," the radioman said. "I tell you they've got some new electronic device that tells them where we are, but nobody believes me."

"You might be onto something there," Jake replied.

The doors to the briefing room swung open. Jake and the others got up to go in.

"Let's hope it's anything but having to go back to Schweinfurt," Okie said as he walked past.

The airmen filed solemnly into the briefing room and took their seats in rows of hard wooden benches. Some sat quietly, while others carried on a conversation with the crewmen seated around them. Cigarette smoke filled the room and the room temperature began to rise from the body heat.

The prevailing mood was that the odds were stacked against them and it permeated their every thought. This morning, the men awoke to empty bunks that only a few weeks ago were filled with fellow airmen. Some had tried to choke down some breakfast eggs, but most with a case of nerves could not even do that.

A neatly dressed non-flying officer, a ground-pounder major, stepped onto the stage and began roll call. Each of the plane commanders answered for his crew over the noise and muffled conversation in the room.

On the wall behind the major, a black curtain covered what everyone knew to be the mission map. When he finished roll call, the major commenced reading the standard statement of instructions.

"From this time forward, you may not converse with any person other than your own crewmen. You may not make phone calls or have contact with any outside persons..." and so on the announcement went.

The crewmen had heard it all many times before. Most kept on talking among themselves until the squadron C.O. stepped onto the briefing stage. At that point, a sudden hushed silence fell over the briefing room.

"Good morning, gentlemen," the C.O. said, as the long black curtain opened to reveal the mission map. "Our target today will be," and several dozen crewmen spoke the word aloud in unison with the C.O. "Schweinfurt!"

Hopes for an easier target were dashed.

A tone of antipathy could be heard in the airmen's voices as mutterings of, "Son of a bitch!" and "I knew it!" and "Damn it, anyway!" drifted across the room.

The C.O. completed a brief pep talk to the men and the Intelligence Officer commenced a rundown.

"Flack enroute will pickup south of Ruhr. Your primary target will be defended by approximately five hundred German 88mm anti-aircraft guns. You should expect to be under heavy fire for the full seven minutes you're on the IP." The officer went on to explain where the bombers might expect to encounter fighter attacks based on the known range and distance from operational Luftwaffe airfields.

The Weather Officer came forward to announce, "The visibility is down to a quarter mile, but will improve steadily between now and takeoff time. Expect overcast and rain over the Channel, but the target is forecast to be clear to partly cloudy."

The men filed out of the briefing room. Many assembled in small groups to kneel before the Chaplain and take communion. These men had learned the hard way aerial warfare was not the glamorous, wild blue yonder epic depicted on the recruiting posters. Today, they would be fighting six miles above the earth with nowhere to run and no foxhole to hide in.

The bombers were dispersed widely around the perimeter of the airfield as a defense against air attacks. The crews piled into jeeps and ammo handling trucks and were delivered to their waiting aircraft. Jake arrived at the *Annabelle Lee* along with his assigned flight crew and walked with Arnie during his once around of the aircraft.

Ground crewmen slowly turning the blades on the four large radial engines by hand to pump out any oil, which may have seeped into the lower cylinders and thus prevent a blown jug on startup.

A damaged engine on start meant their plane would be scrubbed for the mission. Nobody in their right mind wanted to go on this mission, but no one wanted to stay behind either. The group would need all the firepower they could muster if all were to have any chance of making it back.

The gunners went about the task of loading additional boxes of .50 caliber ammunition into the planes as they anticipated heavy fighter attacks. Each crewman went through the motions of running their pre-takeoff checks the same as every other bomber crew throughout the airfield.

Sooner than anyone wanted, the inevitable first flare soared into the air and burst in the sky. Engines began to crank and soon a dull roar overpowered the sound of any one aircraft. The whole airfield hummed in unison as the bombers formed a single-file line on the taxiway like winged monsters doing a Congo dance. The bombers slowly made their way to the single long runway on the airfield.

One by one, the heavily loaded B-17s lumbered down the runway at full throttle and lifted into the air, some barely clearing the tall trees at the far end.

Many of the crewmen feared this part of the flight more than any other. With their planes heavily laden with fuel and bombs, a crash on takeoff offered little or no chance of survival. The burned out airframes of a couple of B-17s that did not clear the trees still remained in the woods as an ever-present reminder.

The squadron climbed slowly to 28,000 feet where they formed up with other B-17 groups from nearby airfields.

Crossing the English Channel and approaching the coast of France, the bombers streamed long contrails in the sky behind them, a flashing neon sign to the German coastal spotters announcing their coming.

Every ten minutes, Okie called out over the ICS, "Oxygen check."

This to insure none of the crew had passed out in the rarified air and the minus fifty-degree cabin temperature. Without oxygen, at high altitude, a crewman would pass out in less than a minute and be dead in twenty.

Each crewmember checked in by identifying his station.

"Tail gunner... navigator... Radio..." and so on over the ICS they checked-in.

With the roll call complete, Okie added his own friendly reminder to the crew, "Keep your masks free of ice and stay alert, you guys."

An hour or so into the flight, Arnie called, "Clear your guns men, fire at will."

The gunners cocked and fired a short burst from each of the machineguns to make sure the weapons would operate properly when needed.

The long wait began and tensions grew higher. Minutes seemed like hours. Impending doom and possible destruction lay ahead. It could take place in the next instant or seemingly take forever to arrive.

Arnie's calm and reassuring voice came over the ICS, "Many and many a year ago, in a kingdom by the sea. A maiden lived, whom you may know, by the name of Annabel Lee. I was a child and she was a child, in that kingdom by the sea. We loved with a love that was more than a love. I and my Annabel Lee."

For some unexplainable reason, the poem Arnie recited aloud seemed to have a comforting effect on the crew.

This poem, which Arnie recited on every mission they had flown to date, not only reminded them of the loves left behind, but it seemed to give meaning to the namesake of the goliath upon which they rode into battle.

Suddenly, Okie from the top turret called out over the ICS, "Bandits ten o'clock high."

Arnie held his heading like he was engaged in some kind of surreal game of chicken, but he knew the fighter would swerve at the last instant. For him to also turn could result in a fiery mid-air collision. Even worse, breaking formation would put their B-17 in the crossfire coverage of the other bombers in the formation.

There remained no other options. Arnie held the *Annabelle Lee* steady on course with nerves of steel.

The fighters came in directly out of the sun diving on the bombers. The airframe of the Boeing Flying Fortress literally vibrated with the simultaneous firing of all fourteen .50 caliber defensive guns.

The engine sound of the Fouke-Wulf 190 echoed with a Doppler effect as it crossed in front of Jake and passed twenty-feet below the Fortress.

Another small speck in the distance came head-on at their plane. Jake swung his gun and fired directly at the oncoming fighter. Okie fired simultaneously at the approaching target from the top turret gun.

The attacking fighter took a hit and smoke poured from the engine. The plane did not explode, but rolled over on its back plummeting earthward.

Jake felt relatively certain he had not hit the fighter. Okie or one of the other gunner's must have downed the plane. No sooner had the fighters arrived than they were gone again. Their luck had held once more.

Every fifth round the fighters' guns fired was a tracer round. This so the pilot could better judge his firing accuracy. All it would take was one tracer round through a fuel tank or into their pregnant bomb-load and the Fortress would become a blazing inferno.

"Everyone okay, anyone hit?" Arnie called over the ICS and all the crew reported in okay.

Jake watched as a B-17 below them took a hit. One of its engines began smoking badly, but so far the damaged bomber was managing to stay in formation.

A crippled bomber could attempt to make it back to England, but more than likely a lone bomber would be easy prey for the fighters and picked off before they made it back. The crew would have to bail out over western France and hope to make contact with the French underground known as Freedom Fighters to escape capture.

Ahead on the horizon loomed flack, the silent killer. Hundreds of small black puffs of smoke, each burst emitting hundreds of red-hot fragments of steel. As the bombers approached the heavily defended primary target, they attempted to regroup into a tighter formation on their steady unrelenting march to the IP.

The flack became heavier as the bombers approached the factory complex far below. The B-17s ahead opened their bomb bay doors and Jake followed suit.

"Okie to bombardier," came the call over the ICS. "Bombs are armed. Racks are cocked and ready. Over."

"Bombardier, roger," Jake replied with his hand on the bomb release and his attention fixed on the B-17 ahead. As the first bombs left the lead bomber's bomb bay, Jake also release. "Bombs away," he reported over the ICS.

As the bomb-load left their aircraft, the normally stable B-17 tossed in the air from the prop wash of the other bombers and the bursts of flack. Arnie fought to hold the plane level with its constantly changing CG as the bomb-load left the aircraft.

They had their orders. Hold the IP seven full minutes for the entire group to release. Every crewman on every bomber knew if they failed to hit their target, they would have to come back and do this all over again.

Jake watched the ground as some of the bomb patterns missed the factories and fell into nearby villages. The thought came to him that his own grandparents were German. If old John Martin's folks had not come to America, whose side would he be fighting on today? Exactly when in the hell was it he had not been paying attention and the whole damn world had gone insane?

Each crewman knew the second wave of fighters would soon jump them, but it came sooner than expected. The aircraft behind them had not yet released their bombs and all were still taking flack when a dozen Bf109s and Fw190s came screaming through the formation.

Normally, the fighters would have waited until the flack stopped before attacking, but this heavily guarded target seemed to demand the ultimate sacrifice from the Luftwaffe pilots.

The lead aircraft started a wide turn to the left and all of the B-17s struggled to move into a tighter formation as they turned with the lead bomber. Things only got worse as the fighters came at them from every direction.

Above and to Jake's right, he heard a couple of dull thuds hit the fuselage as two 20-millimeter shells from one of the fighters hit their intended target.

Over the noise and confusion, Jake heard Arnie call on the ICS, "Jake, can you come up here and give me a hand?"

Jake crawled out of the nose section dragging his oxygen bottle with him. As he entered the cockpit, a blast of cold air hit Jake in the face. Arnie was holding his copilot back in his seat with one hand and trying to keep the aircraft level with the other. The side window and part of the frame on the copilot's side had been blown out where a fighter's round impacted.

The unconscious copilot was bleeding profusely from the right side of his head and his shoulder. Jake grabbed him, unfastened his seat belt and slowly lowered the copilot to the cockpit floor.

Above and to the rear, Okie's spinning turret gun continued to fire at the incoming fighters.

For an instant, Jake was back in the cockpit of the old Boeing 314 flying boat struggling to pull Captain Nelson from his seat and out of the Clipper before it sank into the San Francisco Bay.

He got control of himself and took the white wool scarf from the copilot's neck and wrapped the scarf tightly around the injured flyer's head-wound to stop the bleeding. Taking a deep breath from his mask, Jake unplugged the copilot's oxygen mask hose and attached the hose to his own portable bottle.

The radioman came forward with a first aid kit, opened the kit and handed Jake a morphine syringe.

"Here, sir. You do it," the radioman said. "I can't."

Jake removed his glove and took the syringe from the boy's hand.

"Nothing to it, kid. I used to treat a lot of ol' sick cows this way when I was about your age."

The copilot was starting to come to as Jake shot him in the hip with the morphine to ease the pain.

Jake looked down at his ungloved hand. His fingernails were turning blue, indicating impending hypoxia. He was only seconds away from passing out. He grunted hard several times with his lips held tight to force the remaining oxygen from his lungs into his blood stream and struggled to climb into the copilot's seat where he connected his oxygen hose to the copilot's station. He cleared the ice from his mask and took a long deep breath.

Jake asked the radioman, "Was anyone else hit?"

"Yes sir. One of the waist gunners took a really bad cut from a piece of flack. He wouldn't call for help because he wanted to stay at his gun. I've got the bleeding stopped for now and so far, everyone else is okay," the radioman said straightening the steel helmet he was wearing. "I'll stay here with the lieutenant 'til Okie comes down out of the top turret. You go ahead and give Arnie a hand."

Jake jammed a large seat cushion against the busted out window and buckled himself into the copilot's seat. He looked around the cockpit to familiarize himself. How strange the crew appeared, he thought. They looked like alien monster invaders from another world in their leather suits and strange breathing devices dangling from their faces like an elephant's snout.

The bombers rendezvoused with the Tuskegee Airman in their P-51 Mustangs and soon put the Jerry fighters on the run. The formation turned for home.

There were no winners that day. The Luftwaffe had not won and the lumbering bombers had not won. The only winner to take this day was the Devil himself.

Jake looked over at Arnie whose glazed-over eyes were affixed straight ahead and his leather-gloved hands locked with a death grip on the control yoke.

"Let me take her for awhile, Arnie."

Arnie looked at Jake with a blank stare on his face.

"Come on Arnie, let go. I got it."

Arnie released his grip on the yoke, leaned back in his seat and sat motionless staring straight ahead.

Jake had been at the controls only a short while when he spotted a twin-engine, prop-less aircraft approaching at high speed, the first jet airplane Jake had ever seen.

The German ME262 came streaking through the formation and right across the flight path of the *Annabelle Lee.*

Okie took one or two futile shots at the jet as the fast moving aircraft passed.

The tail gunner's voice came on the ICS, "Look at that puppy go! Those things scare the hell out of me."

"Holy smokes! What was that?" Jake exclaimed, as he strained to look out the side window and watched as the ME262 trailed away.

Arnie also turned to look back and followed the jet as the plane vanished from site.

"We see them every once in awhile. That's the Jerry's new jet fighter. I understand, they'll do close to five hundred miles an hour in level flight, but they only seem to have enough fuel for one or two passes on the formation when they do come. Most of our gunners can't swing their guns fast enough to hit one, but the guys try anyway."

Except for the steady drone of the Fortress' four engines, the rest of the return flight home was shrouded in silence. The crewmen's adrenaline from combat action was slowly wearing off and physical exhaustion began to set in.

Okie tended to the injured copilot, repacking the wound with a bandage from another first aid kit. The copilot was conscious now, but was in danger of going into shock. Okie checked the copilot's oxygen regularly, plugged his heated suit into the flight engineer's station and made him as comfortable as possible.

The bomber squadron was no longer tightly grouped in its defensive formation as on their steady march to the target. The B-17s were now a loose cluster of limping and wounded aircraft. Those with engine trouble were falling to the rear, but all were lumbering toward the sea, headed for the safety of island fortress England.

The weather over the Channel was clear now and only a few scattered clouds covered the mainland. The squadrons were vectored north to come in over a large estuary on the east coast of England the Brits called The Wash.

A flight of RAF Spitfires was in the process of trying to intercept and shoot down some incoming V-1 Buzz Bombs before they reached London.

Before long, Jake saw the smokestacks of Peterborough in the distance. Rested now, Arnie took back the controls. Their smaller group of bombers broke with the larger formation to turn south to their home base.

As they approached the airfield at Huntington, several aircraft, along with the *Annabelle Lee*, fired a flare to indicate wounded crewmen onboard. The crippled B-17s were cleared for straight-in landings.

Jake watched as one of the B-17s went in wheels-up and skidded along on its belly. The bomber's nose plowed a furrow in the soft sod and the plane's tail rose high into the air before coming to a stop and settling back onto the ground. The crew had opted to land on the grassy area beside the main runway so as not to render the only runway un-usable for the rest of the returning bombers.

Fire trucks and ambulances waited alongside the airfield. When the *Annabelle Lee* rolled to a stop, medics boarded and took the wounded copilot and the waist gunner off the aircraft.

Once on the ground and out of the airplane, Arnie said to Jake, "I need to go to the hospital to check on my two crewmen. I'll catch up to you all at the debriefing."

Okie inspected the damage to the aircraft.

"She's repairable, sir. We won't have to donate her to the queen bees yet!" he reported to Arnie referring to a parts airplane that sat around and no longer worked for its keep anymore.

***

Jake sat quietly with the rest of the crew of the *Annabel Lee* waiting their turn to be debriefed. He was nodding off to sleep and it startled him when a WAC corporal tapped him on the shoulder.

"Are you Captain Jake Martin?"

"What! Yes, I'm Martin."

"Sir, there's a gentleman waiting for you in the squadron headquarters' office. If you'd come with me, please?"

When Jake entered the squadron office, an 8ᵗʰ Air Force command officer greeted him.

"I'm General Patterson. You may not remember me. We met years ago at Wright Field when you came to visit an officer named Harkins who served under me."

"Of course, I remember you. Good to see you again. And thanks for the loan of your car and driver when we brought the B-27s in from the States."

The general shook hands with Jake and turned to a tall, distinguished, gray-haired gentleman in formal attire seated in the general's office.

"I'd like you to meet Monsieur Jon Claude LeBourget," General Patterson said. "I believe you two gentlemen know of one another."

"Pardon me for not rising, Captain Martin," the man said making a small hand gesture towards his cane.

Jake did not recognize the man, but he certainly knew the name.

"It's an honor to meet you, sir. I heard so much about you from your daughter I feel like I know you."

Jon Claude spoke English with a thick French accent.

"And I you, Captain Martin. As you know, the French government in exile is based here in England. I'm fortunate to have been able to come here to work with General Charles DeGaulle. However, that is not the reason I am here. I have come specifically to see you this evening."

"You two gentlemen feel free to use this office as long as you like," General Patterson said. "If you'll excuse me, I have some things I need to attend to."

The general left, closing the door behind him.

Jake pulled up a chair facing Jon Claude, the man who at one time might have become his father-in-law.

"Sir, I feel sure you are aware of the relationship between your daughter, Suzette, and myself during the time I spent in Rangoon."

Jon Claude smiled and replied, "Oh, yes and from what she tells me, she also cares very much for you, Jake."

A thick French accent obscured Jon Claude's English and made it difficult for Jake to understand him. Nonetheless, Jake felt reasonably sure Jon Claude had spoken in the present tense.

"You mean told you?" Jake said attempting to clarify.

"Possibly, but I have a message for you from Suzette."

"Sir, I'm still not sure I understand exactly what you're saying. Did Suzette leave a message for me before she died?"

Jon Claude's smile widened, "No, my boy, the news is far better than that. Suzette is very much alive."

Jake rose from his chair and spun around in a circle holding his forehead. He paused and turned to look directly at Suzette's father.

"Where is she? Is she okay? Why isn't she here?"

"I know how you must feel. I will try my best to answer all your questions. She is in good health and living in a small village in occupied France where she has been working with the Freedom Fighters. The message she sends to you is, 'she thinks of you often and wants you to know she waits for you as she hopes you will wait for her.' I believe I have relayed the message to you correctly."

Calmer now, Jake's initial shock gave way to joy. He sat back down and pulled his chair right up in front of Jon Claude and asked, "How come I'm just now finding out Suzette is alive?"

"As I promised, I will try to answer all of your questions. It is my understanding that while you were away at Mangwe, arrangements were made for Suzette to be evacuated with the French Embassy personnel and other French nationals. Suzette told me she sent a written note by messenger to your Clipper docked at the harbor. I must assume neither you nor any of your crewmembers ever received the message."

Jake's face lit up.

"Was she onboard an old LaFrance steamer with a dark blue hull and white deck when she left Rangoon?"

"Suzette's ship passed through the Suez Canal and landed in Algiers where I met her. Yes, I recall the ship. That is the one."

"I saw that vessel making its way out to sea when we took off from the harbor and wondered if they would escape without being spotted. Now it all makes sense."

"It is regrettable you did not know all this time. After we returned to France, the Germans took Paris. Suzette and I were at our country home in Reims, at least we always called my family's old estate home."

"Of course, I remember Suzette telling me stories of her home in Reims," Jake said starting to remember things he had blocked out of his mind because they were painful to recall.

"Suzette, poor child, never spent much time there. She was very young when her mother died and I dragged her all over the world with me from posting to posting. I had to leave France with DeGaulle's provisional government, but I felt she would be safe in Reims. At that time, the Germans seemed to leave the local French citizens alone."

Suddenly, it dawned on Jake to ask, "Then the girl's body found in Suzette's apartment, who was she?"

"I'm not sure, but I believe it must have been a young girl by the name of Maelee," Jon Claude replied with a very solemn expression. "I met her when I was still in Rangoon, a pleasant young girl about the same build as Suzette. She quite often stayed with Suzette at her apartment."

"Yes, I remember her too, now that you mention it. I can certainly understand the mistake."

Jon Claude rose from his chair with the slight assistance of his ivory-handled cane.

"Jake, here is my card. Call me anytime, day or night. My apologies, but my car is waiting and I am expected to attend a function at the American Embassy."

Jake remained seated, staring at the floor until he realized Jon Claude was about to leave. He stood and took the card and shook Jon Claude's hand.

"Thank you for coming in person to tell me about Suzette," Jake said seemingly preoccupied, his mind already formulating a plan, but he was way too tired to think it through right then. "I'll be in touch... Soon!"

Jake returned to the debriefing area, but Arnie's crew had finished and disbursed. He went to the locker he had borrowed in the pilot's ready room where he changed clothes and returned his high-altitude flight gear.

From there he went to the transit barracks where a grumpy old sergeant issued him a sheet and a brown army blanket. The old sergeant told Jake to find an empty bunk wherever he could, which he did. Dinner that night for Jake was a Hershey bar and a cup of coffee.

***

Early the next morning, Jake rounded up a driver to deliver him to the airfield at Northampton where they had landed the B-27s and the home base for a clandestine RAF Mosquito squadron.

Jake continued to operate under the auspices of being a factory technical representative for Martin Aero, which he had cleared earlier with 8th Air Force command. As such, he had been issued an identification card and credentials for access to RAF airbases.

His cover story being that he was studying the flight characteristics of the de Havilland Mosquito bomber for possible incorporation into new U.S. aircraft designs.

The damp morning fog still filled the lowlands at the Northampton airfield when Jake arrived. He got out of the car and walked across the ramp to the RAF Mosquito reconnaissance squadron and into the airborne intelligence squadron office where he had been debriefed a week earlier.

Entering the office, Jake asked the squadron clerk, "Wonder if I could see your commanding officer, Rex Green?"

"Good morning, sir," the clerk said recognizing Jake as the flight leader who arrived with the B-27 Dragon flight. "The C.O. has gone to London to meet with Bomber Harris, our group commander. I expect him to be gone all day. Can I make an appointment for you tomorrow?"

Jake agreed to the appointment and would return the following day. He thanked the clerk and left.

The next order of business was to round up some chow. After that, he contacted Jon Claude's office in London to start the paper work to request a clandestine flight operation into German occupied France.

From that point on, any political opposition Jake might encounter would be referred to Jon Claude's office and quickly dispatched. Otherwise, his plan might have taken months to accomplish.

***

That evening at the officer's mess, Jake struck up a conversation with a young British flight officer at the bar. A U.S. Navy pilot lieutenant recognized Jake's American accent and asked to join them.

During the course of the conversation, Jake mistakenly referred to the young flight officer as an RAF pilot.

"Actually I'm Canadian, RCAF, not RAF," the young flight officer responded. "I'm assigned to ASW, the airborne anti-submarine warfare unit across the airfield."

"Yep, I'm assigned over at ASW too as military liaison officer," the Navy lieutenant said. "Now I not only have to put up with the Limeys, but these Canucks, too."

"Where were you stationed before coming here, Lieutenant?" Jake asked.

"Served on an aircraft carrier in the North Atlantic trying to protect shipping from German air and submarine attacks. Truth be known, those four-engine Condors of Goring's sunk as many ships as the U-boats."

Typical of pilots when they got together, the four began to exchange flying stories.

Jake told them the story Dale Harkins had told about Roosevelt having the Air Corps fly Goony Birds up to Canada and leaving them parked at an abandoned airfield.

"I'm not sure how accurate that story is, but that's the way the tale was told to me."

The Canadian officer smiled smugly.

"Oh, it's true alright. I know because I was one of the pilots who picked up those Gooneys."

"Darned, if it's not a small world after all," Jake said raising his glass. "Here's to the Gooney Bird."

The Canadian raised his glass adding, "And to your President Roosevelt. We thanks you Yanks for the Dakotas and I assure you they are being put to good use."

"Okay," Jake said and turned to the Navy lieutenant, "Now it's your turn to try to out lie us."

The lieutenant thought for a moment and began, "The best story I can think of is about the Americans entering the war. I know the press and the American public think we got into this war when officially declared on the 11th of December."

"Not true?" Jake asked.

The lieutenant paused, mostly for effect and took a sip from his pint.

"Not true. I was assigned to the carrier Wasp in the North Atlantic before coming here. In mid 1941, we were at sea escorting some merchant ships bound for England. Actually, we were shadowing a convoy when we received a radio message from a RNAF Lockheed Hudson patrol plane. We saw one go over earlier in the day. The message alerted us to an incoming flight of Ju87 Stuka dive-bombers headed our way. Dive bombers had attacked our ships before."

"Well, go on, you've got our attention," Jake said.

"We broke 'em of sucking eggs that day. We were airborne and waiting for them at altitude. I was flying an F4F and I got two myself. My squadron shot down about half of their planes and the rest went packing. So you see, we Navy guys flew against the Germans at least five months before the Army Air Corps ever saw combat."

As the evening wore on, the other two pilots discovered Jake had been a flying boat pilot for Pan Am. The two young pilots prodded him to tell them stories about flying the Clippers in the Pacific, which continued until about twenty-three hundred hours when the threesome finally called it a night.

***

The following morning, Jake arrived at Rex Green's office at the appointed hour and the squadron clerk showed him into the commander's office.

Following the usual exchange of formalities, Green reached for a large manila envelope labeled Urgent and placed the envelope on the desk in from of them.

"This arrived late yesterday afternoon," Rex said smiling. "Actually the bloody thing beat me back from London. You have any idea what it's all about?"

"I can pretty much guess," Jake replied.

"I figured you could, Captain Martin. Since I've been in this man's air war, I've never seen a request dated and approved on the same day before!"

"Great!" Jake said smiling because of Rex's use of the word approved.

"If you'll wait here for a moment, I'll locate Flying Officer Herriot who will be assigned to your mission."

Rex made a couple of phone calls and shortly, a pleasant young fellow in an RAF blue dress uniform entered the room.

"Herriot, this is Captain Martin."

"I'm James Herriot. Glad to have you with us, sir," James said extending a handshake to Jake.

"You can drop the sir stuff, James. Everyone calls me Jake."

"We'll combine this operation with your next U4 drop," Rex said handing the mission envelope to James.

"Right, sir," James replied and saluted. "Very well, Jake," James said motioning toward the door to the ramp. "Let's go get you oriented."

"Thanks for your help, Commander," Jake said to Rex as he got up to leave with James.

"You're more than welcome. Always glad to help out a Yank, even if you did kick our tails in '76."

As they left, James looked over the contents of the envelope he had been handed.

"I noticed the commander addressed you as captain. Are you military?"

"No, it's an old title. I used to be a China Clipper pilot for Pan Am."

"Ah then, that explains why you're listed here on the flight manifest as my copilot."

"I assume we'll be using a Mosquito?" Jake asked.

James pointed to a row of aircraft parked on the ramp.

"Yes, it's the best plane for the job. We'll go have a look see at the one we'll be using if you'd like?"

As the two men passed down a row of twin-engine, single pilot Mosquito attack bombers, Jake asked, "How are we going to carry passengers in one of these?"

James stopped at the last Mosquito in the row.

"Here she is, the one we will be using. You'll notice the forward fuselage of this Mosquito is wider. This model has both pilot and copilot crew positions, but more often we fly a navigator or a camera operator in the copilot's seat, as we are short on qualified pilots. For the type of mission we'll be flying, we use an unarmed Mosquito. The only defense we have is speed."

Jake went closer to look over the aircraft.

"Take a look under the plane," James said. "You'll see the bomb bay sealed shut and there is a small access ladder extending down from the hatch in the belly. This enables us to carry two passengers instead of a bomb load. This is the Mk21 version of the Mosquito. There were only two others like this one ever built."

"You Brits think of everything. This is the ideal aircraft for our mission. High speed for evasion and plenty of power for getting out of short landing strips."

"I thought you might like that," James said smiling.

"Let's walk on over to the base pub for a pint. I think you Yanks call it an officer's club."

"Little early for that isn't it?" Jake asked.

"Not when you work nights like we do, but this job is a hurry up and wait job anyway. Got to kill some time somewhere."

As they walked, Jake asked, "You a career officer?"

"No, I'm a Vet," James replied.

"You look awfully young to have flown in the First World War?

James smiled. "No, not a veteran, a veterinarian. You know dogs, sheep and cows, that sort of thing. I joined the RAF when ol' Adolph started this bloody mess. I think I dislike that arrogant fat-ass Goering most of all. Probably the reason I volunteered to go upstairs and harass his fellows. Instead, I was assigned to this airborne Sherlock Holmes outfit."

For the balance of the morning the two flyers visited, discussing the various aspects of their mission.

Gray Ghost

Jake spent most of the day at the aircraft assigned for the mission. Seated alone in the cramped cockpit of the MK21 Mosquito, he memorized every switch and control onboard. He read the flight manual twice and knew how each system operated. As James suggested, he paid particular attention to how the specially installed radios operated.

Along about sundown, James came out to the aircraft and climbed into the cockpit beside him.

"The weather over the Channel has been sorry the last few days, but Coastal Patrol reports the weather is clearing. We're go for tonight!"

"What time is takeoff?" Jake asked.

"We have two outbound passengers. If they're ready, we'll be airborne by twenty-two hundred hours."

Shortly after dark, a small lorrie with dimly lit running lights made its way across the airfield ramp and pulled up to the Mosquito bomber where Jake waited.

James, accompanied by two men in foreign looking civilian clothes, got out of the vehicle.

Jake thought it a little odd that James did not introduce him to their passengers.

The two men went about their business loading equipment into the aircraft through the modified bomb bay hatch and boarded the plane like they knew the routine. Occasionally, they spoke with one another in French.

After a thorough preflight of the Mosquito, James boarded the plane with Jake and squeezed into the cramped quarters of the dual-pilot cockpit.

James sat quietly in the pilot's seat of the plane, looking out across the dark airfield.

Jake cracked the sliding window on his side of the cockpit for a little fresh air and listened for a while to a chorus of crickets chirping in the night.

Their two passengers raised the bomb bay compartment boarding-ladder, closed the hatch and buckled themselves into the two passenger seats.

Jake could see the two men through the small hand passage connecting the flight deck to the rear belly compartment. The small opening was only large enough to pass messages or to hand small objects through, but not large enough to crawl through.

"Who are those guys in the back? Will we have enough room for our pickup on the return?"

James glanced rearward.

"Don't ask and try not to look at them well enough that you could identify them. The less you know the better off you'll be if we're captured. If we are able to effect a landing, our two guests will not be returning with us."

Jake finally got the picture. The men were Allied trained spies disguised as French civilians.

While they waited for departure clearance, the two pilots exchanged small talk. Most of their conversation centered on technical things dealing with the Mosquito and its flight characteristics.

James asked, "Did you read the aircraft handbook and the manual on the radio receiver we'll be using?"

Jake pointed to the odd-looking radio control head mounted in the instrument panel.

"This one? As best I can tell, its pretty simple. I can handle it."

"Yes, it receives the signal from a small pencil antenna, which sends only a cone signal straight up in the air. This prevents the Jerrys from intercepting the signal and using direction finders to locate our people on the ground. The device was invented by one of your Yanks, a guy name Steve Simpson with the Radio Corporation of America."

A green light flashed twice from a small building off in the distance, the signal James had been watching for.

"That's us, we don't use radio transmissions for takeoff clearances. German spies eavesdropping on the tower frequency could alert interceptors to our coming."

James handed the takeoff checklist to Jake and prepared to start the engines.

They were airborne in a few minutes. James took the Mosquito up to six thousand feet and leveled off.

"You take her for a while, Jake. Give you a chance to get a feel for how she flies. We'll hold this altitude 'til we near the coast and then I'll take her down to a couple hundred feet before we reach the Channel to stay under the German coastal radar."

As they passed over the White Cliffs of Dover, Jake could see the phosphorous glow on the shoreline even though there was no moon in the sky and commented, "Pretty sight."

"Even prettier on the way back!"

The speeding Mosquito made quick work of the thirty odd miles across the English Channel and James dropped down to a hundred feet off the deck as they came in over the coast of France.

"I'm going to head northeast and we'll hold this heading until we are roughly in the area of our landing spot. Listen Jake, logic will tell you the reciprocal of this heading is your way back out of here if anything happens to me, so memorize it if you can."

"Sure," Jake replied looking questioningly at James.

"Don't mean to be morbid, ol' man, but you see on my first mission, right after takeoff on our return flight, we took a bad hit on the pilot's side and my plane commander was killed." James made a power adjustment and a slight heading correction and added, "Fine chap, good pilot, too."

"Okay, I'll pay attention!"

"We used the old Avro Anson twins for those early missions. They weren't as fast as this Mosquito."

They were doing close to three hundred knots when a factory smokestack passed by the right wingtip in the dark.

"Good. There's our last checkpoint."

"You mean, there it went."

James smiled.

"If I can nail our time and distance from here, you should get a signal on the pencil receiver in a few minutes. If not, we'll have to climb and circle until we can receive the signal. That's not good because the more we're airborne in the area, the better chance the German patrols have of guessing our landing location."

James commenced a zigzag course to keep from passing over several small-populated areas.

Jake observing how good James was at what he did, remarked, "I can tell this isn't your first time at the county fair!"

"Thanks, but you're not home yet."

At the Mosquito's speed, it did not take long to cover the required distance to their rendezvous location.

"Okay, Jake, we're coming up on our contact point."

James pulled up into a wingover to gain some altitude for better reception and no sooner had he spoken those words, than Jake called out, "Got a signal!"

James throttled back to lessen the engine noise and to play-off their airspeed as he set up a landing approach to an open grass field between two groves of high trees.

Extending full flaps he dropped the powerful twin into the field. As soon as the wheels touched the ground, he cut both engines and the plane coasted quietly to a stop at the end of the field not far from the edge of the grove.

"Look for a torch to flash," James said.

From the black of the grove, Jake saw the beam from a flashlight flicker one time.

The plane had barely rolled to a stop before their two passengers were on the ground unloading the radio gear and several cases of small arms ammunition onto the ground.

Four dark figures, obviously French Freedom Fighters, ran from the woods towards the waiting plane. Jake wondered how long they would have to wait for Suzette to get there. He worried James might opt to depart without her if she missed her rendezvous time.

The first man to reach the plane helped the two deplaning passengers carry the equipment into the trees.

The second man, holding an automatic weapon, appeared to be standing guard.

The remaining two figures approached the plane. The smaller of the two was wearing dark clothes and a short-billed cap pulled down tightly over the forehead. For some reason that Jake failed to understand, the larger man was carrying a small child.

The door to the bomb bay passenger compartment was still open and the ladder remained extended. The smaller person in the short-billed cap climbed the ladder into the airplane helped up by the larger man.

The large man holding the child came partway up the boarding ladder and handed the child into the airplane passenger compartment. He said something quietly in French, climbed down, stowed the ladder and shut the hatch.

Jake watched through the hand passage between the two compartments as their new passenger removed the cap and long black hair fell down over her shoulders.

"Suzette!" he exclaimed and leaned over from the copilot's seat far enough to touch her outreached hand.

She grasped Jake's hand through the narrow opening, still clutching the small child under her other arm and said softly, "Jake! I knew you would come for us!"

Jake heard a sound outside in the distance through the open cockpit side window and turned quickly forward to see the last French Freedom Fighter disappear into the cover of the woods.

Three flashes of light came from the darken grove of woods and James exclaimed, "Three flashes means trouble!"

Jake saw it too and through the open cockpit window, he could now clearly identify the distant sound as heavy equipment in the still night. The vehicles were faster moving than a tank, possibly an armored car or large truck.

James engaged the starter on the left engine and the Mosquito engine cranked with a high-pitched whine.

Jake reacted instinctively and raised the fully extended landing flaps to the ten-degree takeoff position. Turning to Suzette in the rear compartment, he hollered over the noise of the engines, "Sit down and buckle in!"

James released the brakes, allowing the left engine to spin the Mosquito around as he engaged the right engine. He came in with full power and called, "High-boost, now!"

Jake switched the turbo-chargers to the high position.

The craft had a rear-quartering breeze, but no matter, James kept rolling for a downwind takeoff. The Mosquito bounced across the rough pastureland and several unseen chuckholes jarred the aircraft violently as it struggled to obtain liftoff speed.

The end of the tree grove was coming at them fast, but James continued to hold the controls forward and then pulled back hard. The plane, somewhat lighter now from having burned off half of its fuel load on the inbound flight, hurdled its precious cargo skyward.

Jake looked back over his right shoulder and could see a German half-track and a large army truck pull onto the far end of the open field. Nazi storm troopers bailed out of the truck and commenced firing at the plane.

Repeated flashes of automatic weapons fire disappeared behind the Mosquito as it barely cleared the trees at the end of the field.

Holding full military-power setting on both engines, James nosed the plane over to stay barely above the treetops, thus blocking their departure from the gunfire.

Jake was sure he heard the plane's landing gear strike the upper leaves of the tallest tree at the end of the field as the gear started its retract cycle, but no need to worry about damage to the landing gear right now.

Still not breathing easily yet, they sat quietly listening to the drone of the engines until James said, "We should make the coast in about fifteen minutes. Dial in the code I gave you on the IFF transmitter. If coastal radar doesn't see that, we are going to have a swarm of Spitfires on our tail before we can make it across the Channel."

Jake wanted very much to see and hold Suzette, but that would not be possible until they landed. Besides, James could use an extra pair of eyes right now. Still he continued to glance back into the rear compartment to check on Suzette.

Suzette sat clutching her child and whenever Jake did turn to look at her, she would smile proudly back at him.

***

"On course, on glide path," came ground control's reassuring voice over the radio headsets as the runway lights came into view through the early morning ground fog.

The Mosquito touched down as softly as James could make the landing at the Northampton airfield and both pilots uttered a mutual sigh of relief when the landing gear held firm on rollout.

In their hasty departure back in France, Jake forgot to say his usual prayer on takeoff, but he did quietly say, "Thank you Lord," when the gear held up on touchdown.

James swung the Mosquito into its parking space and shutdown the engines.

Jake scrambled out of the cockpit to open the bomb bay hatch and lowered the ladder.

Suzette handed the child down to him and climbed down into his arms. He held her and the child for the longest time. Finally letting go, he gazed into her face.

It had been three long heartbreaking years since they parted in Rangoon, but it seemed more like a lifetime.

Jake held the two-year-old boy up to the dull morning light, smiled and asked, "And who is this fine young fellow we have here?"

"Jake Martin, I'd like you to meet my son, Chen Laun," Suzette said smiling with joy.

Jake could not stop smiling either. He held young Chen in one arm and held onto Suzette with the other as they looked back at the dependable ol' flying machine, which had returned them faithfully from their intended mission.

James came out from under the wing after inspecting the landing gear with a small tree branch in his hand.

"Guess we didn't quite clear the one tree," Jake said and laughed.

"Guess not," James replies with a wide smile.

Jake and Suzette walked a ways towards the squadron office with James.

Jake paused as James went on ahead. "Thanks for everything," he hollered out to James.

"You're more than welcome, all in a night's work for Tree Top Airways. Drop me a postcard, Yank."

"I'll do better than that, we'll send you a wedding announcement."

Suzette smiled and held on tightly to Jake's harm as she waved goodbye to James, "We'll always remember you for this!"

James smiled and waved back.

Looking up into Jakes eyes Suzette asked, "What now?"

"I've arranged to have a car waiting. The *Queen Mary* sails from Glasgow for the States tonight. We've got time to make it if we get going."

In front of the squadron office, two cars waited in the faint dawn light. A uniformed Army corporal waited in an olive brown Packard sedan staff car. Not far behind, a black Citroen sedan with a gray uniformed chauffeur at the wheel and a dark silhouette of a man in the rear waited.

As Jake and Suzette approached the staff car, Corporal Brown stepped out.

"Good to see you again, Brown. Hang loose, we'll be ready to go shortly."

Corporal Brown saluted, "Right, sir."

The chauffer of the Citroen limousine stepped out and opened the rear door.

Jake took Suzette by the arm and led her to the second parked car. "You may want to visit with this gentleman for a few minutes."

"Papa!" Suzette exclaimed as she climbed into the back seat and hugged her father's neck.

Jake stood at the open car door and handed Chen into his grandfather.

"Here's a young fellow you might like to meet, Monsieur LeBourget."

Jon Claude held young Chen on his lap as Suzette and her father conversed in French. Jake could not understand the words, but obviously father and daughter were very happy to see one another again.

A quarter hour passed and Jake stuck his head in the open door to say, "We better get going."

"Yes, you best be going now," Jon Claude said to Suzette in English. "It's 500 kilometers to the port at Gourock and you don't want to miss your sailing."

Suzette was reluctant to leave, but she knew she must.

Jake reached in the car and took Chen from his grandfather's lap. He shook Jon Claude's hand.

"Take good care of her, Jake."

"Don't worry, Monsieur LeBourget, I will."

Suzette kissed her father goodbye and stepped out of the limo. She stood at the open door. Father and daughter exchanged a few more goodbyes and well wishes.

Jake, carrying Chen, walked on ahead to the waiting staff car and stood talking with Corporal Brown while they waited for Suzette.

"I can drive you to the train station to catch the Flying Scotsman," Brown said, "but the train might not get you there before your ship sails. Colonel authorized me to take you all the way to the Port of Gourock if you want."

"You're a good man, Corporal Brown. Let's do that."

Jake looked back to see if Suzette was coming.

Suzette hugged her father one last time, holding onto his hand as though she might not see him again. She turned tearfully and ran to get in the car with Jake and Chen.

The rising sun crested the horizon through the morning haze of the English countryside as their car pulled away.

Suzette looked back to wave goodbye one more time.

***

During the eight-hour drive to the Port of Gourock near Glasgow in northwestern Scotland, Jake and Suzette were as giddy as a couple of teenage kids in love. They held hands and sometimes just sat looking at each other.

"I can't believe that shy, gentle young woman I fell in love with in Rangoon has been fighting with the French underground for the last two years."

"And disguised as a man most of the time," Suzette responded making a sweeping hand motion at the dark, dirty trousers and working man's shirt she still had on.

"Did you kill anyone?" Jake blurted out thoughtlessly.

"More than I care to remember. I watched our men die, too. If I told you the horrible things I saw the Nazis do, you'd find them hard to believe!" Suzette's sad expression turned into a coy smile. "But, tell me now what my handsome captain has been doing and of all the beautiful women you have made love to while you were waiting for me?"

"At least you haven't lost your sense of humor."

"I don't care what you've done in my absence, mister, I've got you now and I never intend to lose you again!"

Regardless of what had happened in Jake's checkered past, he took a personal oath that very moment there would never be another woman in his life. He would marry Suzette and do whatever it took to hold on to her.

He began by telling her about moving to California.

"Lora was nine last June and has turned into quite a young lady, pretty and smart as a whip. Michael will be eight in November. He's a beach bum now like most of the kids in the neighborhood. Chen will probably end up being just like him. All the teenagers are trying out these new Hawaiian things call surfboards."

Jake explained who Lydia was and described to her where they had been living in Santa Monica. He told Suzette all about the new home he was having built in Malibu.

"I've taken Lora and Michael out to see the new house several times while it's been under construction. The place was almost finished when I left. They may have even moved in by now. Lora loves it there and Michael is excited about being closer to the ocean. You can walk down to the beach from the hill at the back of the property."

"Oh, I love the beach. When I attended college at UCLA, I'd go over to Venice Beach on the weekends."

Jake told Suzette about the new bomber plant and explained his plans for building private and commercial airplanes after the war was over.

"There will be such a demand for new planes when all the guys who learned to fly in the Army start coming home from the war."

"It all sounds so exciting. I can tell by the enthusiasm in your voice you'll make it happen."

Jake glanced out the window at the setting sun realizing how far away all that seemed from a world at war.

"Tell me where you went and what happened after you met your father in Algiers."

"From there we returned to the family estate near Reims in the north of France. Father was in Paris when the Vichy government took over and he was evacuated to England with General DeGaulle."

"How did you get tied up with the French underground?"

"I remained at the estate with my aunt and a cousin. One morning, a German Field Marshall arrived with his staff and announced that he had selected our home to use for his new headquarters. We were given until noon to vacate the estate. My sixteen-year-old cousin, Pierre, protested and one of the Nazi officers shot him. He died instantly. The soldiers would not even let my aunt and I go to him."

"I'm so very sorry you had to go through all that," Jake said and held her close thinking she was about to cry.

"I would like to cry for him still. I did cry for him and others too, but it's over now and I've cried all I can. I must go on from here." Suzette moved to the edge of her seat and turned to face Jake. "My aunt knew a man who owned a small townhouse in a nearby village. Chen was born there. My aunt's friend was a member of the resistance movement and that's how I became involved."

"It's okay, you don't have to go on," Jake said realizing Suzette's life experiences these past two years had been very different from his own. He also realized that Suzette was more mature and self-assured now.

"No, I want you to know the things I had to do. I would help the men rig the bridges with explosives, but it wouldn't have done any good to just blow up our own bridges, so the others in our group…"

"There were other women?"

"Oh yes, several. They would set up machineguns on the far side of the bridge and lay in wait for a German convoy. When the first armored vehicles were on the bridge, it was my job to blow the explosives and then run to join the others. The soldiers who became trapped between the stalled column and the collapsed bridge fell under our gunfire."

As she talked, Jake realized it was more than the Nazis killing her cousin, the anger she held in her heart against the Japanese for the death of Chen's father and her friend in Rangoon had manifest itself in an intense hatred of the Nazi occupiers.

"Hell hath no wrath like a woman…" Jake mumbled and quickly changed the subject. "Your father told me briefly what he thought had happened in Rangoon while I was stranded in Mangwe, but I'd like you to tell me."

"Very well. The day of the air raid, Maelee had come to spend the night as she often did. She loved to stay with me because she had her own small area with her own bed to sleep in. You remember the apartment don't you, Jake?"

"Yes, of course I do. I also remember Maelee."

"That afternoon, I received a call from the French Embassy asking me to come in. The man on the telephone told me they were preparing to evacuate French citizens and wanted me to complete the paperwork for my transit visa so I would be ready to leave when the evacuation started."

"Why didn't you get a message to me so I'd know what had happened to you?"

"A message?" Suzette exclaimed with aggravation in her voice. "I was supposed to get a message to you! Where were you? You said you'd be back the next day. I waited. I worried my fool head off."

"Okay, maybe it was my fault."

"And then later, I'm suppose to pick up a telephone and tell an operator in a country we're at war with, 'I'd like to talk to my boyfriend in America. Oh no, I don't know his phone number or where he is now.' Or maybe I should have just asked if I could leave a message for you?"

"I said it was my fault!"

"I did try though. When I arrived at the Embassy, I was told arrangements had already been made for me to leave on a French vessel. I was not being requested to leave, the man at the Embassy had received orders from my father to see that I was onboard the steamer when the ship left port. I was given no choice in the matter."

The car sped northward through the English countryside and Corporal Brown stopped the car to wait for a shepherd to move his herd of sheep from the road.

"Oh look, Chen," Suzette said holding him up to the window so he could see. "Look at all the sheep!"

"Chen understands English?" Jake asked.

"No, but I've decided to only speak English to him from now on. If he is going to be an American, he must learn to talk like one."

When the sheep cleared the road, the car pulled away again and Suzette continued, "I gave a handwritten note to a boy from the same messenger service I had used to send messages to you at the dock in the past. I instructed the boy to give the message to any of the Clipper's crew if you were not there. I can only guess that the messenger must have been delayed in his delivery by the air raid or worse. At any rate, I sailed on the steamer *Champlain* from Rangoon only an hour before the Japanese air attack began."

"Yes, I saw the old LaFrance steamer making its way for the open sea when we took off from the harbor. The bombers were already attacking to the north of town and I remember wondering if that ship would manage to slip away."

"By some miracle we did. I stood on the deck with others. We saw the bombs exploding on the horizon hoping the bombers would not come after our ship. Someone on deck pointed to a large airplane climbing out in the distance. I prayed the plane was yours and that somehow you were onboard. My prayers were answered!"

"I'm sure you're right about that," Jake said with a sigh and they both sat quietly then for a long while.

By late afternoon, the two reunited lovers had filled in most of the missing blanks of their absence by exchanging every story, which came to mind. There would be more to tell and more to talk about in the coming years, but hopefully they would now have a lifetime to do it in.

Young Chen had been standing up looking out the window for some time. He climbed up on the seat beside his mother and fell asleep. She took a wool blanket from the rail on the back of the driver's seat to cover the boy and warm him from the cool Highland air.

Suzette rested her head on Jake's shoulder and fell asleep. Jake sat admiring her as she slept and dozed off to sleep a couple of times himself.

Early that evening, Brown pulled the staff car up to the main entrance of the Gourock shipyard. The guard on duty at the port entrance stopped them to check Jake's identification and papers.

"Thank you, Mr. Martin," the guard said returning the papers to Jake and passing the car through.

Corporal Brown stopped the car on the pier next to the passenger-boarding gangway and they got out of the car.

Jake, with the sleeping boy over his shoulder, went around to the driver's window.

"Thanks for the ride, Corporal. Tell General Patterson how very much we appreciate the loan of his car."

The Corporal turned the car around and waved as he pulled away. Suzette and Jake waved back.

***

The giant *Queen Mary*, tied up to the dock, had been painted a solid battleship gray. Her luxurious compartments stripped and replaced with stacks of bunk beds. The *Gray Ghost*, as the ship was now affectionately referred to, had already delivered thousands of allied troops to the dock here at Gourock.

The ship's crew would sail tonight for New York. After their port-of-call at New York, the ship would sail on to South America before making another Atlantic crossing.

A uniformed British official approached Jake and Suzette at the foot of the gangway. Jake showed the official his identification and transit papers prepared by Jon Claude's people at the French Embassy in exile.

"Good evening Mr. Martin. We were notified of your pending arrival." Raising his clipboard, the official prepared to fill out the required boarding information. "I will need your full names for the roster."

"Jacob Teel Martin, Jr."

"And you, ma'am?"

"Suzette LeBourget and Chen Laun."

To which Jake added, "Chen Laun Martin," and the official wrote it down exactly the way Jake said.

About halfway up the gangway, Suzette turned and asked Jake, "Why did you say that?"

"This will make it easier when we arrive in New York. We won't have to go through a bunch of immigration BS."

Suzette smiled, suspecting that might not have been the real reason. As she started on up the gangway, she said to Jake, "I'll bet that was the quickest adoption procedure in history." Then she turned and asked, "What about me?"

Nudging her gently in the ribs to go on up the gangway, he whispered, "I got that one figured out, too."

At the top of the gangway, the ship's Purser greeted them, "Welcome aboard the *RMS Queen Mary*."

"Thank you," Jake replied.

"We've been expecting you. The ship is nearly empty except for some war brides and a large number of children being sent to the States to stay with relatives. Captain Bisset asked me to make arrangements for you to use the Royal Quarters on the forward upper deck. I see you have arrived with no luggage. Is that correct?"

"Just the clothes on our back. And, oh yeah, we did manage to make it out of France with our asses intact."

"Jake!" Suzette exclaimed.

"It's quite all right, ma'am. Mr. Martin is a man after me own heart," the Purser said smiling. "I suspect he might have been a seafaring lad at one time himself. If you'll come with me, I'll show you to your cabin."

Suzette entered the cabin first and exclaimed, "Jake, look at this place, it's beautiful! Can you believe this, I haven't stayed anywhere this nice in years."

"It ought to be nice. I think this is the Royal family's cabin," Jake said and sat Chen down on the bed.

"Right you are, sir."

"Good of Captain Bisset to let us use the stateroom, but I guess he can bend a few rules, wartime and all."

"Yes sir. Wartime and all."

"I'm assuming this ship runs on steam so there must be plenty of hot water?" Suzette asked.

"Yes ma'am, it does and yes we do."

"Good! I'm going to have a long hot bath. Maybe a shower and two hot baths."

"Enjoy your bath, I mean your voyage, ma'am," the Purser said as he left shutting the cabin door behind him.

Suzette dropped her dirty and well-worn men's clothes on the floor where she stood and crossed the cabin wearing a raggedy old bra and a pair of men's boxer shorts. Jake preferred not to even consider where she had gotten them.

In a moment, the boxer shorts and the well-worn bra came flying out the door and landed beside Suzette's dark and dingy discarded old clothes.

"What am I supposed to do with these?" Jake asked.

"Burn them! Throw them overboard. Just get rid of them," came the reply from the bath.

In a while, the beautiful young Dragon Lady with neatly combed, coal-black hair and shining eyes emerged from the bath in a terrycloth robe she found hanging in a closet. She stopped in the doorway and smiled.

There was Jake, shoeless and sprawled across the bed, fully dressed in the wrinkled clothes he had worn for the last three days. He was sound asleep and curled up under his arm was young Chen, also fast asleep.

She drew the drapes on the window and climbed into bed next to the two fellows she loved so very dearly and fell asleep admiring them.

***

The following morning, a rap on the cabin door awakened Jake. He eased slowly out of bed so as not to wake Suzette and nearly stepped on young Chen. The boy had been up for hours and was sitting in the middle of the floor happily tearing out pages from a magazine he pulled off a nearby end table.

As Jake went to answer the door, he felt the movement of the ship under his feet. The *Queen Mary* had put to sea in the middle of the night and was well underway.

A steward at the opened door asked, "I was wondering if you might like to have lunch served in your cabin? I believe you and the madam missed breakfast, sir."

"What time of day is it anyway?"

"Nearly noon, sir."

"Sure, breakfast, lunch whatever you've got would be great." Jake started to close the cabin door, then called the steward back. "Could you possibly find us some clothes? You see, we left in kind of a hurry and didn't bring much with us," Jake said understating the problem.

The steward returned to the doorway.

"I can see you're a rather tall gentleman," and looking into the cabin at Suzette still lying across the bed in the terrycloth robe, he said, "and the madam, possibly a small to medium? Consider it done, sir."

Suzette woke when the door shut. She stepped out of bed and staggered to catch her balance from the rocking of the ship running at full steam through rough seas in the North Atlantic.

She pulled back the window curtain, flinched from the bright sunlight and turned to Jake with a beaming smile.

"It's a beautiful morning and what makes it so beautiful is that we're together again."

Jake held her around the waist. She put her arms around his neck and lifted her feet off the floor as he kissed her. When he finally put her down, her smile faded slightly as though recalling an unpleasant memory.

"There were times when I began to think this day would never come, but deep down, I never gave up hope."

They stood together looking out the small cabin window, watching as rays of sunlight broke through the scattered clouds and danced across the infinite sparkling waves. There was only ocean as far as the eye could see.

A knock on the cabin door was the steward again.

"I fixed you both a luncheon tray and here are several sets of clothes I managed to round up from the Royal Merchant Marine uniform stores. It's the best I could do."

Jake took the pile of clothes from the steward's arms.

"Thanks, you did great. These will do fine."

"Sir, Captain Bisset extends his invitation to you and the madam to join him for dinner this evening at twenty hundred hours. Oh, and the captain has arranged for one of the Royal Women Marines to come to your cabin and stay with your son this evening."

"Tell the captain we will be delighted to join him for dinner," Suzette replied accepting for them.

"Thank you, ma'am," the steward said and he left.

"You may not like the fashion, but at least they're clean," Jake said tossing the clothes on the bed.

Suzette selected one of the smaller outfits. Her lovely, long olive-tan legs shown between the parted terrycloth robe as she held it up in front of her.

"What do you think, Jake, is it me?"

"My dear Dragon Lady, you'd look stunning in anything!"

Jake went over to carefully pick up Chen from the floor where he had fallen asleep playing. He carried the boy into the small adjoining room, laid him on the bunk and quietly closed the door. He stood looking at Suzette.

"It has been a long time since we were together," she said loosening the waist tie on the terrycloth robe and let it fall to the floor.

"Too long," Jake replied.

***

That evening, Jake and Suzette went to meet Captain Bisset for dinner in the captain's mess topside adjoining the bridge and the officer's quarters. The mahogany paneled officers mess, decorated with pictures and mementos from notable cruises, had a large desk at one end of the room. A giant oval-shaped table, which could seat twelve comfortably, occupied most of the center of the room.

Captain Bisset, a middle-aged jovial, round-faced handsome figure of a man had invited his first officer, a tall, slender, square-bearded seaman to joined them.

Upon being introduced to Suzette, the captain said, "I have been told you are known in some circles as the Dragon Lady, but the name does not forewarn one of such beauty."

"I fear you are a flattering old seadog like my very own captain, but thank you anyway, kind sir!" Suzette replied smiling and everyone in the room laughed.

After an excellent dinner, the four were served cognac in small brandy snifters and Jake inquired, "Are we running alone? I noticed we don't have any escort ships."

"I am assuming you were asleep during our departure."

"Yes we were. We didn't wake until nearly noon."

"Had you been on deck, you would have observed that we picked up a cruiser and two destroyer escorts from the Royal Navy shortly after leaving port. As soon as we were in open sea, I elected to discontinue our zigzag course and proceed full-ahead without them."

"The crew refers to that part of our departure as running torpedo alley," the first officer interjected. "It has not been for lack of trying that a German U-boat has not gotten a shot at us. Das Fuhrer has offered a quarter million pounds and an Iron Cross with oak clusters to any U-boat commander who is able to sink the *QM*."

"You see," the captain explained, "the *QM* can make thirty knots underway and the escort ships can't keep up with us. If we slowed to their speed, we'd become an easy target for a sub's torpedo. My experience dictates that our faster speed makes it almost impossible for a U-boat to get into position, aim and fire even when they are lucky enough to be laying in wait ahead of our course."

"There are a few other good reasons," the first officer said glancing over at the captain as if seeming to ask his permission to continue. "Last October, the cruiser *HMS Curacoa* cut across our bow and the *QM* nearly split her in-half when we collided."

"Of course, we had the right-of-away!" the captain said. "No self-respecting Royal Navy Captain would admit to doing such a stupid thing, so the matter was hushed up. You can see now why it's best for the *QM* to cruise alone."

"You've convinced me," Jake said and finished his cognac.

Captain Bisset motioned to the steward.

"Another round of drinks, but only three this time. Number One here, has the duty tonight."

Suzette had been mostly listening to the three men talk 'til now.

"Thank you, Captain. No more for me either."

"Make that only two," the captain instructed the steward and turned his attention back to Jake who asked a question about the ship's navigation.

The captain stood up from the table and motioned for Jake to step over to a large world chart on the wall.

"Here, let me show you."

Suzette, considerably uninterested in ship's navigation, engaged the first officer in conversation.

"Tell me more about the *Queen Mary*," she said. "No, first of all tell me why you refer to a ship in the feminine gender?"

"I'm not sure I know the answer to that one, ma'am," the first officer replied. "Perhaps it's because ships are high maintenance and demanding of your attention like most women I've known."

"Spoken like an officer and a gentleman."

"Ma'am, I can tell you some of my own experiences onboard the *QM*, if you like?"

"Please do," Suzette said and the first officer began.

Across the room, the captain pointed to the chart and said, "We are right about here now. In calm seas, we can make the crossing to New York in five days easy."

Jake glanced over at Suzette who was engrossed in her conversation about the *QM* with the first officer.

"Captain, I understand you have the authority to conduct a marriage ceremony at sea."

"Yes, of course. However, I don't get many requests to perform them now days. Why do you ask?"

"When Suzette and I were separated in Burma, we had not yet been married. Would you consent to marrying us?"

"It would be an honor to marry the famous flyer and adventurer, Captain Jake Martin to the daughter of a French dignitary."

"I think possibly you might mean 'the notorious' Captain Jake Martin," Jake said smiling.

"Not at all. Would tomorrow afternoon be agreeable? I'll have my personal steward make the arrangements."

Both men rejoined Suzette and the first officer at the dining table.

The first officer rose from his chair.

"Mr. Martin, ma'am, it's been an enjoyable evening, but duty calls. Don't want to make the officer I'm relieving late getting off duty," and to the captain he said, "By your leave, sir?"

"Carry on," Captain Bisset replied nodding politely. As the first officer left, the captain said to Suzette, "I understand congratulations are in order."

Suzette looked at Jake, "You didn't ask me yet!"

"I'm asking now."

"No matter, the answer is yes anyway."

"I know you're Catholic and we'll get a priest to marry us when we get home to California, but Captain Bisset has graciously agreed to marry us now. All kidding aside, this will simplify our going through immigration."

"I didn't intend to give you the slightest chance of backing out on me anyway. The only way your going to get away from me this time, mister, is to jump overboard." Suzette got up from her chair and jumped in Jake's lap. "Pardon me, Captain, while I kiss the man who is offering to make me an honest woman."

The captain gave out with a hearty laugh.

***

A young girl from London recently married a U.S. Army soldier and had packed her wedding dress in a footlocker. She and Suzette went to the cargo hold with the boatswains mate and retrieved the dress.

The wedding onboard the *Queen Mary* the following afternoon was the major social event of the crossing. The war brides and transient children all attended the ceremony in the main ballroom where the bunk beds had been pushed back against the wall for the ceremony.

Suzette wore the borrowed dress and she looked like a princess in the white lace gown with a long train.

Captain Bisset, in his full dress Royal Merchant Marine uniform, performed the marriage ceremony with great dignity.

The steward had arranged for the cooks to bake a giant wedding cake and the reception afterwards was more akin to a birthday party with all of the children running around.

Young Chen, tired from running and playing with the other children all day was put to bed early by his mother in the small attendant's bedroom adjoining the Royal Suite.

The day had been mostly a blur for Jake and Suzette, but their first night together as man and wife would always remain in their memory.

The sea was smooth now and they made love passionately from the heart to the gentle rocking of the giant ship.

It would have been impossible to convince either of them there were ever two people more in love. Both firmly believed God had ordained them to be together.

Suzette fell asleep snuggled up as tight to Jake as she could get and in a while, Jake drifted off to sleep listening to the steady churning hum of the *Gray Ghost's* powerful engines.

***

Early on the morning of the day the *Queen Mary* was to make landfall in New York, Jake stood at the rail on the Promenade Deck having a cup of coffee.

He had gone to the radio shack the day before and asked the operator to send a ship to shore message to be relayed to Dan in California. The message requested Dan to have the company airplane meet him at LaGuardia.

The sun was just coming up and Jake had been watching the flying fish leap from the water and glide for long distances. He could tell the ship was nearing land as the deep blue color of the ocean water was beginning to take on a dark turquoise tint.

Out of the corner of his eye, he glimpsed something off in the distance. Maybe by force of habit or due to his pilot's alertness, he instinctively spotted an airplane on the horizon.

Jake grew a little anxious until he recognized the plane as a long range Navy patrol plane, a Catalina flying boat. The mission of these U.S. Navy aircraft was to spot and rig or identify any ship approaching U.S. waters.

He thought even a one-eyed, dimwitted Navy aircrewman would be able to recognize the *Queen Mary*. Nevertheless, he rested a little easier as the patrol plane circled the ship and headed off in the direction it came from.

Jake went back to leaning on the deck rail. His thoughts were of home and what the coming days would bring. There was no way he could take Suzette to California without first introducing her to Flo and Big Jake.

He poured the remaining bit of cold coffee over the side and went to return the cup.

Jake spent the rest of the early morning in the cabin being a nuisance to Suzette and playing with Chen.

Around ten hundred hours, Jake and Suzette stood at the rail on the Promenade Deck on the *Queen Mary* and watched as they cruised past the Lady in the Harbor.

Two tugboats met the giant *Gray Ghost*, queen of the sea, and maneuvered her into dock at the Manhattan pier.

Rising Sun Also Sets

Jake and Suzette arrived by taxicab at LaGuardia where the *Dragon One* awaited, its familiar pilot and namesake at the executive terminal. Dan and Ida had flown in from California with Harry Hammond, the company pilot.

As Suzette walked past the nose of the C-67 company plane, she looked up and read the name aloud, *"Dragon One*! And just where did that come from?" she asked teasing.

"Yeah, Jake, I don't think you ever told me either," Dan said, but Dan always suspected Jake had named the plane for Suzette having heard enough of the bits and pieces of the Rangoon story to put things together.

"Named her after an old girl friend I met one time," Jake replied. "How you been, Dan?"

"Fair to midlin' as always, Jake."

Ida greeted them smiling.

"Thought we'd come along for the ride and be the first to welcome you two home."

Jake introduced them to Suzette. Dan and Ida both gave Suzette a hug and a kiss on the cheek and of course Ida wanted to hold young Chen.

"Harry has made all the clearances and we're ready to takeoff if you guys are ready," Dan said.

"Where are we stopping for fuel?" Jake asked knowing the *Dragon One* could not make California non-stop.

"Dallas is where Harry filed for. Why don't we go on up to Gainesville from there."

"I figured that's what you were planning. Do you think there's any chance Mom would fly on to California with us?"

Dan shrugged his shoulders.

"All we can do is try!"

The five boarded the Dragon. Jake went forward to the cockpit and Harry moved over to the copilot's seat so Jake could fly. Dan got everyone buckled into a seat and closed the cabin door.

"Haven't seen you since we landed the B-27s at Northampton," Jake said, greeting Harry. "How are things going back at the factory?"

"Running like a well-oiled machine, boss, but you can thank Dan for most of that!"

"That's the kind of good news I like to hear. Crank her up, Harry, and let's head west."

***

Somewhere over southeastern Pennsylvania, cruising at an altitude of ten thousand feet, Jake said to Harry, "You flew all day yesterday coming up here. Go back and sack out for a couple of hours. I'll give out after a while and you can spell me off then. Send Dan on up would you?"

Dan came forward and slid into the copilot's seat.

"Lovely lady, that Suzette."

"Yeah, and she fought with the underground in France."

"She what?"

"Sure did. Get her to tell you about it one of these days," and Jake filled Dan in on events in Europe and told him about his flights in the B-17 and MK21. "I want to incorporate some of those planes' features into the next version of the B-27 and I've also got some new ideas on a post-war commercial aircraft design."

Dan brought Jake up-to-date on work at the factory and then told Jake, "Your builder called about a week ago to say the new house in Malibu was finished and he had a buyer for the beach house. He wanted to know if he could move your stuff from there up to the new place."

"You told him to go ahead, didn't you?"

"I did. Ida and I drove Lydia and the kids out there Sunday with a few of their things. They said they wanted to wait for you there."

"How do they like the place?"

"Lora said to tell you she approves of most of it, but there are a couple of things she would still like to change. However, she and Michael did agree on which bedroom they wanted without arguing."

"Sounds like my sanguine Lora. She makes friends so fast she'll be trying to run things at her new school before they know what hit them. How did Michael feel about moving out there?"

"Said he liked it because Malibu was a small town like Pottsburg and he hoped the people would be as friendly. He seemed neither thrilled nor did he complain about the house. He showed more interest in the beach than anything. Claimed he wanted to learn how to surf like the Hawaiians."

"That's what he told me, too. What did you say?"

"I told him I thought it might be a good idea if he learned how to swim real good first."

Jake laughed.

"That boy! He's got guts. He'll try anything once. Gets more like his great granddad, ol' John, every day."

Jake landed the *Dragon One* at the Gainesville airport and the band of trans-continental travelers arrived at the Flying M ranch late that evening.

They weren't home yet, but as any good Texan will tell you, California is just one of the western counties of Texas, so at least they were in the neighborhood.

***

The following morning, Suzette got acquainted with her new in-laws. Flo was taken with Suzette and immediately began to think of her as the daughter she always wanted. It also did not take long for Suzette to charm Big Jake.

When Jake and Suzette finally got a few minutes to themselves, Jake told Suzette, "I'll make the arrangements to have our wedding in a Catholic church as soon as we get to California, but I'd sure like mom and dad to be there."

"Can't we take them with us to California? There are empty seats on the plane!"

"Mom has never flown before and I don't think I can get her to fly with us on the plane."

"What do you think she'd say, if I'd ask her?"

"You know that's a dang good idea. What the heck? Give it a try when you get the opportunity. Tell her how much it'd mean to you and she'd also get to spend some time with Lora and Michael."

***

Sure enough, the plan worked and the next day, the whole Martin clan was airborne on their way to California. Violet did not come this time as she and her new husband were expecting their first child.

As they approached Los Angeles, Jake requested special permission from the Los Angeles area Army air controller to fly over Long Beach and up the coast.

"Cleared as requested. Welcome home Mr. Martin."

"Understand, request approved," Jake replied. "How'd you know it was me flying today?"

"If your usual request to fly up the coast hadn't given you away, sir, that Texas drawl would have."

The radio receiver speakers were on in the cabin and everyone on board the *Dragon One* laughed. They laughed even harder when Jake protested, "I don't have a Texas drawl!"

Jake flew over the California shipbuilding yards of the Henry J. Kaiser Company on Terminal Island. Long rows of Liberty ships under construction crowded the docks along the piers.

Harry moved out of the copilot's seat so Suzette could sit up front to see out the cockpit window and Dan was seated on the jump seat between them.

Jake banked the *Dragon One* slightly to the right for a better view of the shipyard. Looking down at the vast armada of ships being built, his thoughts drifted back to that day on the dock at Rangoon when Benny first told him about the attack on Pearl Harbor.

"I think they woke the sleeping giant! What do you think, Dan?"

"That they did and maybe that's what we needed. Something to wake us up."

Jake turned the *Dragon One* northwest out over the ocean and soon the Malibu coastline appeared over the nose and off to the right side of the plane.

"There's your new home right down there," Jake said pointing the large, red-tile roofed house out to Suzette. "Let's let 'em know we're home!" Jake dropped the plane down to a couple hundred feet off the deck to buzz the house on the hill. "This'll rattle their windows."

Passing low over their new home, Jake added power for more noise as he turned the *Dragon One* up Topanga Canyon, climbed out to standard pattern altitude and set a course for the approach to the Culver City airport.

"How you doing back there, Mom?" Jake hollered and looked back over his shoulder.

Flo did not care for looking out the window. She smiled and gave a little wave back at Jake.

"We're not home yet, Mom, but we'll be on the ground shortly. Just hang on a little longer."

Jake turned and smiled at Suzette.

She smiled back at him and got up to go with Dan to return to their seats in the cabin as Harry climbed back into the copilot's seat.

"It's all yours, Harry. Put us down at Martin Aero." Turning to look back into the cabin to see his dad who had been watching out the window, Jake said jokingly, "The prodigal son returneth, huh Dad."

Big Jake nodded acknowledging his son's comment and smiled proudly. His son had not followed in his footsteps, but had carved a different path through life.

Suzette hollered back, "But this time, he brought his bride along to keep him on the straight and narrow!"

Flo giggled delightfully at Suzette's little come back and said, "You may have finally met your match, Jacob."

***

Suzette and Jake were wed a week later at the Catholic church in Santa Monica.

Lora served as Suzette's bridesmaid and told her dad later, "It made me feel so grown up that Suzette asked me."

Red was back in the States on furlough from Pan Am flight operations in the Pacific. He and his wife Margo drove down from San Francisco and Red stood up with Jake as his best man. Jake hated the rented tuxedo he wore, but Red looked dashing in his Pan Am captain's uniform.

Later, at the reception, Jake asked Red, "Where's that lucky red tie of yours? Did you ever find the thing again after I saw you at Pearl?"

"Nah, I'm pretty sure I left the thing in a locker at the New Guinea airport, but never got back there to get it. Oh well, the dang thing probably wasn't lucky anyway."

"Can you and Margo stay for a few days? Got plenty of room at the new house or you're welcome to use the house in Santa Monica as long as you want."

"We'll stay tonight, Jake, but we've got to get back to Frisco. My furlough is over in a couple of days and I need to settled Margo in before I leave."

"Back to the Big Pond again?"

"Yep, back to the ol' Pacific," Red said with a smirk.

***

Big Jake spent some time with Dan at the factory.

Flo and Ida helped Suzette and Lydia get settled into the new house as soon as the movers delivered the things they wanted from the Santa Monica house.

Jake told the women, "A lot of that junk isn't worth moving. Leave the stuff there. It can all go with the house when it's sold."

Later, Jake told Dan, "Those four women cleaned that place out to the bare walls. Said they thought they might need some of the stuff sometime in the future."

Even though Jake had finally gotten his mother to fly in an airplane, Flo decided the train would be more comfortable going home.

***

Suzette settled into her new home in Malibu and things began to run on a more or less normal routine.

That was until the flair-up incident with Lydia. About a month after the wedding, Jake got a call at work from Suzette.

"You better come home, Jake."

"What is it? What's wrong?"

"It's Lydia. I can't do a thing with her! You just better come on home."

Jake arrived home to find Lydia's bags packed and stacked by the door.

"What's going on here, Lydia?" Jake asked.

"I'm moving out, Mr. Martin. You have a missus now and no man needs two women in the house. My mother always said, too many cooks spoil the soup."

"You talk to her," Suzette said. "I can't reason with that Spanish Madonna. She's thicker-headed than a Mexican Brahma bull."

He looked at the somewhat bewildered Suzette who waved her hand motioning him to handle the situation.

"Is that what the problem is?" Jake asked trying not to smile. He knew better than to laugh. A little wiser now about the ways of a woman, he guessed Lydia only wanted to be reassured she was still needed.

"Look Lydia, we need you here. Suzette wants you here, I want you here, this is your home. What more can I say?"

Lydia started to cry and Suzette took her arm in arm.

"We can talk in the kitchen. We don't need him butting in anymore, do we?"

"No," Lydia replied, tearfully going with Suzette.

"Women!" Jake said, throwing his arms up in the air. "I give up," and he went to his study to do some paperwork.

In an hour or so, Jake smelled something good cooking in the kitchen. Michael went galloping down the hall on a make believe pony and Jake hollered at him, "What are those two women doing in the kitchen?"

"They're cooking your favorite Spanish cars'aroll. I think Lydia is showing Suzette how to fix it."

"The word's casserole, Michael."

"Right Dad, cars'aroll."

"Well, I guess that problem's solved," Jake mumbled.

Michael remounted his pony preparing to gallop off.

"Whoa there big fellow," Jake hollered after Michael, "Where do you think you're going? Come on back here and help me carry some of Lydia's stuff back to her quarters."

Jake passed through the kitchen with a load of Lydia's bags and said, "Donde nosotros comer?"

"No, Mr. Martin," Lydia said. "You'll never get it right. It's not where, its when. Cuando, cuando! When do we eat? And be careful with my things!"

"Dinner will be ready in about ten minutes, dear," Suzette said and smiled.

Jake was pleased with himself as he left the kitchen with the load of Lydia's stuff and Michael carrying a small bundle right behind him. He had certainly settled that argument, although he was not exactly sure how.

Jake constantly brought home Air Corps personnel, old flying buddies and business associates unexpectedly for dinner. With all that and three young children in the house, Suzette had her hands full. Secretly, she was very pleased Lydia agreed to stay on.

Suzette never mentioned it to Jake, but she was not a very good cook. She had never quite figured out how to cook American food very well let alone Mexican food, Jake's favorite.

***

Christmas of 1943 came to the Martin home in Malibu and like all American families that year, there were shortages of everything.

The aluminum foil strips traditionally used for icicles on the trees were no longer available. Most of the decorations were made of cardboard, but not a problem for the children who enjoyed punching out the icicles, angels and stars and hanging them on the tree. Lydia popped a lot of popcorn and the kids strung it with needle and thread to make chains to go around the tree.

For Christmas morning gifts, Chen got some toy cars, Michael a pair of cowboy boots he wanted and Lora was more than pleased with the junior lady's cosmetic kit she received. She interpreted the gift to mean she now had permission to wear a little make-up from time to time.

The Christmas lights in the living room window formed a wreath around the small cloth flag with a single blue star. The star represented Lydia's boy who was away serving in the Marine Corps somewhere in the Pacific.

Suzette adjusted quickly to her life in Malibu. She was very much in love with Jake and he with her.

Jake traveled a lot on business and unlike Liz, Jake did not have to worry about Suzette. She seldom worried or got upset when Jake was weathered-in somewhere overnight or had to stay over on business.

Suzette could care less if he came dragging in all hours of the night or day. She was just glad to see him whenever he did show up and accepted Jake's lifestyle as simply being the way things were supposed to be.

***

The year 1944 passed quickly. The War in Europe turned in the Allies favor as the British and Americans air forces gained air superiority. Save for the will power of General Eisenhower, Germany would have been boomed into non-existence.

In the spring of 1945, Jake received a phone call from Benny Weston in San Francisco.

"Captain, I'm sorry to be calling you like this..."

Jake knew by tone of Benny's voice, there was a problem.

"What's wrong, Benny?"

"It's Red. Yesterday, his PBM flying boat was enroute to Okinawa with a load of medical supplies. They were jumped by some Jap carrier planes and shot down. A Navy destroyer saw them go in and searched the crash site, but there were no survivors."

Jake thanked Benny for calling him personally and hung up the phone. He sat at his office desk and recalled the time when still a teenager, Big Jake told him about having gone to war. Jake recalled his father saying "war is a terrible thing!"

Jake went home early that evening and finished half a bottle of bourbon before he finally broke into tears and cried like a child. Suzette sat on the couch holding him until he finally fell asleep in her arms.

Jake called Larry a few days later and asked him to set up a trust fund for Red's wife.

"Now days a woman can't hardly support two kids without a husband so make it something she can live on for a while. Oh and Larry, she's not to know where it came from. Set it up where it looks like an annuity Red had purchased for her."

"I'll take care of it," Larry assured Jake.

***

Jake busied himself with aircraft production at the factory and still volunteered one night a week to fly for the Civil Air Patrol squadron. Jake and the other volunteer pilots diligently performed their coastal submarine patrol duties. Except for assisting in a search for an occasional Navy plane downed in the water or an Air Corps trainer up in the mountains, not much exciting ever happened.

Production quickly came to a head at the factory with victory in Europe. VE-Day was declared on May 5th, 1945 and the allied forces began switching resources over to fight the war in the Pacific. The remaining B-27 bombers were loaded onto cargo ships destined for a forward island airbase in the Pacific. The Marines finally fought their way close enough to the Japanese held positions for the shorter-range bombers to be utilized.

The hard won battles were a hollow victory of sorts for the Martin household. On a late afternoon in June, Jake returned home from a business trip to Washington to find a blue star flag hanging in the living room window where the gold star flag hung earlier.

The day before, Lydia had received one of the most dreaded letters from the War Department, which began *"Dear Mrs. Gomez, We regret to inform you…"*

In time, Lydia came to deal with the loss of her son and somehow carried on with her life.

The Empire of Japan was on the run and their defeat was certain, but Jake found himself becoming increasingly anti-war. He came to hate what war had done to his once-upon-a-time innocent homeland and to the lives of his friends.

***

Michael got it into his head that he wanted to spend his summers on the Flying M ranch with his Grandma Flo and Grandpa Jake.

"Look Dad," Michael argued, "I want to be a real cowboy, not one of those drugstore cowboys like these Hollywood movie actors around here. I was born in Texas and that gives me the right to be a cowboy if I want."

Jake was not sure he exactly understood Michael's reasoning, but the week school was out, he finally gave in to Michael's request. He made arrangements for Michael to travel back to Texas and spend the summer.

They only received one letter from Michael that whole summer. The letter read "Having a great time on the ranch. Thanks for letting me come. Miss you all, mostly late at night when it is real quiet here."

Flo wrote often to say how things were going and in one letter she wrote "Your father said to tell you Michael took to ranching like a duck takes to water and that the boy reminds him of your grandfather John."

The summer Michael was away, Suzette was about three months pregnant with Jake's child when she began to hemorrhage. Jake rushed her to the hospital where she miscarried.

The doctor told them later the loss of their unborn child had been caused by Suzette having RH-negative blood and Jake being RH-positive. There would now only be a fifty-fifty chance Suzette could carry Jake's child to term, but the worse news of all was that she could possibly die the next time.

Suzette was depressed for some time, as she wanted very much for her and Jake to have a child together. After a while, she got over the loss and wanted to try again. But after nearly losing her, Jake was very careful not to let her get pregnant again.

***

On August 6th, 1945, the Japanese government officially surrendered ending W.W.II. The factories shutdown for the day and there was celebrating in the streets. Jake made reservations at the Mocambo nightclub for dinner and a small celebration that evening. Dan and Ida met them at the club along with a couple of the company directors.

"You met MacArthur didn't you, Jake?" Dan asked.

"Yes, just briefly in Manila once, but I can tell you one thing, MacArthur understands the Japanese mindset. He plans to add insult to the surrender by sailing the battleship Missouri right into Tokyo Bay. They took General Wainwright prisoner after MacArthur left the Philippines and he intends to make them sign the surrender papers with Wainwright standing by his side."

Percy Mulholland, the stockholder in the California Martin Company who threatened a minority shareholder's suit, showed up at the Mocambo club. Jake had not invited Percy, but he and one of his associates joined them for the evening anyway.

Everyone seemed to be having a good time except Percy, who persisted in maintaining a sour mood.

"What are you going to do at the factory now the war is over?" Percy asked Jake. "Going back to oil equipment production, I hope and give up those cockamamie unprofitable aircraft production ideas of yours."

"I got it handled, Percy. Don't worry about it."

"That's not good enough, Martin. I want some kind of sound business plan from you as soon as possible."

"Maybe I'll close the place down altogether. I understand the old Luscombe plant in Garland, Texas is available after the government closed it down during the war. I'll just move the whole company out there," Jake said sarcastically. "How'd that suit you, Percy?"

"That won't work either. Now the war is over your suspension of our complaint will be lifted and you can't stop us from filing suit."

"Tell you what I'll do, Percy. I'll give you double your money back on your original investment with Martin Company. I'll write you a check right here tonight."

"No way, Martin. Once civilian oil production moves into the profit mode, my investment will be worth ten times that amount."

Jake glanced across the table at Dan, who was giving Jake one of those don't-do-this-now looks.

"Lighten up, Percy, this is a time for celebration. Besides, we have to hold an open house for the public like all the aircraft factories are planning and complete our contracts before we can do anything. After that, I'll get you your business plan."

Suzette and Ida were not paying attention to the men's conversation. They were mostly talking on their own, but Suzette noticed three men at a table across the way were staring at her.

"Ida, who are those men at that corner table? They're kind of scary looking and one of them keeps glaring over here at me?"

Ida looked casually over her shoulder.

"The heavy-set one is a mob boss by the name of Mickey Cohen. He hangs out here a lot. I've also seen him at Ciro's and other nightclubs along Hollywood Boulevard and the Strip. He fancies himself the King of the Sunset Strip and likes for people to refer to him that way. The other two, I'm sure, are probably a couple of his wise guys."

"What kind of stuff do they do?"

"They're into gambling, all kinds of vice, rackets and mostly extortion is what I've heard."

Across the room at Mickey Cohen's table, Cohen asked the two guys who were sitting with him, "Is that the famous Captain Jake Martin sitting over there with the two broads and his cronies?"

"Yeah, boss. The distinguished gray-haired fellow seated next to the slender old broad is Martin Company's president, Dan Parker. The weasely little guy in the black suit is Percy Mulholland. I think he and Martin don't like each other so much."

"Who's the broads?" Mickey asked.

"The older one is Parker's wife and the good looking, black-haired dame is Martin's wife."

"Maybe it's about time we tapped that bankroll!"

His two associates grinned and looked at each other.

Dan and Jake had gone to the men's room and were standing at the washbasin.

"Jake, you were only bluffing about closing the place down weren't you?"

"Sure, Dan, you knew that. You didn't really think I'd let you off the hook that easy did you? I'll tell you one thing though, they'll serve ice water in Hades before I let that greedy SOB Percy tell us how to run Martin Company?"

"Why do you keep putting up with him then?"

"Sometimes, the devil you know is better than the devil you don't," Jake said as he and Dan exited the men's room to return to their table.

In the hallway, Cohen bumped into Jake hard with his shoulder as they passed.

"Pardon me," Jake said as he stepped aside thinking Cohen was just another rude drunk.

Cohen intentionally stepped in front of Jake again. "Pardon you for what, Martin?"

"Well for openers, pardon me for not knowing who in the hell I'm talking to."

"Names Mickey Cohen and I think it's about time you started paying a little respect to the guys who really run this town. Exactly when would you like one of my boys to start coming around to pick up your weekly insurance payments?"

Caught off guard, Jake looked questioningly at Dan, but then it dawned on him this was the mobster who ran the protection rackets along Sunset Strip.

Jake intended this to be a pleasant evening, but with all of the aggravation from Percy and now this from Cohen, he reached the limit of his patience. He grabbed Cohen by the lapels of his suit jacket.

One of Cohen's thugs moved toward Jake.

"Don't even think about it!" Jake said to the thug.

"Back off," Cohen told his man. "We don't want no trouble in here. Its bad for business."

Jake held Cohen up with both hands and left him dangling on his tiptoes. He could feel the .38 revolver in Cohen's shoulder holster as he spoke directly into the man's face.

"In my book, you're just another punk like that guy, Tojo. We kicked his ass and you play in a lot smaller sandbox than he did. I've been shot at by the Japs on the Burma Road and the Jerries over Europe. If you think that little peashooter you're packing scares me, you got another think coming. You can take your small time gangster crap and stick it where the sun don't shine."

Jake let go of Cohen and pushed him away.

As Jake started to walk away, Cohen straightened his jacket and snarled, "You don't know who you're messing with, Martin. I got guys can do things to your business."

Jake paused and stepped back in front of Cohen.

"Maybe it's you who don't understand who you're messing with? Since you don't seem to, let me explain it to you in a way you will."

"Yeah, what can you do to me?" Mickey blurted out straightening his necktie and puffing up his chest.

"That store I've heard about. The one that only has your size suits on the racks. The one you think no one knows is a front for your rackets. Well, those B-27s I build fly right over your neighborhood on their way out to the bombing range at Catalina Island. They carry five hundred pound bombs. One of those can take out a whole city block, your store and a couple of your nightclubs for good measure."

"You'd never get by with a thing like that!" Mickey said with a strange expression on his face and he stepped back away from Jake.

"If you think I can't get by with it, try me! We've had a lot of trouble with those bomb release racks not latching real good. What a shame it'd be if one of them came loose right over your head. Who would believe a thing like that wasn't an accident?"

Jake's use of the phrase right-over-his-head caused Cohen to glance at the ceiling and gulp.

"You're nuts, Martin!"

"Maybe, but I'll bet they wouldn't even find enough big chunks of you to give you a decent funeral. Think about it the next time you're sitting in your office counting your extortion money and one of my planes flies over."

Jake walked away leaving Dan standing not quite believing what he just had just seen and heard. Then he hurried to catch up with Jake who was already headed back to their table.

"What's all this about the Burma Road? You've never mentioned anything about that before and problems with bomb rack releases? Jake, we've never experienced any failures with the B-27 bomb release system?"

"And probably never will. Or Cohen either, for that matter," Jake said and looked at Dan with a big wide grin.

"Got me again, you rascal and twice in the same night!" Dan said and laughed.

Back in the hallway, one of Mickey's thugs said, "He's bluffing, don't you think boss? What do you want us to do with this guy?"

Mickey watched as Jake and Dan returned to their table at the club.

"The guy's crazy. Nah, that guy's totally insane. All them war heroes is like that. Besides, he's one of those stupid Texans who hunts deer and that sort of thing for sport. He'd probably just as soon kill you as look at you. We don't need that kind of aggravation. Come on let's blow this joint."

For better or worse and maybe fortunate for Jake, Mickey Cohen was a poor judge of character. Otherwise, he might have figured out Jake was bluffing. Then again, no one had ever pushed Jake that far before and maybe it would have turned out he was not bluffing after all?

***

Jake arrived at his office on an early July morning in 1946 and had not yet seen the morning papers.

Gertie met Jake at the door with the L.A. Times and handed him the paper. The headline on the newspaper article read "Famed Aviator Howard Hughes Crashes Prototype Airplane, Flyer Seriously Injured."

"What hospital's he at?" Jake asked Gertie.

"Good Samaritan. I already checked. Should I arrange to have some flowers sent?"

"He probably wouldn't accept them. He's funny about things like that. Send him a Western Union telegram wishing him a speedy recovery."

"From the company?"

"No, from me personally. Then get a hold of someone at the hospital in authority and find out how bad he's injured. Try that surgeon friend of Dan's. I think he's on staff there."

"Right, Mr. Martin. Do you plan to go visit him at the hospital?"

"Probably not. I doubt Howard would see me or anyone at this time."

Jake went to his desk to read the rest of the newspaper article. He knew before he started to read which plane had crashed. It was the new XSF-11, a multi-engine, counter-rotating prop, twin-boomed photoreconnaissance plane Hughes was hoping to sell to the government.

The newspaper article quoted an unnamed source as saying "Questions remain unanswered at this time as to whether or not Howard Hughes will be able to complete his giant flying boat planned for the final construction phase at the Long Beach Harbor pier."

Several days later, Gertie took a call from one of Hughes' assistants saying Hughes would like Jake to come to the hospital to discuss a business matter.

When Jake arrived at the hospital, he found Hughes in worse shape than had been reported, but Hughes wanted to talk. He told Jake about the crash.

"One of the counter-rotating props stuck in reverse and I was trying to make it to the Beverly Hills Golf Course to effect a landing. That part of town is solid residential now and I was doing my damnedest not to hit any of those houses."

Hughes knew that Jake, a fellow flyer, would understand his predicament. He also told Jake about the Marine sergeant who pulled him out of the burning plane.

"There's no doubt in my mind that fellow saved my life… I'll have to repay him, someway," and Hughes added sarcastically, "but then again, I don't owe him a whole hell of a lot, do I?"

Hughes more than once complained about how uncomfortable his hospital bed was as they talked. He explained to Jake how he thought the bed might be redesigned.

Jake got a pencil and some paper and made some rough sketches of the modifications Hughes suggested.

"I'm not going to let this accident slow up production on the Hercules flying boat," Hughes insisted. "I want a maximum effort on the parts Martin Aero is producing."

"Don't worry about us. We'll meet or beat all our delivery dates on the HK-1," Jake reassured Hughes.

"Henry Kaiser backed out of the project on me, so I'm going to change the designation to the H-4."

"Howard, everyone calls your flying boat the Spruce Goose behind your back. You know that, don't you?"

"Yeah, damn it, I do. The ship's not even made out of spruce. It's mostly constructed of laminated birch, but Spruce Goose is probably better than some of the things they could think up to rhymes with birch!"

Hughes was not trying to be funny, but Jake laughed anyway and Hughes, seeing the humor in it, finally smiled.

"I don't want to let production fall behind schedule on the Hercules while I'm laid up. I've given instructions that any sub-contractor who falls behind on deliveries, their jobs are to be transferred over to Martin Company."

"You got it, Howard," and Jake made an effort to change the subject as he could see Hughes was getting himself all worked up over being confined to bed.

"Tell me something, Howard, I know the H-1 was the Speed Racer you built to set the world's speed record with, but what were the H-2 and H-3?"

That did the trick and Hughes was off telling a longwinded story about old times.

After Jake left Hughes' room, he located the hospital administrator and told him, "I want to buy one of the hospital beds like the one you're presently using in your patient rooms."

"Why would you want one of those beds?" the administrator asked. "Everyone tells me they're very uncomfortable."

"Yes, I've heard. That's why I want one," Jake replied with a smile. "Here's my business card. How soon can I have a truck pick one up?"

"I'm still confused, but I'll make the arrangements and give you a call, Mr. Martin," the administrator said reading the name off of Jake's business card.

Jake left instructions for the bed to be sent directly to the welding and machine shop when the bed arrived at the Martin factory loading dock.

Using his pencil sketches and notes from Hughes, Jake showed the shop foreman how to add screw-drive motors and make the other modifications to the bed.

Jake told the foreman, "See it's delivered to Hughes' hospital room as soon as it's finished and tested."

***

Lora and Michael were looking forward to getting out of school for the summer in the spring of 1947. Jake had already agreed Michael could again return to Texas and spend the summer on the ranch with his grandparents.

Lora wanted to take some drawing design courses in a summer program at the art institute and Suzette had agreed to drive her there on her class days.

The past ten months had been rough on Jake, complying with the balance of the military contracts for B-27 spare parts and making plans to convert the aircraft division over to civilian aircraft production.

Jake was sitting on the patio at home in Malibu having coffee when Suzette came out with her cup of tea, a stack of mail and the Sunday morning paper.

"You're not going to work again today are you?"

"Got to, only time I can get anything done is when it's quiet out there."

"You need to take more time off, you know."

Jake conceded the point and went on to tell Suzette about driving with Dan over to Long Beach to watch the giant Hughes flying boat's fuselage being moved down the narrow streets by house-moving trucks.

"I'll bet that was quite a sight," Suzette said as she sorted through the last couple of day's mail. "Look here, we've received a wedding announcement from Margo Henderson. She's getting married again."

"Not another pilot, I hope! We won't be able to go, but get her a nice gift and include a note. I told her on the phone not to marry anyone whose profession begins with P... Preachers, painters, poets, pilots, they're all a bunch of bums," Jake said smiling at Suzette who was, of course, married to one.

"That's not nice. You're not a bum." Then she looked at Jake who had not shaved since Friday morning. "No, I've rethought that statement. You are kind of a bum," she said with a grin, not looking directly at him.

"Got to get going, my dear Mrs. Bum. I need to catch up on a bunch of paperwork."

"Jake, you really need to spend some time with the kids. Michael will be gone all summer and they're growing up so fast."

Suzette gathered up the mail, empty cups and went into the house.

Michael came around the corner of the house from the garage carrying his surfboard on the top of his head.

"On my way to meet some of my friends down at the beach. See you, Dad."

"What do you guys do all day at the beach and whoever came up with the idea to call those small floats a surfboards anyway?"

"Ah, Dad, you're just not with it. You've seen the guys from here trying to catch a wave and stand up on their boards haven't you?"

"Yeah, but where'd you all get the idea to do this? I heard someone say surfboarding was a Hawaiian custom. When I used to fly into Honolulu with Pan Am, I don't remember ever seeing anyone using those things."

"I don't know about that, but some Hawaiian guy by the name of Duke Kahanamoku invented them or at least perfected them and I guess it just caught on here in California. Why don't you come down to the beach and watch us?"

Jake had intentionally engaged his son in conversation mostly because of what Suzette said earlier.

"Lay that surfboard down, come over here and sit down for a minute. You said the other day you wanted to ask me about something. What was it?"

"Well, yes I do," Michael said and plopped down in a patio chair across from his dad. "How come my mother left me and Lora back in Texas when we were little?"

Jake always thought the question might come up, but years passed and Michael never asked so Jake began to think he might not.

"Wow, that one kinda came at me out of the blue!" Jake paused to think for a moment. "I've discussed the subject a time or two with Lora, but 'til now you never asked so I assumed you weren't interested."

"Don't get me wrong, Dad, Suzette is the best step-mom a guy could ask for, but I've been wondering for some time what happened to my real mom. All I know is her name was Elizabeth. I can't remember anything about her."

"I don't think I really know why your mother left. I know she didn't like to be left alone and I left her alone way too much when I was away flying for the airline. That part, at least, was my fault."

"Where did she go away to? Where is she now?"

"I'm not sure, Michael. Your Grandma Flo talked to some of her relatives at a church function. You might try asking her this summer. I think Elizabeth, we always called her Liz, is still alive and I think Grandma heard she lives back east somewhere. That's honestly all I know. Do you want me to try to find out more for you?"

"Nah, I guess not. If she wanted to find me I guess she would," and Michael went over to pick up his surfboard. "I'm headed to the beach. Thanks Dad, see you later."

Suzette came to the patio doorway. "There's a long distance call from Texas for you, Jake."

"Who is it?"

"It's Larry. Says he needs to talk to you."

Jake went to the phone and asked, "What's so important you'd call on a Sunday morning, Larry?"

"Good morning to you, too!" Larry replied joking. "You know the summer ranch house you rented to Sarah? Well, Hank is home from the Marine Corps now and he came to my office to ask if he could work out someway to buy the place."

"Larry, you know Big Jake won't sell any of the land that's part of the Flying M. He never has, so why are you calling me about this?"

"Well, something must be different this time because Big Jake told me to call you. Said whatever you wanted to do with the place was fine with him."

"Should have been hers all along, I guess."

"What does that mean?"

"Nothing, just a passing thought. What do Hank and Sarah want to do?"

"Hank wants to buy the house and forty acres of land that the house is on. He intends to build a boarding stable and eventually a veterinary clinic on the property. You know the town's almost grown up to the edge of the place."

Caught up in his thoughts, Jake did not respond for a moment. He never really liked Hank, but also he had never forgiven himself for trying to steal the man's wife.

"Well, what do you want me to do?" came Larry's voice from over the phone.

"Yeah, sell them the place, but put a hundred and sixty acres with it instead of the forty so they can make a living off of it if they come on hard times."

"Jake, I don't think they can afford to pay for a place that big. Do you have any idea what land is selling for around here nowadays?"

"Probably not, but something is only worth what somebody is willing to give for it. Isn't that right?"

"I suppose that's true."

"Find out what the going rate for land is and sell it to them for a little less than that, but put a clause in the contract that Hank can't sell the land except back to the Flying M so long as Big Jake is alive. If Hank can't afford the payments, put a no interest balloon note on the end of the mortgage so he can."

"I understand. Do you want to carry the note?"

"No, run it through Dad's bank. I'll co-sign the mortgage if need be."

Jake visited with Larry on the phone for a few more minutes about a couple of other matters and then hung up. He stood there thinking for a while about what was really important in life and what was not.

Jake walked back out onto the patio and looked out over the distant sparkling ocean admiring the beautiful classic Mediterranean morning.

Suzette settled back into her favorite lounge chair with the newspaper and a second cup of tea.

"You going to work now?"

"No, don't feel like charging anymore windmills this week." Jake sat down, removed his shoes and socks, rolled up his pant legs and said, "If you want me, I'll be down at the beach watching Michael and his friends surf."

Spruce Goose

Mid-morning on a typical workday in late 1947, Jake had been on the phone continually since arriving at work.

Gertie entered Jake's office and waited patiently for him to get off the phone.

Jake hung up the phone and asked, "What is it Gertie?"

"The guard at the front gate is on the other line saying there's a gentleman at the gate in a limousine demanding entrance to come in and see you, Mr. Martin."

"Who is it? Did they ask his name?"

Gertie picked up the extension phone.

"Find out the man's name," she said to the guard and held for a moment. "It's Mr. Juan Trippe."

"Great Scott! Tell the guard to have someone escort him to the lobby downstairs and I'll meet him there."

Jake was glad to see his old friend Juan and took him on a short walking tour of the factory.

"How's the leg, Jake? Noticed you don't hardly favor it much anymore," Trippe commented as they walked.

"Years of practice, I guess. Only bothers me when I'm tired. Pretty handy though, I can always tell when the weather's fixin' to change."

"Jake, you amaze me. You're one of those guys that has the ability to take things as they come and keep on going."

"Well, you never accomplish much by giving up I found out a long time ago."

Back at Jake's office, the two men talked over old times. Jake asked, "What can you tell me about the Pan Am Lockheed Constellation that crashed in June?"

"NC845 was one of our newer aircraft. It departed on an inaugural Around the World Flight from New York. We can do that now with these new land-based transports. They're more dependable and much faster than the old Clippers. Since the war, all kinds of new runways and airports have been built all over the world."

"The crash, how'd it happen?"

"My information is the number one engine failed on the leg from Karachi to Istanbul. The pilot elected to continue on to Al Mayadin, Syria and that's when the number two engine caught fire. They ditched near the shoreline."

"See there, maybe a flying boat would have saved the day. How bad was it?"

"There were fourteen fatalities out of the thirty-six onboard. You might have known one of the younger crewmen, a fellow named Gene Roddenberry. He was credited with saving several of the passengers from drowning."

"No don't think I do, probably one of the W.W.II pilots. Are you going to stay with the Connies?"

"There're the best we can get for now, but we have some of the new Super Stratoliners on order. They'll go into service in '49."

"The new Boeing transports based on the B-29?"

"Yes. They've got a great payload capability, but jets are the answer. We'll get them someday," Trippe lamented.

"I saw one of those twin jet ME-262s over Germany in '43," Jack said. "Maybe I should say caught a glimpse of it. Did you know the Germans flew a jet aircraft as early as August 1939, a Heinkel-178? The British are even way ahead of us with those jet engines designed by Whittle."

"Yeah, the Brits have approached us about buying some of their new four engine jet Comets. They have orders for a hundred now and they'll be available in the early '50s. I think I'll wait and see what kind of a design Boeing comes up with for a new jet transport," and Trippe changed the subject. "Say Jake, what do you know about Hughes' flying boat? I'd like to see that monstrosity."

"That's my old Juan, I figured there was more to this visit than a social call. I think we can arrange it. I'll schedule one of our trucks to deliver a load of machine parts. We'll meet the truck there and that'll give us an excuse for going into the facility. I understand why you had trouble getting in, their security is very tight."

"I've made plans to meet with my old associate Charles Lindbergh for lunch. He's in town for a speech. Why don't you come on along and join us and then we can go on out to Long Beach afterwards."

Trippe walked with Jake out of the factory, past Trippe's waiting chauffer-driven limo to the parking lot.

"I'll drive," Jake said pointing to his new bright red Ford pickup truck with Martin Aero painted in an arc above a winged flying M logo on the door.

"I'm not riding around L.A. in some darn factory pickup truck. I thought you always drove Lincolns. Where's your car at?"

"My old yellow '40 model Continental is at home in the garage with Suzette's new '47 Sedan. I prefer driving myself and kind of like these new Ford pickups we bought for the factory. Reminds me of my old International Harvester pickup I used to drive back on the ranch."

"Forget it," Trippe said and motioned to his driver to pull forward to pick them up. "We'll take my car."

***

Arriving for lunch downtown at the Old Chinatown Restaurant off Broadway Street, Juan introduced Jake to Lindbergh.

"I'm sure you don't remember me," Jake said.

"Captain Jake Martin. I've heard Juan speak of you from time to time. It's a pleasure. You were the Operations Manager at Treasure Island, weren't you?" Lindbergh said, but he did not remember having met Jake.

"Yes sir, back before the war. We met briefly in Juan's New York office in 1936 the day I went to work for Pan Am."

"That'd be about the time I flew one of Juan's old SK-42 Clippers to Hawaii. I live there now you know. During the war, when I worked for Lockheed I use to stop over in Hawaii. I met one of your captains there, nice young fellow by the name of Henderson."

"Yes sir. That would have been Red. Good friend of mine. He was with me the day we met you that time in Juan's office."

"Okay, now I do remember you two."

"Red and his crew were killed when their PBM was shot down enroute Okinawa not long before the war ended."

"Too bad," Lindbergh commented sadly. "We lost a lot of good men in that damned war."

Jake remained somewhat surprised Lindbergh never once during the course of their luncheon conversation mentioned his famous Atlantic crossing flight or the political fiasco of his having been awarded the Iron Cross by Hitler.

Lindbergh mostly talked about his exploits in the Pacific during W.W.II as a technical consultant.

"In mid June, 1944, I was granted permission to investigate some problems with the F4U Corsair," Lindbergh explained. "After that, I proceeded to the Army Air Corps 5th Fighter Command in New Guinea where I flew the P-38 Lightning. I actually saw combat several times flying with the 475th Fighter Wing."

Lindbergh left for his speaking engagement at a nearby hotel, but Jake and Trippe lingered at the restaurant for a while to have coffee and reminisce. They had a couple of good laughs recalling their visit to San Simeon.

Then Jake said, "The truck will be waiting for us at the Hughes Aircraft Long Beach Harbor gate by now, so we better get going."

***

During the drive over to Long Beach, Jake explained some of the more difficult technical problems they dealt with on the Spruce Goose.

"You see, Juan, with the control surfaces being so large, the air pressure would make them impossible to move with conventional cables and bell-cranks. One man and a mule couldn't move those controls at cruise speed. As a result, the aircraft is considerably heavier because of all the lines and actuators running throughout the ship to operate the control surfaces."

"It's all hydraulic then?" Trippe asked.

"That's right. The ratio is about a hundred to one. Every one-pound of pressure the pilot applies to the controls will exert a hundred pounds of force on the ailerons, rudder and so on. I wanted to design a lighter weight system using electrical wires to activate the hydraulics. This would have cut the system weight in half, but Hughes argued it would've taken too much time to develop and test. He called it my fly-by-wire concept."

Trippe mused, "I'll bet he meant 'wire' as in a Western Union telegram. Not an electrical wire, the way you probably took it."

"You know, you might be right!" Jake said and laughed.

At the harbor entrance, they met and escorted the Martin Aero delivery truck in Trippe's limo to the dock where the H-4 Hercules neared completion.

As they got out of the car, Jake waved his hand widely motioning to the Hercules moored to the dock.

"There she is, Juan. What do you think?"

Trippe stood gazing up at the giant flying boat and read the registration number aloud, "NX37602."

"Come on, I'll show you how to go aboard."

Jake showed Trippe to the boarding gangway and went to check on the parts delivery.

As Trippe entered the cargo bay, he found Hughes talking with one of the supervisors. Trippe and Hughes had met previously. Trippe greeted Hughes and being aware of Hughes' diminished hearing, he spook up clearly.

"I'd like you to know that your input on the Lockheed Constellation design has helped produce a really great airliner. We're flying them at Pan Am now and the increased speed has made some of our marginal air routes profitable."

Trippe meant his comments as a compliment to Hughes and he took them that way, but did not reply.

"How'd you like to see the cockpit?" Hughes asked pointing to the bulkhead ladder up to the flight deck.

"I'd like to very much."

Trippe climbed the ladder and Hughes followed him up.

In an effort to make up for Hughes' quiet demeanor, Trippe made small talk by expounding on some of his personal philosophies on the subject of aviation.

"The transport aircraft will replace the bomber in the future world. People pray for world peace. They should pray for better transport airplanes. Once people of all nations get to know one another and do business together, they will become friends."

"And it's hard to make war on your friends," Hughes said finishing Trippe's point for him.

"That's right. You must have heard me say it before."

"No, I believe I said something like that myself," Hughes replied and motioned for Trippe to have a seat in the pilot's crew position as he explained the cockpit layout.

Hughes may or may not have believed the H-4 Hercules would go into production, but being a natural born promoter, he knew an all-metal commercial version of the H-4 could be marketed to airlines like Pan Am. Hughes treated Juan Trippe with all the respect of a potential buyer.

After checking on the parts delivery, Jake boarded the H-4 from the outside scaffolding and crawled into the right wing section up to the first inboard nacelle section.

Jake could hear parts of the muffled conversation between Trippe and Hughes in the nearby cockpit and chuckled to himself recalling that only a short time earlier Trippe had referred to the Hercules flying boat as an Ancient Dinosaur.

***

By October of 1947, Martin Aero completed the assembly and delivery of the last B-27 bomber. With wartime orders filled, Jake and his engineers went to work on preliminary designs for their new non-military aircraft line.

The proposed single-engine design was a low-wing model with retractable tricycle landing gear. Most pre-war aircraft used tail-wheels. Nicknamed tail-draggers, they were difficult for inexperienced pilots to land. The success of nose wheel equipped planes like the Bell Air Cobra, Lockheed Lightning and the Boeing Superfortress proved the utility of the tricycle landing gear.

The single-engine design promised a cruise speed of over two hundred miles per hour with an economical six-cylinder, two hundred horsepower engine. The new four-place monoplane would be named the MA-27 Astar and its airframe design resembled a scaled down P-51 Mustang. Jake considered a similar design concept for the XP-78, which he never pursued building.

The second design under consideration was for a twin-engine executive aircraft based loosely on the design of the B-27 Dragon Bomber. The new light twin would carry sever passengers plus a crew of two. Dubbed the MT-27 TurboStar by Jake, the new business twin would have virtually no competition in the marketplace due to its high-powered turbocharged engines and pressurized cabin features.

With the capability of flying at high altitudes, the new aircraft would be able to cruise at speeds in the three hundred plus mile per hour range and because of the company's recent experience building the B-27, the company could easily re-tool to produce the MT-27 TurboStar design.

The Dragon Bomber had used supercharged engines, but these engines were not economical on fuel or easy to maintain. A smaller, more powerful turbocharged engines would not be available for several more years.

The manufacturing group managers estimated they could have either one of the models ready for first flight within eighteen months from the time they received the firm design from engineering, but not both. The study concluded unless major personnel and facility expansions were undertaken, attempting to produce a single-engine and a multi-engine aircraft at the same time would spread resources too thin.

After several design project meetings lasting well into the early hours of the morning and much deliberation, a consensus began to emerge.

The profit on several executive aircraft would exceed the profit on the sale of several single-engine models. The higher performance of the Astar would place the new plane at the upper end of the market where sales would be limited. Additionally, Cessna and Piper were already offering improved versions of their pre-war, single-engine models and this would make competition even fiercer.

The decision soon became obvious to all involved, so engineering headed back to the drawing board. The Dragon bomber based design would become a lighter weight, non-pressurized version called the TwinStar. Thus, Martin Aero's first venture into the general aviation market would be the non-pressurized, normally aspirated M-27, a six place state-of-the-art executive aircraft.

By entering the lower priced end of the multi-engine business aircraft market, the company could establish itself as a commercial airplane manufacturer and be in a position to develop more advanced models as newer engines and technology came available.

One major obstacle to production remained. Jake had not yet reached a negotiated settlement with the Percy Mulholland group. A minority stockholder's suit seemed virtually guaranteed if Jake proceeded with his plans to produce the TwinStar.

***

Late on a Friday afternoon, Jake was seated at his office desk. In front of his large dark mahogany desk were two matching brown leather guest chairs. Someone normally occupied the chairs registering a complaint or trying to sell him the latest great deal to invest in, but this afternoon the chairs were empty.

Things had quieted down for the week and Jake sat pondering one more time how he might gain control of his company without a long legal battle with Mulholland.

Jake recently had a large ceiling-to-floor window installed in the outside wall of his office, as aircraft factories no longer needed to be blacked-out now that the war was over. The window framed the evening sky as it turned a deep blue in the mountains to the east and it looked a little like rain out over the Pacific to the west.

Jake's office had been sparsely decorated in years past, but as time went on thing seemed to accumulate. Above the old overstuffed leather couch, on which Jake had spent more than one night, hung a large oil painting of Suzette seated with Lora, Michael and Chen seated around her.

He swung his desk chair around to prop his feet up on the desk credenza and pushed aside a stack of old magazines with his boot. On the credenza were several photos in small standup frames and half-dozen souvenirs he had liberated. Things like an old spent .50 caliber shell and his Pan Am captain's wings.

One of the photos was of Michael in the saddle of an old cow pony holding onto the saddle horn. Jake was leading the horse by the reins as Lora held onto Jake's hand. Flo had taken the photo years ago on the ranch with her Brownie box camera.

Above the credenza, behind Jake's desk hung three wooden frames, the ones he asked Gertie to have matted and framed the first day he came to work. In the center, the largest of the three frames contained two rectangle black and white photographs.

In the top photo Jake, Red, Larry and Charley stood shoulder to shoulder in front of Jake's old Fairchild. The bottom photo was of the B-27 on the day of the rollout when Colonel Polaski's wife christened the first Dragon Bomber.

On either side of the large center frame hung two smaller frames. The one on the left contained the *Terry and the Pirates* cartoon Milton Caniff had drawn on a napkin one night in Dayton, Ohio at the Idlewild club.

The frame on the right contained the tattered orange decal Jake removed from the instrument panel of his Spartan Pegasus, which read "Warning: Do not open cockpit windows at speeds in excess of 500 mph." In calligraphy below the decal was Jake's own personal credo "The gods of infinite possibilities are only waiting to be born."

The photo taken in the Rangoon market of Jake and Suzette was not there. Jake had the well-worn, black and white photograph sealed in plastic a year ago and still carried the snap shot in his wallet where he always had.

Above the door to Jake's office hung an old oil stained wood prop with both ends busted and sanded smooth. Jake salvaged the old prop off of one of Charley's early racers. The clock mounted in the hub of the prop no longer kept time. When anyone questioned whether the clock was correct, Jake would reply, "It's right twice a day."

The large drafting table stacked high now with folders and drawings was pushed back against the far wall. The old wooden coat tree still stood sentry duty in the corner by the door. Jake's leather flight jacket with the burn mark from the Browning automatic machinegun he held that day on the Burma Road still hung on the back hook were he placed it the day he reported for work in 1942.

The phone finally stopped ringing for the day, but rang one more time. Gertie, who was leaving for the day, came back to answer it. She entered Jake's office.

"There's a man on the phone asking for Jake. He wouldn't give his name, but I think its Howard Hughes."

"Thanks. Good night, Gertie," Jake said and picked up the phone. "Hello?"

"Jake," the voice on the other end of the line said, "this is Hughes."

"Working late today, aren't you, Howard?"

"Early for me. I just got back from the hearings with those congressman up in D.C."

"Been reading about it in the news. Kind of tore you a new one, didn't they?"

"They'll change their tune after the Hercules proves itself. That's what I'm calling you about. You know the H-4 as well as anyone and they tell me you're the best flying boat pilot to ever set at the controls of a Clipper. How'd you feel about being my copilot on the test run?"

"We going to fly her or just make a taxi run?"

"Depends on the weather and the water conditions, most likely just a high speed taxi test."

"And, when are we going to do this?"

"November 2nd. How early can you be there?"

"As early as you need me, Howard."

***

Jake had not told Suzette he would be testing the Spruce Goose with Hughes that Sunday morning and slipped away before sunup without waking her. He hadn't wanted to worry her unnecessarily the night before.

Jake arrived at the harbor flying boat dock and parked his red company pickup on the fill-dirt nearby. First light was breaking as he walked slowly over to where a group of Hughes Aircraft workers were going about their duties preparing the Hercules to power up.

Tied to its mooring dock at Long Beach the H-4 bobbed in the shallow water and stillness of the calm wind.

The morning air coming in across the harbor was chilly. Jake stood with Hughes, his flight engineer and a radio reporter named McNamara around a fifty-five-gallon barrel with a fire burning in it. Jake warmed his hands over the fire and one of the ground crew brought them all a cup of coffee from the work-shed.

"How are things going over at Martin Aero, Jake? I understand you're about ready to produce that new TwinStar your people have designed."

"Your information is pretty good as always, Howard, but there are some problems other than with the airplane I need to overcome."

"Yeah, I know. That Mulholland bunch is still giving you trouble aren't they?"

"What do you suggest?"

"Why don't you call a fellow in Houston by the name of Melvin Nutter. He might have a solution for you."

"What can some guy in Houston do?"

"Just call him!"

In a couple of hours the crew chief reported everything on the aircraft ready. Howard and Jake had already been over the plane several times. Howard, in his two-tone brown waistcoat and broad-brimmed hat, boarded the Hercules followed by Jake and their put-together flight-test crew.

The giant flying boat was loosened from its mooring ropes and one by one the H-4's eight mighty engines were cranked, warmed up and brought to idle.

The water in the bay was choppy most of the time, but today it was relatively calm and there were no large swells. Jake sat at the copilot's controls on the far right with the large center console between him and Hughes.

Under power and with Hughes at the controls, the Hercules headed into the center of the harbor. Jake monitored and double-checked everything as he prepared to back Hughes up on the controls. Nothing would be left to chance in the event they had underestimated the required hydraulic pressures needed on the flight controls.

The flight engineer, positioned behind Jake, gave a thumbs-up indicating all engines were online.

Jim McNamara, a local radio station reporter, watched over Hughes' right shoulder as he came in with full power and could read the flight indicators from where he was sitting.

With his wire recorder running, McNamara reported the following "This is James McNamara speaking to you from the giant Hughes aircraft. Howard Hughes has just alerted us. He has asked everyone to hold on. All eight engines are moving, tremendous horsepower picking up. Howard Hughes is sitting directly in front of us. Here we go. (Roar of engine noise in the background.) The airspeed indicator has moved up to 25, 30, 35 as he pushes the throttles, 40, 45, more throttle, 50 over a choppy sea, 55 more throttle, 60, 65. Its 70, its 75 and something momentarily. Ah, I believe we are airborne."

From the shore, one of the spectators yelled out, "Look! There's no more bow wake!" as the giant gray colored Spruce Goose rose above the water.

Another onlooker exclaimed, "It seemed to levitate into the air."

McNamara's recording continued. "We were airborne ladies and gentlemen. I don't believe Howard Hughes meant this to be, I don't know? (A pause.) We were airborne for just a moment, we were really up in the air and I don't know whether… Howard, did you expect that? 'Certainly, I like to make surprises.' Were you surprised or what? 'No, I thought I'd make a surprise.' (Laughter in the cockpit.)"

Jake monitored the amount of control pressure Hughes had applied and could tell the H-4 was stable as a kite in level flight, but the plane's lack of response to the slightest control inputs indicated to Jake the aircraft would not recover well from turning maneuvers.

Looking briefly in the direction of Hughes, Jake showed concern as he attempted to read Hughes facial expressions. Hughes looked back at Jake as if seeming to agree and began easing the power off. The H-4 settled gently back onto the water. The two experienced pilots had read each other's concerns loud and clear.

As the H-4 taxied back across the harbor, McNamara continued his transcription into the recorder.

"Well, you certainly surprised the people here. The airspeed was 80 miles an hour when it took off and we were perched up here thirty feet above the floor of the sea, above the surface of the sea rather. It certainly was the greatest surprise, but ladies and gentlemen, the Hughes mammoth aircraft has flown this afternoon. I don't know about the expression on my face, but I looked at the assistant engineer and I have never seen a more surprised character in all my life. He looked like he had bet on the Brooklyn Dodgers in the last ballgame of the World Series."

McNamara leaned forward and pointed the microphone towards Hughes to ask one more question to conclude the interview.

"Why did you decide to fly the plane today, Mr. Hughes?"

"It just felt good, buoyant and good, so I just pulled it up."

The H-4 had been scheduled for only an engine and water-handling tests. Hughes surprised everyone, except possibly Jake, by letting the H-4 lift off the water.

After everyone else had left the flight deck, Hughes said to Jake, "You knew, didn't you?"

"I wasn't sure, not being on the control yoke, but I detected a slight vibration in the airframe when you applied aileron."

"I felt it, too. That's why I decided to let her settle back onto the water rather than circle back for a touch down."

"If we'd of touched wing low, she'd have come apart!" Jake said with a hint of trepidation in his voice.

"At least we proved she'd fly. That's all we needed to do for now. That's enough to get those Senators in Washington off my back."

"That's right, Howard, She did fly and nobody will ever be able to dispute that!"

With the Hercules securely tied up at the dock, Howard exited the aircraft to a reception of a few invited celebrities and a large number of press people who had been admitted to the dock area at the last minute.

Jake managed to stay in the background until one of the newsmen asked him for his opinion of the first flight in the giant bird.

"I'd rather you'd talk to Mr. Hughes about that," Jake told the reporter and at the earliest opportunity, he slipped slowly out of the crowd. He went unnoticed to his pickup and drove away.

***

Jake pulled into the circle out front of his house. Suzette heard him drive up and met him at the door.

"Jake, I thought you were going to stop working on Sunday. My gosh! You look like something the cat drug in. What time did you get up this morning?"

"I'm fine. Where are the kids?"

"They're all spending the night with friends and Lydia went to spend a couple of days with her cousin. Say, did you hear Howard Hughes flew the Spruce Goose today over at Long Beach?"

"Yep, she flew great!"

"What do you mean by flew, who flew?"

"Get dressed up in that sexy black dress of yours, the one I like you in. I'm taking you out and I'll tell you all about it over dinner. I'm headed for a shower and a shave."

"Come back here this minute, Jacob Martin!"

Suzette picked up the habit of calling him Jacob from Jake's mother when she had a bone to pick with him.

Jake knew he had not quite pulled it off as smooth as he would have liked and replied, "Yes, dear?"

"You went flying with Hughes didn't you?"

"Well kind of," Jake said forcing back a grin.

"Jacob Martin! You haven't changed one tiny stubborn bit since I met you and you left me stranded in Rangoon to take off with that Flying Tigers bunch."

"Yeah, but I came back for you didn't I? Besides who could love you anymore than I do or ever will."

"Nobody, and I love you too, you overgrown excuse for an airborne China sailor!"

Suzette took Jake by the hand and led him down the hall to their bedroom.

"I guess this means we're going to be late for dinner. Is that correct, Mrs. Martin?"

"I believe you're correct about that, Mr. Martin," Suzette replied smiling at her husband.

***

Monday morning at the office, Gertie brought Jake the morning paper as he arrived for work.

"Good morning, Mr. Martin. How was your flight?" she asked as she handed him the newspaper opened and folded to the article on the Spruce Goose.

"My name's not in the paper, is it?"

"No, sir."

"Good! Well then how'd you know?" Jake asked realizing he just admitted to what Gertie only suspected. "Gertie, you think you know everything don't you?"

"Not everything. Only what I'm suppose to," she added as she placed a fresh cup of coffee on the coaster at the edge of Jake's desk.

Jake put his suit jacket on a hanger, hung it on the old wooden coat tree in the corner and seated himself at his desk. He picked up the morning Los Angeles newspaper and began reading at the place where Gertie had it neatly folded.

"November 2, 1947, Howard Hughes and a small engineering crew fired up the eight R-4360s engines for a taxi tests, but instead thrilled thousands of on-lookers with the unannounced first flight of the largest airplane in the world. With Hughes at the controls, the Flying Boat lifted 70 feet off the water, and flew one mile in less than a minute at a top speed of 80 miles per hour before making a perfect landing. Congress had demanded proof of the plane's airworthiness. Yesterday in Long Beach Harbor Mr. Howard Hughes obliged them."

Jake sat quietly for a while staring at the telephone. "Gertie, come in here."

"Yes, Mr. Martin," she said as she entered with her steno pad in hand.

"You won't need that, sit down I want to talk over something with you."

"You mean, you talk and I listen."

"Mostly. Do you know anything about sailing?"

"Not very much. I went day-sailing once with some friends," Gertie replied cheerfully.

"Most people think the wind pushes the sail."

"It doesn't?" Gertie asked trying to show an interest in whatever it was Jake was explaining to her.

"No, Gertie, it doesn't. Aerodynamic lift moving past the sail creates a low pressure area on one side and this pulls the boat, not pushes it."

"The same way a wing lifts an airplane. Isn't that correct, Mr. Martin?"

"Correct, Gertie. Now for the sixty-four dollar question, if the Phoenicians used sails on their boats thousands of years ago, why didn't they turn the sail sideways and fly?"

"They didn't want to?"

"Maybe," Jake replied thoughtfully.

"I suppose they couldn't figure it out."

"That's right, Gertie! They couldn't figure it out, but we did and we can figure our way out of this shareholder mess, too. Get me a guy named Melvin Nutter in Houston on the phone. You might have to call a couple of the big oil companies, but someone in that town will know how to get a hold of him."

Scarcely five minutes later Gertie announced, "Mr. Melvin Nutter is holding on the phone for you, Mr. Martin."

Jake picked up the phone. "Melvin, this is Jake Martin in California. We have a mutual friend who suggested I give you a call."

"I've been wondering when I'd hear from you. Howard mentioned you might call. You can skip all the stuff about that rattlesnake Percy Mulholland. He's a major stockholder in Amerada Oil Company like myself. I'm on the board of directors with him."

"Then I guess you know why I'm calling?"

"Sure do! Let me save you some time. Mulholland's group wants to get their hands on the Flying M oil field leases. In order to do that, they need to put your company in a financial bind, thereby forcing you and your dad into releasing some of your holdings."

"I'm not surprised. I guess I should be more aware of what's going on outside of the company here in California. That being said, what do you suggest?"

"I thought you'd never ask!" Nutter proclaimed in a slow Texas drawl. "For some time now, Amerada stock has been losing value. Without something like the Flying M leases they aren't going to become a major producer. I'm gonna tell you right up front here, I don't approve of what Mulholland is trying to do. Don't want to be a part of it. I'm planning on starting my own oil exploration company, but I need my investment back out of Amerada to do it."

"I'm sorry, Melvin. You lost me that time."

"Buy me out! With what I hold and the shares you can pickup on the open market at the current low price, you will hold a major position in Amerada. The rest of Mulholland's cronies will sell out, once they get wind of what's happening. The shoe will be on the other foot then and I'll bet Mulholland will sell you his shares in the California Martin companies for whatever you offer."

Stunned by the simplicity of Melvin's solution, Jake did not reply for a moment.

"You're welcome!" Nutter finally proclaimed kiddingly on the other end of the phone line.

"No, no. That's great Melvin. I'll have my attorney, Larry Wilcox, get right back in touch with you. If it's all as described, you got a deal. Muchos-gracias-mi-amigo."

"De-nada, Jake. Us Texans got to stick together, you know."

"Listen Melvin, if this deal works and you get your new exploration company going, we'll make you a good price on your new drilling equipment. Heck, I'll even carry some of the paper to help you get started, if you want."

In about an hour, Larry called back.

"That offer from Nutter in Houston is even a better deal than he described. We can't lose, Jake."

"Okay, now where do I get the capital to do this deal?"

"Do you ever look at those financial statements the CPAs send you every quarter."

"Sure, Gertie files them."

"No, do you read them?"

"I'll look over them one of these days."

"Jake, your Texas instrument company stock and your Pan Am holdings alone are worth ten times what it'll take to do this deal. Not to mention your trust fund that you've hardly tapped in years!"

"Okay, cash in the Texas instrument stock. I'm not sure those transistor widget things are going to go over that well. Heck, ol' Earl had an idea for making them back in Oklahoma in the 30s."

"Wouldn't do that, Jake, from what I hear, transistors are the coming thing in electronics."

"You're probably right as usual. We own a lot of Pan Am stock. Let's start dumping some of it because if Trippe ever leaves it won't be a good investment. The same is true for the TWA stock if Hughes sells out. Better dump TWA, too. Oh, and Larry when the deal's done I want to attend the next Amerada shareholder's meeting personally."

Larry laughed, "I'll bet you do!"

***

Jake overheard Gertie being very firm with someone in the outer office. "I'm sorry, you'll have to go see personnel. Mr. Martin does not handle that."

"I understand, ma'am, but I need to talk to him."

The man's voice sounded vaguely familiar to Jake and he got up from his desk and went into Gertie's office to find out what was going on.

"Can I help you?"

The medium built, nice looking young fellow with a thick country accent approached Jake.

"You probably don't remember me."

"Well, I think I do."

"We flew together one time. I was the top gunner and flight engineer on Arnie's crew. You flew a B-17 mission with us in '43."

"Certainly I remember you. Everyone called you Okie."

"Yes sir. My given name is Herman Willis, Junior. Back home everyone always called me Junior, but when I went in the service the crew started calling me Okie and I liked that better anyway."

"What can I do for you, Okie?"

"You see, I went to school to become an engineer, but there's no work back home. So my wife and I came out here. I hadn't had no luck finding a job here either. I'm a good engineer and I'm also a darn good machinist. I learned from my dad working in the oil fields."

"I'm sure you are. I remember how you handled yourself in the B-17 that day I flew with you guys."

"Look, Mr. Martin, I'll take any work you got. I'll even sweep floors if you have an opening."

Gertie was staring a burning hole through Jake's back. She considered it her job to try to screen people like Okie from getting to him. She knew Jake would never turn away a Vet down on his luck, much less someone he had flown with.

Jake invited Okie down the hall to the break room and as they walked, Jake explained, "Okie, the company is barely able to keep the employees its got now, let alone hire new ones. Things are pretty slim around here. They should pick up in another year or so, as soon as we get our new plane into production."

In the break room, Jake lifted the half-full glass coffee pot from the hotplate. He poured them each a cup and sat down with Okie.

"You know the thing I remember most about that B-17 mission was Captain Arnett, I guess you all called him Arnie, getting on the ICS when things got tense and reciting that Edger Allen Poe poem."

"I know, the *Annabelle Lee*. Arnie's way of calming the crew down. Anna was Arnie's wife's name. That's who we named the plane after."

"Have you ever read the rest of the poem?" Jake asked.

"No sir, I don't believe I ever have."

"Well you probably shouldn't. The poem ends a lot like war does, in death and sorrow. Whatever happened to the crew of the *Annabelle Lee*? Do you guys still stay in touch?"

From the look on Okie's face, Jake wished he had not asked that question.

"Not really. The crew and me had flown nearly fifty missions together by the end of '44 when I came down with pneumonia. Couldn't stand up let alone fly. First mission I ever missed."

"Arnie and the crew didn't make it back did they?" Jake asked, guessing the worst.

"The way one of the crewmen in the plane next to them told me later they took a hit in the wing fuel tank. The plane broke in half and exploded. No one saw any chutes."

"Wow, that's rough!" Jake said and looked away.

Both men sat quietly as though remembering fallen comrades and then Jake said, "That mission I flew with you guys in '43 reminded me of something I read in *Dante's Inferno*. 'I did not die and I did not remain alive. What I became, deprived me of both life and death.' That was the way I felt on that bombing mission."

Okie took a small yellow piece of paper from his wallet and unfolded it.

"One of the officers in our squadron wrote this. I copied it down and I've carried it with me ever since. Helps me to remember my crew."

He handed the paper to Jake who read it aloud, "The worst thing about an air battle is that there is no battlefield. There is no hill to point to and say, the battle took place over there. There is no hallowed ground on which to build a monument to honor the dead. The sky is washed clean and only those who fought and those below who watched the burning planes falling from the sky have any remembrance of the raging battles that took place there."

After Jake read it, he folded the paper up by its well-worn creases and handed it back to Okie who said, "Makes me wonder, why not me? Why did I walk away from that war and the guys I flew with didn't come home? Why wasn't I with my crew the day the Annabelle Lee went down?"

"I don't know, Okie, but I've talked to a lot of Vets coming back from the war and they all wonder the same thing. Tell you what, we don't have any openings for floor sweepers or engineers right now, but we can always use a good machinist. Come on back to my office and I'll give you a hire slip to take down to the personnel department. As soon as we get into production with our new aircraft, I'll see if we can't find you an opening in engineering."

"Mr. Martin, you don't have any idea what this'll mean to my wife and me. I'll make you the best dang employee you ever hired."

"You don't need to thank me. Its guys like you the rest of us need to thank. Besides, you'll earn your pay out there in the machine shop. Its hot, dirty work making oil well equipment parts."

***

Jake took Dan to lunch at a Chinese joint a block off Lincoln on Venice Avenue to explain the offer from Nutter. Dan did not care a whole lot for Chinese food, but Jake had not bothered to ask.

"Looks like that's the way to go," Dan said after Jake finished explaining it all to him. "Does this mean we're full steam ahead on the M-27 TwinStar?"

"Not only are we full ahead, but I'm going to push for a rollout in fourteen months instead of eighteen. Do you think our people can handle that?"

"We can sure as heck try, but Jake, I need to talk to you about these new hire slips you have been authorizing. You've got to stop hiring people. We can't afford to pay the ones we have on the payroll now, at least until we get into full civilian production."

"Dan, the last time I looked at our checking account ledger, we were four hundred thousand overdrawn. What difference does it make if we're four hundred and ten thousand overdrawn?"

"When you look at it that way, none I guess. Hand me one of those menus and let's see what they've got here for dessert besides these little fortune cookies.

***

The year 1947 turned into 1948 and by the end of summer, the prototype of the M-27 TwinStar had developed into an amazingly advanced aircraft. The shop was in full production on all components engineering had completed.

The new engines for the TwinStar arrived on Christmas Eve and Jake could not have received a better Christmas present. He stood watching like a kid with a new toy as the wooden crates were opened and the engines were unpacked.

Jake went back to his office after going down to receiving to see the first of the new engines arrive on the loading dock. He sat down at his desk to go through the mail Gertie had pre-opened with a letter opener and laid in a neat stack on his desk.

A Christmas card postmarked Minnesota with no return address was on the very top. When Jake opened the envelope, a small color photograph fell out onto the desk, but he read the card first. The printed card read only "Best Wishes for the Holidays, Mr. and Mrs. Bernard Olson."

He picked up the photo that had fallen out of the card and laughed. The photo was of a family of five, a big stout blonde-haired fellow, two young boys about age three and a baby girl sitting on the woman's lap. The only one Jake recognized was the woman in the picture.

Turning the photo over, he read the writing on the back "Dear Jake, Thought you might like to see my twin boys and my new daughter. Fine family, don't you think? Merry Christmas, Maggie."

Jake sat looking at the photo and wished he had remembered to take more photographs over the years. He wished he had a photo of Zack and Sarah when they were kids together. Oh well, what the heck he thought, they were in his memory and in his heart. That was good enough.

He smiled at the photograph and said aloud, "Yes Maggie, that's a fine looking family," as he stood up, reached over the credenza and stuck the small color photo in the corner of the frame with the picture of the B-27 rollout.

The photo stayed there until it turned yellow and curled up at the corners. Jake never bothered to remove it.

End Of An Era

In the early spring of 1949, exactly fourteen months from the day they started work on the M-27, the first TwinStar rolled off the assembly line and went to the flight-test center.

Jake and Dan decided not to make a big ceremony out of the event and so on the day of the first flight, only invited guests, some aviation press writers and factory personnel were in attendance.

Suzette's father, Jon Claude, came for a visit. Big Jake and Flo also came for the occasion and this was the first time Suzette's father had met Jake's parents.

Michael wanted to ride along on the first flight, but of course, Jake would not let him. Suzette did the honors of christening the new plane with a special bottle of champagne.

At the rather small reception in the hangar after the initial test flight, Dan came over to Jake.

"In addition to the ten advance orders for new TwinStars we already had, we've just received twelve more orders by Telex within the last hour. Seems some of our buyers had been sitting on the fence."

Jake turned to those at the rollout reception and announced loudly, "Martin Aero will commence a production and delivery schedule of three aircraft per month starting immediately," and everyone cheered.

An article about the new Martin Aero M-27 appeared in two popular aviation publications and except for that, the birth of the new TwinStar went relatively un-noticed.

***

Early on a fall evening in 1950, a low-lying fog and a slow drizzling rain moved in from off shore on the Malibu coast.

The evening news with Walter Winchell was coming over the large Philco console radio in the living room at Jake and Suzette's home.

"Hello Mr. and Mrs. America and all the ships at sea."

Jake was seated on the large sectional couch fumbling through a stack of flight-test reports when the front doorbell chimed.

"Lydia," Jake yelled out and then he hollered, "Someone, please get the door!"

Finally, he lifted the stack of paperwork from his lap, laid it on the couch beside him and went to answer the door himself.

As Jake approached the large double doors, he could see the silhouette of a woman through the large oval, etched glass door panes. The headlights of a car in the circle driveway backlit the darkened figure at the door.

Jake opened the door to a handsome, middle-aged woman in a black, hooded raincoat standing on the porch water-soaked from the rain. She clutched her coat collar with her right hand and held a large, black leather purse cradled under the crook of her left arm. The car in the driveway was a taxicab.

Jake started to ask if he could help the woman in some way, but she spoke first.

"Jake, is that you?"

He did not recognize the face at first, but he certainly knew the voice. He stood startled for a moment as though he had just seen a ghost and maybe he had.

"Elizabeth, for God's sake, you're soaking wet. Come in, please come in."

Liz stepped onto the white marble entry. The rain dripped from the hem of her coat and Jake started to shut the door, but Liz raised her hand to stop the door closing.

"The cab driver wanted ten dollars for the fare, but I wasn't sure I had the right house and asked him to wait."

Jake took an umbrella from a stand near the door and went to the driver's car window. He paid the driver and the taxicab that brought Liz from the Greyhound bus station pulled away. Jake assumed Liz would be staying for a while to visit with Lora and Michael.

Jake shut the door behind him and yelled, "Suzette, Lora, Michael, we've got company," and turning to Liz, he said, "Let me help you off with that wet raincoat."

Lydia and Suzette came from the kitchen drying their hands on tea towels where Lydia had been trying, once again, to teach Suzette how to cook some sort of a Mexican dish. Neither had the slightest idea as to the identity of their guest.

Michael emerged from his room down the hall at about the same time as Lora came in from the study where she had been reading.

"Well, do you all know who this is?" Jake asked.

No one spoke up until Lora, standing with her arms folded in front of her said, "I guess I do, its Elizabeth, I suppose. I've seen pictures of her, you know."

"You mean your mother," Jake said, correcting Lora.

Lora cocked one shoulder.

"Yeah, my mother, whatever."

Liz turned to Jake and her voice cracked as she said, "I shouldn't have come. I knew this whole thing was a bad idea. Really I should go."

"No, don't go," Michael asked approaching Liz. "Are you really my mother? If you are, I'd like you to stay. I'd like to know more about you."

Liz's face brightened with Michael's enthusiastic curiosity.

"Where do you live now? Do I have any other brothers or sisters?" Michael asked looking over at Lora who glared back at him for the questions he had just asked.

Liz forced a smile and answered, "Pittsburgh and no, in that order."

The tension in the room eased slightly.

"And I'm Suzette. The wife!" she said giving Jake a really stern look for having failed to introduce her.

"I'm pleased to meet you. My, but you're a very pretty lady!" Liz said with a pleasant smile.

"Thank you. You're welcome in our home, Elizabeth. I'm sure Lora and Michael will also want to make you welcome," Suzette said turning to look directly at Lora.

Jake ushered the group into the living room.

"Oh, and the lady over there is Lydia Gomez."

Lydia nodded politely.

"Con mucho gusto, ma'am."

As Lydia passed by the console radio on her way out of the room, she switched it off and muttered something else in Spanish under her breath.

Jake was not certain whether she was commenting on Mr. Winchell's radio broadcast or the present situation.

Suzette went over to the couch where young Chen was seated and motioned for her eight-year-old son to stand up.

"This is my son, Chen. He is named for his father who was killed in the war in Burma."

"Oh, I'm so sorry, I mean about your husband."

"No, that's alright. It all happened quite some time ago," Suzette replied before Chen could say anything. "We'll leave you two to visit," and she nudged Chen to come with her. "Lydia and I need some help in the kitchen."

"Aw, Mom!" Chen complained, obviously thinking he might be going to miss out on something. "Why?" he asked as Suzette ushered him down the hall towards the kitchen.

"Because this doesn't concern you, that's why! Now make yourself scarce. Lydia and I can handle the kitchen."

Suzette busied herself making coffee and suggested Lydia prepare some snacks.

The conversation in the living room was awkward at best. Lora and Jake found it difficult to converse, but Michael kept coming up with new questions to ask.

Jake gathered up the paperwork he had been reading and excused himself to go to the den. As he left the room, he motioned for Lora to show an interest and participate in the conversation.

Lora started to ask Liz a question she had carefully thought up, more like a member of the press doing an interview than as an interested party, but Michael interrupted her before she finished her question and continued to bombard Liz with questions of his own.

Liz seemed a little overwhelmed by the attention. Clearly she was not used to teenagers or for that matter, anyone being interested in her opinion on any subject.

After a short while, Michael asked Liz, "Would you like to see my room and some of the model airplanes I've built?"

"Of course I would," Liz replied with a smile.

Lora reluctantly followed them down the hall for the guided tour of Michael's room, her arms folded tightly in front of her pastel-pink, cashmere sweater.

Suzette noticed several things about Liz, which in all the commotion the others had overlooked. Liz's tailored brown dress suit did not fit well and most likely had been purchased at a secondhand store. Her high-heeled shoes were also scuffed and the sides of the soles badly overrun.

Suzette entered the den where Jake was pretending to read one of the documents he had brought home from work.

"You might turn that report right side up, it'd be easier to read," she said smiling. "What's the plan for our guest? I doubt that poor woman has the funds for a hotel. Is she going to stay here for the night?"

"What do you suggest?" Jake pitched his papers on the desk and leaned back in his chair. "I wish she would have called or given us some kind of warning. Why now? Why does she show up here now, after all these years?"

The private telephone line rang, the number only a few close associates and the factory security officers were privy to in case of an emergency.

Lydia answered the phone on the second ring from the hall extension, as she knew Jake and Suzette were talking in the den and probably did not wish to be disturbed.

Lydia entered the den. "Mr. Martin, it's the security guard at the factory. He says he needs to talk to you."

Jake picked up the phone on the desk.

"Yes, what is it?"

The voice on the other end of the phone explained, "Sorry to bother you, Mr. Martin. There's some guy named Huffman keeps calling the switchboard operator and is demanding to talk to you about his wife."

Jake was stumped. "Tell the switchboard operator to patch him through to this phone?"

In a moment or two, the connection was made. "Yes, this is Jake Martin. What's the problem?"

Both Suzette and Lydia could hear the muffled ranting and ravings of the man's voice on the other end of the phone. The man had obviously been drinking.

Jake would hold the receiver some distance from his ear and then move the receiver back to speak. "I believe I heard you mentioned the name Elizabeth. Just hold on."

Jake laid the phone down and went into the living room where Liz, Lora and Michael had resumed their conversation.

"Liz, do you know someone by the name of Huffman?"

Liz rose quickly to her feet.

"Yes! That's my married name."

Jake thought to himself that he could not quite recall the name of the preacher Liz had ran off with years ago, but he was relatively sure the name was not Huffman. If the years had taught Jake anything, they had taught him to leave sleeping dogs lie.

"I think this phone call might be for you." Jake said and pointed to the den where Liz could take the call.

Suzette and Lydia returned to the kitchen. Jake sat quietly with Lora and Michael on the living room sofa. They could not help but overhear Liz as she spoke on the phone in the next room.

Liz pleaded with the man at the other end of the line, "Please be patient and calm down. I promise I will be home soon. You will just have to understand this was something I had to do!"

Liz hung up the phone and when she returned to the living room, she asked Jake, "Could you call me a cab to go to the bus station?"

"You don't need to leave yet, do you?" Michael pleaded. "You're welcome to stay for a few days. She's welcome to stay isn't she, Dad?"

Lora half-heartedly, but politely supported her younger brother by saying, "Sure, we have a guestroom you can use. We have people stay over with us all the time."

"Oh, I'm sorry, but it'd be out of the question for me to consider staying now. Maybe another time."

Secretly relieved Liz's visit had been considerably shortened, Jake offered, "Suzette and I will drive you. It's difficult to get a cab out here this time of night."

He went to get Liz's coat and handbag from the entry closet and Suzette met him in the hallway.

"What's going on?"

"Liz has to go now," Jake replied speaking softly. "She seems so frail, I hardly recognized her at first. She's afraid to fly you know, so I'm going to take her and put her on the train. She doesn't need to be riding a bus that far. Come along and ride to the station with us."

"No, you go on. There may still be some things that need to be said between the two of you."

Jake handed Suzette Liz's things and went to get the family's Lincoln Cosmopolitan sedan out of the garage.

Suzette helped Liz on with her raincoat and handed her the large black purse. Liz had arrived with no luggage, so Suzette assumed everything the lady had traveled with was in that purse.

The rain had stopped, but the air was still damp and the night foggy as the four waited on the front steps while Jake pulled the car around to the circle drive.

Michael and Lora walked Liz to the car door where she paused and made one simple request.

"Would it be possible to get a small hug goodbye from you Michael and from you too, Lora?"

Both hugged the neck of the woman that bore them and the mother that they had never known, except in name only.

Michael opened the passenger door of the sedan for his mother and said pleadingly, "Please come to see us again when you can."

Lora returned to stand in the doorway with Suzette.

The gunmetal gray, torpedo-back sedan with Jake and Liz pulled away in the darkness and onto the Pacific Coast Highway, disappearing into the fog.

They were past Santa Monica and well on their way to downtown Los Angeles when Jake broke the silence.

"You don't have a return bus ticket, do you?"

Liz shook her head no.

"I know how much you hate to fly, so I won't suggest that, but the Empire Express leaves L.A. late at night for the east coast. Locals here call it the Redeye Special. How about we put you on that?"

"Yes, that will be fine," and Liz smiled politely.

If she did not have a return bus ticket, Jake figured she likely had no money at all.

"I'll buy your ticket for you," but it was fairly obvious Liz had been banking on that anyway.

"Thank you, Jake. That would be very helpful."

The rest of the ride to the train station was shrouded in silence. Jake occasionally looked across the front seat at Liz and she would glance back at him. They were total strangers who, for whatever reasons the gods of fate had ordained, shared a few years of their lives together.

Both tried, with great difficulty, to remember when they were together as man and wife, but it had been too long now. The hurtful memories of those times had faded from their hearts, as had the anger they both once felt.

***

At the ticket counter in the train station, Jake reached in his jacket vest pocket for his wallet.

"A single one-way ticket to Pennsylvania." Turning to Liz with some uncertainty he asked, "Pittsburgh?"

"Yes, Pittsburgh."

"And make that a Pullman sleeper, please," Jake added turning back to the ticket agent.

The ticket agent, a slender old man wearing a sweater vest, glanced up at him over the top of his wire-frame glasses and asked, "Which station?"

Liz spoke up, "The Westchester station, but coach will be fine."

The agent did not have to ask, he could tell by the fact that Jake was preparing to pay for the ticket he should ignore the lady's objection. The agent completed preparing the tickets, placed them in a folder and wrote 3B on the front of the folder with a black grease pencil. He handed the ticket folder to Jake, but addressed Liz to explain, "You will have to make a change to the Penn Central Railway in St. Louis, ma'am."

"Yes, I know. Thank you."

The Empire Express was being called for boarding over the station's distorted public address system. Jake walked with Liz out to the loading platform where the train had backed into the station for boarding.

Pausing at the boarding steps of one of the silver Pullman cars, Liz pointed to the number 3B in the window.

"I guess this is me. Thanks for buying my ticket."

Jake handed Liz the ticket folder and fumbled in his pocket for a money clip containing a dozen or so large bills. He removed the silver money clip and placed the bills in Liz's hand.

Liz looked at the bills, removed a single twenty and handed the rest of the money back to Jake.

"This will be enough to eat on. If I was to show up at home with that much money, it would only cause trouble."

"I understand," Jake said, placing the bills back in his pocket.

Jake stood staring downward. He wanted very much to say something, but he could think of nothing to say.

Liz raised her hand and touched Jake's chin ever so gently to cause him to look her in the face.

"I'll say it because I know you'd never ask me to. I am sorry for every harsh word that ever passed between us. I am sorry for all the pain and heartache I ever caused you. Most of all, I am so very sorry that I never got to know those two wonderful young kids of ours."

Jake started to interrupt her, but she knew he would only try to take the blame for everything that went wrong between them. She placed two fingers over his lips because she did not want him to make excuses for her.

"You have done a fine job raising Michael and Lora. Please tell them that I love them."

She seemed ready to cry, but held it back.

Jake could tell she had recently had a lot of practice learning not to cry. Liz turned to board the train.

Jake stepped back as the engineer sounded one long blast from the locomotive. He thought what a terribly lonesome wail a train whistle makes and how it sounded like a large animal in great pain.

The porter placed the boarding step inside the car and closed the boarding door. The train cars jerked a couple of times and started to roll slowly forward. Jake could see Liz seated by a window about halfway down the car, but she did not look back. He gave a half-hearted wave goodbye, turned and walked away as the train pulled out.

***

The following day, the experience with Liz caused Jake to contact Larry by telephone and invited Larry and Jenny Lou out to California for a week. Jake always felt like Jenny Lou and Suzette got along real well and enjoyed one another's company.

Suzette took Jenny Lou to a fancy tearoom she liked and gave her the Cook's Tour of Los Angeles.

Lora went shopping with Jenny Lou and Suzette on Rodeo Drive. It is likely that it was on this very shopping trip that Lora started thinking about opening her own boutique.

Although Lora's personality was quite different from her fathers, she possessed his same quick mind and his monomaniacal attitude towards accomplishing her goals.

She felt the small Rodeo Drive shopping district, which was growing rapidly in popularity with the locals, had the potential to one day become a major fashion center and began to make plans for the day she would open her own retail business there.

The second day after Larry arrived in town, Jake took him to lunch at Musso and Frank's to discuss the growing number of business alliances in which the Martin companies were becoming entangled.

"Larry, I've got a business proposition I've been mulling over in my head and I want to run it by you. I would like you to consider handling the Martin enterprise's legal business exclusively. Put all the other lawyers in your firm on their own and only retain the staff you need to handle our business."

"Jake, I've never complained about the retainers you pay me. I will admit since my dad retired, the workload has increased geometrically. Are you sure you'd want to do that? A law firm with a single client is pretty darn exclusive, not to mention expensive."

Jake pushed a paper cocktail napkin in front of Larry and held out his fountain pen.

"What do you make a year at your law firm?"

Larry took the pen and wrote the approximate figure on the napkin and turned it for Jake to read.

Jake looked at the amount written on the napkin and drew a line through it. He wrote a figure roughly double the amount and pushed the napkin back in front of Larry.

"Wow, you smooth talker. You are serious, aren't you?"

"Yes, I am. Things are expanding faster than I can keep up with them. And Big Jake, well, he's kinda getting like your dad. He'd rather fool with the ranch and race them ol' quarter horses of his than be involved in the business nowadays."

"Okay, okay. I accept. I'll transfer all my accounts to the other attorneys and close my firm to new clients. It's a done deal," and he shook Jake's hand. "Now what's this other matter you mentioned you wanted me to handle?"

"It's in Pittsburgh."

"Pittsburgh?" Larry replied with some skepticism. "This has something to do with Liz, doesn't it?"

"Your pretty sharp aren't you? Always up on things."

"That's what you pay me those big bucks for."

"Yeah, it does. She's got cancer and it's terminal. She might do a little better if she could get some specialized treatment, but the costs are far above what this guy Huffman she's married to can afford."

"Go ahead, I'm listening."

"I've done some checking and turns out Huffman works for a steel mill in Pittsburgh that Martin companies buy a lot of materials from. I'll give you a contact name there. Arrange to have this Huffman fellow promoted to supervisor. It'll be a raise in pay for him and he's probably not worth it. Drinker I think, but it'll qualify him and his dependents for their company's health insurance plan."

"Listen Jake, I think there's a hospital there that specializes in cancer treatment. How about I contact them and you make a charitable contribution to one of their pet research projects. I'm sure they'd treat Liz then."

Jake looked away out across the dining room, staring off not really seeing.

"Odd how things in life turn out," Jake sighed. "Well, do which ever works or do them both. Like Big Jake always used to say…"

"Yeah, I know," Larry said with a smile. "Money's like manure. Don't do no good unless you spread it around."

"You got it, Larry," and both men laughed.

"Jake, I never understood why you married Elizabeth anyway. Why didn't you marry Sarah?"

"Many a man has left a good woman for a bad one!" Jake said and called for the check.

Larry just grinned and shook his head.

***

A year had passed since Liz came for her one and only short visit to see the kids. Michael, now sixteen, had tried to write to her several times, but the post office always returned his letters as undeliverable.

Jake had come home early from work and was seated at his desk in the study when Michael came into the room with an opened envelope and letter in his hand.

"It's a letter from Grandma Flo. She says Elizabeth, my mother, died. Did you know about this?"

Jake stopped what he was doing and looked up.

"Yes, Michael, I did. I talked to your grandma about a week ago on the phone and she told me then. She visited with one of your mother's relatives at church and that's how she found out. Grandma said she would write to you about it and so I thought it would be better for you to hear it from her than from me."

Michael plopped down on the arm of the nearby couch.

"Do you know what she died of?" and invoking typical teenage melodramatics he added, "I'll bet she died of a broken heart."

Jake got up from his chair and leaned back against the desk with his hands in his pockets. He knew in his own mind he had done everything he could to help Michael's mother, but for better or worse he had chosen not to share those things with his son.

"Might have been, but I suspect she already knew she didn't have long to live when she came to visit you."

Michael rose to his feet and faced his father.

"You don't even care, do you?"

"I do care, Michael. I care very much. Life is a gift from God. I am sad when anyone dies, but you see, I don't know how to mourn for someone like your mother who was never able to find contentment or happiness in life."

Jake reached for a novel on his desk he had finished reading a few days before. He handed the book to Michael.

"Here's a popular new novel you might want to read."

Michael took the book and started out of the room. He paused as he read the title of the book in his hand and asked, "Whom do the bells toll for?"

"All of us, Michael. The loss of one diminishes each of us."

***

In the summer of '52, Michael again returned to the Flying M to spend his school vacation on the ranch with his grandparents.

Flo re-did Jake's old boyhood room upstairs at the main ranch house and Michael now considered it his room.

For several years, Suzette had wanted to return to her childhood home in France for a visit. She also wanted Lora and Chen to see her family's old country château near Reims in northern France.

Jake arranged for them to fly first class to Paris that June in one of Pan Am's new Boeing Stratocruisers. They toured The City of Lights like tourists for three days before Jon Claude met them in Paris and drove them up to Reims where they spent another two weeks.

When they returned home, Lora told her father, "I just loved Paris! There's a fashion design school there I would very much like to attend."

"We'll see," Jake replied dispassionately, but Lora seldom ask him for much of anything and when she did, Jake hardly ever refused her.

Summer vacation neared an end and Michael would be returning home in three weeks to start back to school.

Jake was in the middle of an important meeting when Gertie came into his office. She did not normally interrupt him under those circumstances.

When Jake looked up and saw the concerned expression on her face, he knew something was wrong.

Gertie bent over and whispered, "Suzette is on line two. It would be best if you took the call in the outer office, Mr. Martin."

Jake excused himself from the meeting and went to take the call.

"What's wrong?"

"It's your dad! Michael called from the ranch and he's taken a bad fall from his horse. Michael and some of the other wranglers were with him and brought him to the house. They've called in young Doc Winens, but Michael says he's hurt pretty bad. Jake, maybe you should go out there."

"Okay, I'll have a plane made ready. We'll take one of the new TwinStars, there faster than the Dragon One. You and Lora meet me at the flight line as soon as you can get there."

Jake was just finishing his pre-flight inspection on the M-27 demonstrator aircraft when Suzette and Lora pulled up. Suzette parked her sedan by the hangar and handed the keys to Gene who met her and opened the car door for her.

Gene removed the two small suitcases out of the back seat as Lora and Suzette ran for the plane and boarded. Lora went forward to ride in the right seat with Jake and Suzette buckled into the forward cabin seat behind him.

Gene placed the two cases in the plane's luggage compartment and latched the door. He slapped the side of the fuselage near the cockpit twice with his hand indicating the luggage compartment was latched, backed off to where Jake could see him and where he could see both wingtips. Gene gave a thumbs-up indicating the chocks had been pulled from the wheels and the aircraft was clear to taxi.

Jake was preparing to start the engines when one of the factory security cars pulled onto the flight line ramp. The uniformed guard stepped out of the car and waved an envelope over his head.

Gene ran to get the envelope and took it over to the TwinStar. He passed the Western Union telegram envelope to Jake through the small cockpit storm window.

Jake tore it open and read the message.

"Regret to inform you. Stop. Your father passed away at 12:30pm today. Stop. Travis."

Jake sat motionlessly in the pilot's seat holding the telegram in his limp hand. He said nothing.

Suzette leaned over Jake's shoulder from the rear seat in order to read the telegram. She settled back into her seat and began to cry.

Lora asked, "Grandpa?"

Suzette shook her head yes.

After a few minutes, Jake looked out the windshield at Gene and made a forward open-hand pointing motion indicating he was ready to taxi.

Gene looked left then right and gave a circular motion overhead indicating cleared to crank.

Jake started the engines and taxied out.

***

Typical of August on the Flying M ranch, the days had been hot and dry, but the morning of Big Jake's funeral there came a slow drizzling rain. Ranchers and friends from miles around began arriving to express their condolences for Big Jake's passing.

The funeral was held at the Episcopal Church where Flo and Big Jake always attended, but the little church proved far too small to hold everyone who came. Folks sat in their cars and hundreds stood outside under umbrellas in the misting rain.

Father Kinsley gave the eulogy. He began by telling of Big Jake's many exploits of which most attending were familiar. Big Jake's reputation preceded him, a true icon and celebrity in his own right.

Near the end of the eulogy, Father Kinsley reached in his pocket and unfolded a small hand-written paper.

"I would like to read something Jacob Martin gave to me some time back. I do not know the author. Jacob might have written it himself, I'm not sure, but I believe he intended for it to be read at this time."

Father Kinsley commenced to read aloud, "Oh God, Thy love has blessed me and brought me to this place in time. Your hand has guided me safely along to come to know Your power divine. You found me wondering alone and gave me friend and kin. They have shared my joys and sorrows, but now I must go home again."

Father Kinsley folded the small piece of paper up, returned it to his pocket and concluded the eulogy by saying, "We will miss Jacob Teel Martin. The whole world will miss a man like him. There are ever so few men that when they walk the face of the earth, the earth thunders from their presence. Big Jake Martin was one of those men!"

They buried Big Jake that afternoon at the Martin family plot near John Martin's original cabin on the far north part of the Texas side of the ranch. He was laid to rest near the graves of his father John Martin, his mother and his younger sister who died very young.

Flo barely made it through the service. Jake and Michael held onto her firmly throughout the ordeal. By the time everyone made it over the muddy dirt road to the Martin family gravesite near ol' John's first cabin, the rain had stopped, but the sky was still heavily overcast.

Roy Briggs, Jake's old friend from the Flying Tigers, was now a full colonel stationed at Carswell Airbase in Fort Worth. Roy had spoken to Jake earlier about the arrangements he made for a fly over by the last operational squadron of B-27s. This to honor the man who was chairman of the board of the Aero division of Martin Company when the planes were first designed and built.

Roy was not sure the planes would be able to make the fly over due to the inclement weather.

Father Kinsley was speaking the words, "May his faults be written on the sand and his virtues written on our hearts," when bright sunlight burst through the clouds.

As the gray overcast rolled back, a patch of brilliant bright blue sky shown through and at that very instant three Dragon Bombers passed low overhead in a missing-man formation.

***

By the time all of the guests arrived back at the ranch house, the sun had dried up the morning rains.

So many people came to pay their respects, the fried chicken dinner Flo's friends prepared had to be moved outside. Folks from church rounded up all the large tables and folding chairs they could find and set them up on the porch and under the large shade trees in the yard.

Jake was visiting with some of his father's friends when Sarah and Hank came up to him to offer their condolences.

"I've never had an opportunity to thank you personally for selling Sarah and I your old summer ranch house," Hank said. "Maybe you'd like to come by and see what all we've done to fix the place up."

"Sure," Jake replied politely nodding to some friends of the family as they passed by. "I'd like to see what you've done with the old place," but Jake had no intention of returning even for a visit to the old summer ranch house where he and Elizabeth first made their home and where he had told Sarah he loved her. The memories that dwelled in that place would have to remain there.

"Well Jake, I just wanted to let you know how much Sarah and I appreciate you working it all out for us."

"You're more than welcome, Hank. At least it's being put to good use. I understand you're a full-fledged practicing doctor of veterinary medicine now, that right?"

"Sure am. Used to couldn't spell veterinarian now I are one," Hank said beaming proudly. "Finished my doctor's degree on the GI Bill. We're building a new clinic next to the boarding stables now. Seriously, you need to stop by!"

"If I get a chance while I'm here, I will. Thanks for the invite."

Sarah's two reddish-blonde haired daughters in their pink pinafore dresses with matching anklets and patent-leather shoes stood quietly staring up at the man they perceived to be some sort of a legend.

Hank took his two daughters by the hand.

"I'll leave you two to visit. I know you have a lot to catch up on."

Jake watched as the two little girls walked away with their father.

The oldest one looked back at Jake as if she wanted to have one more look at the man she had heard so much about.

Jake smiled and waved at her and she waved back.

"I know what you're thinking, but she's too young. If you'll add up the years, it doesn't come out."

Jake looked questioningly at Sarah, trying to pretend he did not know what she was talking about, but he did.

"And yes I did," Sarah said sternly, "but I miscarried in the second month and you, my dear Jacob, are the only one I've ever told this to. So you see," and Sarah's expression softened, "some things just aren't meant to be!"

Jake recalled an old passage from Bible school, *thou shall not covet*, and at that moment he was struggling with all his will not to do that very thing.

Jake turned away, mostly to hide the sadness in his eyes. The pressure from the loss of his father and all the old memories were caving in on him. He composed himself, looked back at Sarah and forced a smile.

"You've put on a little weight."

"Well, it's good to know you're still the same ol' silver-tongued romantic you always were, Jake Martin."

"No, no. I meant that as a compliment."

"I know you did. I always was kind of a skinny-Minnie, wasn't I?"

"Yes, you were, but you sure turned out to be a fine specimen of a woman. Those two girls of yours are real beauties. The youngest one looks just like you."

"Thank you, a mother always likes to hear things like that. I've got to tell you that wife of yours is not only gorgeous and charming she's quite an elegant lady. You're a very lucky man."

"I'll tell her you said that, Sarah," and they turned to step away from a group that looked about ready to come over to pay their respects to Jake.

"Funny how things always seem to work out for the best. I couldn't be happier married to Hank and I can tell by talking to Suzette you two are very much in love. She's made you the wife I could have never been. There'll always be a special place in my heart for you and because of those dang airplanes you fly all the time, you will always be in my prayers."

As a small group of old family friends approached, Sarah smiled politely and slipped away into the crowd. This was the last time Jake and Sarah's paths would ever cross.

***

Early the next morning, Jake talked for a long time with his mother.

"Don't worry about a thing, Mom. Travis is more than capable of running the ranch and I'll have Larry handle any problems that come up. What I really want you to consider is moving out to California with us. You can stay with Suzette and I. We'll fix you up your own bedroom just the way you want or I'll buy you your own place nearby. What ever suits you?"

"Oh, Jacob. I don't know if I could ever leave the place here, but I'll think about it," his mother promised.

"Okay, Mom. You know I'm always here for you if you need anything. I'm only a phone call away. We're going to be flying back to California this afternoon. Please think over what we've talked about."

Jake visited with Travis for a while to work out some of the details of running the ranch and then asked to borrow his pickup truck.

Jake went to get in the pickup and Michael followed.

"Where you going, Dad?"

"Out to the gravesite," Jake replied solemnly.

Michael got into the pickup to ride along and Jake pulled away onto the old ranch road.

"Are we moving back to Texas?"

"No. Why do you ask? Do you want to move back?"

"I been thinking someday I would like to come back and run the ranch. I know the ranch doesn't mean all that much to you, but it means a whole lot to me. There's something about this place that's always drawn me here. I can't explain it exactly."

"Well, I can. There's a bit of old John Martin's blood that runs through your veins. Sure, you can come back and run the Flying M. In fact, you can have the whole dang spread, if that's what you want. You're the natural heir to the place and I'm sure Lora has no interest in ranching."

"I know you want me to go to college and I will, but I've also been thinking about learning to fly."

"Whatever you want to do. You're old enough to decide your own future. We just need to keep the ranch going for Grandma Flo for right now. I'm going to have Larry incorporate the ranch along with the oil production companies. You've got your whole life ahead of you and this place ain't goin-nowhere! The Flying M will be here waiting for you when you're ready to take it over."

"Sounds like a great plan to me. Thanks for understanding, Dad."

Jake turned the pickup onto the dirt road and headed north up to John Martin's old cabin.

"I am glad to hear you're going to try to go to college. I never did and somebody from this family sure ought to do it one of these days."

"After I graduate, I'm thinking about joining the Marine Corps and becoming a jet fighter pilot flying off of a carrier."

"High ambition I'd say, but have at it tiger. Never saw anything you couldn't do when you set your mind to it, including learning to stand up on one of those surfboards."

Jake pulled up to the Martin family gravesite on the hillside overlooking the Red River Valley and got out of the pickup. He walked slowly up the hill to Big Jakes freshly covered grave and stood quietly.

Michael followed him and stood off at a distance watching his father not sure whether he was praying or just standing there thinking. After a few minutes, Michael went to stand with his father at the graveside.

Jake felt his son's presence and without turning to look at Michael, he said, "Everything that Texas is or ever was to me, lies here in this small plot of ground. This man gave me birth and this land gave me life on a grand scale. Today, I gave it all back to the land it came from."

Michael seemed to not quite understand what his father meant by those words, but he did not ask.

Jake turned abruptly to Michael and said, "Let's go get the girls and go home!"

***

Flo never came to California. She lived only three more months after Big Jake passed away. She died suddenly the evening of the first snowfall in November.

When young Doc Winens called Jake to tell him of Flo's passing, Jake asked, "What in the world happened? I talked to mom the day before yesterday and she seemed fine."

"I know of nothing seriously wrong with Flo's health. She had lost a little weight and seemed a little frail. Her friends told me she missed your father more than she ever let on. I suspect she no longer had any desire to go on without him. I've seen this in older folks before, they just seem to give up the will to live. I'm sorry, Jake"

"Nothing to be sorry about, Doc. Those two had a wonderful life together. We should all be half as lucky."

***

There is never a good time in the affairs of any family for the loss of one of their own, but the loss of the Martin matriarch could not have come at a worse time.

Lora was away in Paris and Jake told her not to fly home. Michael had enlisted in the Marine Reserve and was on two weeks active duty at Camp Pendleton. Only Suzette returned with Jake to the Flying M to tend to his mother's passing and to wrap up loose ends at the ranch.

Jake did not see Sarah and her family on this, his last return to the ranch. Sarah and Hank were away in Mexico doing some volunteer church mission work when Flo passed away. Sarah did not learn of Flo's passing until she and Hank returned home.

The day after Flo's funeral, Jake and Suzette where sitting in the living room of the ranch house. Jake had selected a small box of mementos, some photographs and stuff he remembered from his childhood.

He asked Suzette, "Is there anything here of Mom's you want?"

"I took the doily from the small round table over there. I remember Flo crocheting it the day you first brought me here to meet her. I also have the brooch with the small ivory cameo she often wore. She offered to give it to me one time, but I wouldn't take it because I knew the locket was one of her favorite things. That's all I need. I just wanted something to remember her by."

There came a knock on the front door and Jake went to answer. It was Travis. Jake had asked him to come by so they could go over some instructions on how to keep running the ranch.

Travis removed his large black Stetson hat when he entered the house and stood holding the brim with both hands.

"You gonna come back and run the place, Little Jake?"

"No, Travis I never will. The Flying M is an empire I did not create and one I never asked to inherit. There is one bright prospect though. Michael says he plans to return one of these days. He'll most likely go to Texas A&M. So maybe a Martin will once again run the Flying M."

"Sounds real good to me, cause I don't know how many more years I can keep on going myself. Hard to find good hands nowadays. Young folks all want to take off for the big cities where they can get those high paying jobs for a half a day's work."

"I'll tell you, Travis, there are some things we can do to cut down on the workload. I'll lease out part of the place and apply to put some of the ranch in the Grasslands Program. Wilcox will continue to handle all the finances, so all you have to do is come up with enough profit each year to pay the taxes."

"We can do that. We'll keep the spread going till Michael's ready to take over."

Jake asked about the Washingtons and told Travis to see to anything they might need. Then he added, "Flo had a lot of good friends. I want you and your Mrs. to see to it that all of Flo's things, particularly her favorite antiques, are distributed equally among them."

"Give it all away, Little Jake?"

"Yes Travis, give it all away and as soon as the house is empty, board it up. The place here belonged to two of the finest people God ever put on this earth and I don't want anyone else ever living here again."

ANOTHER ASIAN WAR

Enrico Fermi predicted in 1940, atomic energy would power everything from locomotives to ships in the future. The newly created U.S. Air Force took Fermi's prediction seriously and in early 1950, asked for development proposals for an atomic powered airplane.

Kelly Johnson's group at Lockheed and some researchers from MIT had already done much of the preliminary studies for the project called the Nuclear Energy Powered Aircraft. The NEPA project, code named Pluto by the Air Force, proposed using a Convair B-36 airframe.

Jake received a request for Martin Aero to bid on portions of the subcontract work for the program. Jake and Dan flew to Andrews AFB at the request of the Air Force brass. The civilian research team presented their findings at a formal conference to brief all of the potential subcontractors on the project.

The NEPA conference was held in a large, theater-style briefing room with the doors to the meeting guarded by heavily armed Air Policemen. Everyone attending had been cleared for Top Secret.

The Air Force general in charge of the project introduced four nuclear scientists who expounded on the various methods by which atomic energy could be used to power a ram jet engine. Long-range bombers using these engines would have unlimited range and endurance.

Jake rose several times from his seat during the meeting to ask questions.

"What is the potential for flight crews and ground crews exposure to radiation?" He also asked, "What are the dangers posed if such an aircraft were to crash into a populated area?"

Each time, he was given an unsatisfactory answer.

During a break in the meeting, Jake and Dan were in the hallway outside the briefing room discussing the project and Jake said, "Can't see it, Dan. Looks to me like they're fixing to kill a bunch of people from radiation exposure. I don't believe we want to be a part of this project."

Jake walked over to the Coke machine and reached in his pocket for some change. As usual, he had none and Dan offered him a handful of change. When Jake looked at the price of the Cokes on the machine, he exclaimed, "When in the heck did a Coca Cola go up to ten cents?"

"Do you want a Coke or not," Dan asked. "I'm buying."

Dan was about to put two dimes in the machine when the general in charge of the project and some of his staff came down the hall.

Jake stopped the general and said, "I need to visit with you privately for a few minutes, General."

The general looked around for a place other than the hallway to talk. One of the general's aides pointed to a small office just off the corridor.

"Certainly, Mr. Martin. We can use this office here," and he motioned towards the office door his aide was holding open.

Dan followed Jake into the office. One of the general's aides and a scientist from the Nuclear Regulatory Commission accompanied them.

Jake began by raising all of the same questions he asked earlier that day in the formal meeting.

The general listened patiently and then replied, "I understand your concerns and I too have many of the same concerns. Unfortunately, we simply do not have all the answers at this time. The best explanation I can give you is that soldiers and airmen are often asked to attack the enemy, even into direct gunfire. From the beginning of any military operations, it is always known there will be a certain number of casualties. We are in a cold war with the Soviet Union and it may be necessary for men to die in different ways during the execution of this war."

"General, that's one of the most eloquent bullshit speeches I've heard in a long time. Seems like I recall Patton saying, 'It's not a soldier's job to die for his country, but to make the other poor bastard die for his.' Maybe you should consider Patton's advice!"

"I'm sorry you feel that way, Mr. Martin. Maybe you and your company shouldn't be a part of this project?"

Jake looked over at Dan.

"No, I don't think we do want to be a part of this project. Do we, Dan?"

Dan shook his head no and looked down at the floor.

Turning back to the general, Jake said, "You'll have to excuse us from the rest of your meetings. We're going to leave now. I have some peacetime airplane designs we need to be working on."

As Jake turned to leave, the general remarked, "I hope we can keep the peace long enough for you to build them!"

"It's hard to make war on your friends," Jake mumbled as he walked away.

"I'm sorry, Mr. Martin, I didn't quite understand what you meant by that last comment?"

"Nothing, General. Just something an old friend of mine said one time," and Jake waved with the back of his hand as he and Dan went out the door.

***

Jake held a strong admiration for Douglas MacArthur, more for his handling of war-torn Japan than the general's military accomplishments.

Jake listened, along with the rest of the nation on April 19th of 1951, to MacArthur's farewell address when the old soldier spoke before congress saying, "It has been said, in effect, that I was a warmonger. Nothing could be further from the truth. I know war as few other men now living know it, and nothing to me is more revolting. I have long advocated its complete abolition as a means of settling international disputes... Armageddon will be at our door and all material and cultural developments of the past two thousand years will not save us. It must be of the spirit if we are to save the flesh."

MacArthur's speech only served to reinforce Jake's belief he had made the correct decision when he pulled his company out of the Pluto Project.

***

The decade of the 1950s proved to be a transition period for the United States as well as for Jake, his family and his companies.

Martin Aero continued to successfully market the TwinStar models. When the new lighter weight, six-cylinder, turbo-charged engines for the new MT-27 became available, production on the pressurized cabin TurboStar commenced.

The new model would cruise faster and higher than any competitor's aircraft in the same class. Orders poured in so fast, the company doubled its production schedule.

Boeing introduced a commercial version of the Air Force's C-135, the new 707 airliner. As a result, Jake grew even more optimistic about developing a small corporate jet for business use in the near future.

If nothing else good came from the modernization of the Air Force, at least the CAP squadrons, which Jake continued to support, got all the used Beech T-34 tandem trainers to replace their old worn out reconnaissance aircraft. The Air Force training command claimed the little T-34s were too easy to fly.

Lora returned from her six months of study at the fashion design school in Paris and attended four semesters at UCLA before coming to her father to tell him she had decided she would like to return to Paris for the summer.

Michael finished high school and during his first year at Texas A&M in College Station, he signed up for Officer's Candidate School. Michael proved to be a better student in college than he had been in high school and graduated early with a degree in engineering. He jokingly told his father, "I graduated in that half of the class, which made the top half of the class possible."

Michael accepted a commission as a 2nd lieutenant in the Marine Corps and completed his officer's training at Quantico, Virginia. From there, he went on to aviation flight school at Pensacola Naval Air Station in Florida to begin his training to become a jet fighter pilot.

Chen was still at home and had not yet finished high school when Lora and Michael left home. He was a good kid and never got into any kind of trouble. He had a great personality and people naturally took a liking to him.

Jake told Suzette, "That kid could sell ice cubes to the Eskimos."

Chen was more into hot rods than surfing. He ran with a different crowd than Michael and Jake taught Chen a lot about working on old cars. Chen wasn't keen on going to college after high school, but promised his mother he would enroll at UCLA and at least give college a try.

On a Saturday afternoon when Jake was out running errands, Suzette got a long distance phone call from Lora in France and when Jake arrived home, Suzette met him at the door to say, "Lora called while you were gone and she is flying home from Paris on the next available flight. She said she has something very important to talk to us about."

"Talk to us about what?"

"She wouldn't say. She just said the she would talk to us about it when she got home."

"What flight is she on? When will she get in?"

"She said not to worry about picking her up at LAX because she wasn't sure exactly which flight she'd be able to book and she would take a cab here from the airport. Jake, quit fretting over her. She's a grown woman now and is used to being on her own and taking care of herself."

"She's still my little girl, I'll worry if I want to."

***

A day and a half later, Lora arrived home.

Jake was out in the far back part of the yard standing not far from the edge of the small cliff overlooking the ocean. He had been watching a small flock of pelicans diving on a school of fish offshore and turned when he heard Lora's voice from the patio.

"Hi Dad, I'm home!"

Lora ran across the yard to hug her father and they walked arm in arm back to the house.

They paused for a few minutes on the patio steps to visit and Lora said, "Daddy, there's someone waiting in the living room I want you to meet."

"Your friends are always welcome here, Lora. Tell them to come on out here on the patio."

"I'd rather you meet him in the front room."

"Oh, it's a him, is it?" Jake commented as he went into the house with Lora.

As Jake and Lora entered the living room, Suzette was seated visiting with a tall, slender young man.

The young man stood up as they entered.

"Daddy, this is Douglas Westbrook. Doug, this is my father, Jake Martin."

"Pleased to meet you, sir. I feel like I already know you. Lora has told me so much about you and Mrs. Martin."

Even though Doug spoke perfect English, Jake assumed the young man was French.

"You and Suzette been visiting? I imagine she enjoyed having someone to brush up on her French with."

"No," Suzette replied in her usual gracious manner, "when Lora introduced us, I greeted Doug in French, but he apologized that he did not speak the language."

"Oh, where were you born then, Doug?"

"Right here in Los Angeles. I grew up over in Palo Alto, but Lora and I met in Scotland," and Doug went on to explain that he would soon be graduating from Harvard law school and would join his father's firm, a prominent local Los Angeles law firm.

Lora interrupted to explain, "My friend and I had gone to London for a few days. We wanted to see the castle at Edinburgh and I remembered you and Mom telling me about your drive through Scotland in 1943. So a girlfriend and I took the Flying Scotsman train from London to Edinburgh."

Lora had called Suzette Mom for a long time now.

Doug excitedly joined in to help Lora tell the story, "I had been to St. Andrews where I met up with my father and some of his friends. He's an avid golfer and it had always been his ambition to play the famous Old Course at St. Andrews. The next day, I was waiting on the train to return to London and that's when I met Lora. I visited with her at the station and on the train back to London."

Lora picked up the story again, "And when I went to take the plane back over to Paris, Doug followed me. We haven't been apart one day since."

"And exactly why am I being told all this?" Jake asked sarcastically even though he already had his suspicions.

"Well, you see, sir. It's that we would like to, I mean I want to ask…" Doug stammered.

"Dad! What he's trying to say is we want to get married. I think its called asking for my hand in marriage, but there is a minor problem Doug wants to ask you about."

"You see, sir, most of my family are of Scottish descent and of course, we are Presbyterian. Lora tells me you've always been an Episcopalian. Is that going to be a problem between our families?"

Suzette looked at Jake and smiled. Jake saw the look and he knew why she had smiled. Even though Suzette had attended the Episcopal Church with Jake ever since they were married, she had never converted from Catholicism.

"You see, Mr. Martin, I know it's traditional for a couple to get married in the bride's church."

"What he means, Dad, is his mother wants the wedding to be held at their church."

Jake looked away so as not to allow Doug and Lora to see him smile. Jake was so pleased his daughter would be living closer to home that their request amused him.

"Lora, you know I believe your grandma's father was a Scotsman. I never knew him. Some claimed he was a horse thief." Jake had made the last part up. "Doug, is this Presbyterian God of yours the same God that marries couples over at the Episcopal Church?"

"Oh, Daddy, I love you!" Lora said knowing that was a yes answer and she hugged her Dad's neck, then Doug's.

Suzette hugged Lora and Doug.

Jake shook Doug's hand and said to Lora, "But don't expect me to play golf with your new in-laws. I hate that game," and everyone laughed.

Douglas Westbrook and Lora Ann Martin were married two months later in a lavish wedding ceremony at the Presbyterian Church where the Westbrooks were members.

Michael came home on furlough for Lora's wedding and after the wedding Lora told him, "You looked so handsome in your full dress Marine Corps lieutenant's uniform!" and jokingly added, "You took all the attention away from the bride. All the ladies were looking at you instead of me."

***

Jake, Suzette, Dan and Ida flew down to Pensacola in one of the new MT-27s for Michael's flight school graduation and the awarding of his Navy Wings of Gold ceremony. Jake had been wanting to try out one of the new fully pressurized TurboStar models on a long cross-country and this seemed like a good opportunity.

At the pinning on of the wings ceremony, all of the cadets in training were in formation dressed in summer khaki uniforms. The graduating pilots were in full dress summer whites standing at attention in front of the reviewing stand. Parents, wives and girlfriends gathered on both sides for the ceremony.

The air station captain gave a welcoming speech to the guests. The pinning on of the gold Navy wings on each of the graduating cadets followed the captain's greeting. The pilot training squadron C.O., assisted by a chief petty officer passed by Michael without presenting him his wings.

When the last wings were pinned on, Michael's name was called to come forward to the podium.

Michael took a position beside the two presiding officers and stood at attention. The training squadron C.O. stepped forward to a microphone on the reviewing stand.

"Would aviation pioneer and veteran China Clipper Captain Jake Martin please come forward?"

Jake was taken completely by surprise and a little embarrassed as he went up to the podium in front of the microphone with Michael and the other two officers. The crowd gave Jake a polite round of applause.

The Commandant spoke into the microphone, "It is not often that we have a pilot cadet with such excellent scores in both academics and flight performance." He turned to Michael and Jake. "However, today we are privileged to be graduating such a pilot. It is my honor to present to you the cadet flying officer graduating at the top of his class, Marine Lieutenant Michael Martin."

The other Navy officer handed Jake a pair of gold Navy aviator wings and said, "Captain Martin, would you do the honor of pinning the wings on your son."

With that, the graduating cadets, officers and men let out a loud cheer and the crowd applauded wildly. A Navy band began to play as the Blue Angels came in low overhead and commenced an aerial aerobatics display.

After the ceremony, Dan congratulated Michael. Suzette and Ida gave Michael a big hug. Ida got lipstick on his cheek and wiped it off with her hankie.

Jake tried several times to tell his son how proud he was of him, but he more or less muffed every attempt.

Michael seemed to understand and everyone laughed when he modestly joked, "Maybe all those hours I spent busting my ass learning how to surf paid off. If nothing else, it may have taught me a little coordination and balance."

The old wounds between Michael and his father over Elizabeth had long since healed. Michael had turned into a fine young man. Jake considered it the ultimate compliment Michael had wanted to follow in his footsteps and become a pilot, but he knew his son's heart and true ambitions lay with the Flying M ranch back in Texas.

"You still planning on returning to ranching after you finish your tour of duty in the Marines?"

"Never more sure of anything in my life, Dad," and Michael asked, "How's the development of the new JetStar coming along. Plans off the drawing board yet?"

Jake explained about the JetStar project and asked Michael, "Where do you think you'll be stationed?"

"Right now, looks like I'll be sent to Gitmo, that's Guantanamo Bay, Cuba. I'll finish carrier qualification there and then it's on to F-4 school.

"Those aircraft carriers looked like a postage stamp when you see their deck from the air. Better a young flyer like you than me trying to hit a moving target like that at high speed. I'm getting too old for that much excitement."

A very attractive young blonde girl walked up and took hold of Michael's arm. Her face beamed with pride.

"Dad, I'd like you to meet Lisa," and Michael introduced Lisa to Suzette, Ida and Dan.

Lisa was a lovely, charming girl, but a little quiet.

That evening, the six of them went to dinner at a seafood place on one of the shrimp boat piers along the Gulf Coast. During the evening, it became obvious to all that Lisa and Michael were a lot closer than just friends.

***

The following day preparing to leave the Pensacola airport FBO, Dan asked Jake, "You want to stop by the Flying M and check on things? It's right on our way and this TurboStar is going to need one fuel stop to make it back to California anyway."

"No, I don't want to stop there. Everything's running fine on the ranch. They don't need me meddling in things. Suzette and Ida have been talking up going to Las Vegas and spending a couple of days at one of those fancy new resort casinos. Hughes recently purchased 27,000 acres out there on what they call The Strip. Vegas is fixin' to boom and I'd like to have a look at the place before it does."

"Yeah, I know," Dan said, cutting his eyes over to Ida standing next to Suzette waiting with anticipation for the outcome of their conversation. "Ida's mentioned it to me more than once. Where we going to stay, the Flamingo?"

"Nah, a bunch of mobsters own that place. I was thinking about the old El Rancho Vegas. They've remodeled the place and I understand the casino is pretty fancy now, kind of western saloon style."

"Yea," Ida cheered, looking at Suzette and clapping her hands excitedly. "That's the place one of my friends told me she saw Clark Gable and said she had seen all kinds of movie stars and celebrities there."

Jake went into the airport flight service office to check the weather and when he returned, he said, "Weather is severe-clear all the way, so if we get going we should be there mid-afternoon. I'll file direct to McCarran and ask for flight level two-two. Air should be smooth up there. A comfortable ride all the way, ladies."

Suzette sat in the back with Ida, so they could visit and Dan rode up front in the right seat with Jake.

As Jake started his takeoff roll from Pensacola, Ida hollered, "Look out Vegas, here we come!"

After two nights in Vegas, Jake announced, "I've enjoyed all I can stand of this place!"

Dan concurred and the foursome flew back to Culver City right after lunch.

***

The Soviet Union put Sputnik in orbit in October of 1957, which placed the United States second in the race to space. America would now have to play catch up. The electronics industry was growing faster than any other field of development and the aerospace industry was right behind it. Jake's Texas instrument company stock had quadrupled in value in the last two years alone.

Lydia stayed on as housekeeper even after the kids were grown and had left home. This gave Suzette more free time to became active in several church related charities.

With no children at home, Jake thought Suzette needed a dog to keep her company. She mentioned one time she thought the little Scottish terrier like FDR's was cute, but she had never actually said she wanted one. Buying her a dog was Jake's idea.

Jake stopped by a pet shop on his way home from work to buy her a puppy. In the process of picking out a Scottish terrier for her, he made the mistake of picking up and holding a furry little golden yellow Labrador pup. He ended up buying both dogs. Now how was he going to explain two dogs to Suzette?

When Jake got home, he left the Lab puppy in his car. He carried Suzette's new puppy into the house and handed the pup to her. After he was certain she liked the little girl pup, he went out to the car to get the other pup he had bought.

Returning with the Lab puppy, he explained, "Can't let a little dog grow up by itself, needs a companion."

The little Scottie puppy grew up with the big Lab and she boxed his ears many times when they were still pups. Because of this, the little Scottie had her bluff in on the big dog after they were grown. Jake contended that was exactly the way Suzette always had her bluff in on him.

***

Late on a Friday afternoon in December of 1961, Gertie came into Jake's office and seated herself in one of the guest chairs in front of Jake's desk.

Jake knew without asking, this was going to be a personal conversation.

"I want you to know what a privilege it's been to work for you these past twenty years, Mr. Martin."

As Gertie began, Jake thought this did not sound to him like a very good opening sentence.

"What's on your mind, Gertie?"

"I've struggled with this for some weeks now, but I believe the time has come for me to retire."

"What will you do?"

"I plan to move to Florida and live with my daughter. She has asked me to come and stay with her until I can find a little place of my own nearby."

"Your daughter! I didn't know you had a daughter. All these years, and you never once mentioned a daughter? Heck, I didn't even know you were ever married."

"I've never been married, Mr. Martin."

"Oh, guess that's the reason you never mentioned it."

"My daughter was raised by her father. I knew very little of her until recently when she came to visit me a few months ago and we got to know one another."

"So, you're going to retire in a couple of years?"

"No sir, if it's okay with you, I would like to go ahead and give my two weeks notice now."

"It's dang well not okay," Jake blustered and then paused to ponder the matter for a moment. "But things have to be what they have to be, I guess. I'll miss you, Gertie. Won't be the same around here without you."

***

On the day Gertie left Martin Aero, everyone who had worked with her crowded into the break room for a send-off. Suzette brought a large cake with "Happy Retirement" on it from the bakery and Jake made a short speech.

"We've all decided that old Chevrolet of yours probably won't make it to Florida, so in lieu of a gold watch, we've gotten you this!" and he pointed out the window to a shiny new white Chevrolet Bellaire in the parking lot as he handed Gertie the keys.

Gertie started to cry, but kept her usual composure.

Of course, it had been Jake who purchased the new car for Gertie even though he insisted the car was part of her retirement bonus.

"I'd have gotten you a Cadillac, Gertie, but I knew your modesty wouldn't have let you drive it."

After Gertie left the company, Jake went through a half dozen secretaries, but never found one he cared for. One week, he sent three in a row packing out of his office.

Jake finally gave up and told Dan, "I'll just use the secretarial pool when I need something typed."

Suzette started coming into Jake's office a half day twice a week to organize things and work on some of his projects of a more confidential nature.

***

Lora opened the dress shop she had always planned to open on Rodeo Drive and it became an overnight success. She kept on working right through her first pregnancy.

When Lora gave birth to a baby, she announced, "If we're going to hang a name like Westbrook on the boy, I'm at least going to pick out the other two names."

She named her newborn son after her dad's grandfather and after her dad's family, as she knew Jake would never have approved of her calling him Jacob Teel. She named the boy John Martin Westbrook, but everyone called him Johnny.

Chen attended college at UCLA for two years, but decided college wasn't for him. While at UCLA, Chen met Sue Lee, a beautiful young Oriental-American girl and they were married the summer after they met.

Sue Lee, Chen's new wife, was a talented artist and worked part-time as a magazine illustrator while continuing her junior year at UCLA working on a degree in Fine Arts.

Jake took care of Sue Lee's school expenses at UCLA and told her, "If Chen won't take the money to go to college, then we'll use the money to put you through."

When Sue Lee became pregnant, Suzette told Chen, "Sue Lee does not need to be working with all her school studies and a new baby coming."

"I agree, Mom, but you tell her. I've tried. She loves what she does, so I just let her do what she wants."

Chen continued his old car hobby and began restoring them, but he still drove an old Lincoln Jake had given him. He took a job in the sales department with a Los Angeles Ford dealer and proved to be a natural born salesman. The owner promoted him to sales manager in less than a year.

Chen and Sue Lee had a daughter, which they named Chena Sue and Jake called her, "His little China Doll."

Suzette loved having the grandkids and kept Johnny and Chena whenever the opportunity arose. Lora continued to be busy with her dress shop and her husband's social activities, and before long her second child was on the way. Lora hoped for a girl this time and if a girl, she intended to name her Kathryn.

Jake told Lora, "There's no point naming the child Kathryn, because everyone's going to call her Katy anyway," and when Lora gave birth to a girl, she named her Kathryn and everyone called her Katy.

Jake and Suzette received a letter from Michael saying he had been promoted to captain. He wrote he expected to be transferred to a new fighter squadron on the USS Ticonderoga CVA-14 and would be deployed to the western Pacific for about six months. After which, he was looking forward to completing his tour of duty and coming home.

***

The summer of 1962 was exceptionally hot and dry in Los Angeles, but good flying weather. As a result the preliminary flight-testing on the prototype of the new eight-seat, twin rear-engine corporate MJ-27 JetStar had been completed in record time. The aircraft would soon be ready for final FAA certification.

Jake was in his office seated at his old wooden drafting table reviewing some JetStar drawings when Dan entered with a Marine major and a gunny sergeant. Dan introduced the two Marines to Jake and excused himself.

"What, may I ask, brings two Marines to my office this morning?" but judging from the serious look on their faces, Jake wasn't sure he wanted to hear the answer.

The officer cleared his throat, "Mr. Martin, it is our duty to inform you that your son, Marine Captain Michael Martin, has been killed in the performance of his duty."

The reality of the officer's statement did not fully sink in and Jake reacted with no emotion. He was in total emotional shock and seemed to be inquiring as though he was only an uninterested party. Denial and his automatic defensive mechanisms had taken over.

"How'd it happen?"

"The details are sketchy, but it happened while flying an unarmed reconnaissance mission over Indo China, some call it Vietnam now, sir." the gunny sergeant replied.

"Was it an accident?"

"No sir, not exactly. Seems the Russians have given the North Vietnamese army some smaller versions of the high altitude surface-to-air-missiles they used to shoot down Gary Powers' U-2," the officer explained.

Jake was only half listening.

"Sir, sir! Are you okay?"

Jake looked up and said, "I'm sorry, please go on."

"Captain Martin was flying a photo reconnaissance F-4 when his aircraft took a hit from a SAM. Some French Foreign Legion troops on the ground observed the incident and reported the aircraft disintegrated in mid-air. There were no parachutes. Michael and his electronics officer are both listed as lost in the line of duty. Because we are not at war, they could not be listed as missing in action."

Jake sat quietly looking down at the floor.

"Is there anything we can do for you, sir?"

"No, but thank you for coming in person."

After the two Marines left, Jake went over to a chair by the window and stared off into the distance where he sat until well after dark.

Dan, of course, had spoken with the two Marines when they arrived and waited before going in to sit with Jake.

"Years ago you told me of a book you read as a boy and of a passage. 'There be dragons out there,' I believe is what it said. Do you remember?"

"You think I no longer need to hunt for them. Is that what you're saying, Dan? "

"I'm afraid they've found you instead, Jake."

After a period of silence, Jake asked, "Would you call Suzette and tell her about Michael? I don't think I can."

"I already have and she's in pretty bad shape. You need to go on home, Jake. I'll drive you?"

"No, tell her I'll be on along in a little bit. I just want to sit here for a while longer."

***

In the weeks and months that followed, Jake threw himself into his work. He dealt with Michael's loss by staying busy. Suzette understood and on nights when Jake worked late at the factory on the new JetStar, she would bring his dinner to him. She would sit their meal on a box or workbench out in the factory and they would have dinner together.

The prototype JetStar passed all of the FAA type certification testing and Martin Aero went into all out production on the new corporate jet. Soon, the first five production JetStars neared completion for delivery.

Those working with Jake kidded him about getting to be as bad as ol' Howard Hughes wanting to do the hands-on development. Occasionally, work would be held up and generally for something waiting on Jake's approval, but Jake would contend he was only double-checking so as to insure they were building the best airplane they could.

Jake was bent over under production model Number One with an engineer and one of the lead foremen. They were discussing a more efficient way to mate the undercarriage to the airframe when Dan walked up with two civilians from the Defense Department.

"Jake, we need you for a meeting. These two gentlemen have a government contract proposal for the company."

Jake came out from under the suspended airframe of the JetStar and stood full up. Wiping his hands on a shop towel, he politely shook hands with the two gentlemen as Dan introduced them.

"I haven't got time for a long meeting right now. What's on your mind, gentlemen?"

The one DOD civilian appeared to take offense at Jake's directness and replied, "As you may already be aware there is an increasing threat of war in Indo China."

"You mean Vietnam, don't you?"

The man let Jake's comment pass and went on to explain, "We need reliable contractors to produce the new airborne rocket systems which we will need for our aircraft if the President decides to pursue military action."

"Not interested."

"What do you mean, you're not interested?"

"We don't do military contracts anymore. We're a civil aviation aircraft manufacturer. Thanks for stopping by," Jake said and turned to go back to work on the JetStar.

"Mr. Martin, I've read your dossier in the FBI file. There were some questions in World War II about your being of German descent. Then in the early fifties, you backed out of the Pluto Project. If you turn down this contract, you'll never get another chance at a government contract again. You'll be blacklisted."

That last remark was all Jake intended to take.

"Look, you war mongering bureaucratic bastard, I flew against the Japanese before they ever attacked Pearl Harbor. I built bombers and delivered them to Europe and I gave my only son to one of your rotten military operations. In the words of that old hymn, 'I ain't gonna study war no more,' so get the hell out of my factory and don't ever come back."

The Setting Sun

On a beautiful no moon night the evening of July 7th, 1963, Jake and one of the company pilots were descending into Los Angeles in the new MJ-27 JetStar demonstrator. They were approaching the city from the north and had not yet been cleared out of their cruising altitude.

The clear black sky caused a billion stars to shine even brighter. The starlit night sky stretched out over the Pacific and disappeared in the distant haze at the edge of the world. Saturn shown brightest of all and was about to set on the western horizon.

With the JetStar throttled back in the still evening air, they seemed as though suspended on a magic carpet above a vast blanket of city lights.

Jake was seated in the copilot position. The newest company pilot, an ex-Air Force officer who had flown F-86 jets in Korea, was flying the aircraft. He had not been with Martin Aero very long.

Jake was returning from Boeing, Seattle where he attended a meeting as a technical adviser for Pan Am. He went to help work out problems with the modifications on the newest 700 series aircraft. Pan Am intended to place an order for ten of the new larger Boeing jets. Martin Aero would be doing some of the avionics and interior work on a sub-contract basis and Trippe requested Jake represent them at the preliminary design meeting.

During the meeting, Trippe's latest request for Boeing to build a Jumbo jet with an upper level flight deck was also reviewed. Trippe held the view that if a cargo version of such a large aircraft crashed, the load might come forward and crush the flight crew.

Jake did not know for sure if Boeing would take the financial gamble and build the 747 now on the drawing board, but he suspected Boeing was going to seriously consider trying.

Although the concept originated as the brainchild of Juan Trippe, after Boeing built the 747, a man named Halaby took over Pan Am and claimed credit for the idea.

Jake was going over the recent meeting in his mind. As he watched out the cockpit window to his right, he marveled at how much the city had grown and spread out. He often flew over the L.A. area in the daytime, but the lights at night lit up the urban sprawl so much more profoundly.

"Los Angeles Approach this is JetStar November Three Six Juliet, flight level two one, requesting ILS to LAX," the pilot radioed.

"Roger, Three Six Juliet. Squawk zero four two five," came the reply from approach control.

The pilot selected the new transponder code.

"Three Six Juliet, radar contact, fifteen miles north of the outer marker. Cleared out of your cruising altitude direct to the approach fix for runway Two Five Right. Advise when you have the airport in sight."

"Three six Juliet. We have the airport. Understand cleared for the approach."

"Roger, Three Six Juliet, contact the tower now on one two five point eight."

The pilot switched frequencies. "Los Angeles Tower, Three Six Juliet is with you."

The blue outer marker light came on and the ADF needle rotated 180 degrees. The pilot lowered the gear and set the flaps for landing.

"Three Six Juliet cleared to land Two Five Right. Your traffic is a light twin on roll out, should not be a factor."

The JetStar pilot continued to monitor the tower frequency as he should have and had not yet switched to ground control.

A separate radio transmission, to which the pilot and Jake were not privy, took place over the ground control frequency and was as follows, "Trans-Continental ninety-five hold short of the active. I have a corporate jet on short final."

The ILS on the JetStar's flight director locked onto the glide slope and their vertical speed indicator pegged at five hundred feet a minute rate of decent.

Ahead in the shadows of the runway lights, the JetStar's landing lights lit up the blacktop and Jake caught a glimpse of an aircraft's silhouette crossing the runway.

The Trans-Continental airliner had misunderstood or not heard the ground controller's instructions. The airliner's crew committed one of the most lethal of all on-airport mistakes, a runway incursion.

"Look out! There's an aircraft crossing in front of us!" Jake exclaimed, but his seat was slid back too far to reach the controls.

With the JetStar's sink-rate already established, recovery from their descent was not an option. The pilot applied full power, but the turbine spool-up time was not sufficient. What partial power the engines did produce, broke the jet's descent just enough to keep the JetStar from settling onto the top of the airliner.

Still there was a horrendous crashing noise as they passed over the tail of the airliner. The right landing gear of the JetStar had struck the upper portion of the airliner's vertical stabilizer.

"I'm going around!" the pilot said to Jake,

"No! There's plenty of runway left. Take what you got. We don't know what the damage is."

Jake had made the right call. Adequate runway remained and the landing gear would not have retracted.

Unknown to Jake and the pilot at that time was that the damaged gear strut would collapse on touchdown and puncture the fuel cell in the right wing.

The pilot made an excellent flare-out to landing, but when the full weight of the aircraft settled onto the busted landing gear, the strut collapsed.

Jake braced himself, but his head hit the sun visor, which broke and scratched his face causing it to bleed.

The pilot reached for the thrust reversers, but as he did he was thrown forward and jammed his right wrist into the instrument panel.

The JetStar veered sideways as the left landing gear fully collapsed, but continued to skid down the runway for about a quarter mile spewing sparks like an Independence Day Roman-candle as it went. The pilot held the plane as straight as he could with nose gear steering and what little rudder control still remained.

Jake's subconscious memory instantly recalled the sickening sounds of crunching metal and things breaking in the old Yankee Clipper. Those sounds are indelibly imprinted forever into any crash survivors mind.

As the JetStar slid to a stop, Jake reached for the all-kill electrical switch and turned the fuel selector switches to off.

"Get out of here!" Jake yelled and the pilot followed him out of the cockpit.

Jake reached the rear exit door first and turned the lever. The airstair door would not open.

The pilot, holding his right wrist with his left hand, gave the door a good hard kick with his foot and the door fell open.

Both men jumped to the tarmac and ran a hundred or so feet from the JetStar before stopping to look back.

There had been no time to declare an emergency, but the tower observed the collision. Two fire trucks and an ambulance were already on their way out to the aircraft by the time Jake stopped to catch his breath.

"I guess we got lucky on this one. Doesn't look like she's gonna burn after all."

"I swear I smelled jet fuel when the door opened!"

No sooner had the pilot uttered those words, than the fuel from the leaking wing bladder contacted the red hot metal of the steel undercarriage, which had ground against the runway surface. The aircraft burst into flames. Both men ducked instinctively and ran further back from the aircraft.

An ambulance pulled up beside Jake and his pilot as two fire trucks passed them up and began spraying foam on the burning JetStar.

***

An employee at the Executive Aircraft Service center where Jake based the JetStar saw the crash and had called Jake's home number and talked to Lora who happened to be there visiting with Suzette.

Jake and his pilot arrived at the hospital by ambulance and Suzette and Lora arrived at the hospital only shortly after they had been admitted.

The pilot's wrist appeared to be broken and they took him to x-ray.

Jake kept insisting he was okay, but judging from the scrapes and cuts on Jake's face from the sun visor, Suzette did not believe him.

Suzette had called Jake's personal doctor to meet them at the hospital and he gave Jake a thorough going over.

After the exam, the doctor said to Suzette and Lora, "I assured you Jake is all right, but I need to talk with my patient in private for a moment, so if you two would excuse us for a few minutes?"

Suzette objected, but Jake asked her to go on.

"I know you asked me not to discuss the matter with your family," the doctor said to Jake, "but that heart murmur of yours is not going to get any better and things like this don't help any."

"You mean that thing with my heart you told me had been caused by a fever I had when I was a kid. Aw, Doc, I'm fine. I've lived with it all my life and I know how to pace myself."

"Jake, I can't revoke your pilot's license because you don't fly commercial anymore, but you're going to have to stop pushing yourself so hard all the time. Modern medicine has no fix for what you have. You're going to have to ease up."

"Listen Doc, I've defied death more times than I can count. I've been thrown from horses, shot at several times and survived two airplane crashes. If a hundred thousand miles of ocean can't kill me, a little heart murmur is not going to do it!"

"Look Jake, take things a little easier. Okay?"

"Wilco! Can I go home now, Doc?"

"Yeah, I'll fill out the release forms. Oh, and you owe me a ride in one of those new executive jets for getting me out in the middle of the night."

"You got it, any time. Thanks for your trouble."

While Jake sat waiting with Lora and Suzette for his release from the hospital, Lora started in on her father.

"Dad, you're getting to old to be flying around in jets. Why don't you leave the flying to the younger guys."

"That's so very like you, Lora, to ask me to stop flying. I've never crashed an airplane in my life." Before Lora could protest, he added, "Although a couple of other pilots have tried to kill me once or twice. Oh, there was the time I scraped a wing tip, but that don't count."

Suzette chimed in, "Lora's right. You shouldn't be flying jets and you shouldn't be flying at night."

Just then Jake's new company pilot walked up with his wrist in a fresh cast and his arm in a sling.

Jake smiled and pointed to the pilot. "I wasn't flying, he was."

Suzette looked at the pilot and then back at Jake.

"Well then, maybe you should have been!" she said disgustedly.

Jake laughed and said to his pilot, "See, you can't win an argument with a woman."

The pilot attempted to apologize saying, "Look, boss, I'm really sorry. I tried my best to miss that idiot who crossed the runway in front of us."

"Don't worry about it. I was there remember? I saw the whole thing. You did everything you could. I couldn't have done any better myself. We can build more planes, but good pilots are hard to come by. Forget it and thank God you'll live to fly another day. Go on home and take a couple days off. I'll see you next week."

Jake went over to the Coke machine and fumbled in his pocket for some change. He looked up and reading the sign on the machine "Please Deposit 25¢" he asked, "When in the heck did Cokes go up to twenty-five cents?"

Lora shrugged her shoulders and smirked.

Turning to Suzette, Jake said, "Let's go home."

"We haven't checked you out yet."

"I'm sure they'll send us a bill. Where'd you park the car?" Jake asked as he headed for the exit door.

Suzette and Lora grabbed their purses and scurried to catch up with him.

***

The morning of Jake's fifty-first birthday, July 28th, 1963, Jake had gone to the office to clean up some paperwork. He returned home shortly after noon because Suzette was planning a birthday dinner and he had been ordered to be home early.

Only family was coming as Jake had indicated he was not in the mood for a big party.

Lydia was cooking all of Jake's favorite dishes for the evening and Jake went to the kitchen to see Suzette who was helping Lydia. Suzette had flour on her hands and leaned over to give her husband a kiss on the cheek.

"Chena is out on the patio playing with your two dogs. Chen dropped her off earlier. He and Sue Lee went shopping at the new mall, but they'll be back for dinner. Go spend some time with your granddaughter."

Jake changed into an old golf shirt and a pair of baggy khaki work pants, which he generally wore around the house and went out on the patio. He found Chena sitting on the ground with the two dogs rubbing their bellies and the two old dogs loved it.

Chena's eyes lit up when she saw Jake.

"Hi Grampa."

Jake sat down on the ground with four-year old Chena and the two dogs.

"How's my little China Doll today?"

"I fine, Grampa."

The afternoon sun loomed high in the sky and Jake soon went over to his favorite chaise longue on the patio to stretch out. He was still a little sore from the crash, but would not admit the fact to anyone.

Jake's favorite chaise longue was the one with just the right view of the ocean between the two leaning palm trees. Lydia had placed a pitcher of sweet ice tea with lemon, the way Jake liked it, on the small patio table.

Jake heard a car pull up out front and he thought it sounded like Lora's car. In a minute, Johnny, Lora's six-year old son, came running through the patio door and jumped on the chaise longue with Jake, but squirmed down when he saw Chena and the two dogs. With Johnny there, the quiet petting soon turned into a game of chase between the kids and the dogs.

Lora came through the patio door right behind Johnny with her almost two-year old daughter, Katy, in her arms.

"Hi, Dad, here's someone who wants to see you," she said sitting Katy on Jake's belly. "I'll go see what Mom and Lydia are up to. Watch the kids for me."

An airliner glistened in the sun as it climbed out from Los Angeles headed west. Jake called Johnny and Chena over to him.

Pointing to the distant plane he explained, "See that big airplane? It's probably headed for Hawaii or maybe to Asia where your grandmother and I first met. The people on that airplane are going to a far off land where they will meet people with strange and different ways."

The children watched the distant airliner leaving a contrail behind its flight path, but soon lost interest in what Jake was telling them. The two dogs had been waiting patiently to play chase again and the kids ran off after them.

Jake put Katy down to go run after the dogs with Johnny and Chena. He leaned back to watch the small armada of pleasure boats making their way up and down the coastline a mile or so offshore.

Lora came back out onto the patio and Jake asked, "Where's your husband this evening, Mrs. Westbrook?"

Lora had become her father's closest counsel the last few years. She pulled one of the lawn chairs into the shade near where he was sitting. She instinctively knew when her father wanted to talk to her about something.

"Oh you know, Dad, he's on the board of directors over at the Getty. They're having some fancy reception for a bunch of the patrons tonight. I'll need to go over there later and make an appearance. Would it be okay if I leave the kids here for a while?"

"Sure, that's fine. Johnny is over here almost every Saturday night anyway. Says he likes our new TV better than the one he has at home. The only way I can get him to go to bed is to turn the television off. How's your dress shop on Rodeo Drive doing?" Jake always pronounced the street's name like a cowboy rodeo to tease Lora.

"Great. In fact, I'm talking with a manufacturing house about starting my own line. How does 'Designs by Lora' sound to you?"

"Sounds pretty highfalutin to me, kid."

"Word on the street is you're cutting back on aircraft production. I thought the new executive jet was so popular you all were backordered for two years."

"They are, but you know Martin Aero lost all its government contracts."

"No, Martin Aero didn't lose them, Dad, you ran them off."

"Same difference," Jake smiled, because Lora always had his number.

"Dad, tell me something. What's the biggest dream you've ever had?"

"I guess I've fulfilled most of them."

"Well then, what would you do if you could start all over again?"

"Probably make all the same mistakes I made before," Jake chuckled.

"No, seriously."

"I'd start a jet cargo airline. A trans-ocean fleet of giant freighters with extended range. They'd have quarters onboard so the crews could fly in shifts like we did in the old Clippers." Jake paused to reflect and then he added, "But these modern airline pilots are a bunch of pansies about long flights compared to the routes we used to fly in the old days."

"All you old pilots feel that way about the new guys. Where would you have gotten the planes?"

"Buy them."

"What if you couldn't buy them?"

"If I couldn't buy them, I'd build them myself."

"Well there you are!"

"Think you're pretty sharp, don't you?"

Lora smiled smugly.

"Listen Lora, you're the executor of the Martin estate and I need your opinion about something."

"Shoot, Dad."

"We've had a couple of inquiries from both Raytheon and North American on the Aero aircraft line, but I'd rather Martin Aero become a major player in the new biz-jet market. To do that we'd have to embark on a major expansion and without liquidating most of my assets, we wouldn't have enough resources to expand."

"What would you do if you sold the company?"

"Selling the company wouldn't be my first choice. Dan is fixing to retire, but he's trained a fine young management team to take over. Halliburton and Schlumberger are interested in making an offer on the drilling equipment companies and Phillips made a standing offer on the oil leases years ago. I think I can raise the capital."

"Then that's what you should do!"

"The real question is what am I going to do with the Flying M ranch. Do you think Johnny or any of the family would ever want to be ranchers or run an oil empire?"

"The only one who ever showed the slightest interest in taking over Big Jake's empire was Michael," Lora said.

"I know," Jake replied with a certain sadness.

"Not me, that's for sure! The happiest day of my life was the day Grandma Flo brought me out here to California to live with you. And Johnny, well, the honest truth is my husband and the West brooks already have that boy's life planned out for him. I'm sure he'll go to Harvard and most likely join the Westbrook law firm after that. Poor kid doesn't have a chance."

"I didn't either, but I went my own way."

"There's not many like you, Dad. Look, it's your money. Do what you want with it. Sell the whole darn mess and start over again if that's what you want."

"Tell me something, Lora. Why were you and I always able to talk while Michael and I always locked horns over things?"

"That's an easy one. You were both too much alike. I've often wondered, am I like my real mother?"

"No Lora, your personality is more like Grandma Flo's," Jake smiled and added, "of course, you got your good looks and brains from me."

"Where did I get my humility?" Lora quipped and Jake laughed.

"Dad, there is something I've been wanting to tell you."

"Hope it's not bad news."

"Not really. It's more about a couple of ol' nosey women needing to 'fess up to what they've been into. I told Suzette I would tell you. The other day we were cleaning out the closets, going through kid's clothes and came across an unopened package from the Navy Department."

"Oh that. Never could bring myself to open it up."

"Well, we did. There were a few personal things, I guess from Michael's locker. Some medals, things of that sort, but we found a photo of Michael and this nice looking young blonde girl." Lora had the photo in her hand.

"Let me see it."

Lora handed him the photo.

"Yes, I remember her. The girl's name was Lisa. We met her in Pensacola when Michael graduated from flight school."

"That's who Suzette said she thought the girl was, too. Mom said you'd probably want to see the photo."

"Thanks. Yes, I'd like to keep it."

"Thought you might."

Jake studied the photo for a moment.

"Wonder what would have happened if she and Michael had married, maybe even had a son? You think he'd have wanted to be a rancher?"

"My guess is he'd probably have wanted to be an aviator like his father and his granddad."

Jake was still smiling at what Lora said as Dan came through the patio door.

"What's going on out here? Is this a private conversation or can anyone join in?"

Dan jumped back to keep from being knocked down by Jake's two dogs with Chena and Johnny right behind them. Katy came waddling past Dan with her diaper nearly down around her knees trying to catch up with the others.

Lora grabbed her up and hugged her.

"I'm going into the house with this one. Is Aunt Ida with you, Dan?"

"She's in the kitchen with your mom and Lydia," Dan replied as he went over to sit with Jake.

"Air's clear today. I can see the pier at Santa Monica from here," he said to Jake as he pulled up one of the patio chairs.

"You know Dan, I wish cars still had fenders, airplanes still had propellers and that damned atom bomb had never been invented!"

"I know. You've mentioned that several times before. I guess, considering what a jet airplane can do, they are magnificent machines."

"Yeah, but they take away the charm of travel and the mystery of far away places. Sometimes I long for the old days."

"Those aren't the times we live in, Jake."

"My ol' friend, Zack, used to say, 'Yous plays the cards yous is dealt.' That's what he used to say and there's a lot of wisdom in that."

"What other choice do you have?" Dan lamented.

"I guess to go kicking and screaming into madness?"

Jake and Dan had worked together now for almost twenty plus years. What they agreed on and what they disagreed on, had long since been established.

For most of Suzette and Jake's married life, the family had always eaten on the run or at the bar in the kitchen. Since the kids had moved out on their own, Jake and Suzette often had breakfast or late evening dinner at the small kitchen table by the bay window that looked out onto the backyard.

For entertaining and for special occasions like Jake's birthday, the formal dining room was used.

When the occasion was family, Jake always insisted on Lydia coming to the table, too. Suzette and Ida had been rushing around to help Lydia get everything ready so they could all sit down together.

Ida stuck her head out the patio door.

"Round up the kids and you all get washed up. Dinner's almost ready."

The dining room table was elegantly set with the good china and the silver, which Big Jake and Flo had given Suzette as a wedding present.

Chen and Sue Lee returned from shopping about the time dinner was ready and the entire family were seated for dinner.

The family sang a slightly off-key chorus of *Happy Birthday* to their patriarch.

Lydia sang, "Mr. Martin."

Lora and Chen sang, "Dad."

Johnny and Chena yelled out, "Grandpa."

All of which led to one indistinguishable name.

Dan offered a toast, "To Jake Martin. May the sunshine always follow you, may the wind be at your back and may you be in heaven at least an hour, before the devil knows you're dead!"

The clinking of crystal glasses with silverware and several saying, "Hear, Hear!" followed.

"Thank you, thank you all, Suzette would you offer the blessing for this fine dinner?"

Suzette bowed her head and crossed herself. "Hail Mary, full of grace…" she began.

When Suzette finished saying the prayer, Johnny yelled out, "Amen, pass the pickles."

"That was a lot funnier when you were littler," Lora said, but Suzette smiled at him indicating her approval.

During the course of the dinner conversation, Jake said to Chen, "Your mom says you have some good news to tell us. What's that all about?"

"Ever since I became sales manager down at the Ford dealer, I have been trying to figure out a way to start my own dealership. Turns out, Los Angeles is growing so fast Lincoln Motor Company has authorized another dealership in Pasadena. I applied for it and was officially awarded the franchise the day before yesterday."

"Congratulations Chen," Lora said, "that's really great news. We're all so proud of you."

The others around the table added their congratulations and good wishes to Chen on his new business venture.

At that point, Dan took the opportunity to make an announcement of his own. The announcement would not come as any surprise to Jake.

"Ida and I would like to let everyone here know that as of a week from Monday, we are going to officially retire."

"Oh, no." Suzette groaned.

"My long time business associate here," Dan smiled and gestured towards Jake, "has kept me here in California for so long it doesn't look like I'll ever get back to Texas to settle down and become a rancher. So Ida and I have bought one of those new GM motor homes and we're off to see the west."

To which Chen smiled and yelled out, "Booo!" Chen being a Ford man and everyone laughed.

"Chen, when Lincoln builds a motor home, I'll come and buy one from you." More laughter. "Anyway, we're headed north to Seattle and plan to come back through Nevada. Probably stop for a while in Las Vegas. I understand they've got a new show at the Sands starring the Rat Pack and of course, Sinatra is one of Ida's favorites."

Everyone applauded.

Chen asked Dan, "Why aren't you going to ranch?"

Dan replied, "Ranching is all too scientific now. They breed and feed cattle a lot different now than what I remember growing up. I think men have started to think they are gods and can create life."

"Reminds me of a joke," Jake began. "A scientist was arguing with God and God said if you're so smart, let's see you create life. So the scientist reached down for a handful of clay."

Lora and Ida yelled out in unison, "And God said, get your own clay," and both giggled.

"Sorry, Dad. We couldn't help it, but you have told that joke before."

"More than once." Suzette added. "Jake, at some point we all know you're going to tell us the story about the day you first rode in the ol' Jenny. Now is as good a time as any. You might as well tell the story now and get it out of the way."

Everyone laughed.

So Jake began, "You know the thing I always forget to tell when I tell this story is the day was my birthday. Over the years I've thought about it and I'm not real sure Big Jake hadn't planned the whole thing?"

The phone in the other room rang as Jake was telling his story and Lydia got up to go answer it. When she returned, she went over to Jake and whispered, "It's Larry Wilcox and he says he's returning your call."

Jake pushed his chair back from the table.

"I'll take the call in the study. What's for dessert, Lydia?" Jake asked as he left to go to the study.

***

"Sorry to be so long getting back to you with the info you requested," and Larry went on to fill Jake in on the details of the largest single business deal the Martin companies and Jake would ever put together.

Larry had been negotiating the deal for several weeks now. A land company that developed property near the Flying M wanted to build a shopping center on the site where the old main ranch house still stood. They also wanted ten sections of land to develop into residential housing and a ranching syndicate had agreed to buy the remaining sections of the Flying M ranch.

"They have raised their offer considerably," Larry went on. "I think this is going to be the best offer we're going to get unless we hold the place for another five or ten years."

"What about the oil portion of the deal?"

"Phillips has agreed to honor their leases even if the property goes under new ownership. I don't know what the estimated gross income will be with the recent increase in the price of crude. Let me see. Crap, my desk calculator doesn't go that high. Oh well, you can round it off from the figures we talked about. They said the offer wouldn't be on the table forever, so what do you want me to do?"

"Sell it!"

"That didn't take long. Thought you'd at least want to think on it for a while."

"Thought on it for forty years now, Larry. That long enough?"

Larry laughed, "I guess."

"Look, as long as we can keep the oil depletion allowance to protect us from the taxes it's a deal we'll never better. Start drawing up the contracts. Oh, and you know the land we deeded to Sarah and her husband?"

"Yes, I was going to ask you about that. Their deed still has the restriction on it that states the land can only be sold back to the Flying M. That property's worth enough now to buy ten ranches that size."

"That's what I was coming to. Go ahead and release the property to them. Say the title office made a mistake in the paperwork. Sarah will know better, but do it anyway."

"We done with business now?" Larry asked.

"Sure, what else's on your mind?"

"Jake, we've known each other thirty years now. Can I ask you something personal?"

"Of course Larry, I can't think of anything you'd ask, I wouldn't answer. If I can, that is."

"You were born to an oil and ranching empire the likes of which most men can only dream. You and Sarah were meant to be together from the day you were born. Why did you want to be a flyer and turn your back on all of that? And, Jake, if you don't want to answer, you're welcome to tell me it's none of my damn business."

"No, no, it's a fair question." Jake paused for a moment because he wanted to give Larry an honest answer. "I don't know! What I do know is every man is born with two lives. The life he could have lived and the life he chooses. We make our choices at each fork in the road, but in the end there was really only one road, the one we took. Maybe, just maybe, we thought we had a choice and we really never did. I don't know. I honestly don't know the answer to your question, Larry."

"I understand. Sometimes I wish I'd chosen differently myself. I wish I'd chosen a life of adventure like you, but I didn't."

Larry was in a better position than anyone to know the many things Jake had done to help others through hard times. He knew because he had carried out Jake's instructions to do them time and time again.

"Been an honor to know and work with you all these years, Jake Martin. Oh by the way, happy birthday."

***

Jake returned to the dining room where a cake with fifty-one candles awaited.

"Put the fire department on standby before you light those," Dan joked.

After ice cream and cake, the kids ran off to the living room to watch television.

Dan and Ida excused themselves to leave.

Chen kissed his mom goodnight and asked, "You sure it's okay for Chena to spend the night?"

Suzette smiled at her son who was now taller than her.

"She'll be fine. She loves to stay over when her cousins are here."

Jake commented to Suzette after Chen and Sue Lee left, "I think that boy took after your father, Jon Claude. He looks more like him the older he gets."

Suzette's father had retired several years ago to his old family estate in Reims.

"That reminds me, I need to write Papa. I'll tell him what you said about Chen. That will please him."

Lora came through after settling the kids down in the living room.

"Got to go meet that social climbing husband of mine, at least make an appearance at the museum reception. Mom, do you want me to come back for Johnny and Katy later?"

"No, you go on. No need to drive all the way back out here tonight. They want to spend the night anyway. I'll let them watch TV and stay up a little late."

***

Suzette joined Jake on the patio that evening. The western horizon was now only a dull glow and the silver light from the rising eastern moon glistened across the ocean waters.

Suzette curled up in her favorite chair and picked up the book she had started several days ago and was just now getting back to.

"I'll relax a little before I go try to put the junior space patrol to bed."

Jake was making some notes on a Big Red Chief tablet with a pencil and humming a tune as he worked.

Suzette soon gave up reading by the dim light from the porch lamp and laid her book aside.

"What's that tune you've been humming?"

"An old hymn that Mom used to sing around the house, didn't even know I was doing it. I think its *God of my Fathers*. I'll stop if it bothers you?"

"Oh no, I just wondered what the name of the song was," actually Suzette wanted to visit. "Lora told me you two had one of your talks and you were thinking about selling either the factory or the Flying M."

"The offer on the Flying M was too good. Looks like it'll go first. I been thinking maybe I need a new challenge. Start an airline, something along those lines."

"Jake, you know anything you want to do is all right with me, but I wish you'd slow down a little. Take a little more time off. Are you sure you want to take on another big project like an airline?"

"In grade school, I was the runt of the litter, littlest guy my age. I made up my mind I was going to be six feet tall. I did and with an inch or so to spare."

"I've never had any reason to doubt your tenacity, Jake dear. I'm just concerned about your well being."

"How'd you like to move to Hawaii?" Jake asked Suzette out of the blue, changing the subject.

"You want to leave the grandkids?"

"No, I guess not."

"Jake, we can fly over and spend a few weeks at Waikiki any time you want. For that matter, we can go anywhere in the world you'd like to visit."

"I know and you're right. I am going to start taking more time off. I haven't been feeling all that good lately anyway," Jake admitted, but he stopped short of saying he was still sore from the crash.

"That does it. You're going to the doctor tomorrow for a checkup. I'll call in the morning and make you an appointment."

"Okay, but make it later in the week. I've got several important meetings scheduled for tomorrow and Larry's flying in Tuesday."

"What else did you and Lora talk about?"

"About the estate and how there is no one to take over the old Flying M empire anyway. Chen's no rancher, Lora could care less and our grandkids, why we'll be older than the hills by the time those kids show any interest."

"I wish I could have given you a son. I understand they've developed something now that keeps the RH factor from being a problem. Too late for us though."

"Wasn't meant to be and wasn't your fault you lost the baby. I have always accepted the way things turned out. You know that. Besides you've got your hands full helping raise grandkids now seems like to me."

"Do you know how much I love you, Jacob Martin? You're one of the finest men I've ever known."

Jake looked over at Suzette and said, "When the angels ask me what I remember, I'll tell them I remember you most of all."

"That's the words to a song! You cad. You heard that on the radio, didn't you?"

"Well, I still mean it. That's what counts, isn't it?"

"You ol' smooth talking charmer. You only say those things to keep me hanging round."

"Worked so far hasn't it?"

Suzette smiled.

"Yes, and most likely always will," and she got up to go in the house. "Guess I'll go get them young'uns ready for bed."

Jake laughed, "Since when did you start talking like a Texan?"

"Oh, sometime after I'd been married to one for twenty years, I suppose," Suzette said, looking at Jake with a smile of demure admiration. "Like Ida told me, you can take the boy out of Texas, but you can't take the Texan out of his wife," and she giggled as Jake looked at her over the top of his reading glasses.

***

On a Sunday afternoon in late November, after Jake's 51st birthday, Thanksgiving had come and gone and Jake was home alone. Suzette had gone with Lora to take the grandkids to a matinee showing of the *Nutcracker* at the Little Theater and Jake had spent most of the day working in his rose garden, pruning and cleaning out flowerbeds.

The sun sank low on the western horizon and Jake came over to the patio to rest for a while. He always liked to stop to watch the sunsets. The sunsets over the Pacific were beautiful, but they never quite compared to the ones he remembered as a boy back on the ranch.

Jake stretched out on his favorite chaise longue and gazed out over the ocean. The two crossed palm trees perfectly framed the sunset at the far end of the yard. As the sun touched the horizon it burst with red rays that shot across the sky like a giant Japanese flag of the Rising Sun.

Jake was having some pains in his chest. Momentarily, the thought crossed his mind he might be having some heart trouble. His doctor had cautioned him about overdoing things and he had been working a little too hard. The pain was not bad, only a bit uncomfortable and after he rested for a moment, the pain went away.

He would rest there on the chaise longue for a while until Suzette came home and then maybe they would go out somewhere for a quite dinner.

Jake closed his eyes and his thoughts drifted off to memories of the past and once again, he remembered that day when he ran to meet the old biplane.

He recalled a time, standing on a hillside looking out over the Red River Valley, holding the reins to ol' Robey. Prince and Scout were at his feet and Sarah on her black charger galloped towards them off in the distance.

He thought of Zack seated proudly at the wheel of that worthless old Model T pickup truck he had given him. He laughed and for whatever reason that reminded him of the time when Red was at the controls of an old Ford Trimotor and they were fighting their way through a blinding Oklahoma snowstorm.

He remembered coming home late one night at the summer ranch house and finding Liz curled up asleep on the living room couch with young Lora asleep beside her and that reminded him of how, when Lora was little, he had to be careful where he stepped back because she was always right behind him like a shadow.

Like a high-speed motion picture, the memories raced through his mind of a Pan Am China Clipper roaring across old San Francisco harbor and gracefully lifting into the air. He remembered peeling off over the mountains of Burma in the Flying Tiger P-40 and that day in the Annabelle Lee with a German fighter coming straight at them with its wing guns blazing.

He recalled Gertie's subtle smile when he cracked a corny joke and Maggie in her worn, dirty tan flight suit climbing down from a B-27, smug-faced and tired, tagging along behind him.

He was able to think of Michael now without tears coming in his eyes and of the day Michael stood at attention in his Marine officer's uniform with the gold Navy wings on his chest and how proud he was when his son saluted.

Foremost in his memory was a day in Rangoon in a small teahouse where a young Eurasian girl was seated at a table. She turned and smiled at him. He would remember Suzette and that day most of all.

He once again recalled Juan Trippe's words, "The airliner will replace the bomber. If people get to know one another, they will find it hard to make war on their friends."

So long as old men dream and build new airplanes for young men to fly, maybe there was hope for the world after all, Jake thought to himself.

He looked off into the fading twilight of the setting sun and saw a vision of a giant new silver airliner making its way across the sky to some far away land.

He realized life itself was really only an adventure. It was all about choices. The choices each of us make in our lives everyday, the big choices that have no effect and the small choices that change the course of our lives forever.

As the sun sank into the distant ocean, the sky turned from magenta to a deep blue. Far from harms way, Captain Jake Martin was taking a nap, resting peacefully in the arms of the God that had always granted him safe passage. The phone in the house rang, but he did not hear it.

The answering machine came on.

"Martin residence. Please leave a message," and then the machine beeped.

"Jake, this is Sarah. The papers for the ranch came in the mail the other day. When I was reading over them, I got to thinking back to the day you jumped out of the hayloft with those stupid batwings on. I got to laughing so hard. No wonder I always thought you were invincible."

Sarah paused.

"Don't know why I called? Probably shouldn't have, but since I did, I'll just say thanks for looking after me all these years. I know you don't think I knew, but I did!"

Sarah's voice became distant, as she placed the receiver back on the hook.

"Love you Jake, guess I always will."

Suzette's car pulling into the drive woke Jake, but he had awakened with a commitment. He made the decision that very moment that he would build it! He would build a new state of the art executive jet and he would see it fly in his lifetime. He would do this, if the venture cost him everything he owned and all that he could borrow.

***

Like other aviation men of vision, Jake Martin went on to build some of the finest planes to ever take to the sky. The new jet transport he helped designed flew faster, further and safer than any that had come before. After that, he built an airliner that flew faster than the speed of sound and could race the setting sun to its destination.

On July 28th 1982, the rollout celebration of the new JetStar II was a major aviation news event. The press, representatives of several large corporations and three thousand guests attended.

The newest JetStar could carry fourteen passengers at a speed of mach point nine eight and fly nonstop from the United States to anywhere in Europe or Asia without refueling. The new jet was an unchallenged aviation technological breakthrough for its time.

Jake Martin was still a handsome figure of a man, graying now and sporting a broad, matching gray mustache. Today was also Jake's seventieth birthday and the second best birthday of his life.

After the celebration, he strolled through the factory feeling pretty good about all he had been able to accomplish at Martin Aero in the last thirty years.

He stopped from time to time to visit with an old friend or introduce himself to a new employee, but in his mind, he was preoccupied with concerns about who would run the company after he retired.

Jake stopped at the airframe jig assembly section of the factory to greet a tall, nice looking, blonde haired young man working there. He seemed familiar for some reason.

"You're new here, aren't you, son?"

"Yes, sir, been here about six months now."

"My name's Jake. Good to have you onboard. What's your name?"

"Michael, sir, but everyone calls me Mike."

"Good name Michael. My son's name was Michael."

"Yes, sir, I know. My mother's name was Lisa and I was named after my father. I'm your grandson."

"Hay, Joe," Jake hollered across to the line foreman, "Going to borrow you man here for a bit." Joe waved his acknowledgment. Jake said to young Mike, "Come walk with me."

The old man with a slight limp and his newly found grandson, moved slowly across the factory floor, visiting as they walked towards the large partially open hangar doors.

As they stood between the open hangar doors, the rays of the afternoon setting sun silhouetted the two men and lit the silver airplanes on the assembly line with a golden glow.

FLYING STORIES
HOW I CAME TO BE A PILOT AND ENGINEER
AND WHAT HAPPENED AFTER THAT
by MARVIN ARNOLD

Lincoln and Continental
Classic Motorcars
by Marvin Arnold

For information about this book
Samco Publishing
www.storydomain.com